The Alcoholic

A Hero Contends for His Soul

T.S. Flanagan

Roscommon Press
2025

roscommonpress@gmail.com

Copyright © 2025 T.S. Flanagan

ISBN: 979-8-9926985-0-3 (Paperback)
ISBN: 979-8-9926985-1-0 (Hardcover)
ISBN: 979-8-9926985-2-7 (Ebook)

All rights reserved. No part of this publication may be reproduced, stored in a retrieval system, or transmitted in any form or by any means, electronic, mechanical, recording or otherwise, without the prior written permission of the author.

The characters and events in this book are fictitious. Any similarity to real persons, living or dead, is coincidental and not intended by the author.

2025

Second Edition

Library of Congress Cataloguing in Publication Data
Flanagan, T.S.
The Alcoholic by T.S. Flanagan
Library of Congress Control Number: 2022922968

To AA sponsors, past, present, and future

Chapter 1
September 30, 2016 - 1:05 AM

Roland leaned a shoulder against the tree in front of his building and frisked himself for his keys. The trudge up the hill, if you could call it a hill, had been slow. Now suddenly the street seemed tilted in the other direction as if it were balanced on a fulcrum and a weight been flung from one end to the other. Woozy, he tottered and reached out a hand to steady himself on the trunk then knelt. On the verge of puking, he swallowed hard to hold it off. Looking at his vomit on the sidewalk when he left for work the next morning would be an ugly way to start the day. He would disgorge into his commode like a proper gentleman.

The street lay perfectly quiet. The lamp overhead shed no light, having spent its last flicker months ago. As tall a man as Roland was, he was barely visible in the dense midnight shadow under the tree. Many nights he'd been grateful for the darkness afforded by the defunct lamp and would sit with his back against the tree and doze off; but now, feeling ill, he rose to go inside. By day he used the more convenient side entrance in the alleyway, but at night, without the streetlight, the alleyway was so dark that Roland, mighty martial artist though he was, chose the safer course and mounted the steps to the front door. Before he went in, he surveyed the length of Sacramento Street, noting the several gaps where lights were burnt out. The addicts had their free government needles, he thought, but the city couldn't manage to illuminate the thoroughfares well enough so pedestrians might avoid stepping in their waste at night.

Roland threw up in his toilet, brushed his teeth, undressed, and crawled into bed without flipping on a light. The only luminescence in his apartment glared from the red display on the clock in his bedroom at the end of the hall. It read 1:11 AM. Early really. Time enough to sleep for a few hours then grab a bite to eat on his drive to work, as long as he could quiet his mind and fall asleep straightaway. He reached down and felt for the bottle of Jack Daniel's on the floor next to his bed and took it by the neck. It sloshed heavily. Still plenty there. 1:15 AM. He lifted his head from the pillow, filled his mouth, and gulped down a few swallows. That should do the trick. *Another industrious day safely logged in the books.*

Roland took another drink, capped the bottle, and lowered it back home. Soon, he drifted off.

He woke to a loud pop. Supine, he opened his eyes and listened. The clock read 1:38. He sat up as if to sense the world more clearly and heard the sound of wood scraping against wood. It came from his parlor, right next to his bedroom. It stopped. He kept listening, now fully alert. There it was again, this time louder. No question, someone was forcing open a window in the parlor and with considerable difficulty. The building was old, its window casings weathered and warped. He knew which one. The steep slope of the alleyway made it possible to reach only the corner window without a ladder. Its crescent latch was misaligned and could not be secured, and the condition of the frame kept it pretty well stuck, but apparently not permanently. *Fuck. This can't be happening.* He swiveled out of bed thinking he might be able to get there in time to stop the intruder from crawling through, but before he could take a step he heard a thump. The man—he correctly assumed—was inside. Roland groped for his Laredos and found one—the right, thankfully—and pulled it on. No time to find the other. Instead, he leaned down quietly and took the bottle by the neck.

The beam from a flashlight panned across the kitchenette just outside his door, across the hall from the parlor. Roland stood just inside his bedroom doorway. Should he call out and warn the man off? *I've got a gun, motherfucker!* Believable in some cities, but not in San Francisco. He remained frozen, not with fear but with indecision. He felt sure that whoever it was had come alone, and Roland soon would have the drop on him. Twenty-five, he'd never been in an actual fight, though he'd sparred with and competed against adult blackbelts of various disciplines since he was fourteen. He'd been the occasional target of drunken men trying to prove themselves but had always been able to talk them out of their stupidity, a skill that proved invaluable to a late-night bar drinker who measured six-foot-six. But now was not the time for a parlay. Sluggish from intoxication and confined to the tight spaces of his apartment, worried the intruder might be armed, Roland raised the bottle and waited, his breathing calm, his heart trilling.

The man appeared before him in profile, short compared to Roland, gloved, wearing a black hooded sweatshirt that revealed only his dark eyebrows and sharp nose. He held the flashlight in his right hand and a pry bar in his left. He turned and shined the light on the front door at the end of the entryway then at the open bathroom halfway up the hall. It was a quality flashlight, producing a powerful beam, with a long handle that doubled as a truncheon. This was no random intruder, he figured, but a working criminal, standing just a few feet away, his back turned. In an instant, as though he sensed being watched, the man spun around and shined his light on Roland just as he stepped out of his bedroom to make room for a swing. He brought the bottle down squarely on the intruder's head. The bottle shattered. The man stumbled backward and dropped to one knee, his hood thrown back, his face wet with whiskey. A line of blood dribbled from his forehead down his nose. He looked at Roland standing there outside his bedroom, naked except for his steel-tipped boot, the jagged neck of the broken bottle still in his hand. He stood up and lifted the pry bar to attack, but before he could aim a blow, Roland delivered a swift side-kick that sent him crashing shoulder-first into the wall. The flashlight rolled away and stopped, providing a steady light. Roland stood back and waited to see what the intruder would do.

The man rose, his twelve-inch steel tool, hooked at one end, gripped firmly in hand. He stared at Roland where he stood, one foot bare in the broken glass, unshaven, hair down to his shoulders, muscled like a well-conditioned athlete and without a stitch of clothing, green eyes steady amid the whiskey fumes. The bottom of the square-shaped Jack Daniel's bottle had landed flat and still held a bit of liquor. Both men glanced at the improbable sight then back at one another.

Roland spoke. "Vete."

The man dropped the pry bar and palmed the blood from his face.

"Vete ahora. Vete andale!"

The man didn't go. Roland dropped the jagged remnant thinking the man was ready to throw down. He'd gladly go mano-a-mano with this stupid little shit, but the man was not after a fistfight. He reached into his pant waist and unsheathed a knife, an Arkansas bowie with a ten-inch drop-point blade polished to a high shine.

"I'm not a Mexican." It was an honest mistake. His olive skin, black hair, and short stature marked him as possibly from south of the border.

"Then get out of here in English."

"I'm going to cut off your cock and shove it down your throat." He spoke in a flat West Coast tone.

Roland looked down at his member and processed the situation. All he had to do was take two steps backward into his bedroom, close the door, turn the lock, and call the police; but he decided that he'd rather not live with that decision. Sure, he was afraid, but more than that he was irritated.

"Guess you'll have to kill me first."

The man studied him and slid forward, tracing tiny circles in the air with the point of the outstretched knife. Roland took a defensive stance, the stance he learned on his very first day in karate class when he was six. *Left arm up to block, right arm tucked to punch, light on the balls of your feet, right leg back and poised to kick.*

"You won't be my first."

"I'm not going anywhere. The door is right behind you. I suggest you pick up your tools and use the door or this will not go well for you."

The two stood facing each other for what to Roland seemed like half a minute but was, in fact, only a few long seconds. He'd finished what he had to say and waited for the intruder to make a decision. He relaxed his arms and opened his palms upward in a gesture that said *What's it going to be?* The man sprang forward and slashed at Roland. Roland blocked the knife with a downward sweep of his left arm and kicked the man in the ribs with the steel point of his boot, driving him hard again against the wall. He slid off the wall and stumbled backward toward the door and fell flat on his back. Roland sprang upon him with a heavy knee to the chest and drove his right fist into the man's jaw. He heard the mandible crack and felt the crunch of broken teeth. The man still clutched the knife. Roland pinned the wrist of the knife-hand and hit him again, this time squarely in the temple. The knife fell free and spun slowly on its brass handle guard. *Son-of-a-bitch can take a punch.* Roland had often scoffed at how in action movies people could batter one another tirelessly without losing consciousness. He knew from experience that even wearing headgear a man could be knocked out with a single powerful blow. So, when the intruder, face bloodied and jaw shattered, patted the floor for the knife, Roland regarded him with puzzled respect. *Adrenaline?* Perhaps. He looked at the gash in his forearm, now throbbing with pain, and saw blood dripping from his fingers.

"Motherfucker." He grabbed the knife with his blood-wet hand.

The intruder groaned and coughed, his eyes ajoggle. Roland shook his head, half in pity for the defeated man beneath him and half in disapproval of what he was about to do. The words of the intruder echoed in his mind—*you won't be my first. Okay, then,* he thought, *you deserve this.* Roland switched the knife to his right hand and plunged it into the man's chest, aiming for the heart. The blade glanced off a rib and pierced the left lung. The man convulsed and spit blood. Roland stood and regarded his handiwork. His victim struggled to sit up and burbled blood down his chest. Then he lay back down and tried to pull out the knife, but the blade stayed wedged between two ribs.

Roland looked at his injury, his blood still dripping off his fingers. In the spray of battery-powered light he could see the gash line, thin, about six inches long, and not too deep. *Idiot*. It was his own fault. When he'd relaxed his arms in a show of mock impatience, he'd left himself vulnerable. Without time to sidestep the thrust, he'd had to deflect it. He looked down at the man on the floor and observed his impending expiration. With both hands on the knife handle, he'd managed to pull it out an inch or two, his coughs growing weaker, blood now flowing freely from one side of his mouth. Roland watched intently as he backed into his kitchenette to get the dishtowel draped through the handle of his refrigerator door. Sobered by adrenaline, he walked back to where the intruder lay dying, careful now to avoid the shards of glass strewn about the hallway.

"Ambulance." The man began to choke. "Call an – am – bu – lance."

Roland stood over him and wound the towel around his arm.

"I gave you a chance to leave on your own, and now you want me to call you a ride."

He spit out a mouthful of blood as though better to form his words then looked at Roland.

"I am Ka-sa-bi-an. Sam-u-el Ka-sa-bi-an." His hands fell from the knife and onto the floor palms up. The handle bobbed, tilted to one side, the blade partially unmoored.

"Not for long."

He went back to his bedroom and found his phone in his jacket and tapped 9-1 before he changed his mind and set the phone on the dresser and went back to the hallway and switched on the light. He knelt before the little miracle. He lifted it gently, careful not to spill any, and turned it to find the safest spot to place his lips then poured the last few ounces of sour mash into his mouth and set it back on the floor.

He went back to his room. The clock read 1:44. He took the phone, sat on his bed, and searched his contact list and placed a call.

The man he called picked up after three rings. "Who the hell is this?"

"You know. You can see my name on your display."

"I mean who the hell do you think you are, calling me at this hour?"

"You told me I could call you whenever I needed to, Denny. I just killed someone."

Denny went silent. Drunks say a lot of crazy shit. He'd sponsored dozens "Mmmhmm," he said.

"Look, Denny, I'm not fucking around here. There's a guy bleeding to death in my hallway. He broke into my apartment and attacked me. I stabbed him in the chest with his own knife."

"You said you killed someone. Now you say he's not dead. How much have you had to drink tonight, Roland?"

"Not so much that I couldn't get out of bed and put up a fight. Listen to me, man. I need to know what to do. You told me not to make any big decisions until I ran it by you first."

"I haven't seen you in months. You stopped coming to meetings when you got my last signature on your court card. You're no longer my problem. Besides, I told you you could call me anytime *unless* you were drinking."

"This is not about my struggle with sobriety, Denny." Roland's phrasing was dishonest. He'd never once confessed to himself or to anyone that he struggled with sobriety. He believed he could stop drinking anytime he wanted to. "I'm a little freaked out here. I just want to know what to do."

"Wait for the cops to remove the body then clean up the blood. That's all I can think of. You're not clergy so you can't administer last rites, though I don't suppose that would do any harm. If he's still alive, see if you can throw together some sort of last rites. Maybe google it. I've got to get back to sleep."

"You think this is a joke? You need to see a picture? If you think this is a joke, I'll snap a picture and text it to you."

Roland waited for an answer. Denny stayed silent. Roland continued.

"Should I? Do you need to see what I'm talking about?"

Finally, Denny spoke. "No. Do not send me a picture. Have you called the police?"

"No."

"Listen to me very carefully. As soon as I finish my next sentence, I'm hanging up the phone. If it's true that someone is dead or dying on your floor you need to call 911 because you've created a phone record that points to me and the longer this call goes on the more the police will have reason to believe that I know about whatever you've done tonight and if they contact me about whatever this is I need to be able to say only that I told you to call the police immediately and hung up on you, you unbelievably stupid idiot." Click.

"Asshole," he said to the phone and set it on the dresser.

"Idiot," he said of himself again.

The man was not yet dead. Roland could see the handle of the knife twinging as its unconscious owner labored to draw his last shallow breaths. His mind suddenly became clear. He had to place the call, but he needed to delay as long as possible. But if he sat there and waited for the man to die, it might take a while, and if the blood on the floor was already hardened when the police arrived, they might be able to prove that he sat around and waited before placing the call. He gambled on an expeditious death.

"911 Emergency Dispatch." It was a female voice.

"I need an ambulance."

"Are you injured or in distress?"

"I'm a little injured but I'm not calling about me."

"What is the nature of the injury or distress?"

"There's a guy in my apartment and he's hurt pretty bad."

"How badly is he hurt? Can he talk?"

"No."

The dispatcher went silent. Roland waited right along with her.

"So, you're sure he can't talk?"

"Yes."

The standoff continued for a few more seconds. Roland figured she couldn't pull his address from his mobile phone and wasn't about to give the address until she asked for it.

"Is that *yes he can talk* or *yes you're sure he can't talk?*"

"If he could talk, I'd put him on the phone."

"Where is the man exactly?"

"Look, lady, if you're not going to send an ambulance I'll just hang up and call back. Maybe I'll get someone who knows how to do her job."

"Sir, I am following the correct procedure..."

"By asking the same question twice? They must recruit you people from the tent village in the Civic Center. If this dude dies, it's on you."

"Have you been drinking tonight, sir?"

"Is that in your script? Maybe stick with the script."

"I need to establish that this is a legitimate emergency."

"How are you going to do that? What words do I need to say? What is your job exactly?"

"Sir, if you could please calm d—"

"You answered the call by saying 911 emergency dispatch. I did the 911 part, now aren't you supposed to do the emergency dispatch part?"

The woman waited again. "What are the injuries?"

"He has a knife in his chest."

"Is he still breathing?"

"A little bit."

"You're calling from a mobile phone—correct?"

"Yes"

"Tell me the address."

Roland gave his address. He could hear her fingers moving rapidly along her keyboard as she silently set the emergency wheels in motion.

"Ok, sir, the EMTs and police will be there shortly. Now I need you to give me some more information."

Roland hung up. Not in defiance of her push for useless information but because he had to get dressed and ready for the authorities. He took off his Laredo and put on his pants and a shirt. The clock read 1:49. He couldn't shake off the invective of his sponsor—*you unbelievably stupid idiot.* Not a phrase our prodigy—champion in all endeavors growing up—was used to hearing. *Stupid idiot* gets tossed around as a term of endearment in the brotherhood of post-pubescent males, but *unbelievably stupid idiot*—

that took conviction. Such a slap was meant to raise a welt. And it begged a question, one he could not immediately answer and did not wish to entertain. *Why did I call Denny?* It bothered him. Calling him was not, as Denny would have put it, the next indicated thing. For drunks and addicts buffeted for years by their own erratic whims, divining *the next indicated thing* in the early days of recovery was often reduced to the most mundane of tasks, such as tying one's shoes or even getting out of bed in the morning. In the most desperate cases, the unrecovered, in despair, decide that *the next indicated thing* is to end one's own life.

The urgency of the moment intruded on his bewildered self-reflection and drove him to his own *next indicated thing*—the bottle of wine in his refrigerator. A bottle of white. He hated white wine and kept it there only for emergencies, but not this kind of emergency. Roland's modus operandi, on a lucky night, was to spend it in the bed of a stranger; but when circumstances, such as her roommate, prevented that, he would bring her to his grubby abode. He found that women were, as a rule, more agreeable to white wine than, say, straight bourbon.

He uncorked the bottle and chugged until he needed air. *I'm alive and you've breathed your last, you murderous son-of-a-bitch.* He set the bottle down and moved over to see if it was true. Of one thing he felt certain—Mister Kasabian would never see the light of day and probably not even hear the sirens that were beginning to awaken the denizens of Nob Hill. He pivoted to fetch the bottle and drove a shard of glass into the ball of his left foot.

"Motherfu—"

He returned to his bedroom and pinched the glass from the wound and double-socked the foot then pulled on both boots and went back to the kitchen and took another pull off the bottle. He set it on the counter and exhaled a deep sigh as the familiar sense of ease and comfort warmed his body from within. *Everything's gonna be fine.* Roland stepped over the dead-enough man—*good luck, Sammy*—opened the door and went down to the lobby.

A police car escorted the ambulance. Both vehicles parked in front of his building. The sirens went quiet. Red and blue lights splashed through the glass front doors and circled the foyer, bouncing blindingly off the array of aluminum mailboxes. Roland propped the front door open and went outside to greet the civil servants, raising his right arm and waving it side-to-side. Two officers approached him shoulder-to-shoulder, hands on their holsters.

"He's in apartment two on the floor in the hallway right behind the door."

Two EMTs pulled a stretcher from their rig and one of the officers led them into the building. The other officer approached Roland. He took a step backward and leaned heavily against his tree. He'd hit the white wine a little too hard—a little too fast.

"Please step forward into the light, sir." The officer removed the flashlight from his service belt and pointed the beam at Roland's face.

"Please don't shine that thing in my eyes, officer."

"It's not just for shining. Please come out from under the tree so I can see you."

Roland complied and made sure not to walk directly toward the policeman, whose other hand hovered above his sidearm.

"Don't worry. I'm not going to take a run at you."

The officer nodded and smiled smugly. Roland angled his steps unsteadily to the mouth of the alleyway. "As you can see," he said, swirling his right arm above his head, "the streetlight is out. This is where the whoooole thing started."

"How much have you had to drink tonight?"

"Wait a second." Roland pointed to the dark passage behind him. "Shine your light up there so I can show you where he broke in."

"Let's start with your name."

Roland slumped his shoulders in defeat. He wanted to sit down in the street and recount the night's sequence of events, beginning with when he slid into bed. It seemed the officer wanted to go back much further.

"Roland Hazzard."

The officer stepped away for a brief exchange with someone on the radio hooked to his epaulet. He returned with a black leather notepad in hand.

"Spell that for me, please?"

Roland spelled his name.

"You live here? In apartment number two you said?"

"Yes. That's right."

The EMTs came down with their gurney unoccupied and collapsed it and rolled it back into the ambulance.

"Where are you going, guys?" Roland sounded like a disappointed child whose new friends were about to run off. The men ignored him, didn't appear even to have heard him.

He turned to the officer. "What's going on? They shouldn't be leaving."

"They transport the living."

"The man up there is dead?"

"No. Vital. Signs."

Roland held up his left arm to show the now thoroughly blood-soaked towel wrapped around it. "Can you ask them to look at this at least?"

"Stay right where you are." He went over and spoke to the EMTs.

One of the medical men came back with a kit and took a look at Roland's wound. He spoke to the officer as if Roland were not there. "It's a knife wound. Sharp blade—that's pretty clear."

That annoyed Roland. He sat down on the curb and presented his arm for treatment. "*Defensive* knife wound," he said.

People in the nearby apartment buildings had come to their windows to observe the proceedings, and Roland's neighbor, Astrid, a young woman, late twenties, in a purple terrycloth robe, came outside and stood next to Roland's tree with her arms crossed, wearing the satisfied expression of a queen about to witness the execution of a disloyal subject.

The officer repeated his previous question, but this time in the form of a request. "Tell me how much you've had to drink tonight."

Astrid voiced her opinion. "He's a drunk. Whatever else he is or did, he's a daily drunk. I've seen him asleep against this tree in the morning. Now why would anyone walk home drunk and sleep outside instead of coming in?"

Roland thought about explaining that he found the cold midnight air salutary during slumber but instead belted out in his best Mick Jagger country drawl. "Wontcha come on, calm down, sweet Petuniaaaah. Come on, calm down, I'm beggin' yoooo." The medic gave his elbow a tug to remind him to keep his arm steady as he dressed the wound.

"Please go back inside, ma'am. We'll talk to you later if we need more information."

"Well, I've got plenty to say. I live in unit three right next door to him. I'll fill you in on the questionable habits of Roland Hazzard." With that, she walked back inside.

"I see you're pretty popular around here, Mister Hazzard."

"Actually, I am, neighborhood-wide. No one likes her though. She did try to get me to sleep with her once and I probably should have done it just for good community relations, but that can backfire as you probably know. Besides…"

The officer cut him off. "Mister Hazzard, if you're too drunk to answer my questions, then you're going to have to sleep it off tonight in lock-up."

"Hold on. Hold on." Roland collected his wits. "I've done nothing wrong here, sir. I just got stabbed in my own apartment and now you're talking about taking me to jail. I don't think so."

"If you don't quiet down, I can do just that."

Roland realized that he should probably shut up. He needed to get to work tomorrow for his three-month probationary review. He liked this job. Denny had hooked him up with the initial interview through one of the other AA members and he didn't want to go back to cleaning fish down on the docks. He looked at the officer.

"Fine. What exactly do you wanna know?"

"You've had a lot to drink tonight, right? I just want to establish that first."

"Yes. For most people. But by my standards, I'm pretty far from drunk, not drunk like that silly woman was sneering about. She has seen me drunk, but this ain't it."

"Slow night, huh?"

"I got to bed alright, but after I called 911, I chugged most of a bottle of wine. I can still feel it coming on."

"Why did you do that?"

"To stop my heart from pounding." The truth, should he have sought it, would've been too hard to formulate. The medic completed his work on the injured arm and stood up to leave.

"Thanks, mate," Roland said. The officer thanked him as well, and the medic jumped into the vehicle and his partner hit the gas.

"Let's go inside and take a look at your friend."

"Not my friend. Let me show you where he broke in, just up here." Again, Roland pointed to the alley.

"We'll get to that later. First, let's go take a look at the man in your apartment."

Roland led the way. The door to his place was wide open and all the lights inside were on. The other officer stood over the body and spoke to someone on his radio. He looked a few years younger than his partner and more physically fit.

"We'll need a van for the body and a forensics team." He buttoned off his radio and looked at Roland. "I've been waiting for you."

"They were taking care of my gash." Roland held up the freshly dressed arm.

"Looks like a knife wound," the senior officer said.

"Which one of you guys is in charge?"

The officers looked at each other. The younger one spoke first. "He seems pretty drunk. Can we interview him?"

The senior officer shrugged. "Let's give it a try."

Roland looked down at the decedent. Anyone, he reasoned, could see that, whoever the guy was, he had it coming. He seethed inwardly with self-righteous impatience at the rigors of process.

"I need to get to bed. You guys look smart enough to take a look around and figure out what this is." He moved toward his bedroom.

"Not so fast, cowboy."

Roland turned around. "I'm not asking you to scrub off the blood and sweep up the glass."

"We're not a body removal service," said the junior officer.

"You can call yourselves whatever you want, but if this body is still here when I get up tomorrow morning, I'm going to brush my teeth then drag it out onto the sidewalk because I am not a body storage service. The city must have those big, refrigerated drawers in the morgue like you see in the movies. I think that's where it belongs, but I'm not going to jam it into the back seat of my car and take it there myself. I'm sure you find guys dead on the street all the time in this jewel of a metropolis so we can just let it be another one of those." He turned toward his bedroom again.

"Stop right there," the senior said in a threatening tone.

"What are you going to do—shoot me for going to bed?"

"We should just take him in," the junior officer said.

"On what charge?" Roland laughed.

"Suspicion of murder," the junior officer said.

Roland looked at the senior. "Let's go. Let's go book me for murder."

"Why don't you just tell us what happened here."

Roland looked down and pointed to the pry bar on the floor and cocked his head to the side like he was giving a silent demonstration. Then he pointed into the parlor and did a pantomime of someone jimmying open a window.

"We know how he got in, asshole," said the junior officer. "What about all this glass?"

"I hit him with my bottle of bourbon, standing right here in front of the kitchen, naked as a jaybird."

The senior officer teased out the narrative with a series of questions. "So, you came from the bedroom?"

"Armed with nothing but my johnson and a fifth a' Jack."

"You hit him with the bottle—then what?"

Roland decided to omit the blow-by-blow account. "Well, his hood was down and that must have softened the blow a bit. He stumbled backward and got up and pulled out his knife."

"Then?"

"I asked him to leave."

"You could have gone back into your room and closed the door."

"And locked it," the junior officer said. "The door has a lock."

"Castle law."

"So, you're a legal expert?" the senior officer said.

"Just the basics."

"What's he talking about?" the junior officer said.

"He doesn't have to retreat to the bedroom—that's what he's saying."

Roland crossed his arms. "So, we good here? I really do have to get some sleep."

The senior man continued. "How did the knife get in his chest?"

Roland grew visibly annoyed. "Let's be precise here—*his* knife—the one he cut me with." Roland lifted his bandaged arm to emphasize the point.

"How did you get the knife?"

"I never said I got the knife."

"He didn't stab himself."

"We fought. I got in a kick and a few punches, then we grappled with the knife. I turned it around on him."

"Turned it around on him?"

"He wouldn't let go of it, so I bent his wrist around and when the point was on his chest, I leaned on it. He made that necessary."

"And then you drank wine."

"I called 911, then I got dressed, then I drank wine." Roland stepped into his kitchen nook where the bottle stood uncorked on the counter and picked it up by the neck. "This wine."

"Is there anything else you'd like to tell us?" The younger officer sounded a bit sarcastic.

"Before he died, or when he realized he was probably going to die, he said his name—Samuel Kasabian." He tilted the bottle and drank from it.

The senior officer took out his pad and pen. "Say that again."

Roland finished his quaff and held out the bottle to eye how much remained. "Samuel Ka-say-be-an."

The officers stared at Roland and Roland stared back. He saw in their identical expressions a mutual incredulity, not of his veracity, necessarily, but of wonderment at this behavior. He pursed his lips and squinted to assure himself that, contrary to the looks on the officers' faces, there was nothing wrong with him.

"So," he said, "if there's nothing else."

"The homicide forensics team is on its way," the senior officer said. "Why don't you keep us company until they get here?"

Roland wavered and rolled his head in a circle, exaggerating his condition. He took his wallet out of his pants and removed his driver's license and set it on the kitchen counter.

"No can do, Magoo. I've had enough of today. Tomorrow has begun and I'm already chasing the sun. My name etcetera are here on my license and my prints are on the bottle in case you need them." He drained its contents and set it on the counter with a thunk. "Now, if you gentlemen will excuse me, I've got to lie down and pass out. I'll leave the door unlocked in case you need to arrest me, but I'm going to be a hard man to wake up." He turned around and stepped into his room and closed the door behind him. He took off his Laredos and stripped off his pants and collapsed onto the bed with his shirt still on.

Outside he could hear the officers moving around. To muffle the noise, he pressed in his earbuds and put Beethoven on shuffle. The clock read 2:00. The bars were just now closing. He wished it were 1:59.

Chapter 2
September 30, 2016 - 6:00 AM

The antiquated steel doorbell did not produce a pleasant ding-dong but sounded more like a fire alarm. It jarred Roland awake at 6:00 AM. On the dot. The reporters outside, in a perverse nod to civility, must have decided that waking Roland at 5:59 would be wrong, but 6:00 AM was acceptable. The building, being very old, had no intercom, so Roland had no choice but to get out of bed, dress quickly, and limp out to find out who the hell had his thumb on the bell. Morning twilight had just begun to seep through the blinds in the parlor and made the hallway visible. The body was gone. On the wooden floor where it had lain was a thick bloodstain about two feet across, still soaking into the raw old floorboards. He crunched over broken glass with his boots as he swore his way to his door and opened it. Light rushed in from the foyer below. Roland squinted. His mouth was dry. His face flushed. *They'd better be selling gold ingots at half price.* Who was he kidding? Roland was practically broke, living mostly off a credit card. Worse than broke, really. He had gambling debts to the tune of thousands. Other than the few twenties in his wallet, he had only the promise of a paycheck next Friday.

Outside the building stood a group of some ten reporters and a few cameramen, all jostling for position in front of the glass door. They had a clear view of the steps leading down to the foyer and were able to see Roland's slow approach, legs first, then the torso, then the man himself, unshaven with hair splayed in several directions. The fresh white bandage stood in contrast to the dirty black t-shirt from which swung his long, muscular arms. From their red-ringed sockets glared his most fearsome eyes growing wider with his mounting rage as he flung open the door.

"What the fuck you think you're doing? There are people sleeping here." He might as well have said *I have blueberry muffins fresh from the oven.*

They all talked at once. He could make out his name repeated in their breathless excitement.

"Yes I'm Roland Hazzard, goddamnit." He lowered his voice. "Now slow down so we can have a conversation." They looked at him mutely and raised their electronic devices toward his face as if they were observing a well-practiced ritual.

"Does anyone have a smoke?" They all started talking again, this time in a somewhat more orderly fashion.

"Do you think you'll be arrested? Did you know the man you killed? How many times did you stab him?" Roland wrenched the phone from a hand shoved too close to his face then carried it aloft out into the street to get the crowd to move away from the building. He turned to them and repeated his request. "Someone gimme a cigarette. I know at least one of you must still have the nerve to smoke." One of the cameramen took out a cigarette.

"Should I light it?"

"Yes please."

"Give me my phone back," a woman said.

Roland backed up until he was leaning against his rusted yellow Nissan Sentra. One would have doubted that a man his size could squeeze into such a runt of a vehicle. He handed the phone back to its owner and took the lit cigarette from the man.

"Thanks—my brand." He took a drag and exhaled the smoke in their direction and watched them jerk away in unison like a school of fish. "Now what do you unruly early-risers want?"

"Did you know the man you killed?"

"Do you know who you killed?"

Roland thought for a second, parsing the two different meanings. "No. I didn't know him. Was he someone important?"

"The Glendale Butcher—that's what we're hearing."

Roland had heard the moniker. Most of the country had. The Glendale Butcher was blamed for the murders of seven women in California and the Southwest in the space of a few months several years ago and was still on the loose. Technically, he was only a suspect, but the evidence collected left no room for doubt.

"Whoever he was, he ruined my evening." Roland exhaled another cloud of smoke.

Questions came again in a flurry. "What happened to your arm? Did the Butcher say anything? How many times did you stab him?"

Roland fished his keys from his pocket.

"All I can tell you is the good guys won." He deftly unlocked his door and squeezed himself into the driver's seat. "Gotta run, kids—can't be late for work," he said with the cigarette clenched between his teeth. He yanked the door closed and started the car and pulled away from the curb.

Their shouts trailed off as he drove away. His exhilaration from the impulsive escape carried him for a few blocks until his hangover returned full force. Pouring a bottle of wine on top of a belly half full of whiskey—God, Evolution, whatever was behind it all—was no way for the human being to treat itself. Regret was built into the system.

He needed to kill the few hours before work. He needed a shower. Hadn't showered since Wednesday morning. In the testing lab at the video game company where he worked, you could get away without bathing for a day, maybe two; but even under that loose standard Roland was unpresentable. He had a solution. At the local 24-hour drug store he bought shampoo, a towel, a new bandage for his arm and, to slake his monstrous thirst, a jug of water. A few miles west, just south of the Golden Gate Bridge, lay Baker Beach, a popular destination for the clothing-optional set. Not that it mattered. In The City by The Bay, one could go naked just about anywhere without attracting legal attention. Hell, people were known to defecate on the steps of City Hall and in the planters outside the towers in the Financial District. Such was progress.

~~~~~

The beach was empty. That suited Roland. Neither exhibitionist nor prudish when it came to public nudity, Roland nonetheless would have felt uncomfortable performing his morning ablutions for the world to see. Before he undressed, he gorged himself on water. Over-gorged, in fact. Recalling what he'd read about the indomitable Comanche preparing for a raid, he drank until he vomited. He had no idea why the savages did that, but he figured a good purging would accelerate the detoxification process, so he dug a hole in the sand and puked into it and covered it over. He felt better immediately and took off his clothes.

He bundled them inside his new towel and set them with his boots, water jug, and bandage kit twenty yards up from the shoreline and carried his shampoo bottle to the surf and waded in. The frigid Northern California Pacific took his breath away momentarily and he needed a dozen rapid shallow pants to regain his normal respiration. After a minute or two his body adjusted to the shock, his skin tightened, and he felt a strange sensation of warmth in the cold water that encased him. The ocean breeze bit his exposed flesh, so he kept his body immersed, appearing as little more than a head sticking out of the ocean.

He sudzed his hair and rinsed it several times until it squeaked between his fingers. As he wiped his eyes clear of residual soap, he saw a woman standing on the shore watching him. She wore tight black yoga pants and a light blue t-shirt soaked with sweat and her forehead was wrapped in a yellow headband. She'd finished her morning run on the beach, it appeared, and had paused to take in this unusual spectacle.

"Is this the new thing—homeless bathing on the public beaches?" She spoke with a playful Irish lilt.

"If it is, I'm sure I didn't invent it. I don't qualify as homeless."

"Oh, I see—you prefer to wash your hair in salt water. Makes it silky smooth, does it?"

"It's a sad story that led me to resort to this." He rose from the water to display his full height. "I don't intend to make a habit of it."

The jogger took stock of the magnificent masculine specimen standing naked before her, his broad shoulders tapering to a slim waist accentuated by a stack of hard abdominals. The muscles of his arms and upper torso, taut from the cold water, showed the definition of a latter-day Adonis. His powerful legs and buttocks, his ample mane, might have conjured the image of a lion on the savannah. Whatever diminishing effect the cold water had on his genitals, they yet made an impressive display in the cradle of his loins.

"Oh my. You certainly don't have the body of a typical homeless male."

"Is that your lay opinion, or do you have some expertise?"

"I'm a nurse at SF General and I've seen my fair share of naked homeless." She walked over to his belongings and picked up the towel and brought it to the surf line and held it out, careful not to let the tide splash her running shoes. Roland kneed his way through the surf and strode up the sand and tossed the shampoo bottle in the direction of his things.

"Thank you." He took the towel from her hand.

"It's a wee bit small for you."

"Best I could do on short notice." Roland dried his torso and arms as they spoke.

"Who worked on that arm?" she said. "It looks like a professional job. Even sopping wet it's still holding tight."

"You're not going to leave, are you—not going to respect my privacy?"

"I will if you tell me to. Do you want me to move alone?"

"I do not. I could use your help re-dressing my arm."

She didn't reply. To his surprise, she took the towel from his hand and walked behind him and dried off his shoulders, back, and buttocks. Then she buffed his thighs and patted down his legs, finishing at his ankles. "There y'are." She stood up and stepped around to face him. "You can do the rest." She handed him the towel.

"Thank you again." He smiled, drying his groin with the towel. "Now I guess I should know your name—Nurse...?"

"You didn't answer my question." She smiled back. "Did you even hear it?"

"Maybe not. I've been standing here thinking you were overdressed for the occasion."

"That's the standard come-on, love. I jog here in the early morning when there's usually no one around just so I don't have to hear that."

"I was minding my own business. And here you are."

"I'm not opposed, in principle."

"To helping me re-do my bandage or to taking off your clothes?"

"I'd like to know a bit more about you. You're awfully cagey."

"Me? You're the one. You just now dodged *my* question."

"You dodged mine first."

Roland was enjoying the back and forth with the attractive Irish woman and decided to see how much fun he could tease out of her.

"What does it matter? You either will or you won't."

"Won't what?"

"Take your pick."

"I'm not about to shed me clothes right here, darlin'."

"But you don't mind standing here making me feel naked. You have me at a distinct disadvantage."

"Hardly. You're the one who caught me off guard, rising out of the ocean like an ancient sea god."

He held up his wounded arm as exhibit A. "As you can see I'm a mere mortal."

"Mortal, yes—but hardy mere."

"So you like what you see."

"Not enough to fornicate with you here on the beach."

"No? Law enforcement is pretty lackadaisical in this city." He glanced up at the parking lot, empty but for his clown car. "If the police rolled up, they'd probably park and watch." He was bluffing. If she'd stripped off her knickers then and there his slightly tumescent member would have withdrawn. Like most men, he leaned toward exhibitionism, but performing on the beach with a stranger in broad daylight was out of the question. He sensed that she too was disinclined and so felt confident in the flirtation.

"I wouldn't do it here if we were madly in love."

The words—fornicate, madly, love—the images they conjured aroused him visibly. He wrapped the towel around his waist but the tent he made in the cloth declared the fact he would conceal.

"Wouldn't *madly* include just about anything?"

"Most men are half-mad to begin with, so I see how a man might think that."

"How about on a warm night under the stars on a soft blanket with no one around?"

"If you want me to help you with that arm, put your clothes on."

Roland shrugged and picked up his dirty laundry and jug of water and handed her the drug store bag. She opened it and looked inside as he began to dress.

"What's your bandage covering—a burn, a cut? If it's a burn, then the worst thing you could have done was take it into this filthy ocean."

"It's a cut."

"How fresh?"

"Five hours or so."

"There aren't any scissors in here, no antiseptic cream. This won't do a'tall."

"I don't need scissors to remove this bandage."

She looked at him appraisingly. "You still haven't answered my question."

He knew the question she meant but decided to play dumb.

"I can't keep track of them all."
"Who took care of that arm for you?"
"You were right. A professional."
"An EMT?"
"Yes. It was a house call."
"What happened?" From her tone, Roland sensed she wasn't going to brook another evasion. The rising sun warmed his shoulders and cast a thin orange sheen on the choppy Pacific stretched out before them. He turned his head and looked directly into her eyes—his emerald greens against her limpid blues.
"A fight—I got into a fight."
"Five hours ago you say—shortly after midnight?"
"What is this?
"Is it a knife wound?"
"It is."
"Big bowie knife with a wooden handle and a curvy brass guard?"
Roland cocked an eyebrow. "It was well above cutlery."
"Because last night around 2AM they wheeled in a corpse, a man dead from such a knife stuck in his chest."
"I see. You're connecting the dots."
"Or taking a shot in the dark."
He'd finished dressing. He looked at her again and nodded.
"Is that a yes?"
"Sounds like my attacker."
"Black hair, swarthy?"
"The knife in the chest says enough. I can't imagine there were two like that last night."
"You did the world a favor."
"So I've gathered. But how do you know?"
"The SFPD showed quite an interest. Then the FBI arrived and printed the deceased. I'd never seen authorities fingerprint a corpse before. And I heard them talking. Looks like you took out a serial killer. The Glendale Butcher."
"That's what brought a gaggle of reporters to my door this morning. I fled the interview looks like straight into your jogging path."
"Imagine that."
"I am. I certainly am. So, will you take care of my arm, Nurse…?"

"Deidre. And what's your name?"

"Me llamo Roland Hazzard."

"Goes well with the cowboy boots." She handed back his bag of supplies. "This won't do a'tall. You're not very bright, are you?"

"I get by on my lonesome. A lot of smart people don't."

"True enough, Roland. Anyhow, let's get your arm cleaned and re-wrapped. I've got proper supplies up at my place."

~~~~~

Deidre lived in a walk-up apartment building in the Sea Cliff neighborhood a few blocks from the beach. She led the way. The streets were still quiet. He followed her as she padded up the hill in her neon orange training shoes. The clop of his boots on the sidewalk made him keenly aware of the silent buildings and rows of idle cars wedged tightly against the curbs. He guessed she was just one side or the other of thirty. Viewed from behind, her body could have been that of an athletic teenager, with no sign of a bulge in her hips. Roland took stock of her oscillating buttocks as they flexed in time above the gap between her thighs.

She turned her head and noticed his limp. "Are you faking a hurt foot so you can lag behind and ogle my bum?"

"No, ma'am. I stepped on a piece of glass."

"On the beach?"

"During the fight"

"That's unlucky."

"I should have been more careful."

"You've bits of glass lying about your flat, do ya?"

"I smashed a bottle over his head."

"Just like in the movies."

"Yeah, except it wasn't stage whiskey."

They continued their uphill march without further conversation until they reached her address and veered in. The front of the building was landscaped with acacia trees, poinsettias, and morning glory. The stairs up to her floor were painted seafoam green and each apartment door had its own custom color. Potted flowers abounded, so much so that one could not tell which flowers went with which apartment. Or was it simply one happy community where everyone tended the marigolds? Communism at the local level, apart from the individually painted doors.

"Your place is beautiful."

"That's easy to say when you're not the one forkin' out the rent."

"And you're beautiful."

She turned and looked at him. "Not even close. My face could barely launch a kayak."

"You're way too modest, Deidre. A good-sized yacht. I'll settle for nothing less."

"People sometimes say *hot*. *Beautiful* is too complicated—a curse I think."

"I get it. I think I get it. Anyway, you're damned good lookin'."

She unlocked her bright green door and they went inside. The place was amply furnished, tastefully decorated and remarkably tidy, as though its occupant wanted always to be ready for guests. The little air-freshener plugged into the wall imparted a mild vanilla smell. Roland could not imagine living this way, but he imagined it would be nice to live with someone who liked to live this way.

"The shower's in there. I'll wash those clothes in my little unit."

Roland went into her bathroom and undressed again. He beheld his dirty clothes and was ashamed to have to hand them over to such a fastidious person, intuiting perhaps for the first time a moral dimension to bodily cleanliness, something touched on by his martial arts instructors over the years but in recent months completely forgotten. For the moment, his embarrassment softened his priapic impulse.

"How you doin' in there, love?" she said through the door.

This was her idea, he reminded himself. *I'd have settled for first aid on the beach*. Even so, he didn't want to open the door with his arousal on display, nor did he want to have to cover it with his hands or clothes. He wanted her to see that he was not prematurely aroused, so he drew upon the most unerotic image he could recall, that of a man he witnessed in Union Square a few days ago squatting against a wall and sucking the blood from the neck of a pigeon whose head he'd just torn off.

"You having trouble working the shower?" Roland could hear her smiling. He reached into the shower with his free hand and turned the knob and adjusted the temperature then opened the door.

"I'm not in a terrible hurry here." He handed her his dirty clothes.

"Keep the bandage on until after the shower and keep this door open. It gets too steamy in there."

Roland stepped into the shower and slid shut the clear glass door. He could see her in the hallway loading his clothes into a miniature washing machine stored in a utility closet. She didn't look over at him but lowered her head for a moment as she started the machine and closed her eyes as if in contemplation.

"How long do you think it will take? I'm not in a rush but I was planning on going to work this morning."

She looked at him. "What line are you in—waste management?"

"Video games."

"Oh, I've heard about you guys. Sounds like a fun place to work."

"Yep. And the dress code is pretty lax, but not the hours."

"I'll have you out of here in a jiff. I need to get to bed anyway. I got off work at five this morning."

He wiped a hole in the fog on the glass. "That's perfect. You are very kind."

"I am—'tiz true. You needed help."

"I guess I did, but I didn't know that until you showed up."

"Tell me again why you felt the need to bathe in the ocean, other than you being just plain strange."

Roland spoke slowly and loudly so he could be understood above the rushing water. "Reporters camped outside my building and woke me up at six. I gave them a good thrashing then jumped into my car."

"A good thrashing—Americans don't say that."

"I like old movies. My TV doesn't even have service. I use it just to watch movies on DVD."

"I like that." Deidre opened the shower door and climbed in. Her body was as gorgeous as he'd imagined, stunningly white, hard, and virtually hairless.

"What's this all about?"

"You wanted to see me naked so here I am?" She cocked an eyebrow. "No point in wasting water."

He wanted to reach out his hand and touch her but resisted. "This isn't a very safe space to get engaged."

"Engaged?"

"Physically coupled."

"You're not going to shag me in here, love."

Roland laughed to conceal embarrassment. "Certainly not. The cut on my foot smarts under my own weight, so holding you up..."

"Shhhhh." She touched her finger to her lips in case the shower had drowned out her sibilant. She handed him a bottle of shampoo and told him to wash his hair then she pumped out a palmful of shower gel and began to lather his body. "Raise your arms higher." He stood nearly motionless as soapy water cascaded over his shoulders and down his chest while she ministered to every inch of his body, including the bottoms of his feet.

"Nasty little puncture there. Now rinse out your hair." She got behind him to give him room to stand under the warm stream and caressed his back and buttocks.

By the time she was finished, his head was spinning, his hangover in full retreat.

"You have a gorgeous body. It begs to be touched." She looked at him with shy civility and began to wash herself. He stepped to the side and made way for her to stand under the stream and leaned against the opposite wall facing her, watching, trying not to slip on his heels. In the whole of his short life, Roland had never been more aroused, and he knew it. He had ceased to be Roland, son of so-and-so and so-and-so, born on such-and-such date in Saint Whatchamacallit's Hospital somewhere in the Milky Way. He was simply the man in Deidre somebody's shower watching Deidre rub fragrant soap all over her perfect white body with steam rising around them.

"You should see the look on your face." Words failed him yet. He drew her close and kissed her, not savagely as he might a temptress, but cautiously, inquiringly, exploratorily, with his lips only slightly parted.

"That's lovely."

"Why are you doing this?"

"I had to make sure you were perfectly clean."

"For what?" Roland believed he knew what for but wanted to hear her say it.

"Your reward."

"It was self-defense."

"Whose knife was that sticking out of his chest?"

"The dead man's."

"You mean the Glendale Butcher's." His lust was beginning to flag. "Killing a psychopath with his own weapon is a feat that warrants a show of appreciation."

"I like the way you think," was all he could manage.

"Consider this a cosmic reset. Last night you defeated the worst of evil, and this morning you've been blessed with the best of good."

"Golly." Roland had never used that expression before in his life, and he said it without irony.

"Not another word."

When she'd finished rinsing her hair she stepped out of the shower and set a dry towel on the lid of the commode. "Have a seat, Roland. You look a bit unsteady." Roland complied. Water dipped off his body onto the floor.

Deidre wrapped her hair in a towel and cinched it tight and then proceeded slowly, carefully, to straddle the prodigious grateful mute. "You'll be stretching the edge of my envelope, love, but let's give it a try." Roland reached around and took the small of her back in both hands to provide maximum support as she cautiously lowered herself onto him.

"That's good so far. Now hold still."

She regulated the depth and speed of their intercourse with precise muscular control and narrated each adjustment with squeals and sighs and rolling grunts while he kissed and tongued her breasts. By the time they were finished, the water from the shower was replaced with sweat. Neither of them had spoken a word, though both discovered guttural sounds Roland had never known. She draped her arms over his back and rested her forehead on his shoulder and caught her breath, satisfied, then she stood up and pulled him to his feet and they embraced in the tight confines then toweled each other dry.

"My neighbors probably heard that. I'm certain they're home."

"I hope you won't promise them it'll never happen again."

~~~~~

They lay side by side atop her spacious bed. He stared at the pale blue ceiling as though it were a movie screen upon which their just-completed coupling was projected.

"Your clothing will be dry in a little while."

He fought the urge to sleep, his hangover returning.

"I'll be out of here as soon as they're ready."
"I think I misjudged you."
"How so?"
"You're not such a dim bulb."
"What changed your mind?"
"You work in high-tech, for one thing. What's your job in video games?"
"I test the games for defects. Today is my ninety-day review. They'll either make me permanent or let me go."
"You must have to be pretty sharp to do that job."
"I'm the smartest person I've ever known."
"Are ya now?"
"Have you ever heard of Elon Musk?"
"Vaguely."
"He launches rockets and builds electric cars and is currently developing neurotechnology. He might be smarter than I am."
"Well, I'll let you two sort that out. Now rest your eyes."

The two slept until the dryer buzzed. He touched her hand and swiveled off the bed. She got up and brought back his dry warm clothes and stood naked in front of her mirror while he dressed. He wanted to take her again but knew that would seem greedy, ungrateful, would debase the gift he'd already received. She left the room and came back with a medical kit and cut off the wet bandage.

"The man you killed—did he say anything?"
"He asked me to call him an ambulance."
"I mean beforehand."
"He vowed to choke me with my own castration."

She gasped. "Well, I guess it's good we gave it proper use today."

She inspected the gash on his arm then led him to the living room and set him on the couch and went to a cabinet and brought back supplies. She disinfected and salved the wound and applied a fresh bandage then set his heel on the coffee table and knelt on the carpet and dressed the cut on his foot. Watching her there naked, on her knees, tending to his injury, projected him back to an earlier time, somewhere in Ancient Anatolia it seemed, where he imagined he was a warrior returned home from a victory, there to be pampered by a devoted maiden. The image seemed more memory than fantasy, and he shook it out of his mind. She stood up and put the first-aid kit away and went into the bedroom and came back wearing a bathrobe and holding a comb.

"Put on your boots and tell me how it feels."

He went to the door and pulled on his Laredos and raised himself up and down on the injured foot and nodded it felt ok. She took him by the shoulders and faced him away from her and combed his long damp hair until the comb went smoothly through.

"You truly are the best of the good."

"I take pleasure in healing. In uniform or out."

Chapter 3
September 30, 2016 - 7:45 AM

Roland pulled into the drive-through lane at the first McDonald's he saw and bought a sack of breakfast sandwiches and devoured the greasy fodder while he drove, until his stomach seized. He set an uneaten portion aside and finished his commute to the fractious chatter of sports talk radio. The parking lot was still half-empty when he pulled in, early for a change. Michael, his manager, was already there, as was Gina, the only coworker he genuinely liked and could call a friend. Since he was early, Roland sat in his car and checked his texts and voice messages. Unlike most of the electronically connected population, Roland suppressed all notifications on his mobile device so that he had to delve into it to retrieve communications. The only time the device sent an alert was for a phone call and, in that case, it didn't ring but simply vibrated; so, unless Roland was carrying it on his body or in close proximity, he wouldn't know when someone was trying to reach him. He scrolled through a few text messages he could ignore for now then found a single voice message, left that morning while he was engaged with Deidre. It required his immediate attention.

The voice was that of Taras Andruko, a Ukrainian who with his brother, Oleg, owned and operated the little grocery market on the corner down the street from his building. Taras kept things short and to the point.

"Roland, five small by Sunday or the door is closed. Peaches are a steal."

Andruko's Market fronted for a syndicated sportsbook from which the brothers earned a cut. Roland owed $4800 and had just been reminded that he was expected to pay ten percent of the debt every week for the privilege of being permitted to keep playing. *Five small* meant five hundred dollars—Taras was rounding up. If he didn't show up by close of business Sunday with the cash, the book would be closed to him, and he'd have to pay interest on top of the principle going forward until the debt was fully paid. Only then would he be allowed to bet again, and then under more stringent limits. The consequences of not paying were never discussed, and since Taras and his brother would not get their cut unless Roland paid his debt, Taras had thus far remained cordial.

"Christ," he inveighed, but not against The Redeemer. Roland knew he had only himself to blame. He rolled his eyes upward and frowned at the rips in the car's headliner before punching in the numbers for another call. A mechanical female voice answered and prompted him to leave a message at the tone.

"Chow, it's me. Let's do this thing today or tomorrow. I've got the latest beta on a thumb drive. Call me."

The die was cast.

~~~~~

The headquarters of Pacific Gameworks, a three-story affair entirely windowed in blue reflective glass, stood perched on a spit of land at the edge of the bay in Foster City, just south of the airport. Roland worked on the first floor in the Quality Assurance department, the most secure space in the building and also the largest, occupying roughly half of the floor. Once behind the keyless, code-lock door, one was treated to a workplace arrayed with massive wall-mounted flat-screen monitors on swivel arms, long tables laid out with smaller monitors, gaming consoles and their associated control devices. Also laptop computers, headphones, and whimsical personal items that signified who worked at the individual stations. The backs of the ergonomic chairs bore all sorts of custom insignias pasted there by their owners. There were no cubes and only one office, that of the QA manager, Michael, situated in one corner of the room.

Roland concealed his limp when he entered the floor by walking slowly to his chair and sitting down immediately. Gina was already there testing the latest beta version of a basketball game that was destined to shake the foundations—or shatter the backboard—of the video gaming world.

"Morning, Rolo." Gina was always in a good mood. "You're here pretty early."

"I've got my three-month review with Michael this morning."

"You look good. I'm glad."

"What's that supposed to mean?"

"You know what it means." She swiveled her chair and looked directly at him. "Why are you always deflecting? Just say thank you."

"Sorry, Gina. Thank you."

"Boooll-shit." She crooned a high-pitched tone as though he'd set off her bullshit detector.

Gina had an unblemished, ovular face, a dainty nose, a slightly crooked mouth, and a crop of auburn hair concealed under a baseball cap. She let a ponytail stick out the hole in the back. Her most striking feature was her green eyes, like thick glass, the color of a Jameson's Irish Whiskey bottle. Though not a head-turner, Gina was pretty enough to feel secure in her looks while letting her natural poise carry the load.

Roland turned his attention to his computer for a minute to log himself in.

"You wanna go to get lunch with me today? I'm thinking tacos." He toed the water.

"What happened to your arm?"

"Now who's deflecting?"

"You are. That's a big-ass bandage. It looks brand new."

"First let's talk about lunch."

She glanced sidelong at him. "What does lunch mean, exactly?"

"Comida solamente, senorita." Roland knew only a little Español but made up for his modest vocabulary with an exaggerated flair for pronunciation.

"When's your meeting with Michael?"

"No idea, but I bet not during the lunch hour."

"True."

"So?"

"First tell me about the arm."

"I guess what we have here is an old-fashioned Mexican standoff."

"I'm not sure what that means. No one ever says that in Iowa."

"Iowans watch movies, do they not?"

Gina googled it on her computer and read aloud. *"A confrontation between two or more parties in which no participant can proceed or retreat without being exposed to danger. As a result, all participants need to maintain the strategic tension, which remains unresolved until some outside event makes it possible to resolve."*

"Sounds about right."

"Ok, I'll go to lunch with you. There. Mexican standoff resolved." Then she added, "But only as a friend."

Roland looked over at her. "Were we ever more than that?"

"Asshole." She paused. "Forget it. I changed my mind."

"Sorry, Gina. You're right. I should shut up."

They worked in silence side by side for nearly half an hour. Roland was testing a golf game midway through its development and still full of bugs, so lately he'd spent more time logging defects than maneuvering through the lush green replications of Donald Trump's signature courses. The NBA title that Gina had been assigned was approaching completion, scheduled to be released just before Christmas and bound to set a new standard for graphical realism and tightness of player control.

Finally, Roland spoke.

"I had to fight off a burglar in my apartment last night. He had a knife."

Gina stopped what she was doing and swiveled around and looked at him squarely, as though to assess his sincerity.

"You're serious."

Roland held up his bandaged arm and gently pressed the inside of the forearm with the fingers of his other hand to show how tender it was.

"Yes. Big long gash."

"Whaaat haaaapened?"

"He came in through my back window while I was sleeping. I heard the window pop and jumped out of bed. I smashed a bottle over his head."

"Oh my God!"

"He got up off the floor and pulled out a knife."

"Jesus, Roland. You could be dead."

"That was his intention, or so he said."

"Is that the only place he cut you?"

"Yep, and it was my mistake. I cut myself actually when I deflected the blade."

"Then what?"

"I threw him into the wall and gave him a good beat down. Then I called the cops. They took him away." Such half-truths came easily to Roland.

"You better not be lying to me because I'm totally freaked out right now."

"You can come by and see for yourself. The glass and blood are still in my hallway. I haven't cleaned any of it up yet."

"What kind of bottle?"

Roland knew her well enough, knew how closely she'd observed his alcoholic decline since he'd joined the testing group three months ago. He cursed himself inwardly for divulging the identity of his weapon. To lie now would be to risk contradiction by the police report.

"Jack Daniels. A fifth."

"You just happened to have a fifth of Jack handy?"

"I keep it next to my pillow like a Teddy Bear."

"Are you trying to make me hate you? You might as well spit in my face."

Roland lowered his eyes. She was right. It was a thoughtless remark disguised, poorly, as a joke. He thought himself unworthy of her affection and, he observed with self-disgust, would just as soon dynamite whatever it was they'd been working toward than show any sensitivity over her concerns. Before he could formulate an apology, she preempted it.

"How can you ask me to lunch and then joke about being an alcoholic? I thought you were smart."

"I hate that word."

"Most alcoholics do."

"Forget the tacos."

"No. We're going for tacos if Michael hasn't fired you first, and you're going to tell me about last night. Start to finish. No bullshit either."

"WHY—" Then Roland lowered his voice. "Do you think I'm bullshitting you?"

"Because it doesn't sound like a burglary to me. Burglars don't fight. Have you played The Hobbit game we put out last year? Bilbo had the lowest combat rating."

"Bilbo carried a blade."

"There you go, deflecting again."

He held up his bandaged arm. "That's how I got this."

She gave a defeated harrumph. They both swiveled back to work. Roland's fingers began to twitch from alcohol withdrawal. He hadn't advanced to full-blown shakes as yet, but the fine motor skills necessitated by his occupation suffered noticeably on the days after he'd drunk excessively, increasingly more often in recent weeks. The cause of his trembling digits was not lost on Roland and being confronted about it by the woman to whom he was drawn, in whose presence he felt unworthy, compounded his agitation. He clenched both fists as if to physically resist an aggravating truth. The arm throbbed. It would be hard to concentrate on work.

After a few minutes, Roland spoke. "I can't say for sure."

"Can't say what for sure?"

"That the intruder was a burglar."

"What do the cops think?"

"They let me get back to bed after they took my statement. I was in no condition."

"So, what's next? I'll guess you'll have to testify."

"I have no idea. If I'm lucky I'll just clean up the mess in my apartment and eventually forget all about it." Roland hoped that would end the interrogation.

Gina wasn't convinced. "I couldn't forget something like that."

"I don't mean literally. I mean just let it recede until I stop thinking about it."

She laughed. "Yeah. The mind can drive you crazy."

He laughed with her. "I've got it worse than most."

The moment of shared jocularity helped Roland relax a bit and pay attention to the task at hand. The other testers had begun to take their stations.

Roland turned to Gina and whispered, "If anyone asks about my arm, I'm going to say that I cut it climbing over a fence to get a frisbee. I don't want to go into it anymore."

"Roger that. I'm glad to hear you're out there getting some exercise."

~~~~~

His computer knocked. The sound of knuckles rapping three times on a wooden door. That was the alert he had chosen for an incoming instant message. Michael was calling. The message read *Good morning, Roland. It's time for our sit-down.*

As Roland stepped into Michael's office gingerly on his tender foot to find out whether he would be canned today or, hopefully, converted to a regular full-time employee with all the applicable benefits and possibly stock options, it occurred to him that, had it not been for this morning's momentous probationary review, he would have closed the bar last night as usual and probably avoided the combat with the supposed Glendale Butcher or whoever the hell it was. The bottle of wine he chugged after the killing had made him just as drunk as he would have been had he stayed at the bar and lurched his way home, so the net consumption was the same. And now the anxiety of a job evaluation. The morning's hangover, sent in retreat by the sexual rush an hour earlier, had returned with renewed force.

Roland closed the door behind him and sat down, eyes forward and smiling. "Good morning, Michael."

"Good morning, Roland." Michael, mid-thirties, short-haired and outfitted with a dress shirt and loosely cinched tie, peered into his face appraisingly, a bit too long for Roland's comfort. "You look pretty good—well rested."

"Big day for me."

"If you'd shown up today looking trashed, I'd have shown you the door."

Roland wondered if it was a lie for him to let Michael believe he wasn't suffering from a hangover or if maybe he was foolish to think he was hungover since Michael was the one taking his measure.

"I need you to know I really want to keep this job."

"You took it easy last night so I wouldn't let you go—is that what I'm hearing?"

"Is it that close?"

"What do you mean?"

"A call—is it that close of a call?"

"Yes. My decision won't be a reflection on your job performance."

"You haven't decided yet?"

"I've decided not to decide."

Roland raised up a few inches in his chair and quickly sat back down. "You're keeping me on probationary status?"

"*Provisional.* We call it provisional."

"For how long?" He wanted to ask on what, if not his job performance, was the non-decision decision being based—though he knew the answer—and decided it was wise not to insult or antagonize Michael by playing dumb.

"Another three months." Michael held up his hand to stop Roland from protesting. "Look, Roland, let me be perfectly honest—I need you to finish the golf title. I can't hand it off to anyone else. You're an extremely observant tester. Not everyone on the floor has what it takes to spot the tiny defects that the golf audience will notice and complain about. Golf titles are like luxury autos—low volume but very discerning buyers. So as long as you keep showing up and submitting the kind of quality bug reports that challenge the developers, I'm going to keep you on for the good of the product."

"The game is supposed to ship before Christmas, so I figure it has to be signed off and sealed before the end of November. That's two months max."

"I'm not going to haggle with you, but I will make you a promise."

"Oh?" Roland let a hint of sarcasm seep through.

Michael leaned back and folded his arms. "Remember how you got this job."

"What do you mean by a promise?"

"I'm getting to that. First let's revisit how you got here."

"Of course I remember."

"More than a hundred applicants. A lot of them offered to work for free on a provisional basis just to get their foot in the door, but that's not how we operate around here."

"I see your point," said Roland.

"Do you?" Now it was Michael injecting sarcasm.

Roland lowered his chin and looked down. "You did me a favor."

"No. Not you. I did a favor for a friend of mine who vouched for you, who said you'd come out of a rough patch and needed a fresh start. And after your first few weeks, I thought I'd made a good decision."

"I'm grateful. I do a good job, you said so yourself. What more do you want?"

"Are you still going to meetings?"

Roland knew better than to lie. The job had come, indirectly, through Denny. The friend to which Michael referred was Victor, a kindly old-timer with nearly half a century of sobriety and Denny's own sponsor. In the parlance of Alcoholics Anonymous, Victor was Roland's *grand-*

sponsor. One might say that in the larger scheme of things the AA fellowship got Roland the job.

"I completed my court card."

"So that's a no?"

Roland nodded his head, not in assent to the question but in a show of broader understanding.

"I get it. If I go back to meetings, then I can keep my job."

"No." Michael shook his head. "If you stop showing up for work wrecked from the night before, then in three months' time I'll make you permanent."

"But I can work baked to the gills like half the guys on the floor."

Roland didn't use marijuana, but that was beside the point.

"As long as you smoke it in your car, it's none of my business. What happened to your arm?"

Roland glanced down at his wounded limb where it rested on the arm of the chair. He raised it slowly, chin-high. "Knife wound. Guy broke into my apartment last night."

"Uh-huh." Michael twisted his lips in a show of skepticism.

Roland nodded in the affirmative, not inclined to elaborate.

"Tell me why you want to keep this job."

Roland lowered his arm. "I'd like to make my way up to producer. I've got big ideas."

Michael nodded soberly then leaned back in his chair and looked at the ceiling then leaned forward again. "So, you fought off a burglar last night?"

"Gina doesn't think it was a burglar."

"Oh, why's that?"

"Because he brought a knife."

"So where is this non-burglar now?"

"Cooling his heels."

"Sounds like you think you're in a Humphry Bogart movie."

Roland, already perturbed with Michael for putting him in occupational limbo, was in no mood to convince him that he'd been involved in a violent confrontation last night. To divulge that the man he'd fought was in fact dead would have expanded the conversation beyond the meeting's original purpose.

"If you don't believe me, you can call the SFPD. They took him away."

Michael shook his head in resignation and set his hands flat on his desk.

"So, is there something I need to sign?"

"What do you mean?"

"An agreement—the extension of my probation."

Michael lifted his hands and pressed them together in the attitude of prayer and brought them to his chin. He appeared to be thinking, eyes pointed up, though his chin was still lowered. Then he pointed his eyes at Roland and spoke.

"You're here at my discretion, Roland. I want you to succeed. You're an excellent analyst. But, to be perfectly honest, if I didn't need you to finish the testing cycle on Trump Resorts, I'd have let you go already. You can call this a second chance. What happens after the product is finished will depend entirely on you. I'm not going to keep a drunk on staff."

Roland nodded his understanding and stood up. "I guess I'll get back to work then."

~~~~~

Without a word to Gina, Roland sat down in his chair and resumed his testing activities. The game consisted of six of Donald Trump's most picturesque courses, three in the US, two in Europe, and one in Dubai. At the moment, he was studying a graphical stutter he observed when the ball was soaring high against an ocean backdrop. His task was to record the defect and document the steps necessary to reproduce it. While he worked, he found himself distracted by the beauty of the course, Trump National Golf Club, snugged into the cliffs overlooking the Pacific Ocean in Rancho Palos Verdes, California, and thought he might like to take up golf one day.

After a few minutes, he spoke, not taking his eyes off the screen. "Have you ever golfed?" There were a few other testers in earshot and he kept his voice down so it was clear he was addressing Gina.

"I see you still work here."

"Not an answer."

"Yes. I have *ever* golfed."

"Not a friendly answer."

"I'm good at it. My dad taught me when I was young. Now tell me how it went in there."

"Can we talk about it at lunch?"

"What's to talk about?"

"He's extended my probation."

"Ouch. Did he say why?"

He gave her an incredulous look that one might give an intelligent person for asking a stupid question. "Naturally."

"Sorry. I'll wait to hear about it at lunch then."

Roland nodded and turned back to his screen. After a few minutes he spoke again, again without looking at her. "Maybe you can teach me sometime."

"Do you have any clubs?"

Roland shook his head. He realized that to ask a friend for golf lessons before you'd obtained clubs meant you weren't serious at all. A serious person would get the clubs first and then seek lessons.

"I guess I'd need help picking the right ones."

"I don't know." She showed him a pessimistic look. "Golf lessons? That would almost amount to a relationship."

"Tell you what—first let me get the clubs. Then I'll ask you again."

"Fair enough."

They worked in silence as the floor filled up with testers, producing the general din of a typical day. A few of his coworkers asked Roland about the arm and he told them he'd gashed it climbing over a fence to retrieve a disc during a game of ultimate frisbee. After a while, Gina got up and left the floor to use the restroom. He watched her glide to the door. She could sense his watching and turned around. He smiled. She shot him a phony frown and flashed her emerald eyes, stern but sympathetic. As soon as the door shut behind her, Roland quickly, but without hurrying, slid his thumb drive into her computer and with a few clicks of her vulviform mouse copied the pre-release version of the eagerly awaited NBA game onto the thumb drive, smaller than a pack of gum. He put it into his pocket and stood up to get a cup of coffee as a pretext to scan the room to see if anyone had spotted his larceny. Everyone appeared to be hard at work and none the wiser.

Gina returned to her station. "I thought you didn't like the coffee here."

"I need the caffeine today."

"Those power drinks in the vending machine work much better."

He shrugged and drank the black, sugarless liquid and, with an exaggerated gasp of satisfaction, pretended to like it. Then he donned his headphones and continued testing, as was the normal practice for the dozen or so analysts on the floor. Otherwise, the room, filled with an electronic clamor, was liable to bring on vertigo or some form of temporary insanity. But wearing cans over his ears made Roland feel isolated and freakish, amplifying the noise in his busy head. The golf game offered very little in the way of sound effects that could be checked for accuracy. Was the whoosh of the swing synchronized with the motion of the club? Did the sound of the ball hitting the bottom of the cup come too soon? Too late? Roland removed his headphones, sat back, and decided to enjoy a relaxing morning knocking the ball around the gorgeously manicured landscape before the room got too loud. Yes. He would have to learn how to play this decadent game in real life and enjoy the peace and serenity it might afford.

His computer knock-knock-knocked. Michael again. "Please come in." Roland froze. His fingers quivered over the keys. He wanted to reply, "What's up?" but that would be avoiding the request. Roland rose from his chair and walked slowly to Michael's office, kicking away a miniature foam basketball that lay in his path. The various toys and juvenile paraphernalia draped and strewn about the office, often freely tossed around the room—the trappings of a *cool place to work*—struck him as so much silliness, a pathetic attempt by young adults to perpetuate their childhoods after college and on into the workforce. He reflected on his former job, the one he'd left for this one. Processing fish fresh off the boats for sale at a fluctuating market price was a far more legitimate way to develop one's appreciation for the value of hard work, he thought, as he crushed a paper airplane with the sole of his boot. Still, he didn't miss it.

~~~~~

He sat. The chair was slightly warm from his first visit. Michael looked relaxed, even smug.

"The police just called—someone from the Homicide Division."

Roland couldn't conceal his surprise. He thought maybe Michael had summoned him to say he'd changed his mind and decided to terminate him immediately or, hope against hope, bestow upon him the coveted blue badge of a permanent employee. Or perhaps someone had seen him monkeying around Gina's computer and ratted him out. Not so.

"Yeah?" He sounded worried.

"He wants to see you right away." Michael reached out and handed Roland a sticky note. Roland read it. *Inspector Spelman—Homicide—Northern Station*. It held the address and the inspector's phone number as well.

"Did he say anything else?"

"Just a few questions to make sure he had the right Roland Hazzard?"

"Like what?"

"Did you have a cut on your arm."

"Why didn't you let me talk to him?"

"He didn't ask to talk to you."

"So that's it?" Roland held up the sticky note on one finger.

"He'd like you there in thirty minutes."

"I guess I'd better get going then. Thirty minutes is about how long it takes without traffic."

"Right. No need to come back. I'll pay you for the whole day."

"Thanks, Michael."

On his way out, he stopped to talk to Gina. "I've gotta run. We'll have that lunch next week."

"What's going on, Roland?"

"I don't know. The SFPD found out where I worked and called and wants me to come in—right now."

"Any idea why?"

"Whoever talked to Michael didn't say why, and I think I'm glad about that."

~~~~~

Roland jumped on the freeway and headed back to The City. He turned on the radio to slow his thoughts, but to no avail. He looked at the note still stuck to his finger. Inspector Spelman—*Homicide*. He said the word aloud again and again. Fair enough. A man was dead. It didn't mean murder. Necessarily. But his lie was exposed, to Michael anyway, and would be soon enough to Gina and the rest of the office. He bounced his forehead gently on the steering wheel as if that might help him understand why he'd felt the need to give Michael and Gina the impression that the police had taken away the intruder alive. They were bound to find the truth out anyway, even if the man were only an ordinary burglar. He recalled the look on Michael's face—a look of deep distrust and wished he'd waited until after he'd left the office to look at the note. To be caught in a lie was one thing, but to have to face the man who'd caught it the moment he knew you knew you'd been caught was a novel humiliation for Roland. And then to suffer the further indignity of Michael not even bothering to call him a liar—that was more than he could bear.

Chapter 4
September 30, 2016 - 11:45 AM

The City, as San Francisco denizens preferred to call it, lay just behind San Bruno Mountain, which loomed closer as Roland drove. Traffic was light as expected. He'd make it to the station within thirty minutes, plenty of time to calm himself down. He rocked back and forth like an autistic child. Still, his psyche squirmed. The voices on the radio made no sense, each word unrelated to the next. He switched it off and picked up his phone and placed a call to Denny.

Denny answered on the second ring. "I kinda thought I'd hear from you today. How's your head?"

"It's bad, Denny. Will you talk to me?"

"Come over now. You remember where I live?"

"I'm in my car on the way to North Beach Station. Some inspector called my work and told my boss to send me up."

"You still have that job?" Roland held his tongue against a violent outburst. *Didn't I just say I was called away from work? Are you determined to irritate me?* The sheer stupidity, or worse yet, accusatory nature of the question made him squeeze the wheel.

"Yeah, why wouldn't I?"

"Rumor has it you've been showing up late and drunk." *Rumor my ass.* He knew who'd sold him out. Michael had been talking to Victor.

"Can we talk about my work situation later, or never?" Roland's tone revealed his annoyance. He swallowed hard and leveled his voice. "I'm in a jackpot, Denny."

"What do you mean?"

"Serious trouble. I'm a little white ball bouncing around in a bingo hopper."

"I know what jackpot means. What I meant was *how do you know you're in one.*"

Roland pulled the phone away from his ear and held it at arm's length. To the motorist behind him it might have appeared that he was being yelled at and choosing not to listen, but it was just the opposite. Roland was keeping himself from telling Denny to shove his impertinent questions up his ass.

His effort to maintain emotional control caused him inadvertently to decelerate below the speed limit. In his mirror, had he looked, he'd have seen the man behind him, in a low-slung midnight blue Mercedes, toss up his hands in exasperation.

He returned the phone to his ear. "I don't." The question was, after all, eminently pertinent.

"What are you afraid of?"

"Do you have to be like this? Can you drop the sponsor routine?"

"Look, dipstick, you called me—TWICE now in less than a day—because, I think, somewhere in the fizzle and pop of your haywire brain you believe I can help you, that consulting with me will help you see things more clearly. The first thing you said was that you wanted to talk, but what has to happen is for you to decide to *listen*."

"You're right, Denny. I'm sorry. I'm listening."

"What are you worried about, Roland, specifically? Be very specific."

"The police. The homicide division."

"How can the homicide division hurt you?"

"I'm not sure, but I can't imagine a good outcome here." Roland continued driving very slowly and not in the rightmost lane where he belonged, but in the middle of the freeway, oblivious to traffic, aware only of the sound of Denny's voice and his own replies, unaware of the consternation welling in the driver behind him, though the man was tapping his horn.

"Let's walk through it. What happened after I hung up last night?"

"I called 911 like you told me to. Then I watched the asshole bleed to death."

The Mercedes changed lanes and passed him on the left. The driver thrust his hand through the moonroof and shook his middle finger at Roland for all the world to see. Roland hinged his foot down on the gas pedal, moved over, and fell in behind the peevish fellow in his splendid German car worth more than Roland had ever earned in his young life. The paint job alone cost more than the current bluebook value of Roland's redoubtable Japanese rattletrap. *World War Two did not end well*, he reminded himself.

"Okay, but that's not necessarily a problem. He broke into your place, right? In the middle of the night, right? You stabbed him with his own knife, right?"

"Yeah, but…"

"But what? Believe it or not, this kinda shit happens in the world. It just happened to happen to you. Are you hurt?"

"Only a little—a knife cut on my arm."

"Then you've got nothing to worry about, Roland, unless there's something you're not telling me." Roland had begun to calm down, his focus now directed on the prick in front of him trying to get away.

"I just can't imagine what a homicide inspector wants."

"Well, it's a homicide, dumbass, and they probably want to interview you again, when you're not loaded. Any drugs in your place? Could they have found any drugs?"

"No. I've told you I don't do drugs."

"And they didn't haul you in last night, I gather." Denny confirmed the obvious again.

"No. I went to bed and let them finish their business."

"And they processed the crime scene."

"Yes—his crime, not mine."

"You were probably too loaded to be interviewed."

"I wasn't too drunk to talk to you, was I?" Roland neglected to mention that he guzzled a bottle of wine after the call. "They took my statement."

Roland narrowed his vision on the Nazi speeding forward. Fresh haircut, dark suit, getting away. He set the phone on the passenger seat next to the half-eaten Sausage McMuffin and maneuvered to keep up. He could hear Denny speaking.

"No big deal. Just meet with the inspector and tell the truth. How could you possibly be in trouble over this? Your mind is just trying to fuck with you."

Roland picked up the phone. "Okay okay. I'll just see what happens."

"You can't control it, anyway, can you?"

"You're right."

"And you'll probably get your name in the paper."

"A few reporters buzzed me out of bed this morning."

Roland was driving fast now and needed to end the call to maintain his hot pursuit of the Spawn of Satan.

"Don't worry about that. Don't think about anything," continued Denny. "Just do…"

Roland interrupted him. He'd set his phone in his lap in keep both hands on the wheel. "YES! YES! YES!" he shouted. "THE NEXT INDICATED THING. YOU GUYS NEVER QUIT."

"And pause before you act. Don't just react."

"I GET IT DENNY. HAVE TO PUT THE PHONE DOWN NOW. TRAFFIC GETTING HAIRY."

Denny kept talking. "And get to a meeting. You know where they are. And call me after you talk to the inspector."

Roland picked up the phone. "Thanks Denny I will I promise," then dropped it back in his lap.

"Don't promise, just do it. When someone says they promise…" Roland hit the button to end the call and tossed the device back onto the passenger seat.

The freeway narrowed to three lanes as it ran the gap between the mountain and the bay, bunching the cars together as it fed the flow of traffic into The City. Roland cranked down his window, changed lanes and nudged the Sentra forward until he was crawling side by side to the right of his enemy. The man looked over with his eight-hundred-dollar prescription sunglasses and shook his head with a disgusted smirk. Holding his stare, Roland reached over with his right hand, wadded the Sausage McMuffin into its wrapper, switched it to his left, and with a quick flip of his wrist tossed it into the open moonroof of the luxury sedan. The sandwich came free of its wrapper and broke apart, the bulk of it striking the driver's face, the rest strewing across the front of his shirt and into his lap.

Herr Benz, in a panic, swerved and almost collided with the car on his left and came to halt. Roland continued forward, found a gap between cars, and drove down the restricted emergency lane to the next exit. When he came to the light at the end of the ramp, he checked his mirror to be sure that he hadn't been followed then took his time getting back onto the freeway, exhaling to enjoy the adrenal euphoria of his herculean triumph. A flaming home was collapsing behind him, his hair was singed and smoking, and he carried a squalling baby safely pressed to his chest to the outstretched arms of its hysterically grateful mother. Denny was right. There was nothing to fear. *Let inspector whoeverthefuck snap a bag over my head and force me into an electric chair. Guide my hand to the panel. I'll flip the switch myself. The whole municipal grid will blow.*

Chapter 5
September 30, 2016 - 12:15 PM

By the time he found a place to park, it was a quarter past noon, late if the thirty-minute target mentioned by Michael was firm. But for Roland, the clock had stopped. He took his time walking to Northern Station, paused in front of Lucky Spot, a neighborhood hole-in-the-wall, and considered ducking in for a quick double. Not to relieve anxiety or muster courage—he felt as calm as a demolitionist-in-training disarming a look-alike bomb—but only to cure his lingering hangover, the rush from his battle on the freeway having worn off. He extended his right hand and studied its reflection in the window. It was steady, but not perfectly steady. He checked his face in the glass and ran his fingers twice through his hair. The door was open, but the place sounded empty. His mouth watered at the thought of a slug of whiskey. He ran his tongue across his lips. The image of his own thirsty face smacking in the window of Lucky Spot took him aback. Call it a moment of sanity. Roland shook his head no, concluding it would be unwise to show up at the cop shop at half past noon smelling of liquor. The drink could wait. He leaned his head through the doorway and took a deep quaff of the fermented air through his nostrils to tide him over. Then he moved on.

Arrows led him to the entrance of the station. What lay beyond its darkly tinted doors concerned him not. Roland paused to regard the butt of an unfinished cigarette poking erect from a sand-filled ashtray set atop the cover of the concrete trash container at the end of the walkway. The filter bore the red lipstick of the woman who'd lit it, taken a few quick drags, and jabbed it in the sand before going inside. True, he thought, it could have been a man, or a woman with a penis, or even a man with a vagina. The rapidly evolving categories were hard to keep track of. He remembered that the only time he'd entered this building he'd worn handcuffs and been led through the back door directly into the booking room. That arrest had started outside a bar when he'd invited a red-lipsticked woman outside for a cigarette. Roland patted his pockets for a lighter he knew wasn't there, and there was no one around to ask for a flame. Smoking was a dying practice. Sadly, he turned away from a perfectly good Salem that no one would ever finish and entered the building.

The officer standing behind the desk, tall fit and trim in his well-pressed uniform, followed him with both eyes the moment he stepped into the lobby. The man, Roland observed, had a friendly enough demeanor, though his steady gaze informed the rangy visitor that he was not impressed with his greater size and would stop him with a bullet if he had to.

"What can I do for you, sir?"

"I'm here to see Inspector Spelman."

"What's your name?"

"Roland Hazzard."

"The officer picked up the phone and pressed a button. "He's here." After listening for a few seconds, he nodded and hung up. "The inspector will be right out."

Roland nodded and began to whistle contentedly as he turned around to view the formal portrait photographs of high-ranking current and former mayors and chiefs that arrayed one wall of the waiting area. After a minute or two, the inspector assigned to handle the city's most recent homicide, its most newsworthy in decades, walked up behind him and interrupted his musical interlude.

"Mister Hazzard?"

Roland turned abruptly and instinctively held out his hand. The inspector shook it. Roland looked at Spelman's face to assay it for any predisposition or judgment and nodded and stop whistling.

"Follow me." The inspector led the way to his office and closed the door behind them.

"Please have a seat, Mister Hazzard."

His thirst remained forefront. He hadn't taken water since he'd left Deidre, and the few gulps of coffee he'd taken at the office did more harm than good. The hangover pleaded for water.

"Can I get a glass of water?"

"How 'bout a Coke?"

Without waiting for an answer, the inspector reached into a small fridge behind his desk and pulled out a red can. Who wouldn't want a Coke instead?

Inspector William Spelman of the SFPD was a mostly bald, shiny-skinned Jamaican who looked about fifty but was in fact sixty. He retained only a slight accent, having resided in the States for nearly forty years. Roland could tell he was Jamaican by the way he elongated the 'o' in 'Coke,' caressing the vowel.

"That'll do." Roland accepted the can and opened it.

"Here. Use this to wipe off the top." Spelman handed him a napkin. "I should have done that for you."

Roland circled the top of the can with the napkin before opening it. He did not say thank you, as he normally would have.

"What should I call you, sir?"

"Whatever you like, but before we're through today, I hope you'll want to call me Bill."

Roland drained the Coke in one tilt, wiped the dribble from his chin with the napkin and stuffed it partially wadded into the spout of the can so that it puffed out like a bloom. He set the object back on the desk as an example of modern art. All the while, he kept his eyes locked on the spectacles of his genteel interrogator.

"Can you tell me why I'm here, Inspector?"

"You're aware that you killed a man last night."

Not a good start. The inspector didn't appear to be stupid. On the contrary, he bore the mien of an intelligent party. Furthermore, the crucifix on his wall gave Roland a hunch that the man he faced was, more likely than not, well educated.

"He was dead when the officers arrived. You must have known that."

"That's good. Just making sure you remembered. How's the arm?"

"It's fine. Am I under arrest? Should I get a lawyer?"

"That's the wrong direction to take this, Mister Hazzard. But, to answer your questions—No, you're not under arrest. You're free to go at any time. A lawyer won't be necessary, though some sort of professional advice might be wise as this thing plays out."

"Fine. So back to my first question—why am I here?"

The inspector picked up the file folder on his desk and held it up for Roland to see. "I want to add your statement to the casefile."

"I gave a statement to the officers last night. You should know that too."

"Do you remember what you said?"

"Why wouldn't I?" Roland's memory was only a little fuzzy.

"Look, Mister Hazzard, I'm a patient man. The chief assigned me to this case because he knew you would be difficult and that I possess—how do I say it?—a suitable temperament. But my patience has its limits. If you persist in playing the hardass we can end this interview right now and you can muddle through on your own. The SFPD has no obligation to help you."

"To help me? To help me how? Just tell me what this is about."

"You're about to become a famous man."

"So, it's true—the motherfucker was a serial killer."

Inspector Spelman removed his eyeglasses and set them on the desk so he could look Roland directly in the eyes.

"I don't like that sort of language, especially not in my office, no matter who it refers to."

Roland shot another glance at the crucifix mounted above the window behind the inspector.

"My apologies, sir. But is it true?"

"How did you come by that information?"

"A bunch of reporters ambushed me outside my building this morning. They were pretty excited. They asked me if I knew he was a serial killer, or if I knew the serial killer. I'm not sure which, maybe both. They were talking pretty fast."

"It looks like things are moving faster than I thought. We haven't spoken officially with the press, so someone must have leaked it. Yes. He was a serial killer—The Glendale Butcher, Sammy the Butcher, a few other names I think."

Roland tugged on his earlobe. "I'm sorry, Inspector Spelman, but I'm still confused. You said the SFPD is under no obligation to help me—what does that mean? What sort of help do you imagine I might need? And why do you want another statement?"

"Because of how you behaved last night."

Roland blinked. A jolt of fear raced through his nerves.

"I didn't break the law," was the best he could come up with.

"You acted like a drunken fool—can we agree on that?"

At least Bill wasn't asking about how the knife wound up in the intruder's chest. "Ok. Let's say that's true. What difference does it make?"

"It's part of the public record—the 911 transcript, the police report. Are you starting to get the picture, Roland?"

"No. I think the serial killer thing is a bit more newsworthy than, I dunno, *how I treated the civil servants*. Anyway, I'm here. I came like an obedient citizen. What now?"

"The chief asked me to get your statement—your sober statement. It's normal procedure for a serious case like this to do a follow-up interview when a critical witness was impaired at the crime scene." Bill removed a sheet of paper from the folder and held it up. "This," he said, "is short on details."

"Oh, how so?" Roland bristled like a superior given direction from a subordinate.

"Are you saying you won't give one? Because if you won't give one, you can leave right now."

"I just want to understand the rationale, Inspector, and the urgency. Why did you tell my boss I had thirty minutes to get here if all you wanted was a written statement?"

"There's a press conference at two. The chief needs time to read it."

"You're telling me that's normal procedure." Roland dropped the defensive tone, suddenly curious.

"It is not. But if what you say now doesn't match what you told the officers last night, then the department can't stand behind you."

"Which means what?"

"That the chief is not pleased. If your statement today lines up with the police report, then at the very least…"

"Excuse me—not pleased? I killed a prolific murderer. How is he not pleased?"

"Again, it's your behavior—your blatant disrespect for authority. If your statement lines up, then at least he can call you a reliable person. Your arrest a few months ago—the circumstances surrounding that—added to how you acted last night, puts you in a very poor light."

"I fail to see how that matters."

"I appreciate that. Again, you're free to go. I've explained your situation as well as I can."

Roland mulled it over, shifted in his chair, crossed and uncrossed his arms, and decided to delay his decision. He looked up at the crucifix again and gestured toward it with his wounded arm. "Is that thing kosher?"

"This hardly seems time to jest?"

"I'm serious as bunions. I thought religious symbols were a big no-no in government buildings."

"You can file a complaint at the front desk on your way out." Bill stood up as though to escort Roland from the room. Now he must decide. Truth is, he had decided already. The curiosity presented by a Jamaican homicide inspector in the SFPD was too great to dismiss. Besides that, the man was kind and seemed interested in Roland's welfare. To walk away as superior to the situation, thought Roland, would be unwise, a missed opportunity perhaps. He decided to stop pretending that he couldn't care less.

"Ok then. I'll prove I remember what happened last night if that will make the department happy."

"Good." Bill picked up a yellow pad and two pencils from his desk. "I've got a room where you can write in private."

"Do you have any cigarettes? I like to smoke when I write."

Bill went into a drawer and pulled out a pack of Marlboro then picked up Roland's empty Coke can. "This way."

Roland followed the inspector to an interview room that locked from the outside. Bill set the legal pad, the sharpened pencils, two cigarettes and a book of matches on the table. "No one will bother you in here." He set the Coke can on the table. "You can use this for the ashes."

Next to the table stood three chairs, one outfitted with shackles. Roland pulled one of the normal chairs next to his writing supplies. Before he sat down, he turned to the inspector, now with a tone of complete seriousness.

"This room makes me want to call a lawyer."

"How many times do I have to say it, Roland? You're free to go at any time. This is for your benefit."

"Can I see the police report first, before I write?"

"That would make your statement worthless. If you don't remember what happened, just say so and we'll conclude that you were in a blackout. But that won't do you much good. I've made a copy of the police report to give you when you've finished here."

"You swear on the blood of Christ, on your mother's immortal soul, that this is not a trap?"

"I will not. If you can't understand how much you stand to benefit from making a sober statement, then you might as well leave now. I'm through trying to persuade you."

Bill held the door open, poised to leave, waiting for Roland to sit or exit the room. Roland sat.

"What do I do when I'm done?"

"Knock on the door."

Roland took up a pencil and began to write, making sure his hand was legible. He delivered his narrative slowly and sparely. *I went to bed at exactly 1:15 AM. I know because the only light in my bedroom is the red numbers on my clock.* He continued methodically, in sequence. *When I heard him come in, I put on one of my boots. He was in the hallway outside my bedroom before I could find the other boot.* Then he began to fudge. *The light from his flashlight was enough that I saw the bottle on my dresser and picked it up.* The next lie made perfect sense. *When he spotted me at my doorway, he rushed me, and I hit him over the head with the bottle.* Roland proceeded to describe the fight much as it had happened until he reached the moment where he committed murder. *I grabbed the handle of the knife and we struggled for it. I managed to turn the point toward him and force it into his chest.* The rest wrote itself. He ended with *I greeted the officers in front of my building and directed them to my apartment before seeking attention for my arm.* He did not mention the call to Denny or setting a new personal best for downing a bottle of wine or the dialogue with his victim, other than to say that *the man said his name before he died. Samuel Ka-say-bee-an.*

Roland read his statement over while he finished his second cigarette and felt satisfied that it would not contradict the police report. Then, as an afterthought, he decided to write a separate statement, one to keep for himself. He tore a page from the back of the pad lest the inspector detect the impression it would leave on the page behind it. He wrote *I killed him because he deserved it.* There it was, the truth he could not acknowledge to the civil authorities, let alone to the world. He folded the page twice and slid it into his pocket. If God exists, thought Roland, at least He knows I have not deceived myself.

~~~~~

Roland rapped on the door with the his knuckles. A few seconds later a young officer pulled it open.

"Mister Rolawwwland Hazzard, the man of the hour."

Roland sensed that the officer wanted to shake his hand. Roland smiled instead of reaching out. He had no idea what to say so what fell out of his mouth felt to him like an accident.

"Ha, my first fan."

"We're just glad you're alive."

"Thanks. The bad guys don't stand a chance."

"In San Francisco, bad guys rule. They have their own t-shirts."

The officer walked him back to Inspector Spelman's office. Roland set the pad and pencils on Bill's desk.

"That was fast."

"The fight lasted only a few minutes, so there wasn't much to write."

The inspector read from the pad.

"You have excellent penmanship."

"Too bad all the monasteries are shuttered. I'd fit right in."

Inspector Spelman shook his head and looked like he was mulling over a reply but let it go.

"If you want to go back to work, don't let me keep you." Roland got the impression that the inspector was toying with him.

"You promised me a copy of the police report."

"Of course. You'll need to read it before you call your parents. I don't imagine you've done that yet."

"My parents? Why do you care about my parents?"

"Because I'm a parent. If my son was about to become national news, I'd like to know before…"

"How bad is it?"

"In and of itself, not so bad. It says you were drunk and uncooperative. But then there's the 911 tape and your prior arrest record. Altogether it's a pretty unflattering picture. The press can be vicious."

"Let me have a look." Roland reached out a hand and Bill gave him the report and watched him scan the first page then the second. As soon as he finished, he looked up. "Tell me about Kasabian."

"That's not his name. His name was Barsamian. Samuel Barsamian. You got that wrong."

"I'm sure I didn't."

"How can you be sure? You'd had a lot to drink."

"I have an excellent memory. Born with it. Off the charts."

"You have a photographic memory?"

"It's in that range, yes. Besides, I made a mental note of it."

"Mental note?"

"Casaba melon. I do that, especially when I hear an unfamiliar name. He said *Kasabian*. My brain said *casaba melon*."

Bill looked at Roland's statement. "I see you mentioned it here at the end, but I assure you that's not his name. If he said that, he was lying."

"Tell me about him."

"I don't know much more than you can find on the internet. Armenian kid from Glendale, California somehow got it in his mind to start throat-cutting young women. Started in his hometown then took his act to Glendale, Arizona. Then he headed to New Mexico and butchered a few women in a place called Glendale Canyon. The New Mexico murders cemented his nickname. Before those, they were also calling Sam the Butcher and a few other things."

Roland remembered the flurry of news about those murders and the fear it engendered in young women in the western states. Several had joined the campus karate club where he'd been an instructor to learn how to ward off a knife attack.

"That was three years ago. Nothing since then?"

"No. Not as far as we know. He managed to disappear. The FBI assumed he fled to Mexico."

Roland felt relaxed now, not under suspicion or scrutiny, satisfied that his statement matched what he told the police. If the inspector could be trusted, that's all that mattered. He decided to stick around and talk to the man since he had nowhere to go except back to his apartment to deal with the bloody mess.

"I'm wondering why he broke into *my* place. That doesn't seem to fit his pattern."

"I'm wondering why he gave you a phony name while he was bleeding out. In my experience, people generally tell the truth when they think they're dying."

"You have a lot of experience in that area?"

"More than anyone in this department. I worked Chicago's Southside for years. This job practically feels like retirement."

"You said the chief assigned you this case because your *temperament* would help you deal with a guy like me."

"Is that a question?"

"Yeah. How would your experience dealing with gangbangers in Chicago make you the right man to interview me? I've committed no crime."

"You've made a careless logical leap there, Roland. My guess is that the chief knows I have a calming influence on people, but you'd have to ask him. As for the killing…"

"I don't want to meet the chief."

"Then I'd suggest you be on your way." Bill took a card from his jacket and extended it to Roland. "If you ever feel like talking, don't hesitate."

Roland stood up and took the card. "Thank you. But I'm not sure what we'd have to talk about."

Someone tapped on the door and didn't wait for an answer before entering the room. Bill stood up for the visitor.

"Chief Maruyama, meet Roland Hazzard."

Roland turned around to face Takahara Maruyama, chief of the San Francisco Police Department. He towered over the civil servant and bent down to shake his hand. "Good afternoon, Chief."

"Sit down sit down." the Chief spoke in a cordial but hurried voice. Bill handed him Roland's handwritten statement.

"Is it cogent?"

"Yessir. And it corroborates."

The chief removed his octagonal hat and placed it on the inspector's desk then backed up until his shoulders braced the adjacent bookshelf. It appeared that we wanted to regard both men as he addressed the room. Roland noted the perfect tailoring of his pressed navy-blue uniform, replete with patches, gold braids, and the emblems of his rank. Short as he was in stature, the chief wore the demeanor of a man in charge and might as well have just stepped off the bridge of a World War II Japanese battleship. Chief Maruyama's perfect American English, then, stood in stark contrast to the scenes Roland conjured from his mental inventory of old war movies. The man stood stalk-straight and let his arms hang loosely at his sides.

"Mister Hazzard, let me congratulate you. You made a few of my highly trained professionals look like idiots."

"That was not my intention, sir."

"Perhaps not in retrospect, but that hardly matters. What you say sober about what you did drunk is, may I say, unreliable at best. The fact of the matter is that you appear to have acted within your rights when you thrust a knife into that man's chest."

"Excuse me, sir. Not *a* knife—*his* knife."

The chief looked over to Bill. "Have you gotten through to him yet?"

"Not all the way. I was making progress. Progress, not perfection."

The chief turned back to Roland and continued.

"Let me speed things up a bit, *Mister* Hazzard. Regardless of the provenance of the knife, under ordinary circumstances I would put you through the paces. My position would be that you acted recklessly and probably with malice. I'd publicly acknowledge your history as a local drunk and abuser of women…"

"ABUSER OF WOMEN!" Roland startled himself with his spontaneous outburst.

"That's how it looks to me. Your recent arrest for drunk and disorderly includes a statement from witnesses at the bar who claimed that you were making unwanted advances toward a certain vulnerable female. And your treatment of our female dispatcher last night can be taken as misogynistic. Then we have the woman in your building who spoke to the police, who you verbally abused. The press would round out the edges and play with the perspective and render you as a fully three-dimensional antediluvian throwback."

"Antediluvian?"

"It means…"

"I know what it means. Primitive. Before Noah's flood."

"And I even might have referred your case to the DA for manslaughter charges. It probably wouldn't stick, but I might have put you through that process."

"Because I made your people look like idiots? Is that how the justice system works around here? Malicious prosecution? I bet I could sue."

"Fuck with me at your peril, Roland Hazzard." Chief Maruyama looked over at Bill as though to acknowledge the inspector's objection to profanity. "I still have options. You *want* me not to despise you."

"What can I do to prevent that? I thought I'd crossed a forbidden line."

"Has Inspector Spelman explained the situation to you?"

"Yes. He says I'm free to go."

Bill cleared his throat to get Roland's attention. "There's a news conference at two, and the press is going to ask a lot of questions about you—about the *hero* who ended the career of the Glendale Butcher."

Chief Maruyama chimed in. "I'm not going to go along with the hero business. The media will get its hands on the 911 tape and the police report. It won't take them long."

"They already know who I am."

Chief Maruyama looked at Bill. "What's he talking about?"

Roland shot the chief a glance that said he didn't appreciate being referenced in the third person.

"Reporters showed up outside Roland's building this morning. That's what Mister Hazzard told me."

Roland kept his eyes on the chief.

"Yes. That's what Mister Hazzard told him. And they knew Mister Hazzard's name, first and last. And they knew the dead guy was a serial killer."

Chief Maruyama shook his head miserably at Bill. "You don't know who leaked it, do you?"

"No. The hospital was swarming last night. Could have been a lot of people."

Roland smiled and felt like blurting out that he ran into a nurse that morning who knew the score but thought better about having to back up that assertion with details. Still, he insisted on keeping his voice in the proceedings.

"Excuse me, sir." Roland stared at the chief. "What do you want from me here? I don't have any control over the press. No more than you it seems."

"Tell the truth."

His chair suddenly felt too small, like it was squeezing in on him. He wanted to stand up and display his full height over the self-important authority figure and ask him where he got off implying that he wasn't telling the truth, but he realized that the chief had been careful with his words. For Roland to infer an accusation of dishonesty in a simple call for *the truth* would cast doubt on his veracity thus far. He turned to Bill with a look of perplexed consternation then turned back to the chief and cocked his head to one side.

"Why would I do otherwise?"

"No need to get defensive," said Inspector Spelman.

"Oh no?" said Roland. Then, to reciprocate the third-person treatment, prodded. "What does he mean, *tell the truth?*"

"You murdered him. I can't say that publicly, but the facts don't point to self-defense."

Roland stood up chest out and pressed his shoulders to the door. "Is that why you called me down here?" He addressed both men. "To accuse me of murder?"

"Settle down, Roland. There's murder and then there's *murder.*"

"I didn't do either."

Chief Maruyama took his octagonal hat from Bill's desk and put it on. What he was about to say apparently required him to be in full uniform. "Listen, kid, I'll break it down for you. If I come out this afternoon and badmouth you, it will look like I'm not glad the Glendale Butcher is dead. You lucked out. But don't think for a second that we believe your bullshit self-defense story. You broke two ribs, shattered his jaw, gave him a brain bruise—a *subdural hematoma*—about this big." The chief made a circle with his thumb and forefinger about the size of a silver dollar. "There's no doubt he was unconscious or nearly unconscious when you stabbed him in the chest, unless you beat him about the head immediately *after* that. Man your size—no way he had the power to attack you with the knife after the beating you gave him. But that doesn't matter, does it? Even if I thought I could prosecute you for murder, it wouldn't make sense. You lucked out, son. You murdered a most-wanted murderer."

Roland kept his eyes locked on the chief the whole time he was speaking. Not a flaw to be found in his logic. For Roland to open his mouth in denial would indict his own intellect, but he had to say something, for mute acquiescence was unmanly.

"The man said—no, he *declared* with very precise enunciation—that he was going to *kill me* and then he took a whack at me. That's *after* I told him to pick up his flashlight and prybar and leave. The good guys won. That's truth enough for me."

Chief Maruyama took a step toward the door then stopped to wait for Roland to move aside and let him pass. Roland crossed his arms.

"Since you can't publicly accuse me of murder without charging me, what are you going to say?"

"That your statement at the crime scene was sloppy due to your drunkenness and that we interviewed you this morning and have since found no cause to call this anything but a justifiable homicide. The department will not applaud your actions."

Roland turned the handle and opened the door a few inches and stepped aside as though he was in charge of the egress and content now to allow the chief to leave the room. "I'm sorry I put you in such a tough spot, sir. Next time I need a body removed I'll remember to be more friendly."

Chief Maruyama left without a reply and clicked off down the hall. Roland closed the door and returned to his chair and looked at the inspector.

"So, where were we?"

Bill frowned. "You're far too cavalier."

"I don't appreciate being treated like a criminal when…"

Bill interrupted. "When you should be lauded as a hero?"

"I didn't peacock in here like a hero, but the officer who let me out of the interview room treated me with respect at least."

"Word got around about your snoring."

"My snoring?"

"The forensics team could hear you snoring through your door while they processed the scene. You'll be remembered by the rank and file not just for who you killed but as the guy who called the police to, as you put it, *have a body removed*, so you could get back to bed."

"That's not how it happened exactly."

"Legends have a way of condensing themselves."

Still suffering from alcoholic dehydration, Roland asked for another Coke and got it and thanked the inspector and opened it and drank it down.

"So, what's your story? You were telling me you came to Chicago via Jamaica. How would you distill your legend?"

"We're not so unalike as you might think."

"I doubt it. Apart from our XY chromosomes."

Bill reached into a drawer and took out a manilla folder and opened it flat on his desk. It contained several newspaper clippings. He unfolded one of them gingerly, almost reverently, as a medievalist would handle a precious manuscript.

"I've had my name in the newspaper too—like you will soon. But when I was the story, there was no internet. You, young man, are about to enter a world that magnifies your flaws and never forgets them."

Roland raised himself forward out of the chair and leaned over to peer at the open news page, not so much to read it, but to show curiosity. "What did you do?"

"I killed a few men—notorious men, wicked men." Roland could see in the inspector's face that he was remembering.

"You're shitting me. Let me see."

Bill spun the folder around so Roland could read for himself the frontpage story in a yellowed edition of *The Gleaner*, a Jamaican daily. It showed a photograph of a young, uniformed Constable Spelman under the headline: *Hero Cop Clips Coke's Assassins*. The article gave an account of how the rookie officer managed to outwit two killers sent to his home by their boss, Lester Coke. A drug kingpin, Coke distributed cocaine and marijuana on an international scale. Spelman had uncovered evidence against Coke that could send him to prison. An arrest was imminent. Spelman's testimony would be critical. As a precaution, Spelman trained his parrot to squawk when a stranger entered his dwelling and dug a deep pit just inside his front door and set a bear trap at the bottom and covered the pit with a rug.

On the day of the incident, the parrot raised a racket. Spelman crawled through a back window. He heard the trap snap shut, followed by the cries of the intruder. Instead of going back inside, he hid in the bushes and ambushed the partner, shooting him dead. Then he went inside and killed the assassin still stuck in the trap.

"Nice work. Where'd you get the bear trap? There aren't any bears in Jamaica."

"An antique from the slave trade."

"Oh." Roland closed the folder and slid it back to its owner. "That makes sense."

"Provided slavery makes sense."

"It's probably older than marriage."

"Civilization needed only the one."

Roland thought about that and figured it was the inspector's office and not his place to offer any further wisdom on such a serious topic.

"So, did you testify against this Lester Coke character?" Roland lifted his can to show the logo. "Is that his real name?"

"Yes. I think of him every time I open a can."

"Where is he now?"

"Dead. Burned alive in his jail cell prior to extradition to the US. He had the goods on a lot of powerful people."

"You put him there? Your police work?"

"Noooo." He lapsed into his native vowel. "That was later, 1992. I got him as far as a mistrial, a Jamaican mistrial, which means he bought his way out."

"So that's why you're here—you had to skedaddle."

"My life was forfeit once he was released."

Roland dragged his fingers through his hair and transported himself back to Deidre's shower, nodding the while, showing a faint smile.

"I see. So you came to the USA?"

"Yes. As a refugee. The only asylee from Jamaica in 1985. The rules were much stricter then."

"Let me ask you—the guy in the pit with his leg in the trap—you just shot him? Hiro Hito comes barging in here calling me a murderer—sounds to me like you're the murderer. Heck, that bear-trapped-pit-under-a-rug stunt would put you in hot water here in the states, even if you didn't execute him."

"Jamaica was like the Wild West, still is to some extent. Someone breaks into your home—all bets are off. British Castle Law."

"I see. There's murder and then there's *murder*." He glanced up at the crucifix. "I wonder what our Lord and Savior would have to say about that."

"My conscience took a harder beating in Chicago than in Jamaica, more about things I didn't do than things I did; but I didn't call you in here to talk about me, about my life. I will say that the remedy I used against my moral struggles turned out to be my worst enemy."

"Don't tell me—you drank. Now I see why the chief picked you to be my investigator."

"The chief has no idea that I'm a recovered alcoholic."

Roland had no reason to believe the inspector was lying, but he couldn't suppress his glib incredulity. "Dogged by the cosmos once again."

"The cosmos leaves no stone unturned."

"You really believe that? Fate brought us together? Sounds more like Caribbean voodoo than Christianity."

"It was you who dragged in the cosmos. But I will tell you one thing I believe from my years working among criminals and crime fighters—and they are sometimes one and the same. Every crisis large or small forces a decision, and our decisions in those moments lead us toward or away from who we were meant to be. For the alcoholic, the bottle itself is a crisis, and his decision to drink or not to drink comes before all other decisions. People who still have the power of choice can achieve great things while drinking and using. Take artists and musicians for example. But at a certain point, the power of choice begins to weaken, and the alcoholic knows in his soul that to continue will destroy his day, then his week, then eventually his life. Will destroy his ability to achieve what he was gifted to do. Young man like you still has the choice."

Roland had heard this spiel before said in various ways in the rooms of AA, but here in the inspector's office it somehow carried more force than before, and he was defenseless to rebut it.

"So that's it then? Go forth and drink no more?"

The inspector shook his head and rolled his chair back a foot or two but didn't stand up. It was clear to Roland that the conversation would soon be over.

"I cannot make that decision for you. Just do the next indicated right thing." Twice in the space of an hour, thought Roland, the same venerable aphorism from recovery scripture.

"Right now, Inspector, I can't say I know what that is."

"At the risk of sounding like a sponsor—*call your parents*. They're bound to hear about this on the news, and I think you owe it to them to soften the shock."

A minute ago, Roland had waived off that suggestion as one would a housefly, but now he knew the inspector was right. Still, the prospect of having to call home, and soon, sent another jolt of panic through his limbs. He hadn't spoken to his parents in weeks.

"I guess I'd better get to it then."

"I've got a hunch you come from a good family, that your parents raised you well."

"You're right. All three of us. My brother, my sister, and me."

"What happened to you?"

"My mother says I came out with a twinkle in my eye and mischief on my grin."

"And your father?"

"He liked to say I was too smart for my own good and my mouth would get me into trouble."

"Now here we are."

"I don't see this as trouble."

"It hasn't started yet. How you handle your accidental celebrity will…" Bill paused as though to complete his thought, as though he needed to make sure he phrased it just right. "…will determine—may determine—the course of your entire life, perhaps even the status of your very soul."

Roland let out a scoff. "How do you mean, Inspector?"

"You're a cork on the ocean, a bobber with a twinkle in his eye and a mischievous grin, but all alone on the wide-open seas."

"And how should one handle such a distressing state of affairs?"

"Look for a friendly vessel, a helping hand." Bill gestured at the card in Roland's hand. "Call me anytime for any reason. But I fear you'll need more help than I alone can give."

Roland looked at the card, not sure how seriously to take the inspector's warning. He put the card in his left hand and extended his right and they shook, then Roland followed him out the door.

"I'm going to let you out the back in case there are any reporters at the front."

They made their way through corridors, past the locker rooms, to the rear of the building into the parking lot with its idle police units, fuel pump, and assorted private automobiles. Bill stopped and pointed toward the booth at the exit, secured by a mechanical gate.

"The man in the shack will let you out."

Roland twiddled the card, suddenly embarrassed by his presence there and unsure of how gracefully to set forth and face the slings and arrows of the outrageous fortune the inspector promised awaited him.

"I feel like I should thank you." He slipped the card into his pocket. "Not just for your number, but for your basic sense of kindness and decency. I'm still a bit shaken at having just been called a murderer." Roland wanted sympathy.

"Why? Is it true?"

"He was trying to kill me. I'll leave it at that."

"So why do you care what anybody thinks?" Bill paused. "Anyway, it will all get sorted out on the other side."

"You really believe that? You'd shout that from a mountaintop?"

"It's the only way my life makes sense to me. Now I should be getting back to it."

He gestured to the man in the booth then shooed Roland away with a playful hand. The man in the shack hit a switch and the gate rolled open. Roland walked, the inspector's words buzzing in his ears. He was forced to admit inwardly that his life made no sense to him. He turned around, hoping to see the inspector there watching him go, but the man had gone. Now he stood on Green Street, the sun overhead reminding him of the celestial monotony we call the days.

Chapter 6
September 30, 2016 - 1:20 PM

The clown car had baked in the sun for over an hour. He rolled the driver's window down to vent the heat and hoped vaguely that the oven was hot enough to exterminate the insects that married in the garbage underneath his seats. It would take a good cross breeze to cool the interior enough so he could sit comfortably and study the police report. The crank for the passenger window was broken and in its place he'd clamped a vice-grip. As Roland turned the tool slowly counterclockwise to lower the window the jaws popped off before he made a few inches' progress. *Christ!* he said, though not to blame the Redeemer. The vice-grip still in his fist, Roland fought against the impulse to smash out the window with a few powerful strikes and let the breeze pour in.

It took all of his patience and a few painstaking minutes to rotate the slippery plastic post with the oversized pincers, and with each measure of progress his desire for a drink increased. Roland knew himself well enough to battle that desire for it had become impossible to predict where the first drink would lead. *What about a nap?* Yes. That sounded like a good idea, but first he had to make the call. *Read the report and then call my parents*—those were the next right indicated actions in the proper order. On a Friday afternoon at their home in the Idaho Panhandle, surely they would be puttering about their property, attending to the upkeep of the house and surrounding acreage. *Hell, they're always home. But what about me? I'm hard to find, a sorry excuse for a son, running amok in a decadent metropolis while Harold and Millicent Hazzard go about their pleasant routine nestled in a happy marriage on their plot of earthly paradise under clear blue skies to the music of chirping birds and scurrying squirrels, unaware of what a colossal fuck-up has become their baby boy.* His frustration with the window left him vulnerable to a tear, and now self-pity nearly brought it forth. But a single tear leaked from the corner of one eye could release a flood strong enough to carve a channel into his fragile psyche, a runnel that could force his rudderless life in a new direction, toward a course to redemption or to suicide, he dared not contemplate which. All he knew at the moment was that he must not cry. It had been too long. All he allowed himself to feel was the gentle breeze his labor had provided.

Roland moved the Sentra to a shaded space under a tree across the street and unfolded the report. He wondered which officer had written it. He hoped it was the older, easier-going one with whom he'd conversed outside his building, but he quickly realized it was the younger, more earnest one who'd composed the narrative.

…. The resident, described by the 911 operator as belligerent and later identified as Roland Hazzard, met us in front of the building. He had a bloody rag around one arm and was agitated and clearly intoxicated…. Officer Gates remained with Mr. Hazzard while I led the EMTs into the building….

Clearly erring on the side of hyperbole, thought Roland, as he continued to read.

…strong smell of alcohol in the apartment…

Gratuitous detail.

…Hazzard engaged in a hostile verbal exchange with a woman who'd come out of the building…

Seriously? How is that relevant? Roland felt a surge of anger.

…showed no concern for the victim and continued drinking during the interview…

His anger became dismay.

…slurred speech…blatant disrespect…

Now disbelief. Not so much at the inaccuracy—for perceptions, he allowed, are largely subjective—but at the obvious attempt to discredit him. Is this the job of the police—to badmouth the victim of a crime? Roland fought the urge to rip the report and half and throw it on the floor, but he composed himself and continued.

…uncooperative…arrogant…reluctant to give a statement…tried to tell us how to do our job…just wanted to go back to bed…dared us to arrest him…

Roland searched his memory to corroborate that last assertion and shook his head at what he concluded was quite possibly true.

…we agreed to let Hazzard go to bed…blah blah blah blah blah…forensics team arrived to collect evidence….

He was nearing the end of this travesty of a public document.

…could hear Mister Hazzard snoring loudly through the door of his bedroom.

There it was, the final flourish, the pièce de résistance, the kick in the schnoz.

Roland read the signatures at the bottom. Officer Brian Dempster, the author, co-signed by Officer Aaron Gates. He set the report on the passenger seat. *Officer Dempster. What an asshole.* It had a certain bounce. He sang it like a nursery rhyme. *Officer Dempster—what an asshole. Office Dempster—what an asshole.* But the incantation quickly lost its power and gave way to a flood of concerns. The forty-eight hundred he owed to the Ukrainians was money he did not have. Not yet anyway. The contents of the thumb drive in his pocket might fetch enough to defray that debt. *Does the network keep a record of the download? And why didn't I tell the whole truth about last night to Gina and Michael?* He couldn't fathom the reason, for he had none, other than wanting to avoid an uncomfortable moment. *And who's going to fix my window—the landlord? Should I pay for it myself then deduct it from my rent? Why did he pick my window? Will reporters be waiting when I get home? How long before the news reaches my parents, my brother, my sister?* His breathing quickened as his mind diverged in the opposing directions of fight or flight with neither option promising a resolution to his present discomfort. Fight whom? Flee from what? *I'm the victim here.* He'd never thought of himself as a victim, not even when he got kicked off the college volleyball team for showing up drunk to practice. On it went, an onslaught of unstoppable thoughts, until Roland began, unconsciously, to rock back and forth in the clown car. Its chassis bounced gently under his shifting weight.

    Underlying his accelerating panic was the desperate truth that a drink would make it all go away, and buried beneath that truth was his experience, the oft-repeated routine which exposed that *truth* for what it was, an insidious lie. Not the lie of a proverbial lipsticked pig, but the prevarications of an educated pig, straight-toothed and fluent in English, sober and mellifluous, a silver-tongued swine who crooned *I am not a pig, for I can say I love you.* Yes. A drink would make it all go away, but only for as long as he kept drinking. After that would come, inevitably—today, tomorrow, or after a good long run—the dread moment of awakening. No. Not of awakening, but of *coming to.* And in coming to he would reel from the physical sickness brought on by alcohol withdrawal and suffer still more the mental torture of knowing that he had, once again, entertained the coaxing of the cloven-hoofed beast, having known from the start, and consciously denied, that to drink would solve nothing. The problems he'd escaped would be there still, only magnified. Would

Roland add to the numberless count another lash of incomprehensible demoralization born of willful self-deception? No. To take a drink now was unthinkable, but so was the act of calling his parents. Not in his present condition.

What to do when KFUK is blaring in your mind? How to pull the plug? Relief lay only in drink or sleep. Sleep it would be. The call could wait. He levered back the seat to make himself as comfortable as possible and put in his earbuds and set Brahms on shuffle.

He awoke an hour later, forehead damp with sweat. The sun had moved past the tree and was beating down on the car. Brahms still seeped into his ears. He'd come to rely on soft classical melodies to ease him into slumber when he needed a car nap, lately a frequent requirement on workdays. His pungent body odor clung to him despite the light breeze wafting through the vehicle.

Roland picked up his device and silenced the music with the swipe of a thumb. He'd not spoken to his parents in weeks. Hardly an unprecedented state of affairs, except in this case he'd failed to return several of his father's calls, and he knew that his mother must be worried. The last message his father had left him ended, "I assume you're alright, Son, but your mother is concerned. Every day you fail to call puts a pebble in the shoe of my marriage." Roland understood the implications of his father's complaint: *My marriage is more important than you. A man that cannot command respect from his son will lose the respect of his wife.*

He looked at his phone, grimaced at the crack in the screen. He'd discovered it there a few mornings ago and had no memory of how or when the damage had occurred. Now it stood as a sharp reminder of his drunkenness, as if his avoidance of his parents were not enough. If only they'd joined the modern age, the thought, and purchased a mobile phone that enabled texting, he might have been able to allay their concern with an occasional reassuring text. Suddenly, he resented them. Could they not be happy that he was finally off the docks, no longer gutting fish for a living? He had a *real* job now, with a company listed on the NASDAQ, soon to have medical insurance, stock options, a 401K—the American Dream.

His mind began racing again. *Should I come clean—give them the whole story? Where would I begin? The first arrest or the second?* Either way, it would be a long conversation, an unnecessary one perhaps if the press failed to dig up his criminal record or, finding it, decided not to share it with the world. By now it had finally sunk in that he was about to be tossed into the public arena to receive all manner of treatment. The urgency of the forthcoming call took on a moral weight Roland had failed to appreciate when the inspector had advised it, and he seriously wondered if he'd have made the decision on his own that day, and if not, how long he would have waited. The chatter from the committee in his head began slowly to grow in volume. At least in talking to his parents he'd only be dealing with two voices, and they would take turns on their separate landlines.

The moment had arrived. His mouth was dry. Roland rummaged around the car in search of water and found a plastic bottle half full among the trash in the back seat. He squeezed the hot water through his teeth and took a breath. It tasted of plastic but felt good going down. Cancerous? Maybe. But he'd survive today. He crushed the empty in his fist and tossed it devil-may-care over his shoulder into the back seat and placed the call.

The phone rang and rang, seven, eight, nine times before his mother picked up the old-fashioned receiver at the Hazzard household and breathlessly said hello.

"Hi, Mom."

"Rowwwland! I'm so happy to hear from you, sweetheart. We were beginning to get worried."

"I know, Mom. Dad left me a couple of messages. I'm sorry I didn't call back."

"You don't sound like yourself. Is something wrong? Shouldn't you be at work? Do you still have that great job?" He'd traded the committee in his head for this, but at least his mother said one thing at a time.

Roland cut her off before she could ask another question. "Is Dad there? Can you put him on the other line?"

While he waited for his mother to fetch his father, Roland stared through the windshield and deliberately slowed the pace of his breathing. It had been so long since the glass had been properly squeegeed that the dirt line marking the radius of his wiper blades seemed etched. A colorful splinter of sunlight refracting through the grime caught Roland's eye and spun the gears of his intellect. In that instant, as if on cue, an excretion from a bird in the branches above fell splat onto the windshield. His momentary trance was broken. He watched the viscid, speckled guano drip down the glass and wondered if there still existed a bone-nosed shaman or wild-eyed haruspex somewhere in the world who could divine the portents encrypted in the seemingly fortuitous dropping.

Howard Hazzard picked up the extension upstairs. "Hello, Son, and to what do we owe the pleasure?" The tone was sarcastic.

"Sorry, Dad, no excuses. I've been a little off my rails lately."

"I have no idea what that means."

"It means I fell off the wagon."

"Why not just say that?"

His mother's question saved him from having to respond to his father. "Did you lose your job, Son?" She sounded more than a little worried.

"No, Mom. I went to work this morning and my boss…"

"Millicent, Honey, just let him tell us what he's calling about."

Roland seldom heard his father address his mother by name. The man of the house was annoyed, apparently, with both wife and son, and Roland knew that he was to blame. Over the entirety of his upbringing, he'd never once witnessed his father mistreat his mother, and he was pretty sure that the presence of children in the home had nothing to do with his father's good behavior. Until he heard him say her name in a tone of irritation, Roland had almost forgotten it was Millicent. What a name! Old fashioned to an absurd extreme. Laughable. Millicent? One-thousandth of a penny? Unlikely. He'd have to google it later.

"Son? Roland? Are you there? We're waiting."

"A man broke into my apartment last night while I was asleep. He attacked me with a knife. I killed him."

Millicent gasped. Roland waited for his father to react, but he did not.

"With his own knife. I killed him with his own knife."

"Oh my God. Are you hurt, Son?"

"No, Mom, not badly. I got cut on the arm during the fight. Just a long scrape, no stitches. I made it to work."

Harold began his own line of questioning. "Have the police cleared you?"

"Yes. Like I said, I made it to work."

"You didn't say you called the police."

"Do you think I would kill a guy and just go back to bed, then step over the body on my way to work this morning?"

"Depends on how drunk you were."

"Harold!"

"It's alright, Mom. I see his point. Yes, Dad, I called 911. They took the body."

"I didn't ask that—I asked if they'd cleared you. The scales of justice in San Francisco are a little wonky."

"And I said *yes*, Dad." If Roland had been looking for an opening to tell his parents—his father, really—about his arrest record, the window had snapped shut for now. "I've been cleared of any wrongdoing. In fact, I'm a bit of a hero as it turns out."

"Best not get carried away."

Millicent broke in, fairly shouting by her mild standard. "You shouldn't be living there, Roland! You need to come home!"

Roland lied, reflexively. "Believe me, Mom, that was my first thought." But he'd known she would say that, so it didn't seem like a lie to him.

"When did this happen?"

"Last night, just before two."

"Had you ever seen the guy before or was he just a random burglar?" Harold would have made a competent cop.

"Neither."

"Neither?"

"He wasn't a burglar, Dad. He was a killer, a *murderer* to be precise."

Millicent gasped.

"Did he have a gun?"

"No."

"A murderer with no gun? How do you know he was a murderer?"

"The police told me, just now. Have you ever heard of the Glendale Butcher?"

"WHAT!" Millicent topped her vocal register. It was not a question.

Harold answered her anyway. "Samuel Barsamian—Armenian." Then he spoke to Roland. "You killed Sam the Butcher? Don't be screwing around here, Roland."

"He sounded American to me."

"You spoke to him?"

"I tried to convince him to leave, but he wouldn't. He came at me, he thought he could kill me."

"Tell us what happened."

"He pried open a window in my back room. The noise woke me up. I got up and confronted him outside my bedroom. Hit him in the head. He went down but didn't stay down. Pulled out a knife. Attacked me with it. I managed to turn the blade around and push it into his chest. He died on the floor in my hallway."

"That doesn't make any sense. He killed women, only young women."

"That's right! We watched a show about him not too long ago. *America's Most Wanted.*"

"He came from a family of insurance defrauders. City of Glendale opens its arms to refugees of the Armenian genocide and a few generations later they've figured out easy ways to scam the incompetent government. There's gratitude for you."

"That has nothing do to with psychopathic murder, Dad."

"You sure?"

"You tell me. You seem to know a lot about this Glendale Butcher fella."

"Like your mother said—he was profiled on TV recently. Before the murders, his parents and a bunch of his clan were sent to prison for their medical insurance scams. He was left alone. It appears he joined a mosque in Los Angeles. Then the bloodletting started."

"They used the word *radicalized.*"

"Still. It doesn't make sense that he would come after you. All his victims were women—young white women."

"How many was it, Harold?"

"Seven or eight, I think. He started off near his home in Glendale, California then took his act to Glendale, Arizona where he killed three or four more, just randomly in rest stops and trailer parks as I recall."

"That's only two Glendales. And not that far apart. Could have been a coincidence."

"It was the third one that…"

Millicent interrupted. "Stop it Harold—the man tried to murder our son last night, and you two sound like you're playing a trivia game."

Roland exhaled audibly. "Mom, it really wasn't that scary. The guy didn't stand a chance."

"I guess your martial arts came in handy."

"No doubt. Besides, he was a little shit. I warned him too—told him to get out. He made his choice. And now that I know who he was, I'm glad I pushed it all the way in."

"Pushed it all the way in?"

"The knife."

"You mean you didn't have to?"

"He did the right thing. In California, burglars have rights so it's best not to leave them alive to assert those rights."

"I wasn't thinking about the law."

"In my book, man breaks into a home ought never to leave it."

"Lord and Savior. I'm going back to my gardening."

"Wait, Mom. I need to tell you two about the chief."

"The chief?"

"The chief of police—San Francisco PD. I just got through talking to him. He's not too happy with me."

"Why not, Son? What else is there to know?"

"Let him finish, Harold."

"He doesn't like how I treated the cops."

"That doesn't make any sense. He called you down to the station today to tell you that he didn't like how you treated the cops?"

"How did you treat the cops?"

"Hold on, Honey. Roland, tell me—tell us—why did they call you in today?"

Roland paused to formulate an answer. He wanted the call to be over, and he wasn't sure how he could tell the truth without inviting more questions.

"I was pretty drunk last night, Dad. They called me in—the lead inspector did—to redo my statement, to make sure it matched what I told the officers last night."

"Did it?"

"Yeah, well enough."

"Your sister said you'd quit drinking."

"I did, for a while. I never told her it was permanent."

"So, you were drunk and acted like an asshole. I don't see why the chief of police has to get involved."

"Me neither. Except that—except that he wanted me to know—to know that he doesn't have my back—that I was lucky who I killed."

"Lucky?"

"If it'd been just anyone—just a burglar—then he'd..."

"Then he'd've done what—prosecuted you?"

"He didn't say it outright, but that was the drift."

"I still don't see the problem."

"There is no problem, unless you want to count my local police record."

There, he'd said it. Like lighting a fuse. Would it detonate a bomb, a firecracker, or wind up a dud?

"Oh," his parents said in unison.

Roland paused to let them—either one of them—continue, but they both remained silent.

"Nothing serious—nothing felonious. Just drunk in public."

"Really?" said his father.

"Is that a question or an accusation?"

"You're telling me that the police in San Francisco, where they hand out needles to junkies and let street crime go on unchallenged, arrested you for drunk in public?"

"Twice." Roland added the hint of irony, as if to say that the facts of the matter were not only absurd, but doubly absurd.

"And you didn't think to tell us about it? Does Sandy know, or Phillip?"

"No. But it will all come out. Chief Hiro Hito will make sure of that."

"Hiro Hito?" Harold said.

"The chief of police. Japanese gentlemen. Maruyama. Real high strung. Real martinet."

"And yet you still drink? Arrested twice, and yet you go on drinking? You don't see the problem? It's not the arrests, Son. The arrests, the police record, are not the problem. This runs in families. It destroyed your grandfather. You know that." The tone of compassion in her voice pierced his ego and he hung his head as though he were sitting across a table from them. Roland had no rebuttal and remained silent, and his silence was an acknowledgment of the truth in what she'd said. Had it been his father who brought up Papa Merrill, he'd have considered it a cheap shot. But coming from his mother, Merrill's daughter, he was forced to look within. Papa's death was still fresh, less than two years past. He still loved the man. Papa Merrill often showed up in his dreams.

"Your mother's right. Maybe you should come home. His old Jeep is still in the garage. You said you wanted it. Now might be a good time to come fix it and take it away. And there's a few other things I could use your help with around here."

"I don't want to quit my job. I really like what I'm doing. I'll take care of that over Thanksgiving."

"Are you sure they're still going to want you there?"

"My boss knows why I came into the station this morning. He gave me the rest of the day off. I'll be back to work on Monday."

"Your boss knows you were too drunk to give a proper statement?"

"That's not what I said."

"That's why they called you down, according to you. Right? Give it to me straight, Roland."

"He knows about the break-in and the killing. That's all I meant."

"I guess by Monday he'll know the rest, once the press gets a hold of it."

"Yeah. Whatever's coming, there's no stopping it."

"Just don't make it worse. Don't play into it."

"Of course, Mom. So, Dad, what more do you know about this guy?"

"I'm going back to my garden. You're in God's hands now, Roland. I did the best I could." It wasn't just an expression. Roland knew she meant it—*God's hands*. They were real to her. Whole edifices of theology were built to honor those hands. The scientific method was devised to understand the physical manifestations of those hands. If it was true—if he was in God's hands—the implications were too great for him to contemplate.

"I'll ride this out, Mom. Don't worry about me." She hung up the phone. "Dad, you still there?"

"Yeah, I'm here. I've told you most of what I remember. The New Mexico murders were particularly gruesome. Hacked up two women in a remote campsite in some obscure little gouge in the desert near the Mexico border—Glendale Canyon—left a horrific mess. Authorities assume he crossed the border after that, through El Paso, but I could'a come up with that."

"The inspector gave me the same basic story on the guy. Glendale Canyon—that surpasses coincidence."

"I'm not like your mom, as you know, as far as religion goes, but one thing I'll tell you is I don't believe in coincidence."

"What do you mean?"

"There's a reason he broke into your apartment. I doubt it was a random act. Whether or not he was after you, you're at the center of this now. I don't know what grand forces might be at work, but they decided to work on you. There's one school of thought that says we bring everything on ourselves. I don't necessarily buy that either, but you never know."

"Well, he definitely broke his MO—no Glendale, no female…"

The silence hovered over more than an incomplete sentence. It contained the unspeakable distance between a father and his extraordinary yet ungovernable son.

"You're a killer now—that will never go away. That will stay with your name long after you're dead."

"I'm glad Mom isn't here to hear you say that."

"I wouldn't have said it if she'd been on the line."

"I gotta go, Dad."

"One more thing." Roland clenched his hand around the phone. His dad was going to tell him to stop drinking. He could take it from his mother, for that was her job, but for his father to say it would be a humiliation.

"Yeah?"

"Be careful who you talk to, especially reporters and such. If you're going to talk about this thing, make sure you're in your right mind."

That was tolerable. Good general advice under any circumstance. While *right mind* certainly included sobriety, it didn't point a finger right at it.

"I will. I'll give 'em the ol' Buddha treatment."

"Whatever that means."

"You know—*What, me worry?*"

"Don't make a joke of it, Son." Harold said *son* not in the way of a devoted father addressing his beloved child, but as an avuncular stranger—in an earlier time, perhaps—might reproach a petulant teenager. Roland had never heard him take that tone. He listened to the dead air knowing that his father was waiting for him to speak. He knew he had to come up with something that at least orbited sincerity.

"I won't. But between me and you, I'm glad. It's going to be hard not to say that publicly, so between me and you, I'm glad. Even before I found out who it was, I knew when he faced me that he was a bad hombre, but I gave him a chance to go. He had a clear pathway to my door, but I didn't want him to take it."

"You weren't afraid?"

"I could have killed him without raising my hands."

"Don't repeat that. Promise you won't repeat that."

"I don't plan on boasting, Dad."

"Good. Now go face whatever it is the press has in store for you. And don't mouth off about the police chief. Leave that alone. And call your brother. He might have some good advice."

The call ended. Roland picked up a piece of trash from the floor of his car and stepped outside to wipe the bird poop off his windshield. All he managed to do was smear it around and make matters worse. He shook his head and thought of what to do next—*the next indicated right action*—and decided that was to go home and scrub the bloodstain off the hallway floor. *Scratch that. No TV service there.* He wanted to watch the local news, to see what the journos had to say about him, and he knew just the place that would welcome him.

Chapter 7
September 30, 2016 - 2:40 PM

The Gutter, a decrepit waterfront tavern, lay nestled between two of the many piers that fingered the bay in a section of The City dubbed The Barbary Coast in the Gold Rush years when all manner of seamen, fortune-seekers, gamblers, cut-throats, opium-dealers, prostitutes, wastrels, and missionaries peopled its overcrowded warrens, streets, and saloons. It was here, amid depravity and corruption, that an impecunious tippler, Mark Twain, not thirty years old, was sacked from his job as a newspaper reporter for practicing his fanciful brand of inebriated journalism. He hit bottom, then wrote the short story that launched his literary career. Though San Francisco travel brochures and tour guides still traded on his nautical nom de plume, The Barbary Coast had long since lost its anarchic charm and was now a purely mythical place. Twain had left no ghost behind. Yet the fishermen remained—the fishermen and their haunts—as nearly every day on that corner of the bay, tons of fresh catch were unloaded, processed, and sent to market. The few cafes and bars that serviced the piers subsisted almost solely off the patronage of the men who worked the boats, docks, and processing houses, often called *gutteries*. The men—most all of them men—who processed the fish were called *gutters*, naturally. After graduating from Berkeley with a degree in English, Roland spent two years working as a gutter and became a regular at the watering hole that shared the name of his occupation. No self-respecting tourist would poke his head through the door of such a place. It was here that Roland decided to repair after the uncomfortable conversation with his parents.

Establishments of its ilk were, quite literally, permitted to exist, despite their myriad health and safety code violations, under the tacit immunity enjoyed by dives of local color. Only nearby Chinatown received a similar—some would say much greater—administrative leniency. Truth be told, The Gutter could ill afford to comply with all the regulations. Its owner and fulltime bartender, Gerry, earned barely enough profit to keep fresh paint on its weathered exterior to combat the corrosive salt air. Almost any color would do. When a drunken Roland last lurched out the door of the place six months ago, it was coated with an inoffensive, peeling, brown. Today it wore a fresh, belligerent red, no doubt procured at a significant discount, if not purloined.

Roland parked his car two blocks away and ambled up the sidewalk toward the door, working up a tang in his mouth in anticipation of his first drink—it would be whiskey—in the only bar he considered a haven, and, as it happened, one of the few in San Francisco where the smoking ban was not enforced. But he felt a little nervous, like a defector returning to his unit having found no place to hide. *How will I be received?* he wondered. The regulars at The Gutter, he thought, must have noticed his absence as soon as he'd stopped coming, since many of them worked alongside him in a guttery a stone's throw away. That had job ended after a week of Roland calling in sick from jail when, finally, he had to admit to his supervisor that he was incarcerated. He had no idea how much his coworkers and fellow barflies knew about his circumstances, but he correctly assumed they had teased out something of the truth from the traffic of scuttlebutt and conjecture that swirled at the bar. But, by now, he was all but forgotten, like the AWOL soldier gone for several months. He folded the police report and slipped it in his pocket then opened the door and went inside.

The stench in the air consisted of alcohol, smoke, urine, fish guts, body odor and air freshener. It was strong enough to alter one's mood even before one took a drink. Unlike its shiny new exterior, the bar's interior remained unchanged, its walls festooned with fishing nets adorned with all manner of retired gear—rods and rusty reels, harpoons and gaff hooks, and a few dozen deep-sea lures of every description. On the back wall was bolted a mahogany captain's wheel showing the distress of decades on the open seas. From one of its handles dangled a yellow rain bonnet, the emblem of the fishing trade. On either side of the wheel hung more than a dozen framed photographs that featured heroic fishermen smiling as they held out their defeated quarry on steel chains at the lengths of their muscular arms. It was almost as if showing off their strength was more important than displaying their impressive fish. The obligatory marlin mounted above the bar measured eight feet long, not counting the spear. Its brilliant dorsal blues, its long band of yellow, and its tapered vertical stripes shone muted beneath years of residual grease and smoke. Unconcerned with the dust strings that clung to the tips of its fins, the marlin glared predatorily from its black glass eye, alive as ever it appeared. Roland noticed the menacing eye as if for the first time and, distracted, caught his hip on the corner of the plywood plank that rested atop the pool table, now serving as a buffet table. Empty steam pans rattled from the impact. Soon they would hold hot dogs and beans, hamburger patties and buns, potato salad, maybe even breaded fish fillets. He stopped and fitted the lids snugly back in place. Gerry looked up and said nothing. Roland stepped toward his usual stool at the end of the bar next to his favorite piece of decor, an erotic poster advertisement for Red Hook Ale. The leather soles of his Laredos peeled and smacked across the sticky floor.

The place was empty except for a pair of dedicated underachievers propped on their stools at the bend in the bar watching television, and Gerry, shielded behind a newspaper near the register, standing far enough away so as not to have to engage the peculiar customers. The unemployable pair, in their late middle age but looking much older, sat side by side, there to dispose of their disability checks or whatever form of government largess kept them going. They stared at the television, nursing their drinks sparingly. Roland took his seat next to the Red Hook poster on Gerry's side of the bar. The advertisement depicted a mermaid reclined on an outcropping of rocks in a serene oceanscape, holding a bottle of Red Hook Ale on a serving tray. Her perfect, youthful breasts glistened wetly under a necklace of sparkling seashells, and her sea-green eyes lured the viewer to her lascivious mouth, which taunted with the caption: *Nowhere else to set your hook*? Roland had explained the ad numerous times to his fellow drunks, who saw in it little more than soft-porn titillation. It was a triple entendre, keying off the angling vernacular, 'set your hook,' which means to secure a catch by tugging the line when you feel the hook is inside the fish's mouth. Here it also meant, *place your beer on my tray* and, luridly, *find purchase for your penis in my body*. Since mermaids lack vaginas, unfortunately, the only option was to set your bottle on her tray.

The poster brought to mind his last night at the bar, the night of his second arrest. Arturo, a regular, had prompted Roland to explain the poster to a buddy of his who was new to The Gutter. A small group bunched around to hear Roland deliver his now half-memorized spiel about the clever play on words as it pertained to the deficient anatomy of the otherwise desirable mermaid.

Roland remembered how he'd summed it up. "She's trying to torment us with the fact that we can't fuck her."

The stranger replied, "I'd rather have a blowjob anyway. She's fully equipped for that."

The bar had laughed, and Roland had to suppress his irritation, resolving never again to edify his fellows with his keen intellections. Indeed, he'd decided not to grace the cretins with his presence any longer that evening.

"You guys can keep drooling over the pretty picture. I'm off to reel in the real thing." With that, he'd departed, head full of booze but not too drunk to make good on his promise. Roland had honed his practice of landing a species he called *Femina Solitariam Inebriabitur* once he spotted her in her natural habitat.

Taking a seat on his favorite stool, Roland realized that the sexual allure of the poster had, on several occasions, touched off his pursuits. He pulled his eyes away from the image as Gerry came over and set his newspaper on the bar in front of him. He bore the pallid complexion of a man who spent most of his time indoors, with the wrinkles of a man who used to spend a lot of time in the sun. His skin showed all its imperfections.

"I thought I'd seen the last of you." Roland searched Gerry's eyes for a glimmer of humor and found them void of emotion, dulled by years of occupational monotony.

"I'm guessing you'll be seeing a lot of me now."

"You guess? Maybe I can help. Maybe I can eliminate the guesswork." He sounded antagonistic now.

"How's that, Gerry?"

"I think you shouldn't drink here anymore."

"May I know why?"

"You're the smart one, right, the one with all the penetrating insights?"

"Let's take a step back here, Ger." He spoke with a forced whisper, lest the strangers overhear him. "I didn't mean you'd be seeing a lot of me *in here.*"

"What—you running for president?"

Roland wanted to postpone the chit-chat until he had a drink in front of him, but it was clear he'd need to pass this interrogation before Gerry would serve him.

"I'm going to be on the news today."

"Oh?" Gerry glanced at Roland's bandaged arm. "You still in trouble with the law? You been in a fight?"

Roland pursed his lips and with his good hand scratched the back of his neck to show his irritation with the question.

"Can I get a shot of Jack first?" He raised his wounded arm. "I'll tell you about this, and maybe you can tell me what you've heard about my *trouble with the law.*" He made the quote sign with his fingers and flexed them twice.

"You should know I don't lean into gossip. What I know about your trouble with the law *came straight from the law.*"

"*Straight from the law?* What does that mean?"

"It means you told them you'd been drinking here when they picked you up at Bix a few months ago."

Walking distance but a world apart, Bix Supper Club, a swanky jazz bar in the Financial District, was the scene of Roland's second arrest.

"The police came *here?*"

"Two police to be exact. I don't need that kind of attention. The city could shut me down without a hearing we're so far out of compliance."

"I know it doesn't matter, Gerry, but I don't remember telling them I'd been here."

"They showed me the police report in case there was any doubt. You told 'em alright." He kept his eyes fixed on Roland as they spoke. His focus made Roland nervous. He considered getting up and walking out, but curiosity kept him put. He glanced furtively at the bottles arrayed behind the bar.

"Why would they care if I was here, or did they just want to see if I'd been telling the truth?"

"They wanted to know about you—what kind of a person you are."

"And what kind of person am I?"

"I gave you a good character reference. I told them it didn't sound like you."

"What didn't sound like me?"

"Arm-twisting a woman."

"I didn't lay a hand on her. They say I did?"

"No. But they implied it."

"What did you tell them exactly?"

"You worked the gutting houses. Always cleaned up before you came in. Never caused any trouble. Only one thing unusual about you besides your height."

"Only one? I'm insulted."

"You know you're overeducated for the crowd that drinks here. That's all. I'm surprised you could stand it, Roland. Frankly, I was glad when you stopped coming in. You're made for better things than this."

"You're not mad? Just now you seemed mad."

"More like disappointed. I'd hoped I'd seen the last of you, for your sake."

"Can I get that drink? I'll tell you what brought me in here today."

Gerry turned around and made Roland a double Jack over ice and set it in front of him. "Just the one." He nodded toward the drink. "Now, tell me what happened that night that was so serious the police had to pay me a visit. All I know for sure is you wound up in jail and lost your job."

Roland put a twenty on the bar and wrapped a hand around the drink. He wanted to gulp it down in one tilt, to flood his brain with a rush that would instantly ease his discomfort, but he knew he had to make the serving last. He took a sip and then another quick sip. His words came slowly but not to relish the memory.

"You're right. It came down to a woman. I'll tell you what happened. I got sick of holding court over the knuckleheads in here and I was sober enough to navigate polite society, so I walked down to Bix to find myself a companion for the night."

"It's that easy for you, huh? Like picking fruit."

"As long as the stars are aligned. It doesn't take long for me to spot my mark or spot no mark at all. That night it took about a minute. She was sitting alone at a table near the jazz trio, practically sliding off her chair."

"Good looking, or do you care?"

"It's Bix, so she's pretty upscale. Mid to late thirties, expensive coif, wearing a loose dress. Good body. That's the main thing." He took another drink, the glass half empty now. "So I buy a cocktail at the bar, walk over and sit down at her table without asking permission, crack a few jokes, ask her a few friendly questions. I don't remember what I said. It's all standard patter for as long as it takes for her to get comfortable. Then I put the question to her."

"You just ask 'em if they want to have sex—to go home with you?"

"Patience, grasshopper. You ask them if they want to go outside and have a cigarette. Drunk women love to smoke. If she says yes, you're almost there."

"I assume she said yes."

"Yes. We finish our drinks, she grabs her purse, and we walk outside to smoke. I had to loop my arm around her waist to keep her steady as we sashayed out the door into the alley."

"Sounds innocent enough to me."

"It was it was. We were just smoking and talking, then she takes out her phone and is about to call us a cab when these two dicks come strolling out of the bar, shoulder to shoulder like they're on a mission in their shiny shoes, four-figure suits, neckties loosened, twiddling their fat cigars."

Roland's memory returned with full, photographic clarity, and he suddenly began to enjoy the retelling.

"But they didn't light the cigars. Clown one asks the lady if she's alright or am I bothering her, but I don't give her time to answer. I tell him to mind his own business, and he gives me an obvious macho comeback, something like *I'm talking to the lady* or *the lady can speak for herself*. So, I take a little step toward them, and I say *First answer me one question—Which one of you gives a better blowjob?*"

Gerry chuckled. Roland took another drink before he continued.

"That sets them off, as if I'd slapped them both across the mouth with one swipe. They look at me and I look at their limp hands and drop my cigarette and wiggle my fingers so they can see them wiggling. Not fists, just my open hands with fingers itching to clench, fingers asking *Whaddaya gonna do about it?* I didn't say that. I didn't say anything. But that was the question. *What are you overdressed financial district stooges going to do about it?*"

By now Gerry was smiling broadly. "I don't need all the dialogue."

"Men would have fought me or walked away, but these two pricks started yelling. *Who the fuck do you think you are? You're in the wrong part of town, motherfucker.* False bravado, impotent anger, but loud enough to bring out the bouncer just in time for him to see me feint a lunging jab at the taller one just to see him flinch. I guess that counts for assault these days. I don't know. I should have walked off. That would have been the end of it. But I still wanted the lady. I'd worked for it, and she was laughing now, all in my favor."

"You got arrested for that?"

"They told the bouncer I'd grabbed her and she'd resisted and they were just being good citizens. The bouncer called the cops. She wobbled off. I could've followed her, but I wasn't gonna be scared off by a lie. Then the flashing lights rolled up and the cops got out and the suits told their story first and the bouncer mentioned he saw my aggressive posture. The woman—Jada, I'm pretty sure—wasn't there to back up my side of things, so they called it *drunk and disorderly* and put me in the car and booked me into jail. North Beach Station."

"You'd never seen these guys before?"

"Nope."

"Why you think they did it?"

"Territorialism—didn't wanna see a long-haired lowlife miscreant make off with one of their tipsy Betty-Sues."

"Hard to believe."

Roland drained the drink and showed Gerry a querulous eyebrow. "What's?"

"That you spent time in jail for that. You can set a cop car on fire in this city and the mayor will bail you out the next morning."

Roland swirled the ice at the bottom of his glass. Gerry's incredulity merited an answer. "Second offense. They picked me up a month before for sleeping on a couch in the Fairmont Hotel."

"Don't you live just a few blocks from there?"

Still staring at the bare ice cubes, Roland nodded exaggeratively, like a show horse bobbing its head.

"Will you pour me another?" He kept his head down because he knew Gerry was looking at him and didn't want his bartender to catch the hint of desperation in his eyes.

"Why would you curl up in the lobby of the Fairmont? That's just asking for trouble."

"The police asked me the same question." Roland slid his glass forward. "Wish I had an answer. Last thing I remember about that night was sitting at the bar in Li Po's."

"That's a scary way to live. How long did you do?"

"The first time? Just the night."

"No. After the Bix arrest."

"I pled guilty to avoid a trial. Spent three weeks in city lockup." Roland omitted to mention the alcohol diversion program appended to his jail sentence, still anxious for a refill.

Gerry shook his head. "I haven't changed my mind."

"It's not like you've got too much business." Roland glanced over at the two ciphers on his left then looked back at Gerry's impassive face. He didn't want to beg and he didn't want to leave. "Look, Gerry, I'm not here to resume my patronage at your illustrious establishment. I need a place to watch the local news. I did something newsworthy last night and I want to see how they cover it. I could have picked a lot of places, but I wanted to watch it here, to say hello, to be on friendly ground. But if I'm not welcome, I'll be on my way."

"Let's ask the Magic 8-Ball." Gerry reached underneath the bar and pulled out the black globe of divination.

"You're shitting me. There are twice as many yeses as noes in that ball."

"Say the question any way you want."

"Ok. Gimme that stupid thing."

Gerry handed him the plastic orb. Roland looked at it and said, "Should Gerry pour me another shot of whiskey and keep pouring as long as I don't cause any trouble?" He gave it a vigorous shake and handed it back to Gerry.

"What's the verdict?"

"It says *Ask Again Later.*"

"Fuck it." Roland got up to leave.

"Okay." Gerry relented. "But promise me—if you get picked up…"

"I've been known to blackout, Gerry. That would be like promising someone I won't snore when I fall asleep."

"You sure do have a pretty fair recollection of the arrest."

"I wasn't exactly blacked out then; but even when I am, sometimes I can piece things part-way back together if I really want to—if I have a reason to—and not too much time has gone by." He reached into his back pocket and removed the police report and flattened it on the bar.

Gerry took the empty glass and turned around to refill it.

"Pour me a beer back too. Please?"

Gerry brought the drinks back and set them in front of Roland. "What's that? I'm guessing that arm has something to do with it."

Roland slid the police report over to Gerry. "It's all in here."

He carried his drinks to the other end of the bar near the TV to see if he could bum a cigarette from the two wastrels glued to *The Andy Griffith Show*, as if absorbing the glow of its innocence might somehow restore the virtues they'd discarded. To be polite, Roland watched along with them for a few seconds, waiting for a likely moment to beg a smoke. Barney gesticulated wildly in righteous indignation over the liberties Otis, the town sot, was taking with the Mayberry hoosegow, using it as his personal flophouse to sleep off last night's bender. The show had held up well over the decades, he had to admit. The comic antics on the screen drew Roland in, and he took a stool alongside the two idlers.

Gerry stood next to the register reading the police report.

Roland took a mouthful of whiskey and let it slip down his throat. The fumes overwhelmed his nostrils and caused him to sneeze.

"Science!" the man next to him said.

Roland turned his head, looked at the man, and said in a warning tone, "*Silence?* Really?"

"Noooo. I said *science*."

"Ok—science. I've heard of it. What's your point?"

"That's all there is to it, stranger. It speaks for itself."

His confederate snickered.

"We're both strangers. But I'd say you're the stranger stranger."

The man motioned with his thumb toward his companion, like a guy trying to hitch a ride. "He's even stranger."

The other man spoke up. "You're s'posed to say *thank you*."

"Am I?"

"Yes. You sneezed. My friend here acknowledged science. Now you say thank you. That's the polite response."

"Which one are you, Rosencrantz or Guildenstern—or are you both just waiting for Godot?"

"What?" the first man said.

"Who?" said the other.

"I think he's calling us Jews."

Roland leaned over the bar and turned his head so he could address both of them. "People used to get shot in this town for talking your level of nonsense."

"The Wild West rolled up its tent a long time ago," the first man said.

"We wouldn't get shot in Mayberry," said the other. "Andy doesn't carry a gun and Barney's only allowed one bullet and usually shoots himself in the foot."

"You guys are too broke to be drunk this early. So, I'll go with crazy."

"You got it all wrong, stranger," the second man said. "*Science* has replaced *God-bless-you* in the new trans-humanist world order. I guess you didn't get the memo."

"It's the atheist way." The first man—the one who'd exclaimed *science*—gestured *there you have it* with an upturned hand.

Roland smiled with understanding. "I see. You're a couple of evangelicals."

"Satanists," nodded the sidekick. "He's the chief warlock. I just clean up the blood."

Clean up the blood. That stopped Roland mid-retort. He took another drink and withdrew from the repartee. *Clean up the blood*, he repeated the phrase in his mind. *I'll need supplies.* All Roland had to work with was a bottle of shampoo and a few bath towels. *When will it start to smell?* he wondered.

The pagans resumed their private conversation.

"I can't believe how stupid Barney is. Why doesn't Andy can his ass?"

"Because they're cousins. All those hillbillies are related."

"Mayberry is not a mountain town, you know."

Roland interrupted before they could delve any deeper into the subject. "I'll buy you devils a drink if you can spare a few cigarettes."

The transaction was approved and the cigarettes handed over. Gerry moved slowly down the bar, not taking his eyes off the report. He set an inverted shot glass in front of each man to indicate the bar owed them each a drink. Then he motioned to Roland to rejoin him at the other end of the bar. He poured a shot of whiskey for himself and another for Roland.

"This is some serious shit. How come you have a copy of the report when it happened last night?"

"They called me in this morning to go over it again."

"What makes you think this is going to make the news?"

"Ever heard of the Glendale Butcher, a.k.a Sam the Butcher?"

"I've heard a' Sam the Butcher, you know, from the Brady Bunch. Allen Melvin. He and my dad went to the same high school in New York City. He did a few Andy Griffiths, come to think of it. I think he ran the town grocery store."

"You've spent too long in close quarters with these simpletons." Roland tilted his head in their direction. "I'm talking about a psychopath, a throat-slitter. FBI most wanted. They identified his body last night."

Gerry picked up the TV remote. "I wanna hear about this."

"I've told the story too many times already today."

Gerry switched to a local station.

"Hey, no. NO!" the sidekick said. "Barney was just about to accidentally lock himself in the pokey."

"Shut the fuck up, Donny," Gerry said.

The alcohol filtered through Roland's liver and into his brain replacing his irritation with a familiar sense of contentment, buoying him with confidence in his own unimpeachable rectitude. Then the magic kicked in, the lifting of a curtain that revealed the limitless world of his exceptional mind. The room around him disappeared as he transported himself back to the garage of his youth in his parents' Idaho home. He was thirteen years old. A pivotal moment, he'd come to realize, as he saw himself opening an unmarked box to discover its contents. A trove of old periodicals, all bearing the smirking mug of the gap-toothed ginger with the *what-me-worry* grin. Alfred E. Neuman, the insouciant mascot of *Mad Magazine*. In consuming that boxload of American satire, Roland at once validated his own seemingly inborn iconoclasm and gained a welcome insight into his otherwise straight-edged father. Whoever he was now, Harold Hazzard had once been a free-spirited young man. When his father bristled at his choice of college curricula—Literature, Philosophy, History—Roland often reflected on that day as critical in his decision to pursue a life of a mind and maintain an attitude ever suspicious of established authority. He savored the memory as he saw himself holding up a copy of the magazine and studying the cover—an elephant and a donkey locked in combat. Much as now, in the current acrimonious election cycle, the wild-eyed donkey chomped down on the trunk of the furious elephant. He opened the magazine in his mind and began to read, as though the thing were actually in his hand. Gerry jarred him from his musings.

"Here it is, Roland."

The station cut away from an inane daytime talk show to tease the lead story in the upcoming evening news. A theatrically serious male voice reported that *a home invasion in a Nob Hill apartment last night by one of the nation's most wanted serial killers resulted in the death of the killer at the hands of a very alert and fortunate resident.* Cut to a clip of the chief in front of Northern Station addressing the press. *We have confirmed the identity of the deceased as Samuel Barsamian, known in the media as the Glendale Butcher and other descriptive nicknames. The department continues to investigate the circumstances surrounding the encounter between Barsamian and the resident.* Now back to the station announcer. *We'll have the full details on the story for you at five.*

Full details, thought Roland. *They don't even know when they're lying.*

"Looks like we'll have to wait till five," said Gerry.

Roland felt happy now. It was all coming together. He had a place to drink. Some of his old buddies would show up after work and be there when the news came on to marvel at what he'd done. Amazing what a few ounces of whiskey could do for one's perspective. The gents at the end of the bar were no longer a pair of shiftless degenerates but a couple of affable bon vivants. And who could deny that Don Knotts as Barney Fife was a comic genius? All Roland needed was a little food in his belly to keep himself from getting smashed.

"I'm going to get something to eat. I'll be back before the news comes on."

"I'll save your stool."

Roland lit a cigarette and moved toward the door. The idlers followed him with their eyes. As he reached for the handle, he heard the sidekick say, "Can you change it back to Andy?"

"Shut the fuck up, Donny." Gerry raised the clicker and changed it back to Andy.

Chapter 8
September 30, 2016 - 3:20 PM

The best clam chowder in The City, by popular opinion, came ladled from a steaming kettle in the outdoor market at Fisherman's Wharf. New England style, of course. Ladled into a sourdough bread bowl. And the plastic spoon provided was strong enough not to snap when a famished consumer scraped clean the inside of the bowl. The Wharf lay several blocks away, a long enough walk to afford Roland a phone call as he strode.

The inspector picked up right away. "Hello, Rooweland." As before, his oos were lushly Caribbean.

"Hellooo, Inspector Kingston. That's my name for you now."

"Whatever amuses you. I didn't expect to hear from you so soon."

"I'm going to be on the news at five." Roland normally followed a coherent conversational thread when he talked, but now he was simply an exuberant child delivering good news.

"You sound like you've been drinking. Where are you?"

"Headed to the wharf for somma dat good chowda." Roland tried his best Boston accent, mimicking Ben Affleck in *Good Will Hunting*. Spelman kept silent for a few seconds, long enough for Roland to get the impression that the silence was purposeful.

"Why have you called, young man?"

Roland recalibrated his attitude to match the inspector's officious tone. "Well, sir, I was wondering if you know if, or how much of, my history—my extensive criminal history—the department has shared with the press."

"I do not. Are you asking me to see if I can seal those records? Is that what this is about?"

"No. Certainly not. I just thought you might know how things are moving along."

"Those wheels are turning; I can assure you. I couldn't stop them if I wanted to. But, as far as I know, nothing has changed since you left my office a few hours ago, nothing, that is, except you. If you're worried about how you're going to come off in the media, I suggest you sober up and be prepared to make a good presentation of yourself, because they're not going to leave you alone. Or else you could leave town and hide out in a motel in the desert somewhere."

Roland felt the sting of humiliation, of being caught thinking he could manage a situation far beyond his control. That the inspector had detected his intoxication didn't bother him, for the alcohol inoculated him against any shame its effects could produce. He slowed his steps and leaned against the nearest wall.

"I'm sorry I bothered you."

"Before you go, let me give you a piece of advice."

"Alright."

"Whatever you do today, don't get yourself arrested."

"I think I can manage that, sir. One day at a time, right?"

"When you mock the program, it makes it hard for me to care what happens to you."

"I know I'm in turbulent waters, sir, but I promise I'll tie up to my slip tonight."

"You might need more than a decorative promise, son. Good luck to you."

The call ended. Roland ambled on. *The Internet. Christ!* He pulled out his phone and checked a few national news sites and didn't find anything about the killing, but he knew it was coming. He'd have to call his brother and sister before too long, lest they read about it first. Or maybe Mom and Dad would tell them. Hard to know. He slid the phone back into his pocket and quickened his pace down Jefferson Street toward Fisherman's Wharf and Ghirardelli Square, which offered tourists a wealth of kitschy pizzazz. Even now, a few blocks away, a living statue—a 19th Century English gentleman—worked the sidewalk in front of Madame Tussaud's Wax Museum. Slow day for the dandy, Roland observed, with only a few dollars swirling above a splash of coins in the bronzed top hat at his feet. Roland wondered how much it took for the performer to break even once he'd sprayed himself from scalp to spats with metallic paint and paid for parking, not to mention the cost of the ruined tuxedo and oxfords, amortized over a period of, say, five years. Or maybe he rode the bus looking like that and didn't have to spring for parking. Roland's mental percolations distracted him from his concerns, and he entertained them as far as they would go. *How long has the calcified fop been able to maintain this particular pose? Of course, the cane is a cheat. No self-respecting human statue would incorporate a prop to assist him in remaining motionless. Maybe I'll go over and snatch the money out of the hat—that might put a spring in his step! But I promised the inspector I wouldn't get arrested tonight, though I could always plead post-traumatic stress disorder.*

At the end of the block, Ripley's Believe it or Not Odditorium still managed—after how many decades?—to extract disposable income from the overawed tourist set. One window display pitched an exhibit about twins conjoined at the armpit who suffered from a tragic abnormality whereby the sibling on the left could utter only adjectives and nouns and the one on the right only verbs and adverbs. The struggle to complete a sentence was monumental. Roland slowed to a halt and thought about submitting his own story for consideration but thought better of it. The violence of last night remained much like a dream, not a fuzzy memory, because of the sheer otherworldliness of the sequence of events and the speed in which they took place.

When he reached the outdoor food vendors, Roland bought a sourdough chowder bowl and carried it to the Maritime Garden next to the Hyde Street cable car turnaround. He joined a ring of tourists to watch two men perform the necessary and time-honored function of securing the cable car to the circular terminus and then, with nothing but the strength in their backs and legs, slowly haul it counterclockwise on its platform until it faced the direction from whence it came. A two-man job to be sure, but one he imagined he could accomplish alone. He found an empty bench and sat to enjoy his meal. He studied the vacationers moving around him, some leisurely and others with hurried purpose. What archetypes possessed their personalities—trickster, sage, hero, shadow? He eyed them for clues. Was it possible to divine such things, or were such categories mere inventions of the overly educated? A young father kept a firm grasp on the ponytail of his four-year-old daughter as she tossed her head from side to side, smiling the while, in a mock attempt to break free of daddy's hold. His wife kept pace and urged the two elder offspring forward, two boys in crisp, black pirate hats, content to strut with elbows out behind the family.

The afternoon sun began its descent, pulsing fatly in the particulate haze that rose from the Pacific Ocean. The wooden bench had been soaking in heat all day and pressed through his clothing a perfect warmth that counteracted the chilly breeze just kicking up in the hours before dusk. When Twain said that the coldest winter he'd ever spent was a summer in San Francisco, he was undoubtedly referring to the marine layer that enveloped The City at end of day, regardless of the season. Roland closed his eyes and lifted his face toward the sun to better receive its warmth and, with a deep breath, drew in the medley of odors that competed in his nostrils—chowder, crab meat, cotton candy, caramel corn, putrid bay water, cut grass, machine oil from the cable car, his own body odor, and the sourdough bread in his hands. Never, as far as he could remember, had he given himself over to the luxuriant occupation of dissecting and identifying each and every recognizable smell on an odoriferous breeze, and he smiled at each one just as Adam must have smiled when he named all the animals. Tobacco smoke, roasted peanuts, a woman's perfume, coffee, even pigeon feathers. Meanwhile, the chowder cooled. Then he took on the cacophony of sounds, too fast and numerous for his brain to isolate and identify, but worth the effort, nonetheless. For what else, he thought, was life meant, except to savor every moment as deliberately as possible? You couldn't, he imagined, experience life in such a way and, at the same time, be a serial killer. Yet Roland failed to reflect on the question of whether he could relish the here and now—each exquisite sliver of infinity—without the fleeting serenity afforded him by alcohol.

Roland devoured the chowder then scraped the inside of the bread bowl clean with the sturdy plastic spoon. He tore off a hunk of bread and wiped his mouth with it before eating the makeshift napkin. Then he began slowly to dismantle the bowl one savory gob at a time until he was left with only his fingers to lick clean. *What now? Did I smell coffee?* Unlike half the people in The City, Roland was not a coffee addict, and he liked it best when augmented with whiskey. Just across the street, on the corner of Beach and Hyde, the Buena Vista Café, home of America's original Irish coffee, sold its famous elixir hand over fist, sometimes with lines out the door, as fast as the bartenders could make them. From his vantage, he saw that the place was not overcrowded and as he crossed the street toward the entrance the fumes of whiskey mixed with hot coffee overpowered the other odors in the air. Roland decided that the celebrated concoction would settle nicely in his belly on top of his hearty lunch. He needed to maintain his euphoric buzz.

He took his place in line. His pocket vibrated. He fished out his phone and looked at the display. It was Chaoxiang, his recent acquaintance from the underworld of international software piracy who claimed to know people in China that would pay thousands of dollars for the code to the pre-release version of NBA Shootout, whose job it was Gina's to test. The thumb drive that held the code was in his pocket, a much safer place than the glove compartment in the clown car. Roland had stopped locking his car long ago to keep the windows from being smashed, theft in The City had become so rampant.

Roland was skeptical that Chaoxiang—who he called Chow—was the real deal, as they'd met late one night in a bar where most of the conversations were a mixture of ninety percent bullshit diluted by cubes of dissolving hope. Still, being on the wrong side of the Ukrainian bookies' ledger gave him more than enough reason to take a chance when there appeared to be nothing to lose. They'd agreed in advance not to use names over the phone.

"Hey there, Charlie."

"What, you racist?"

"In this country everything is racist, so I don't fight it."

"You come see China. I show you racist. Chinese racist to Chinese. Hard do business in China except you know the best Chineses."

"I'm open for business right now, down at the wharf. I'm about to get a drink where the cable car turns around. Do you know where that is?"

"Can't come now. We meet tomorrow."

"Is that a question?"

"No. Me telling you. You hear me right?" Chaoxiang spoke rapidly, as though he spoke English well enough to talk fast without caring that his grammar was defective.

"Ok. I'll cancel my plans for tomorrow."

"You got no *plaanns*. Drunk got no *plaanns*. That always true everywhere."

"I forgot what a rude little fucker you are." Roland was feeling too good to resent the sketchy criminal.

"USA make people rude, that right Joe?"

"I'm in no position to disagree. When do you want to meet?"

"You tell me when. Me be so good to you because you got your booshit plans."

"Okay. Two o'clock then. Two o'clock at…"

"Don't say it, stupid. The poet house, right?"

"I'll see you there at two."

Roland ended the call. Poet house was a reference to Li Po's, a dive bar in Chinatown where the two first met. Any government agents listening in would have a hard time making the connection since Chaoxiang said 'house' and not 'bar.' *Clever little…* Roland couldn't decide which epithet to choose.

He ordered two Irish coffees. The barman, dapper in his black and white get-up, mixed them continuously in rows of bell-shaped glassed with practiced alacrity, topping each drink with a thick layer of chilled cream. He handed two to Roland. Roland paid the cashier and carried them to an empty corner at the back of the café and slugged the first one down with a double gulp that seared his throat.

"Thirsty, I see." It was a woman. She stood alone near the wide front window watching him.

She rated a definite *yes* on his scale of instantaneous sexual appraisal. Slim, youngish, smooth brown hair, sharp-boned, face lightly rouged. Her tight green short-cut dress pulled his eyes down to her well-toned legs. Ordinarily, Roland would have set about to ascertain her level of willingness, but he'd been lucky already today and, besides, he had to get back to The Gutter

"Just warming up for a swim to the rock." He gestured with his eyes to the historic prison island visible in the window.

"Alcatraz? Wouldn't it be easier to take the ferry over?"

"I plan on spearing a shark along the way. The fins are a delicacy."

"I'm pretty sure that's illegal."

"I'm pretty sure swimming to Alcatraz is illegal. Like jogging on the freeway. The freighters own the shipping lanes."

"I see. What's a dead shark tacked on to the rap sheet?"

"I'll just claim it attacked me. Man's got a right to defend himself."

"Won't the spear get in the way? How're you going to swim all that way with a spear in your hand?"

"It straps onto my back. And I carry a knife on my ankle in case the shark tries to sneak up on me."

"In case the hunter becomes the hunted. Very cunning."
"I live yet."
"Live to tell your tall tales." She pointed to his injured left arm. "What ferocious creature did that?"
"The most ferocious one of all."
Roland set down his empty glass and stared straight through the lenses of her sunglasses, nodding slowly in agreement with himself. If the conversation was to resume, she would have to keep it going. She gestured toward the untouched drink in his other hand.
"Are you going to drink that one too, or are you holding it for someone else?"
"I can do what I want with it."
"Are you thinking of offering it to me?"
"Normally, I'd hand it to you now and get myself another while you waited for me to come back. But today that would present a problem."
"Buying me a drink would present a problem? How so?"
"*Today* it would. Such a transaction would begin a relationship, and I have somewhere I have to be in a little while. One drink leads to another and then you know where that would lead."
"You're confident of that?"
"I wouldn't want to disappoint you."
"Oh I'm sure I'd get over it. I get a lot of attention. But I'm curious—what's wrong with today?"
"Tell you what. If you meet me tomorrow, I'll tell you what was wrong with today. It's a tale best told in an Italian restaurant in North Beach over a checkered tablecloth with pasta and a carafe of Chianti."
"You've got it all figured out."
"Sodini's on Green Street."
"Give me your number. I'll call you by two o'clock unless I change my mind."
She handed him her phone and he keyed in his phone number and handed it back.
"What's your name?"
"Same as yours."
He raised the glass. "To incest, then, and good health!" He drank the Irish coffee halfway down and handed her the rest.
"What a prince."

"You'll meet the prince tomorrow. I'm playing the pauper today."

"The pauper or the fool?"

Roland touched her hand to forgive her little jest then turned and left the bar.

~~~~~

He found a market and bought a pack of cigarettes, which expense depleted his resources substantially. The cost of a pack of twenty little doses of delicious poison was skyrocketing. The state had recently heaped yet another punitive tax on the product to further discourage its use. Cigarettes were a luxury item for all but the rich. Roland winced before he handed over the cash. Now he needed a patch of shade where he could sit, smoke, and make one last phone call before heading back to The Gutter to catch the local news.

"Hello." Deidre sounded groggy. He'd woken her.

"I'm sorry, Deidre. It's Roland. It sounds like I woke you up."

"I would have bet I'd never hear from you again."

"I'm tempted to let that hurt my feelings."

"Feelings—you have more than one? I sensed only the one."

"I thought we left things pretty well."

"Don't misunderstand me, sunshine. That one feeling—I liked it very much."

"I thought so. You matched me blow for blow."

"But that doesn't mean I hoped you would call, and it doesn't mean I didn't. What happened between us was just one of those rare moments sent down from heaven. But that one magnificent shagging will have to hold you indefinitely. We were outside of time, on the earthly plane, but outside of time."

"I see. So, the angels were up in heaven munching popcorn, delighting in our little romp, but now the show's over and they've moved on to staging their next entertainment?"

"Yes. And you and I—we're back to the usual humdrum."

He held the phone away from his mouth and whispered. *"Not I. No. Not I."*

"What did you say?"

Roland snapped himself back into the moment. "I don't get it. I know our little interlude felt like a dream, but in Earth time it lasted a little over an hour. Are you saying our time is up? You don't want to see me again?"

"We'd have to go through a process. We'd have to completely put aside what happened today. I've never done anything like that in my life. Right now, I'm thinking I must have caught myself up in the fairytale of the grateful maiden rewarding her dragon slayer. I'm glad I did it and I'm scared that I did, if that makes any sense."

"I don't have anything you could catch, if that's what you mean."

"I'm glad you said that, but I doubt you know that for sure. I took a chance. Anyway, that's not what I meant. I don't think a man—a man like you—could understand the kind of scared I mean."

"Let's slow this down a little, Deidre. I think you have the wrong impression. I mean, it makes sense, your misimpression, if I'm right about what you're thinking."

"And what do you think I'm thinking?"

"That I want you to be my plaything. You're thinking that I might think you're willing to be that. And I don't fault you if you thought that. It's totally understandable. "

"What are you calling for, Roland?"

"Because I can't go back to my humdrum. The humming and drumming are about to get a whole lot louder for me."

"Yes. I guess they are. But now you're being cagey again. Just answer my question."

"I'd like to know if I can..." Roland wasn't sure how to say it. Deidre waited for a few seconds then spoke.

"If you can what? We've eliminated *shag me again*."

"The press has my name—verified by the chief of police. I'm the officially recognized killer of the Glendale Butcher. The few early birds that showed up this morning outside my apartment—I think that was just the first trickle from a crack in the dam."

"Of course."

"You understand?"

"You can stay here if you need to dodge the press."

"Thank you. Thank you for making that so simple."

"On the couch. You will sleep on the couch."

"Yes of course. It's part of the process."

"You really are an idiot."

"Not part of the process?"

"You're a bit young for me, and a wee bit large. I'm terribly sore."

"So, what's this process you're talking about?"

"The situation you've gotten yourself into is very alarming, but it's not going to last very long. A week or two at the most…"

"That I've gotten *myself* into?"

"I'm not saying you did something wrong or that you're not the victim here, but sometimes even victims play a part in their fate."

"You sound like an insurance adjuster assigning contributory negligence."

"More like the night nurse in the trauma ward at city general. Only the very young and the very old are innocent victims, but I'm sure you're not in the mood for that debate."

"Ordinarily I'd love to stroll down that conversational road with you. But you're right—now is not the time. Maybe we can pick it up later? Can that be part of the process?"

"You won't know if you want the process till your life gets back to normal, and that shouldn't take too long. The kind of fame you're facing is so fleeting that it isn't even fame, more like sudden attention."

"I hope you're right."

"Do you want my couch tonight?"

"I just want to know that it's there if I need it."

"If I'm at home and you're not drunk, you can sleep on my couch. All you have to do is call."

"I was joking about angels before, but you really are one."

"Now is probably a good time for you to thank me and hang up."

Roland thanked her and hung up. When he stood up to walk, he felt a familiar pressure in his pants and, looking down, took note of how aroused he was. *Till my life gets back to normal.* Walking back to The Gutter, he rolled that phrase around in his mind as he would a multi-faceted gemstone. Might it pertain to most people? To most people his age? Had someone done a study? Would the study merely confirm—as he had come to learn most studies did—the wisdom of common sense? A baby screaming its head off on a passenger plane has a normal routine to return to. School kids too and working people and retired folks. The elderly and infirm certainly. When did he, Roland Hazzard, last have a normal life to go back to? How would he face the unpredictable and abnormal stretch of days or weeks that lay ahead without a foundational normal? His mother knew instinctively that he needed to get out of that city and take refuge, if only temporarily, in his parents' normal life in bucolic Northern Idaho. *Should I go back to the bar?* By the time he'd gotten around to asking himself that question, he'd come upon the clown car a few blocks away from the place. An unwelcome voice in his head let out a mocking giggle, not of the impish demonic variety, but that of an avuncular stranger offering advice to a child he knew would ignore it. The dreaded next indicated right thing, the giggle said, was to hop in the Sentra and urge it up Nob Hill to his own personal one-bedroom crime scene, glass-strewn and blood-spattered. The hallway, to be sure, needed to be returned to its normal condition. All the more reason to stroll past his pathetic little automobile and silence the voice with a few shots in the convivial company of his old drinking buddies—his own *back to normal*. Roland patted the keys in his pocket, pointed his nose toward the bar, and quickened his pace.

The place was partially filled, mostly with men just released from their shifts on the boats and nearby docks and gutteries. Plenty of familiar faces among the laborers crowded around the bar, with Sal now tending to business. Sal was not his name— perhaps no one there but Gerry knew his real name—but as he cut the perfect profile of a *goombah* and hailed from the Italian section of North Beach, the nickname landed on his head and clung like a squid. Gerry moved around the pool table lighting the Sterno cans underneath the steel serving pans. The lids would come off at five o'clock, only minutes away. He nodded hello to Roland and glanced over to the stool where he'd been sitting, now draped with Gerry's jacket to reserve it. Roland nodded thank you and took his spot next to the poster of the impenetrable female.

Roland held up Gerry's jacket and Sal came over and took it from him. "Good to see you back at your post." It was clear Gerry had told Sal that Roland had reemerged and would be taking that stool.

Before Roland could reply in kind, half of the patrons turned their attention in his direction and began to greet him. "Roland, Roland, Roland," sang his old buddy, Cesar, to the tune of Frankie Laine's "Rawhide," except Cesar was aping Dan Aykroyd. Roland laughed and grabbed the bar rail and leaned back on his stool and raised one of his

Laredos above the bar in salute. The stool tilted back on two of its four legs and balanced precariously when Roland let go of the bar, swirling his hand in the manner of a bull-rider. "Yee Ha!" He saved himself from spilling over backward with a split-second spin and caught the upended stool as he landed with both boots on the floor.

"Couldn't stay away, I see." It was his old gutting mate, Martin.

"Like a dog returning to its own vomit."

"Musta missed the smell." It was Chuck, another friend from the docks.

"No. But I'm sure it's the only place strong enough to mask your stench."

Carlos chimed in. "Not if he's standing next to his sister. The two together can fog up your glasses."

"Are you dating them individually or as a pair?" Martin said.

His old drinking crew carried on with their raillery—none yet too drunk to be anything but friendly—and peppered Roland with questions. Judging by their line of inquiry, none appeared to know much about why he'd been absent from the bar for so long, which bolstered Roland's trust in Gerry's confidentially. They knew he'd lost his job at the guttery because of an arrest and subsequent incarceration, but nothing more concrete than that. Roland had so compartmentalized his former working and drinking life that his pals had but a general idea of where he lived, and only a few knew his last name. That's how it was between most of them—friends of a sort, but only in this limited way. He could tell them whatever he wanted to, make things up as he went along. But today he was decidedly reticent. As adroit a fabricator as he was, no story he could conjure now would match the drama about to be revealed to the bar by the local TV news.

Sal set a whiskey on the rocks in front of him. Roland paid and sucked half of it through his teeth.

The anchorwoman appeared on the screen. "Quiet down. I want to hear this."

Sal raised the remote and touched up the volume a few bars. The anchorwoman began in earnest.

"FBI most wanted serial killer, Samuel Barsamian, the notorious Glendale Butcher, was killed last night in a home invasion on Nob Hill..."

The crowd around Roland was still making a lot of noise.

"Shut up. I said I want to hear this." Roland's eyes remained glued to the tube.

"...and after a violent struggle, the resident killed the intruder with what the police say was the attacker's own knife..."

They were still too loud. "Hey Sal, can you pause it?" It was meant as a request but received as a question. Sal shook his head. The bar had not invested in a DVR.

Roland erupted. "EITHER SHUT THE FUCK UP OR EXIT THE GODDAMNED BAR!"

The place went quiet. They'd never seen that side of him. Gerry shot him a disapproving look. Roland shrugged and shook his head with his mouth half-open in a plea of innocence, as if to say *what am I supposed to do?*

"...wanted for several murders across California, Arizona, and New Mexico over the span of two violent months in 2012. Federal and local agencies lost the trail of the fugitive..." The screen showed what looked like a high-school yearbook photograph of Barsamian. It was he. No doubt about it.

"Why do you care so much about this guy?" Cesar said. "Did you know him?"

"For a few minutes. Just listen."

"...SFPD Chief Maruyama in a press conference earlier today identified the Nob Hill resident who managed to kill the notorious serial murderer as Roland Hazzard, a twenty-five-year-old Berkeley graduate, himself no stranger to the law."

"That you? You killed that sonofabitch?"

Roland nodded and turned his head so Cesar could see the truth of it writ large on his face. A few others gathered around.

"...Mister Hazzard has been unavailable for comment. We can report that he left his apartment in a hurry shortly after daybreak this morning and has not returned home since..."

"Is that how you got that arm?" Martin said.

Roland held up his good hand to reinforce his command for silence. The co-anchor, a mid-wit named Xavier, had some follow-up questions.

"So, Jasmine, do we know what brought this Butcher character to our fair city? Or if he had some relationship with Mister Hazzard? Was this just a random break-in? Are we even sure it was a break-in?"

"According to the police report, it appears to have been a break-in through an alley window, but as far as the motive or any history between Mister Hazzard and the serial killer, that's unknown at this point, according to our sources in the police department..."

"Bullshit."

"What's bullshit?" said Cesar.

"*Unknown at this point.* She's trying to make it sound like I might have known that psychopath."

"You just said you knew him, knew him for a few minutes," Martin said.

"Yeah. Starting when he broke into my place and ending when he died in my hallway a few minutes later."

The news piece continued, providing more information about Barsamian and his murder spree. Roland turned away from the screen. He'd heard what he had come to hear, had seen the first ripple from a bolder flung into a deep lake. Had felt the first flutter from the wings of a moth emerging from its cocoon, a flutter that would precipitate a devastating hurricane. No. What the hell was he thinking? Nothing that extreme. Deidre was probably right, he thought. Certainly right. The ripples would flatten out soon enough. No tsunami would crash into his life and smash it to splinters.

"That's badass," said Martin.

"You're a goddamn hero, Roland," said Cesar.

"How badly did he cut your arm?" said Chuck.

The questions started piling up, from the sensible to the idiotic. "How long did it take to kill him? Did he beg for his life? Could you smell his blood? How big was he? What if he'd had a gun? Did he tell you who he was? How did you get the knife away from him? Did you check his wallet for cash?" It irritated Roland to think that he would have to field some of these same questions and slews of others in the days to come. He spun around on his stool to face the cohort and leaned his back on the rail and propped one elbow on the bar. He sipped the remnants of his drink and bore the questions with terse, monkish patience. "Tell us what it feels like to kill someone." Holding court had already lost its novelty.

"I feel like Socrates instructing a bunch of neophytes."

"What's that supposed to mean?" Martin said.

"Picture baby birds packed into their nest with their greedy little beaks gaping open."

"Right. That clears it right up."

"What did you come down here for?" Chuck said. It was an excellent question.

"Did anyone hear what the newslady said? Was anybody listening?"

No one dared venture a guess. Roland drained his glass, leaving only whiskey-flavored ice. He shook the cubes audibly, waiting. At the far end of the bar, the two itinerant Andy Griffith fans remained on their stools and craned their heads to hear the conversation. Beside them, next to the wall, a clean-shaven, bespectacled man with a newspaper spread out on the bar nursed a pint of beer and kept to himself.

Finally, Chuck answered the question. "To get away from the press."

"And why would I want to get away from the press?"

"I can think of a bunch of reasons."

"What's the most obvious one?"

"They ask a lot of questions," Sal said from behind the bar.

"No spoilers, Sal. I was addressing my disciples."

"Because reporters ask a lot of questions," Chuck said.

"Correctomundo! But no cigar for a secondhand answer."

"What's your point, killer?" Martin said.

"He came here to avoid a lot of questions," Cesar said.

"Can I get an amen?" Roland said.

"An amen and a bottomless glass," Cesar said, looking around the room to elicit the assent of the others. "This man drinks for free tonight, and no more questions."

"What a bunch of bullshit," said Martin. "He can't just disappear for months and then show up to hear his name on the evening news and tell us to mind our own business."

Roland let his air of condescension expire and resumed his normal posture. Since he was nearly out of cash, the prospect of an everlasting refill struck him as a cosmic boon.

"Martin, buddy, hear me out. In the first place, I've already answered a shitload of questions, which I don't begrudge. And you're right; I can't just show up out of the blue and expect the royal treatment." He was beginning to resent the mutinous son of a bitch. "But considering I've told the story about five times already today, including a long drawn out second-by-second recap to the police, I'm begging your forgiveness and asking for a little respite." He turned to Sal and held out his empty glass. "If you would be so kind, my good man."

"Have it your way," Martin said. "But one more question."

"Sure, Marty—one more, one that needs only a simple answer."

"Did you really graduate from Berkeley?"

"That's where I met Socrates."

The assembled regulars and sundry others dove into the buffet and stuffed their faces with hotdogs and beans and washed them down with beer. Roland refused the food and kept one hand wrapped around his whiskey glass, which Sal kept full. The subject of the killing had subsided, though here and there one of his buddies would look at him and, with an admiring shake of the head, express solemn admiration. "God love you, brother." "Roland fucking Hazzard." "Dude fucked around and found out."

Gerry came up from behind and put a hand on Roland's shoulder. "You seem satisfied."

"I'm in that general vicinity."

"You're starting to get that look."

"I guess I'm supposed to ask—*what look is that?*"

"Are you going to make this difficult? All I have to do is nod at Sal and the glass goes away."

"I agreed to not get out of hand."

What Gerry was observing in Roland might be called his slipping from gray to black. Roland wasn't drunk exactly, but his consciousness had begun to close in around the edges, evidenced by a glazing of the eyes and a drooping of the chin. On his mouth was affixed a feeble smile. Contentment void of content. The look of an idiot.

"Another drink or two and you'll be nowhere at all."

"Is that your professional opinion?"

"I'd go so far as *diagnosis*. I've been practicing for years."

"So, what do you prescribe, doc?"

"No more than one more."

Cornered, Roland had the good sense to surrender. He accepted the concession in the form of a pint of draft beer and floated around the bar proffering thank-yous, take-it-easys and see-ya-laters to make the appearance of a voluntary departure. He drew Cesar forward with an affectionate yank on the back of the neck and planted an exaggerated kiss on his forehead in appreciation for all the free booze his friend had arranged. "You're a real prince, Cesar, and I bet you've got the papers to prove it."

Nearing the door, he stopped and glared at the two dawdlers. "I sent *your prince* another soul to torment."

"You told the whole bar you didn't want to talk about it," the warlock said.

"I just thought you should know the good guys are winning."

"Thou shalt not kill," the sidekick said.

"It's a bad translation. The Hebrew—*ratzach*—means murder."

"Did he just call me a rat sack?" the sidekick said.

"Let me handle the professor," the warlock said.

"I see why you're in charge," Roland said.

"I bet you had a choice."

"I bet he was drunk and doesn't remember."

"In that case, not a choice. An action true to his nature."

"That, or he chose the darkest path."

"Why don't you ask him?"

"He doesn't seem very friendly."

"Keep it up and you'll both be picking teeth out of your own shit."

"I'm glad we didn't chip into the get-our-local-hero-shitfaced fund," the warlock said.

"You deadbeats were broke to begin with."

With that, he pushed the door open and with one arm swam through the flood of light that poured in, holding his bandage up to shield his eyes. The stranger, sitting alone next to the adversaries, let the door close then got up and slipped out after Roland.

Chapter 9
September 30, 2016 - 5:45 PM

Walking to his car, Roland forgot why he'd parked two blocks away or if he'd even had a good reason. If he understood his progressive disease, he'd have admitted that he had no reason, only the reflexive secrecy of a typical dry alcoholic. Carefree in his intoxication now, he felt unnecessarily inconvenienced by his own mindless decision. Parking was easy down here, after all. But in his neighborhood up the hill a mile or so away the window for street parking was rapidly closing. He quickened his pace accordingly, began to list, then slowed his steps to steady his gait. He knew he was well above the legal limit, but in his inebriated estimation still not too drunk to drive. He stopped to frisk himself, first for his car keys—check—then his cigarettes—check—and finally his wallet—check—empty except for his driver's license, library card, ATM, and credit card. The internal echo of the inspector's admonition to not get arrested tonight gave way to the sound of footsteps behind him. He surmised by their proximity that whoever it was had come from the bar. Without turning around, he stepped sideways toward a parked car and leaned against it. A glance confirmed his suspicion. The loner sipping beer and reading the newspaper next to the third-string devils had followed him out.

The man stopped and looked at him. Roland fished out a cigarette and lit it, ignoring him in such a way that the man should know he was being ignored. He would have to speak or move on.

"Roland Hazzard?"

The man took a step toward Roland, who had the setting sun behind him, and reached into his coat and took out a pair of sunglasses and slid them under the brim of his Giants baseball cap to shield his eyes. He looked around forty-five, on the short side, well-muscled under his tight-fitting polo shirt. Roland observed that his was not a working man's or an athlete's physique, but that a man who lifted weights a couple of times a week.

Roland stretched out his legs and balanced the heel of one boot on the toe of the other and spread his arms wide like a wire-walker to demonstrate his impressive physical coordination.

"I like old movies." Roland gave it a Humphry Bogart snarl, letting smoke seep past the cigarette clenched between his teeth. "Do you like old movies?"

The stranger pulled his chin up as though struck by the oddness of the question. "Um, hmm—no. Not especially."

"Well, if this were an old movie, the guy in my boots might say something like, *you have me at a disadvantage, sir*. It sounds better with a British accent."

"You're right. People don't talk like that anymore."

Roland switched to a slurred Peter O'Toole. "Civilization is lost, IRRETRIEVABLY."

The stranger, visibly flummoxed and unable to parry, bided his time by glancing at his wristwatch. A few seconds more without a reply and he would have to keep walking. Roland smiled, having turned the tables and put the stranger at the disadvantage. But only for the moment.

"Oh. I thought it was gay marriage that killed civilization."

"Ha!" Roland maintained his British accent. "You've touched upon the very heart of the matter. There was a time when gay marriage meant nothing more than happy matrimony."

"I see you've given this some thought."

"Not a wit. I'm gifted with an unnaturally agile mind." He dropped the accent. "Or maybe it's a curse. Anyway, you get the point."

"I have to admit I've been lost from the start."

"Lost? Is that why you've been following me, hoping I might be able to help you find your way?"

"Forgive me, but I wasn't exactly following you. I just want to talk to you."

"You could have talked to me in the bar."

"Alone—that is if you don't mind."

Roland was determined to outlast the man. He set aside his parking concerns in favor of the present delay, not eager to return to his apartment and deal with the wreckage of his recent past. Killing time on the sidewalk in chat-chat with this curious, harmless fellow seemed as good a way as any to avoid doing the next indicated thing. The man would have to declare his business eventually, for Roland would not ask it. Only one question weighed on his mind—had the man known his name before he entered the bar, or did he learn it there amid the revelry?

"Have you ever seen the Flintstones?"

"We're jumping from old movies to old cartoons now?"

"I don't use an umbrella."

"Umbrella?"

"I don't block the raindrops, man."

"I see. It's raining inspiration."

"The Flintstones—do you know it?"

"I would hope so. I'm a good bit older than you."

"Did you know it was a kid's version of The Honeymooners, which starred the great Jackie Gleason? Have you heard of him?"

"My head is spinning, and you're the one who's been drinking."

"Pull up a fender." Roland motioned to the rear section of the car he was leaning against.

The stranger did as suggested and settled against the fender.

"The Flintstones had a theme song. It went: *When you're with the Flintstones/ Have a yabba-dabba-doo time/ A dabba-doo time/ We'll have a GAYYYY old time*. And then they repeated it. *We'll have a GAYYYY old time*. Gay—real loud and drawn out."

"I see you can carry a tune."

Roland was glad the stranger could spar. While he had no clue as to why the man had followed him, he was content to dance around the subject until he decided whether he liked him or not. If he decided he didn't like him, it wouldn't matter, and Roland would walk off.

"Do you know those two assholes sitting next to you?"

"No. But it seemed like *you* did?"

"Only well enough to completely dismiss them."

"Then why are you asking about them?"

"Because they embody the very nihilism that harbingers the fall of Western Civilization. Don't lose the plot, Sir Lancelot."

"I'll guess I'll have to take your word for that."

"Can we take anyone's word for anything anymore, when we're shoving our language into the shredder one word at a time?"

"I see I see—like the alteration of the word *gay*."

"*Alteration* does not quite capture it. More like *redefinition*. You see, whoever owns the re-run rights to the Flintstones has seen fit to dub the word *great* over the word *gay*; so now it goes, *we'll have a GREAT old time.*"

"Wow. I can hear the Parthenon crumbling as we speak."

"Mock away, monsieur, but if you google *Gay Paris*, I'd bet you won't get much information about the artsy café culture in the capital of France—you'll get a list of male sex clubs."

"Seems you've made an odd choice of cities to call you home if you have issues with…"

"Hold your horses, Geronimo. You're the one who dropped the gay bomb. I'm talking about the corruption of language. The examples are legion."

"What makes you think I disagree?"

"That doesn't mean you agree."

"Am I required to—required to agree with you?"

"Of course not." Roland decided he was a good sport and opted to like him. "But if you want to keep talking—if you want to get around to telling me why you followed me out of the bar—then give me an example, one from your own observations. Otherwise, I'll be on my way."

"I should be able to think of one. I make my living as a writer."

Aha, Roland rejoiced inwardly. *A journalist—this guy's a journalist.* "Well. I'm a gifted listener." Roland watched the Giant's fan search for an answer. The pressure was on. He watched the man squint with concentration and twist his lips with worry.

"Ok. I've got one—*adult.*"

"Bingo! What used to mean *mature responsible person* now doubles for *dirty sex*. An assault on the psyches of English-speaking *a-dol*-escents everywhere. Gold star for you."

"Are you like this when you're sober?"

"I'm sober now. Sober enough."

"Not sober enough to drive."

"I'm pretty sure that's none of your concern."

"You're right. I'm not a cop."

"No. Your job is writing."

"Seriously, is this your normal personality? I'm asking as a writer now."

Roland fought against anger, an emotion he, as a martial artist, had necessarily worked hard to control. Where did this impudent prick get off questioning him on the peculiarities of his personality? He knew how quickly a surge of wrath could morph into a rage that only an act of violence could assuage. It struck him as odd that the violence he committed last night was driven by something else entirely, from an emotion he did not recognize and found impossible to name, whether remembered in tranquility at The Wharf or in his current state of genuine pique.

"Why the hell did you follow me out here? Declare your business or fuck-off or declare your business *and* fuck-off."

"I want to make sure you get home alright."

"And why should you give a shit?"

"I'm not sure I do. I'm doing a favor for a friend, a mutual friend actually."

"Gerry? Did he call you down here to be my guardian angel?"

"Who's Gerry?"

"He owns the bar. You saying you don't know him?"

"Bill Spelman sent me. I didn't know that place existed before today."

"You're friends with Inspector Spelman?"

"Yeah, I've known him for years. He's a very good man."

"You said *mutual friend*—he's not my friend. I met him just a few hours ago."

"Whatever he is, he's got your best interests at heart. Of that I can assure you."

Roland stepped away from the car, turned and stood on the sidewalk to face the man squarely.

"By having me followed? How did he even know I was here? Let's start there."

The man took off his sunglasses and met Roland's stern demeanor with his own seasoned fortitude.

"You called him a couple hours ago, right?"

"Yeah."

"And you told him you were down by the wharf."

"Did he tell you what I had for lunch?"

"No. But he said you'd been drinking."

"This isn't the wharf. We're six seven blocks from the wharf."

"I said the same thing when he gave me the address. I said that's a long walk from the wharf."

Roland intuited the solution to the mystery but did not utter it and let the man continue.

"Bill said you've been known to drink here, that you were arrested a few months ago after leaving this bar. He said he'd be surprised if I didn't find you here. The man's a police detective, a very good one."

"He called you?"

"Yeah. He wants to help you. You made a good impression on him. You're lucky because I think you're a goof, but then again you were sober when you met Bill, so I'm assuming this is not your normal personality. That's why I asked."

Roland lit another cigarette and exhaled straight up into the air and watched the breeze disperse the smoke.

"Okay. The conspiracy is out in the open. I'll be sure to thank the inspector for the ride home. Parking where I live is a bitch at this hour anyway. I'll get my car tomorrow. Where are you parked?"

"That's not the conspiracy. There's a much bigger conspiracy. I work for *The San Francisco Chronicle*. I want to write your story for tomorrow's paper. I'm here to get the scoop as they used to say in old movies. And, of course, I'd be happy to give you a ride home."

"Let me get this straight—your friend Bill is doing *me* a favor by helping *you* get the scoop?"

"I guarantee you, when we get to your apartment there's going to be a bunch of reporters hanging around, and when they see me with you, they'll know it's time for them to go home. I'm fairly well known in this town." He stepped forward and extended his hand. "Joshua Goldberg—pleased to meet you."

Roland shook his hand. A bus roared up and stopped at the light, forcing them to pause their conversation. Roland noted that the public conveyance was nearly empty at an hour when a bus should be packed with people coming home from work. One of the few passengers, a young woman seated at the window facing them, stared into her phone. Her spiked hair, a variegated splash of purples and greens, looked like a prize-winning sea anemone. Four or five stainless steel piercings clung to her face, ornamenting her eyebrow, nose, and lips. Roland found himself, unconsciously, transfixed on her face, as a pygmy would at the first helmeted white man to hack his way into his corner of the Congo. She noticed him watching her and stuck out her studded tongue then aimed both middle fingers at him as the bus lurched forward and roared away.

"She voted twice."

Joshua Goldberg laughed. "Not counting her tongue."

"Maybe she was trying to catch a fly."

His laughter ebbed to a chuckle that flattened to a smile meant for Roland, who accepted it by smiling back. The moment passed. Roland was softened but not satisfied. He'd never heard of this Joshua Goldberg, but then again, he seldom read the newspaper.

"I'm waiting to hear how giving you an interview is supposed to help me. I dealt with a gaggle from the fourth estate this morning, and I can easily push my way past them again."

"I know you just met him, but do you trust Inspector Spelman? He knows what kind of press you're going to get, and he knows I'll give you a chance to speak for yourself. He knows me well enough to trust that I'll give you a fair shake."

"Tell you what. You come help me clean up and we'll talk. Then write whatever you want. I don't care one way or the other, as long as you're polite."

"What do you mean by *clean up*?"

"There's a lot of glass and blood in my hallway. I'll take care of the blood."

"Fair enough. I'll sweep up glass. I shouldn't be touching blood so close to the Sabbath." He pointed to his car and walked toward it. Roland followed.

"Josh, huh? That's an unfortunate name for a journalist."

"How's that?"

"*Josh*. It's folksy for *kidding, spoofing, lying* even."

"No one's ever pointed that out to me before."

"I'm gifted—gifted, underpaid, and unappreciated."

Joshua opened the passenger door to his silver Volvo. Roland climbed in and settled into the fragrant leather seat while Joshua took his place behind the wheel.

"Can I smoke in here?"

"You just sucked down two cigarettes."

"I just wanted to hear you say no."

"Buckle up."
Roland took out his phone and checked it for recent activity. Two voicemails and seven text messages. Unprecedented. It vibrated. The name 'Sand' appeared on the display.
"I've got to take this. It's my sister."
"Don't mind me. I know the way."
"Hi, Sand." Roland forced a sober voice.
"Roland, Roland." Her tone was a mixture of panic and relief. "Where are you?"
Roland paused to ponder the question. Surely, she did not want to entertain his speculations as to the location of his consciousness. Did she want merely to know at which Earth coordinates his body was located? Maybe, but probably not. Before another second elapsed, he came up with, "I'm in a car on my way home."
"A car? Whose car?"
"I met a newspaper reporter, a friend of the police inspector working my case."
"That's kinda weird. Why is there a case? Mom and Dad said you weren't in any trouble."
"I'm not, not with the law anyway. I should have said *the* case."
"What's the reporter for?"
"He wants to write the story."
"The story's already all over the internet."
"That must be just the usual noise. He wants to interview me and tell *my* story."
"What's his name?"
"Joshua…" Roland turned to Joshua to make sure he got the last name right."
"Goldberg."
"Goldberg."
"Let me talk to him."
Roland offered the phone to Joshua. "She wants to talk to you."
"Put it on speaker."
Roland set his phone to speaker mode.
"Sandy, meet Joshua Goldberg. He drives a sleek silver Volvo."
"Hello, Mister Goldberg. What paper do you work for?"

"Hi, Sandy. It's nice to meet you. I've been writing for *The San Francisco Chronicle* for more than ten years."

"Are you observant?"

"Well, yeah. It's kind of job requirement."

"I mean *religiously*. Are you an observant Jew?"

"I don't see what difference that should make."

"I've got no use for atheist Jews. An atheist Jew is not a Jew at all, not in my book."

"I see the mouth runs in the family."

"Easy there, fella," said Roland.

"Well, I don't wear a yarmulke or spend a lot of time in synagogue, but I do honor the sabbath in my own way."

Roland laughed. "He's going to violate it today by helping me clean up the blood in my apartment. I think I remember something in Deuteronomy prohibiting that."

"I consider this an emergency, so I get a pass."

"Emergency?" she said. "What's the emergency?"

"My deadline."

"That doesn't sound like an emergency."

"Speed is everything in the press cycle. Roland needs to get out in front of this thing, to get on the record before speculation becomes reality."

Sandy paused as though to consider the situation. "Roland, do you trust this guy?"

"What's the worst he can do?"

"I could do a lot of damage, actually."

"Don't tempt me to dare you."

"Have you been drinking, Roland? Scratch that. Let me ask the Jew. You won't bear false witness, will you Mister Goldberg? Has my brother been drinking?"

"Yes. But he's holding up pretty well, working me over pretty good, actually."

"Don't start on me, Sandy. I had a pretty rough night last night, but you knew that already."

"You should get on a plane right now, Roland. Fly home. Let Mister Goldberg write a nice little story about you but get out of that godforsaken city. Mom and Dad would love to have you up for a good long visit. Let this thing blow over."

"I can't just leave my job."

"Have you asked them? I'm sure they'd give you a week or two off, considering the circumstances. Tell them you've got the PTSD."

"It's a good idea, Sandy. I think I might just do that." His tone was insincere.

"And you could dry out too. Help out Mom and Dad with some honest labor."

The car began the steep ascent up Nob Hill toward home. Roland levered back the seat and shut his eyes and muttered, "Yes. Dad suggested that." He waited for a reply and hoped it would be goodbye. While he loved and respected his sister, now was not the time for her tender ministrations. The image of his blood-soaked hallway appeared in his mind, producing a shudder of horror. Horror—but not that of a child being dragged to a house haunted by poltergeists that tormented no one but him. Rather, the horror of a man being conveyed by a stranger back to the confines of an apartment he no longer wished to inhabit, indeed, back to a life he did not want to resume. To a life over which, though he did not especially enjoy it, he'd maintained until now at least the illusion of control. Like a poisonous gas seeping through the vents, a foreboding crept over him as from some villainous source he couldn't identify. All his life, Roland had been immune to fear, and given the idyllic circumstances of his upbringing, his physical stature and beauty, quick intelligence and carefree temperament, the demon fear had never found a place to sink its claws. He clenched his eyes against the dread while his brain automatically tracked the location of the Volvo on the grid of San Francisco. He knew from the pitch of the streets exactly where he was, intersection by intersection. His ears transmitted to his brain the easy back and forth between his sister and Joshua, who seemed to be enjoying the chance to get acquainted. How dare they be in the moment, so comfortable with one another, so naturally personable, so full of unpretentious good humor, when he, the man of the hour, had ten plates spinning in the middle of a hurricane with a blindfold cinched around his eyes and both feet hobbled by ski-boots? "All the king's horses," he whispered. The alcohol had stopped working.

"What was that, Roland? Did you say something?"

"He said *all the king's horses.*"
"What the hell does that mean?"
"He's half asleep I think."
"ROLAND!"
He sat up and opened his eyes. "Sorry, Sandy. These hills are making me a little woozy. I was imagining Humpty Dumpty rocking back and forth on a castle wall."
"Sober up and call Phillip."
"I love you, Sis."
"You have to love yourself first for your love to be worth a damn."
"That won't make the country charts."
"You really are an asshole."
"Have you talked to Phillip?"
"Yes. Just before I called you. He's not going to play the big brother role. You need to call him if you want to talk to him."
"Thank you, Sis. Thanks for calling." She ended the call with her unsatisfied goodbye.

Roland directed Joshua to stop a few blocks from his building at the CVS Pharmacy where he'd bought his necessaries that morning. Next door to that was Trader Joe's, the largest market in the Nob Hill district. The little corner grocery, Andruko's Market, a few steps away from his building, was owned and operated by the Ukrainian brothers to whom he was in serious arrears. It didn't stock the required cleaning products—buckets and brushes and such—anyway; but even if it had, Roland had no intention of crossing its threshold until he carried an envelope of some respectable weight to hand Taras Andruko.

"I've got to pick up some cleaning supplies."

Joshua pulled in and found a parking space. Roland thought about tapping Joshua for a bit of cash but decided that might be pressing his luck. His credit card had yet to give out, God bless America.

"Stay alert. This is the getaway car."

Roland got a bucket from the CVS and filled it with detergent, brushes, a mop, and some rags then took his purchases next door and bought a bottle of Trader Joe's Kentucky Bourbon, which he concealed at the bottom of the bucket under the rags. As he turned to leave the store, the effeminate cashier sang a few bars from the Disney tune, "Whistle While You Work," except he improvised. *"Tipple while you work.*

Tipple while you work..." Roland shot the clerk a hateful backward glare that did not change the demeanor of the jolly assailant. But was he an assailant, or just a happy fellow wishing his customer a pleasant evening with innocent good humor? Warranted or not, there was plenty of untapped resentment in Roland's reservoir, and he decided to pass along one of the two fingers flashed at him by the pagan bus rider. He held it aloft as he turned toward the door, loath to see the clerk's reaction.

The throng of reporters Joshua had predicted turned out to be only a minor assemblage. As the two approached Roland's building, the unsteady hero limping along on his injured foot with the bucket of supplies in hand, three journalists—two women and a man—all holding recording devices, leapt from their cars and ran to intercept them before they could reach the entrance. "Let me handle this," said Joshua. Roland set down the bucket and stood behind his protector. The three reporters reminded him of frenzied school children reaching out their hands for the first ball at a dunk-the-principal booth.

"Roland Hazzard," said one of the women. "Channel Four would like to put you on the news tonight. Would you be willing to come down and talk to our producer?"

"He's all booked up for tonight, Melissa,"

"Are you in charge of his dance card, Goldberg?" said the male in the group.

Roland leaned on the mop handle to demonstrate his patience.

"Mister Hazzard has agreed to sit with me for an interview. You'll find it in *The Chronicle* tomorrow morning."

"Are you two friends? How long have you known each other?"

The other woman stepped forward and thrust her recording device at Roland. "Roland Hazzard, we just want to ask you a few questions. How much do you remember about last night? Were you too drunk to remember what you did? Why did you rush off so fast this morning? Where's that little yellow car you were driving? Are you hiding something? What do you have to hide?"

The others heaped on more questions. The male reporter, from Channel 5, offered to drive him down to his newsroom right then and broadcast a live interview. "We can get something to eat along the way if you want."

"Look, you guys, Mister Hazzard has been through a harrowing ordeal. Leave me your numbers and he'll call you if he wants to be a carnival attraction. But it won't be tonight."

The male reporter piped up again. "Can you confirm that, Roland? Is Goldberg from *The Chronicle* speaking on your behalf?"

Then the second woman, very loudly. "Are you impaired right now?"

Now the first woman. "Can you even speak? Can you say anything at all?"

Roland put his hand on Joshua's shoulder to stay his intercession. He would handle this question himself. With a sweep of his injured arm he said in a stilted professorial tone, "In the words of one of the greatest characters in all of American LIT-ra-CHA, *I would prefer not to.*" Then he picked up the bucket, mounted the steps, keyed open the door, and stepped into the lobby. Joshua followed him inside and made sure the lock clicked shut behind them.

"You went to Berkeley I heard you say."

They spoke as they moved toward the stairs.

"Is this the start of the interview?"

"Everything is the interview unless you tell me to keep something off the record. I'll be happy to respect that."

"Yep. My degree is in English, but I earned a lot of units in History, Philosophy, Linguistics, Archeology."

"Archeology?"

"Yeah. Ancient archeology. The entire field is a fraud. A racket. A complete waste of time. Those guys have no idea how human civilization came into being."

"Is that the booze talking, or do you really believe that?"

Astrid appeared at the top of the stairs. She'd been glued to her computer screen when the sound of the conversation—leastways Roland's boisterous voice amplified by the stone-tiled lobby—drew her out of her chair and onto the landing. She seemed practically out of breath, not from walking too fast but from heart-racing excitement.

"Good evening, Zinnia."

"Roland. I'm so glad to see you. I really need to apologize for the way I acted last night."

"Forget it. I always enjoy your theatrics."

Joshua reached the landing first and held out his hand. "Hi, Zinnia. I'm Joshua Goldberg from *The Chronicle*."

"Hi, Joshua Goldberg. My name is actually Astrid." Joshua looked at Roland for an explanation.

Astrid came to his rescue. "Every time he sees me, he pretends he can't remember my name and picks the first flower he can think of."

"Is astrid even a flower?"

"No. I guess that's…"

"The difference between silly and droll," said Roland.

"He's been turning me in circles since I met him today."

"You look a little discombobulated, Buttercup. Why not come inside and have a drink? Better yet, you can fix the drinks. Josh and I have work to do."

Astrid took a step back to assess the situation. She pointed to the bucketful of cleaning supplies he was carrying. "Is that what I think it's for?"

Roland ignored her and turned toward the door and extended his key toward the lock. She shot Joshua a look of emergency bewilderment as though to seek his advice.

"Let me peek my head in first, Astrid. I'll let you know what it looks like in there."

"We'll have to step over the big blood patch by the door…"

"Wait a second—both of you. I have something horrible to tell you, something horrible and wonderful."

Roland withdrew the key from the lock. Something about the tone of her voice and the strange combination of adjectives—horrible *and* wonderful—made Roland turn around and take her seriously. Her mouth was half open, her phony red hair a mess. *Haven't you been to work today?* he felt like saying. *Did you lose whatever thrift shop job has been keeping you afloat? Drawstring burgundy hospital pants, tie-dye t-shirt, no bra, slippers—clearly you're not going anywhere tonight. Have you been putting on weight you don't want anyone to see? Slipping maybe? Maybe you don't need a drink. Maybe you've been drunk all day or stoned or both.*

Her eyes darted between the faces of the two men as though deciding which one to tell her important revelation. Roland observed her panicked expression and after a few seconds concluded she was more crazy than sane. The thought that she lived next door to the scene of a homicide, he figured, must have sent her over the edge.

"Do you want to be part of my interview?" He spoke as if coaxing a reluctant child. "Josh is going to write up a story in tomorrow's paper…"

"He was going to kill ME! The man you killed—I think he was after MEE! I think he made a mistake and broke into your apartment instead of mine." Her body was trembling.

"What makes you think that, Astrid?"

"I saw his picture on my computer. I was just reading about him when I heard you guys come in."

"The sound from the lobby really carries up. You can hear a mouse fart."

"Shut up, Roland. Astrid, just because his history was killing women, that doesn't mean…"

"I *knew* him. I mean I talked to him before, a few times over the past couple of weeks. I talked to him *yesterday*." She looked like she was about to faint. "He asked me if he could help me carry my groceries up to my apartment."

Roland reinserted the key and opened his door. "Let's talk inside. I want to hear more."

"I'm not going in there if there's blood all over the place."

Roland set the bucket down and picked her up by the waist. "Close your eyes. I'll carry you into my sitting room." He hoisted her onto his hip and proceeded down the hallway, her arms around his neck and her face buried in his shoulder. Joshua picked up the supplies and followed them, closing the door behind him.

Roland eased Astrid onto his couch in the parlor next to the window Barsamian had pried open. The police had shut the window but left the yellow crime scene tape in place. "Let me get you a drink."

"I don't drink much. I'm more of a weed girl." The light went on in the hallway. Joshua was taking stock of the scene.

"Marijuana paranoia is the last thing you need right now, Tulip."

"Stop doing that, Roland. It's way past being funny."

"I'm sorry, Astrid. You're right. But I think a stiff one would calm you down a bit. The fact that the sonofabitch is dead should give you some peace of mind."

Joshua came in and held up the pint of whiskey. "This work well on blood?"

"I had to replace the bottle I broke last night." Roland got up and took it from Joshua and went into his kitchen nook. He listened to their conversation while he threw together a makeshift cocktail, mixing the booze with flat lemon-lime soda and the last few cubes in his ice tray. He heard Joshua ask her to tell him about her encounters with Barsamian.

"I talked to him at least four or five times. He said he was new to the neighborhood. He was very friendly, but not in a hungry kind of way, so I didn't have to push aside advances. Every time I saw him I was near the corner by Andruko's, and once or twice inside the market. He was very polite. Once he put out a freshly lit cigarette just so he could talk to me without the smoke bothering me. He even put the mangled-up thing in his pocket instead of throwing it in the gutter."

"Are you sure he knew you lived in this building?"

"Not just in this building—on the first floor. I told him yesterday. I almost let him in. He caught me halfway up the hill, came up right behind me, kinda scared me. He offered to help me carry my jug of laundry soap. I was lugging it with one hand and a bag of groceries in the other..."

Roland gulped down a few slugs of bourbon straight from the bottle since no one was watching. "You should shop at Trader Joe's," he shouted from the kitchen. "Those Ukrainian fuckers are getting rich off the foot-bound renters on this crowded little hill. I told you I'd drive you whenever you asked, or you could borrow my wheels and I'll do pushups in the parking spot until you bring the car back."

"Is he always like this?" Joshua spoke loudly enough for Roland to know that he didn't care that Roland could hear him.

"When he drinks, which lately is all the time. Earlier this year he was on the wagon and never once called me a flower. Seemed kinda shy and likable. But even when he's drunk, I'm not scared of him. I can tell he's a good person deep down, but when he's drinking, he's totally self-obsessed."

"So, did you let that serial killer lug your jug of laundry soap up the hill for you? I'm losing the thread here. Forget it, don't answer. I can fill in the rest myself based on what I've heard already. Then you tell me how drunk I am."

"I'd rather Astrid say what happened."

"No. Let Roland say what he thinks happened. If he's not correct I'll say so."

Roland came in with the drinks and set them down on the coffee table, one for Astrid and one for himself. He looked at Joshua. "None for you, Shakespeare. You've got to drive home and write."

"You were saying?" Joshua put his phone on the table and set it to record.

"Here's how I see it. Barsamian offers to lighten Astrid's load, but Astrid tells him no my apartment is only one flight up. She actually *gives* him that information. It's been bothering me all day, but now it makes perfect sense. He was after Astrid. It wasn't a random break-in." He turned to Astrid. "You're lucky you didn't let him in."

"I almost did. That's why I can't stop shaking." Her eyes welled with tears.

"He might not have killed you right then. It's impossible to say. He might have made a gametime decision and come back later."

"So why did he break in here? What's your theory on that, Roland?"

"If you look around the building..." Roland made a circular motion with his wounded arm, then in one swift and dramatic gesture, as if he were a magician, pointed his hand at the parlor window. "...you'll see that THIS is the only window you can reach from the street, and the only reason you can reach this window is because the alley slopes up sharply to the rear of the building. The only other way to get in is to break the glass in the front door or scale a ladder. The side door has no window and is bolted like a safe."

"So, you think he broke in knowing this might not even be Astrid's apartment?"

"He had a fifty-fifty chance. It's easy to see that there are two units per floor in this quaint little firetrap. Three floors, six mailboxes in the lobby. I'm sure he made that calculation."

"And what if you weren't home?"

"Then there's nothing to stop him from walking out my door and trying his tools on Astrid's door. He'd have her trapped and there'd be no one in my unit to hear anything. And if he can't jimmy open Astrid's door, or if he gets spooked, he can leave out the side door into the alley. Or he could come back to my place, piss on my toothbrush, and climb back out my window."

Astrid cradled the cocktail in her lap and leaned into the sofa. She'd sucked down half of it already. Roland couldn't tell if she was laughing or crying because she was alternating between the two with a sort of mewling giggle. Given a thousand takes, probably no actor in the world could have conjured the emotion coming out of her.

"I'm so sorry, Roland, but I'm so happy." Joshua turned off the recorder. "I was so mean to you last night when the police came, and you'd just killed the man who'd come to murder me."

"You'd better give me that thing." Roland extended his hand to take back the drink.

"No. I like it. It's good." She took another swallow.

"Astrid, I think you should talk to the police." Joshua had already placed the call.

"I was just about to call them right before you guys walked into the building."

Bill answered. It was his personal line.

"Hello, Joshua. Did you find him?"

"I did. We're in his apartment right now. There's someone else here you'll want to talk to."

"Put it on speaker," said Roland.

Joshua shot Roland an irritated look but complied and set the device on the coffee table.

"Hey, Bill. Nice detective work."

"You practically gave me the name of the place."

"Oh, I see. You think I was sending up a cry for help…"

"Give it a rest, Roland. It's not about you now." Joshua made the drinking motion as if to tell him might as well shut up and drink. Roland was glad he hadn't yet touched his drink and thought how wise he'd been to knock back a strong belt in the kitchen so he could appear indifferent to the cocktail.

"Roland's nextdoor neighbor is sitting here with us. Her name is Astrid."

"Who's Bill?"

"Hello, Astrid, my name is William Spelman, inspector, SFPD homicide division."

"He's the one assigned to this case."

"Barsamian was coming for HER! Tell that to Maruyama. Tell that sonofabitch that I'm a PROTECTOR of women."

"Shut up, Roland, or we're gonna clear out of here and you can be alone with your bloodstain and your bottle."

Roland made a what-the-fuck-did-I-do face and leaned back in his chair to salve his phony wounded feelings with a nice long swig. He listened while Astrid confirmed to the inspector that she'd been acquainted with Barsamian and had nearly allowed him into her apartment the afternoon of the break-in. Bill told her he would send up a squad car right away to take her down to the station so she could give a formal statement, and Joshua walked out with her so they could wait together for the car to arrive. She let out a powerful gasp when she saw the dried puddle of blood just inside the door.

"I guess I'll get started on that right away, Mister Goldbricker."

"I'll be back up as soon as she's on her way." Joshua gave Roland a look that said he was growing tired of his antics.

Roland left the door open and grabbed the broom from the kitchen. The glass had to be cleared aside before he could get to work on the blood. He swept the shards and fragments into a pile away from the blood at the far end of the hallway near his bedroom door and left it for Joshua. Then he filled the bucket with hot soapy water and soaked a few towels before laying them out over the blood patch to loosen it up. He knelt down with the scrub brush and eliminated the spatter on the floor and along one wall. He rose from his labors to take a few swallows of Trader Joe's finest straight from the bottle. *Not bad for grocery store whiskey.* He wiped away the dribble on his lips and let out a sigh of relief. Smoother than Jim Beam, but not quite Makers Mark.

By the time Joshua returned, most of the satellite drops were removed so all that remained was the pile of glass and the massive stain where Barsamian had bled to death, still soaking under the wet towels. He found Roland sitting in his parlor next to his bookcase listening to Beethoven and reading from the Bible. Second Book of Samuel. The few hundred books on his shelves, categorized and neatly arranged, stood in stark contrast to the general untidiness of his apartment.

"I see you've been busy."

"The death spot is softening up. I figure if it won't scrub off, I can always use sandpaper." Joshua brushed the glass into a dustpan and emptied it into the trash bag in the kitchen.
"You're a very strange man, Roland Hazzard."
"I've got nothing on this David character."
"Yes. He was a complicated figure."
"I've never understood how he got away with offing Uriah the Hittite. Maybe he'd stored up a lot of credits for taking down Goliath and winning all those battles against the Philistines."
"Is that what you're doing now, trying to get to the bottom of God's inscrutable justice?"
"That and enjoying a bit of the old Ludwig van."
"The Ninth, right?"
"You're plum ready for Junior Jeopardy."
"By the looks of this place, I'd be willing to bet you don't have a girlfriend."
Roland ignored the reporter's impertinent observation, inwardly applauding his own powers of restraint. The conversation continued for more than an hour, Roland measuring his sips throughout to show that he could drink like a gentleman. It didn't occur to him that the amount of alcohol he'd consumed already that day would have knocked out—even poisoned—the average grown man.
Joshua recorded the interview, which centered mainly on Roland's past, particularly his adolescent and teenage years. Roland cleaved closely to the facts in his responses to Joshua's questions, but after a while his answers expanded into personal anecdotes whose details triggered old memories that fed into more stories until Roland found himself delivering full-blown soliloquies, such that, apart from the occasional prompt of "what happened then" or "how many touchdowns did you throw," Joshua had only to listen and gesture with his hands to keep his subject talking. Roland enjoyed talking about himself, delighted to recount the many victories and exploits of his young life.
"The blue jay dropped like a rock in mid-flight and when we went to pick it up, we couldn't find where the bee-bee had entered until Stewart noticed a perfect little red hole right where its eye had been. That was before everyone was carrying camera phones or I would have taken a picture."

"Which eye?" Joshua sounded skeptical.

"I was facing south, the bird was flying west, so that would have been its left eye."

"So, you did a lot of hunting as a kid?"

"Not when we graduated to actual firearms. Too much work for not enough action. Too much waiting around and trying to be quiet. And if you were lucky and brought something down, you had to clean the kill and bury the guts, and then you had to clean the gun. My brother was the hunter, but I was the better shot. When it came to shooting targets—paper targets on hay bales or cans on a fence rail, whatever it was—no boy or man in the county could beat me. Pistol, rifle, it didn't matter, as long as we had equal guns."

"But you needed more action."

"Yes. Sports. I loved sports."

"What else besides football?"

"Whatever they had. Basketball of course, and volleyball, state wrestling champ one year. I quit baseball in the middle of my senior year when I broke three ribs on a pitcher with a line drive straight up the middle. No one would pitch to me after that. Had to chase pitches way outside the strike zone just to put the ball in play, so I figured what's the point?"

"What was your greatest athletic achievement?"

Roland thought about it and nodded to himself with a satisfied smile four or five times before he gave the answer. "Winning the Long Bridge Swim three years in a row."

"Long Bridge Swim?"

"It's a yearly one-mile sprint next to the Long Bridge, a span of Highway 95 across Lake Pend Oreille in Northern Idaho. It connects the town of Sagle to my hometown Sandpoint. Serious swimmers come from all over, and I would train for two or three weeks before the event and then go wire-to-wire. I'd stand there on the beach at the finish smoking a cigarette with a towel draped around my neck while the rest of the field dragged themselves out of the water. I kept my pack of smokes and matches wrapped inside two zip-lock baggies tucked under my swim cap. Kinda like Brando with a pack rolled up in his shirt sleeve."

My other favorite sport was girls, which led to a lot of skiing and snowboarding. I wasn't very good on the snow because I didn't really like it, but it was an activity I could do with the ladies, and it meant sitting around in hot tubs after. I'm sure you get the idea."

Joshua avoided any questions about drinking and Roland stayed away from the subject. After listening to him reminisce about his seemingly endless run of female conquests until the details began to verge on the lurid, Joshua pricked the bubble of his reverie.

"Being a sports hero gets you your pick of the ladies—I get it—so then why did you give up sports?"

Roland could not stare down that question as he would a human opponent. Before he could stop himself, he glanced at his nearly empty glass where it sat perspiring on the table just within reach. Next to it was Joshua's mobile phone with the red recording light blinking.

"Who said I gave up sports?"

"A guy like you could have easily gotten an athletic scholarship, probably to a really good school. I assume you had the grades to go with the brawn. Swimming, wrestling, football, basketball, baseball—seems like you could have gone a lot of different ways."

As a high school senior Roland had carried the volleyball team to the state finals where they lost, but not before Roland sent the opposing team's middle-blocker to the bench bibbed in his own nose blood. The scouts had smelled that blood and come circling.

"We haven't talked about last night. I thought that's what you were interested in."

"Of course, but it's an obvious question."

"Are you saying you don't believe me? Some of the stuff I did—the bridge swims, the wrestling awards, the state finals—you can find on the internet."

"Not at all. I believe every word. The question is why you stopped. Thousands of guys, maybe hundreds of thousands, work their asses off every year in the hopes of receiving an athletic scholarship, and it sounds like you could have had one easily."

"I could have played for many of the best football teams in the county, and of course I was offered wrestling scholarships, a few for baseball too."

"What stopped you?"

"In a word, *coaches*. I don't like being pushed, being yelled at, and spending all my time at practice. I play because it's fun, and when it stops being fun, I make other plans."

"You refused football offers just because you don't like being pushed by coaches? Sounds like a cop-out to me. Sounds like you didn't want to face tough competition. Dominating your peers in Idaho was a breeze, but the NCAA would have demanded a lot of work, dedication, commitment." Roland was glad he didn't add *sobriety* to the list.

"I went to Berkeley on a volleyball scholarship. I wasn't even that good at it, compared to guys from California and other places whose parents spend thousands on clubs and private coaches; but I can jump out of the gym and crush the snot out of the ball, so based on that they thought they could work on my passing and setting and turn me into an All American."

"A college volleyball scholarship is nothing to be ashamed of."

"Can we go off the record here?"

Joshua reached down and turned the recorder off.

"My parents don't know about this, but I got kicked off the team." He paused. Joshua looked at him and shrugged to ask why.

"I got kicked off the team for showing up to practice drunk. Twice. I got a warning, and I did it again. Satisfied?"

"It's not going into my story, Roland. I only have room for a few hundred words. It's not going to be a biography."

"Good, or else I'd have to get into my years of service as an altar boy, my knack with the violin and piano, and my numerous poetry and essay contest prizes. There is literally nothing I put my mind to that I did not get good at very quickly." Roland paused again and thought for a second and decided to omit his multiple black belts in several disciplines. "I was born with a phenomenal memory, which helps a lot."

"Well, that doesn't explain the athletic prowess."

"You'd be surprised. I mean, not in something like swimming, but in basketball for example, and wrestling too, remembering your opponent's tendencies is a huge advantage. People tend to repeat the same moves that have worked before, and if you can frustrate their strongest moves you've gotten inside their heads. Then the battle is all but won. A good memory helps with that. Half of intelligence is recall."

"Why didn't you tell your parents?"

"I didn't need to. I worked out a deal to keep my scholarship money."

"You worked out a deal? Pardon my skepticism."

"You can check it out. I became an instructor in the martial arts club, an actual university employee. They waived my tuition and even gave me a check every month."

"How'd you swing that? You just walk in and tell 'em you're a karate master and bingo you're hired?"

"I've mastered three disciplines—karate was the first."

"By the age of—what—twenty? That's astonishing."

"Memory again. To get through the belts you have to master the forms, and the forms are like a language, a kinesthetic language. If you memorize the forms and execute them perfectly—perfectly and powerfully—you get the corresponding belt. For the higher belts you need to prove you're fit to fight, that you can withstand the attacks of multiple masters. Yes, I earned three black belts before I was twenty. Karate, Jujitsu, Taekwondo. And I'm well versed in a few others."

"So, you're basically a superhero."

Roland chortled at the wisecrack and decided to play along. "I didn't have to play all my cards. I met with the sensei in charge, and we did the pebble snatch."

"Like in Kung Fu?"

Roland opened his hand and tapped the center of his empty palm with a finger to show where the pebble would be. "As quickly as you can, snatch the pebble from my hand."

"Seriously, what did you have to do?"

"The only part that's off the record is me getting kicked off the team. If the internet trolls uncover that fact, then so be it. But don't print it."

"I won't. And I won't have room for any of this backstory stuff either. Still, I'm just curious—how'd you jump from disgraced volleyball star to martial arts instructor and get a paycheck thrown in?"

Roland reached down and lifted his glass and finished his drink and exhaled forcefully. "I fought and I won."

"Fought the sensei?"

"No—that would have been a mismatch. He's way too small. Yeah, he had me work the bag, do a few spinning kicks—tornado, 540 roundhouse, both legs—he made me work up a sweat. Then he entered me into the next tournament and promised me the job if I won the black belt competition. But first I had to put him in touch with my dojo back in Idaho just so he could make sure I had the proper credentials."

"I'm assuming you won."

"Easily—too easily. I had to hold back to keep from hurting my opponents."

"That's amazing. He gave you a job just like that, knowing your issues with…?" He pointed to Roland's empty glass.

"He told me if he ever smelled alcohol I'd be out."

"I guess your parents bought that story. That's pretty remarkable, lucky even."

"We make our own luck."

"You're pretty young to be drawing such grand conclusions."

"I don't mean for you to write it, but there is one thing I do want you to put in the piece, something I want the chief of police to know."

"Let's hear it—I make no promises."

"See if you can work in that I started the first women's self-defense class at Berkeley. Taught them how to fend off a male attacker."

"Why?"

"The chief thinks…"

"Forget it—doesn't matter."

"What do you mean?"

"There's no time to verify it."

"Just write that I said it. *Roland Hazzard claims etcetera.*"

"That's not the way print journalism works, not the way I do it anyway. You'll have plenty of opportunities to say whatever you want if you decide to give live interviews."

"I want nothing to do with all that."

"That will be your choice. Let's get back to your athletic scholarship. I'm curious how your parents took the news that you were leaving the volleyball team to teach martial arts."

"My dad didn't care, as long as my tuition was covered. My mom told me to follow my bliss."

"Ahh, your mother reads Joseph Campbell."

"I forgive her. Campbell was only half an idiot. I like my Jung served straight, not watered down with psychobabble."

Joshua checked his watch.

"Your sister mentioned you had an older brother Phillip."

"Major Hazzard."

"Major? As in the military?"

"Yes. You'd be wise not to mention him either."

"Agreed. Your family is off the record, but that sounds like a warning."

"He's a decorated Marine Corps combat veteran. Works at the Pentagon in the intelligence world. World, galaxy, universe—I'm not sure which. Anyway, I'm sure he wouldn't want to see his name in your article."

"Someone will dig him up, anyway. I can practically guarantee it."

"As long as he knows his name didn't come from me or my sister."

"Like I promised, I won't be writing about your family. But it strikes me as odd that you think your brother would not want to be associated with you. You killed a notorious murderer with his own weapon in hand-to-hand combat. That would earn you some kind of medal in the Marine Corps I imagine."

"You've read the police report."

"Of course. And it's going to be posted on the internet if it isn't there already."

"You didn't see anything embarrassing in there? The police chief was furious. He went banzai on me."

"Roland, you're not the first person to get drunk and act like a dick to the police. And taking out the Glendale Butcher outweighs your childish behavior afterward, at least in my view."

"What about the other police report, from months ago? Have you seen that?"

"Bill mentioned two other arrests—misdemeanors, drunkenness—but I haven't seen the reports and don't want to. I don't see what you're worried about."

"One misdemeanor, officially. The first arrest was just an overnight catch-and-release. Anyway, do you think the hacks and trolls in the newsrooms and chatrooms are just going to ignore that shit?"

"You can't control that, Roland. You can only control what you say in a public forum if you choose to say anything at all. You're good at playing the unruffled tough guy. You did what you did. Own it. Laugh it off. Maybe you're a drunk, but you're not a criminal, not as far as I can tell."

Roland held up a hand. "What are you going to write? What's the point of this conversation? We haven't even talked about last night."

"What happened last night, apart from what's in the report? Imagine you're speaking to a massive crowd of people. What happened last night, in a few words?"

"I did my job, thank you very much."

"How'd you feel about it, after it was done?"

"I didn't feel much of anything except maybe relief it was over. It's hard to say. I was jacked up on adrenalin."

"What about now?"

"I'm disgusted there are people like him—both arrogant and stupid—that force us to kill them. It's a grim inconvenience."

"Us?"

"The mighty."

"There's a community? A League of the Mighty?"

"I doubt I'm entirely on my own."

Joshua adopted a grave expression and took a serious tone. "You're not on your own, young man. I may not be one of the mighty, but I am definitely one of the good guys. I'm surprised you haven't figured that out by now."

"I don't trust journalists. It's a dirty profession."

"Tell you what—if you don't want me to write your story, just say so. I'll leave here now, satisfied that I kept my promise to Spelman."

"Will you send it to me before it goes to print? Email it."

"Then I might as well let you write it yourself. Besides, even if it were ethical for me to let you review it before it went to press, there still isn't time. Unless it hits the stands tomorrow, there won't be much point to it. The law of good first impressions applies very much here."

"Why would you want to help me make a good first impression?"

"It's not just that. I must admit I like the idea of getting the scoop on a national news story, and the revelation by Astrid makes it all the more scoopish."

"So, if I tell you that our entire conversation is off the record, you'll still report that Barsamian was after Astrid?"

"I will. It's legitimate news—that it probably wasn't a random break-in—that you probably were not the target. Just as you explained it. It makes perfect sense."

"Go ahead and write whatever you want. Just don't mention anyone in my family."

Joshua fitted his Giants cap back on his head and slid his phone into his pocket then removed a little cloth and buffed the lenses of his sunglasses. "I have one more question."

Roland got up to see him out. "Ok, one for the road."

"Did you pray for him?"

Roland showed a perplexed face and pointed two fingers at the towels soaking up Barsamian's blood. Joshua nodded yes.

"The fight brought me briefly to my knees, but not to pray. When would I have prayed for him—between what and what?"

"His soul, I meant to say. You're a religious man I take it."

"Why, because I read the Bible?"

"You mentioned you were an alter boy."

"Emphasis on *boy*. Your question assumes that I believe in something that can be prayed to."

"You can pray to an idea of God, or to the God that you wish you believed in, or to the God that someone you know professes a belief in, or to…"

"I get the point. The answer is no; and for the record, I did not refrain from praying, either. It never even occurred to me."

Joshua nodded conclusively, the way one nods when a matter of some small importance, like the price of a used bicycle, is settled between the two parties. He fed his eyeglass cloth back into his pocket and saw himself to the door, careful to avoid the blood-soaked towels.

Roland followed him.

"I've enjoyed meeting you, Roland Hazzard." He extended his hand. Roland shook the hand. "Thanks for the ride, Mister Goldbricker."

"That's not fair. I whisked up and dumped the broken glass."

"That you did. That you did."

"Be sure to check the paper tomorrow morning."

"You bet I will." Roland tapped the brim of Joshua's baseball cap. "Go Giants."

Back in his parlor, fresh drink in hand, the killer, drunk on top of an endless hangover, switched the music to Mahler—disgusting, hateful, Mahler—and set it to loop to punish himself. *In this corner, spurting blood from his eyes, sporting jet-black trunks with bright red SS trim, the baleful Teutonic giant, Gustav the Mauler!* He drank deeply, gasped loudly, frowned scornfully at the object of his sardonic imagination. "Go Giants," he muttered. "Who gives a damn about the San Franfuckincisco Giants? The Antediluvian Giants—now them was some badass giants." He reclined on the couch, stuffed a pillow under his head and closed his eyes to Kindertotenlieder. In English: Songs on the Death of Children.

Pray for him? Pray what exactly? What words? What intentions? Be my guest, mister half-assed Jew. You pray for his goddamned soul.

Chapter 10
September 30, 2016 - 8:03 PM

A persistent knocking carried down the hallway into the parlor and penetrated the music, waking him. The windows had darkened with the evening, but not all the way. Roland summoned his consciousness up from a cavernous realm he'd been exploring, an undiscovered stronghold built within a complex of caves that reached deep inside a wall of the Grand Canyon, a prehistoric subterranean citadel ceiled with celestial maps embossed on enormous sheets of hammered gold, a maze of chambers furnished here with vertical echelons of ten-foot mummies, each soldier housed in a separate alcove scooped flawlessly out of the granite walls, here with galleries adorned with exquisitely crafted artifacts from Africa, Asia, the Amazon—who knows where?—objects fashioned millennia before the continents had names. Altogether, the spiritual and scientific headquarters of the original human race built below ground and accessed only through an entrance hidden inside a fissure in the vertical face of a towering cliff. The complex did not surrender him easily, but as the knocking continued he managed to throw off his spelunking helmet which, he suddenly noticed, took the form of an ornamental jackal's head, silver-snouted, jowls enameled in mother of pearl, its dogface studded with opal, agate, turquoise, and lapis lazuli, its brow fitted with a miner's lamp. He watched it spiral downward, the electric bulb tracing circles until it disappeared into a bottomless crevasse.

Roland raised himself off the couch to face the dim confines of his drab apartment. *Who the fuck is it now?* He flipped on the light as he walked to the door. The smell of body lotion—blackberry forest fire or some such—seeped through the gap between the door and the frame. It was Astrid. She left a trail, a pleasant contrast to the odors in the space around her, and now, standing outside his door, to the stale smell of his living quarters.

"Who is it?" he said through the door.
"It's Astrid."
"Half the city is named Astrid."
"Astrid Venus Fly Trap."

"Ahh, the one and only."

"Will you please open the door?"

Roland opened the door. "Hi, Astrid. I need to be cautious with all the reporters out trick-or-treating."

"Can I come in?"

"I guess so. Whaddaya want?"

"Another one of those drinks. Let's start with that."

Could it be? No. Unthinkable in the extreme. There'd always been some sexual tension between them, but Roland excluded her from the domain of his possible liaisons more than a year ago, shortly after she moved into the building. She wasn't bad looking, young of face for a twenty-seven-year-old, with gender-neutral, red-tinted, easy-care hair, body thin and pert enough to fall squarely within his standards for physical desirability. But she displayed an emotional fragility that warned him from ever taking her to bed. Vulnerability was one thing, a quality that promised both a high degree of arousal during the act itself and then a mess of hurt feelings after the woman realized she'd served her limited purpose. Still, *that* woman would land on her feet and eventually see the interaction for exactly what it was. But a woman of Astrid's emotional fragility was likely to turn her disappointment into victimhood and thus be able to absolve herself of any act of retaliation. Anger was the flame in her candle shop, the cinnamon stick that stirred her herbal tea, and Roland had long sworn off that treacherous concoction—the passively angry female. To his way of thinking, his alternate indifference and teasing of Astrid ensured that he would never be swept up by the tempest in her teacup. Still, he led her into his parlor.

"I didn't think you could handle booze."

"Not the way you do. But that first one calmed me down a lot. I'm sure I would enjoy another. Besides, I want to talk to you."

Roland picked up her empty glass and took it to the kitchen to fix a refill.

"What's this awful music?"

"Gustav Mahler."

"Gustav? It sounds like a woman screaming in pain."

"He's the composer, circa nineteen hundred," Roland answered loudly from the kitchen. "I don't know who's screeching the libretto, but she's singing about the death of some children caught alone in a storm who never made it back home."

"You actually like this?"

"It serves a very specific purpose."

"Well, do you have something else? Anything but this would do."

Roland came in and handed Astrid her drink. His own was still half-full on the table, diluted by melted ice. "I have thousands of songs in my database." He picked up his device and keyed in the name of another song. The sound of a Gibson hollow-body electric guitar filled the parlor. "Do you recognize who this is?"

"B.B. King?" She listened for a few more seconds. "Yes. It's B.B. King."

"The unmistakable Lucille."

"It's not exactly soothing."

"Give it a second." After pinching out a few more bluesy notes from his famous guitar, B.B.'s voice broke in.

Nobody loves me but my mother, and she could be jivin' too.

Roland amused himself with a laugh. "Please turn it off." She sat down in a chair next to the coffee table. "I didn't come here to be entertained." He complied and sat down on the couch across from her.

"What then?"

"The reporters outside, before I left, they were asking questions about you. And then, just now, on my way back in, one of them was still there."

"So?"

"He saw a police car pick me up and then bring me back."

"Patient man."

"Stop it, Roland. He wanted to know what the police wanted with to me."

"That's his job."

"I didn't tell him. I told him it was none of his business and not to write about me."

"Why are you telling me this, Astrid?"

"Cuz then he switched the subject back to you. He wanted to know what kind of neighbor you are."

"I don't want to be rude, but I don't really care what you said about me."

"But *I* care—I want you to know."

"Ok, since it's important to you—tell me what you said."

"I told them that you're a very good neighbor. Polite, quiet, helpful."

"So you lied."

"Sometimes you are. You're two different people."

Roland gritted his teeth to keep from rolling his eyes.

"What was the point of all that yelling last night?"

"I can't stand to watch a beautiful man like you destroy himself."

The way she said *man* caught him off guard. She was, of course, a little older than he, and at his age he wasn't used to being called *man* by anyone but a little kid.

"Is that what you and the inspector talked about, my drinking?"

"It never came up, I swear. We talked just about Barsamian. There was an FBI agent there too."

"Well, thank you for your concern, but I think you're overreacting."

"If I am, then so be it. But I've seen the progression of the disease in my own family, and it's not pretty. If you're an alcoholic and you don't learn how to stop and stay stopped, your future is bleak. A few months ago, after you came back from wherever you were, I was really happy to see you sober. You were a very nice person. I really like that person."

Roland preferred the German screeching. Gina had said similar things too, but when it came from her it assumed the form of glib, matter of fact, remarks, as in *your stock is falling, Roland. I guess you're not trying to attract investors.*

"Let me get this straight. You came out last night thinking I was in trouble with the law, and you tried to make things worse for me because you *care* about me? Do I have that right?"

"If I didn't like you, or care about you, I would have stayed inside and hoped they took you away for a long time and you never came back again."

Her logic fell short of Roland's exacting standards.

"So, coming out and actually *expressing* that sentiment, at the top of your lungs no less, means the sentiment was *in*-sincere?"

"Yes. I'm sorry I did that."

Astrid sipped her drink and watched Roland with her birdlike face as though assessing his expression to see how well her apology had sunk in.

"Of course I accept your apology. After all, whatever the intent, your actions were harmless."

"And I know that you and me…" She swung her finger back and forth between them. "Not a good idea. You don't seem like the type of guy who could…"

"How do you know I'm not gay?"

Astrid had to cover her mouth to keep from spraying her drink. Her eyes bulged wide as she forced down the mouthful before she was able to speak. "Same way I know the difference between this…" she held up her drink, "…and a glass of water. Your look, when you want to use it, has a powerful kick. But it wouldn't work on a man. You know how to *look* at a woman."

Roland thought about how, with his eyes, he'd drawn in the nameless delicacy at the Buena Vista a few hours ago and gave Astrid a nod. Not exactly a nod of agreement, but one of understanding.

"Am I supposed to be flattered by that?"

"Only if that's what you're after. I don't believe you seriously thought I couldn't tell that you're straight. Straight and strong. A hundred proof."

"You're right about at least one thing—you and I would not make a very good match."

"You'd toss me around like a rag doll, tear me limb from limb, split me right up the middle."

She'd made a serious dent in the cocktail and clearly had reached her limit. He'd have to cut her off if she asked for another.

"I don't know where you're getting all of this, Astrid, but since you brought it up, I'm actually very gentle when it comes to that."

She wasn't listening, swept up in her own narrative.

"A man with your looks, your charm, charisma, your sexual magnetism—picking up girls must be like picking shirts off a rack. When you don't come home at night, I've got a pretty good idea where you must be. And I notice that you rarely bring them here."

"You're a pretty girl, Astrid, and way too decent for me. I'm a bit of a bottom-feeder if you want to know the truth. But if I spotted you drunk at a bar I'd pick you off the rack, in theory—I mean a woman who looked like you. Your identical twin let's say."

"I haven't always been decent. If you want to know the truth, I've been reckless too many times and kind of sworn it off."

"It?" Roland knew exactly what she meant.

"Easy sex. Most women can have sex whenever they want. That's one reason I didn't consider letting that—that—monster in the building. I didn't want him to think I was available."

"Your good sense—your decency—saved you."

"Maybe. But if I lived in this apartment instead of mine, or if he managed to get by you—I don't want to think about it."

It dawned on Roland that Astrid didn't want to be alone, was too freaked out by the thought of what might have befallen her to go back to her apartment and sit with it. He didn't know what to say but knew he had to manage a reply.

"I'm glad I put a stop to him."

"I want to thank you. You've already taken off your boots, like a soldier coming home from war. What's the first thing that soldier wants to do?"

"I don't want to seem ungrateful, Astrid, so please don't take this the wrong way, but I don't think you're in any condition to be making that offer. I can't accept in good conscience."

"I made up my mind on my way over here, before I took this drink."

"I don't doubt it, but that first drink was pretty strong."

"I haven't had a man in a long time, and I've never had a man like you. Never even close."

"Tell you what—when you wake up tomorrow morning, you'll either heave a sigh of relief that I didn't take you up on your offer, or you'll still be in the mood. If it's door number two, then we can have this conversation again. But either way, I'm in no position to fall in love, not with you or with anyone. As long as that's clear."

She picked up her glass and drank, not in sips but in gulps, and slowly landed the glass back onto the table, swaying in her chair. Then she stood up and kissed him where he sat, a sweet soft kiss on his cheek just at the corner of his mouth. You shouldn't have carried me in here before, across your threshold. You've no idea what effect that had on me. I was light as a feather to you."

"I didn't like standing in limbo in front of my own door."

"Yes. You like to make decisions. A man of action. You size up a situation and make your move. I bet that's how you were able to kill that guy. You probably saw him and said *you're you—but I'm me. No contest.*"

"I gave him a chance to fold, but he pushed all in. I really don't want to talk about it."

His phone vibrated on the table. Roland picked it up and looked at the display. Denny. He set the phone down and let the call go to voicemail.

"I've got to call this guy back."

"You're going to be a *very* popular man." She steadied herself with a hand on the back of her chair.

"Astrid, you should have told me you were a lightweight. Do you need some help getting back to your place?"

"Yes. I'm a lightweight. All the better for you to carry me back across the blood puddle." She was laughing now. "I bet there's a culture out there where that means something, like in a sacred ritual. We'd be blood spouses. You kill my murderer and then carry me over his blood puddle—now we're blood married."

Roland bared his teeth and scratched the back of his head wondering how to respond to such lunacy.

"I really gotta call this guy back—right now." He stood up and moved toward the hallway to guide her out. She frowned through her smile.

"I'll let myself out, Roland. You can go back to your deadly German opera."

~~~~~

The phone showed three messages, which was unusual, as Roland was very stingy with his number and seldom had more than one voicemail in the queue. Without checking to see if one of the messages was from Denny, he called him back. Denny picked up right away.

"Ro-land Haz-zard." He enunciated the syllables slowly and precisely.

"Hi, Denny. I didn't forget about you."

"That's quite a name. Is that one zee or two?"

"I'm not trying to be famous here."

"I'm not saying you are, but your name…"

"People have been making fun of my name since I was a kid."

"Is that why you never told me the second half of it?"

"I don't know *your* last name. I went by Roland H. You're Denny M. Isn't that proper AA protocol—the anonymity part? What am I missing here?"

"Page twenty-six."

"Page twenty-six? You must mean in the Big Book."

"Yeah, we went over it in Step 1."

"Went over what exactly?"

"Patient zero—Rowland Hazard the Third."

"No, Denny—I'd've remembered seeing my name in the Big Book."

"The book doesn't give his name, but the story is well known. I guess I never took you through it."

Roland took a drink and let Denny hear the gulp go down. "Look, Denny, I've been drinking since two o'clock, drinking to crush a hangover. It's not a good time for a Big Book study."

"Look here kid, I'm not trying to pull you back in. You're clearly not ready, but at least you know we're saving a seat for you. In the old days, they'd never let someone your age join. You'd have had to show a lot more damage. Only reason I called was to make sure you knew—you're not the first Roland Hazzard to make history. Rowland Hazard the Third touched off an improbable sequence of events that resulted in the founding of an organization that has since then saved probably tens of millions of people who would otherwise not have been spared the death and or depredations of alcoholism."

"Almost like God had a hand in it, right? Sounds like a pitch to me. You think if you'd known I shared the name of the indispensable Rowland Hazard the Third, you might've been able to save me?"

"No one can save you from booze, hotshot. Alcoholism is the only foe that can be defeated by surrendering. Let go and let God—He'll meet you more than halfway."

"Not a pitch? Really?"

"Just the truth. Your case might require the gift of desperation, and that's not something anyone can give you. Only life can give you that." Denny's voice itself betrayed a tone of surrender, as if he'd stopped caring what happened to Roland, as if, as far as he was concerned, this might as well be the last time they would ever speak. It put Roland on his heels.

"You wanna hear about my sit-down with the police? You made me promise to call you after."

"You were flipping out this morning, slick. I was trying to calm you down. Now it sounds to me like your fears were a little out of proportion with reality. Is that safe to say? Anyway, you sound better than you did before. I'm glad you're not in any trouble. Hell, I saw the news—you're something of a big deal. Congratulations."

Roland took a drink and waited to reply to build suspense.

"He was after my nextdoor neighbor."

Now Denny remained silent and waited for Roland to continue.

"She just left my place—she's pretty freaked out."

"You know this for a fact?"

Always a troublesome question.

"No. But my neighbor, she was sure enough about it when she saw his face on the news that she ran straight down to the police station."

"Ahh. It's beginning to make a lot more sense."

"What makes you so sagacious?"

"His MO was women, of course. But more than that, it adds to your mystique." He paused. "Remember earlier you said you're in a jackpot like you were in some kind of gangster movie?"

"Yeah. I used that word."

"Well, kid. I've been in this carnival long enough to tell when a game is rigged. You're in a jackpot alright, a cosmic jackpot."

"What the hell are you talking about?"

"I don't believe in accidents or coincidences, unless the entire universe came into being by accident, unless you yourself are an accident."

"Ok, I get it—Chapter Four. God is everything or nothing."

"Go ahead and brush it off, killer. Keep drinking. See how that works for you. I'd wish you good luck, but I think you've crossed into a place where luck can't help you."

Roland tired of Denny's cryptic goodbye but still suffered a pang of guilt, a pang he needed to alleviate before Denny ended the call. He changed the subject to get the matter off his chest. Whatever else was true, Denny, through the old-timer Victor, had set him up with a good job, and he wanted to let him know that he was mindful of that fact.

"Have you talked to Victor lately?"

"What about?"

"I don't think I ever thanked him for setting me up with the job."

"It's a little late for that. You quit coming to meetings as soon as he did you that favor. But it really doesn't matter. We don't expect very much from our court-ordered visitors."

That stung, being reduced to a statistical unlikelihood not only of success in recovery but of success even in the exercise of common human decency.

"I've still got the job, and I have every intention of keeping it, and not just to show my gratitude and respect for..."

"Stop right there. I've heard more than I can stomach. I was prepared to tear you a new one about letting down the program if I ever heard from you again—but we're way past that now, considering your circumstances. In the rooms, we're always saying *there are no big deals*."

"Heard it a hundred times."

"Any idea what it means?"

"Only in the abstract. It means don't drink on resentment. I don't invent *big deals* as a reason to get loaded. I'm just easily bored. Alcohol eases that some."

"Yeah, you told me that before—but have you ever considered that life tends to be boring, that we all experience it? Your low tolerance for boredom might be a low tolerance for life."

"What's your point?"

"You might not have any personal resentments to drink against, but resentment of life itself boils down to resentment of God, and that, slick, *is* a big deal."

"Chapter Four again."

"More like Chapter Infinity."

"That's a long slog. I guess I'd best get started."

"Best not go it alone."

Denny, perhaps without knowing it, had touched the heart of the matter. Roland was alone, catastrophically alone, and hearing Denny's admonition left him with neither rebuttal nor course of remedy. How does one who finds himself alone resolve to not go it alone; and even if that resolve could be formed, how then to conjure up a friend?

"I'll be at work on Monday." His voice was reduced to a growl.

"Good. And remember we're saving a seat for you. There's plenty of love in the rooms."

Roland hung up without saying goodbye or thank you or see-ya-later or take-care or fuck-you. He simply pressed the button with the self-satisfied finality of a commander incinerating an enemy stronghold with a single enormous airborne weapon. *Boom! There goes my seat along with your entire society of folding chairs. You fucks don't even know how to brew a decent pot of coffee.*

Tears welled up. *Love.* He recalled the words *I love you,* spoken in his own voice to his sister just a few hours ago. Then he heard Denny say it, say it to him as he had many times, even as he questioned Roland's pathetic imitation of a sane twenty-five-year-old man in charge of his own future. He took a drink straight from the bottle to feel the bite in his throat that would quell the emotion. But he heard it still, heard it in the voices of so many sober AA regulars, grown men attempting to pierce the resistance of the wretched newcomer.

I love you? What had he meant when he said it to Sandy? Was it his craven way of bowing out of the conversation? He wanted not to hurt her, that much he knew. But was that an actual feeling, a heartfelt sentiment, or just dutiful regard for the sincerity of her feelings? Was his statement a necessary formality expressed merely to assuage any doubt she might have that he did actually love her, or was it a statement of truth? Roland did not know, and his uncertainty filled him with shame. The responsibility incurred from being loved brought with it much more than a social convention requiring one to say certain words in response to certain other words. It required actions that demonstrated those words so that, even when they were not expressed verbally, the feeling was expressed nonetheless and perhaps even more powerfully so. Often Roland had debated inwardly—*Why should they care? I'm only hurting myself*—and he had believed his argument so well that he bristled at any rebuttal. As for what to make of the I-love-yous shared by participants in the recovery rooms, Roland remained at a loss. Those declarations were real and in no way sinister, but he knew not their source and merely intuited their purpose. He could have recited and defined the three words for love in Ancient Greek, but he'd never understood *agape.*

Now, sitting alone in his ill-lit parlor, he felt himself pulled into the black hole of a facile nihilism, which emptiness had always kept him safe.

But that emptiness, formerly a product of his mind, had metastasized to his stomach and there expanded. He was safe alright, but only in the way a prisoner is safe—not an ordinary prisoner, but a prisoner in solitary confinement on death row, safe under suicide watch. *No—It's not that bad.* He still had half a bottle left of Trader Joe's Kentucky Bourbon, which had its own gravitational force, its own immutable laws.

He gulped down another mouthful and waited in his chair for the effects that he craved, but the hole in his gut gripped more tightly and his mind raced on. His father was speaking now. It was the speech he'd heard since adolescence. *Freedom scares the hell out of most people. When given a choice between a secure poverty and an insecure freedom, people most often choose security.* This maxim was recited as a sociopolitical conclusion about human nature. Rolling it over in his mind at that moment, Roland sensed that it might contain for him a deeper, more personal lesson, one his father had not intended to convey. To drink, or not to drink, that was the question. The security he found in alcohol felt necessary, but there was no freedom in it. He'd tasted a morsel of freedom during his few dry months after his second arrest, when he'd been forced to deal with life on life's terms; but it was a freedom whose uncertainties led eventually to a restlessness and irritability that could be alleviated only by alcohol. As long as he could control his drinking, he saw no reason to quit. *After all,* he found himself arguing, there alone in his chair, *did I not stop short of drinking myself into a stupor last night? Did I not retain enough of my wits to emerge victorious in a fight for my life? Am I not now able to think clearly, and speak calmly and rationally even after drinking all afternoon?* He assured himself that he was in control, and to prove it capped the bottle and carried it to the kitchen, satisfied that he was done for the evening.

In the hours that remained before bed, Roland busied himself in his apartment by cleaning the kitchen and bathroom and straightening up his bedroom and the parlor. He even changed the sheets on his bed, which he hadn't done in months. He organized his meager collection of silverware and cooking utensils, polished his boots, boiled his toothbrush, changed the water in his goldfish bowl, which was so green and murky that he could barely see its occupants, and completed a dozen other little tasks that ordinary, self-respecting people take care of without much effort in the regular flow of life. This flurry of activity, which transformed his apartment from a pathetic mess into a dwelling that advertised its inhabitant as a man who had learned how to manage his life, distracted Roland from his pressing apprehensions concerning the machinery his actions last night had set in motion.

Knowing that his name had been broadcast to the world accentuated his long-felt but, until now, unarticulated, passion for privacy. That he would be held up to public view as a hero mattered not at all, regardless of the picture painted of him by the police report. Those details could be brushed aside as insignificant in light of the villainy of the man he'd killed, the monster he had permanently stopped. What disturbed him more and more, even as he fought against his mind's insistence that he contemplate the future, was the undeniable realization that he would be tied forever to the killing. Earlier that day in Inspector Spelman's office, still impaired by his brutal hangover, he had managed to make light of this truth by weighing the catchiness of a likely label—The Butcher Slayer—but alone in his apartment with the curtains drawn against the mounting cupidity of another San Francisco Friday night, the illusion of control his ferocious attachment to privacy afforded was unveiled as fraudulent. Roland forced himself to accept a truth about himself—*I do not like people.* The implications of that truth remained hidden from him, though not like a fossil encased in the substratum or concealed like seams of ore in rock, but hidden like a coin flipped into a well and resting safely at the bottom, a wisdom that simply could be retrieved—if one was willing—though not without effort.

And what of the original Rowland Hazard that had Denny all excited? Roland slid his Big Book off the shelf and turned to page 26. *A certain American businessman…floundered from one sanitarium to another…placed himself in the care of the celebrated physician, Carl Jung.* The hollowed pages of AA's recovery manual did not supply much more detail. Roland took his laptop from a drawer and hunched over it to learn what he could. In a matter of minutes, he found what looked like a credible source of information. The article referred to Rowland Hazard the Third as a Yale graduate and tenth-generation *scion* of a prominent colonial Rhode Island clan of considerable wealth, largely from the chemical industry. Roland smiled at the word. He knew what it meant—*an offshoot, a branch, a descendent, an heir*—but he had never dared to use it. Fits nicely with the family tree metaphor, he mused, but it had less to do with who begat whom and more to do with who's in line for daddy's money. Roland quipped to himself—how many scions does it take to trim the sails on a yawl? In his hometown of Sandpoint there were no scions. Hell, you could probably count all the Yalies in Idaho on one hand.

This particular scion was falling short of expectations, underachieving to an alarming degree. It's hard to apprehend the vagaries of the industrial chemical production business from the interior of hospital alcohol wards and insane asylums, which is where Rowland Hazard the Third spent much of his time. The family, well-heeled as it was, at their wits' end, sought out the best psychologist in the world—but Sigmund Freud was busy, either that or he turned them down. Next call was to Alfred Adler, second in renown only to his teacher Freud—again, no dice. So they turned to Freud's other famous protegee, Carl Jung, who agreed to see the patient. Then off to Zurich went the scion for a year's worth of treatment, during which the doctor applied his esoteric craft to tease the atavistic demons from Rowland's troubled mind, guessing that might do the trick.

A sober Rowland bid Jung farewell and a week or so later, somewhere in Paris, the drunken scion found himself in a state of incomprehensible demoralization. He crawled back to Jung in shame—what now? *There's nothing I can do for you—you're beyond my skill—a lost cause.* Rowland Hazard the Third wouldn't accept that determination. What's money for anyway? *Two choices then—hire a bodyguard to protect you from yourself or check into a sanitarium.* Despondent. Is there nothing else? *I've read of a few rare cases where men like you have undergone a life-altering spiritual experience and lived sober, virtuous lives thereafter, like the drunken fornicator who became Saint Augustine.* Sign me up for that! *Sorry, it can't be done. I'd sooner call down a bolt of lighting. But there's an evangelical movement—The Oxford Group—that appears to be helping people turn their lives around, based solely on foundational Christian principles. You might look into that.*

Enter scion #2, one Edwin Throckmorton Thatcher. The one and only. Descended from Bostonian colonists, one ancestor being the first pastor of the Old South Church in 1635. The Albany native, known as 'Ebby,' inherited a tidy sum at a young age and cast about for years, burning up his reserves through profligate living, unable to establish himself. The life of this spectacular underachiever came to a head when he was arrested after an incident at the family's summer home in Manchester, Vermont. He'd gone up to Vermont to dry out and paint the outside of the house, and after the job was done, he decided to get drunk and pull out the shotgun to take care of the pigeons roosting on the roof. It was raining, of course, the wet grass slippery, and Ebby went down before he could squeeze off the first shot. There, flat on his back, he started blasting at the unwelcome fowl. A neighbor witnessed his insane behavior and called the police—*there's a drunkard on his back blasting a shotgun into the pouring rain.* Unfortunately for Ebby—but fortunately for the world—Vermont had a three-strikes law. Three convictions in a calendar year meant a mandatory six-month sentence, and Ebby had been arrested twice already for public drunkenness.

The old boys' network kicked in. Vermont was a favorite vacation state, where many upper-class East Coast metropolitans *summered.* Roland composed another quip—*the scions summered in the scintillating scenery of New England*—before reading on. It turned out that the judge presiding over Ebby's case was the father of Ebby's golfing buddy, scion #3. (Ebby's father, George, had played for twenty-two years in a regular foursome at a local course with Abraham Lincoln's son Robert) Scion #3 invited scion #1, Rowland Hazard the Third, to attend the hearing of scion #2, Ebby Thatcher. The reason—Rowland's enduring sobriety since joining the Oxford Group presented a bona fide example of recovery with which to persuade the judge that there was an alternative to incarceration. And so it was decided. The state released scion #2 into the custody of scion #1 under strict conditions and an enforceable threat of jail time if Ebby strayed.

Roland closed the laptop. He remembered the rest of the story in as much as it was recounted in the Big Book. Ebby joined the Oxford Group. One of his tasks was to *carry the message to another alcoholic who is still suffering.* Ebby thought of his ol' drinking buddy, Bill Wilson, a native Vermonter but scion of no one. Bill's bickering parents had sloughed him off on his stern and exacting grandpa when he was still a child. Now Ebby's fellow carouser was on the verge of physical and financial collapse in New York City—a perfect candidate. Bill Wilson sat at his kitchen table one morning over a glass of gin when Ebby, six-months sober, appeared at the door. Lois, Bill's long-suffering wife, was away at work at the local department store, earning just enough to keep the two afloat. Bill offered his old friend a drink. Ebby declined and got right to the point—*I've got religion.* Bill, a modern thinker and studied agnostic, scoffed. The reunion lasted for hours with Ebby evangelizing and Bill politely listening. Ebby departed, message delivered and rejected, but not forgotten. Though Bill's drinking continued—he'd long since lost even the illusion of control—Ebby's serene sobriety, preternatural enough so as to make him seem almost a different person, nettled Bill in the ensuing days and weeks. He wanted what Ebby had. Ebby showed up again, this time at Bill's hospital bedside in an alcoholic ward. The drunkard lay there defeated, out of options, one spree away from commitment to an asylum. Again, the message—*ask and you shall receive, seek forgiveness from those you have harmed, etc.*—offered with compassion. Then Ebby left.

Completely alone, as a child lost in the wilderness, Bill arrived at a rare moment of humility. *Who am I to say there is no God?* he cried out. *If You're there, show Yourself.* Then ensued his storied mountaintop experience. The metamorphic spiritual awakening that Carl Jung could only report through inexplicable anecdotes had never descended upon his patient, Rowland, nor upon Rowland's sponsee, Ebby Thatcher—and both returned to alcohol before their days were done. But, for some unknown reason, Bill Wilson was chosen. The room lit up. He was propelled into a psychic stratosphere. The warm wind of grace stirred him to the bone. His mind was flooded with a liberating ecstasy that beggared hyperbole. Yes. It defied exaggeration, for he was never the same, not to say completely transformed; for the admirable attributes that drove him so hard to succeed in business remained. From that day forward, it was Bill Wilson's sole mission in life to help fellow alcoholics recover from their common fatal affliction. The indomitable drive that had brought him so close to success in the cut-throat world of Wall Street—his charm and optimism, qualities that kept his wife, Lois from abandoning him to desuetude—enabled him against great odds to found the society that Roland Hazzard of Sandpoint, Idaho had forsaken. Hazzard of Sandpoint could, if asked, tell you how Lois was the unsung heroine of the movement. He could regale a listener with paragraphs of AA lore, so prodigious was his memory; and if he hadn't closed the laptop on his research just now, he'd have found that Lois Burnham, a girl of Vermont, had once lived across the street from the Thatcher home and remembered visiting baby Ebby soon after he was born. Even had Rowland read of that extraordinary fact and added it to the improbable confluence of events that lead to the creation of the book resting there beside his computer, it would have moved him none the more. The world is filled with strange and wondrous things, and he'd be damned before he put stock in a fluke about his name.

Roland returned the book to the shelf and picked up his phone. The messages were piling up. He hated the device for the obligation it imposed, like an itch on an unwanted appendage that nonetheless needed to be scratched. To delay, he took a shower. The hot water poured over him. The ion-charged air freed his mind of concerns and let it wander. He wondered at the difference between *what a man does* and *who a man is* and concluded that *who a man is* cannot be known, not in life. Who a man *was* might be knowable in a disinterested sort of way, if his or her life impacted the world in some meaningful regard. If he dropped dead there and then, Roland surmised would be remembered only for what he'd done the night before, but as to who he'd been—that would remain a matter of speculation if not indifference. Could he *be guilty* if he did not *feel guilty*? After all, he reasoned, if I told the truth I'd be liable for a murder charge. So then is guilt determined by legal statute? Hardly. A murder in the USA might be a culturally sanctioned honor killing in another country. Withholding the truth—keeping it folded in his pocket on a handwritten note—was merely a matter of self-preservation.

He dressed for bed then went back to the parlor and picked up his phone again and sat down with it. Gina had dropped him a text message: *Be good to yourself.* Roland replied: *Thanks Gina I'm safe and sound.* He ignored a few others, from acquaintances who knew him well enough not to expect an immediate reply. Then came one from Phillip, his brother, the major. Sandy said he wouldn't call, and she was right. But it appeared the major was willing to text. *Remember Polonius.* That's all it said. Roland set the phone down then picked it up and read the text again. *Phillip, you sly dog,* he said aloud. Roland thought he knew what to make of it, but he wasn't sure. He got up and retrieved the Collected Works of William Shakespeare from his bookshelf and flipped to *Hamlet* and found the passage he was looking for, one his mother quoted from often when the subject of money came up. She liked to recite the first two lines as though they were enough to settle any question about finances.

Neither a borrower nor a lender be;
For loan oft loses both itself and friend…

Though he owed his brother a lot of money, he believed it was the verse which followed shortly after that Phillip wanted to impress upon him as an admonition relevant to his current situation.

This above all: to thine ownself be true,
And it must follow, as the night the day,
Thou canst not then be false to any man.

Roland resisted the impulse to call his brother and make sure he understood the cryptic message, but the thought of having to deny his intoxication, which Phillip would notice right away, rightly struck him as contrary to the purpose of being true to oneself. Besides, the day's consecutive dramas, were he to divulge even half of them to Phillip, had sapped his will to endure what was sure to be the blunt assessment of his battle-hardened bother, even if the Major was willing to deal with an intoxicated Roland. No. He would leave that conversation for tomorrow.

He rifled through the tome until he found *Henry V* and searched the scenes to find the quote—the raindrop—that had struck him as a fitting, if flippant, reply. He wanted to be sure to text the words exactly as the Bard had composed them. There it was.

I would give all my fame for a pot of ale, and safety.

He noted with no small chagrin the character's lowly name. Mister William Shakespeare, the Swan of Avon, had chosen to refer to Falstaff's young page simply as Boy. More or less like naming a dog, Dog. Phillip might not even bother to look up the quote, Roland hoped, before he pressed send.

All that remained was to sleep. The vigorous fornication of the morning, plus the naps he'd taken during the day, had kept him going, just barely. Now he would burrow into his unconscious mind and careen through whatever phantasmagorical dimension would invite him. He would read cuneiform from original clay tablets and find meaning that other scholars had never imagined. He would sit bestride the polished limestone cap of Giza and apprehend the perfect geometric network that connected many ancient megalithic structures on planet Earth. He would hear echoes both of catastrophic violence and melodic serenity from civilizations, extant and extinct, on worlds in distant solar systems. He would inhabit as a visitor the unfathomable emptiness of a godless death.

Wherever his astral projector would send him, he'd mastered the trick of coming awake once there, of enjoying the power granted by a lucid dream. Had he drunk too much to gain access to that power tonight? God knows in recent months he'd hampered that gift, and many others besides, through constant excess of alcohol. Yet he'd tasted a vivid dreamscape just hours ago before Astrid had yanked him loose by knocking on his door, so perhaps he would be free to roam again tonight.

Reading from the Bible seemed to grease the skids. He took it to his bedroom and climbed in and opened it to the First Book of Kings. The folly of Hebrews never ceased to amaze him. Thumbing your nose at Yahweh for the pleasures of cavorting with Baal—what could possibly go wrong? For background music to score his reading he played Beethoven, a deaf man who heard music in this mind clearly enough to write it down. If Ludwig could do that, how could Ahab fail to take direction from God? He smiled at the farce that is the human race. As he turned the pages, sleep gently pulled him in. Tomorrow would arrive at its own pace and Roland would make use of the day however he saw fit, without a plan, confident that his instincts would take him in the right direction. From earliest youth, never for a moment had Roland Hazzard considered that his decisions could lead to disaster, for as he surveyed the blundering world, there was no crisis from which one such as he could not recover.

Chapter 11
October 1, 2016 - Morning

Roland awoke from an abysmal sleep and got dressed and pulled on his Laredos. The cosmos had not blessed him with a journey as he'd hoped, so he'd have to face the day without the residual thrill that shimmered at the edges of his psyche after a night of lucid dreaming. He stood before the mirror to brush his teeth and assess the disarray of his hair, which was long overdue for a chop. There was more than enough in the back to gather into a respectable ponytail, though such a phrase would have struck him as oxymoronic. He wet a particularly stubborn tent on the top of his mop and tried to press it flat. No fixing that, he conceded. Only a hat would do, and the only one he had, a baseball-style cap he rarely wore, would clash with the boots. He avoided his eyes while he weighed his options. To meet his own eyes in the mirror would force upon him a self-judgment he did not welcome. The baseball cap it would be, that and an old pair of sneakers. After all, as well broken-in as his Laredos were, walking the distance down to the docks to retrieve his car needed more comfortable footwear.

He sat on the edge of the tub and took off his boots and socks and examined the bandage Deidre had applied to the cut on his foot. Pressed his thumb against it. Not too painful. It was healing already. She had ministered well. He got up and found his sunglasses and hat and saw the whiskey bottle in the kitchen and picked it and up went back to the bathroom. He poured a few ounces from the bottle into the glass on the sink and put on his glasses and began the process of shaving. He heard cars roll down the hill outside his building, then the rumble of a bus. Saturday was underway. He dragged the razor down his cheeks and along his jaw and up his neck, taking a sip each time he rinsed the blade. Flecks of shaving foam floated on the brown liquor.

Roland drained the glass and wiped his face with a towel. He capped the bottle and put on his hat to complete his disguise. To avoid any journalists that might be lying in wait at the front door of his address, he pulled off the crime-scene tape and climbed through the damaged parlor window and made his escape through the alley. He grabbed *The Chronicle* from the first coin-operated box he passed. The feature story commanded most of the space on the front page. *Local Man Slays Glendale Butcher.* Joshua's contribution took up a single column on page two. Another article reprised the details of Barsamian's seven suspected murders and sketched flattering portraits of his alleged victims. Roland gleaned all of this while scanning the pages afoot on his steep descent down Sacramento Street eastward toward the bay. His nose buried in the daily, he tripped over the lip in the curb and almost fell sprawling flat on his face. Regaining his balance, he folded the paper and stuffed it in his pocket, deciding to find a café where he could read it thoroughly over a cup of coffee and whatever looked worth eating.

Peet's Coffee on Sansome Street served the sort of high-octane brew that could contend with a hangover. The few sips of bourbon in the bathroom had served only to motivate him out the door with a sense of purpose, and now as he sat over his coffee and extravagant blueberry muffin, symptoms of physical withdrawal from alcohol began to manifest as a dull pulsing in his cranium and a slight trembling of his fingers. He held out his right hand and stared it steady.

First order of business: Get a load of what exactly his new best buddy, Joshua Goldberg, had been so eager to publish in the morning edition. Or maybe, he thought, Joshua was just itching to get in on the action, to see his by-line attached to the biggest crime story to hit The City in at least a decade. Roland looked at the paper and unfolded it slowly, reluctant to do what he'd come to do. He peered into the words like a cryptologist pouring over an enemy intercept.

An Accidental Hero
By Joshua Goldberg

Most of us were asleep an hour after midnight on Friday, including Roland Hazzard. Then occurred a confrontation in his apartment that would awaken the country and indel his name in history. The police report submitted by the officers dispatched to the scene describes a situation so peculiar that I decided to seek out the subject of the report and speak to him privately.

Indel? Seems a bit precious. I'd've gone with something more immediate, more visceral, like thrust. And clearly he's never heard of this other, this profoundly consequential Rowland Hazard the Third. Roland smiled at his own sarcasm as he did not fully trust it.

The report depicts Hazzard—the man who slew the Glendale Butcher—as an uncooperative, even belligerent, victim of a home invasion who, having been wounded by the knife-wielding intruder, managed to take the weapon and dispatch his attacker before calling the police. When they arrived, Hazzard told the officers that he needed to get back to sleep and bid them to conduct their business without his cooperation.

This is America, or was, last time I checked.

Unknown to him at the time, he had just excised from the rolls of the living a fugitive who had for three years avoided capture by several law enforcement agencies, including our vaunted FBI. While Hazzard slept, authorities would discover the identity of the deceased intruder as being Samuel Barsamian, the alleged murderer of seven young women during a killing spree in 2013 that lasted several weeks.

Excised from the rolls of the living? Did this guy go to a writer's workshop? Vaunted? Are you sure you want to poke a sarcastic finger into the chest of the FBI?

After a little detective work of my own, I found Hazzard at a local bar in the early evening, where he watched, with his bandaged arm on display, the story of his heroism unfold on the local news and entertained the high-spirited congratulations of his drinking buddies. When Hazzard left the bar, I followed him to his car and introduced myself with an offer to drive him home.

Prick. Sly way of saying I was too drunk to drive.

…It took some cajoling on my part, but after establishing my bone fides and agreeing to help him clean up the floor where Barsamian bled to death, Hazzard invited me into his humble abode. The hallway of his apartment still bore the evidence of the fight that resulted in the death of Barsamian and a knife wound on Hazzard's arm. Glass from the whiskey bottle Hazzard smashed over his assailant's head lay scattered about the hallway. Blood spots dappled the walls. Near the door, a large thick stain where The Glendale Butcher drew his final breaths.

Just one wall. Blood on just the one wall.

...before we could commence with our janitorial labors, Hazzard's nextdoor neighbor in the building came in and told us that she had just seen the picture of the dead man on a website. She explained with trembling excitement that just the day before he had asked her if he could help her carry her groceries up the street and into her apartment.

With trembling excitement. Wow, you're giving me goosebumps.

...The police sent a car to take her down to the station so she could provide her statement...and when I returned to the apartment after walking her to the street and waiting with her for the squad car...

Such a gallant gentleman journalist.

...Hazzard sat on his couch reading the Bible, having already scrubbed off the blood spots and placed a wet towel on the thick blood patch...we resumed our conversation, Hazzard doing most of the talking. Other than expressing relief in finally understanding why Barsamian must have chosen his building and his satisfaction that his neighbor was not murdered, Hazzard did not discuss the killing. When I asked him about it, all he would say was, "I told him to leave. Twice I gave him a chance to leave."

Good. That's all I needed to see.

During the time I spent with Roland, we were constantly engaged in conversation, and I found him to be intelligent, witty, a bit sarcastic, sometimes deadly serious and, above all, completely unimpressed, at least outwardly, by the fact that he had just hours before killed someone so notorious that it would make him an instant celebrity. That is one thing I took away from our meeting—Roland Hazzard does not court fame. I predict he will eschew it.

Roland Hazzard's name is part of the public record as it should be in a country where governmental institutions, such as police departments, are required to be transparent except in extraordinary circumstances. My agenda yesterday was to be the first reporter to obtain an interview with Roland Hazzard, and after meeting him and getting to know him, my further agenda is to admonish the media at large to respect Roland's penchant for privacy and not bedevil him with bevies of irrelevant questions. Take him for what he is, an accidental hero who simply wishes to go on with his life.

Roland paged through the other articles while he finished his coffee and muffin. Barsamian was a legal immigrant from Armenia who came to Glendale as a young teenager with his parents to join his extended family already established in that largest of the Los Angeles suburbs. He graduated from Glendale High School and earned a few credits at Glendale Community College in computer science and public administration but fell short of an AA degree and withdrew to work full-time in one of his uncle's medical device supply stores. His pursuit of the American Dream came to a screeching halt when his uncle, father, and mother were arrested for their involvement in one of the largest medical fraud schemes ever perpetrated in California, and he was left to fend for himself, working mostly minimum wage jobs in the Glendale area. Apparently, his criminal relatives had not set aside any of their illicit gains in a safe place for Samuel.

The lead story claimed that Barsamian, born into a nominally Christian family, converted to Islam after his relations were incarcerated and joined a Los Angeles mosque. The article was quick to point out that the mosque was not one known for radical jihadist views or activities but that it probably provided Samuel with much-needed fellowship. He drifted away from the mosque shortly before his first murder, committed less than a mile from his small, rented apartment in Glendale. The article laid out the details of each of the seven murders, including the evidence linking Barsamian to each one. The gas station video from Glendale, Arizona stood as the most conclusive and damning of all. The common elements in all the murders were the weapon and how it was used—a straight cut across the neck from ear to ear—and the profiles of the victims, all young white or Hispanic women, all murdered in a place named Glendale. He left no footprint on social media.

Roland scanned the photos of the victims, reflexively evaluating them on his scale of desirability and, catching his indiscretion, shook his head in self-disgust, reminding himself that they were dead and, in case they were watching from the unseen realm, asked their forgiveness. Another article featured a photograph, most likely gleaned from the archives of the *Daily Californian*, that showed a group of smiling karate champions holding a trophy, with Roland in the back row, taller than the rest, looking sober and satisfied. He scanned the copy for any mention of his prior encounters with the law and found nothing. He folded the paper in half and got up to leave. None of the other patrons even glanced at him.

~~~~~

The clown car was just as he'd left it. He drove to North Beach for a proper morning meal at Caffé Trieste and ordered the Tom Waits 'Raindogs' Breakfast—eggs and sausage and a side of toast, coffee and roll, hash browns over easy, chili in a bowl. He hummed the tune as he devoured the feast. It would tide him over for most of the day. On his way out of the door he stopped and went back in to retrieve his newspaper, not because he wanted to read more of it, but to remove it, as though it were a piece of incriminating evidence. It went into his back pocket as he stepped onto the sidewalk. The neighborhood had begun to awaken, beginning with the older generations and the business owners. With so few people on the street, he noticed that the trees and lawns were trimmed and manicured, most of the windows clean, the railings shiny. The younger folks and most of the tourists were still asleep, waiting for the morning fog to burn off. An attentive ear would have heard a snippet of Italian here and there. North Beach at this hour might have reminded those up and about of how it looked and sounded decades earlier before it became the nightly haunt for aimless children of drinking age and a neighborhood impossible to park a car after noon.

Roland looked up and beheld the white spires atop the basilica on Vallejo Street—The National Shrine of Saint Francis of Assisi. He watched the pinnacles cleave the thick ocean mist as it pushed eastward off the bay. It had been a few weeks since he'd been inside, one of his favorite places in The City. A place he went alone. A refuge he kept secret from his few acquaintances. He had no real friends—Gina was the closest thing to it, and she was both more than a friend and less than a friend. Call it a relationship postponed—*romanza interrotta*. Postponed by Gina after Roland interrupted his sobriety by picking up a drink once his court card was completed, just a few months after he started at Pacific Gameworks. *Picking up a drink* is parlance in the recovery community, for when it comes to them a single drink usually portends the resumption of a downward spiral of abuse. He'd kept the AA meetings secret too, but they were far from a refuge. He tolerated them as a child tolerates going to church, not hating it exactly but certain that he would never go unless forced to. As for Mass, Roland hadn't been since he was a teenager.

The national shrine of the world's most popular Italian saint, the eponym of The City, while it was certainly a church and held religious services, served Roland as a concert hall. He made regular visits to the sanctuary to enjoy the madrigal groups that occasionally performed there, usually on Saturdays. The sometimes-breathtaking choral arrangements, all without the accompaniment of instruments, made time stop for Roland and left his mind cleansed of all psychological debris. He called these madrigal concerts his *reset respite* and partook of them as often as he could during his stretch of court-ordered AA meetings. Roland made his way up the stairs to the venue where his personal one-step program congregated and read the signboard—*Santa Barbara Madrigal Singers-Saturday, 7 PM*. He remembered them well, an award-winning group of high-school students. They'd rocketed him into the fourth dimension.

The tall wooden doors were open. The place appeared to be empty. Removing his baseball cap, he stepped through the doorway and crossed the vestibule into the church. There was Jesus, suspended above the altar, bolted to the wall, larger than life, taking one for the team, the whole human team, from the owners on down to the groundskeepers, top to bottom, beginning to end—the alpha and the omega. The wound on his arm tingled under the bandage. *Jesus got a bandage, a full-body bandage, but only after he gave up the ghost. The Shroud of Turin—is that near Assisi? I wonder if the best and brightest scientific skeptics with all the latest machines are still trying to figure out that little mystery. At least it gives them something to do. Idle hands, as the saying goes.* There was no one in the pews, no one in the shrine at all. Roland felt like he was trespassing. A snatch of the Lord's prayer came to mind—*and forgive us our trespasses as we forgive those who trespass against us.* A tall order indeed, taller than the gothic arches that reached to the ceiling of this venerable establishment. Taller than any cathedral, he surmised. *Why did he call himself Kasabian? Why would a man go out with a lie on his lips?*

He took a seat in the nearest pew. Agnostic though he was, Roland did not hold religion in contempt. He'd sooner sneak a drink of whiskey in church—alcohol was served there, after all—than open a newspaper in one. He set the folded *The Chronicle* beside him next to his sunglasses and hat, closed his eyes, and took in the smells. It was so quiet he could hear the flames in the votive candles licking the air. The place smelled not just of burning wax, but of the oil rubbed into the wooden pews, lingering incense, and Italian marble. After a few minutes he heard the rustling sound of someone approaching, not from the street entrance behind him, but from the business end of the church, from the sacristy behind the altar.

He opened his eyes to regard a familiar figure, a Franciscan monk dressed in the brown robe of his order, cinched at the waist with a knotted white rope whose ends reached nearly to his sandaled feet. The monk's shaved head made the identification certain. Roland had seen him at every choral performance hosted by The Shrine, acting as a sort of master of ceremonies, introducing the program and offering a prayer to set the mood. Roland remembered his name—Farther Bartholomew. The two had never spoken. Roland wasn't sure whether or not he wanted the monk to recognize him or if he should make his acquaintance now. Before he could decide, Father Bartholomew raised his eyebrows and gave him a knowing smile and came over to say hello. Roland rose to his feet as the friar approached, and Father Bartholomew motioned for him to sit back down.

"Good morning, young man. It's good to see you again."

"Good morning." Roland couldn't bring himself to add the title, *Father*. It would have rung false; would have meant he'd signed on to the crew and recognized the man as a bona fide fisher of men. *To thine own self be true. Ain't that right, Polonius?* "Good morning," he tried again, "Friar."

The bald man grinned with genuine humor. "Bartholomew. Father Bartholomew as far as the post office is concerned."

"Not Friar Bartholomew? You've kinda got that whole monk thing going on there." He motioned up and down with his bandaged arm to indicate the friar's religious garb.

"Only when I'm in trouble with my superiors."

"The place looks shipshape to me."

"You don't look so shipshape. What brings you down here so early in the morning? Atoning for whatever mischief gave you that arm?"

"Breakfast at Caffé Trieste. Then I thought I'd check to see if the angels would be singing tonight."

"Yes. I think it's been a while for you. I'm here for every performance."

"I think I'll come tonight. Maybe grab a bite at Sodini's before or after."

"I see. I'm sure you saw the announcement on the board outside, and yet you came inside and sat down."

Roland appreciated the friar's tact in pointing out his lie without shaming him for it. "If you're asking why, to tell you the truth I don't know. The place seemed empty, and I guess I wanted to feel what it was like to be all alone in here. That's the best I can say."

Father Bartholomew sat down in the pew in front of Roland and hooked his elbow over the pew to face him. "I rarely sit down in here myself. We're lucky to have this place. I don't take it for granted." He looked at Roland's arm. "That was rude of me. Your injury is none of my business."

"It was an innocent question."

"Maybe not."

"It made the morning paper." Roland handed it over the pew then stood up and took a little stroll around the church, taking in all the murals, stained glass, and statuary that celebrated the miraculous saint, while Father Bartholomew paged through *The Chronicle*. He was in charge of the place, so he could read the paper if he liked, or spread out a game of solitaire if the spirit moved him.

When he finished his tour of the furnishings, Roland returned to the pew. "I've heard that if you want to be sure to sell your house, it's a good idea to put a little statue of Saint Francis in the front yard and that usually does the trick. Have you heard that before?"

"Not Francis. Saint Joseph."

"How does that work?"

"You bury the statue upside down."

"Who came up with that idea?"

Father Bartholomew folded the paper and handed it back over to Roland. "I was thinking about you this morning, just a few minutes ago actually, and then I come out and here you are, sitting alone in the pews, just like you were waiting for me. Can you believe that?"

Roland raised his chin and squinted down hard at the friar in an expression of incredulity that under ordinary circumstances might be considered rude.

"That surpasses odd. Frankly, I'm surprised you recognized me in the first place. What could possibly have put me into your mind?"

The friar nodded appreciatively. "The Madrigal Singers, naturally. You're one of my more memorable customers. You can't be surprised that a man of your bearing leaves a lasting impression."

"So, we can rule out a Higher Power then."

"Do I detect a note of sarcasm?"

"I mean no disrespect, Padre."

"A church is not a bad place to be, after what you've been through. I'm happy to leave you in peace if you'd like to be alone." He held up the newspaper. "I'm curious why you would show me this."

Roland sensed he was facing a clever one, one who would volunteer to leave him alone and in the same breath pose a difficult question. His skeptical expression changed when he saw how sympathy weighed on the friar's face in a look that said—*You don't have anywhere else to go, do you, young man?*

"I don't know, Padre. You asked about my arm here—I guess I wanted to see your reaction."

"You wanna talk about it?"

"That's not why I came in, however aesthetic the coincidence seems to you."

"You're a very intelligent person. I could tell from watching the way you listened to the music we enjoy in here."

"I've never met anyone more intelligent than I, at least not obviously so. A few writers have challenged my mind, but no one I've ever talked to. What does my intelligence have to do with anything?"

"I just wanted to acknowledge it, to let you know I wouldn't dare think I could bullshit you."

"But for some dim bulb, you might trot out the clerical bullshit."

The compassion in the friar's face hardened to annoyance. "It's up to you." He glanced back toward the sacristy from whence he'd come. "Something brought me out here, and not to tend the candles." He breathed deeply through his nose as if getting ready to stand.

"As long as you think it's important, I guess we can…"

The friar laughed, not derisively but merrily, as though entertaining the innocent stupidity of an earnest child. They'd been speaking softly, but the friar relaxed to his normal register. "You killed a man yesterday, a man who was trying to murder you, and this morning you stroll into an empty church and tell the priest on duty you just happened to be in the neighborhood."

"Would you rather I pretend otherwise?"

"Yes. If that's what it takes. Sometimes acting a part can transform you."

"Yeah. Fake it till you make it. Problem is, I don't feel any particular way about what I did except maybe a little proud. He had it coming. I gave him a choice."

"So you're all squared away?"

"I don't think so. People will say I could have shut my door and locked it, called the police, let it play out that way. There's a narrative where I'm still a bad guy—a lesser bad guy—but still a bad guy."

"I meant square with the Higher Power—I prefer the term *God*."

"I'm not so sure there is one such as God."

"Were you raised to believe it?"

"Roman Catholic. Served as an altar boy at Saint Joseph's in Sandpoint, Idaho until my career was cut short."

"Caught chugging the sacramental wine?"

"I outgrew the uniform. My sixth-grade growth spurt shot me up to six-one. Even if they'd bought one to fit me, it would have looked ridiculous—a sixth-grader towering over the priest at Mass."

"So, you were raised to believe. Most kids don't question it. But now, if there was a God—I mean your own hypothetical God—what would He have to say?"

"Let's stick with the God of Abraham—Yahweh. He sanctioned a lot of righteous violence and allowed for extensive collateral damage. Yahweh would probably just stroke his beard if he even took notice. Jesus, on the other hand, drove a harder bargain."

"Have you ever heard of the Baltimore Catechism?"

"Yes. But I wasn't indoctrinated with that text."

"The first question in the first lesson is: *Who made us?*"

"Slam dunk. The ever-popular *God*."

"That's all you really need to know. If you can wrap your mind around that astonishing claim, you can't veer too far off the path."

"What path?"

"Decency—right action."

"It wasn't the church that soured me. I have fond memories of my time assisting at the altar. It's people that did it, people who claim they know what is and what is not God's will. Anyone who says they believe in God and does not give himself over in service of God is no more than a gorilla who's learned a few words of sign language."

The friar chuckled. "Well, I'm glad to hear you had a good experience as a boy." Then changed his tone. "I've met a few former altar servers who were badly damaged—criminally damaged. The Church bears a great ignominy for hiding those crimes. Satan does his greatest harm when he works through members of religious institutions."

"I'm much more inclined to believe there's a Devil than a personal, all-powerful, loving God."

"God shows Himself subtly in the vastness of creation, in its countless irreducible complexities, and in small acts of human kindness. The Devil's blunt approach is easier to recognize."

"Yeah. I spotted him the other night."

"Don't be so sure. Whatever he was guilty of, he was still a child of God, like the catechism says."

"That child of God was evil." Roland pointed to the newspaper article that enumerated his multiple murders. "It's there in plain English, in black and white, slit women's throats for sport."

"He may very well have deserved to die—though you can't be sure of that. But make no mistake, you did not kill a demon or decrease even by a tiny fraction the sum total of evil in the world."

"I didn't have time to weigh the matter, Padre. I guess I settled for reducing the sum total of evil in my apartment."

"As you say. And you appear to be satisfied with the way it ended."

Roland searched the placid face of the friar for any sign of smugness, for there was no mischief in his voice. If the friar harbored any in his heart it did not surface in his countenance. *True enough*, he thought. *I'm satisfied with the way it ended.*

"To tell you the truth, I've gotten used to killing."

The friar went silent and twisted his lips.

"Before you say more, I need to caution you you're not in confession, not protected by the seal."

"Don't worry, Padre. You couldn't turn me in if you wanted to."

"You've lost me, son."

"I can't be held to account for what I do in lucid dreams."

"That's dangerous territory."

"I never feel safer, more at home, than in the land of lucid dreams."

"There's the seduction."

"You sound like you know what you're talking about, but do you? Have you much experience?"

"Enough to know I should stay away from altered states of consciousness. Recall what happened to Jesus in the desert after an extended fast. His mind was altered, and who showed up promising limitless power? The power you possess in your lucid dreams is illusory, and frolicking in that illusion can be dangerous. How long have you been doing it?"

"It started when I was ten. Osama bin Laden was hiding out in Tora Bora, and we needed to put him down. I prayed in my bed that our troops would capture him, kill him, and when I fell asleep, there I was alone in a cave with a bow-and-arrow and a purpose."

"And you killed him."

"Had to kill a mess before I got to the boss. It was like a video game."

"That must have been a thrill."

"Later, when I started reading Tolkien, I had a field day in Middle Earth. Couldn't wait to get to bed at night. My point is, I used my powers for good."

"Used? You're saying you don't use them anymore?"

Roland grew suspicious of Father Bartholomew's curiosity. Did the cleric truly believe that Roland's lucid dreaming put his soul at hazard? He felt like confessing that the gift was severely diminished by alcohol and in recent years often he hadn't been able to access his astral portal. His tour through the ancient subterranean headquarters in the walls of the Grand Canyon—that was the most vivid experience he'd had in a month, since he'd resumed his drinking habit, and he recalled his pique when Astrid's rapping on his door yanked him out of it.

"Let's cut to the chase, Padre. Do you think I'll be held accountable for the sins I commit during my astral adventures?"

"Not as long as you knew you were dreaming. My concern is that you might be held accountable for what you've let your little hobby do to you. Killing that man was no big deal—you said as much."

"None of it matters if there is no God, right?"

"Even atheists have consciences, whether or not they choose to believe it comes from God."

"Conscience or non conscience, without God the conclusion is the same—cessation of consciousness."

"How you lived matters, even if there were no afterlife."

"I believe that at least. I'm not an atheist, Padre. Atheists are believers, the most devout I've ever met. I ran into a few of 'em yesterday. You can't get a word in edgewise."

"I know the type, though they seldom darken my door. To tell you the truth, I prefer talking to souls like you. You're an example of what I call a traditional non-believer, a mainstream Christian agnostic."

"And why do you find them interesting?"

"Because they struggle, and struggle is always interesting. We can't take our eyes off a baby bird pecking its way out of its shell because it's life or death for that little creature and it's giving its all. It doesn't even know why."

"That's not how I see myself."

"How do you see yourself, Roland?"

"I don't know. Just another lapsed Catholic who still likes religious music."

"That's the second largest religious denomination in America—the Lapsed Catholic. So many of them poke their heads in here when they visit our fair city."

"And what do they say that lets you know they've lapsed? What do they confess?"

"If we get to talking, they tell me how the Church let them down in some way, after a divorce perhaps, or because of a political position, or the child abuse scandals, and suddenly they find the question of faith overwhelming."

"Faith in God, you mean."

"Faith in a personal, loving God."

"So they let it drop."

"Yes, in a word. But it keeps coming back up."

"Like a bad chili cheese dog."

"No. More like a fond memory."

An elderly woman pushed through the door. A slash of morning light glanced off the friar's bald head and illumined the altar. She looked around like she owned the place and fixed a puzzled stare on the two men conversing. The monk smiled at her and nodded hello. Roland was glad he'd resisted the impulse to leave and shot her a look that said *mind your own business*. He knew the conversation might soon be over and wanted it to continue.

"Except for this bit of mischief," the friar held up the newspaper, "I've met a hundred men like you in my years as pastor at the Shrine, men who came in to tell me they lost their faith. Some even call themselves atheists."

"I see. But they're not, because they're still searching—they walked back through the door. What do you tell them?"

"To stop seeking answers outside in the world, or in the latest spiritual book or fad, and to avoid the subject at parties."

"Where to look then?"

"I said before—in the subtleties. The whorl of a baby's ear, the kindness of strangers. Such signs are ubiquitous and infinite, but you have to tune your mind to notice them. It's a skill, like learning how to control your dreams, but with neither the thrill nor the peril."

Roland remembered the subtle changes in Barsamian's breathing as life ebbed out of him, then the healing sexual kindness of Deidre.

The friar continued. "God sometimes intervenes directly in an unholy life, but it's very rare, and there's no way to call it forth."

"Like with Saul of Tarsus."

"Him of course, and Francis of Assisi too. He lived a life of luxury until he heard the call to poverty and service. The rest of us just muscle through—trudge the road—as long as we are willing."

"And what if we're not willing?"

"We find less satisfying gods—false gods—to adore."

"People like Barsamian—what do they worship?"

"Only God knows—the power of their own rage, perhaps. And you, the smartest man you've ever known—you worship your own intelligence. You mentioned there were a few writers that have challenged you. Who, for example."

"Friedrich Nietzsche."

"Why him?"

"I don't understand how he knew so early on that Christianity would devour itself—that the Church would unleash reason, and that reason would destroy faith, and that loss of faith would unleash horror. It's an uroboros."

"I'll steer clear of Nietzsche. Anyone else?"

"They weren't writers, of course, but the Neolithic architects and builders. No one can explain how they quarried thousand-ton stones and moved them fifty miles without heavy machinery and shaped them to perfect flatness. Then how do you set it crossways fifteen feet up on top of two standing stones?"

"You mean Stonehenge?"

Another regular entered the church. Father Bartholomew made a sign with his hand to say that it was time for him to tend his flock. "May I put my number into your phone?"

Roland reached for his pocket to extract the device, then stopped. "You want me to call you?"

"It's up to you. But I wouldn't be serving my ministry if I let you walk out of here without at least offering my number."

The two exchanged phone numbers. "Thanks. You can notify me whenever there's music on the calendar. If I want to continue our discussion, can I text you?"

"The Franciscan Order does not permit texting. The Benedictines and Augustinians can text, but they're not allowed to use emojis or send images. The free-wheeling Jesuits, on the other hand…"

"Okay okay. You've made your point. I won't text."

"Call me if you need to talk. I check for voicemail often."

"I'll see you tonight. I mean—I plan on being here."

"I look forward to seeing you, Roland." He stood up and handed Roland the newspaper.

Roland took it and used it to salute the friar before returning to the street. North Beach had lost its early morning charm, but removing his battered yellow Nissan Sentra from the curb would improve its appeal.

He drove up the hill unconsciously, the several themes of the conversation whirring through his mind. Suddenly, he felt happy, felt himself smiling irresistibly, his obstreperous ego muzzled. The clown car seemed to park itself—landed a spot right in front of his building. *A miracle*, he laughed. The still small voice within him laughed along. When he opened the car door, the spell was broken. *What next?* His mind intruded. *Where now?* To go inside was to face the question posed by the presence of the bottle on his sink still holding a few swallows of whiskey. The still small voice said nothing but whistled a carefree tune. Father Bartholomew had something he wanted, a sense of ease and natural good humor that life seemed not to have worn away. Something had to change. *No--it's not that easy. For me to achieve that kind of peace, everything would have to change.* Freedom, he understood, could not be achieved by taking half-measures.

Chapter 12
October 1, 2016 – Afternoon

Roland turned his back on his apartment and began a vigorous walk. He figured he'd cover six or seven miles by the time he returned to the building—hard, steep, San Francisco miles that pounded the knees and burned the thighs. He was about to join the tribe of ear-budded arm-swingers, piping music into his brain to lessen the monotony of prolonged perambulation. It was a tribe whose members never interacted, rarely even acknowledged one another, like zombies, but much more vigorous and alert in their own myopic way. On the pretext of going to a bank machine to withdraw what remained of his net worth, the mood had struck him to hoof it out to the Presidio to test his physical endurance, to assure himself that he was still in good athletic condition. Anything to keep him out of his domicile.

On the flat streets of the Marina District, he broke into a jog. His long, powerful strides took him to verdant Chrissy Field which flanked the San Francisco Bay just east of the Golden Gate Bridge. He took a seat on a bench to rest and watch a few expert sailors contend with the whipping winds and buffeting surges just inside the iconic bridge. He could barely make out the figures of the sailors, but as he'd lent a hand on a few boats in the bay he knew how difficult it was to sail well under those conditions. The lakes of the Northwest were much more his speed and he thought that if he never again set foot onto a sloop in the ocean, he'd be fine with that. Unconsciously, he removed his shoe and checked the wound on his foot, which, though throbbing, was not inflamed or bleeding. Before turning back toward home, he walked to Fort Point to admire the surfers riding the swells that emerged in quick succession just under the towering vermillion span. The sailors, he thought, were impressive to be sure, but far too serious. The surfers, on the other hand, abandoned themselves to exhilarating pleasure, avoiding a prominent outcropping of rocks as they carved the rapid left-to-right break, darting, doubling, twisting, and spinning around to go back and do it again. He knew a man of his size, however athletic, never could control a surfboard so nimbly. With a twinge of envy Roland nodded his respect. Their minds, he thought, were empty, their hearts abrim.

Now, standing outside his building, heart thumping under his drenched t-shirt, self-satisfied after the lengthy exercise, he pulled the buds from his ears and went inside. It took him twenty minutes to shower and shampoo using the one free arm, and after he put on clean clothes and combed out his long squeaky hair, he noticed just how ragged the bandage had become, fringed with grime and wet with a mixture of sweat and shower spray. He sat on the edge of his bathtub to affix a new band-aide to the cut on his foot before slipping on fresh socks and lacing up his walking shoes again. On the sink stared the bottle, still holding its last few swallows. It seemed powerless—did not beckon to him. The still small voice said *dump it down the drain*. Roland looked away and went outside.

As he passed Andruko's Market, Taras appeared in the doorway and stood with his arms crossed over his greengrocer's apron.

"Roman, did you get my message about the peaches?"

Roman was a nickname he'd chosen for Roland, likely based on his physical appearance, as though he were a strapping young Roman soldier. Other times he called him cowboy.

Roland barely heard Taras's voice, as was apparently intended, like a comment passed through the teeth of a cigar-chewing Clint Eastwood in a crowded saloon directed at a man at the bar with his back turned. Roland stopped, turned around, and walked back to face Taras. He stood a little too close so that Taras would have to look up at him or take a step back. Taras stepped back.

"You said tomorrow."

"I'm just checking. I know you've been busy."

"No more than usual."

"Oh? You must be unlucky."

"How so?" Roland was in no mood to bandy words.

"If last night was not unusual, you must run into a lot of trouble."

Roland nodded. "I'm no stranger to violence. Last night was not the first time I've lightened the workload for the police. First time I've helped the FBI, though."

"My brother and I have been lucky. We've never had to get rough."

"Must be you've put the fear into your customers."

"Maybe we've been lucky enough to have customers who don't let their grocery bills get out of hand."

The elder of the two Andruko brothers, Oleg, emerged from the store and stood just behind Taras' right shoulder so that Roland could see him hefting a cleaver in his right hand. His white apron was speckled with blood as he'd been hard at work behind the meat counter.

"You come for peaches?" his English was not nearly as good as his brother's. "Taras left you message about awer dewlicious peaches."

"Do I dare to eat a peach?" Roland grinned insincerely.

"What? They're perfect."

"I'll try one tomorrow."

"Not as good tomorrow. Not so dewlicious."

"I'm sorry, Oleg, but I won't have a hankering for peaches until tomorrow."

Roland turned to walk away but Oleg spoke loudly to stay his departure. "I hear you good with a knife." He spun the cleaver deftly, not twirling it like a showman but spinning it with a quick twist of the wrist so that it flashed and finished edge down, just as he'd been holding it to start with, once, twice, three times, like a tennis player at the service line.

"Not good enough to impress a master like you." He was lying. His months as a gutter had made him proficient with several different kinds of blades. "But I'm good at taking them away from people when I have to."

"Dat's good trick tew have."

"It's one of many in my toolbox."

"Slow down you guys. You're going to be here tomorrow, right, cowboy?"

"What happened to yuwer pretty boots?"

"There's a row of human teeth stuck in the toe of the right. I'm having it repaired."

"Why not leave the teeth in the boot to show yuwer meester badass?"

"I already put them under my pillow so the tooth fairy will bring me the money I owe you."

"I think you like lotta fairies. They help you with yuwer football picks."

"Easy, Oleg. I gave him till tomorrow."

"I'll bring either five hundred or the whole nut." It occurred to him to ask them what might happen if he failed to show up tomorrow or showed up with less than the required five hundred dollars, but he wanted the conversation to end so he kept silent and continued his descent down Hyde Street.

Oleg wasn't finished and followed him with a holler. "Tomorrow is the day that's coming after that one that is today."

Roland walked until the street flattened out in the Tenderloin district. A few blocks ahead, Tina, his fondest person in The City, conducted an honest business along with other hardworking, mostly immigrant shopkeepers in the neighborhood, all forced to tolerate an ever-shifting tide of human detritus, mostly drug addicts and washed-up prostitutes of every persuasion that roamed or lay crumpled on the streets. No matter how fast they died or were arrested, there were always more to replace them, making for a certain constant density of broken individuals. Nature abhors a vacuum. It was not uncommon in that quarter to come upon a used needle or a deposit of human feces, evidence of a headlong, hell-bent progressivism. It was no place to raise children, yet Tina and her husband were doing just that, and rather well as far as Roland could tell. He'd seen her son and daughter grow from toddlers to school children over the past three years from the vantage point of a seat in her little two-chair salon, one occasional weekend haircut at a time. Indeed, hers were the only scissors in The City that had ever snipped his locks.

By the time he reached her door, Roland had exorcised himself of his murderous ruminations concerning Oleg. No one had forced him to wager on football games through the Andruko's sportsbook, he conceded to himself, and he allowed that they'd been more than patient. Still, that didn't excuse Oleg for being an asshole, though it put his behavior into perspective. Roland knew that he'd put himself in a vulnerable position, had behaved in such a way as to force the Andrukos to confront him. Just the same—*Fuck Oleg. Bugger him with an electric cattle prod.*

Brass bells jingled as he opened Tina's door.

"Hi, stranger. I thought maybe you move away and forget to say bye-bye. You like to break-a my heart."

"I'd have to be dead or in jail. You should know that, darlin'."

"Maybe yooo getting close. Yooo not look so good, my handsome man."

"I still abide above street level. Keeping body and soul together."

"Well, I see you washed your hair for me. It grow too long. You look-a like-a hippie. Come in and tek-a seat."

Roland sat and set the wounded arm gently on the padded leather armrest.

"What can I do today for you, sir."

"Let's go all the way, baby."

Tina, a tallish, hard-eyed beauty, was in her mid-fifties, but as with some Asian women, it was hard to get a fix on her age. She easily could have lied it down to forty. Of her husband, friends, and neighbors, Tina held the distinction of being more than a common immigrant, though some might say less. Tina was a refugee, a genuine escapee from the Vietnam War, one of the tens of thousands of Boat People, as they'd been labeled by the press.

"Don't play with me."

"I'm serious. Take it off. Take it all off."

"You must be drunk, but it too early."

"No. You can smell my breath if you want, or give us a kiss."

"Don't be so silly."

"I'm not joking, Tina. I need to lose the hair."

"People pay money for thick, long hair like-a you got. Wig makers—I mean it."

"Then sell it of course. My contribution to your kids' college fund. Where are they, anyway?"

"At their soccer games with daddy. He coaches."

"I thought you escaped Communism. You own your own business, speak a bunch of languages, your English is perfect, and now you're letting your children join a Communist collective? Why not an American sport—baseball or stock car driving?"

"Don't be stupid. It fun for them. Baseball too hard for little ones."

"I dunno...but soccer? It's a slippery slope. Next thing you know they'll be on the Che Guevara Strikers, running around the pitch with black berets and red jerseys showing the face of that psychopath."

"You joining the skinheads? That's not my idea of America. I won't help make you a skinhead."

"Skinheads are ignorant fools. I'm going for the monk look."
"What kind-a monk—Buddhist?"
"Catholic maybe. Franciscan—San Franciscan."
"Catholic? They don't have to be bald."
"Yes. They don't. That's true. But I know *one* that is. He's in charge of a nice little church in North Beach. I talked to him today." Roland held up his mobile device. "I got his number. You can call him and ask him if you want."
"I believe you. I give you the monk cut. Do you want me to chop off your penis while I'm at it? You'll be number one monk first day."
"I doubt you're licensed for surgery. Besides, I'm going to need it. I've got a date tonight."
"No license for that, but I've done surgery before. Maybe I told you that story already. Yes?"
Roland had heard her tell it twice before but wanted to hear it again.
"Yeah. You lanced a nasty boil."
"What that mean?"
"Nothing. I was only kidding."
"You maybe kidding, but I wasn't kidding. I cut off a lady's foot. No one wanted to do it. We were crowded on the boat and she had a rotted foot. Gang-green—it had to go. She begged and begged but no one wants to cut it off. It smelled very very bad, worse than dead body. I got sick of it. I did it to stop the smell and to shut up the lady. I was fourteen years old. Grown men, big pussies, they wouldn't do it. I told them they could do it in one or two hits with the machete we had. I said it's gonna take me three or four whacks and I'll make a rough cut, an ugly stump, or make her bleed to death. But they said no. Big pussies. Men are what? You know the word."
"I don't know—big pussies?"
'No. The book word. Use your fancy English."
"Squeamish."
"YES—a bunch of big squeamish pussies."
"So you hacked that bad boy off."
"Three whacks. It look-a pretty good—pretty clean cut."
"And she lived?"
"Yes. She passed out and woke up later. We wrapped the end and kept it from bleeding her to death."

"Yes. I remember now."

"True story. I threw the foot at the biggest pussy and told him to eat it."

"Not that part. You just made that part up."

"No boosheet. He would have thrown me off the boat into the ocean, but I keep the machete. The whole trip I keep the machete."

"Did you tell your kids that story?"

"Never. All they know is that I had to leave Vietnam because of the war, and I had three choices: Australia, Canada, USA. No brainer. And I make sure they know they're Chinese, not Vietnamese. I don't even speak Vietnamese anymore. Chinese, English, French I still like to speak, and I'm learning Mexican."

"You mean Spanish."

"Spanish you get at community college. Mexican you get on the street. At the farmer's market. Many, many friendly Mexicans I've met. They should stay."

"Believe me, I'd have a better chance of being kicked out of this state than your Mexican friends."

She opened a drawer and took out a pair of narrow scissors and showed them to him.

"If I'm going to sell the hair, I need to cut it very carefully. There's a special way. I need to cut it right at the scalp. It take longer. No charge of course."

"I'm in no hurry. But when you're done, I'm thinking I could use some of your medical expertise."

"You want me to look at that arm, give it a new wrap?"

"How are you getting along with your husband?"

"Should I lock the door and turn the sign? You want to take me back in the potty?"

"Now who's playing? I'm talking marriage. If he burps and doesn't say excuse me, just call me and we'll be off to Vegas."

"Sorry. You too young. You too poor. Quickie nookie or nothing. Last chance. I'll leave some for your date tonight."

"Before the cut or after?"

"Before, of course, tiger." She let out a laugh. "No can do it with a shaved head monk. Even a phony monk. Forbidden by my culture."

The flirtation had played out.

"Sorry, darlin', too late. I'm starting my afternoon San Franciscan monk meditation. No more sexy talk or I'll call your bluff, take you in the back and give you a big hairy white baby."

"Can't grow watermelon in the desert, Mista Goo-Roo."

"Please wake me when you're finished, princess."

Tina wrapped a cape around her placid patron. "You call *my* bluff?" She muttered cheerfully. "Maybe I call *your* bluff."

She used the precision scissors to snip off small pinches of his hair as close to the roots as possible, carefully draping each little yield over the crossbar of a wooden coat hanger she had hooked to the knob of her comb drawer until she had harvested the entire crop. It took nearly half an hour, and Roland did not move or make a sound. She would have known if he'd slept, as a slack neck would have made her job more difficult. All that was left was to shave the head. The scrape of the razor along his virgin dome roused an almost erotic sensation—no, it was a real erotic sensation. He shifted in the chair to readjust himself.

"It feel good, huh?"

"Little bit."

When she was finished, she turned him to face the mirror.

"Nice handsome head. Good round shape. No moles. No blotches. You think your girlfriend will like it?"

"If not, I can talk her into it."

"Maybe without your hair you not so powerful. Maybe I'm Dalilah. Think about that!"

"Your Chinese Bible is all fucked up. Dalilah had to nag Sampson into giving up his secret, and she wasn't the one who clipped his wig—it was her servant. Plus, Dalilah was a whore who betrayed him for money."

What Roland left out was that Sampson, a Nazirite, had sworn off alcohol. One gulp of wine would have had, he surmised, the same result as the shaving of his head—the loss of his superhuman strength.

She handed him a little tube of sunscreen. "Rub this on every day if you going to walk in the sun."

She went into the back of the salon to retrieve her medical box.

"Can't you rub it on?"

"Need special permit."

"So, you're licensed to do the bouncy-bouncy in the potty, but you can't rub sunscreen on my head?"

"In the potty with the door locked and the sign turned, you're not a customer. When you're in the chair during business I can only do so much."

"Is that a city or a state thing?"

"It's all the same to me."

He stared at his shiny head in the mirror as he applied the lotion. The erotic sensation was lost because the fingers were his own. *Damn*, he promised the head, *I'll get someone to take care of you later.*

She turned him back around and sat on a stool to work on the arm. "Stay away from children. You could scare them."

"Don't you think the kids around here have already seen their share of freaks?"

"Not big like you, especially when you wear your boots."

She cut the bandage off and cleaned the wound with iodine. "Is a knife cut, right?"

"Yes. Only a few people have seen it, besides me."

"Are you running from something? Shaving your head is no way to hide when you taller than all the other flowers."

"You can't run from the internet. My picture is part of a big news story, and I don't want to be so easily recognized."

"What did you do?"

"Killed that man—that murderer."

"The Glendale Butcher? That you who got him?"

"Yep." He said it like he was admitting that he was the one who dropped the big fat strawberry ice cream cone splat in the middle of the public library or, better yet, that it was he who released the mylar balloon that got tangled in the power lines and blacked out the eastern seaboard. Like he'd made a mess he could not undo.

"You shouldn't hide from that. You a hero."

"I'm not a hero just because he turned out to be a villain. If I'd tracked him down like a bounty hunter and killed him in a fight to the death then you could call me a hero, but Friday night I simply got out of bed and completed the task set before me."

"I see. Okay then go. Take your monk brain that's in your new monk head and go think your big monk thoughts. You come back anytime. Free head shaves and shiny buff job. No kidding. Remember sunscreen every day and get out of my store. Get out so you can get to work hiding if that is—how you say?—*the task before you*. Come back soon anytime."

"Thanks, lover. I knew you'd understand. And remember, if he drops dead let me know and we'll catch the next boat to Las Vegas and practice planting melon seeds in the desert."

"I don't understand nothing, except you crazy and the world needs you—people like you. The world don't need most people."

"The world needs you too. There's a one-footed lady somewhere who'd testify to that. You know a little something yourself about doing the task set before you."

"Never tell my kids that story."

"Je te promets." He jingled himself out.

Roland took a right and walked down Hyde to Eddy Street then crossed at the light to the northeast corner where the doors to the Brown Jug Saloon were flung wide. Not so much to invite business, he supposed, but to let out the lingering smell of bleach and detergent used every morning to remove the unsavory residue from the night before. It wasn't one of his regular haunts—far from it—but he was thirsty and remembered that the Jug sported a free glass of draft beer with the purchase of a shot.

The only patron in the place sat at the dark end of the bar and held his beverage cupped between both hands and stared at himself in the mirror in the studious manner of a stray pioneer trying to solve the puzzle of his wayward past before taking a stab at his future—tomorrow, always tomorrow. The bartender stood nearby the man under the silent flickering television. Unlike Tina, whose indeterminate years were the blessing of her porcelain complexion, the chronological age of the woman manning the bar was hard to appraise because she'd drained the elixir of youth prematurely, her face florid from decades of boozing, cheeks sunken and pock-marked, wiry hair stuffed under a red bandana to advertise her long-since dissipated biker-mama chic. Whatever the series of missteps that dogged her ill-starred birth—the betrayals, misplaced loyalties, bad investments, failed exams, misdemeanors, and miscellaneous bad decisions—and had led her here, to this place, on this day, perhaps were recorded in some horoscopic ledger, or nowhere at all. The God of her childhood did not blame her, bore her only goodwill, but she carried herself as though damned.

Roland sat on the stool nearest the sunlit doorway so as not to engage in requisite small talk with the solitary castaway. The bartender walked toward him, speaking before she reached his chosen spot.

"Good afternoon, young man. What can I get you?" Tips were scarce in The 'Loin, so it paid to be friendly to a strapping lad wandering in off the street.

"Blackjack and a beer back."

"Short back? It comes with."

"Yes, ma'am. I've been here before."

"You're from the neighborhood?"

"Walking distance. I have business this way sometimes." He wanted to give the impression that his business was something more important than a haircut, something nefarious perhaps. His bald head, he imagined, might help in that regard.

She brought the drinks and he put a twenty on the bar. A couple of rounds and he'd be ready to call Phillip, his brother, the major. Without warning, a man outside began shouting at the top of his lungs. Too late to reverse the purchase and move on to another bar. Roland took a sip and listened. The voice was stationary, its owner apparently having decided to stand in one spot to issue his rant.

"I WANT A WHOLE NEW WORLD. I WANT A WHOLE NEW WORLD." Over and over again. Then a pause, perhaps to flip the broken record in his brain.

"IF IT AIN'T A FIST IT ISN'T LOVE."

Roland had heard enough. He set a napkin on top of his beer glass and went outside. The man's face was raised, nose pointed upward to the sky as if he were beseeching God Almighty and believed that Almighty God was actually listening. He walked straight toward the man, whose appearance left no doubt that he lived on the streets. As soon as the man saw Roland he stopped yelling, as one might do when a bald man of Roland's height and bearing was approaching so briskly. Roland stopped as soon as he smelled him and spoke before the man could open his mouth.

"What's the problem?" It rated high on the scale of stupid questions. Clearly, the problem amounted to nothing less than the entire world because, as the man had declared, the only trustworthy form of intimacy was violence.

"What's your problem?" The man displayed his rotting mouth. His chipped greenish teeth looked like they'd been jammed into his gums by a feeble-minded child.

"You're my problem. I'm in the bar enjoying a drink and some peace and quiet, putting the finishing touches on the blueprints for my reverse-gravitational hyper-dimensional timeshuttle, and you're out here breaking my concentration. You want a whole new world? Maybe if you shut up and let me finish my work with any luck pretty soon we'll have a vehicle that can take you to a whole nuther universe. We'll go together. You can be the skipper. I'll pencil in a little shower just for you. But first, you gotta shut up already."

"This is America, man. Ever heard of freedom of speech?" If he'd ever possessed the power of reason, the poor creature had long since abandoned it.

"Freedom of speech? That's only for American citizens."

"Fuck you. I AM a goddamned YOO-ESS citizen."

"Really? You can't even speak English."

"You're crazy, man. We're speaking it now."

"Not true. You seem to understand a little English, but right now you're speaking fluent bullshit."

"So, what are you going to do about it?"

Roland pulled out his wallet and withdrew a twenty. "How about you take this little fortune and stumble your show on down the road?"

The lunatic snatched the bill from Roland's hand with astonishing speed. The motion sent a waft of body odor up his nostrils so fast that Roland reflexively waved his hand in front of his nose like a prissy aristocrat.

"You win, man. Money talks."

"And bullshit walks."

Mollified, the cosmically disgruntled complainant ambled toward Civic Center Plaza to rejoin his bedraggled herd. Roland went back inside the bar.

The bartender nodded appreciatively. "Whud you do, threaten to kick his ass?"

"I took a shower this morning, so I made sure it didn't come to that."

She set an empty shot glass upside down on the bar in front of him. "Whatever you did, it's worth one on the house."

Roland nodded. Two shots of whiskey and the appended beers would suffice to embolden him to place a call to Phillip, his brother, the major. He drank them slowly, letting the feeling of ease and comfort swell within him. He made a show of looking at his phone so as not to have to stare at himself in the mirror or at the cigarette burns on the wooden bar. When he felt ready to make the call he stood up and spoke to the woman.

"The night man lets me smoke in the patio out back. Are you cool with that?"

"I'll save your stool in case we get a big rush." She refilled his beer glass and set a napkin on top of it.

Patio was a kind word for the gated space outside the rear door, which housed a few open trashcans, a stack of milk crates, empty kegs, and a small rusted folding chair surrounded by cigarette butts. It would have been cruel to leave a dog out there, which people did, judging by the urinous odor that permeated the bricks. The smoke from his cigarette blunted the smell.

Phillip answered after a couple of rings. "Hey, little brother. I was hoping I'd hear from you."

"Major." Roland offered a deliberately formal tone.

"What time is it over there—one o'clock? Are you gassed already?"

"I don't sound gassed. You know I'm not gassed."

"Then don't call me major. It's disrespectful."

"It wasn't sarcastic."

"Coming from you, it might could a' been, and I'd rather not sift for the difference."

"*Might could a'?* Have you dropped down on the evolutionary ladder?"

"Too many years humping around with good ol' boys. I've sprinkled in a little dialect just to add some flavor."

"Did you get the gist of my text last night—*My fame for a pot of ale and safety?*"

"Damn clever, as always, Roland; but I don't think I read that play, assuming it's Shakespeare."

"Henry the Fifth, his best military drama. Should be core curriculum in the Corps."

"Speaking of reading, I read that bit of hagiography in *The San Francisco Chronicle* by that Goldberg fellow. You lucked out there."

"I read it too, but I don't see what good it does. It's just one guy in one paper."

"Well, it's a good opening shot across the bow, if what you really want is to be left alone by the press."

"I don't care about that right now. I just want to tell you what happened, Phillip. I haven't really talked to anyone about it, not honestly. I haven't even rolled it over myself."

"No. Not here. Not now."

"Why not?"

"We have to assume this conversation is being recorded, even if no one is actively listening in. Computers transcribe telephone conversations automatically these days. So never assume you're on a secure line."

"Isn't this your personal phone?"

"Doesn't matter. Nothing's private anymore, little brother. If there's something about what you did that you need me to hear that's not in the stories all over the internet, you best keep it to yourself until the next time we see each other, which will be Thanksgiving as long as you show up."

"There's something else. I've got myself into a little financial trouble."

"Don't tell me. You hurt yourself playing football again and can't afford the doctor bills."

"That's right."

"How much?"

"Forty-eight hundred."

"Ouch. When do you need it?"

"It's already gone to collections."

"Ok. Ok with reservations. Same account as before?"

"Yes. Thanks, Phil. I owe you."

"Quite a bit, actually. I'm keeping track."

"I've hung up my cleats, just so you know."

"Don't say that. I mean it would be great if it were true, but I'd rather not hear your promise. But there is one thing I do know is true."

"You gonna get on me about my drinking? I'm sure Sandy told you I was pretty well lit yesterday."

"Before we get to the life-or-death issues, let's talk about this Goldberg article. How'd he get the idea you wanted to be left alone?"

"By listening to me express my aversion to the press."

"I don't think that's the way to go with this, Roland. For one thing, isolation and alcohol are a lethal mixture."

"I never spoke of isolation."

"I know you. You checked out for a month earlier this year. No one could get a hold of you. I call that isolation."

Phillip had rapped at the door of his secret. Roland put on his poker face, trusting that the impassive expression might lend calmness to his voice.

"What are you getting at, Phillip?"

"Milk this pig for all it's worth. It's not going to be lactating forever. And put some lipstick on it while you're at it."

"Are you talking about money?"

"Yeah, dumbass. Ride it all the way to a book deal."

"You can't be serious."

"It's a serious sum you owe me."

"I wouldn't know how to get that started."

"Call your newspaper buddy. Tell him he had you all wrong or that you've changed your tune. Maybe he can hook you up with a TV interview."

"Yeah, then what? I'm still not seeing the dollar signs."

"You gotta make it happen. Any interview you give on local TV potentially goes global, so make it a good one. Just keep at the top of your mind that you're speaking to the entire world, not just everyone living now but everyone who will ever live. If you go viral, there's no telling where it will lead."

Roland pondered the implications. What Phillip said sounded true enough, or at least possible. The story would quickly fade from the news in this world of constantly swirling events and he and only he could keep it going.

"I got my head shaved today."

"Perfect. Sounds like you're way ahead of me."

"I was thinking the opposite. There's a photo in the newspaper showing me in my gi with my old karate team. So I removed the hair, thinking maybe…"

"Doesn't matter what you were thinking, little brother. Bald is dramatic."

"I'll give it some thought."

"Don't think too long. Fortune favors the bold."

"What did you mean by *Remember Polonius?* I'm guessing *To thine own self be true.* Was that your point? Or did you mean *Neither borrower nor lender be?* That might make more sense, except you had no idea I needed money."

"Your response was right on the mark. *I'll trade everything for a drink.*"

"I was just fucking with you."

"Then you were fucking with yourself as well, because that's what I was pointing at right there, and your wiseass text confirmed it."

"You've lost me, Phillip. You'll have to spell it out."

"Look kid—and I hate calling you kid—but for someone as smart as you, you really do act like a fool sometimes. Of all the people I've ever known and probably ever will know, no one was born with more on the ball."

"You're starting to sound like Dad."

"He's given up trying to get through to you, so you'll have to hear it from me, and just this once. You can pull the phone away from your ear if you want to, but I'm going to say what I think needs saying."

"I'll listen." Roland figured his brother had paid for the right to dress him down.

"There's a thousand things you could have been, and most of them you still could be. Professional athlete is off the table, I guess. Twenty-five is probably too old for a no-name to show up at training camp, but I swear to God you could have been an All-Pro tight end or defensive end or even a quarterback. Or a starting pitcher in the big leagues. Do you have any idea how few guys are born with what you've already thrown away? God, I can't tell you how much I wished you'd had the character and discipline to take your natural talents to the top level. Shit, you didn't even have the discipline to make it on a college volleyball team. You know why volleyball players don't make any money, little brother—because you can take an average basketball player and train him for a couple months and turn him into a competitive volleyball player. It's a club sport, a family sport. Fifty-year-olds play it on the beach."

"I don't mean to be rude, Phillip, but you've circled this quarry before, so unless you're going to rack one in the chamber..."

"You're working an entry-level job at a video game company, and that's a step up for you, a step up from cleaning fish. A genius of your IQ, your world-class memory, your gift of gab—you could get a PhD in a dozen areas or breeze through law school. Work a little harder, and you're a doctor. Or make a zillion on Wall Street. Hell, even open a string of dojos. I'm just scratching the surface, Roland. I'm sure you could come up with possibilities that would never even occur to me."

"I'd never have landed on writing a book."

"The book has landed on you, if you've got the sense to maximize your publicity."

"I don't know, Phillip…"

"Think about it. You can work both sides, the hero and the scofflaw. Embrace the press, show 'em who's boss, generate an online following, then comes the book deal. There's only one thing that can stop you."

"Don't tell me."

"At least Papa Merrill lived a life before the bottle caught up to him. People in Panhandle mourned. You remember. Musta been two three hundred people at the funeral, and half of 'em total strangers. People don't show up for an ordinary drunk. It's not crazy to say that if he'd stayed on track he could have run for governor and had a shot if he'd wanted it. But he gave up at fifty and faded away for twenty years. You're lucky in a way—you're catching it early. You get a handle on it now; it won't hamstring you when you're in full stride."

Their mother had taken him aside before he went off to college and hinted that she thought he might have a drinking problem, and she mentioned her father as a tragic example, but she hadn't brought it up again until yesterday. Now Phillip was declaring it, preaching God's holy truth. Roland wished he hadn't left his drink on the bar. This conversation had taken an unexpected turn and would go longer than he'd anticipated.

"There are things you don't know, things that are bound to come out."

"Let's have it."

"I've been arrested a couple of times—exactly two times. I did a few weeks in county lockup for the second one. The local news hasn't dug it up yet as far as I can tell, but it's bound to come out."

"Arrested? For what?"

"Drunk in public and drunk and disorderly. Court ordered me to do thirty AA meetings."

"Is that all? If that's all, then use it to your advantage. Everyone likes a good recovery story, but first you have to sober up. Go back to the meetings. You've got a choice here, little brother, a very stark choice—a long happy life or a slow unhappy death. Only a fool would choose the latter. Remember what Dad used to say? *Intelligence is not a virtue. Wisdom is.* So make the wise choice. Keep your eye on the prize. Be bold, and mighty forces will come to your aid."

He fought back a tear. He'd never heard this tone from his brother. Not a hint of irony in his voice, just a pleading, and in the pleading Roland sensed a waning of hope. He wanted to comfort his big brother by assuring him he would be okay, but he knew that any words in that vein would ring false. While Roland searched for a reply, Phillip got a hold of himself.

"I'm sorry, little brother. We all just want what's best for you."

"I thought we were going to talk about the killing. You're the only one I want to talk to about that."

"What's there to talk about?"

"I don't feel anything. You've never told your war stories, but I know you've killed men in combat."

"Combat is a different animal. Soldiers fight for God, country, and family in varying orders of importance. Killing is part of the training. You took out a criminal, a notorious public enemy. You should be happy about that."

"It was up close—I watched him die. It took minutes. I mocked him."

"Good. So what? Wasn't he trying to kill you? Don't get sentimental about it. Don't use it as an excuse to drink. Is that what you're trying to tell me—you're all torn up about killing that motherfucker so now you can't function?"

"No. But there's a little more to it."

"Keep that to yourself for now. We can talk at Thanksgiving. In the meantime, you can talk to a priest or a therapist. Or get on your knees and talk to The Man himself."

"I'm not sure I still believe."

"Well. If you don't get your act together, you'd better hope that God is just a childhood fiction."

"Why's that?"

"Remember the parable of the talents? You don't even rate with the guy who buried his share for safekeeping and got his ass kicked when the master returned. Jesus didn't mention your type. You're the guy who took his share to the next town over and spent it on liquor and whores."

Roland laughed. "So, it's the outer dark for me."

"The way you're going."

"You think it would make God happy if I cashed in on killing a guy?"

"Whatever else He wants, it's safe to say He wants you not to be a drunk breaking the heart of our mother. What you do with your accidental celebrity is up to you. Anyway, it was just a thought. You owe me a shitpot of cash, and one way to get square would be to leverage your notoriety. People monetize their cat videos, for Chrissakes. You could figure out something, and if you go viral enough you can shop a book. Such a thing was never possible, not until now, so just think about it."

"I suppose that's true. I'll mull it over."

"Ok. It's done."

"What's done?"

"The money. Transfer confirmed. I did it while we were talking."

"Thank you, Phillip."

"You can thank me by turning things around, Roland."

"I'll see you in Sandpoint."

The call ended. Roland went back to the bar.

"Can you call me a cab, please?"

He drank his whiskeys and beers while he waited for the taxi to appear outside the door. When it arrived, he thanked the woman and left a tip on the bar. She gave him an appreciative nod and sank back into her existence.

~~~~~

The driver wore a burgundy turban expertly wrapped. He turned his olive-brown face toward his passenger. The nose was beautiful, a bit too large but perfectly curved so that its excessive size was a statement about its perfection, not an accident of disproportionality.

"Where we going?" His Indian accent had a vaguely British character.
"Li Po's."
"I'm sorry, sir. I'm new to The City,"
"Just drop me at Chinatown Gate. Bush and Grant."
"Ahh. Two American presidents."
"What, you studying for the citizenship test?"
"Why not?"
"Waste of time. Couple of years it won't make a difference. I'd give you mine if it was transferable."

The driver turned up Jones Street and began the ascent toward Bush.
"You're far too young to be so cynical."
"Why'd you leave jolly old England if you figured out the secret to happiness."
"Simple—San Francisco, California."
"Ahh. Baghdad by the Bay."
"I'm not Arab, though I'm not offended by your mistake."
"I know you're not an Arab—you're a Sikh. As such, I may address you as Singh. That's culturally correct, no?"
"It is—it is. You may. Very good."
"So how do you like it so far?"
"It's a very friendly city."
"Slap an American flag decal on your rear window. See if your tips go up or down."
"You sound angry. What have you to be angry about?"

Roland thought about it and decided an honest answer was too complicated to formulate in a brief reply, so he said the first thing that came to mind.

"I stabbed a guy to death yesterday. Left a bad taste in my mouth."
"That's not something to joke about."
"The Glendale Butcher."

Singh pulled over and stopped the taxi in the bus lane and turned around and looked at Roland. He took his copy of *The Chronicle* from the passenger seat and found the page with the karate team photo and looked hard at it, then looked at Roland again, then back at the photo, then back at Roland. Roland removed his sunglasses.

"You'll have to imagine the hair."

"Jesus. Where I come from, you would be covered in flowers and kisses. There would be a parade. And you say you have a bad taste in your mouth?" He turned and set one hand on the wheel and the other on the shifter and shook his head, but instead of putting the car in gear and resuming the drive he pulled back his hands and swiveled again to face Roland. "You grouse about people not respecting the flag, but that's only a symptom of the problem. What will destroy a society is contempt for justice. Be proud of what you did." Roland thought to defend himself by way of explaining that his remark contained more style than substance, but he decided that a taxi driver's misapprehension would do him no harm over the next few blocks.

"So, from what stouthearted nation do you hail?"

"Not a nation—a region, a people. I am Punjabi." He said it with enough pride that Roland wondered again what he was doing here, coming from England no less. But he let it go.

"Ahh. I see. But after the little tribal parade, wouldn't I be looking over my shoulder for the rest of my life?"

"It's true. Punjabi families are large and steeped in honor, so it would depend on who you killed. But this man I think not even a brother would avenge." Singh returned to the wheel and set the car in motion.

"I'm not worried or angry."

"You should thank God for granting you such a great privilege."

"I'm having a hard time following you." The Chinatown Gate lay only a short roll down Bush Street if the lights cooperated, so he'd be free of this character soon enough.

"A man bent on murder breaks through the wrong window and is slain by an able warrior with his own weapon—that is a cosmic event. You are an agent-protector, not an accidental hero as the paper says."

"Is that proper Sikh dogma or your own personal theology?"

"Only a fool makes life more complicated than it has to be. We are here to seek the truth and enjoy each day while we serve one another."

"Is there a limit?"

"For what?"

"The amount of truth a man should be asked to stomach in a day."

Singh didn't answer right away. "No. The only limit is how much you can stomach. The world is not obliged to respect our limitations."

"You don't charge extra for wisdom, I hope."

"See, you've got your sense of humor."

They reached the destination and Singh snugged the taxi to the curb. "Here we are."

"Let me ask you something. Why exactly did you leave England?"

"Well, it's better here for the Sikh than it is in London where I have no proper place. Ignorant whites think I'm a dangerous Muslim and the dangerous Muslims treat me as a non-believer, a kafir. Here I'm just a guy with a bright red towel on my head."

"Must be hard to wrap that thing on every day and keep it tight."

"I'd rather do that than shave my head twice a week."

The man refused payment and gave Roland a business card. "You call me directly whenever you need a cab. Now I'm going to phone my brother and tell him who just got out of my car."

Roland thanked him and walked through Chinatown Gate down Grant Street to Li Po's Cocktail Lounge, wedged between two sparsely stocked gift shops—some would say junkshops—on the main tourist drag. Its mud-colored façade was built, molded really, to resemble the entrance to a cave whose bright red doors, when opened, revealed a small dive bar furnished with the requisite televisions and mirrors, decorated haphazardly with Chinese paraphernalia—tasseled lanterns, gongs, drooping sashes, calligraphed wall hangings, various accouterments of war—the general theme being redness, faded and worn.

Roland knew a dozen street bars within walking distance of his place on Nob Hill and, except for The Gutter, frequented none of them often enough to be known by the bartenders or regulars. Recognized, yes, but seldom acknowledged in more than a perfunctory, even cautious way. Prone as he was to blackouts, the young man seldom went to the same place twice in a row unless he had a clear recollection of having left it in a relatively sober, amiable condition. More than once he'd sat down clear-eyed on a stool and been refused service before he ordered his first drink, whereupon he'd left without troubling himself to find out why. Li Po's, he knew, was safe. The only red flags here, as far as he was concerned, were hanging on the walls. His last visit, less than a week ago, had started and ended courteously when he'd met his new acquaintance, Chow, and agreed to purloin the pre-release video game code he held in his pocket. He and Chow had not discussed financial terms, only Roland's access to the product and Chow's access to foreign buyers who might be interested in paying for it.

Twenty minutes early, he went inside and found a stool at the elbow of the bar that would allow him to watch the door. Two men drank beer from bottles and studied the baseball game on the flat screen. The bartender came over.

"A glass of water please."

The bartender made a disapproving face.

"Ok, a Coke. Make it a Coke."

He took out his phone, found the name, and pressed the call button. Joshua answered after a few rings. "Roland, hey there."

"I read your article." Roland put on a merry tone. "The prose is excessive but very precise. I might say passionately precise. A tad grandiloquent."

"*Grandiloquent* is grandiloquent "

"Over the top then. But in a good way."

"I'll take that as overall approval."

"It is it is. Except you got one thing wrong."

"Just one?"

"Your main thesis."

Joshua paused. Roland sensed him thinking.

"What—you don't want to be left alone?"

"You judged my temperament correctly yesterday, but I've changed my mind. Can you get me on the local news tonight?"

"You're kidding, right?"

"Nope. I want to control the narrative."

"That's not what I meant. You think I can just book you a spot on the local news?"

"I'm sorry if that's how it sounded, but it's a sincere question. A question and a request all rolled into one. Can you?"

"I know a few people I can call. Is there any particular station you'd like to be on?"

"Look. I realize this is out of the blue and short notice. You'd really be helping me out. Otherwise, I'll have to do it myself and I wouldn't know where to begin."

"Why the change, Roland?"

"A friend of mine…" Roland was thinking about his early AA conversations with Denny. "…once told me to apply contrary action to my first impulses since my first impulses were leading me astray. So, since my first impulse was to eschew publicity, contrary action would be to embrace it."

"Strangely logical, I guess. Where are you now?"

"Chinatown."

"Are you drinking? Tell me the truth, because if I set something up for you and you show up drunk, you won't get on the air and, when your name fades from the public memory, people in my business will still be laughing at me. I'm taking all the risk here."

"I'm sober and plan to stay that way. Call me as soon as you can, one way or the other."

"You want this today, not tomorrow?"

"I'm in a good frame of mind right now. I have no idea how I'll feel tomorrow."

"Alright. I'll get on the horn. It shouldn't take me long."

The call ended. Roland sipped his Coke and fiddled with his phone. Inimical little device, he thought, and wondered what about himself prevented him from becoming a slave to the thing, as had so many people he saw every day walking around with their eyes riveted to their little screens. To him, it was a telephone and a timepiece that housed his music collection. The countless free applications available for use seemed nothing more than enticements to distraction. Occasionally he played chess against anonymous opponents from around the world, but that was the only game in which he indulged himself. He opened up the chess app and returned to the match he'd started weeks ago, which required one move per 24 hours. That was not too onerous a demand on his precious time. He studied the board and sipped.

Chow entered the bar a few minutes early and parked his backpack on a seat at a little table near the back of the lounge and came over to the bar. He stood a few feet from Roland and gave no indication that he recognized him. While the Chinese national ordered from the bartender, Roland moved to the table and took the seat opposite the backpack. Chow came directly.

"Why you cut down all your hair?" He set the backpack on the floor and sat down. "No one tell you you can kill the head bugs with special soap?"

"Not so. Not for Chinese super lice. Those little buggers need the napalm treatment. Complete deforestation."

"You mean devastation, right Joe?"

"Forget it, Charlie. No time for English lessons today."

"The lice attack your arm too? Very, very unlucky."

"Unlucky, yes. But not because of lice."

"What, juggling knives at the wharf for spare change?"

"Tattoo gone wrong."

"You call me next time. I know best tattoo maker in Chinatown."

"Yeah—but can he make a picture of my face on the back of my shaved head?"

"Izz a lady. She can do anything you want excep' fix stupid."

"You made this bullshit sandwich, Chow. Don't expect me to eat it."

"So serious today. Maybe you need a drink."

"What do you call this?" Roland touched his glass.

"Look-a like-a straight Coca-Cola."

"I came to do business, not to shoot the shit."

"Ok ok. So serious." He pulled a laptop from his bag and set it on the table. "Lemme see what you got."

"How much money did you bring?"

"I shit a gold brick if I need it."

"You might need more than one." Roland took the thumb drive out of his pocket and held it up.

"Ok, lemme see it."

"Hold on a sec. How much are you prepared to pay? What's the highest you'll go?"

"I have to see it first."

"I don't think so. Before you stick this thing into your box, I need to see some money."

"If I like it, I go get you money."

"Like what? What do you need to look for?"

Chow spoke slowly. "Production release certificate."

"Dude, this won't run on a production game console. We run these beta builds on test boxes. I assumed you knew that."

"You told me the game was finished."

"It is, essentially. I mean there are no critical bugs or even serious flaws. The only thing that's left is a little tuning and some minor smoothing of the graphics. This game is set to hit the market before Christmas, so it's pretty much good to go."

"No production release certificate. Can't pay much."

"I won't take less than ten grand. I risked my job to smuggle this out."

"Lemme tek-a look."

"I don't like repeating myself."

"I bring no money here."

"I wish you'd've said that right out the gate."

"Out the gate?"

"When we first spoke. You've wasted my time." His phone rang. Roland assumed it would be Joshua and stood up and took the phone from his pocket.

"I've got to take this." He moved toward an empty space near the bar and looked at the phone. The screen displayed a phone number, not the name Josh as he expected. He answered anyway.

"Roland here."

"So that's your name?" It was a female voice, the woman from the Buena Vista. "I was going to call you Nimrod."

"That's generally considered an insult or at least a playful dig."

"No. I meant it as a compliment, the fearless hunter ready to brave shark-infested waters."

"I find Biblical literacy irresistible. Especially when it's Genesis."

"Oh. A religious gentleman."

"Not really. More a student of pre-history."

"Well, I know I'd like to know more about that."

"Well, I'm not sure I'm qualified to lecture on the subject, but I'd be willing to explore the topic with you."

"It's a date then. You said Sodini's in North Beach. What time?"

"Actually, if you're willing, we could meet before dinner near the restaurant for a little concert."

"A concert? Like a concert in the park? Washington Square?"

"No. It's a choral group. The Santa Barbara Madrigals. Truly mesmerizing."

"How could I pass that up? I can't remember the last time I was truly mesmerized."

"You're halfway there already, then. It starts at seven. Meet me outside the church on Vallejo and Columbus about six forty-five."

"A church? You said you weren't religious."

"They won't be doling out any sacraments at the show."

"I must admit, Roland, I'm more than a little intrigued. I'll meet you there, six forty-five."

"One thing I need to tell you—I look a little different than I did yesterday."

"Moving from intrigue to mystery. Will I recognize you?"

"I got a pretty drastic haircut today. A complete hair removal actually. But I'm still tall and still have the bandaged arm, so you'll spot me. There won't be a big crowd to search through."

"Yes—the bandage—I remember. You promised to tell me how you got that wound. I'll be on time."

"What shall I call you?"

"Alison. My name is Alison."

"I'm glad you called, Alison. I'll see you then."

The call ended. Roland went back to the table, where Chow sat staring at him like the parent of a disobedient child.

"What are you looking at?"

"This *business*. No more phone calls."

"This *business*? Really? Cuz I know for sure that call was business, business that was concluded successfully. This here what we're doing…" Roland moved his outstretched hand in a circular motion to stir the air between them. "…I'm not sure what to call it, but *business* is not the first word that leaps to mind."

"You got to show me the files on the thumb drive. You not doing it. So sorry this not good business. Right?"

"Tell you what. I'll show you. Just let me sit and do it while you watch. That's the only way I can be sure that you don't copy it over."

Chow moved the laptop over to Roland's side of the table. "Go ahead."

Roland inserted the thumb drive and opened up the file navigator. One by one he clicked open the folders, scrolling down the list of the files contained in each one.

"Too fast. Wait. Open that. No not that. Scroll up. Sort the list by size. Click that one. Not that one. Double-click. Try again…" He followed Chow's prompts as well as he could until, frustrated by the pace of the process, he finally gave up and surrendered the laptop to its owner. It was clear to Roland that Chow understood computer code and architecture better than he did, so he stood behind him and watched him do his thing, one criminal distrusting the other.

His phone rang again. It was Joshua. Roland stepped back a few feet but kept an eye on the screen, for it would take only a few seconds for someone of Chow's speed and skill to initiate a command to copy everything over to his hard drive and quickly switch back to the file browser.

"Hey, Josh."

"Ok, Roland. It's all set."

"I'll be damned."

"The jury is probably still out."

"What are you talking about?"

"Nothing. Forget it."

Roland took a step back and turned away so Chow couldn't hear him. "No. What did you mean by that?"

"Nothing. I'm just messin' with you. What's the big deal?"

"You guys don't believe in that shit."

"You wanna know about the interview I just got you or about the differing Jewish perspectives on the afterlife?"

"Your perspective. You think if there's a Hell, then I might be going?"

"It was a joke, Roland. I'm not worried about the state of your soul. I'm sorry if I touched a nerve."

"Yesterday you asked me if I prayed for him. That was a little irritating, and now the eternity jury is out—so you see…"

"I'm sorry. Can we move on? They want you there at five. I can pick you up."

"Good. I'll be in Portsmouth Square."

"Where's that?"

"Kearny and Clay."

"You're sticking around Chinatown?"

"I'm going to grab some noodles and then elbow my way into the chess rotation with the old men under the shade trees."

"They know you?"

"We've passed the bag."

"The bag?"

"Baijiu. Chinese moonshine. Made from sorghum."

"Ok. Look for me at four-thirty. I won't be late, and you won't be dru—" He stopped himself. "…you won't have liquor on your breath."

"I won't."

"Or we don't go and the station and my contact there will remain a mystery to you."

"I get it, Josh."

"Four-thirty then."

The call ended and Roland returned to his hovering position over Chow's shoulder. "How much longer is this going to take?"

"You got somewhere to go?"

"No. I'm getting bored."

"Someone else want to buy this? You have some friends call to make me think I not the only one?"

"Nothing like that, Chow. I just want to get going."

"No. You gotta stay here."

"Sorry, excuse me?"

"I go get the money. You sit tight."

"Ten grand."

"Seven."

Roland reached down and pulled the thumb drive out of the port. "Ten. If it's worth a dollar, it's worth ten grand."

"I tek-a big risk here. It might be no good. How you say it—*worthless?*"

"You know it's not worthless. If you were worried, you'd be gone by now. Eighty-five hundred. How soon can you be back here?"

"Seventy-five."

"Eight."

"Ok, Joe. You win. I'll be back."

"When? How long?"

"You gotta be somewhere?" He put the laptop back in his bag.

"I told you yesterday, I got plans. Either way, I'd rather not hang around this dump any longer than I have to."

"I come back twenty minutes, little girl. Daddy buy you nice new Coke while you waiting. Watch the Giants baseball. Buster Posey on fiya this year!" He set a ten-dollar bill on the bar, said something to the barkeep in Chinese and left with his backpack slung over his shoulder.

Roland asked the barkeep to spike his half-depleted Coke with ten dollars' worth of Jack Daniels. He was served without a word. Two hours, a bowl of noodles and a few cigarettes would mask the liquor before Joshua arrived. He sipped his drink. Buster Posey jacked one over the right field wall into the bay, a tremendous feat for a right-handed batter. A pod of knuckleheads in their kayaks raced frantically to the splash to capture the bobbing ball. The lengths some people will go to get themselves on TV, he thought. *You wanna see a splash?* he promised no one. *I'll show you a Got-damned splash.*

Chapter 13
October 1, 2016 - Evening

Two bowls of pho, a Vietnamese beef noodle soup topped with bean sprouts, basil leaves, green onions, and a squirt or two of hot sauce, served steaming at the Golden Star Restaurant across the street from Portsmouth Square, settled peaceably in his belly while he sat hunched with his elbows on a cement table assessing his current predicament in a game of Chinese chess. He was out of his depth, in over his head, flying blind, and happy as a major league bat boy to be accepted as an apprentice by the council of elders that convened daily in the little plaza to pass the time in their native tongue, smoke tobacco, and swig from a bottle of baijiu, always wiping it clean with a handkerchief before passing it.

These men, all family patriarchs, possessed no mobile phones, wore no sunglasses, drove no cars, spoke little English and, for all intents and purposes, lived outside the United States of America in the shadow of the Transamerica Pyramid. That they smoked within smelling distance of the little playground in the square was proof of their insularity, for smoking near a playground in any other district in The City could bring an armed response.

The phone rumbled in his pocket. Joshua had arrived. Roland pulled a crisp hundred-dollar bill from his pocket and set one of the chess pieces on top of it before standing up to address the assemblage.

"This set is too faded for me. I can't see the difference between the pieces." They nodded appreciatively, for not only were the circular wooden pieces identified by Chinese script, but the paint on many of the characters had been all but completely rubbed off.

"My ride is here. Maybe you guys buy a new set so I can learn faster. Maybe buy three or four new sets." They nodded politely and one man shook his hand. No one reached for the c-note. Before he walked to the waiting car, Roland took the seventy-nine-hundred-dollar bulge from his front pocket and divided it into two stacks, folded each one, and fitted them separately into his back pockets where they would go unnoticed.

Joshua shook his head and gave him a despairing look when he climbed into the seat and attached the belt. "What? I promised to be sober, which I am."

"I'm curious about your thought process."

"Do you know that little Byzantine church in North Beach?"

"The Shrine of Saint Francis."

"Do you know the head honcho—Father Bartholomew?"

"Yes and no."

"What does that mean?"

"Means I know who he is, but he doesn't know me."

"I saw him today—spoke with him."

"What? You got your head shaved because you spoke with a bald man—that's your story?"

"Not your run-of-the-mill bald man, Mister Goldberg. He set me thinking, so I took a ten-mile jog to the bridge and back and decided to make some changes, big changes. Dropping the hair is just the beginning."

"You're a strange man."

"I won't ask you what you mean."

"You're not curious?"

"That would be like wanting to know the sex of an abortion."

Joshua stopped at a red light and lowered his sunglasses and looked over at Roland. "What are you talking about?"

"*Strange. Weird.* Kids, people who haven't mastered the language, use words like that. When someone like you, a supposed writer, says I'm a strange man, all it tells me is that you don't know what you mean, and instead of squelching the thought and keeping your mouth shut you belch up a verbal abortion. No need for me to probe it with tweezers to find out what it might have been."

Joshua stared at him. His jaw slowly dropped. The car behind them honked. He put a forefinger on the nose bridge of his shades and pushed them back in place and shot off the line.

"Don't act offended after you insult me. Where are we going?"

"I can tell you exactly what I meant. Yesterday you said, with a Bible in your hand, that you weren't a religious man, and today you tell me you just talked to a priest and had your whole world rocked. *Strange* is generous. I could call you a liar."

"That would be getting a little too personal."

"Fair enough. I'll make a point to stop trying to understand you."

Roland scrolled mentally through his ready list of terse rejoinders when he caught sight of the KGO-7 sign on Front Street, the local ABC Broadcast center, just a few blocks from where they'd started. Joshua saw that Roland was suddenly aware that they'd reached their destination and let the reality of the situation amplify the silence in the car. He parked then turned to Roland. "Let me shepherd you through this. Resist the feeling that you need to say anything until you're in front of the cameras."

As they walked toward the entrance to the building, Roland switched on his name catcher. Despite his excellent memory, he still had to make a conscious effort to recall the names of strangers shortly after meeting them, and since he knew he was about to meet new people he wanted to be sure he did not have to hesitate over their names or, God forbid, ask them to repeat them. A news producer met them inside the lobby and after the requisite formalities ushered them toward the makeup room behind the broadcast studio. He introduced himself as Sheldon Fischer. His blazer hung open around a paunch that would have stressed the buttons. He seemed a bit tense, like someone expecting to be struck suddenly from behind.

"We don't have a lot of time, Mister Hazzard, and that head of yours will blind the camera, so we need to get that thing powdered up." He led them down a hallway.

Roland nodded at the producer then turned to Joshua, who shrugged *what did you expect?*

"We've carved out a ten-minute segment to end the broadcast. It'll be here before you know it." He opened a door and stood aside to let them in.

The makeup man stood behind his chair ready to get to work. He smiled. The kind of smile that suppressed a ready laugh. Roland gave him a little wave.

"One more thing. I need to see your ID."

"What?" Joshua sounded peeved.

"I personally have no doubts," Sheldon said to Roland. "But the only picture we have of you shows a full head of hair, and I know that management will want to be sure you're…"

"My word isn't good enough? I spent more than an hour with this man yesterday."

"I have to be able to tell my management that I verified his identity. They need to justify their existence."

Before Joshua could repeat his objection, Roland produced his driver's license and handed it to Sheldon. "Don't take it personally, Joshua. We can't waive the process, not even for you." Joshua just shook his head and sat down in the nearest chair. Sheldon glanced at the license. "Same name, even the same address." He looked at Joshua. "See how easy that was?"

"What now?" said Roland.

"Rodger here will get you prepped and before you know it someone will be back to walk you to the set. We have a little space on the side of the news desk where our anchor will conduct a face-to-face interview. Thank you for coming down, by the way."

"Who's the anchor?"

"Don't you watch our broadcast?"

"Not on purpose."

"Then it'd just be a name to you."

"I'm just wondering if it's a man or a woman."

"What's the difference?"

"I don't know. Let's start with a tendency toward aggression."

"In that light, she's a man."

"Right. I'll ignore the pelvis."

Sheldon shook his head. Roland looked over at Joshua just to make sure he wasn't shaking his or else Roland would have had to join in, and then the make-up guy would have to make it a foursome. "Her name is Penelope. Penelope Torres. Let's keep it civil."

"Roland *Civil* Hazzard."

Sheldon left the room and Roland smiled at Rodger and took a seat in the makeup chair then turned to Joshua and increased it to a wide grin.

"I'm starting to wonder if this was a good idea."

Roland turned to Rodger, who stood over his tray deciding on a brush. "What do you think, Rodge?"

"You're going to be on live TV." He giggled. "What could possibly go wrong?"

He set himself to the task at hand. Roland closed his eyes so the man could work freely about his face and head, applying the necessary cosmetics and powders that would befriend the lights and lenses on the set. To keep his mind at bay, Roland concentrated on the sound of the fan turning slowly above them then turned his ear to Joshua's breathing, the scuffing of his shoes on the floor, the turning of magazine pages, on every little sound that emanated from his presence across the room. He then presumed to read Joshua's thoughts and intuit his emotions, while the fastidious homosexual continued with his work. It was a species of meditation, a means of getting out of his own head by claiming the space of another's. Joshua's mental condition, as assayed by Roland, consisted of a mixture of fear and regret, a desire to speak coupled with an incapacity to find the right words. Something like—*what am I doing here?* The make-up man hummed a whimsical, improvised melody, pretending not to sense the apprehension of the spectator and at the same time teasing the tension in the room.

After several minutes Roland broke the silence.

"Hey, Josh."

"Hey, Roland." Joshua replied swiftly as if batting back a ball.

"I need you to know something before they come for me."

"Yeah, what's that?"

"When I go out there, I intend to topple domino number one, touch a match to a skyrocket—take your pick—and I'm hoping you'll come along for the ride. I realize you signed your name to the prediction that I was inclined to—how did you say it?—*eschew fame;* well, you were right when you wrote that, and I'll vouch for you till the end, so you don't have to worry. But I've done a complete about-face. Now I'm marching toward the enemy, heading back into the burning building, steering straight for the vortex."

Joshua looked at Rodger as if to gauge what impression, if any, Roland's grandiose pronouncement had made, but Rodger remained impassive. "I don't exactly know what you have in mind, so why don't we see how it goes out there? We'll talk about the future once the present has passed."

Rodger picked up the remote and un-muted the television used to monitor the program taking place in the studio just steps away. "There's a fifteen-second delay. This is the next to last commercial break. Sheldon should be back any minute now."

"Am I good to go?"

Rodger tapped him playfully on the top of the head with his little brush. "As long as you don't start sweating from the scalp."

Roland got out of the chair and looked at himself in the mirror. His head and face belonged to a fresh cadaver, a cadaver with deep sea-green eyes.

"I suppose I'd better get used to this look."

"You have a marvelous cranium. I see a vast rebellion rallying behind it."

Roland turned to Joshua and shook a thumb at Rodger. "He gets it."

The door opened and Sheldon entered. "Time to go."

Roland turned to Joshua, "I'll meet you back here?" He wanted to be certain his driver would not run off.

"Sure. I don't want to miss this."

"Knock 'em dead, killer."

"We'll have a gay old time." Roland shot a glance at Joshua. "Right, Goldberg?"

"I haven't agreed to this *we* business."

Sheldon led Roland to one of two chairs at a table just one side of the anchor desk where the two news leads, a man and a woman, sat silently while the sports reporter finished up his segment by extolling the prowess of Buster Posey. The cameras cut off for the commercial break and Penelope Torres came over. Her beauty was forced. She wore a tight blue skirt and a loose magenta blouse with an egg-shaped hole cut just above her cleavage that framed, like a cameo broach, a traditional Mexican skull—a calavera—with yellow glass eyes. It looked like it was glued to her chest, but on closer inspection he saw that it hung from a thin silver chain. Her shiny brown hair, streaked with golden highlights, swished at her shoulders. She took her seat silently across from Roland, each behind a glass of water. Otherwise, the circular table was bare. She glanced at Roland. Her reptilian eyes blinked mechanically. The cameraman adjusted his viewfinder and waited for the signal. Roland felt his palms begin to perspire. Penelope glanced at him again, this time lingering on his dapper head. The interview by now had been thoroughly promoted throughout the show, so there would be no introduction. After a long couple of minutes, the red light on the camera went on.

"Thank you for coming in, Mister Hazzard. You certainly are a hard man to track down."

"Man? I prefer *guy*. Man is too gender-definitive."

"You don't identify as a man? Should I call you Rolanda instead of Roland?"

"No. The masculine and feminine endings to which we've become so accustomed in Western cultures are themselves a capitulation to the oppressive heterosexist paradigm. You're Latin-x, are you not?"

She ducked the jab. "I'm confused. Does that mean you do or do *not* identify as a man?"

"I identify today, now, relaxing in this comfortable chair, as a killer. You can call me killer."

She cleared her throat. "I know you're having fun with me, so I'll just call you Roland."

"You're the boss." He took a drink from the water glass.

"Just so our viewers are aware, *you* contacted *us* for this interview. I'm told that several reporters were unsuccessful in getting you to stop for their questions out in the field."

"Yes. That's true. I asked Mister Goldberg from *The Chronicle* to contact the TV news, and he chose your station. He's the only reporter I've spoken to so far."

"Good. First question: Why did you decide you wanted to talk to us now, after your earlier refusals to engage the press?"

"I like to fly first class."

"I see. No slumming it with beat reporters for a guy like you."

"There's nobody like me."

"Well." She cocked an eyebrow. "Whatever it is that makes you so special, running from cameras and microphones isn't it. We see that all the time."

"Let me be clear—I like a comfortable controlled environment. That's what I mean by first class. In the chaotic world at large, I'm a dangerous man, especially when I'm hungover. Accosting me on the street for any reason is a bad idea."

"You felt threatened?"

"The English language lacks words for what I feel most of the time."

"What about Friday at 1AM? Did you feel threatened then?"

"Not until the knife came out."

"Yet, before that, you hit Samuel Barsamian over the head with a whiskey bottle, but not because you felt threatened?" Her voice betrayed a deep skepticism that verged on sarcasm. Roland rolled with it.

"I did that to save his life, but I hit him in a bad spot." Roland touched the top of his forehead. "Right here. The skull is very hard right here. He went down but he didn't go out. He'd'a gone out, he'd be alive. Should'a hit him sidelong right above the ear." Again he demonstrated with a tap. "But that can be fatal if you miss and catch the temple. Anyway, I crowned the sonofabitch to prevent a fight, not to start one."

"You apparently know a lot about fighting."

Roland propped his chin on one hand and gave her a thoughtful look, waiting for a question.

"Is that true?"

"Hand-to-hand combat against a human—I'll generally come out on top. Against a lion, a tiger—any of the big cats—what I know about fighting wouldn't count for much. I'd want a sharp sword."

That didn't crack her veneer. "What I'm getting at, Roland, is that you're a martial artist and a very good one. You were a karate instructor at U.C. Berkeley. Your team won trophies. That man didn't stand a chance against you."

Roland showed his bandaged arm. "The knife in his belt might have been a gun. Hell, the crowbar and tactical flashlight he was carrying could have presented a problem if he'd known how to use them in combination. My students won because I taught them to attack when physically threatened, to not *feel* threatened, and I'm not talking about sparring matches."

"What do you mean? What did they win, then?"

"You haven't done your research, Penny—since we're on a first-name basis. A few of my female students won actual fights against actual rapists. I taught a class specifically for women, specifically on how to fend off men."

Penelope cocked her head to one side and looked impressed. "You're right, I did not know that." But her tone gave the impression that she thought he might be full of shit.

"Taught 'em how to stomp the patriarchy right where it lives." He took another drink of water.

"Well, I guess the world should be happy that Mister Barsamian ran into you."

"I don't know about the world, but I know this country should be ashamed of itself."

"What for?"

"For producing a media—no, for tolerating a media—where a monster like that is referred to as *Mister* Barsamian without a hint of irony. If he'd had a PhD, you would probably have called him *Doctor* Barsamian. Instead, I'm the curiosity."

"Why'd you shave your head today?"

"Sympathy with the autumn trees."

"Sympathy—interesting. Is that an English word that falls into your range of feelings? Did you have an ounce of sympathy for the man dying on your floor from the knife you stuck in him? You had no idea who he was or what he'd been accused of."

"Why, because he was once someone's precious baby boy? No. If I'd thought about it, I might have worked up a little sympathy for my landlord who's out the cost of repairs to his window."

"That seems so cold. Is that why you invited yourself to be interviewed, to tell the world just how cold a badass you are?"

"Let's quit dancing around the elephant. The only reason I'm on tonight, the only reason reporters have been camped in front of my building, is that the man I killed was already famous. I wouldn't be here if it was some nameless burglar that pried his way into my apartment and paid the price for coming at me with a knife. I'm here to say that that shouldn't matter. It should always be news—every time a violent criminal dies at the hands of the person he attacked there should be a parade."

"Maybe we should return to the days of public hangings."

"I could think of something more effective, if you want to get the state involved."

"But not for burglary."

"No. But he didn't die from burglary—he died from trying to kill me."

"Understood. But I want to explore your reaction to finding out he was the Glendale Butcher. Did that make no impression on you at all?"

"When I found that out, and particularly when I found out he'd been cozying up to my neighbor, I wished he'd suffered more than he did. I'd like to think I'd've gone full Comanche on him."

"At the risk of offending our Native American viewers, what do you mean *gone full Comanche* on him?"

"Given him a slow, painful death. I mean, I couldn't exactly bury him up to his neck, scalp him, and let the insects take over, or roast him alive on a campfire spit; but I could have tied him up and burned him with cigarettes, maybe thumbed out his eyes and poured cleaning products in the empty sockets."

She cracked a smile. He nodded to affirm this small victory. "I know you're just trying to shock me."

"It sounds sadistic, but I don't mean to suggest that I would take any pleasure in the administration of torture, so instead of sadistic I'd call it justice."

"He lost his life—is that not justice enough?"

"Each person has to decide that for himself, what justice is and what it isn't; but if you ask me, he got off easy. Hitler bit down on a cyanide capsule to *avoid* justice, at least that's the story."

"People—your friend at *The Chronicle* included—have labeled you a hero, but you just told me you identify as a killer. Do you see yourself as a hero too?"

"The lady who shaved my head today—known her a long time—she called me a hero too. She's a war refugee, and even she doesn't get it. I had to explain to her that a hero has to put his life at risk in service of a selfless cause, like diving into a frozen lake to save a child that has fallen through."

"I see."

"No. There's more. The hero has to succeed, has to save the child, whether he lives or dies in the process. The greatest heroes knowingly sacrifice their lives to save the lives of others, and the biggest idiots throw their lives away for a lost cause."

"I guess you got it all figured out."

"I'm not a hero, just a damned good example."

"I don't know about that. You started this interview boasting that you are a *killer*. I understand that a man broke into your home with what looks like homicidal intentions, and you apparently killed him in self-defense. But does that make you a killer?"

"I was a killer before he broke in. It's a mindset—a Bronze Age mindset. And his mindset was not homicidal, it was *murderous*. There's a big difference. Homicide is a morally neutral term—each one is either right or wrong. I'd go so far as to say either necessary or evil. When homicide is wrong, it's murder. When it's necessary, you'd better hope there's a competent killer on hand to take care of business."

"A killer who might throw in a little torture under the right circumstances."

"It takes a special breed of cat, one with a lot of guts, a lot of will toward self-sacrifice, to torture the guilty."

"Here we go again." Roland kept his poker face. He could tell he was getting to her.

"Nothing comes for free, Penny. You can't delete your memories. The torturer carries a heavy burden, but even the cleanest executioner has to live with his resume. When the state used to execute people by firing squad, they put a blank charge in one of the rifles—softens the guilt a tad."

"I'm convinced. You are *one* righteous killer."

"You think I'm kidding?"

"I think you're seeking attention."

"But not for attention's sake."

"Why then?"

"To wake people up. We have too many sheep and not enough shepherds, and the wolves aren't going anywhere. The staff is as much a weapon as a walking stick."

"That's all very neat—all very Biblical. But what about *Thou Shalt Not Kill?*"

"Bad translation. The King James team did some beautiful work, but that egregious mistake has rippled through the ages, right up to the question you just asked. The Hebrew word—*ratzach*—means murder—*Thou Shalt Not Murder* is the correct translation. But I guess people back in the Seventeenth Century had enough common sense that the inaccuracy didn't bother them."

"You're a Bible scholar!"

"No. Just quick on the uptake."

"I'll have to take your word for it."

Roland nodded appreciatively, "No need for that, let's ask the viewers." He turned to the camera and stared straight into it. "Y'all out there let us know what you think. Does the Sixth apply to murder or all killing in general? Should we all be prepared to take out the bad guys, even if it means killing them? The phone lines are open. Let your voices be heard. Kick off a Twitter storm. Stick your head out the window. Honk your horn if you're listening in your…"

Penelope broke in. "Mister Hazzard, this broadcast is not on radio, and it's not your place to use this forum to poll the viewers."

"Sorry, Penny. I got carried away."

"On that unfortunate note, it's time for me to say *we're out of time*. It's been very interesting meeting you, Roland Hazzard. Alarming actually. I had a lot more questions to ask you, but it seems like you stole the show. Perhaps we'll do this again with more success."

"Mister Joshua Goldberg of *The San Francisco Chronicle* is handling all my press requests, so anyone who'd like to talk with me should contact him."

The camera cut off the second he finished his parting pitch, and the feed technician chose not to use the power of his fifteen-second delay button to squash it. Roland stood up, towering over Penelope, still seated in her chair.

"That went way too fast. I wish we'd had more time."

"At least one of us got off. I hope your girlfriends fare better."

Roland had to refrain from matching her crass-for-crass, and instead of saying *I'd be glad to let you find out for yourself* or something along that line, he extended his hand. "I'm sorry I used your time to blare my personal views, but this might have been my only chance."

She did not shake his hand and only wished him a half-hearted *good luck* before she got up and walked away.

~~~~~

Roland opened the door to the make-up room to find Joshua and Rodger much as he'd left them, except now each was holding a paper cup. He noticed that there was no water cooler in the room. Before he could give himself an atta-boy, Joshua stood up from his chair.

"What the hell was that?" His anger was genuine. Roland thought it best not to feign innocence.

"Uhhh, you can always say no."

Rodger piped up to forestall a verbal escalation. "Would you like a drink, Roland?"

"Is that alcohol?"

Rodger opened a cabinet and reached in and took out a bottle of vodka and showed it to Roland.

"They let you drink on the job?"

"The show's over. My day is done."

"I don't think so. You've got to wipe this stuff off my face and head."

Joshua would not be ignored. "You can't just announce to the public that I'm your agent. The time for me to say *no* is *before* you invite the whole fucking world to call me."

Roland moved over to the makeup chair and sat down. "It wasn't planned, but you know what the poet said."

"You're not on stage anymore."

Rodger ventured a guess. "All the world's a stage?"

"No. Fortune favors the bold."

Rodger found a cup and held it up and wiggled it at Roland.

"No. I'll pass. I'm on my way to church." Then he looked at Joshua. "Can we talk about this in the car? I'm not proposing you do it for free."

"I've heard all the bullshit I can stand for one day."

"What? And here I thought you guys were toasting my victory. I was on fire out there."

"I told you before; I don't think I want my fortunes tied to yours."

"You're not gonna spoil my buzz, Josh. I wasn't bullshitting out there. Meant every word of it."

Rodger got to work with his moist towelettes. Roland stared at Joshua, who stood by the door, apparently on the horns of the decision whether to stay or go. Roland's assumption that Joshua would drive him thence had rankled Joshua to the brink of desertion.

"Cool your jets, amigo. Sit down and finish your cocktail. I'll explain myself on the way to The Shrine."

"Are you going to hear the madrigals tonight?"

Roland tapped the tip of his nose with his forefinger then pointed to Rodger.

"They're spellbinding."

"Some even might say divine."

Rodger finished cleaning off Roland's face and head and bid them *bonne chance*.

~~~~~

They walked to the car and drove away. Before Joshua could say a word, Roland pulled out ten c-notes and fitted them in a circle inside the cup holder near the gearshift.

"There's a thousand dollars, yours to keep, whether or not I see you again."

Joshua remained silent.

"Give it to the Jewish boy scouts if you don't want it."

"I have no idea what to make of you."

"There's a certain beauty in that. I can't disappoint you."

"What's with the cash?"

"A gesture of good faith. The appearance you got me tonight should launch the boat, and if you want to help chart the course, then…"

"So, you want me to be your publicist, your press agent?"

"Put it whatever you want, but I'm not asking you to make any calls. I'll spin up an online presence in the social media spaces and keep my fan-base riled up, and I'll direct all media inquiries to you."

"Why don't you pull your own weight?"

"You've got a trailer hitch."

"You're paying for my cachet—is this what I'm hearing?"

"Well. I'd never heard of you, but it seems the right people know you."

"I'm not going to take your thousand dollars unless I agree, and if I agree, then it's not a retainer. A retainer is credited toward the bill."

"Then call it hazard pay, and I'm not trying to be funny. On top of that, I'll give you a percentage of any fees I collect, whether you booked me or not."

"What kind of percentage?"

"What do jockeys make—what percentage of the purse?"

"I think it's ten percent. I'd need more than that. Agents can make as much as twenty. For a Jew, tack on five. So twenty-five percent."

"I'll pay the Jew rate for everything above a hundred grand—call it an incentive."

"Appearance fees won't get to that. Your celebrity won't last that long in my professional opinion."

"Remember what you said when I first got into your car—*I don't know what to make of you.* Let's agree that's true—I'm inestimable, *incalculable*. You can't know what you'll make off me."

"Roland, come back to earth. TV news spots seldom pay anything. I doubt you'll earn enough to get me a thousand in commissions. I'm talking a gamble here."

"Come join me on Mount Olympus. I'm thinking book deals, acting gigs—full-service celebrity. You'll look back on today and wonder how you could stand to be so poor."

"I'd be putting my reputation at risk, and if you know the Hebrew Bible as wall as you say you do, then you know that killing a man's reputation is tantamount to actual murder."

"Anything else?"

"How about a sobriety pledge—a solemn oath?"

"I kept my word today. That's a good start."

"You're not drunk. Not like yesterday anyway. I'll give you that. But it doesn't mean you didn't drink."

"If you see me losing control, then cut me loose. You don't even need a reason. As far as I'm concerned, we're both on an at-will basis. You have your hazard pay."

On the way up Columbus Street, a few blocks from The Shrine, Roland spotted Vesuvio, a historic North Beach hangout and former headquarters of San Francisco's legendary Beatniks. Spitting distance away, across the narrow and brightly muraled Jack Kerouac Alley, stood their propaganda ministry, City Lights Bookstore.

"I'm early. Drop me here at City Lights."

Joshua pulled into the red zone across the street and looked at Roland for the first time since they'd left the TV station.

"The only thing I'll promise you is this: If I get a call from someone wanting to book you for an interview, I'll probably take care of it."

"Probably? You don't know. That's not a promise."

"I think I will, but if I get a sudden spasm of conscience or sickening qualm, I'll give them your number and, of course, set the money aside. We'll deal with that later if need be."

"Fair enough." Roland swiveled out of the car. "Thanks." He shut the door and noted the air-tight thud it made, unlike the clank and shudder of his decrepit car. He loped across Columbus Avenue ahead of oncoming traffic and entered the bookstore. He had no business to conduct at City Lights. It was a convenient ruse to cover his lie about not wanting a drink before going to church. His true destination was the bar at Vesuvio. He looked out the window and saw that Joshua was gone. The coast was clear. To make his entrance into the store look credible to the man at the register, Roland picked up one of the free tabloids in the rack near the door and turned around to make a quick exit.

"Excuse me."

Roland froze, thinking for a second that the tabloid in his hand was not free for the taking and he was being stopped to pay for it. He turned toward the voice, half agape.

"You were just on."

Roland squinted at him, a tall, skinny recovered hippie burnout with rectangular reading glasses, clean-shaven except for his gray goatee.

"On the tube, man, the local news, just a few minutes ago." His tone was insistent, as of a prosecutor refreshing a witness's memory.

Roland saw a small TV strobing mutely in a cabinet behind the counter.

"Oh. Yeah." Roland sounded a little embarrassed. "I was there. The station's just down at the bottom of Broadway."

"That was wild, man. Like intellectual theater. Are you for real?"

"As opposed to what—an acid flashback?"

He laughed and took off his glasses. "No. I mean was that a put-on? Were you just fucking with her?"

"She brought out the best in me."

"Roland, right? Roland Hazzard."

"Yeah. Pleased to meet you." He did not extend his hand.

"She didn't know what hit her, Roland. You hosed her down petty good."

Roland grew pensive, lowered his head, and flexed his toes inside his boots.

"I wasn't really thinking. I was kinda watching it all happen myself."
"Wild shit. *Crazy* shit. You had me glued."
"Thanks, I guess. I wanted to make a big impression."
Roland started to leave.
"Why'd you come in here? I'm here almost every day and I've never seen you before."
"I came to grab a drink next door and wanted to flip through this rag at the bar." It was a transparent lie, for Vesuvio had its own stacks of the same free tabloids, but the clerk let it pass.
"I get it. You deserve it. I'd be happy to have one with you, but I can't step away. But if you give the bartender my name, he'll put it on my tab. It would be my honor. Tell him Lawrence is buying."
"Lawrence, as in Ferlinghetti?"
"No. He does have a son, though—Lorenzo. I'm just another Larry."
"Is he still kicking—Lawrence Ferlinghetti?"
"Still holding on, pushing a century."
"Well, when I publish my memoir, maybe he'll stock it on the shelves in here."
"He's not involved in the purchasing anymore; but even so, from what I just heard, your message might be a little too far right for this location."
"Ok, you want to buy me a drink?"
"For the righteous kill, yeah man."
"Can you hop over and tell the bartender? Save me the explanation?"
"That's fair. Just watch the register."
Lawrence Anonymous left his post, crossed Jack Kerouac Alley, and returned to the store in less than a minute.
"It's set. There's a shot glass on the bar for Roland."
"You didn't tell them why, did you?"
"No, man, that's your business."
"Good. Thanks. I just want to have a quiet drink."
"Vaya con Dios and damn the torpedoes."

~~~~~

Vesuvio Cafe maintained the character of a shrine all its own, complete with stained glass windows, venerable iconography, prayerful verses in faux graffiti, and faithful pilgrims from far and wide working daily the hinges on its doors. At bottom, though, it was a local bar that served a visibly aging—one might say threadbare—clientele in one of the hipper tourist quarters in The City. But Hemmingway's French Quarter this was not.

"Stoli kamikaze please." That meant vodka, Triple-Sec, and a splash of Rose's lime, shaken with crushed ice in a tumbler and strained into a rocks glass. A strong frigid drink that didn't linger on the breath.

He sipped it, marking time, head forward, eyes down, not wanting to draw attention to himself. When the alcohol reached his brain, he felt secure in what he'd said and done, satisfied that the posturing and hyperbolic portrayal of himself on camera in the studio represented his sincere attitude and beliefs. He could, he believed, carry this off, this role he was scripting for himself on the fly. He would, he resolved, become the image—the *type*—he was inventing. *Courage* he whispered before draining the glass. The citrus-laced vodka filled his nostrils. It was what the British might call a healthy snort. The fumes from the drink fairly floated him from the bar and up the street toward his rendezvous with— *what was her name?*—Alison. Yes—with Alison.

He arrived on time at the steps of The Shrine and did not have to find her. She was taller than he'd remembered and a little older, maybe thirty-five, dressed in a pleated skirt a bit too short for church, white tights, black lace-up boots, and a red blouse covered by a brief, very pricey-looking black calf-skin jacket. Most of her long, lush hair was neatly bunched over her head by some kind of magic, and several strands were left to hang down on either side of her exquisitely feminine, lightly powdered face. His fingernails were manicured to sharpness and painted with a glossy lilac polish. He'd hoped she were a bit younger, but he allowed she was more beautiful than he expected and dressed like she aimed to please. Roland felt embarrassed in his street clothes.

"Look at you. You oughta warn a fella."

"Oh, I'm just dressed for dinner." She looked him up and down. "And you're dressed for paying the check, I guess."

"I guess all I'd need is a deerskin toga and a strong tree branch. Picture that?"

"I'm still trying to picture you from yesterday at the bar when you had all that gorgeous hair, bragging about your speargun and ankle knife. You've made quite the transformation."

"I've made a big career move, and this…" He smoothed his head with his right hand. "…is part of the uniform."

A car coming down Vallejo Street slowed when the driver saw Roland, and the passenger popped his head out the window and yelled, "SLAYAH!" Roland waved to him.

"Slayah?"

"I've recently become a bit of a celebrity."

"Actor? Musician? I guess I could see that."

"Not exactly. It's a long story. I'll tell you all about it at dinner."

She took a step backward and looked up at him then let out a quiet gasp. She pointed to his bandaged arm. "Was that you? Are you the Roland in the news?"

"Roland Hazzard, above ground and at your service."

"Oh my GOD."

"That subject will take several dinners."

"I'm not sure I want this one."

People were climbing the stairs and entering the church.

"You can decide inside." He cocked his head in the direction of the upward flow. "Shall we?"

Father Bartholomew appeared at the doors, greeting people as they filed in. "Good evening, Roland. Normally you get the haircut *after* ordination, and only if you finish at the top of the class."

"Father Bart, meet Alison, my date for the evening. As for the shave job, I'm getting out ahead of a lice epidemic that's thundering this way."

"Hello, Alison. I'm glad Roland brought a friend. He usually comes alone."

"Alison is my first recruit."

"The acoustics are best toward the front." He turned away to greet another incoming guest.

The pews were not crowded, the small church being less than half-full, so the two familiar strangers were not forced to sit closely and did not.

"I never knew this place existed."

"I come here to quiet my mind."

"I'll shut up then."

"That's not what I meant."

"I'll shut up anyway."

Roland stole a glance at her, a glance he hoped she'd notice, a glance meant to confirm that she truly looked as attractive as she had a few moments before outside on the steps.

"This was your idea."

"That didn't last very long."

She locked her lips with an invisible key and gave him a concessionary smirk that said *this is more than I bargained for* or *I guess this is my fate*. His eyes revealed only that he felt perfectly in control, the indomitable hunter with his quarry slung over his shoulder.

Father Bartholomew welcomed the audience and introduced the Santa Barbara Madz, who had by then taken their stances in rows up in the choir loft at the rear of the church. He gave a brief rundown of where they were from, notable places where they'd sung, and the awards they'd received. Before taking his seat in the front pew, he pointed to the donation box in the vestibule and assured everyone that all the money went to the choir, not to his humble church.

As the female voices rose, Roland relaxed his frame against the pew and closed his eyes, letting his breathing slow to a steady respiration. Before long, his skin began to erupt in tingles down to the follicles in his scalp. The music, interwoven with separate but coordinated voices, enveloped the audience, and Roland received it not with his ears but through his entire body where it rippled even the fabric of his bones. The song, *Oh Shenandoah*, proceeded as the male voices joined in to increase the volume. The words did not matter, nor the sentiment, just the sound of fellow human beings in full-throated celebration of their shared vocal gifts. It propelled him into a state of ecstasy. The power of their singing signified—no, testified to—an essential, changeless quality of the species that reached back to the original tribal communities. Evolution could neither account for it nor change it. These were not birds chirping for mates or canines howling at the moon, but human souls rejoicing together at their common participation in eternity.

Roland heard and felt the enthusiastic applause but pressed his hands flat down on the pew and kept his eyes shut to maintain his inward trance. The program continued with a medieval canticle to show the Madz' versatility, then back to the American songbook, then on to an English refrain. By now he was out of his body, swimming in a tide of melodic strains, rolled under by the contrapuntal rejoinders, rescued by the gentle interceding harmonies, his vision suddenly possessed of a three-hundred-and-sixty degree perspective, a disembodied eye with circumferential vision now in perfect control of its trajectory, commanding the horizons of the earth below, the sea beyond, and the sky above, now suddenly buffeted and reeling, now plummeting into darkness, now soaring again to the shimmering edge of the universe. Yet his breath remained steady and his body still. This was no lucid dream, for his body was not with him, but a majestic survey of the vastness that surrounds us all.

She touched his hand. He opened his eyes and looked at her and smiled, a smile she did not return. They clapped politely and the program continued. He remained alert until the end and when it was over Father Bartholomew thanked them all for coming. Roland slipped a hundred-dollar bill into the donation box as they left, with Alison behind him, still not having uttered a word since the start of the concert.

~~~~~

Sodini's lay just a short walk around the corner on Green Street where, with its unpretentious menu and lively barroom atmosphere, the hundred-year-old trattoria maintained, almost single-handedly, the old-world character of North Beach, long since depopulated of its majority Italian community. Alison followed him out of the church and when he slowed down in an attempt to walk side by side with her, she stayed behind him, on his right shoulder, at one point even straight-arming him forward to insist that he keep up his pace. He realized that walking in unison would have invited conversation and that she was not prepared to engage. *Ok*, he decided, *I'll lead you to dinner if that's how you want it.*

The hostess guided them into the cozy dining room adjacent to the bar and showed them to a square table draped with a checkered cloth that had as its centerpiece, like all the tables in the place, a wicker-clad wine bottle stoppered with a candle and covered with rivulets of dried wax. She lit the candle and, with an ingratiating remark, stepped away. He made sure to take the seat with its back to the wall, just beneath an autographed photo of Frank Sinatra that bore the caption: *You may be as brave as you make believe you are.* He and the blue-eyed Italian crooner surveyed the comings and goings at the bar.

"Ever been here before?"

She cast her eyes upward and scanned the ceiling. "No one has."

Roland looked puzzled, but only for a second.

"I see. You can't step in the same river twice."

"Nothing that deep."

"So, enlighten me."

"No one has ever been in my seat, sitting across from a practical stranger who just—after learning what he—no not about you—about what you did. When we met yesterday you acted like—I don't know what you acted like, but not like you'd just—" She couldn't manage to finish a sentence.

"Why can't you say it?"

"Like you'd just killed a man, the worst man, the worst kind of man."

"How was I supposed to act?"

"I have no idea, but not like a guy out looking for a—" Again she did not finish.

"Looking for a what?"

"A good time. Out at a bar playing at banter."

"I was there for alcohol, two quick doses of hot Irish whiskey, nothing more. You were the one who…"

"Yes. That's true. I spoke to you first."

"And now here we are. You called me. You sat with me. You followed me up the street. You pushed me forward."

"I don't care about dinner. I'm not sure I can eat. I followed you up here to find out what happened in there."

"In where?"

"Don't act stupid—the church."

"I thought the singers were amazing."

"You went into some kind of altered state. There was some kind of energy pulsing around you. Your face glowed and went dark then glowed again. It was like your soul was trying to get out of your body, and I'm not sure I even believe in the soul. For a moment it came over me, swallowed me, then spit me out. That's when I touched your hand. When I touched your hand, it stopped. You were human again."

"I apologize. I should've reined that in."

"Reined in that? What is *that*? What do you mean by *that*?"

"I don't know if there's a word for it. I go places sometimes, mostly when I'm asleep, but sometimes when I'm wide awake and perfectly at peace, like tonight under the spell of all those voices."

"Go places?"

"Nowhere you could find on a map—places where time works differently."

"That's not normal."

"Funny, I've been doing it since I was little. When I realized most people couldn't do it, or didn't do it, I considered them *sub*-normal. But I've since learned that it's not so unusual, it's just that people don't like to talk about it."

"It freaked me out. You weren't even there."

"Best I can explain it—I was *with* the music, or *inside* it, riding those thick notes woven together by all those separate but intertwining voices, swinging from vines and dropping into nets and bouncing up to grab more vines. But it's probably just brain chemicals. I think I was born with a shaman's brain. Truth is, I was there, sitting next to you the whole time."

"Some brain chemicals. Other people noticed it too. The priest turned around and looked at you. You had your eyes closed and your face practically buzzed. He looked at you, then he looked at me. He could tell I was afraid."

"Fear. Not a good trait for a woman like you."

"A woman like me?"

"I've got a feeling I know what you do."

"Really? I'm in private equity, mostly commercial real estate, the only female VP at my firm."

"My apologies. I was thinking of a different kind of private equity."

"What are you saying?"

"I'm saying you've got a lot of it, and you turned it on thick in the bar yesterday." Roland figured if he was wrong she might get up and leave and he'd chalk her up in the loss column. "I don't think I can afford to invest."

"This place isn't that pricy. If money's the problem…"

The waiter came over and welcomed them and gave them his name and asked if he could take their order. Roland asked her if she liked seafood linguine, and she gave him a shrugging nod that said she was not opposed or it didn't matter.

"Due di mare."

"And to drink?"

Roland deferred to Alison.

"Whiskey. Two double Manhattans."

Roland smiled. "That'll work."

The waiter returned them to their privacy.

"You think I'm a prostitute." It was not a question but a formal assertion, almost an accusation.

"I'm sorry. After my little ecstatic adventure, I'm connecting dots that might not even be there."

"I see. Like people who wake up with psychic powers after getting struck by lightning."

"Well, I'm not about to play the lottery."

She smiled faintly and lifted her hands off the table and set them in her lap. He looked across the dining room into the bar to see if the drinks were forthcoming. She would speak if she chose to. He didn't care. She would eat her meal when it came, or not. He'd box up her portion and take it home if need be. The evening could end in any number of ways, all of them satisfactory as far as he was concerned.

She broke the silence. "*Prostitute* is not the right word."

"Then choose another. Do we need the thesaurus?"

"No. I just want you to know that I didn't come out tonight thinking of you as a client."

"So, I was right—whatever word you want to use. At the bar yesterday you were looking for clients."

"I don't want to be rude, Roland, but you don't fit the profile of my typical client."

"Still, though, I'm right, right? I'm not judging you, but I just want to know if I'm seeing things correctly."

"Yes and no. I have accepted money from men in exchange for my *private equity*, as you call it, but it's just a hobby. I considered this an actual date."

"You must be expensive."

"I am. But I don't do it for the money, really. I've got plenty of money. It's complicated."

"So why am I paying the check?"

"I'm traditional that way. Like I said, this is a real date, the strangest one I've ever been on."

"There's a long tradition for the other business too. The oldest profession, right?"

"It's not my profession." She sounded irritated. "I finance multi-million-dollar acquisitions."

"Personally?"

"No. Right. I broker the deals."

"I'm much more interested in this hobby of yours."

The drinks arrived with a basket of bread. He sucked down half of his in one tilt and bored in on her, the candle flame glittering in his eyes.

"I like to play the role."

"Sounds kinda dangerous, more dangerous than sitting in a church concert next to a man with his eyes closed."

"I wasn't afraid of *you* per se, just disturbed by what was going on inside you, but that's over now. You seem normal now."

"But picking up strangers in bars…"

"No."

"No? I'm confused."

"Can we drop it? If I explain it, can we drop it?"

"You don't have to. I just don't get why a woman like you would…"

"I want to explain it. If you'll just shut up for a second."

Roland raised his hands in mock surrender then took his drink and leaned back and sipped. It was getting low.

"I gave up dating a few years ago. The men in this town are like spoiled children, at least the ones in my tax bracket. They know how to go through the motions to get you into bed, but in the end, that's all they're after—a conquest, a story to tell their buddies. I knew if I kept dating the men in my field it would ruin my career. A woman can't negotiate with men she's slept with or who know who she's slept with."

He nodded astutely to say he understood her logic.

"So, I made a decision—reject them all. But politely, not like a bitch. Deflect their advances gently, like the old Chinese women doing tai chi in Huntington Park. They were my inspiration."

Huntington Park was two blocks from Roland's building. "I know the ones."

"I decided to test the market, see how much I was worth. I wasn't giving up on men, per se, just on the fantasy of a healthy relationship. Call me cynical, fine. I like men very much, actually. Fascinating animals.

I like the power I can have over them, not to hurt them or take advantage, but to give them pleasure, to transform them into grateful pets."

"I think I get it." Roland didn't want to hear any more. He liked this Alison, not as a possible sexual conquest, but as a genuinely good sport. Details of her mercenary dalliances might well diminish her in his estimation.

"Do you? Tell me—what exactly do you think you get about it?" She wasn't hostile, simply incredulous.

"The money preserves your dignity—something like that."

She drank while she mulled that over.

"Not to a fifty-dollar whore—I highly doubt that."

"I wouldn't have put you in that category."

"Good, because I'm not. I'd call myself a freelance lover, more in the geisha tradition. Wives, girlfriends—they're not free to give themselves completely. A man can do for a woman without feeling humiliated, but a woman in a relationship can't go all the way. There's always that little thing that he did or said yesterday or a year ago, not cleaning up after himself or dismissing one of her worries—something he can't really be blamed for. Yet it holds her back. If she gives whatever he wants to receive and puts her imagination into it, the man has that on her if he wants to have it on her. She understands that even if she doesn't fully realize it. If a billionaire marries a woman and sets her up with all the finest things, but he's an asshole once in a while, she's not going to give him her best. But the freelance lover operates above that subtle power dynamic and, in a strange way, is free to be perfectly intimate and creative, because, in the end, it's her show, not his. That's what he's paying for. Without the money, her devotion to his pleasure would make no sense."

"What kind of money are we talking about?"

"That's not what we're here for."

"I know. I'm just curious how it works."

"I've done only it a few times—nine times exactly."

"And always men from out of town—men here on business, or tourists."

"Yeah. That's right. The Wharf is the perfect place."

"And?"

"It's just a matter of being friendly. Starts like any business deal."

"Thousands, then. Not hundreds."

"A few thousand, if I like you. Your hotel. Totally safe."//
"One more question."
"One more question."
"Why did you talk to me? Like you said, I don't fit the profile."
"And just when I thought you might be different."
"What do you mean by that?"
"Typical man, begging to be stroked."
"Tell me anyway."
"You were a sight to behold, true enough. The gorgeous hair—the now tragic gorgeous hair. But what did it was the two drinks. Walking toward me alone with a drink in each hand. That invited a comment."
"One for me and one for him."
"Him?"
The waiter came over and spoke to Roland. "There's a gentleman at the bar who would like to buy your next drink."
Roland looked over at the bar and locked eyes with his benefactor. The man put his right forefinger up to his lips with his thumb cocked back like the hammer on a gun and blew away his imaginary smoke. Roland touched the brim of his invisible cowboy hat and nodded respectfully then spoke to the waiter. "I'm not drinking alone."
"I don't need another one."
Roland looked at the waiter. "He should buy for the table, just to be polite."
"I'll take care of it."
If he'd been honest, he'd have said he'd drink the second one if she didn't want it. He felt comfortably in control, well short of the gray zone that preceded a blackout. He'd learned to see it coming and usually plowed on through, though two nights ago he'd been able to stop and weave his way home, mindful of his need to be sharp for his job review. He thought about that and wondered if it might have saved his life, and Astrid's too. That crowbar was probably strong enough to pry open her door, the only other apartment on his floor in the old wooden building. *Would he have killed me if he'd found me passed out cold and recognized his mistake? I wouldn't move on to Astrid and left me there alive.*
Alison stalled his cogitation. "I get it now."
"Sorry. What?"
"*Him*—you bought one for *him*. You weren't really drinking alone."

Roland remained confused. "When?"

"At the Buena Vista? Did you just go off on another one of your brain journeys?"

"Oh yeah. One for me and one for him." Roland hadn't meant her to take it literally, but he rolled with it. "A toast to the loser, in case he was on the flipside watching."

"You really believe in that—the flipside? Or is it just brain chemicals?"

"I guess both can be true. You're asking the wrong guy."

She turned around and glanced in the direction of the sport who'd bought the drinks. "How did he know you? And the guys in the car?"

"I was on the news tonight, channel seven, just before we met up. Nice long interview."

The waiter arrived with the drinks. Roland took his from the waiter's hand before he could set it down and took a drink then set it down.

"Why would you do that?"

"To control my own narrative. The press answers to no one, so I wanted to get out in front of this thing, plant my flag so to speak."

"What are you worried about?"

"I'll settle for nothing less than grateful admiration."

"Good start so far. Judging from the little I've seen. You've already got at least two admirers."

He checked her eyes for insincerity, but she was unreadable, and he stayed on them as one would watch a cloud floating above an empty plain, the alcohol swaddling his brain. He saw that his fixation on her eyes wasn't making her uncomfortable, but himself instead. "Why did you call me?" That was all he could come up with.

"I couldn't help myself. Your raw animal magnetism—I was no match for it. You could have written your phone number on a napkin and stuffed it in my mouth and walked away with a grunt, and here I'd be."

"Do I deserve that? I don't think I deserved that."

"Are you enjoying my company, Mister Roland Hazzard?"

"Immensely. I'm really glad you came out. This has been an amazing day, in no small part because…"

"SHHHHH." Several diners in the room stopped chatting and looked at her. She leaned toward him and said in a whisper, "Don't ruin my appetite."

He got the message. Her presence there alone should be proof enough that she liked him, and for him not to understand that instinctively was a turn-off. He'd almost screwed the pooch. It was time to shut up and let silence effect repairs.

The meal arrived and was set before them, its steam bearing the aromas of garlic and seafood rising from the pasta on their plates. He ate deliberately lest he gobble it down, and the care he took assembling each bite heightened his awareness of the other diners around them. He sensed that some of them recognized him and were buzzing about it, but he couldn't be sure, and he dared not glance around to confirm his suspicion. He kept his attention on Alison. She was using the table bread to sop up the sauce between bites of linguine. He did the same. His attention to the food and her enjoyment of the food expelled his preoccupation with being watched. After a while, without thinking, he blurted out a question. It was almost as though the question fell from his mouth like a lottery ball.

"So, you'll never get married?"

She looked at him with linguine draped over her lip then slurped it in and dabbed her mouth with her napkin and took a drink.

"Isn't that the whole reason for dating?" Again, he couldn't tell if she was serious, and he liked that. She possessed the demeanor of a practiced negotiator, a good poker face.

"Fifty years ago."

"You're right We're all just flailing around these days, swinging wildly, nursing our wounds, wondering whether or not our injuries were self-inflicted."

"What about children?"

"What *about* children?"

"I'm not the one supposedly born with a maternal instinct. You've got a few miles left on your tires."

"If this were an old-fashioned date, it seems I'd already know what you do for a living. We skipped that step. Before we talk about the tread-life of my uterus, let's hear about your prospects. I know you can fight off the enemy, but can you hunt the buffalo?"

"I'm a great hunter alright. I track down bugs in video games. But I swear to whatever amounts to God I'm not trying to impress you or marry you. I don't even care if you sleep with me. I just think you're a fascinating subject. In the mythical olden days slick-haired boys would have lined up on the sidewalk to knock on your daddy's door. So I asked, not for myself, but for all those mythical boys with their pressed collars and polished shoes."

"When I bank twenty million, I'll retire, buy a nice home on a beach somewhere and get married, have a few kids, and be a mommy. The man, the one I choose, can go to work, pay the bills and be the daddy; but the house will be mine, my investments in my name, my finances completely secure."

Whether she was telling the truth or inventing, it was a good enough answer as far as he was concerned, and he decided to suspend his interrogation and raised his glass to salute her good sense and drank it down. They finished the meal and declined dessert and he paid and they got up to leave. "So, tell me, what do you plan to do with your newfound notoriety?"

"No idea. I lit a fuse on the news today. Only a matter of time to see if the bomb goes off."

~~~~~

The clear, dark night sharpened the lights from the buildings downtown, providing a romantic backdrop to the revelry of North Beach which, at this hour, remained relatively civilized. Roland and Alison stood on the sidewalk in front of Sodini's with no agreed-upon plan, either to part company or to continue their evening together. The temperature had dropped about fifteen degrees since they'd entered the restaurant, not counting the wind chill. The sensation of cold on his scalp alarmed him.

"Rub your hands together."

She gave him a suspicious look. "Why?"

"C'mon, real fast." He showed her. "Like you're trying to start a fire."

She did as instructed.

"A little faster. Good. Another couple seconds."

She brought her hands close to her nose and rubbed them together furiously, then stopped and looked at him. He'd taken a knee, as a man would in the olden days to solemnize a marriage proposal. He offered her his dome. "There. Clamp them on my head. Warm it up."

She pressed her hands on his head and held them firm. "People are looking at us." He let the warmth from her palms sink in for a few seconds then stood up. Indeed, a couple of people, two young men about his age, were staring. He looked at them. "It's fresh off the assembly line. Needs the occasional adjustment."

"I thought she was giving you some kind of blessing."

"Every day above ground is a blessing, boys. Every day above ground." He turned to her and thanked her.

"What was that all about?"

"Just experimenting."

"To see how fast your head gets cold again?"

"They didn't recognize me—notice that?"

"Well, I guess you've got your work cut out for you."

"Can I use your phone? Mine's dead."

"What for?"

"To call us a ride."

"What for?"

"To take you home."

"There's cabs all over the place."

"If my guy's in the area he'll be here in a jiff."

"Your guy?"

"Yeah. Very reliable. C'mon, it's cold out here."

She gave him her phone. He called Singh and told him where they were and gave the phone back to Alison. "He said five minutes."

"Nice to have your own personal driver."

"Oh, he's much more than a driver."

"Feels like I'm in a movie, a thriller maybe."

"I ordered fog, but all I got was this stiff breeze."

"What do you have in store for me?"

"Hard to say. The guy I—*ended*—last night. His soul leaped into me. The disturbance in the church—our two souls battling for possession. The outcome of the contest is uncertain."

"I've been enjoying myself. You're about to spoil it."

His impish impulse retreated. He put his arm around her and she leaned into him. He looked down at her in the hope she would raise her eyes to his, but this was not a movie, neither a thriller nor a romance. She kept her face forward.

~~~~~

Singh arrived and they climbed in his cab. He turned and smiled at both of them and let out a timid giggle.

"Ahh, the hero has found a fair maiden. Things are looking up for you already."

"I don't go by hero, Singh."

"Forgive me. I speak too freely."

"Well. I don't mind fair maiden."

"Where to tonight?"

Roland looked at Alison. He sensed her indecision and understood that she might not want him to know where she lived, and he half-expected her to tell the driver to drop off Roland first. But that would not solve her problem since the driver was his confederate and could report it back to him.

"The Blue Bottle."

"I don't know it." Neither did Roland, but any place with the word bottle in its name was alright with him.

"Pacific Heights. Fillmore and Jackson."

Singh hit the gas. "How was your dinner?"

"The food was good. But the conversation was better."

"Does the lady agree?"

"He's in charge of how well we get along."

The ride proceeded with little more conversation. Singh jerked the taxi through traffic at an uncomfortable rate of speed, timing the lights as best he could, gassing it to beat the close decisions. When stopped by a red he jammed on the brakes and Roland flung his arm across her waist to keep her from launching headfirst. She slid forward on her skirt and her knees nearly hit the front seat.

"Jesus, Singh."

"My hero indeed. This movie comes with a chase scene."

"This is how I roll on Saturday night."

Roland realized it was peak business hours for a taxi driver and the ride to Pacific Heights was taking him out of his prime hunting grounds.

"Just take it easy."

He put on his seat belt and looked at Alison for her to do the same. Her legs had parted when she slid forward. Her skirt was hiked up nearly all the way. She put her hand on his shoulder and pulled herself up straight and fixed her skirt.

"We're almost there." She left herself unbuckled.

Singh dropped them in front of The Blue Bottle, where there was no booze on the menu after all. It was a fancy coffee and dessert house, its artistically crafted confections on display in the window. Roland gave him a c-note.

"No. No, please, sir. I'm at your service."

"Keep it for the lost business. I insist."

Singh took the money and thanked him and sped off as soon as he'd shut the door. The City was popping with fares at this hour. Boughs bent with low-hanging fruit. An energetic driver could pull in a nice haul on a night like this.

"Coffee and dessert? None for me, but I'll watch you."

"Me neither." She made a rabbit face. A face, he thought, to show her indecision.

"You live nearby, don't you?"

"Yes. I come here often."

"Were you thinking I'd stay in the car? Do you want me to call him back? I'll need your phone again. I'm sure he'll turn right around."

"What are you expecting from me?"

"A decision."

"And if I invite you up?"

"A drink, if you have one to offer."

"Nothing other than that?"

"Are you afraid of me?"

"No. But you're a lot more than I bargained for. You didn't answer my question."

"How about this—how 'bout you drag those finely crafted talons across my virgin scalp?"

She looked at him, studied her nails, and touched the corner of one eye to consider the request. "That's one of the more peculiar desires I've ever heard."

"Have you ever entertained a bald guy?"

"No. Not in the way you mean."

"So you can't say it's peculiar. Far as I'm concerned, any bald guy who doesn't want his head tickled—and often—is an embarrassment to the tribe, a veritable apostate."

Alison giggled the giggle of the willing. "Ok. I think I can roll out a tactile buffet for your hungry scalp. I might even be able to find a feather."

She lived around the corner on Jackson Street in a tall Victorian walk-up where she occupied the third and uppermost floor. She unlocked the door and let them in. He scanned the place. The standing lamp in her parlor was dimmed but cast enough light so that he could ascertain the floorplan—two bedrooms in the back, a kitchen off to the side, closets, bathroom, space enough for three or four, depending on the sleeping arrangements. An opulent apartment for one. The Oriental rug in the parlor nearly covered the entire floor and her richly stained, heavy wooden furniture created a warm mood. He pulled off his Laredos and took a seat on the couch and watched her move to the kitchen.

"I have some pretty good brandy, kinda orangey."

"That sounds fine." It didn't, but it was strong liquor, far preferable to wine or beer. He didn't want to sound overly particular in any case. "Can I plug my phone in somewhere?"

"There's a cord under the side table at the other end of the couch."

"Thanks." He found the cord and plugged in his phone. It had died while he was playing Chinese chess in Portsmouth Square and he was curious as to what he would find once it got some juice.

She set the drinks down on the coffee table in front of him and sat in the chair on the opposite side to unlace her boots. He watched her as she carefully removed each one to reveal her dainty feet inside her sheer white tights. He peered at her toes to see if he could count them five to a bunch under the stocking fabric, just to make sure she didn't carry some sort of monstrous gene. She fidgeted under his scrutiny and spoke to break the silence.

"You said something on the phone today that puzzled me."

"Tell me. Maybe I can clear it up."

"When I asked if you were a Bible scholar, because of that Nimrod business, you said no but that you were a student of *pre*-history. I've been thinking about that. How can someone call himself a student of something that hasn't even been written down?"

"Let me ask you this—who discovered America?"

"I guess the Vikings got here before Columbus."

"That's right. But they didn't *claim* the continent. Probably had no concept of claiming continents. History records what people claim."

"What's your point—who discovered America?"

"It's a stupid question. But fifty years ago, if you'd said anyone other than Columbus you couldn't get a teaching job."

"I get it. But as a student of pre-history, what's the truth? Who got here first, besides the natives?"

"It's hard to say, but probably not the Vikings. Probably copper miners from the Mediterranean."

"Copper miners? Like whom?"

"Minoans. Divers have discovered sunken ships in the Mediterranean loaded with raw copper of the kind found only in a particular area of Michigan, on Lake Superior. And lo and behold, there's evidence of ancient mining there that can't be traced to the natives."

"Sounds pretty thin."

"I'm not saying it's iron clad—I should say bronze-clad—proof, but it's not whacko either. They had the ships to make the crossing, ships every bit as seaworthy as Columbus' little fleet. So, until someone can explain where else that grade of copper came from, I'm saying the default is Michigan."

"Bronze-clad?"

"You need copper and tin to make bronze, and bronze can be pounded into a sword sharp enough to cut your head off. Iron came later. Much harder. Much sharper edge. Total game changer."

She got up and took off her jacket and put it in the closet and closed the closet door and sat back down. He watched her every move, would not drink before she did.

"But who really cares, anyway. Who really cares who got here first?"

"I care when someone in authority says a matter is settled. Chances are that authority is wrong and isn't even sure that he's right but is damn sure not going to budge off his spot. The job, at that point, is to hold onto the job."

"And the world needs guys like you to keep the questions open."

"Yeah. Guys like me, without a rooster in the pit, need to look at the anomalies and evaluate them without fear or favor. That is the job of a student of pre-history. Satisfied?"

"No. Give me your best example. Convince me, and I'll come over there." She raised her snifter and sampled the brandy.

He took a drink and thought about it. *My best example.* There were too many good ones, out-of-place artifacts filled volumes, and with the advancements in ground-penetrating radar and methods for dating stone, the dam was breaking. The orthodox narrative around the rise of homo sapiens was soon to be debunked.

"There're some very old maps of the world, ones that shows Antarctica, which was officially discovered around 1820. Not Antarctica with the ice, mind you, but Antarctica the landmass, beneath the ice."

"Maps—how old?"

"Sixteenth Century. A few hundred years before the British mapped it on the Nimrod Expedition."

"There's Nimrod again."

"We're in a regular circus of synchronicity."

"You're saying that there's proof that long before Columbus sailed the ocean blue someone was able to map the whole world—there's evidence of that?"

"Not the whole world exactly. The guy who made the map, an Ottoman Turkish admiral, said he made his map by copying older maps that were disintegrating into powder, maps maybe thousands of years old. It even shows a landmass that looks suspiciously like Japan."

"And you saying this is legit, not some hoaxed-up counterfeit bullshit?"

"Its provenance is unassailable. It would hold up in court. What it means is subject to debate, I guess, but the map is legit, and others too. Global maps with accurate continental coastlines were created, somehow, long before the Europeans set sail into the great unknown."

"I thought the early sailors were afraid that might fall off the edge of the Earth."

"Pure fiction—American fiction. Washington Irving made that up, except he published it as fact in *The Life and Voyages of Christopher Columbus.* You see how it works? The elites control the narrative."

She got up and turned on the space heater in the corner of the room. "So, what are we gonna *doo* about it?" Her voice cooed as with motherly concern. He took off his jacket while he formulated an answer and set it next to his boots. He understood she was making light of his skepticism, but all the same her question merited consideration.

"One of my first days in college I was walking around campus and saw this huge graffitied slogan sprayed onto the side of a building— *Subvert the Dominant Paradigm*. Didn't give it much thought initially. But there it was, day after day, a bold command in black letters two feet tall on the side of a beautiful old white building right next to the central plaza—Sproul Plaza. How many thousands of people must have walked by it every hour during schooldays? Then one day, after I pretty much stopped noticing it, it occurred to me—and normally I'm pretty quick to spot irony—occurred to me just how absurd it was, how pathetic really." He looked at her to make sure she was paying attention.

"I've heard the expression. Kind of a Marxist rallying cry."

"Decorating one of the most left-wing universities in the world."

"Berkeley. Sproul Plaza. I get it." She went into her bedroom and left the door open.

"What are you doing?"

"I'm changing. You still haven't answered my question."

"I'm getting there. The vandalism—the Marxist rallying cry—it took no courage. The university just ignored it."

"Like preaching to the choir. So?" She projected her voice through the doorway of her room.

He raised his voice a little to make sure she could hear him. "And even if the dominant paradigm was meant to be the university establishment, the fact that they let it stand is like a lion not brushing a fly off its nose. But if someone wrote *Darwin was Racist* or *Jesus Loves You*, that would be removed overnight." She emerged barefoot in a t-shirt and a pair of sweatpants. He saw that her breasts were unharnessed.

"You're babbling now. You made your case. I'll give you your reward." She took her glass off the coffee table and set it aside and pulled the table out a few feet to make room on the rug for him to sit. He drained his glass and put it in her hand and sat down on the rug with his back against the couch. She set his glass on the table and stood facing him, playing the air with her talons. "Don't be afraid. These things are sharp, but I'll be gentle." She climbed in behind him and sat on the couch so that his shoulders rested between her knees. *Really?* He wavered internally. She'd called his bluff. He was nervous as a maiden and wanted to delay, to continue the conversation.

"So, what are we as a species going to do about it? Let's start by acknowledging our ignorance and atoning for our arrogance. Otherwise, we're doomed."

"Speak for yourself." She rested her ten fingernails on his scalp and moved them gently down to his temples then drew them back up to his crown. "I like what I do. I like what I'm doing."

"The world is supposed to be a self-correcting enterprise." She applied a little more pressure, causing the sensation to travel farther down his neck. His body relaxed. "Too much evil going on in Quadrant B, the good set down their books and paint brushes and pick up their machine guns."

"You got it all figured out."

"Not enough crops to feed the people in Sector G, folks put together a better irrigation system." She combed his skin, reaching down his face and dragging her fingers up his jawline. "Rockets keep splashing in the ocean—not for long. Mathematicians to the rescue." She changed to a swirling motion, the pleasure so general he couldn't track where she was tracing until she moved down the nape of his neck and then up to dawdle on the cusps of his ears. "Grandma fumbles a jar of preserves, clean up on aisle nine."

"Murderer breaks into your home…"

"Clean up at checkout." He moaned.

"Yes." She massaged his earlobes. "I bet you enjoyed it—winning the fight. Taking the life."

"If I'd enjoyed it I'd have something to feel guilty about, something to correct." His head felt so loose on his shoulders he thought she could lift it off with a gentle tug. She reached down his shirt and explored his pectorals.

"Still feeling like we're doomed?"

"You must be a very high-ranking devil." He pulled off his shirt and tossed it aside. Alison didn't deny it, so he figured he was near the mark but nonetheless submitted himself to her tender ministrations. Her touch produced sensations so subtle and exquisite that it sapped him of his strength. Her power lay not in the paranormal, but in her utterly selfless devotion to the task of giving tactile pleasure. He enjoyed a quality of humanity he'd never known. His gratitude came out in groans.

"Shhhh, or I'll have to stop."

"Don't stop."

She continued. His body limp and listing, his mind divorced from will, drunk on euphoria, his weight too much for her thighs to support. She let him fall to one side onto the floor with a thud.

"I've turned you into a sack of sugar." She took a pillow from the couch and slid it under his head.

"Ferment me into a barrel of rum."

She rolled him prone and straddled the small of his back and continued to caress and titillate his hide—elbows, shoulders, pits, lats, down to his ticklish sides—touching each area very deliberately, now very slowly. He could have drifted off except he felt the pressure of her pelvis grinding on his spine. She was pleasuring herself against him. He listened as her breathing quickened, felt the warm swell of her excitement. Then a wet secretion through the fabric of her sweatpants. Now a grunt. She'd stopped scratching his back and dug in her nails to steady herself for leverage and she pressed her business harder and gyrated. Another stronger, more urgent grunt. Almost a growl. Any more of this and he would have to turn over and put the question to her.

His phone chirped. The battery was renewed. It sounded off again, this time with a xylophonic phrase. He had a voice message.

"I need to see about this." He bucked his hips to disrupt her rhythm.

"You're a monster" She climbed off of him. "I was almost there."

"Sorry, darlin'. My belt buckle was gouging me anyway."

She went into her bedroom. Roland picked up his phone and read a text message from Joshua. *You were right. Call me.* Then a voicemail, left after the text. *Roland, I agreed to a spot on a local TV station in LA tomorrow. We fly at noon. If I don't hear from you by 9 AM I'll call it off.*

Roland texted him back. *Good news. I'll call you in the morning.* He set the phone down.

"Was it important?"

"Another TV interview, tomorrow in Los Angeles."

"The TV station called you?"

"I hired an agent. The agent called."

"Wow, you're really serious about this."

"Can I pour myself another drink?"

"Sure. Finish it. Then come in here."

Roland took his glass to the kitchen and found the bottle on the counter and emptied it into the glass and drank it and set the glass down and went back to the parlor and looked at the open doorway to her bedroom. Shadows of candleflames dueled about her silhouette on the interior wall. He weighed his options. Flight to LA tomorrow—he might want to call it a night.

"Is it safe?"

"What are you worried about?"

"Enchanted forest in there. I might lose my way."

"I'll be sure to send you home, but you'll never be the same."

Let's find out. He stepped through the door. She stood naked at her dresser lighting the wick on the last of three clear glass oil candles. He loved that women liked such things. The candle oil was scented to smell like wax.

"That's a very nice bed." A casual observation meant to conceal his surprise at her nudity. It was a four-poster model, finely carved, sporting a fluffy duvet and a phalanx of decorative pillows. To make such a bed every morning, he thought, knowing that you didn't need to, meant you'd figured out something most people didn't even know to value.

"Roland Hazzard."

He looked at her and said nothing.

"Pay attention."

"I don't think I deserve you."

"That's why I charge a lot of money."

Her slight frame bore the well-defined musculature of a gymnast or even a bodybuilder. Biceps, abs, quadriceps, perfect glutes.

"Do you know how to fight? A girl like you could do some damage."

She pointed to an armchair in the corner. "Put your clothes over there." What warmth he'd perceived in her before had all but dissipated. He sensed that her will was stronger than his own and that his intoxication put him at a disadvantage. He was in her lair and under her control, and with no clothes on he couldn't flee into the night if things went sideways. She viewed his body.

"You're barely going to fit on the bed."

"We don't have to do this. This is your idea."

"You're not going to have to do anything except be still and keep quiet." She removed the pillows to clear the duvet. "Before you climb aboard, let's get one thing clear."

He nodded ok.

"You're not going to put that in me. I don't have a condom to fit it and even if I did, I'm not about to traumatize my little coochee—not for a plate of linguini."

He nodded again and lay down on the bed. For the next half hour, Alison did things in the furtherance of sexual science for which there are no ready euphemisms. Suffice it to say that she endeavored, in a series of rolling climaxes achieved through much the same method she'd employed on the rug, to slather his body with her fluid. Prowling over his sturdy physique, she managed to work herself into a state of rapture that alarmed him. As he lay there with his eyes closed—half in fear, half in concentration to heighten his sensation—a vision intruded on his mind. He viewed, as from above, an Ancient Babylonian sex cult staffed by garishly adorned harlots servicing their devotees with obscene abandon. The temple priestess, bangled to the elbows, lashed the orgy from her throne. Images so vivid they seemed more of memory than imagination. He sensed that he and Alison were not alone, that some external power inhabited her being, enabling her to sustain such a prolonged and energetic performance. He opened his eyes to flee the scene just as she mounted his pate to complete her debauch in a prodigious liquid release. Panting with exhaustion, she dismounted him and stood beside the bed.

"What are you, some kind of succubus?"

"I didn't get that far in demon school."

"Well, you got far enough to…"

"Did I say you could talk?"

Alison opened a drawer in the nightstand and produced her aforementioned feather, though the deft use of which she teased out his long-postponed release with remarkable efficiency. She stood over him and smiled.

"You did well." She left the room.

He knew better than to ask what she meant or even to wonder at it. His consent to her will had been completely nonverbal, even unintentional. It was the lowest form of consent he could think of, akin to that of a domesticated animal. A moment later she returned clad in a robe, carrying a bath towel. She tossed him the towel. He sat up and wiped himself clean of her. The odor was not unpleasant. He patted dry his head and face, for she'd been there too.

"What do you call that?"

"Call what?"

"What you just did."

"Let's call it a wax job."

After he dressed and pulled on his boots, she walked him to the door. He figured at some point she might toss in a kiss, but the date had ended the moment she put on her robe. Perhaps the date had ended the moment they'd entered her apartment. He stood there confused, looking at her hand on the doorknob, feeling a little betrayed and not sure why.

"I'd like to call you."

"Don't you know that would ruin it?"

"Not even for a drink?"

She took her hand off the doorknob and reached up with both hands and drew his face toward her and gave him a firm kiss on the lips.

"You're a spectacular man. But our little encounter tonight should stay trapped in amber."

"I don't understand."

"Yours is a turbulent soul, Roland Hazzard. Further relations with you could blow me off course."

"May I say thank you, then?"

"Here's how you can thank me. Go down to LA for your TV interview and tell the world about the giant pyramids under the ice in Antarctica." She opened the door and stepped back to let him pass and he left the apartment without turning around to see her close the door. He heard the lock click. On his way down the stairs, Roland weighed her proposition. Was she mocking him? *I never said anything about Antarctic pyramids.*

~~~~~

His building was not too far, fifteen blocks or so, roughly half on a downslope and half on the upslope. He picked a route deliberately to avoid passing the bars around Van Ness Avenue and Polk Street, worried that he might not be able to resist the urge to go in. Joshua would not tolerate a fuckup—that much was clear. Besides, he was eager to get to sleep still possessed of his faculties and process this most unusual night. When he reached the corner of Sacramento and Leavenworth and began the final climb to his building, as he had so many nights before, he saw that the streetlight above his alley had been replaced, illuminating the tree where he had so often rested or snoozed in a stupor. *I guess it takes a break-in or worse to get a bulb replaced in this Godforsaken town.*

Astrid heard him ascend the stairs and peeked out her door when he reached the landing. She let out a yelp. He turned and looked at her. She saw that it was he, not a tall, bald stranger, and stepped out her door.

"What have you done?"

Roland wondered how Astrid could know that he'd just let a naked sex-witch do the python dance all over his body and gave her a skeptical look. She reached up and touched the top of her head.

"Oh. Yeah. I got religion." He smiled the smile of the liar.

"I know better than to dig into that."

"Goodnight, Astrid." He aimed his key toward the lock.

"Wait a second, please."

Roland opened his door and put a foot inside to keep his distance, lest she smell Alison. He turned and waited for her to speak.

"I want to thank you for saying no to me last night. If that has anything to do with your new religion, then it's a good thing."

He was relieved to surmise that she had not seen his bit on the local news broadcast, being in no mood to discuss it.

"Don't press your luck. You try that again and you might…"

"Stop." She raised a finger. "You don't always have to use your smart remarks."

"You're right. Point taken."

She said goodnight and he mumbled the same and flung up his good arm to indicate exhaustion and went inside. As he climbed into bed, he heard her words again—*you don't always have to use your smart remarks.* As wise a piece of advice as that was under normal circumstances, she could have no idea how off the mark she was, as far as Roland was concerned, in light of his plans for the days ahead. *I'll need to be in top form if I'm going to shoot my mouth off to the world. I'll need a round in every chamber. Hell, I'll need a bandolier.*

Chapter 14
October 2, 2016

Roland pulled both wads of c-notes from his jeans and counted out the bills on the bedspread, sixty-six in all, and stowed a stack of fifty in his sock drawer. He folded the remaining sixteen hundred into his pocket and dialed up Joshua as he walked down the hill to Andruko's Market.

"Hey, Josh, it's me. Thanks for the call last night."

"Hey, champ. Ready for your next dog and pony show?"

"Champ? You're mighty chipper."

"The morning sun brought a fresh perspective. I've decided that if I'm going to do this, I'm going to be more than a secretary. I'm going to promote you, like a fighter."

The sun was, in fact, uncommonly present for a fall San Francisco morning and strong enough to dull the nip of the ever-present breeze.

"I like the sound of it, but I'm not sure who my opponent is."

"The way you come off, you'll have no shortage of detractors."

"Seriously, Josh, what changed your mind?"

"Prayer and meditation. And I wouldn't say it changed my mind, rather it opened it. Something that you said kept echoing, and I finally let it sink in."

"Oh?"

"You said that your purpose is not criminal, so I didn't need to understand it."

"What about your precious reputation?"

"I look at it this way; you've already admitted, on camera no less, that you drink too much, and then there's your arrest record that shows a history, which is sure to come out. If you crash and burn, all I have to do is shrug you off. Admitting to knowing what you've already publicly acknowledged does me no harm. I'll spin it that I was only trying to help a troubled soul, which would be true."

Roland bristled inwardly. *Troubled soul. Who the fuck does he think he is?* He let it slide.

"I'm glad you've got your scruples all in a row. I suppose you talked to Inspector Spelman."

"Yes. But not to ask his advice, only to let him know what you're up to—what *we're up* to."

"And what are we up to? How would you phrase it?"

"We're up to making Roland Hazzard, the Butcher Slayer, a national celebrity. How you're received is entirely up to you, and the bigger you get, the more light you throw off, the more is reflected on me. I never thought I'd say this, but there's no such thing as bad publicity."

"So I'm the whore and you're the pimp."

"To reduce it to the most cynical of metaphors, yes."

"Tell me what you've got lined up in LA."

Joshua explained. A local network affiliate wanted to introduce Roland to some of the family members of the serial killer's victims, nearly half of them from nearby Glendale, and broadcast it live. The station agreed to pay for transportation but not an appearance fee. He gave Roland the terminal and the airline.

"Meet me at SFO at noon at the ticket counter. The flight leaves at one. Make sure to bring your ID."

Roland thanked him again and ended the call outside the door of Andruko's Market.

He walked in and turned to the little produce section along the wall near the door and grabbed a peach. Oleg observed him from the meat counter at the rear of the store.

"I see they pulled the teeth out your boots, meesta killa."

"Good morning, Oleg. Can I get a couple of paper towels please? This peach looks ripe and juicy, exactly as advertised." He hoped to antagonize Oleg with his most cheerful, unflappable personality.

Oleg tore off a length of paper towels and handed it across the counter. Roland took it and ripped off a sheet to hold the peach then turned his back and wrapped the stack of ten c-notes in the remaining sheet. He took a bite of the peach and turned back around.

"You're right. This is dewlicious." He slapped the parcel of cash on the meat counter and slid it forward.

"Give to Taras. Taras keeps the book."

"I'm giving it to you since you gave me a hard look yesterday."

Oleg took the packet and peeked inside. "Only a thousand."

"That's twice what Taras requested."

"I would tell you all of it. All or nothing."

"Maybe that's why you don't manage the book."
"When d'you get de rest?"
"My hair doesn't grow that fast, Oleg. I had to sell what I had just to get you this."
"More shit talk from your asshole mouth."
"Wow. Your English is really coming along."
"Shit-talker."
"How much are shitakes going for these days, and are they fresh? But how would you know? You're just the salami slicer."
"D'you get out now."
"What's your problem with me, Oleg? Don't you know that hatred poisons the soul?"
"You act like al'amir, but d'you just a drunk."
"I know enough Arabic to say that's not Ukrainian."

Taras appeared behind Roland. "We are from Ukraine originally, but we came here from Georgia, from T'bilisi. That is where most of our family still lives."

"I'm guessing you guys are Muslim."
"Sunni, yes."
"I wish I'd known. I'd've bought my liquor somewhere else."
"Oleg never touches the alcohol. He's very devout."
"Still doesn't explain why he has a hard-on for me."
"You killed a brother. You—a kafir."
"Barsamian was an Armenian Christian. At least that's what I read."
"Read more. He joined the brotherhood. He served Allah. He was not kafir."
"I'm sure he didn't break through my window to serve Allah in the great jihad. The man was a psychopathic murderer. Not a holy warrior."
"Oleg knows that. He's just never liked you, and he was friendly with Mister Barsamian."
"That's okay with me." Roland fixed his eyes on Oleg. "Wish me dead. Just don't pop off with some bullshit religious reason for it."
"I use more than soap on d'yur eyeballs. Maybe d'you like acid."
"Ahh, you saw the news last night!"
"Izz on YouTube. You izz a dead man, a dead shittalker with a mushroom head."
"I'll get the rest of what I owe you in a week or two."

"Come directly to me or call me and I'll come to you."
"Agreed. No sense in agitating your pious brother."
Taras took the money from Oleg and walked Roland to the door.
"Just one more thing. I need a pint of vodka. Smirnoff blue will do."
Taras sold him the bottle and didn't charge him for the peach. Roland put the bottle in his jacket and left. He occupied the remainder of his morning in his apartment at his computer reading up on the prolific career of the inexplicably murderous Samuel Barsamian. If he was going to meet members of the victims' families, he thought it wise to familiarize himself with the unfortunate women and the details of each murder, in as much as he could find credible information on the internet. He trained his exceptional memory on the women's faces and connected them with their names. After reading a few accounts of each of the slayings, he lost his appetite for the research and linked to a live NFL broadcast to watch a football game in one corner of his screen while he pursued his favorite subjects: Ancient Megalithic Structures and Archeoastronomy. As the hour for his departure to the airport approached, he returned to his list of victims and quizzed himself on their names by looking at each face, and he found that his memory was true. Then it occurred to him to do a little research on the name *Kasabian*. After a few seconds he found the meaning: Armenian for 'butcher'. Another citation said 'son of a butcher'. *Not a lie after all. You renamed yourself after what you had become.* 'Barsamian' took a little more time, but less than a minute: 'Son of a priest,' related to the Assyrian word for fasting. He wondered if there was a word in Armenian for 'son of insurance defrauder.'

It looked like the Browns, a fourteen-point underdog against the Eagles, were finally going to cover a spread. He shut off the computer and went down to the street to wait for Singh. As the taxi pulled up, Roland patted his pocket to make sure he had his wallet. The bottle weighed snugly in his jacket next to his ribs, but he patted it anyway as one would pat the shoulder of a sidekick as they embarked on a mission together.

Today Singh's burgundy turban bore gold-colored threads woven intricately in some ancient design and sported a heavy, gold-plated kalgi pin on the forehead with a large red stone at its center.
"Wearing your Sunday best, I see."
"Sikhs do not have a holy day. No Sabbath you might say."

"Tell me that's a ruby."

"Garnet."

"Darnit!"

Singh smiled but held back a laugh. Roland sat back and drew into his nostrils a peculiar odor; one he remembered from his previous rides but only now decided to notice.

"Why no bag?"

"I'll be back tonight."

"Sounds like a business trip, except it's Sunday and you're not dressed for business."

"It's in that general vein. Did you see me on the news last night?"

"I do not watch it. I get my information from overseas."

"Well, I gave an interview on local KABC, and now a station in LA wants to put me on camera along with family members of the victims—the women Barsamian murdered."

"You are being honored. It's important to act honorably when being honored."

Roland suddenly felt relieved that his self-appointed driver-counselor had not seen his display of bravado last night.

"What's that smell—" He quickly corrected himself. "—that *fragrance* in your cab? It's very mild. Pleasant. Inoffensive. Nothing you'd pick up at a carwash."

"Sandalwood. It keeps me from forgetting where I'm from and the people who brought me into this world."

They crossed Market Street and drove down Sixth toward the freeway. A hooded figure layered in clothing that had absorbed the color of the street, a human male only by dint of his chromosomes, stepped off the curb and walked very slowly into traffic. Perhaps it was his last form of protest, forcing the traffic either to give him the right of way or run him down. No glance in the direction of the windshields from which stared the cars' perturbed occupants, no swing of the arms to indicate conformity with the living, nothing but an ambulatory mortal entity auditioning for invisibility. Singh came to a complete stop instead of swerving to avoid him. The man passed silently inches from the hood of the obedient taxi.

"What do you make of that?"

"He's given up. If someone hits him at least he'll get some attention. A ride to a bed where people will inquire after his wellbeing, people paid to care."

"And maybe a lawyer to gin up a lawsuit for him."

"He's well past plotting such a connivance."

They drove on. The City had long since scaled back its street sweeping schedule South of Market. Roland imagined that the job had been delegated to the infrequent, seasonal rain.

"Are you worried I might not act honorably?"

"A man of your great physical stature and powerful sense of personal sovereignty might find it hard to keep himself right-sized. I'm not saying you will, but then again, you're in uncharted waters and the horizon is vast. The wave that could swamp you might already be speeding imperceptibly in your direction from far, far away."

"At the risk of ruining your lovely and ominous metaphor, are you warning me to not get too big for my britches? That would be my father's translation."

"Yes. Keep yourself right-sized."

Roland thought about considering what all of that meant; but knowing that it took a dozen smart people to find two that could agree on the point of such a folksy whip of wisdom, he decided to let it go. At bottom, though, he knew where he stood in Singh's metaphor. He'd already burst his britches and was standing on the deck of a crewless sloop bobbing out of sight of land, holding nothing but a single oar, not for rowing, but for fanning its bedsheet of a sail, and with no destination toward which to bat the air.

"It's good advice, Singh. I'll keep my words right-sized. Short and to the point. I think I can manage that." He was lying, not in the sense that he knew he couldn't maintain a dignified reticence, but that he intended to do the opposite.

Roland closed his eyes and felt the sun flash across his face as the car hummed along the freeway toward the airport. Singh hummed as well, first very quietly, and then, when he sensed that it was not disturbing Roland, pressed the billows of his lungs a little harder to increase the volume. Then his lips started forming words. Singh was singing in his sandalwood-scented cab. Roland recognized the tune, then caught the words. An old 70's hit from the Beach Boys.

"What's that song?"

"It's way before your time, I'm afraid."

"I know it's the Beach Boys, but what's the name of the song."

"*Don't Worry Baby*. One of Brian Wilson's lovelier melodies."

Roland found it on his phone and pressed play. "Do you mind?"

"Not at all. Let's hear the real thing."

"Go ahead. Belt it out!"

"I can carry a tune, but not well at full volume." He sang the song perfectly in time, note for note, just loud enough to mute the traffic. Roland's impulse to chuckle at the cultural incongruity was squelched by his appreciation for the man's truly decent voice. Wilson's acapella got up pretty high, and Singh kept right there with him.

"Do the harmony. It's easy."

Down the 101 they sped, Singh doing a credible Brian Wilson and Roland backing him up with the harmony. The driver's turban bobbed side to side: "I guess I shouldn't a' shot my mouth off when I started talking about my car." Roland crooned in time. "Don't worry baby. Don't worry baby…" Singh came in over the top: "Everything's gonna turn out alright."

When the song was over, they shared a jovial laugh. A Punjabi Brit regaling a cowboy millennial with one of the finer delicacies of 1970s Southern California pop. Never happen. No matter how many parallel universes the powers lined up, that little episode got left out. Score one for the two-legged creatures powered by oxygen.

"Why are you doing all of this for me? It can't be the hundred-dollar bills."

"You called me Singh. You jumped into my cab and addressed me as Singh."

"It was actually kinda racist, by today's standards anyway. Kinda like calling an Irish guy Mick."

"However you meant it, it was correct. I am of the warrior caste. Somehow you sensed that, unless you are in the habit of addressing all men with turbans that way."

"No. You're the first. I know my way around the map of the world, and you struck me as a Sikh. So I took a chance and called you Singh."

"When you told me your story, I knew that I was meant to meet you, to be of service to you. One warrior, in name only of course, attending to the needs of a greater warrior, a man with the role of warrior thrust upon him."

"I'll have to defer to your cosmic connections there. But I certainly won't disparage the thought. Yours will be the last word on that subject."

"Which airline?"

Roland told him the name of the carrier, a low-budget outfit specializing in short domestic hops, and Singh dropped him at the curb.

"Will you need a ride back tonight?"

"I'm traveling with a friend. I'm sure he brought his car."

"Be kind to everyone you meet, even when they don't deserve it."

"Don't worry baby. Everything's gonna turn out just fine."

~~~~~

The check-in lines were jammed. The extra two inches supplied by his Laredos gave him an even greater vantage over the heads of the average travelers, and he spotted Joshua easily, standing alone in the queue, dressed in a thin wool blazer with a soft brown leather computer bag slung over one shoulder and sporting a pair of rimless, circular eyeglasses. Thusly clad and bespectacled, his agent looked like a professor. A tenured professor no less.

"Smart get-up."

Joshua eyeballed him for signs of inebriation. "Thanks for being on time."

They checked in, got their boarding passes, and walked toward the security funnel. Roland ducked into the bathroom before they got in line and went into a stall, took the pint from his jacket, shoved it down the front of his pants inside his underwear and untucked his shirt. He posed in front of the mirror to make sure the bulge was not obvious, then smiled approvingly at himself in the mirror, satisfied that he'd been sharp enough to know, although he'd only flown once, that he'd have to put his jacket through the scanner on his way through security.

Joshua was waiting for him outside the bathroom. They walked.

"So, tell me what this is going to be. What's the setup?"

"A townhall type thing. There'll be family members in a sort of gallery, and you'll be on stage with the interviewer, a woman, Felicia Burbank. She's been in the business for a while."

"Sounds pretty bizarre—like gawking at a freak."

"The focus will be on the stories of the victims. The family members will do most of the talking, I think. You'll be there to accept their gratitude."

"Hugs?"

"I would bet on it. Tears and hugs."

Joshua pulled his laptop out and set it on top of the empty satchel in a plastic tub along with his personals and set the tub on the conveyer belt to be scanned. Roland put his keys and cellphone in a small round container and did the same. As he walked through the metal detector, he felt the pressure of the bottle on his groin and entered the terminal in violation of the law.

Side by side they strolled to the gate. Knowing that he would be attached at the hip with Joshua for the rest of the day suddenly made him feel like a stranger. He to Joshua. Joshua to him. He to himself. His clothes didn't seem to hang correctly. His Laredos felt ungainly, a bit loose. His domed head announced itself to every gawker in the terminal. He sensed that Joshua felt no such unease, seemed perfectly satisfied with their partnership. *He's got nothing to worry about, nothing to lose. He's not escorting a prisoner on an extradition job. Right. Nothing criminal about it.* Such rationalizations comforted him only briefly.

"I wish I'd brought a book."

"It's a short flight."

Roland knew that Joshua knew that Roland knew it was a short flight but had chosen to state the obvious anyway.

"When you're six-six in the cheap seats there's no such thing."

"It's no worse than that cracker box of a car you drive."

"That's low. You're trying to make me feel small."

"I don't think that's possible."

Roland spotted the sports bar. An array of televisions inside monitored the early NFL games, now nearly over.

"We've got more than half an hour. I'm going to watch football and have a beer. Wanna join me?"

Joshua nodded and followed him into the bar and sat at a table while Roland purchased two large glasses of beer and brought them back to the table. In silence, the two watched the garishly uniformed multi-millionaires collide with one another on the field to the swaying emotions of a hundred thousand spectators.

"I can't help myself," said Joshua. "Questions keep rising in my brain, kinda like the bubbles in this beer. It's the journalist in me."

"On the record or off?"

"We're always off the record now, Roland. If I plan to write another story about you, I'll let you know, because then I can't represent you. And while we're on the subject, I can help you with that book you mentioned, if you ever land a book deal."

"You can ask me whatever you want, but I'll write my own book if you don't mind."

Joshua sipped his beer, probably to show solidarity with Roland. They were just drinking buddies now was the sense he conveyed.

"Why didn't you stay in college, pursue a graduate degree, work your way up the ladder in the citadels of academia? A kid with your brains, the photographic memory you claim to have, you could breeze through most any course of study."

"That's a sore subject."

"Why, because you got kicked off the volleyball team?"

"If I really wanted to play volleyball I would have transferred to another school. Even football. Hell, even baseball. I can light up the gun."

"So, what was it then? Why not pursue an academic career, become a professor or lawyer or something? That would have been easy enough for you. You certainly talk a good game."

"The Indians of the Great Plains—when they put their ear to the ground—they could tell the size of a herd of buffalo and where it was headed. Or if it was a bunch of horses, how fast they were going and if there were soldiers aboard. Then when the railroads arrived, well that was just too easy."

"You believe your own bullshit. You'd fit right in."

"You don't know me very well, Comanchero."

"Wait. I thought you were the Indian."

"I am. You're the Mexican. The Comancheros were Mexicans who brokered deals for the Comanche. Tobacco, whiskey, cattle, guns, slaves, ransoms for abducted white girls. Businessmen with no scruples."

"You're right. I shouldn't have asked. Forgive me."

"For what, being yourself? People pretend they can retract the things they say, but they can't. We're not gods. We're not even good umpires."

"Right. If you apologize to someone, then you need to make amends. You can't just say forget it and let bygones be bygones. Nothing is forgotten."

"Gimme a break, Roland. *Forgive me*—it's just something people say. I'm sorry I asked—sorry for myself."

"Forgiveness suborns pity—it takes the verb 'to beg'. I would never use the word so casually, because it involves a moral transaction."

"Uh-huh." Joshua took a sip of beer then bobbed his head in mock understanding. Roland stared as though to take his measure. He would complete his thought and complete it out loud, and there was nothing Joshua could do to stop it, except perhaps to get up and walk out. Not that Roland was unaware of the excessive liberty he was taking with his captive audience, but his overriding concern was making himself properly understood by the man who'd chosen to represent him.

"And once the transaction is complete, the offense is expunged. It's a coin that's lost its value. Now the letting go of resentment—that's a horse of a different color."

"You mind if I interrupt?"

"You don't need to ask."

"What has any of this got to do with not pursuing an advanced degree?"

Roland drank half the schooner in one tilt. He was, indeed, thirsty from his night out. He set the thick-bottomed glass down with a deliberate thunk. He leaned back, raised his eyes, and in a show of contemplation brought his ten fingertips together to form a cage. "It has everything to do with why I crossed the bay to gut fish on the pier instead of gliding into the life of a graduate student."

"Everything? Well, I guess that settles it."

"Annihilation. What the old Arapaho heard when he pressed his ear to the ground was not the rumble of a train—it was progress, progress toward annihilation. I heard the same thing, and I didn't want to participate, to accept life on the reservation of cultural annihilation. When people do things that are wrong and refuse to admit it, refuse to beg forgiveness and change their ways, they leave a whole lot of resentment in their wake. I'm not cut out to swallow my resentment even if it means that I can flourish among the destroyers. So I lit out on my own."

"Annihilation of what?" Joshua appeared to be taking him more seriously now, as a doctor might give ear to a patient describing his symptoms.

"Meaning."

"Meaning?"

"The meaning of words—we've been over this."

"Now it's your turn to give an example. Indulge me."

"Violence. Most of the kids and teachers in universities, especially the top universities, have never been in a fight. Never been punched in the gut so hard they fell down and rolled around unable to breathe. Never been cracked on the jaw to where their vision narrowed and blurred. Never experienced genuine fear of being subjected to lasting pain or even death."

"Isn't that a good thing?"

"Not if you don't appreciate it. Not if you don't study it."

"Who says they don't?"

Roland grew annoyed and looked up at the orchestrated violence of the NFL arrayed on separate televisions above the bar. Then he looked back at Joshua and gestured with his chin at the football games.

"When those guys were in college, do you think they needed safe spaces to protect them from harmful words? Don't answer. Obviously, they didn't. When I started hearing that words, simple ideas, even mathematical principles, could be construed as violence, I knew the university was not for me. I'd've been able to grind my way through to an advanced degree, but at the cost of my molars and my dignity."

"You were born in the wrong century, I'm afraid."

"Precisely. I found myself in the wrong century—in the kiddie pool of the wrong century."

Joshua rolled his eyes a flick. "I had no idea that Berkeley had devolved so precipitously."

"You wouldn't know the difference; you're a journalist. You're soul's already in hawk."

"Then tell me. They won't be calling our flight for a while yet."

"A prestigious university is like a beachfront resort with a swimming pool right up next to the ocean. The kids are splashing around with their inflatable toys, fighting over their isms and their ologies. *It's my turn to play* with the Derrida! Ok, but you have to let me use the Foucault. Marcuse me, but I can see the crack in your Butler. You get the idea."

"Is there a lifeguard in this metaphor? Maybe you're the lifeguard."

"No. A lifeguard would be too much patriarchy. I'm standing in the shallow end looking out at the ocean."

"What's out in the ocean?"

Roland scanned the football games to delay his answer. While he had no action today, he was preoccupied with what might have been. So, he made Joshua wait. *What's in the ocean? The whale? Ship-swallowing vortices? The precipitous edge of the Earth?* He would make him wait the way Melville made the reader wait for the big showdown with the great albino sperm. Chapters and chapters of waiting—and was it worth it? For the patient reader, certainly. Whalers on the hunt had to wait for days, even weeks, sometimes months. Readers—students—have it easy, he thought. Too easy. He tapped the butt of his glass on the table, annoyed at what he was seeing—no, at what he was feeling. He could have made a killing on some of these games, but he'd lost the privilege to play against the Andruko's book, and he had no other means of placing a wager. He'd been greedy and those shady Ukrainian Muslim booze merchant bookies had let him get in over his head.

"You look pissed off. I'll drop it."

Roland looked at Joshua and allowed his thoughts to coalesce. Once his mind was right, he drained his glass. He could tell that Joshua was pretending not to notice that Roland was trying to irritate him.

"Wild Bill."

"Oh, so we're back in the Ol' West now. Wild Bill Hickock is riding the waves?"

Roland put on a Texas twang. "Procure me another drink there, pard, and I'll bring my speculations to a satisfactoral conclusion."

"You break your leg since we sat down?"

Roland lifted his chin and exposed his neck to show respect and got up and went to the bar and bought another beer and came back and sat down and drank and nodded a few times before continuing.

"Not Hickock, Shakespeare—the ocean is Wild Bill Shakespeare. Might as well toss in the whole Western canon. It's a terrifying prospect, to leave the kiddie pool and dive into the tumultuous unknown. Great literature can reject you that way the ocean spits you out when you don't know how to swim. I knew that college was not for me when I could get the same number of credits for deconstructing cis-gender oppression in the *Brady Bunch* as I could for studying the full raft of Shakespeare's sonnets."

"Like I said, born in the wrong century."

"Maybe the century is just plain wrong. Maybe the current millennium gave birth to an imbecile of a century."

"How could anyone—especially someone your age—know enough to say that? Sounds a tad narcissistic."

"I have a bullshit detector."

"Everyone says they have a bullshit detector."

"Mine is state of the art."

"Mine is at least standard issue, and you just now set it off."

"I'm speaking empirically."

Joshua looked amused. "So, we've stepped out of the metaphorical into the scientific? You're saying you can prove it."

"Not in a laboratory. But I can explain how it works and you can judge for yourself."

"I'm game." Joshua lifted his glass and leaned back in his chair. "I'd love to know the inner workings of your mind."

"Not my mind—my brain."

"Oh, there's a difference?"

Roland gestured toward the football games. "The brain crunches the data. The mind decides whether or not to bet and if so how much."

"We were talking about your advanced bullshit detector—you're saying that's brain, not mind."

"Yes. My brain will remember anything I tell it to. As you said, a huge advantage for a college student—any kind of student. It doesn't store everything I see or read or hear. That would overload the memory. It would be impossible to get anything done."

"That makes sense."

"So, I have a choice. I can select what I want to remember. My mind is what decides what it wants my brain to retain."

"I'm following you so far."

"Now here's where it gets interesting. When I read something or even hear something that is very well constructed or crystal clear in its brilliance, my brain will remember it all on its own, sometimes perfectly, without me prompting it. Shakespeare is a perfect example, but it happens with all great poetry. It sticks to my brain with little or no effort. Yeats once wrote to his countrymen—*Irish poets learn your trade, sing whatever is well made.* He understood. But my best example is the Bible. I've read any number of translations, but the *King James* sticks. And it's probably the least authoritative when it comes to literal accuracy; but the gents who worked on that venerable tome were trained lyricists. The brain doesn't lie. The mind is a fabricator."

Joshua stood up and took out his phone and snapped a few pictures of the TVs arrayed above the bar. "Take a look at the games and remember as much as you can—tell your brain to do its best."

"How long do you want me to remember it for?"

"At least until we get back."

Roland studied each of the six screens for about five seconds. "Done." He sat back down.

"I'll test you later." They sat in silence for a minute or two before Joshua spoke again. "So, that's why you gave the Heisman straight-arm to the academic world—because your mind didn't like the bullshit that your brain would be asked to retain. Is that fair to say?"

"Let me put it this way. No university needs a tall chiseled white man waxing rhapsodic on the masterpieces of English literature. I'm a ready-made symbol of patriarchy and white oppression, so Shakespeare's genius, professed by me, would be diminished by my very presence."

"Sounds like a cop-out to me."

"I won't deny it. I'll cop to the cop-out. Maybe I'm wrong—maybe it wasn't the iron horse I heard rumbling across the distance plain. Maybe it was just a few bison out for a jog."

The call came to board the aircraft. "That's us."

"You gonna finish that?"

Joshua dumped the remainder of his beer into Roland's glass so it raised a high foam and walked rapidly to the line now forming. Roland drank it down and wiped the foam from his nostrils then took his place in line next to Joshua. The low-budget airline did not assign seats, so the passengers were eager to jostle their way onto the aircraft and squeeze themselves into the available confinements. Roland found a seat with legroom in the emergency exit row and signaled Joshua that he was situated. They wouldn't sit together. This was not an extradition run.

~~~~~

KTLA Channel 5, the TV station that sprung for the flight, had reserved a car in Joshua's name. He had a choice between a Suzuki Vitara and a Kia Sportage and gave Roland the decision. Roland glanced at the two models. They both looked stamped from the same mold.

"I'll go with the Korean product."

"Why, because it's Korean?"

"Because it's not Japanese."

"Not happy with your Nissan?"

"Not happy with the chief of police—racist little fucker."

"How do you mean?"

"He called me an *antediluvian*."

"When? Friday afternoon?"

"I met him only the one time."

"Well, that's hardly racist. And you're still chewing on it?"

"Oh, it was racist. He definitely meant it as racist."

"Antediluvian isn't a race."

"The mighty men of old, men of great renown—they came down and mated the human women, the ones they liked the best. Genesis six, verse four."

"Because of that arrest outside Bix?"

"You know about that?"

"I'm pretty tight with the inspector—I asked for the background on you, and he gave me what he had."

"That was a bullshit arrest."

"Fine. I don't care. I'm trying to figure out what you're saying here. He compared you to the pre-flood giants in the Bible, and you're saying that's racist."

"We nuked his county, deposed its emperor, reduced his island to economic servitude. Those Nephilim characters were the ones who brought advanced technology to the human race. He was calling me the Prometheus of atomic weapons—because I'm a big white man. That's racism."

"You think Chief Maruyama knows the Bible that well? Maybe he just has a good vocabulary. Maybe he just meant primitive, like someone would call someone a Neanderthal."

"No. It's just like Farrakhan calling us the blue-eyed devils."

"Us?"

"You're right. He's a lot harder on the Jews. You guys are cockroaches."

They got into the car and entered the strangle of minibusses, vans, and taxis competing for the exits out of LAX. Roland sat in the passenger seat, his head jerking left and right, distracted by the vehicular chaos, until Joshua found the freeway entrance he was looking for.

"You ever been to Los Angeles?"

"Never been south of San Jose."

"I was born and raised down here. Most of my family is still here."

"I don't see a city anywhere."

"Downtown is a few miles away. Los Angeles isn't really a city in the usual sense. It lays out more like spilt milk on a wrinkled tablecloth. There are even separate little cities inside Los Angeles—Beverly Hills, West Hollywood. When people say LA, they generally mean LA County, which is vast."

"Where's the TV station?"

"Hollywood, just west of the city."

"Where's Glendale?"

"North—other side of Dodger Stadium."

"Where are we going now?"

"Old Los Angeles. Chinatown. There's an old café I'd like to go for lunch. You'll dig it."

Roland fiddled with the radio, made a game of identifying all the different languages up and down the band. To Joshua, it might have looked like another effort to annoy him.

"What are you doing?"

"Do you think that's Korean? I know it's not Japanese, and I'm pretty sure it's not Chinese."

"I haven't driven a child around in a long time. Never one as clever as you."

"I've already counted five different languages: English, Spanish, Chinese, Persian, and probably Korean. I doubt there's another American city with more radio diversity. Heck, I bet you there's a Hebrew program for your ancient people somewhere on the dial in some obscure time slot."

"I'm glad you're in a multicultural mood. We're going to a French café in Chinatown just down the block from a Mexican open-air marketplace. You might call it the birthplace of LA."

"I see a lot of construction up ahead. I'd settle for a basket of tacos from a food truck."

The car headed north on the Harbor Freeway, the 110, approaching Staples Center. Beyond that lay a sun-drenched cluster of high rises interspersed with construction cranes. In the background, the brown and barren San Gabriel foothills dwarfed the little metropolis.

"It's more for me than for you. I haven't been for a very long time."

"Where'd you grow up—Beverly Hills? I hear there's lots of Jews in Beverly Hills."

"A lot of rich Jews. I'm a lowly Sherman Oaks Jew. That's in the north valley. My dad used to take us kids into the city all the time."

Roland wasn't listening. He peered through the chemical haze into the distance to the east, where rose the southernmost peaks of the Sierra Nevadas, yet to receive their annual snows. His squint became a wince, a pang of regret. His missed unblighted Idaho. This place had no natural right to exist, he thought. It fed off water diverted from the Colorado River. A few hundred years ago it was all but desolate. No wonder Mexico let it go with barely a fight. Now it supported ten million people. Someday something had to give. Perhaps the San Andrea Fault.

~~~~~

They passed the LA Courthouse and headed up Hill Street then made a quick right turn on Ord and drove down the narrow road to their destination. Its sign, in florid red cursive, read *Philippe the Original, since 1908*, one of the oldest continuously operating restaurants in Los Angeles and self-proclaimed originator of the French Dip Sandwich.

"Is this it? I like it already."

"Everything is good. I recommend the pig feet."

"So much for Leviticus."

"You remember, I told you sister I wasn't strictly observant."

"One can forgive the occasional bacon burger, but chomping down on the cloven hooves of Satan's herd—won't that touch off a little lightning storm over your yarmulke?"

"You've watched too many cartoons. I just thought you might give me the gentile's perspective on the delicacy. I've actually never tried them."

"No feet for me, no feet of any kind. I tried chicken feet at a dim sum brunch not long ago and swore off feet. By the way, where's Chinatown? You said this place was near Chinatown."

"We went through it. There were a few seafood buffets back on Hill Street you might have missed."

"I spotted a pruned-up Chinese man with a pushcart sitting on a bus bench. I guess he's the last man, and he wasn't even standing."

"A lot more coolies settled in San Francisco than down here for some reason."

"I wonder if China knows about this insult. If I were running China I'd drone in a handful of tactical rockets on this lame-ass excuse for a Chinatown, just on principle. Not enough to touch off a full-scale conflict, but enough to put the other Chinatowns of the world on notice."

"If you were running China? You're not even running you."

~~~~~

Philippe the Original had that old-world feel. Sawdust floors, pickled eggs on display in enormous glass jars soaking in purple brine. Aproned, paper-hatted order takers. Lightning-fast busboys with bulging forearms. The café was built below street level, furnished with long Formica-topped tables surrounded by tall four-legged stools, a newsstand in one corner, several small dining rooms partitioned off from the main hall, lines of customers queued up at the long glass display counter where the meals were speedily assembled on plastic trays and carried away to the tables. The kind of place where you're expected to know your order once you get to the front of the line.

Roland carried his tray of French dip sandwiches and two bottles of Budweiser to the table where Joshua was waiting with his sandwich and a lemonade. It was three o'clock and Roland had to be at the KTLA studio by four to get ready for the five o'clock Sunday special broadcast.

"Are you nervous? I would be."

"I get nervous only when I go to the dentist."

"Why's that?"

"Because I rarely go to the dentist. I used to get nervous before a competition."

"Competition? You mean a volleyball match?"

"A fight—a martial arts competition. You can progress through the rainbow belts without sparring."

"Rainbow belts?"

"The brightly colored ones—yellow red green blue. Strip mall dojos hand them out for demonstrating proper forms. I'm not knocking it—it's great exercise. But anyone who puts on a black belt and hasn't had to fight for it is a disgrace to the tradition. I don't care what discipline it's for."

"Getting nervous before a fight sounds pretty normal, though I wouldn't know from experience."

"It's not what you're thinking."

Roland opened one of his sandwiches and squirted hot mustard on the roast beef and closed the roll and dipped it in the bowl of au jus and wolfed it down in a few bites. He wiped his mouth with a napkin. "I understand the big huge sign on the roof and the long lines inside. It's warranted." Half of the sentence was garbled by the mouth of his beer bottle as he washed down the food.

"It's a regular culinary landmark. Dodger Stadium is just up the hill. My dad would take us here before the ballgame. I have great memories of this place, of those days."

"Is your father still alive?"

"Yes."

"How's he doing?"

"Not bad. I check in regularly. I'll see him over the holidays with the whole clan."

"Do you tell him that you love him?"

Joshua filled his mouth with a huge bite and sucked down his lemonade through a straw, letting the question pass. Roland saw he'd overstepped. Joshua looked at him, but Roland would not meet his eyes.

"Why did you get nervous before a fight?"

Roland could look at Joshua now, thankful for the reprieve.

"I didn't care about losing, about getting hit, or even getting hurt."

"Then why?"

"Most fights, I mean real fights, out in the world, street fights, bare knucks; most of those fights end up on the ground. In real life people—men—don't bounce around on the balls of their feet jabbing and swinging. The stronger guy tries to take down the weaker guy and sit on his chest and pound his face in."

"Yeah, but you weren't talking about street fights. You said competition, sparring matches."

"I was always worried I might hurt someone—hurt 'em bad."

"You trying to tell me you've got a bad temper?"

"No. Anger—*wrath* as it's known on the list of deadly sins—that's the one I have the least."

"So, what were you worried about?"

"My focus. Speed, power and execution all marshaled by my superior focus. It goes back to the mind-brain thing. My brain is in charge when I fight—there's no emotion, no fear or anger or joy."

"Is that how it was?"

Roland shook his head, not to answer no, but to signal that the question was off-limits. "I was loaded. All I can tell you is that he would have survived if he hadn't put that knife into play."

Joshua let the matter drop. They finished their meal. He doled out tidbits of LA history—the sordid politics, the graft. "We had nothing on Boston, New York, or Chicago when it came to corruption, but when a city grows as fast as LA did, the people that paved the way to progress made sure they got fat."

"I've seen the Polanski movie. Always wondered why he called it Chinatown when the story had to do with crooked land deals in the San Fernando Valley."

"It signifies the inscrutable. *Don't try to understand it—it's Chinatown.* I'm gonna start calling you Chinatown."

"Fine. Whaddaya wanna know?"

"Deadly sins—what's your chief deadly sin?"

"I bet you don't even know what they are or even how many. I could say perfectionism and you wouldn't know the difference."

"You're making my point. That's evasive—Chinatown."

"Lust then—the ever-reliable lust."

"You're twenty-five—that's too easy. How about gluttony?"

Roland leaned back and opened his arms to display his physique. "Do I look like a glutton to you?"

"No. But you drink like one."

Roland tilted his second bottle of Budweiser and drank it down. "Where to next?"

"Olvera Street is just a short walk. We have time. Be a shame not to at least take a peek."

"You're the guide. I like this town so far."

They bussed their trays and headed for the exit, Joshua leading the way. He opened the door and stopped and turned to Roland. "Perfectionism—that would come under Pride. The sin that rules them all, my precious."

Roland nodded and raised a forefinger and brought it down in an empathic stroke. "Score one for the cunning Jew."

~~~~~

They walked down Alameda Street. Roland felt the sun on his head as though for the first time since he'd had it shaved and remembered the warning words of his saucy coiffeuse. No sunscreen had he. The nerves in his scalp were beginning to sizzle.

"I'm gonna buy a hat if I can find one I like."

"They'll be a lot to choose from."

Olvera Street lay a few blocks away. The entrance, at the junction of Alameda and Cesar Chaves, was angled in such a way that it fairly funneled in the foot traffic. It was a walk-street, a tourist trap, not open to cars. Vendors' booths were squeezed together on either side of an esplanade that led the browsers south into a wider shopping plaza. A comic book could not have clashed its colors more violently, the impossibly bright greens, blues, pinks, yellows, reds, and purples making it hard to focus on a single object. Dopy-faced marionettes, un-tunable half-sized guitars, serapes, huarache sandals with tire-tread soles, terrifying skull masks in keeping with the upcoming Day of the Dead, painted wooden tops, and countless other overpriced items of remarkably cheap manufacture. The shade beneath the awnings and trees provided Roland temporary relief from the offending rays.

"I'm amazed this is legal."

"What are you talking about?"

"Cultural stereotyping gone berserk. If you showed up on a college campus decked out in this crap, you'd be torn limb from limb."

"Well, I don't suppose you can stop Mexicans from being excessively Mexican."

Roland watched a kid of nine or ten practicing with a cup-and-ball toy. The wooden device, painted red, yellow, and green, consisted of a long handle affixed to a small wooden cup, beneath which was tied a string, sixteen or eighteen inches long, that was threaded through a wooden ball. The little fucker caught it every time, his role there evidently to demonstrate mastery of the toy. His father or uncle or whoever was running the booth observed disinterestedly. The boy caught the ball then caught Roland watching him.

"You wanna try it, mister?"

"No hablo Ingles."

"¿Quieres probar?"

"No hablo Español."

"That's all I got."

"No Chinese?"

"You don't even speak Chinese."

"I bet I speak more Chinese than you do."

"I don't believe you. You lied once already."

"I come all the way to the world-famous Los Angeles Chinatown to practice my Chinese, and all I get is a Mexican kid who speaks perfect English."

The proprietor laughed quietly, but the kid remained serious. Joshua took a few steps backward and pretended to peruse a display of horrific skull masks at the adjacent booth.

"Then go to China then, mister. No Chinese here today." He pointed north to indicate there were Chinese people in that direction.

"I want one of those ball-catcher toys. It's one of the last things on Earth not made in China."

"I don't know where things are made."

Roland reached out his hand. "Lemme try."

The boy handed Roland the device, the human race's perfect test of eye-hand coordination. The cup was not much larger than the ball. Roland failed on his first attempt and screwed his lips to one side in exaggerated consternation.

"It's not hard."

"Are you the cup or the ball?"

"I'm a boy—Julio."

"Julio, you're the Yoda master of this thing and I'm the young Jedi. Would you advise me *to become one with the ball* or *one with the cup?*"

Julio puzzled over the question and looked to the man, almost certainly his father. The man tilted his head to one side and widened his eyes to say *you're on your own, son.*

"Be the string."

"How do you say *I'm the little brat* in Español?"

"Soy el pequeño mocoso."

"Never forget it. Say it to the mirror every morning."

"Eres un gran pendejo."

Roland looked at the father to see if he approved of such language, and the father apparently thought that Roland was asking for a translation.

"He say you're a big pussy."

"Most men are. It's an international fact."

"Five dollars." Julio beckoned with his fingers.

"How about ten dollars and you give me five chances? Two dollars off for every time I get one in."

Joshua moved in closer to witness the negotiations.

"Start at eleven dollars."

"Eres el gran diablo. Just like those masks."

Julio ignored the slight. "You make four, you take us. Three we break even. Less than three, we take you."

"What if I make all five?"

"Then you're a gran timador and I'll kick your nuts so then you can speak Chinese." The boy demonstrated by bending over with both hands clamped over his groin and letting out an HOOOOOOOOAAAA in mock agony. His version, apparently, of a Chinese exclamation of pain.

"I'm pretty sure that's Japanese if the old karate movies can be trusted."

"You like to sound smart, but I don't buy it."

"Well, I'm buying this, for one price or another. Here goes." He tried and missed. He concentrated harder and missed again, but this time the ball rimmed out of the cup.

"Be the cup. I'm going with *be the cup.*"

"You look more like the ball." Joshua sprayed spit from his own sudden laughter.

Roland made the next three. "I could do this all day. Maybe I'll come back sometime, and we can have a showdown."

Julio's adult demeanor melted into a child's grudging disappointment. "That was pretty good if this was your first time."

"I promise you it was." Roland handed him a five-dollar bill and took the toy and put it in his pocket.

"Come back tomorrow and we'll have a showdown."

"I'll see what I can do. Do they have any cowboy hats around here?"

Julio pointed him toward the plaza, where the quality merchandise was sold—purses, belts, hats, jackets. In a matter of minutes, the new cup-and-ball apprentice, a hundred dollars lighter, strode back tall in his Laredos under a white, wide-brimmed, Alamo hat curled up at the edges with a forward sloping *gus* crown. He weaved through the crowd up Cesar Chaves Avenue where Joshua was still browsing and stopped to show Julio his purchase.

"Whaddya think of my Pancho Villa hat, little jefe?"

"You'd be the first one I'd shoot." The boy blew imaginary smoke off the tip of his pistol finger.

"Good boy. Take out the big dog first. End the war before it starts with one decisive shot."

"Come back when you get five in a row. Then we can talk. We'll use the two-foot string."

Roland removed his new gaucho chapeau and swept it low across his ankles as he bowed to the child and, upon that flourish, departed the scene with Joshua in tow.

"I have a question."

"You've exceeded your daily quota already and we still have a long day ahead."

"You don't seem the least bit drunk, but something tells me you wouldn't act like this if you were perfectly sober."

"That's not a question."

"The question is: *Am I right?*"

"You are. I drink to make life more interesting. And I can hold my liquor."

The first part was true, but the appended boast rang false to his ears, like the words of a coach urging his team to victory at the tail end of a lost cause.

Over the past year or two, more times than he cared to remember, he'd woken up in various places, *come to*, really, from a blackout, come to from blackouts perplexed at his whereabouts and frightened that he could not, try as he might, recall how or when he got there. Had, in fact, come to behind bars.

"You can't fault me for trying to understand you."

"You're right, I can't. And you can't fault me for asking you a favor."

"What's that?"

"If at any point along this journey upon which we have lately embarked someone should ask you—I don't know—ANYTHING AT ALL about something I've said or done, please do me a favor and tell them that you don't understand me and that you've given up trying. And since you don't want to compromise your veracity, I suggest you start right now."

"Giving up trying?"

"To understand me—yes."

"Agreed. I understand you perfectly."

"Asshole."

"Careful there, you might smile and ripple that stern demeanor."

~~~~~

KTLA 5 headquarters occupied an entire city block on Sunset Boulevard in Hollywood, just west of Little Armenia. Joshua circled the adjacent blocks in search of a parking spot and passed the Museum of Death just north of the station. A twelve-foot-tall painting of a grinning human skull marked the entrance to the place.

"I don't suppose your pop took the kiddies to that little attraction."

"No. Not remotely kosher."

He found a spot about half a block from the station entrance. The owners had decided to let the station's antiquated and long-since obsolete broadcast tower stand at one corner of the property as a symbol, or maybe an advertisement. Halfway up, where the tower began to narrow to a point, hung an enormous number five.

"That skull face belongs up there."

"Why's that?"

"They're broadcasting some scary shit tonight. A regular death pageant."

"I don't think that's how they see it."

They made their way through the gate into the main building and checked in with the guard, a black man who gave Roland a friendly look. *Is that his celebrity smile, the widest one he'll crack without spoiling his professional cool? Or is he just an amiable fellow approaching the end of his shift?*

"You think he recognized me?"

"When his shift is over, he's going to tear out that page of his sign-in book and sell it on the internet. Take his wife out to dinner on the proceeds."

"I'm actually a little nervous, since you wanted to know."

"Look, Roland, this is just a warm-up. Remember, you're not the center of attention tonight. You can get away with saying very little."

He followed Joshua down the hallway. He seemed to know where he was going.

"You're kidding, right?"

"No. I'm sure I already told you. We talked about this—about the victims' families. You were invited just to…"

"Stop."

Joshua slowed but kept walking.

"Goddamnit, stop."

Joshua stopped, turned around, and looked up at him mutely, genuinely confused.

"Are you pretending to be stupid just to piss me off, or are you actually an idiot?"

"No, and, I guess, no."

"Most idiots don't know they're idiots. They die peacefully in their mechanical beds thinking they acquitted themselves admirably in life."

"I'm not sure what you're talking…"

"I'm a little nervous not because I think I'm about to be the center of attention. I'm a little nervous because I know I'm going to have to *make myself* the center of attention. Up ahead is an occasion to which I must rise, my friend. The delivery boy is going to try to steal the scene from Lucille Ball."

"You're right. I guess I'm an idiot."

"Thank you. Now I'm not nervous. Not anymore."

Joshua found the door he was looking for and rapped on it lightly. A woman opened the door.

"I was just about to come looking for you two."

Felicia Burbank stood five-foot-six in her heels, not counting her trussed-up russet hairdo. She wore a black suit that emphasized her slim waist. Pinned to one lapel was a white porcelain rose with a silver stem, finely crafted. The bridge of her nose bore dents from her absent eyeglasses. A thin colorless down covered her upper lip, rouged red to match the other. It was a mouth well-practiced in the forming of words, her face feminine and stern, though her eyes offered the compassion of a grandmother. She was thirty-seven, by now a second-stringer at the station, and no one knew her given name, but no one thought it ended in Burbank.

She extended her hand up to Roland. "Felicia Burbank. Thank you for coming down."

Roland bent to shake her hand. "Thank you for the free ride, for me and my friendly driver."

"He's a driver, alright—drives a hard bargain."

Roland dropped her hand and looked over at Joshua for him to say something about that. Was there a stipend he was not aware of? *Are you skimming already?*

"The car. I pushed for an upgrade to get you some legroom."

She led them to the makeup room where a silent Asian woman performed the same ministrations on Roland's face and head as he'd received the day before, though to a lesser extent since the set would not be brightly lit.

"How's this going to work?" he asked the host.

"We'll use our public meeting room. It seats about thirty. The victims' family members—the ones who've joined us—will sit in the seats on the floor with me in the center and you next to me. There'll be two empty chairs. I'll call the family members down, no more than two at a time, to eulogize."

"In what order?"

"In the order their loved ones were murdered."

Roland had another question in mind but held it. He'd already asked two and the second one was of the stupid variety. He sat and gave Joshua a look that said *quit staring at me*.

"I don't want to sit right next to them. I want to sit on the other side of you."

"You'll be to my right, and they'll be to my left, next to the screen where we'll project the pictures they've given us."

"Okay. I'll just let it unfold."

"You're the guest of honor. We won't be profiling you."

"I'm glad to hear you say that."

"Someone will come for you shortly." Felicia Burbank left the room.

Roland closed his eyes and tried to empty his mind, tried to shut out all sensations: the sound of the air conditioner, the touch of the brush on his head, a buzzing from who-knows-what, the smell of the cosmetics, the smell of the woman attending to him. He conjured a memory of himself as a youth on his back in a rowboat in the middle of Lake Pend Orielle, eyes closed and listening to the soft water lick the sides of his craft, the breeze fluttering a distant sail and the chopping sound made by a fiberglass hull cleaving the skin of the lake, the shadow of bird passing over his sun-warmed face, the sound of his voice humming through pursed lips. It was the meditational ommmmm of a monk releasing his soul for a welcome respite outside the body so beholden to the Earth. But Roland's soul stayed put, refused to leave the office while there was still a remnant of anxiety left to measure. He opened his eyes to find that Joshua had gone. *Good.* He hadn't even heard him leave.

A man entered the room. "It's time to go, Mister Hazzard." Roland thanked the woman and got out of the chair.

"I need to use the men's room please."

The man pointed to the bathroom door. Roland went in and leaned his back against the sink, but he was too tall to use it that way, as it was more the height of a stool, and he was not about to sit on it. He stood with his back to the mirror and took out the bottle and unscrewed the cap and drank a quarter of its contents in one pull. He was glad he'd specified the hundred-proof blue label Smirnoff or else he might have had to drink the whole pint. Smirnoff blue was not too harsh and even warm was guzzleable. His eyes watered a little, portents of the promised sense of ease and comfort that would quickly follow. He tipped the bottle into his mouth again and drank, then gave it a square assessment. Exactly half remained. He reduced it again with a third swig and returned it to his pocket with a few ounces left for future use. Then he flushed the urinal, washed his hands, and looked into the mirror. The running water made him have to pee, so he took care of that, flushed again, and went out.

The lights angled toward the stage made it hard to make out the faces in the audience. He could sort the women from the men, the thin from the portly, the collars from the crew necks. His head bobbled from waves of euphoria. He saw Joshua in the back row and had to stop himself from smiling and waving. Felicia Burbank touched his hand a second before the red camera light went on.

"Good evening viewers and thank you for tuning in to our live broadcast for what promises to be an emotional and, we hope, cathartic experience for all concerned. We've opened up our town hall space tonight and invited the families of the victims of the notorious Glendale Butcher to memorialize the young women they lived with and loved and whose loss they will feel for the rest of their lives. Our guests come from nearby Glendale, where the now-deceased savage predator embarked upon his murderous spree, and also from cities and towns in the Southwest, Northwest, Midwest, and as far away as Florida. Many of the families understandably moved away from the places where their daughter, or sister, or niece, or cousin was killed, killed for no apparent reason, to distance themselves from reminders of their pain. We will celebrate the lives of each of the innocent victims with family photos and personal stories and, in doing so, we hope, empathize with their grief and celebrate their courage in moving forward with their lives."

Relaxed as he was, Roland squirmed a little at the lachrymose effusions of the seasoned professional. She continued.

"And here beside me is a different guest, a man some of you might recognize if you've been following the news lately, the man who, by apparent happenstance, killed the Glendale Butcher in self-defense and possibly saved the life of his neighbor, a young woman who, like most of his unfortunate victims, was stalked by the psychopath." She paused to breathe and assess the attentiveness of her audience.

"Roland Hazzard…" She motioned toward him with her open palm, "…has agreed to meet the family members who've joined us today to perhaps more firmly solidify the closure that, at least for some, his actions have provided."

A smatter of clapping was interrupted by a whoop from one of the males in attendance. Roland squinted through the lights to mark his admirer but made no gesture of acknowledgment. Other members of the audience turned and looked at the man who had whooped.

"There won't be time for a lot of applause tonight with all the people we have to meet. Would Mister and Missus Penland from Glendale California please come join me in the chairs?"

The graying parents of the first victim, one Sarah Penland, came forward and accepted the embrace of the host. The father shook Roland's hand with a sort of obligatory formality but with little pressure or warmth applied. His wife, Mrs. Penland, regarded Roland with a vaguely contemptuous cursory appraisal. He understood with telepathic certainty that the couple considered his appearance there as the kind of exploitative, self-serving fame-grabbing that, far from honoring the memory of Sarah, pissed a smiley face on her grave. He could not permit such unconcealed judgmental piety to go unredressed and listened closely to the dialogue that ensued between the host and the still grieving Penlands for an opportunity to interject.

"I know she was close to graduating from, where was it...?"

"The UCLA nursing program. She was carrying a brand-new pair of nursing shoes to her car in the parking lot of the Glendale Galleria when the vicious coward walked up from behind and, well, I'd rather not say it. It was a great loss not only to her family and friends but to society as a whole. Her ambition was to be of maximum service."

Mrs. Penland, at first alarmed at Roland's rudeness in answering a question meant for her and her husband, was forced to hold her tongue and nod in solemn agreement. In the trailing silence, before the host could re-take the reins, Roland added, "I am truly sorry for your loss. I have a sister about the same age a she would have been today."

A few more expressions of condolence and gratitude between the host and the parents brought to a close segment number one in the hour-long pageant of young, throat-slit white women dispatched in or around places named Glendale. *That went well,* he told himself. *One down and six to go.* Roland felt confident he could recall something noteworthy from each case. The hardest part, he figured, is sliding it in at the right time. Not forcing it. Not showing off. *The last thing I'd want is for people to think I'm here to make this all about...* But before he could finish the thought, Felicia Burbank advanced the proceedings.

"Would the loved ones of Deborah Lathower," she read from a card, "Missus Patricia Lathower and her sister, Deborah's Aunt Genevieve, come join me now please?" Felicia Burbank would more than earn her pay tonight, maintaining a solicitous yet professional compassion, all the while moving things along so everyone would receive roughly equal time. Of course, she had not figured on Roland eating up minutes by inserting his voice very often, but her schedule was not in jeopardy as yet. The women took their seats and looked up at the photograph projected on the screen.

The mother spoke first. "So kind of you to invite us to remember our dear Deborah."

Felicia Burbank welcomed them and briefly recounted the basic facts of the crime.

"She was discovered in the morning by the groundskeeper at the Chevy Chase Country Club, hidden behind a toolshed if I recall, not far from the parking lot where her car was left with the trunk wide open."

"The police think he must have followed her there," the mother said. "Her credit card shows that she filled her tank on Verdugo Road just before heading up the canyon for her golf lesson. He may have seen her alone pumping gas and followed her."

Felicia Burbank chimed in. "The police did not initially connect the two cases."

"If he'd stopped with Deborah, they still couldn't be sure. It's impossible to say that two cuts came from the exact same knife, but after five or six, with all the other similarities, the odds go way up."

"Mister Hazzard, I had no idea you were so familiar with the cases and had such expertise in criminal forensics."

"Most science starts with common sense, but more to the point I've spent some time reading about these cases. And since I don't know the names on those note cards, I bid you proceed." He gestured with his hand in an exaggerated display of courtesy when he said the word 'bid.'

From the gallery a few hesitant chuckles and a muttered exchanges as of: *Did he really just say that? Who does he think he is? Is he trying to take over the show?* His remarks took the camerawoman by surprise, and by the time she reacted and began to pan his way, he'd zipped his lip and settled back into his chair with his legs crossed.

"Are you sure, Mister Hazzard? Nothing else to add?" Evidently, she'd taken a course in interrogative sarcasm at some distinguished school of broadcast journalism or other.

The camerawoman took the cue and pivoted to him. "Yes." He straightened up. "She had the most gorgeous eyes, a rare beauty in my opinion. Could have strolled the wide red carpets."

Felicia Burbank finished the segment and thanked the women for coming. Roland rose with them and offered his hand. The mother shook it limply and the aunt clasped it tightly with both of hers. Roland nodded to her obligingly and glanced at the host to make sure she was watching.

Victim number three had not been blessed with pulchritude, and unlike the relatives of Deborah Lathower, Jenny Breining's father and sister were not so stoic. As soon as Felicia Burbank seated them and clicked on the image of their slain beloved, the two clutched hands and began sobbing. One got the impression that the murder of Jenny had brought them far closer than they might otherwise have become and that they shared an unspoken satisfaction in this. Roland thought that someone could have found a better picture of the poor thing, one where her hair was at least combed and she was smiling at the camera. The image projected on the screen showed her slumped on a couch not trying hard enough to conceal her annoyance at being photographed. While Felicia Burbank talked to the aggrieved in an effort to restore their composure, Roland put himself in the shoes of The Butcher who, after the third murder, had exhibited what turned out to be a pattern. The booze had kicked in and fueled a speculative daydream.

For some reason, whatever it is—maybe I'm bored, maybe some white bitch rebuffed my advances—I decide to murder a woman in the parking garage at the mall. And it was easy, almost too easy, and I enjoyed it. The people around here feel too safe in their middle-class routines, and I'm going to change all that in a hurry. But how to find another one? Stake out gas stations until I spot a female that fits my profile, a white woman, young, there are thousands of them. Then what? I follow her to wherever she's going and if she parks in a quiet spot then close in and…

"If only the lock on the laundry room door had been fixed," the father said. "There was no sign that he dragged her in there from her car, so I think after she parked in the apartment garage she got out of her car and spotted him coming and ran to the laundry room. And without a working lock on the door, she was trapped. All she had to do was get to the stairwell. He probably wouldn't have followed her up into the building."

Roland broke off his musings. "I hope you own that building."

"Outrageous! If I owned the building, I would have fixed the lock."

"No. I meant own it *now*. I hope you sued the owner and got a hefty judgment."

"Mister Hazzard, this is hardly the time or place…"

"I was sharing in his anger, ma'am. If the lock could have saved her, then the owner of the door should be held to account."

A few in the gallery clapped and Roland nodded toward them appreciatively then looked over at Felicia Burbank. She was ready to move on.

Next came the Arizona victims, the first of which met her untimely end at a rest stop on the Christopher Columbus Transcontinental Highway, otherwise known as Interstate 10, just west of the most populous of the more than twenty cities or towns in the United States of America named Glendale. Roland resumed his private speculations while the mother and brother of Kelly Stolrow came onto the stage.

Ok, so I've murdered three white girls in three weeks. This city is flipping out, calling me The Butcher of Glendale. Maybe the cops have a snap of my car from a gas station camera, but probably they don't. And they're not splashing around any photos or a sketch of my face, but just to be safe I'll leave town. Mom and Dad are locked in prison so what's keeping me here? Due east the desert is vast.

Kelly's family provided a middle-school yearbook picture of the girl. She looked about twelve, fourteen at most. Hard to tell behind her spectacles and orthodontic smile. A perfectly gleeful smile, nothing flashy or alluring, just an innocent girl yet to reach the first fork on her road of many forks and, against all odds, select the wrong path often enough that she found herself alone at a rest stop along the highway for a purpose no one was indelicate enough to utter in public—the place where Barsamian just happened to pull off the road.

The mother explained. "We lost track of Kelly after high school. She would show up every so often to get some of her things or wash her clothes or spend the night, but she never stole anything or abused us in any way. She just wanted to be on her own, and we had no right to stop her and no good reason not to help her when she asked for help." The brother remained silent, simply nodding.

"Of course, there were drugs in her life. We don't know what kind or how much and she never showed up trashed at the house, but we were always worried when she left that we would never see her again. And she always said *I love you*. That last thing she said was *I love you, Mom*."

The brother spoke. "I knew there was trouble when she dropped off the radar."

"Dropped off the radar?" Felica Burbank said.

"She mostly stayed down around the river, or near the casino, 91St Ave around Foxdale. I could usually find someone down there who'd seen her if I didn't catch sight of her myself. When a few weeks went by with no contact I started handing out my cell number. But the first call that came was to the house, from the police."

The brother's words, his tone of resignation, moved Roland. Having that morning read studiously about the crimes on the internet and heard the relatives of the California victims express their suffering, it was the contrast of the matter-of-fact, humbly spoken sadness of Kelly Stolrow's brother that finally made Roland suck in his breath. The brother's pain was of one who'd tossed a rope to a drowning child too weak to hold on and be pulled to safety, too simple-minded to think of coiling the rope twice around one wrist before grasping it. She was dead the moment she decided to leave home. That's what Roland heard. No anger toward the murderer, if ever there had been any.

But Roland was angry, far angrier than he'd been the night Barsamian forced him to fight, and though no one on Earth knew the circumstances leading up to this particular murder, Roland played it out in his head.

I'm pulling into Glendale Arizona. Long drive. Maybe I need to take a piss. Maybe I don't want to pay for a room and instead just sleep in my car. Maybe I'm sleeping in my car and wake up and see there's a girl there, alone and looking to make some sort of deal. White trash slut. Redundant human being. Allah—peace be upon him—you have delivered me an easy kill.

Roland suspended his excogitation lest it foment a spluttering of profanity. They were all—each of the murders—all unnecessary of course, but this one was gratuitous, opportunistic, un-worked-for, obscene in its offhandedness, like a man walking down the street with a hammer and spotting a pie on a windowsill and walking up and smashing it to bits. Just because he had a hammer.

Roland hated Barsamian, not for what Barsamian had done, but for what Roland imagined he had done, the presumed homage to Allah drawn solely from the scant information supplied by the Andruko brothers. For all he knew, Barsamian had picked her up in town and taken her out there on some illicit pretext or other and then done the deed— slit her throat and dragged the body into the bushes behind the cinderblock bathrooms.

"I'm so sorry," Roland said abstractedly, detached from the conversation he was interrupting.

"What was that, Mister Hazzard?"

"The pain he's feeling—that you're all feeling—it suddenly hit me. It lasts. It never goes away. And it's worse when it's someone you were already trying to save. That's what I meant."

"Thank you, Mister Hazzard," the brother said.

"Roland will do. And I'm barely even that."

Number five followed the MO of two and three—the victim, Aryanna Pedrini, selected at a gas station and followed, in this case to a mobile home park just outside of town. Truth be told, the two Arizona victims were technically not murdered within Glendale's city limits, but the coin had been minted and put into circulation. If he'd murdered in Phoenix, the journalists would have had to regroup and come up with something new.

Ms. Pedrini's relations flew in from Florida, drawn by the allure of television and the glamor of Los Angeles. Seemed like the whole clan was there, four generations worth. The baby in attendance was cared for by her twenty-year-old mother, and when the infant became too fussy, great-grandma took her outside into the lobby.

The camera cut off for a commercial break. Roland's rush had abated. He wanted a cigarette. His mind replayed clips he'd seen of Johnny Carson in a dizzying plaid sports jacket seated at his desk behind his microphone smoking a cigarette and bandying sexual innuendos with the bombshell de jour. *What has the world come to? And what is it coming to? And how fast?*

An argument broke out in the gallery. The Pedrini's had not yet settled on which two of their clan would take the stage. For them, the world had whittled Warhol's fifteen minutes down to six or seven, and the scarce supply accounted for the frenzied demand.

"You didn't even go to her funeral!"

"I was in county."

"Osceola County has berrrEEEvement release. Remember when Dad died and the sheriff got me out and drove me to his funeral?"

"They might do it for parents and children, but not for sibs."

"Did you even fucking check?"

"The sheriff what got you out that day was a friend of Dad's. It was totally off the books. Probably illegal. Sheriff McDaniel actually came in and sat down for the service if you'd shut up and remember."

"Did you even fucking check?"

"Did you even fucking like her? You're just here to sling your skank ass all over Hollywood. I'm doing you a favor by keeping you away from that camera. You'd never live it down. You're dressed twenty years younger than you are. Thirtyier than you look."

Roland could see why Aryanna fled this shitshow of a family to dwell in the desert on the opposite side of the country. He got out of his seat and walked over to the squabbling siblings.

"Easy there, pilgrims. You can use my chair. Just don't sit next to each other."

The sister wheeled around. "You can't just do that. Did you even fucking check?"

Roland looked over at Felicia Burbank. "Is it alright that she takes my place for this segment?"

Felicia Burbank nodded. It was the best way to keep the peace, with the added benefit of not having to be upstaged by the unpredictable outbursts of Roland Hazzard.

The show resumed with the mother and brother on one side of Felicia Burbank and the skanky sister on the other.

"We knew something bad would happen when she left for California all on her own," the mother said.

"She never made it to California," the brother said.

"She couldn't make it *in* California," the sister said. "She had to settle for Arizona."

"It's too expensive in California," the mother said.

"I knew some illegal Mexican would get her when she moved to Phoenix," said the brother.

"It was Glendale, asswipe, and you were worried about her marrying a Mexican, not getting murdered by one."

"Not that big a difference. The first often leads to the second."

Felicia Burbank tried to establish control. So far, no one had even looked at the photograph projected onto the screen, one taken at Disneyworld.

"The killer wasn't Mexican. Let's not use this solemn occasion to debate illegal immigration."

"There's no such thing as illegal immigration."

Now the mother was crying. Not over the loss of her daughter three years ago, but over the behavior of her present children.

"No such thing as illegal immigration?" Felicia Burbank rose out of her chair a few inches.

"Immigration is a legal process. That's why we have a department of it."

"We're wasting valuable time, Mister Pedrini."

"That's why they used to be called illegal aliens until the hippies took over. Saying illegal immigrant is like saying intelligent retard."

"I can't believe I need to say this, but Samuel Barsamian was an American-born citizen. His grandparents came here to escape genocide. Glendale, California extended its arms."

"Stop it, all of you!" The camerawoman trained her lens on the mother. "It doesn't matter where the killer was from. All that matters is that Aryana was innocent. She never did harm to anyone, so if there's a Heaven, she's gonna be up there. The jury is out on the rest of us."

"And God didn't let her life go to waste." The sister drew the camera in her direction. "The SOB got caught on a gas station camera stalking Aryanna. Without that, we'd never have found out for certain who he was."

Roland shut his ears to the Pedrini family and let his mind drift back to the psyche he'd invented for the serial killer.

Now they have my picture and my plate. Not a clear photo, though—too grainy. Still, it's me, and the plate's enough to seal it. I should have stolen a car. Maybe I don't know how to steal a car. Then I should have stolen a plate, stupid. Everybody knows how to use a screwdriver. Pretty soon they'll dig up a clean photo of me even if they have to go back to my high school yearbook. *I'm fucked. I'm fucked because I'm too stupid to know I needed to steal a license plate. Was I born below average? Probably was, but aren't most people?*

The drama on stage flared up again.

"...and that's why I'm voting for Señor Trump. He'll keep those dirty Mexicans from doing the cha-cha across the border with their filthy grins on their greasy faces."

"The cha-cha is Cuban, you idiot!"

I'll be headed the other way—the only American sneaking into Mexico. The bedraggled desert-crossers will stop and scratch their heads. I look like I could be one of them. At a distance anyway. But if they catch me there, I'm truly fucked. California death row is easy street compared to the Mexican system, and extradition might take a while. I could become a political bargaining chip or—who knows?—I might get the royal treatment for slashing up a bunch of American white girls.

Felicia Burbank raised her voice. "Is there anything more anyone would like to say about Aryanna before our time is up?"

"Yeah," said the brother. "If she'd stayed home and kept the baby everyone would be a lot happier now."

"You don't know she was pregnant."

"Hateful boy," said the mother.

"The guy I supposedly robbed. The crime that landed me in county…"

"Don't you say it," the sister said.

"Aryana sicced me on him for abortion money."

"She'd'a told me if she was pregnant."

"Why? You didn't even like her."

"Hateful boy."

Roland missed the rest of the quarreling, adrift in his fantasy.

I could kill myself. That's a reasonable option. I'd just have to find a way of doing it so that no one found my body. Mom and Dad would rather I was in jail for murder than find out I killed myself. The Grand Canyon's not too far from here. I bet I could find a deep crevasse somewhere in there and take the plunge, but I'd much prefer a watery grave, row out a few miles with a hatchet, float all night, wake up with no land in sight and then just hack a bunch of holes in the skiff. Sink down into nothingness. I've heard drowning is pleasant, drowning in cold-water especially.

Roland remembered a teacher he had the first semester of his freshman year at Berkeley, a real wild hair, who liked to just sit and talk to the class. A graduate student teaching assistant assigned to Freshman Core Lit. Galley slave duty, he called it. Promised a B to anyone who could write a coherent paragraph about anything at all. He'd pick passages from the books on the syllabus and wax philosophical on whatever it was. He'd tell you you were stupid if you said something that qualified. He said he couldn't make anyone who was disinclined to read read anything at all, so why bother? He could create only gratitude or resentment, and he chose gratitude. One day he came in and wrote a question on the board and handed out index cards for the students to use to answer the question, which was: *Would you sooner commit murder or suicide?*

"I'm conducting a study," he's said.

Hands shot up with qualifying questions. "Do we get to pick who we kill? Does it have to involve physical violence? Can we hire someone to do the job?"

"No. You have to do it yourself, and it doesn't have to involve violence. You can't presume the victim is a bad guy or that you have a painful terminal illness. Don't overthink it or impose conditions. Simple choice—kill yourself, or kill a stranger?"

On one side of the card, the students were to write the answer: Either 'murder' or 'suicide.' On the back: M for male or F for female. When they were all collected and tallied, the result was definitive. Most of the females in the class would sooner kill themselves than commit murder, and the results were the exact opposite for the males: 25% to 75% vs 75% to 25%.

"What's the point?" Roland had said.

"Men are more violent than women."

"I don't think you need a study to convince most people of that."

"Academics are not like most people."

The Pedrinis left the stage still bickering while Felicia Burbank called down the father and sister of the sixth victim, Carol Vadeen. Roland returned to his chair, a little disoriented from his sojourn into the fabricated animus of the late Samuel Barsamian. He closed his eyes to summon what he could remember of the details he'd read about the unfortunate young woman. She'd been murdered along with her friend in a remote spot in Glendale Canyon, New Mexico, about four hundred miles from Glendale Arizona, just north of El Paso, Texas, a short hop to the Mexico border. The two young women had been camping alone when Barsamian found them, apparently still sleeping, or just getting up, that last morning of their lives. Roland listened while Felicia Burbank referred to her notes to recount the details. Carol hailed from Alamogordo. She and her friend had met at the University of Arizona.

On one finger of Carol's sister, Avery, Roland spotted what he guessed correctly was the antique diamond ring found on Carol's hand and mentioned in one news report as proof that Barsamian killed for no reason other than to kill, as if that had not been perfectly obvious by then. Avery extolled the virtues of her free-spirited, lovable little sister, Carol, especially how she loved working with horses.

Roland interrupted the host and leaned over to point to the ring. "That must be your grandmother's ring. You are very brave to wear it."

Avery lost her composure and slumped rubber-boned in her chair and cradled her face in her trembling hands. "It b-b-belonged to my gr-gr-great-gr-gr-gr-grandmother first." Her words came out in staccato gasps between gulps and sobs. "She wa-wa-was sh-sh-shot through the n-n-neck wi-wi-with an arrow by an A-pa-pa-pa-chee."

Roland widened his eyes in genuine surprise at such an image, mute to reply. *A caravan of settlers? How long ago was that? They must have repelled the attack since the Indians didn't get the ring and her progeny survived.* He recalled a scene from a movie set in the Old West where a band of natives, after slaughtering a party of settlers, rode off with as much as they could carry, one brave galloping away under a stovepipe hat in a wedding dress synched tight with a string of dripping scalps. *How old was the unfortunate woman when she died? Was she your father's grandmother, or your mother's?*

Roland tried to follow the dialogue proceeding to his left, but his imagination—or his will, it's hard to say—persevered. He resolved to make an effort to find, if he could, some historical record of the incident that would corroborate the arrow-in-the-neck account. But that might, he thought, require him to gather a bit more information—names, places, dates—perhaps from the sister—*what's her name? Avery?* But now was not the time, certainly, to begin his research project, what with the circumstances of Carol's murder being the current focus of attention. He shook off his thoughts and tried to pick up the thread of the narrative now coming from Carol's father.

"I knew before the police confirmed the forensics on the wounds that it had to be him. I mean, Glendale California, then Glendale Arizona, and a few days later Glendale Canyon. That was no coincidence."

Of course, he was right. And once the authorities determined that the knife wounds on the canyon victims were consistent with those on the necks of the previous women, the press at large felt safe in confirming Barsamian's nom de tueur. *Sam the Butcher* and various other appellations became, once and for all, *The Glendale Butcher*. And what a perverse individual he was, this Armenian-American! The only serial killer in the history of the world to limit the domain of his victims, as far as anyone who'd bothered to plumb the database of all known serial killers could ascertain, to locations that bore the same name.

I am ONE sick fuck, thought Roland on Barsamian's behalf. *I'm out in the middle of the New Mexico desert headed south toward the border to make my escape. I see a sign pointing to, low and behold, Glendale Canyon. Ok then, journos, you settled on Glendale after just two sprees. I'll give you another Glendale, a Glendale no one's ever heard of. I'll send a shiver down the spines of all the gentlefolk in all the little Glendales in this comfortable nation, from the mountains to the prairies, from sea to shining sea.*

"I've long since resigned myself that it was nothing less than the worst of all possible luck," said Carol's father. "The animal drove into that remote, barren canyon and found two isolated females sleeping in a tent, almost like it was pre-ordained or he had some kind of sixth sense that led him there."

Roland recalled the facts he'd read about the crime scene, from which the police had pieced together a rough chronology. The tent was flattened, the cooking gear outside it in disarray. Carol's body was found some fifty yards from the campsite. Barsamian had dispatched her swiftly and easily, with one conclusive drag of the blade after pulling back her head by the hair—a patch was missing and the corresponding handful was discovered at the scene—to better expose her neck. Her friend, Matilda "Matty" McCabe, was murdered at the campsite.

"I'm sure she didn't suffer, except for that moment of surprise frozen on her face when she knew she was about to be killed. That's what I read in my daughter's eyes."

Avery sniffled, nearly back to her normal composure. "I'm so glad he's dead. I'm so glad he was killed with a knife." She looked over at

Roland. He wanted to correct her. It took him every bit of self-restraint to keep from saying *His own knife. His own knife. It was not just a knife.*

The final victim, Matilda McCabe, had been harder to dispatch. She shed her mortal coil with arms and hands scored with defensive wounds. She alone of the seven women was stabbed, and not just once. Barsamian, in an apparent effort to end the struggle she put up, stabbed her abdomen repeatedly before delivering his characteristic slash to the neck, which, in her case, was not deep enough to have been the cause of death but was more or less drawn there as a finishing touch—his signature. And she alone had managed to embed her fingernails into his flesh, thereby providing the authorities with DNA enough to make a positive match to samples taken from his apartment.

The Vadeens concluded their public grieving and departed the stage, perhaps a little relieved that Felicia Burbank had shown enough tact not to ask them what their daughter was doing out in the middle of nowhere sharing a tent with another woman. That woman, Matty McCabe, had only her brother, Timothy—the one who'd sent up the whoop—there to commemorate her untimely and senseless death. A rugged fellow in his thirties, Timothy appeared only slightly smaller than Roland as he leapt from his seat when Felicia Burbank said his name. He bounded onto the stage straight to Roland with arms stretched out wide to deliver an enthusiastic embrace, as though Roland was a long-lost brother or cousin. Visibly amused, Roland stood up and obliged him with a chest bump that segued into a full-bodied hug that lasted several seconds, a clench that brought him back, momentarily, to the rooms of AA, until Felicia Burbank broke in.

"Mister McCabe, may I call you Timothy?"

"You can call me Grateful Timothy. I've been climbing out of my skin to meet this man."

"I see you're well past grieving for your sister."

"Well past the public display of it, ma'am. With all due respect, I think this little presentation you put together is way over the top, a morose exhibition to be perfectly honest. I came here to celebrate the descent of an evil soul into the Lake of Fire and to honor the man who plunged him down there."

"That wasn't exactly what we had in mind."

"Well, I doubt you'd have thrown this party if the butcher was resting his head on the taxpayer's pillow under the presumption of innocence waiting for a trial. His being dead makes this even possible. Frankly, most of the viewers out there wouldn't be watching if Roland wasn't here. I for one wouldn't have made the trip out."

"I can appreciate your sentiments, Timothy, I surely can. But I was hoping you would want to share a few memories of your sister, Matty." She gestured toward the picture on the screen which captured Matty with a wide smile wearing an Arizona Wildcats softball uniform and holding a bat on one shoulder. "I understand she was quite the athlete."

Roland spoke before Timothy could respond. "She was All-American, and I'm not just talking softball. An All-American badass. She fought that sonofabitch. Her arms were all slashed up with defensive wounds and most of her fingers had his skin under the nails. My sense is that she tried to keep him busy so her friend could escape. I don't think she was killed last. Look how far away from the campsite Carol's body was found. The report I read said Carol was probably out taking a pee when the attacker showed up, but I think she was there and took off running. I think the butcher managed to stab Matty and left her there bleeding while he chased down Carol. Once he did her in, he came back and left his mark on Matty's throat. She left a long blood trail before she finally collapsed. No—Matty was killed last."

"That's exactly what I told the cops. If Carol would have helped her, picked up a rock and smashed him in the head maybe, then maybe they'd both be…"

"Gentlemen gentleman. This is not the forum to be speculating and laying blame."

Mister Vadeen shouted from the gallery, "Are you saying my daughter was responsible?"

"I'm saying my sister fought him all by herself. All by herself. That much is known. It's a self-evident fact."

Roland stood up and raised his arms to call for silence. "Listen listen. All that really matters—the only self-evident fact that matters—is that Matty is the exception. People nowadays have been conditioned not to fight back. Earlier today I was down on Olvera Street looking for a cowboy hat and I started messing with a little Mexican kid, maybe a third-grader, and he made it clear that if push came to shove, he would shoot me dead with a pistol. He showed me just how he would let me have it and then blew the smoke off his pistol finger."

"Mister Hazzard, we didn't invite you here so you could..."

"Pardon me, Mizz Burbank, but there were no rules of engagement, so I'm going to finish." He checked the camera light to make sure it was still on. "I'm here to inform everyone watching and listening that what little Julio on Olvera Street doesn't know is that once he's properly educated in the public schools in these here United States, blowing smoke off his pistol finger on the playground will get him into trouble. That will be his first taste of government. They don't care so much whether or not he can solve an algebra equation or write an intelligible essay, as long as all the aggressive impulses he was born with, that most boys and girls are born with, are neutralized, and shamed out of him. He'll be allowed to slack off all day long and disrespect his teachers, as long as he doesn't pull out that pistol finger."

The red light went off and Roland looked around for Joshua, who was nowhere to be seen. Roland smelled her perfume a moment before Felicia Burbank stood before him with her chin raised to his. Instead of offering him a rebuke for commandeering the attention of her audience, she touched him gently on the forearm. "You've got a gift, young man, but watch your step. Whether you know it or not, you're walking a high wire."

Roland would have liked to ask her to explain that to him, but she minced away before the vibrations from her voice subsided in his eardrums. Besides, he needed to find Joshua and get the hell out of there before anyone else could approach him. He made his exit apologies to Timothy McCabe to prevent the inevitable conversation with him and fairly skipped to the nearest door. He found Joshua waiting on the other side. Joshua looked at him and shook his head with a mixture of amazement and admiration. Roland put a claw around the back of his neck and pulled his agent toward him to celebrate their victory.

"That went well. Now let's take this show on the road."

~~~~~

Outside the building, a small crowd had gathered, some holding cameras, some carrying signs, some just there to speak their minds. There did not appear to be anyone in charge nor an organizing principle, just a rabble of locals without a common purpose. One sign read, "An eye for an eye makes the whole world blind." Another, "Roland Hazzard is a hazard." And, predictably, "I want to have your baby," with an email address scrawled beneath it. When they saw Roland come through the doors, the people raised their voices, and some began to move forward.

Roland turned to Joshua, "My public has arrived."

"Let's go back in and find another exit."

"You go ahead. I don't want to disappoint them."

Joshua stayed next to the building while Roland descended the steps.

A man came forward with his hand outstretched to shake Roland's hand. Roland took the hand. The man pulled him forward and withdrew a large blade from his belt with his left hand. The blade, a short machete, was yet too long for easy use at such close range, and before he could position it for a thrust Roland shoved him backward and faced him. The crowd pulled back. Screams. Gasps. But no departing feet.

"You're under arrest. Drop the weapon and get down on your knees. Interlock your fingerers behind your head."

The man rushed forward and aimed a blow at Roland's chest. Roland stepped to one side and pivoted like a dancer. The momentum of the swipe took the assailant past him. Roland drove the butt of his right hand into the man's nose then grabbed his head with both hands and spun his body with a violent twist. The sound of a snapping neck, like the sound of someone stepping on a bag of broken glass, was audible to all. The attacker dropped his landscaping tool. It clattered on the sidewalk as he fell dead on the spot.

Roland regarded the mostly horrified onlookers.

"You folks think I'm kidding around. Everyone needs to know how to do that." And with that, he walked off to find where they'd parked the car. No one followed him.

~~~~~

He leaned against the red utility vehicle, lit a cigarette, and finished the bottle. A low orange sickle moon—an Islamic moon—sharp and vivid, commanded the Los Angeles basin. Joshua ruined the mood with his hurried footsteps.

"You gotta go back there." Joshua was out of breath, not from overexertion but from raw excitement.

"We have a plane to catch."

"I'm not driving you away from the scene of a crime. I just watched you break a man's neck."

"Give me the keys, then. I'll go alone."

"No. You're going to deal with this." Sirens approached from the distance. "You're going to talk to the police. Walking away makes you look guilty."

"But you know I'm not guilty. Everyone who saw it knows that, and anyone who sees the video will know it. It's a crime scene, but the perpetrator is dead. There's no criminal to prosecute."

Joshua led an acquiescent Roland by the elbow back to the front of the building while they talked.

"Just talk to the cops. Give them a piece of your legal mind."

The witnesses had retreated from the corpse to make room for the police and stood close by. Joshua walked to the top step at the entrance to the building and stood in front of the doors with a dozen other people from the TV station who'd lined up to observe. Two officers stood over the decedent. Both of them looked over at Roland with the same bemused expression. Roland shrugged and stepped toward them.

"Where did you think you were going?" the veteran officer said.

"I lost track of my driver and had to make sure he was still around."

"You're Hazzard, correct?"

"Yes—Roland Hazzard."

"And you did this?"

"I wouldn't put it that way."

"The witnesses here said you snapped his neck."

"His neck did snap, but it was his doing. I'd classify it as an accidental suicide in the commission of an attempted murder or aggravated assault at the very least. I'll leave that up to you. But it doesn't much matter now, does it?"

"I smell alcohol on your breath."

"And I'd classify that as a non sequitur."

"If you're intoxicated in the commission of a homicide, it makes a difference."

"I took a drink afterward, out by the car, waiting for my driver, my agent, who drove me here."

"Your agent?"

Roland gestured toward Joshua with a quick motion of his finger, not pointedly enough to single him out from among the others atop the steps.

"Goldberg, up there by the doors. He booked me for my appearance tonight."

"I see. And you felt the need to leave the scene to go have a drink by the car while you waited for your agent."

"You have summarized it correctly, officer. Is there anything else?"

"I'll need you to come down to the station and give a formal statement."

"These good people saw it all and I'm sure someone has the whole incident on video, so my statement would be just to attest that I am not the identical twin of the man in the video wearing the same clothes, the same man just interviewed on television in that building."

"Do you know the attacker?"

"I did not."

"Did not?"

"He's dead. He's past tense."

"You're going to make this difficult, aren't you?"

"Seems to me that *you're* making it difficult. Clearly, I am innocent of any wrongdoing, yet you persist with your questions."

"I'm just asking for you to give me a statement for the police report."

"No. You're asking me to come to your police station, and I have a plane to catch."

"How about you provide a statement here, or in my squad car."

"I'll do you one better. I'll make a public statement here for all the assembled video cameras to capture." Roland climbed halfway up the steps and turned around and raised his voice. "I, Roland Hazzard, in the course of attempting to effectuate a citizen's arrest on this stranger who attacked me with a machete without warning or provocation, did evade a potentially fatal strike from said lethal weapon and in self-defense did stun the man with a blow to the nose and promptly snap his neck. If any witness here has any evidence or testimony that would tend to contradict my description of the events, then please offer it now."

"You didn't have to kill him," yelled a woman.

"Perhaps, not. But I wanted to set a good example for the children."

"I hope to God you don't have any offspring."

Roland gestured in the direction of the woman who'd been holding the amorous sign, "You might want to have a talk with her, then. She's eager to keep my chemistry brewing in the gene pool." But the woman had disappeared. His accuser made an angry face and the crowd pressed forward a few steps, except for a man in the back who stayed put and laughed and raised a triumphant salute. Roland realized he'd nudged a hornets' nest and heard Astrid's voice—*you don't always have to make a smart remark*. One more poke would set them to swarming.

Roland turned in Joshua's direction. "Goldberg!"

"Here I am."

"I need some professional corroboration here. Can you tell this officer that we have a plane to catch?"

Joshua came down and shook the officer's hand. "He's right. Roland and I were on our way back to the airport when this lunatic came out of nowhere. Neither of us said a word to him or to anyone. It was totally unprovoked."

"Your man Hazzard here seems pretty willing to pop off now."

"He wasn't a lunatic. I'll bet on that."

"Keep your mouth shut, Roland."

"I could take him in now for public intox, the way he smells."

"Let's do it. Let's push all the chips in the middle."

"Calm down, Roland. Officer, I've been with him all day and he had a beer at the airport and another at lunch. That's all I saw."

"He said he drank just now, waiting for you at your car."

"Quite possibly, but he's not drunk. We can both see that for ourselves, so either arrest him now and raise his profile even higher or let us get back to LAX so we can catch our flight."

"Don't you even care who this man is?"

"Who he was."

"Ok, who he was."

"My caring isn't going to speed up the process of you finding out."

"Have you received any death threats?"

Roland decided not to mention Oleg's open hostility or his assertion that Roland was a dead man, for he considered it less than a threat. More of a hope. Whatever it was, mentioning it to this LAPD officer would only prolong the conversation and do nothing to shed light on his attacker's identity.

"No, sir, can't help you there; but if you ask me, he looks like he comes from the same stock as Samuel Barsamian."

The medical personnel arrived with the tools of their trade.

"Is there anything else, officer?"

"Are you his lawyer too? Goldberg, is it?" The officer was writing. Joshua gave Roland an irritated look.

"I told them your name. So what?"

"Can you keep your mouth shut for more than two seconds?"

"Only if I'm told I have the right to remain silent."

"Is he free to go, officer?"

The officer looked at Roland. "You're living on the edge, kid." Then he dismissed them with a wave. More police had arrived by now and the officer and his junior partner walked toward their colleagues on the sidewalk where they stood conversing with the witnesses.

"He's right, schmuck—playing chicken with the police."

Roland pictured the smirking, gap-toothed mug of the ginger-haired Alfred E. Neuman and recalled his clandestine pleasure at discovering his father's box of old magazines. It took him some small effort to restrain his tongue from uttering the slogan: *What, me worry?"*

"He may be right, but we've flown the coop."

~~~~~

Traffic along the downtown corridor at night, even on a Sunday, bunched tightly and squeezed like blood through the clogged artery of a bloated limb. Roland leaned back in the passenger seat and squinted so that the thousand red brake lights inching ahead blurred into a solid band, as of a slow-motion time-lapsed photograph. A sidelong glance to the left revealed a flood of oncoming headlamps that proved too bright to view. He reached for the sunglasses clipped to Joshua's visor.

"Hup, hup. Hands off."

"Can't I even look at them?"

"I don't trust you. You'll try to force them onto your head, then they'll be useless to me."

"Useless is a bit of an overstatement. My head's not that much wider than yours."

"You think you can pretty much do anything, say anything, don't you? Grab a man's expensive sunglasses, break a man's neck, talk down to the police, make sweeping pronouncements to..."

"Easy there, pard. I know the question is rhetorical, but I'd rather answer it than suffer through a speech."

"Okay. Go ahead."

"I don't think I can do or say anything I want to—I'm obligated."

"By whom, or by what?"

"Providence—whatever it is that put me here. Did the prophets have a choice? Did they volunteer to speak the truth?"

"So, you're a prophet now?"

"Got no choice in the matter. I'm going full Jeremiah now and as often as possible. Balls to the wall."

"I'm not sure the One who pressed Jeremiah into service would have approved of that profane image."

"It's got nothing to do with testicles. It's an air force expression, meaning push the throttle all the way to the cockpit wall. The throttle was a double-handled stick will balls on top. My brother, the major, told me that."

Traffic eased up a bit and Joshua pressed on the gas and drove. He evidently knew the way. Roland reclined his seat a few inches and trained his eyes on the blinking airplanes that appeared to float in the distance, spaced safely apart but close enough that they formed a discernable line, an order of approach to the runway several miles west. Roland suspected that the pilots of those commercial jets, with all their automation, couldn't fight their way out of a heavy fog in the saddle of an old-fashioned fighter plane. He closed his eyes and tried to execute one of his out-of-body maneuvers, but his soul stayed firmly anchored.

"I don't think the prophets of the Old Testament needed booze to rise to the occasion."

"Who said I needed it?"

"I doubt you go a day without it. Can you remember the last day you didn't take a drink?"

"Not the specific day, but it's been a few months. Yesterday I kept my wits about me. Most days I do."

"Why do you drink?"

"I like the effect. Same reason as everyone."

"Except most people stop before the effect gets too strong, before they start to get sluggish. Most people can handle only a little bit."

"Look, Josh, I appreciate what you've done for me. And you've made your feelings on the matter abundantly clear. So, unless you think I've crossed the line, whatever line you've drawn, then let's not talk about my drinking again. I plan on having a few more on the flight home, and me thinking about what you're thinking about will put a screech in my buzz."

"Where did you get the alcohol you had at the station? It's a stupid question I realize because I've been with you since we checked in at SFO, so maybe I'm asking..."

"I carried it in my jacket. A pint of Smirnoff has no metal parts, so I just walked right through the metal detector."

"I guess people do that. I guess why not. They find it they take it."

"Right. Couldn't be easier." He removed the bottle from his jacket and peered into the bottom corner at the few remaining drops then opened the cap and shook them into his upturned mouth then let out an exaggerated gasp. "Now you're legal. They can't get you for an open container if we get pulled over."

"Gee, thanks."

"*Gee*...you know what that stands for?"

"Jesus, I guess."

"You're treading on thin ice there, aren't you Mister Goldberg?"

"You can't get enough of yourself, can you?"

"You want me to shut up? Let's listen to some music. Let's make a little musical wager."

"The radio game? Who can name the song first? That's not very original."

"Nothing like that. I've got a massive library of songs here in my little device. You name me an artist, any recording artist—but it has to be someone you like, someone you want to hear in this car right now—and if I can play that artist for you, then you buy me as many little bottles of booze as I want on our short flight home."

"Okay, you're on. Let me think for a minute." Roland pushed a few buttons on the Audi's display screen and paired his phone to the vehicle's sound system.

"Ready to rock."

"Django Rinehart."

"Fuckin' A. Great choice. The man with missing fingers plays a strange guitar. Comin' right up." Roland searched his catalog for one of his favorite Rinehart offerings. He chose *Georgia On My Mind* and, true to his word, kept his mouth shut while he curated the music the rest of the ride.

~~~~~

On the plane, Roland drank four miniature whiskies, all that the flight attendant would serve him and just enough to keep him situated in the boundary that separated self-conscious boredom and erratic exuberance—in short, contentment, serenity. Or so he thought. In truth, only a chemical facsimile thereof, for by the time they'd made it a mile up the freeway toward The City, Roland's counterfeit serenity succumbed to sleepiness. He rode the rest of the way passed out with his earbuds seeping music into his ears.

~~~~~

Joshua turned up Jones Street and climbed the hill. As he approached Sacrament Street near Roland's apartment, he gave Roland's shoulder a shove.
"Rise and shine."
"We here?"
"Pert near, pard."
"My cowboy hat in your backseat doesn't make us cowboy buddies."
"At least you know who's car you're in."
"What time is it?"
"Open your eyes. The time is staring right at you." The dashboard display read 9:58.
"In case I forget, thanks for the ride."
Joshua turned down Roland's block. A few reporters waited in front of his building sitting on the steps and leaning against the cars parked along the curb.
"Time to put on your game face again."
"Just roll on past. I'm not in the mood."
"Whores don't have that luxury."
"Whores get paid. No more freebies. Just roll on past, turn right and up two blocks. My car is there."

"You're going to hide in your car?"

"I've got a few options, a couple of safehouses."

Joshua found Roland's car and pulled over and put it in park. He turned to Roland. "You can avoid those reporters, sure, but I have something to ask you."

Roland reached into the backseat and picked up his fancy new purchase and set it in his lap. "What is it?"

Joshua took out his phone and opened his photos. "Remember those game scores you memorized at the airport—let's have 'em."

Roland laughed. "I thought you were going to ask me about the citizen's arrest. I knew that guy wasn't going to stop."

"I want to check that superhuman memory of yours."

"I'm half in the bag."

"All the more worthy a test."

Roland reeled off the game scores as easily as reciting the A-B-Cs, even providing the times remaining on the clocks. "Satisfied?"

"Remarkable. You should be on a TV game show."

"Whatever you can come up with, but no more free appearances. Next time I'm on TV, we get paid."

Roland opened the car door and paused for Joshua to say something.

"I wouldn't worry about that. You've raised your profile more than I can calculate."

Roland got out and closed the door and waved goodbye and climbed into his faded yellow rust box. The contrast in smells between the two cars jarred him back to the facts of his life. *A couple of safehouses* sounded good, but all it meant was Deidre might be home and if so might let him crash there. He turned the key as a test. The old Nissan, he trusted, would probably go forever, or for at least as long as it could pass the smog test, but the battery was weak and had to be rejuvenated by the engine every three days or so or it would fail. The engine started and thrummed. He plugged his phone into the cigarette lighter adapter to give it a boost and checked the web for news about himself.

It didn't take long. *Killer's Killer Kills Again,* ran the headline on the Drudge Report, followed by two brief paragraphs. Just the facts, the most important of which was the assailant's name—Arman Barsamian, first cousin to the serial killer. And then the last sentence, which veered into editorial. *By witnesses' accounts, Mr. Hazzard appeared to be indifferent and casually walked away from the man whose life he'd ended with a powerful twist of the neck.*

~~~~~

He called Deidre before he could evaluate the wisdom of that decision, which is to say that he knew it was not a good idea and did not want to look squarely at his predicament.

Deidre answered. "Hi." Just that. Like she was expecting him.

"Hi. It's Roland."

"I know it's you. My phone knows your phone."

"Good so look I hope it's not too late but..." Roland spoke more quickly than usual. He seldom sounded hurried or ruffled even if he was.

"You're back from LA I assume."

"What? Do you have one of those apps that tracks the location of all your contacts?"

"Don't be stupid."

"You don't sound happy to hear from me."

"I don't even know you, Roland."

"You didn't delete me or block me. That must count for something."

"Why did you call?"

"I just returned from Los Angeles as you surmised, and..."

"Surmised? Did you turn into a proper English gentleman when you landed?"

"Forget it, Deidre. I'm sorry I bothered you."

"Oooh, poor little Roland. Did the mean lady spit on your lolly and rumple your cravat?"

"Cromwell should have cleansed that little island of you inbred hobbits."

"That doesn't fit with your image Roland. You're all about the justifiable homicide, aye?"

"Can we talk in person?"

"Only if you know the password."

"Don't tell me—*please*."

"Speak the truth. That will be good enough."

"There's a bunch of reporters outside my building."

"That's a factual detail. I'm looking for truth."

"I'd rather avoid them. I'm afraid to face them."

"You're getting closer."
"Because I don't want to face them alone."
"And?"
"I want to sleep at your place tonight."
"Why?"
A trick question? Roland had to think about it. "Because I'd rather not sleep at my place?"
"But why my place?"
"Why are you humiliating me?"
"There's a difference between humiliating and humbling."
"I don't have any other friends."
"You're almost there. Just one little tweak."
"Ok. You're right. I don't have *any* friends. You're the last house on the block, my only friendly direction, or so I thought."
"Do you remember the way?"
"Thank you. I'll be there in twenty minutes."

Roland knew his blood alcohol level exceeded the legal limit to a large degree, but his brake lights were working, and he judged himself sober enough to operate the car. Any car. Not too drunk to operate any sort of motor vehicle that traversed land or sea. Not drunk at all in his own estimation—and that assertion would have passed a lie detector. The psychological beat down delivered by the mellifluous Hibernian, however, rendered him reluctant to stop at a bar or buy a bottle on his way to her apartment. Her one express provision for extending him hospitality was that he not show up drunk, and Roland felt cowed enough not to test her resolve. He gripped the wheel and navigated across the city to her apartment complex, the Skinner Dipper Arms, on secluded Pershing Drive in the Sea Cliff district. As dark as it was in that narrow neighborhood on a misty overcast night, his finding his way back to her building, back to her very door, confirmed once again to Roland that he could excel when drunk where sober men would fail.

She heard his approach and opened the door before he could knock. Roland jumped back, startled. She wore light blue cotton pajamas that covered her head to toe. His memory still held the image of her sensual naked body, the alluring shape of which was nowhere in evidence.

"You sure you don't have that stalking app?"
"You're heavy-footed tonight."

"In case I forget, I want to thank you. And I apologize for the Cromwell remark." Roland took a step forward as if to enter.

She stood in the way, holding the door half open, not inviting him in. "You can't apologize for your character."

"My character?"

"Something blurted out like that, the emotional behavior—that's your character. Unless you're drunk. Drunks get to apologize. They rely on that little loophole."

"This fog has crawled up my ass and is freezing me from the inside out."

"I can't tell if you're drunk, so I guess I have to assume you're not."

"I had a bit on the plane, but nothing since."

"And a bit before the plane too, by all accounts."

"I'll find a motel before I'll beg."

She let him in. The couch was fitted with a sheet and there was a blanket and a pillow stacked at one end. He sat on a chair to remove his boots, taking stock of his bed for the night.

"How's the arm?"

"It's healing nicely I think." Roland removed his jacket. "The lady that shaved my head—I could almost call her a friend, really—rebandaged it yesterday. I got it all wet again."

"I won't ask what possessed you. But if I'd seen you like that bathing in the surf Friday morning I would have hurried on past."

She began cutting away the existing bandage with her medical scissors.

"I'm going for maximum shock value."

"I should say so. Causing multiple spiral fractures of the cervical vertebrae to sever the spinal cord in front of a live audience is quite dramatic all by itself. Traumatic even."

"It wasn't planned."

"Of course it wasn't, but you did it so swiftly, so expertly, that it looked like you'd done it before."

"I'm a martial arts expert, yes. A master actually."

"Well, that was masterful. I watched it several times. I slowed it down. He was dead before he hit the sidewalk." She pressed her fingers gently on the skin alongside the scab line of his cut. "I'm not sure you need the bandage anymore. A few sutures should keep it closed until it heals."

"You're the doctor."

"I have no idea what you are."

"Do I have to be something?"

"What kind of person, I mean."

"I'm following the path laid out for me."

"No. I think you're trying to blaze a trail."

"Well, something gave me a shove, and I'm…"

"…trying to make a big deal out of it. You said so yourself on the news last night."

"What kind of person does that? I'd like your opinion, Deidre."

"A desperate one."

"Desperate how, or for what?"

"To take charge of his life, perhaps."

"I'm desperate for a drink if you want to know the truth."

"I can give you that, but not in the spirit of conviviality."

"Now who's got the high tone? Just say you won't drink with me."

"You prefer to drink alone, I'll wager."

"What makes you say that?"

"Your story is all over the internet, and drinking is a big part of it. You've killed two men in three days, and both times you went to alcohol before talking to the police. That LA cop ratted you out."

"Yeah. I stood too close to him. What about that drink?"

"Is that all you came here for? I highly doubt it."

"You've been kind to me, more than kind, spectacularly kind. That's why."

"So, if you want the drink and the couch, then the price is more of my kindness, but of the unspectacular variety. Otherwise, you can toddle off to some motel with a bottle and get blotto."

He raised his hands in surrender. "I'm not stopping you from talking."

"You've been sober before, correct?"

"Court ordered."

"That's a load a shite. The court can only make you go to meetings. They can't follow you around. You must have, at some level, wanted to stop."

"They can't even make you go to meetings. No one checks the signatures on those court cards."

"Well, did you get sober or not?"

"I did, and so I know I can stop whenever I want to. Right now, I prefer to drink. It's that simple."

She got up and went to the kitchen and retrieved a bottle from the cupboard above the stove. "Have you ever tried Powers?"

"Probably not."

"It's Irish whiskey, single pot. Much different than Jameson or Bushmills. I've only got a few fingers here, so show some respect and don't shoot it." She poured some into a glass and added a splash of water. "The water brings out the aroma." She set the drink on the coffee table before him and the bottle next to it.

He lifted the glass in the hesitant manner of a broker receiving stolen goods, or perhaps of a famished man receiving a crust of bread snatched from the grimy fingers of a starving urchin.

"I'm not sure I can enjoy this after the browbeating."

"The first swallow will anesthetize your guilt."

He swirled it and sniffed it as she'd suggested, just for form, then took a sip. "It's very peculiar. Earthy. Very good."

"That's the peat."

"I could develop a taste for it."

"You know that old joke—why did God invent whiskey?"

"To help the cowboys beat the Indians."

"That's a cynical indictment of God."

"It's my own variation. Of course I know the punchline—*to keep the Irish from taking over the world.*"

"It's a tart bit of humor, a vainglorious self-recrimination."

"Yes—a pathetic ethnic boast."

"And who tells that joke?" He shook his head in slow amazement. This woman, with whom he'd had one of the most astonishing, indelible sexual experiences of his young though prolific career, had transformed herself into a scold of a schoolteacher.

"I'd guess Irish drunks for the most part. Where are you going with this?"

"Drunks that don't think they have a problem, and when they get together, they think their drinking is a tribal virtue, a heroic tribal virtue."

"I'm a quarter Scottish, so."

"Yes. But I think you're part of a larger tribe, though it's not my place to claim that. Yours is the only claim that matters."

"I'll claim one thing, just one thing, before I take another drink."

"I've got to get back to bed."

Roland smiled sheepishly, remembering how he said the same thing to the officers in his apartment.

"What is it, then? You look like a crazy person sorting out the voices in his head."

"Just this, Deidre. Two men have attempted to murder me in the past three days. I'd rather contend with a case of whiskey and a drinking problem than be lying on a slab in some hospital."

"Fair enough. You haven't hit the jumping-off point."

"What's that mean?"

"The point where the booze stops working and you can't imagine yourself with it or without it."

"No. I'm nowhere close to that."

"You have no way of knowing. Good night, Roland Hazzard."

She went into her bedroom and closed the door. He removed his clothes and folded them neatly and set them on the chair next to the couch. He emptied the bottle into the glass and set the drink where he could reach it, stretched out under the blanket, and put in his earbuds. Something soothing. Handel. Soft violins with a playful, lilting flute thrown in. Peasants dancing barefoot after a Sunday evening feast, printing the rake-combed dirt. He drank. She'd ruined it. The peasants ignored the peaceful music and the soft breeze and started fighting. He drank again. Someone raised an axe and aimed a blow. Roland breathed out the tension stored up from the day. *Tried to. Tried to. You can't try. There is no trying. Only doing. And the doing must come easily or the trying makes it worse.* He flipped his mind back to the moment when the fool with the machete made his charge. He froze the memory at the instant when he'd formed the intention to kill him, or more precisely had ignored the commandment not to kill him, had elected not to refrain, had let his body follow the impulse from his brain, had not allowed his mind to intercede and block the reaction. He'd been told somewhere along the line, or heard rather, in some class or other…no, he remembered who'd said it, the course, the classroom, the sound of the professor's voice, each particle of dust floating in the slats of light that jutted through the louvered blinds. *The highest form of action is refrainment.*

Chapter 15
October 3, 2016

He parked his car next to Gina's and got out and put a hand on her hood. Warm, not hot. He guessed she'd parked it twenty minutes ago. Michael's car sat nearby but he had no curiosity about the temperature of his hood. As he walked toward the building, he realized he had no idea why he played the detective on Gina's vehicle. He'd never done anything like that before. *Am I becoming someone I don't want to know or finding out who I really am?*

He walked into the building and swiped his badge and entered the testing lab. That they called the testing facility *the lab* struck him as absurd, a childish aggrandizement. Through the window, at the far end of the room, he saw Michael behind his desk with the door closed. Gina sat at her station alone with the NBA game flashing on her screen. A surge of guilt churned his guts. Then, from a different source entirely, a blush of embarrassment bloomed on his face. *What the hell am I doing here?* But Michael had seen him. *You can't walk into work and then just turn around and call in sick,* he told himself, and it didn't occur to him to knock on Michael's door and tell him that he'd made a mistake coming in and needed time off after the harrowing episode of the night before. No. It was pride that brought him there and pride that demanded he remain, a desire to be thought of as someone self-possessed enough to kill someone before a live audience and then stroll into work the next day as though life should proceed as normal. Yet the moment he walked into the room and saw Gina—seeing her car was not enough—he knew this was not so, knew that he was not so cavalier, that he should not even want to appear to be so cavalier, that he'd made a mistake, that he should have called her before showing up for work, that he should have called her either way, and that there was no way to fix it now. As much as he felt like turning around and walking out, the only reasonable thing to do was to be first to speak.

"Good morning, Gina."

He sat down as quickly as he could. They sat a few feet—smelling distance—apart. She swiveled toward him with an expression worn by someone much older than she was, someone who'd suffered too much at too young an age, not the same Gina he'd had to break a lunch date with last Friday. The look on her face chilled his flesh. He knew he was the cause of her apparent distress and wished he'd opened with *I'm sorry*, though he wouldn't have been able to articulate what for.

"What are you doing here?"

Myriad snappy responses, running the gamut from sarcastic to wounded, fanned across his mind. He decided that the question was not clear enough for him to answer accurately.

"Other than the obvious, I don't know what you mean?"

"Don't be obtuse. I'm afraid for you."

"You can see for yourself I'm doing just fine." He turned on his computer to begin the day's work.

"Then maybe I'm afraid *of* you."

"I should have called. I'm sorry."

"Why? There's nothing between us."

The way she said *nothing* sounded like a declaration of divorce. He winced with shame and forced a squint to suppress any tears that might be preparing an ambush.

"To make sure you would have lunch with me today. I still owe you lunch."

"You came to work so you could take me to lunch? Are you fucking kidding me?"

He'd never heard her swear. The testing lab was more or less a profanity-free zone, and mostly because the other testers, all of them male, observed decorum on her account, so hearing her drop the f-bomb was all the more jarring.

"I was looking forward to it. I haven't spent a normal hour with someone in what seems like a long time."

Her computer beeped as an instant message from Michael appeared on her screen.

"Michael wants to talk to you."

Michael hadn't even waited for Roland to boot up his workstation.

"Must be important. Maybe he's going to give me the ax. That'll settle everything, won't it?"

~~~~~

Michael motioned for Roland to close the door behind him. Roland sat down and waited for Michael to begin the conversation, to explain why they were sitting in his office with the door closed. Michael looked at him, glanced at his computer screen, then back at Roland, then back to the screen, tapped on his keyboard, clicking his mouse and so forth, until Roland couldn't stand it any longer.

"Good morning."

"No." Michael's tone was sharp, a tone one might use when rejecting an unreasonable demand.

"Whaddaya mean, *no*? No to what?"

"Good morning won't cut it. Good morning isn't true. I won't accept your good morning."

"You want me to shove off? If so, just say so." He took the badge from his shirt pocket and held it up. "If this is what you want? All you have to do is ask for it." Roland smiled at himself. It was too much—the exaggerated rectitude—even for him to pull off with a straight face. Like an insubordinate cop daring his chief to fire him, except he had no pistol and shield to slam down on the desk, just a plastic sheath on a lanyard.

"We didn't think you'd show up this morning."

"We? You and who else?"

"My bosses—you know their names."

"And what did they boss you to do if I did? Don't keep me in suspense, Michael."

"Nothing. You're my problem—they consider you to be my problem. They barely knew who you were before Friday. If the CEO told me to fire you, we wouldn't be sitting here talking about it."

Roland tried to look and sound offended. "Problem? What do you mean? Do you think they're testing you, seeing if you'll do the right thing? You thinking the easiest way for you is to persuade me to quit? More to the point—why would I quit, other than to do you a favor?"

"You've made a spectacle of yourself. We can chalk up the violence to bad luck, but the public statements, the—I'm not sure what to call it—the *glorying* in it. Don't you think that might make people—people at work—uncomfortable?"

"I don't think luck is the right word. I'd call it destiny, even certainty. There'd have to be something wrong with you if you weren't awed by a

The Alcoholic—A Hero Contends for His Soul

man of certainty. If people can't stand themselves in my presence, then…"

"See, that's what I'm talking about. We can't have you spouting your moral philosophy around here."

"I can't sue if I get canned, but I'd be glad to sign anything you want. Say the stock drops when my name is associated with the company—you'll have to let me go. In the meantime, I'll keep my mouth shut and do my work. I want to finish the golf title. If by some miracle Trump wins the election, it will fly off the shelves."

Michael fiddled with his mouse again, tapped on his keyboard, glanced up and down, scratched his nose, looked at Roland, rolled back his chair and leaned his head over the backrest so that he was staring straight up at the ceiling, then he let out a long, measured exhalation. Roland studied him. The drama seemed a bit forced. Finally, Michael straightened up and spoke.

"Okay, you can stay, as long as you keep your head down and, of course, show up clear-eyed. And don't get too excited about Trump Resorts. We won't be publishing it."

"Then what will I be working on?"

"Trump Resorts. I didn't say we're going to scrap it."

"I should hope not. It's nearly finished, and it looks great. Plays great. Why won't we publish it?"

"I don't think you'll find a Trump supporter in this building, at least not one that would admit it."

"Then why license a game that promotes his little empire? Why license it in the first place?"

"We bought that license several years ago, long before he announced his candidacy. Paid enough for it that we need to recoup our investment."

"Why not wait? If he wins, the sales will be phenomenal."

"Yeah, we can take our minds off the smoking ruins of our planet by playing a video golf game that honors the man who authored our destruction."

"The addicts will twitch so long as there's still juice in the walls."

"Anyway, I doubt we'll find another distributor before Christmas, so there's no urgency here."

"I'm surprised the company would put politics before profits?"

"If you owned a bookstore in Jerusalem, would you sell copies of Mein Kampf?"

Roland jerked his head back a bit, startled, as though he'd been rammed in the forehead by a housefly.

"If they thought he was so evil, why did they license his name in the first place, let alone produce the game?"

"I don't know, and I'm not going to be the one that asks that question. All I know is that we're going to finish it and find a buyer, probably overseas."

"Since the schedule's been pushed out, I've got a few twists on the gameplay, something totally original. If I put them in writing, maybe you can run it up the flagpole."

"Give me the short version."

"I'd add a fictitious course that butts up against the Texas-Mexico border, and half the holes, naturally, would be flanked by the famously promised Trump border wall. The golfers would have stun guns to zap any illegals they see climbing over the wall or hiding in the bushes or behind trees."

"Very amusing." Michael clearly was not the least bit amused.

"Yeah. How many golf games have been crossed with a shoot-'em-up?"

"You're not serious. Shoot par *and Mexicans* on the Texas border."

"Now you've got the hang of it. *Mein Golf,* if we want to stick with the Hitler thing."

"I think that would get boring after a while."

"There's more. Some of the border-jumpers will be carrying kilos of heroin or abducted slave-babies, and if you get one of those you can cash it in for upgrades on golf clubs, a better stun gun, tax deductions…"

"Tax deductions?"

"I'm just spitballing here. How about a target practice range where you pick off the wokescolds in the parking lot?"

"Wokescolds?"

"The enlightened enraged. The gang of oxymorons."

"You realize, if I proposed any of this, I'd be the one to get fired."

"Just pitch it as a South Park rip-off. In fact, we could call it, *Southern Park* or *South Golf Park* and probably get away with it."

"You had me going there for a second, Roland."

Roland glanced at the furnishings in Michael's office to create a pause that might allow for a change of tone and a reordering of his thoughts. Michael danced his thumbs on the screen of his mobile phone.

The two remained silent until Roland spoke. "Are we done here? If we're done here, I should get back to work."

The door opened and two men came in. Michael looked up and stood as though he'd been expecting them. Then he looked down at Roland. One of the men was on the short side and the other was alarmingly short, too short to joke about, though it would not have been unreasonable to ask if he needed a booster seat to safely drive a car or if the charcoal suit he wore was purchased in a children's boutique.

"These men are here to talk to you."

Roland skooched around in his chair to see what *these men* referred to but kept one eye on Michael. "Sounds ominous."

The shorter one spoke first. "Good morning, Mister Hazzard."

Roland ignored him and turned back to Michael. "The two of them might stack up to one whole man. You kept me here yapping until these two halflings showed up? Is that what just happened?"

"They went to your apartment last night. They saw you drive off. This morning they called and asked me to let them know when you got here. If you got here."

The taller one adopted a sterner tone than his partner to get his attention. "Mister HAZZARD."

Roland jerked his chin around to respond. "You're some kind of cop, right? In that case, you work for me, and I give you permission to wait quietly until I'm finished talking to my boss here."

He turned back to Michael. "So, this was all a put-on? The execs *haven't* been talking to you about me? My job isn't hanging in the balance?"

"Everyone is talking about you, Mister Hazzard," the shorter one said. "In the forests of Borneo, they're talking about you."

Still facing Michael, his head partially turned, Roland threw his words over his shoulder. "They'd better be. I flew down there just last year and showed those swamp monkeys how to make fire. Now you're telling me they've already learned how to surf the internet?"

Michael intervened before the exchange could devolve any further. "Roland, you're on a short leash already…"

"Oh?" Roland exaggerated his surprise. "I thought this was all a ruse. I assumed that as soon as these gents were through with their business, you'd show me the door."

"No. I admit I kept you here until they arrived, but I didn't lie about the job."

Roland stood up. "Then I guess I'll get back to work."

The taller man edged over to the door but didn't exactly block it. "We need to talk to you, Mister Hazzard."

"Are you sure all school children have safely crossed the street this morning?"

They produced their badges as if on queue, as if the timing of such a gesture was rehearsed or part of their training.

The shorter one spoke. "I'm Agent Dennis Mitchell. My partner is Agent Healy." FBI was printed in bold blue letters on their badges.

Agent Healy took his queue. "We didn't come down here to joke around."

"That doesn't mean I can't joke around."

Michael put his head in his hands.

"True. But I'd advise you to take this seriously."

"If I'm not in handcuffs, it's not serious."

Agent Mitchell spoke to Michael. "Do you have a room we can use?"

"Sure. Use our team meeting room. Roland can show you where it is."

"I'm going to bring Gina with me if that's okay."

"Why?"

"Who's Gina?" Agent Mitchell said.

"My moral support."

"She's in the testing lab outside. Sits right next to Roland."

"Moral support, huh?" said Agent Healy.

Roland kept his true reason to himself. He wanted a witness to anything improper the agents might say or do, and Michael hardly seemed neutral. Besides, he thought it might impress her to see that the Feds had taken such an interest in him.

"It's for your protection."

"Our protection?" said Agent Mitchell.

"If Gina's in the room, I'll be much less inclined to hurt your feelings. Her empathetic nature rubs off on me. Whoever sent you down here for whatever bullshit reason, you two seem happy to carry out their fascist bidding. Without Gina in the room, nothing would stop me from making this very personal."

"Lead the way, killer," Agent Mitchell said.

Roland showed them to the meeting room and then went back to talk to Gina. She had her headphones clamped on her ears and ignored Roland so that he had to tap her on the shoulder.

"What?"

"Those guys are FBI—I need a wingman?"

"What do they want?"

"I have no idea." Roland spoke rapidly in a hushed tone. "But it's two-on-one and I'm thinking I could use a witness to whatever they have to say."

"I don't understand."

"It's physics. Atoms, people, behave differently when being observed."

"Let me ask Michael." She tapped on her keyboard to send the boss an instant message.

"I asked him already. He said it's okay."

"Okay. But I can't guarantee it's not going be three-on-one when we get in there."

"That's the spirit." He stepped back to let her pass then followed her to the meeting room.

~~~~~

Roland and Gina took their seats at the long oval table opposite the agents. Roland sensed that Mitchell, the puny one, was the senior agent. He turned his head toward Gina and gave slight nod before he spoke.

"Gentlemen, this is my friend Gina. Gina, this is Agent Mitchell and his partner Agent Healy—FBI. They've come to intimidate me."

"Why would you say that?" Agent Healy said.

"What other reason could there be? You're not here to congratulate me."

"You don't need us for that."

"You're doing a great job of congratulating yourself."

"Why shouldn't I? I kept myself from getting murdered and took out a psychopath at the same time."

"I assume you've registered yourself as a lethal weapon?" said Agent Mitchell.

"We're not in Guam."

Agent Healy looked at Agent Mitchell as if to check whether he had any idea what Roland was talking about. Gina showed Roland the same perplexed expression.

Agent Mitchell looked back at Agent Healy. "I wasn't exactly serious."

"If lethal people had to, I'd have to."

"You're saying in Guam they have to?" Agent Healy said.

"Look it up."

Gina gave him a sidelong glance. "How would you even know that, Roland?"

Roland kept his eyes fixed on Agent Healy as though he'd asked the question. "I looked into it. When you can do what I can do, it's important to know the law."

"We didn't come here because we think you broke the law," Agent Mitchell said.

"How many blackbelts do you have?"

"Three, not counting Krav Maga."

"Is that what you used to snap his neck?"

"I used his head to snap his neck."

"So, you're saying you did it on purpose?" Agent Mitchell said.

"Are you accusing me of a crime?"

"No. I'm just curious."

"Good. I broke his neck but not the law. Now—what the fuck are you doing here? State your purpose if you have one. Or maybe your superiors told you to come down here just to make faces at me."

Gina touched his arm. "Do I really have to sit through this?"

Roland kept his eyes locked on Agent Mitchell.

"It won't be much longer—these clowns have nothing to say. They're just eyeballing." He glanced over at Agent Healy to let him know he should pay close attention, then looked back at Agent Mitchell. "And let me tell you something about eyeballing—it's not recommended when you're facing a wild animal, an apex predator like a wolf or a lion or a bear. You want to look off to one side. It's not a good idea either when you're being addressed by an Emperor or a Pharoah. But a junior G-man—any man can go eye-to-eye with that sort of creature all day long because a junior G-man wakes up every morning ready to receive his daily orders. He's a man with no natural power and is not to be feared."

"I'm too amused to be insulted," said Agent Mitchell.

"It makes for a good illustration of why we came here," Agent Healy said.

Roland rotated his forefinger to say let's get on with it.

"We came to offer you some advice. Maybe we could have been more friendly about it, but all we're here to do is advise."

Roland's phone vibrated in his pocket. The room was quiet enough that everyone could hear it buzzing. He took the device out and looked at the screen. It read *Josh*. "I've gotta take this." He got up to go. "I'll be back in a minute or two. That'll give you guys a little more time to figure out how best to salvage your dignity."

~~~~~

He closed the door and stepped a few feet down the corridor.

"Hey, what's up?"

"You busy between noon and two?"

"I'm at work today."

"How are they reacting?"

Roland decided to keep the visit from the FBI to himself. He wanted to get back to the conference room as soon as possible.

"Not with the usual playful chatter. Showing up bald would have provoked some amusement, but not under the circumstances. Anyway, I'm still drawing a paycheck. They can't afford to lose their best tester. The stock would tank on that press release."

"Tell me. Are you busy or not?"

"Depends on what you've got in mind. I've already made lunch plans."

"The Peter Jordan show. He'd like to have you on for a couple of segments. No more than half an hour. Between noon and two."

"How much?"

"I asked the producer about that—they've never paid a guest in the history of the show. But you'll reach a few million listeners, and it won't be a hostile interview. You can hang up anytime you want."

"Okay. How's this going to work?"

"They'll call you. Just give me a time and be ready for the call. You'll need to find a quiet place, no background noise."

"One o'clock then."

"Good. I'll be listening."

The call ended and Roland put his phone back into his pocket.

~~~~~

He reentered the room. The three stopped talking.

"So where were we?"

"You were belittling us," Agent Mitchell said.

"I guess I'd better quit that. Anymore belittling and you guys'd be garden gnomes."

"Just listen to what they have to say, Roland." He noted her exhausted sigh.

"You obviously enjoy all the attention you're getting," Agent Healy said.

"We can't tell you to stay in your hole, but when you're outside the hole we'd advise you not to…"

"Who's we?" You can't mean just you and Agent Healy here."

"The FBI. The FBI doesn't want to waste its time on you."

"What do you call this?"

"If you keep it up, this will have been a waste of time," Agent Mitchell said.

"Keep up what?"

"The vigilante talk. Your name is trending off the charts. Views of you spouting your message are in the millions. It will die down after a while, but if you keep adding fuel to it, we predict a spike in the kind of vigilantism you seem to be promoting."

"That's why we're here," Agent Healy said.

"Self-defense—self-reliance—is not vigilantism."

"That's true," Agent Mitchell said. "But we're not talking philosophy here."

"We didn't come here to parse words, to talk about *meaning*. We're concerned with the *effect* of what you say publicly, not your deeper motivations. Do you understand?"

"Yeah. I understand perfectly well what you want, but what I don't get is what you plan to do if I don't comply."

"We can inject a little information into the narrative, cast some doubt on your character," Agent Mitchell said.

"What is he talking about, Roland?"

Roland turned to her and spoke in a low voice, not to keep the agents from hearing, but to lend his words only enough volume to match their importance. "Public intox. Hardly a federal case."

"There's enough in the public record for us to paint an unflattering portrait."

"I don't plan to run for office."

"What *are* your plans, if I may ask?" Agent Healy said.

"I plan to have lunch with Gina here this afternoon, then go home and study my Bible."

"We need to get some work done before we go to lunch, Roland."

He could hear in her voice that her sympathies had turned in his favor.

"So, no more interviews?" Agent Healy said. "Do we have your word on that?"

"I will not relinquish my sovereignty as an individual, my right to free speech. Even if I could promise it away just to ease your fears—to ease the fears of the FBI—my conduct going forward would violate that promise. I know how I'm made. Besides, there are certain financial considerations."

"What are you talking about?" Agent Mitchell said.

"Speaking fees, monetized clicks, that sort of thing."

"Are you suggesting that we pay you to stay out of the media?" Agent Healy said.

"Only a corrupted mind would go in that direction."

That agitated Agent Healy. "You took two human lives, the second one unnecessarily in my estimation. Only you know about the first. And you bragged about it because you were apparently within the law, and you seem determined to continue to brag about it for your own financial gain. And you're calling *my mind* corrupt?"

"Police don't aim for the leg when someone's coming at them with a knife or a baseball bat. If someone wants to commit suicide by cop, all he has to do is jab at one with a broken lollipop."

"I must have missed that little news item," Agent Mitchell said.

"I'd love to sit here and trade sarcasm with you guys, so unless you gentlemen have anything of substance to tell me, then I think Gina and I should be getting back to work."

Agent Healy glared at Roland and fairly bared his teeth. "As long as you're clear that the FBI won't stand behind you if you try to leverage your celebrity into some kind of social movement."

"We're a long way from High Noon."

Agent Mitchell checked his watch. "Hours away. Sun's barely cleared the horizon."

"It's an old Gary Cooper movie."

"My dad made me watch that one. Me and my brothers."

"What's your point?" Agent Healy said.

"Forget it."

"No. What's the point of High Noon?"

Roland looked at Gina. "You wanna tell 'em?"

"Gary Cooper is the town marshal. All set to go on his honeymoon. What was the actress' name?"

"Grace Kelly. They're all set to go. He's about to hang up his badge and gun and set off into a bright new romantic future with an absurdly young wife."

"Yes. And then the bad guys show up."

"The Frank Miller gang, loitering at the train station, anxious for their leader to arrive."

"The train gets in at noon and Frank Miller is on it, fresh out of prison."

"Vowed to kill Gary Cooper, the marshal that sent him up, and he's returning to keep his promise."

"Don't tell me," Agent Mitchell said. "The marshal sticks around to face down the threat. Sounds like standard Hollywood formula. What's the point?"

"I'm not finished," said Roland. "He has to do it alone. None of the menfolk will step up. He goes around town while the clock is ticking trying to find men willing to be deputized, men willing to stand up for the law. All of them tell him he'd be wise to take off while he still has the chance. It's a story about cowardice."

"I see. Agent Healy and me are the cowardly townspeople."

"No. You're the Frank Miller Gang. Right, Roland?"

"Yes. You want to punish a man who stands for law and order."

"That's a bit extreme," Agent Mitchell said. "All we're asking you to do is not get people all riled up. There's no way you can foresee, let alone control, the ramifications of your rhetoric."

"Tell you what. If I'm invited on another program, I'll steer the conversation toward archeoastronomy."

Agent Healy looked at Gina "You realize your boyfriend is a nutjob."

"What's *archeo*-astronomy?" Agent Mitchell said.

"Stonehenge, crop circles, ancient aliens—crazy shit like that."

"Not exactly. Now you see why I need to get out there and educate the public."

Agent Healy looked at Gina again. "You do know that, right?"

"He's not my boyfriend."

"We're done here." Roland got up out of his chair. She hadn't answered the agent's insulting question and her silence, then, nullified it. Gina got up and moved toward the door. Agent Mitchell got up and went to the door to open it for her in what was, it seemed to Roland, an unnecessary display of gentlemanliness. Roland stood with his eyes fixed on Agent Healy, who remained in his chair. He wondered if the man chose to remain seated so as not to draw attention to how little difference is made when he stood up, but he kept that observation to himself. Restraint of tongue, a principle touted in AA that he seldom honored.

"You got anything else to say?" Roland looked over at Agent Mitchell. "Or you?"

"I'm not worried about you," Agent Healy said.

"You could have told me that over the telephone."

"No. I had to see you for myself. People like you are bound to self-destruct."

"People like me?"

"The hard-drinking lone ranger type."

"The Lone Ranger didn't drink."

"A kid with your mouth needs four black belts."

"The guys who ratified the Bill of Rights were intellectual black belts. That's all the self-defense I need."

"Don't lean too heavily on the First Amendment," Agent Mitchell said. "What you're doing might come close to yelling fire in a crowded theater."

"That's the right thing to yell when the theater's on fire, Holmes."
"I'm not your homey."
"I meant Oliver Wendell Holmes, Junior."
Roland left the agents to find their way out of the building.

~~~~~

He sat at his station and turned on his game machine. The thought of having to negotiate a digital golf course in search of defects in order to document the exact steps required to reproduce them struck him as the most absurd of all occupations, yet there was a knack to it at which someone with a mind of his fastidious sort naturally excelled. He glanced over to his right at Gina, twice, three times, enough to make sure that she was ignoring him, then set about his punctilious task as the other testers gradually trickled in.

The collegial brotherhood of game testers that occupied most of the floor had not warmed to him over the past few months for several reasons: He was a few years older, a head taller, and built like an athlete. Besides, he was not yet a bona fide employee. That he spoke more fluently, with a broader vocabulary and finer diction, might have put them off as well. And he could horse around with Gina, could make her laugh—that set him apart, perhaps made him the subject of their envy. However they felt about Roland, when he left the building abruptly before noon last Friday and did not return, no one made mention of it. Now he sat at his station, in their midst again, head shaved and radiating the aura of an unrepentant killer. The video they all had watched showed that he could end the life of any one of them with little effort—a chop to the Adam's apple, an elbow to the temple, a punch to the heart, or of course a quick twist of the neck. On the internet, his legend was growing—he could stare you to death or, at the very least, liquefy your bowels.

After an hour or so, the workplace, by all outward appearances, assumed its normal routine amid the buzz of electronic machines and constant flashing of animated graphics. Yet even with most of the testers ensconced in their myopic work with the aid of headphones, the mood among them lacked the characteristic contentment of young people playing games for a living, for the tension given off by Gina's clenched jaw pervaded the room. Gina wasn't laughing today. No, no, no. Gina was angry with Roland, that much was clear. The why of it was anyone's guess. So, when she got up around lunchtime and shouldered her purse to leave the office, heads turned when Roland followed her out.

He was determined to find out what had turned her sour if only to understand how he could have misread her during the interview with the agents. For all his prodigious mental gifts, the behavior of women often mystified him. One thing was clear enough—she hadn't invited him to follow her. The lunch date he'd assumed was still on meant nothing to her. He was starting from scratch.

~~~~~

Gina drove them in silence to a little Thai place not far from work, half empty at 11:30 with the lunch crowd yet to arrive in numbers. The little rectangle of a table forced them too close together for his comfort and exaggerated his size. The cheap wooden chair wobbled a bit and he thought he might tilt it back and balance it on one leg and see if his full weight would collapse the frame. He couldn't look at her, only scan the space around her head like he was assessing the color and luminosity of her aura.

"What are we doing here?" He began to open his mouth to reply, but she cut him off. "And don't say it's because you owed me from last Friday."

"I don't have a good answer."

"Well, you'd better come up with something before we order or I'm not staying."

"You mean you'd just walk out? Leave me here?"

"Like it was a medical emergency."

He chuckled uncomfortably. "You're the only thing about work I look forward to. I care about you."

"I believe you believe that."

"But you don't believe it."

"I'd've believed it a few months ago. But you never said it. Now I don't like hearing it, whether it's real or not. I'm sure you *want* to care about me, but that's as much as I'm prepared to believe out of you right now."

Roland knew better than to probe what she meant by a *few months ago*. He had too much respect for Gina to feign ignorance about the obvious purport of her observation, and since she'd been polite enough not to come right out and call him a drunk, he was not about to invite her to be so blunt. He closed the eyes in his by-now bristly head in a show of genuine shame.

"You're right. I don't blame you."

"Don't blame me for what?"

"Not wanting to be around me."

"Can you even stand to be around yourself?"

They ordered their meals. When the waitress disappeared, Roland didn't remember what he'd ordered, so heavily did her question weigh upon his mind. The chair creaked again as if his mass had suddenly increased and threatened its integrity, as though the stress of his simply being increased the force of gravity on his body.

"I have to do this."

"No. You don't. It's not a duty."

"It feels like it is, like the universe, or fate, call her the Great Stage Mother in the Sky, has shoved me scrambling into the spotlight, and I either have to give a memorable performance or run back and hide behind her skirts."

"Or you could fall flat on your face."

"That's a risk I'm willing to take."

She took a sip of water. "If you plan to continue what you're doing I don't think you should stay at this job."

"Are you speaking just for yourself, or have you polled the office?"

"You should know me better than to ask that question."

"Just tell me to quit and I'll do it."

"It's not about me, not about what I want."

"Then what it is about?"

"I'm suggesting that if you really want the job, really want to succeed in this company, go in and tell Michael that you need to get this media thing out of your system and ask him to hold your job. I bet he would do it. But don't trade on his good nature. He likes you and doesn't want to fire you, but if you become too big of a distraction, he won't have a choice. So think of him. If you do what's best for him, it will probably be what's best for you too."

After their meals came, they ate largely in silence, which suited Roland as he was hungry and wanted to concentrate on the spicy comestibles while he contemplated Gina's advice. As the minutes passed her face softened, as though, having said her piece, she had somehow managed to turn the matter over to a power greater than herself. When they were both nearly finished, she put down her fork and crossed her arms in a frank display of skepticism. "What possessed you to shave your head? It looks ridiculous."

It took a second for Roland to digest the question. "I wasn't drunk if that's what you're wondering."

"I wasn't hinting that. I mean, that wouldn't explain the timing of it."

Roland thought about it. What was the truth, after all? Did he even know for sure why he'd had his head shaved? Did he need to have a reason or, more to the point, did he need to know what exactly, if anything, had motivated him to do it? If it was just a spur-of-the-moment reckless act, did that expose a weakness in his character or perhaps a dangerous quirk in his personality? The more he mulled it over, the more he realized how serious a question it was, how truly it deserved an honest reply, even if that amounted to *I really have no idea."*

"I'm not entirely sure, Gina. Maybe I wanted the world peering in at me to see someone I would not recognize."

"I'm not sure what that even means."

"Maybe I wanted to create a public image that would disappear as soon as I regrew my hair."

"Sounds like you gave it a lot of thought." If she meant it sarcastically, he couldn't detect it.

"None, actually."

"People—men in their twenties—don't just shave their heads on a whim, at least not ones I'd want to know."

"Saturday morning I walked into a little chapel in North Beach and wound up having a good long talk with a priest, a bald Franciscan. If it hadn't been a good talk and he hadn't been bald, I wouldn't have gotten my head shaved afterward. That's as truthful as I can be about it."

"You're a Catholic? You went to confession?"

"I don't do the sacraments. But I used to when I was a kid."

"Did you tell him the truth? Cuz you didn't tell me the truth."

Roland wasn't sure the half-truth he'd told her Friday was what she was talking about. "Remind me."

"You said he was a burglar. When I asked you about your arm, you said the man who cut you was a burglar. You knew that wasn't true. It didn't ring true at the time. Burglars don't stick around to fight when they've been caught."

Of course, she was right. It was a stupid lie, one he'd blurted impulsively, perhaps distracted by the urgency and difficulty of his plan to copy the NBA files from her computer. A stupid lie, yes, but not so egregious that he couldn't wriggle out of it. "You're right. It was the wrong word. I meant it only in the sense of an intruder, not thief."

"Not likely. Not for one so good with words."

Now he grew annoyed. "Look, Gina. I didn't want to talk about it, so I punted. And I don't want to talk about it now either."

"Why, cuz I'm not pointing a camera at you? I watched that little performance you put on last night after you killed that—person. The man I was watching was you, not the man I thought I knew. And then you come to work and sit down like it's a normal day until the FBI shows up, at which point you drag me in to make yourself look like a normal person."

"What do you mean, normal person?"

"One that has friends."

Roland flinched. "You are my friend. You had my back in there. I don't understand this."

"Those guys were there for no good reason—that was pretty obvious to me. I had your back out of basic decency. As to friends, whether or not we are, you definitely are *not* a normal person."

"If I'm going to make myself a media personality, then it can't hurt."

"And I wonder why you would want to make yourself into a media personality."

"I have a message, a distinct point of view, and I think I can make a little money if the demand for my message is great enough."

"I had feelings for you too, you know. I know you know that, Roland. Now I don't know what to make of you."

"I see. So, it's not just about me making things easy on Michael. You sincerely would prefer if I were not around any longer, for your own comfort."

"Once my feelings are turned off, you'll be just like the rest of them."

"I'm not sure what you mean."

"You used me like a prop in there with those FBI goofs."

"You're one of the few people in the world I trust, strangely enough. I felt more comfortable with you there."

"All I witnessed was you taunting them, letting them know how dangerous you can be."

"It's not an act. I am dangerous."

"That's fine. I'd rather be with a dangerous man than a wimp, but only if he has his dangerous powers under control, which I'm not sure you do."

"You may be right, Gina. I stopped sparring a few years ago when I caught myself going too far, well past victory, trying to finish people off."

"Maybe that was a step in the right direction."

"No. The right thing to do was get my mind right and keep sparring—to exorcise that demon."

"You think going out and making a spectacle of yourself will help you get your mind, right? I highly doubt it. Your mind seemed alright when I first met you, and you and I both know what's changed since then."

"I was hoping we could avoid that subject."

"We're avoiding it. That much is clear."

Roland studied her face for a hint of derision. Even a trace of pity would have done. But he found nothing but tired compassion. He drank from his water glass and deliberately let a few ice cubes slip past his teeth so he could crush them loudly with his molars instead of making a reply. Gina remained silent. The ball was in his court.

"I lied to those guys. I want to make sure you know, so you don't think I was trying to lie to you too."

"Lied about what?"

"I implied that I didn't have anything lined up, media-wise. That wasn't true. The call I took was an invitation to do a radio interview today, in less than an hour actually."

"Well, at least you'll be sober, if hungover counts as sober."

Roland started to speak in his own defense but could scarcely mount a respectable stammer.

"Don't. I saw the video of you last night. Should we watch it together right now?"

He had no choice but to submit. She'd made it easy, left him room for self-effacement.

"You're right. I imagine I looked like a lunatic. I hope the radio host goes easier on me than you do."

"I hope he cuts you into little ribbons then rips the ribbons to shreds."

Roland thought that went too far. "He came at me with an effing machete!"

"You and God can sort that out. I'm talking about the spectacle you made afterward. The internet is forever, you know."

He accepted her final dig in silence as they stood up in unison, then he dropped too much money on the table before following her to the door.

~~~~~

Gina pulled into the company parking lot and found Roland's car where it stood out like a rotten tooth in an otherwise flawless dentition. He got out without a word and looked at her and smiled to see if she would smile back. She pursed her lips and drove off. Roland got in his car and left the lot and found a quiet spot in the neighborhood under a tree and parked and rolled down the window and lit a cigarette and stared at his phone. The time read 12:55. He texted Joshua, *I'm ready.* Joshua texted back, *Good. I'll be listening. Jordan just teased your spot. Sit tight.* Roland opened a browser on his phone and searched for Peter Jordan to find a picture of his face. He'd heard of the popular talk radio host, of course, but had never tuned in to his show, and he wanted to see what the man looked like before he went on the air with him. The photo he found showed a man in his late fifties or early sixties with thick, black-rimmed glasses and a full head of grayish-white hair. It was a posed media shot for which Peter Jordan put on the jowly smile of a well-fed man.

Roland put in his earbuds and cranked back the seat and waited, hinging his arm in and out of the window as he finished his cigarette. The phone rang at 12:59. He pressed the green answer button. "Roland Hazzard speaking."

"Hi, Mister Hazzard." It was a woman's voice, a young woman's. "Thanks for agreeing on such short notice. We're in a commercial break right now that will end in exactly five minutes."

"I understand."

"I'm gonna put you on hold—you'll hear some music—and when the break is over, Peter will open up the line and you'll be live to our audience. There's a few seconds delay, so don't have the show on your radio while you're on the air. The quieter the better."

"Got it." With a flick of the wrist, Roland sent the cigarette spinning on an arc toward the far gutter. It was a damned good shot, especially with the left hand. The butt hit the side of the curb with enough impact that the ember popped off and sizzled out in the dirty trickle. He waited. Time had never ground so slowly. He thought of his fight with Barsamian, how those few minutes had passed in a flash. The music stopped. He heard a brief buzzing sound, then a squelch, and then a voice.

"Mister Roland Hazzard, this is Peter Jordan."

"I'm here."

"We're live in five, four, three, two…. Welcome back, sports fans. As most of you know, we reserve the final hour on Mondays for questions and subjects pertaining to universal wisdom and, lacking even one creative bone in my rather gangly skeleton, I decided to call this hour—can I get a drum roll, Audrey?—the Universal Wisdom Hour. Normally, I pick a topic and give you my perspective and then open up the phone lines for the lucky few of you who get past our redoubtable screener to give your thoughts, and we mix it up in between the commercial breaks, and the ratings are always strong, so we know it's good radio.

But today we're going to do something different. We're not going to have any callers—we're going to have a guest. We might have done this once or twice before but whatever the case not for a long time, so it feels like a novel departure from the normal format. I'm going to introduce the topic of course and then spend a few segments discussing it with a young man who has become—very recently become—that topic's poster boy. We have on the line Mister Roland Hazzard. Say hello, Roland, if I may be so bold as to use your first name."

"Glad to be here." The spontaneity with which the professional radio talk show host spoke to his national audience and then pivoted to him set him at ease and he told himself that all he had to do was follow along, speak when spoken to, and let Peter Jordan run the show. *I'll breeze right through this.* He resolved to pay attention to Jordan's art as he himself would, and very soon, need to set himself up as the host of his own internet channel.

"Tell us, Roland, if you'll venture a guess, what is the topic for today?"

"Didn't I just hear you say that's your department?"

"Work with me here, Roland—play along. At the end of the day, we're here not just to edify but to fascinate and entertain."

"All due respect, Mister Jordan, but I've never listened to your show. I don't surf the AM dial."

"But you've heard of the show—at least give me that satisfaction."

"Yeah. I've heard of you and Limbaugh, a few others, the local boy Savage. But I don't know what makes you guys different from one another—except I'm sure there's no one like Michael Savage. He keeps my hand off the dial."

"Now, now—we're not here to pump the competition." Peter Jordan sounded amused. "Anyway, I have only three million listeners. You can be forgiven for not being one of the three hundred twenty-seven million who don't tune in."

"That makes me feel a whole lot better."

Peter Jordan chuckled at the good-natured sarcasm. "Now, seriously, what do you think the topic is for today? Remember, this is the Universal Wisdom Hour."

"Killing bad guys."

"That's a little pedestrian. We have a very well-educated audience here."

"Killing bad guys afoot, then."

"Give him a rim shot, Audrey. That was a good one—he earned himself a rim shot."

Audrey, the show's engineer, obliged with a canned snare drum backbeat.

"RIGHTEOUS VIOLENCE. The topic today is righteous violence, for which our special guest is a perfect exemplar, at least by his own description. Unless you've been living in a diving bell for the past few days, you're familiar with his recent exploits. I'd venture to guess that Roland Hazzard holds the modern record for self-defense homicides in a two-day stretch. Have you reflected on that possibility, Roland?"

"No. But I guess it depends on what you mean by modern. If you mean ever since the FBI started keeping homicide stats, you might be right. But over the span of human history, two righteous killings in a couple of days is practically nothing."

"So, you're a history buff?"

"Yes. It's a necessity. Everyone should be a history buff."

"Oh? And why is that?"

"People who don't know history go around flinching at every little thing."

"What do you mean? You'll have to expand on that."

"Up until fairly recently—historically speaking—everyone grew up hearing stories and legends of what had gone before, and most of it was pretty violent or tragic. People expected bad things to happen, and when bad things happened nobody freaked out. The ancient myths kept people from having PTSD. Nowadays, if someone cuts you off in traffic you grid your teeth all day about it. If someone oversteps his authority, you call him a Nazi. Anyone who knows what the Nazis did would never call anyone a Nazi. Not knowing history makes people prone to irrational behavior and easy to manipulate."

"I see. People no longer appreciate that life is nasty, brutish, and short. We've turned into a bunch of whiners."

"The full quote lays it out. Hobbes wrote: *In a state of nature, the life of man is solitary, poor, nasty, brutish, and short.* Now, the better we learned how to manage nature, the richer we got, the longer we lived, and the more tightly we packed ourselves together. But the nasty and the brutish part will never be solved. Case in point, The City—I mean San Francisco—is so densely populated that this butcher character—this cold-blooded recreational throat slasher—picks a victim and breaks into the wrong apartment. He couldn't even be sure where she lived. And then what does he do—admit his mistake? No. I asked him to leave, did everything but open the door for him, but he was a nasty little brute, and short to boot, not that that matters. He'd opted out of the social compact long before he pried open my window. And so, he stayed. Rather than admit his mistake, he stuck around to get killed. Little bastard had to know he stood no chance. I was wearing next to nothing. He could see how well put together I was."

"So, the Glendale Butcher—you think he knew history?"

"Yes of course. His people were Armenian refugees. He'd heard stories, stories that hit very close to home. He had to know the meaning of the word *brutality.*"

"I get it, now. You two both understood history—the human condition. He didn't flinch and you didn't flinch, and you put him down like the mad dog that he was and haven't lost any sleep over it."

"In an orderly society, bad people need to be killed *instead* of being arrested and arraigned and tried. In a confused society, people lose sleep over that thought. There's a whip of universal wisdom for you."

"What about last night? How did you sleep? The man you dispatched yesterday—a kid, practically—a cousin of Barsamian or so I read—he wasn't a psychopathic serial killer. You could have escaped, could have run back into the building."

"I don't care if it turns out he was a mental retard AWOL from his group home. A fighter doesn't run from a threat when he can stop it. I slept the sleep of the good."

"And just shot right out of bed this morning, huh? Not a care in the world. Clips of your precision self-defense and taunts to the police whizzing all over the world. Everyone seems to know who you are. What are you going to do with all this fame?"

"Tell the FBI, as often as possible, to kiss my ass, all the way up to the director."

"What's your beef with the FBI?"

"Two agents—Tweedle Dee and Tweedle Dum—showed up this morning at the office where I work, took me into a conference room, tried to intimidate me."

"You're putting me in a bad spot here, Roland."

"How so?"

"I don't know you. I can't be sure that what you're saying is true. My reputation—the integrity of my radio program—is more important to me than just about anything."

"I can't prove it over the phone, but I'll give you the names of the agents if that will lend to my credibility."

"Stop right there, Roland. True or not, I won't let you level accusations or pour scorn on particular FBI agents on my program. Let's talk about it hypothetically."

"I don't understand."

"Supposing they did what you said—showed up at your work and tried to intimidate you—why would they want to do that?"

"To keep me off programs like this."

"And you think the director—James Comey I believe—would know about this?"

"The two chumps who showed up this morning were not programmed to act independently, so I have to assume it came from higher up, and the buck stops at Comey if not at his boss."

"Do you think you're making even President Obama nervous?"

"We live in a post-constitutional age. The sovereign individual is a threat to governmental authority in this once great experiment of a country."

"What does the government have to be afraid of?"

"They're afraid I might inspire some sort of vigilante movement. People are basically cowards. You want a piece of universal wisdom—there's one for you. People are basically cowards, Americans included. The government doesn't want ordinary citizens taking the law into their own hands."

"I know you're not a regular listener, Roland, but most of those that are are aware that I'm a bit of a history buff myself. Got my degree in history from Yale, as a matter of fact—and I'll take issue with the statement that Americans are basically cowards. That's one thing that distinguishes us, historically speaking, from other nations."

"Yale, huh? Then you know the history behind the illustrious Elihu Yale, one of the richest slave traders of his day. That school should've been named Dummer University, but that wouldn't have sounded so good."

"Is that supposed to be funny? If so, I don't get it."

"It's not a joke. A man named Jeremiah Dummer ponied up most of the dough for the university—a hell of a lot more than Yale—but they named it after the great slave trader instead because it sounded better. So much for courage."

"Ok, fair enough—we'll fact-check that. In any case, that hardly proves your point. Americans fought a civil war to end slavery. Isn't that a bit more important than the name of a university?"

"The Civil War is a perfect example of national cowardice."

"You've lost me again, Roland."

"Look, Mister Jordan, it often takes only one man or one woman to rally the people, to make them act courageously. There was Lincoln. Sure, he had a lot of support from a few Radical Republicans in Congress, but ultimately it was Lincoln's call. He was a man of vision, of courage, because he knew how bloody things would get, but he went ahead with it anyway."

"I agree with all of that."

"But then what happened?" Roland lit another cigarette and waited for an answer."

"Go ahead and tell us. I think I know where you're going with this."

"We didn't—the nation, what was left of it—didn't dare to win the peace. Lincoln was dead and buried, Senator Sumner—a Harvard man, sorry—was alive but would never see straight again after getting his skull bashed in on the Senate floor by a thin-skinned, pro-slavery Democrat—and the North had officially won. But so much for the newly freed slaves. No places to live, no money, largely illiterate. The victors left them at the mercy of their enemies. And it took a hundred years for the Republicans to button down the law enough so that you could no longer legally oppress the Negro. Is it any wonder there are still a lot of pissed-off blacks? Sad to say, but it's pretty easy to be a race-hustler these days when you can hold up legitimate grievances still fresh in the national memory."

"So, what would you have done if you'd been Lincoln, assuming you hadn't been murdered?"

"After the South surrendered?"

"Yes—after the South surrendered."

"Indefinite martial law. Place the successionist states under some kind of territorial status. Make them earn the right to rejoin the Union. No. Instead, it was: *Recite a loyalty oath and all is forgiven and you're good to go with your Confederate flag."*

"I mean with the slaves—the emancipated slaves."

Roland thought about that. The car was heating up as the sun slipped past the shade tree. He reached over and cranked down the passenger window to let in a breeze.

"I'd've given 'em guns—guns and lots of ammunition."

"Get a race war going right away—that the idea?"

"The forty-acres-and-a-mule thing was a good idea, and Lincoln would probably have implemented something like that across the

South—not just in Georgia and the Carolinas. But without guns, the blacks couldn't really be Americans, couldn't fully practice the American right of lethal self-defense, the right to commit Righteous Violence."

"Seems like you've given this a lot of thought. I had no idea we'd be in for a dissertation today."

"I'm hearing the tinklings of a commercial break coming."

"You're right as a matter of fact. Friends, we'll be back with Roland Hazzard after we pay a few bills."

~~~~~

Roland watched a line of ants march across his dashboard. Five or six of them carried the carcass of a larger insect to a destination he could not ascertain. Did this small contingent have a whole colony to feed somewhere in his car? He gently blew a stream of smoke at the troop to test their resolve and noticed the carcass-bearers did not waver in their duty. He checked the time, a few minutes left before the break would be over. He reached into the back seat and found an empty water bottle and uncapped it and maneuvered himself to piss in it and filled the thing and screwed the cap back on and set the hot receptacle on the passenger seat. He thought about the breakfast sandwich grenade he'd tossed into the sleek Mercedes a few days ago. *Would I have used this bottle of piss instead?* He smoked and waited. When he finished the cigarette, he uncapped the bottle and dropped the butt in. The liquid doused the ember with a fizzle and he capped the bottle again and watched the unburnt tobacco slowly bleed into the dark urine. The last commercial concluded—an advertisement for a nutritional supplement that would eliminate joint pain—and he was back on the air.

"Welcome back, sports fans. For those just tuning in, we're continuing with the Universal Wisdom Hour, and we have on the line a special guest, Mister Roland Hazzard, who no doubt most of you have heard about. We began the hour with the topic *Righteous Violence*—appropriate, some would say, to his recent actions—but Mister Hazzard has nudged us over to the subject of *Human Cowardice*, asserting that human beings as a species are, by nature, cowardly. Before the break, Roland gave, I believe, a rather convincing example in the post-Civil War Reconstruction which, most would agree, put the former slaves in a precarious condition. The victors—the North, the Republicans—did not do enough to stop, let's say, the depredations of the KKK. Is that a fair summary, Roland?"

"You left out one important detail—probably the most important detail."

"That being?"

"Lincoln. One man of courage, in the right place at the right time, is sometimes enough. My point was that Lincoln was the spine that stood the Union upright, and once he was dead—murdered for his courage—the will toward Righteous Violence was vastly diminished. We won the war because momentum was on our side and we had better guns and supplies and more Irish, but once it was over, we were left with Andrew Johnson in the White House, a Southern Democrat, a coward, and a traitor. He openly opposed federally guaranteed rights for blacks, so not only a coward but a villain. A stain on the presidency. Lincoln would have worked hard to set things right, and the racial tensions that have existed ever since would not have become nearly as severe. Few bullets in world history have had a greater ripple effect than John Wilkes Booth's."

"Best I can come up with is Gavrilo Princip."

"Even Princip is debatable. A lot of things could have touched off the Great War. The plans had been drawn, the forces marshaled, the railways laid. Princip just happened to tip the first domino."

"Much as I'd love to have that debate with you in a coffee shop or cigar lounge, I need to re-focus the topic. Back to cowardice, American cowardice. How about the boys who stormed the beaches of Normandy, wading through a literal bloodbath with machine gun rounds whizzing past? No one disputes that the US forces tipped the balance in World War II. Does America get credit for righteous violence in that instance, national bravery even?"

"Are there still Germans?"

"What?" Peter Jordan sounded genuinely confused, as though he'd either misheard Roland's question or didn't comprehend it.

"Germans walking around in this world—is it acceptable to you that Germany still exists?"

"That's ridiculous. Not all Germans were Nazis. Are you suggesting we should have wiped Germany off the map?"

"When we conquered the Hittites, did we say *these are the good Hittites and these are the bad Hittites?* No. We got rid of them all."

"We? We were talking about the Allied forces. Who's *we?*"

"Sorry. I have a vivid imagination. Sometimes when I dig into history I can picture it—sometimes I'm on the winning side, sometimes on the losing. I was—I'm sorry—marauding with the Assyrians just then."

"Now that you're back with us in the 21st Century, tell us why we should have exterminated the Germans. You were sounding almost rational up to that point."

"I didn't mean exterminate, exactly. There's an easier, softer way."

"You're on thin ice, Roland. I don't think this meets the lofty standards of the Universal Wisdom Hour."

"We're talking about righteous violence—right? Well, I'm talking about righteous resettlement. We should have occupied Germany, taken all the assets, handed the country over to the Jews, and methodically relocated every German family—non-breeding groups—to far-flung locations around the globe. Sprinkle them around sporadically so that their genes would be subsumed by the local pools or just die out. No more Germany and, in a generation or two, no more Germans. That's the price you pay for trying to establish a Thousand Year Reich. Who could argue against that approach?"

"The Russians—Stalin."

"We had the bomb. I'd 'a told that sonofabitch to suck beets or we'd decorate the skies above his onion domes with mushroom clouds."

"You'd have been a hoot at Yalta. But really, we're getting too far afield. I'm sure you weren't thinking about the great historical injustices when you snapped that young man's neck as easily as opening a jar of pickles."

"The pageant of human history runs freely in the back of my mind like an Indonesian shadow play."

"Sounds pretty distracting. How do you manage to get anything done?"

"It is. Sometimes I just close my eyes and break out the popcorn."

"And you're there, in the pageant, a man of courage, a hero even—is that the context in which you place your actions, your killings?"

"If it wasn't for the internet, no one would have ever heard about me. My actions would be of little more consequence than opening that jar of pickles. People have been killing bad guys in self-defense or vengeance since we could walk upright, and without a lot of fanfare. I won't pretend that I'm not glad to enjoy a little fame, but I haven't succumbed to delusions of grandeur."

"Well, you've certainly used this platform to show off your education. May I ask how old you are?"

"Twenty-five."

"How many twenty-five-year-olds are there running around quoting Hobbes or opining on the buildup to World War One?"

"It's a gift, Mister Jordan. Ever since I could read—as far back as I can remember—certain books, certain authors, just stuck. When I picked up Hobbes for the first time and started paging through it, it was as though I'd read it before. The Universal Wisdom you celebrate every Monday for an hour—I download that stuff straight from the source."

"What you're telling me—what I'm hearing—is that you're some kind of savant, some kind of super-genius, that you're so dialed in to the human condition that killing bad guys, as you say, is just another day at the office. That's quite a lavish mantle to strut around in."

"You invited me on this program to be a symbol of righteous violence—I don't wear it like a mantle, lavish or otherwise. I see it more as the simple tunic of, say, the shepherd boy who stepped forward when the soldiers were afraid. He never intended to wear the mantle of a king, but the forces that shape history had something else in mind."

"You talking about David—David who slew Goliath?"

"The very one."

"That was just a lucky shot, the way I read it."

"It might have been a lucky shot, but the stone didn't kill him."

"Whaddaya mean *the stone didn't kill him*? That's the narrative. Book of Samuel. I don't even need to fact-check that."

"You're treating it as a work of fiction, in which case you'd be correct. The text must be the last word as to matters of *fictional* fact. But it's not meant to be a work of fiction. We were talking about history, were we not? And as work of history—ancient history at that—it needs to hold up under scrutiny."

"And I guess you're qualified to reinterpret the book of Samuel."

"*First* Book of Samuel, to be exact. Yes—the facts don't add up. It's pretty much impossible to kill a giant, a Nephilim, by hitting him in the head with a stone, even a really smooth hard river stone. It's much more likely that David knocked him out. At any rate, there's no way anyone could have been certain Goliath was dead when he hit the ground. So, what do you do when you knock out a giant?"

"Are you asking me?"

"Yeah. What's the sensible thing to do after you lay out a giant sonofabitch with a stone?"

"I dunno—run like hell?"

"That's why you'd never be a king, why you'd never wear the lavish mantle. If David had fled the scene, the Philistines would have slaughtered the Israelites, and there'd have never been a Jesus."

"I'm sticking with the text, that the stone killed him like it says in the Bible."

"You're getting lost in the weeds here. Whether the stone killed Goliath or not—and like I said, there was no time for a medical examination—it's clear that David wasn't taking any chances. He did what a king would do. Where Peter Jordan, proud alumnus of Yale University, would have taken off running, David the humble shepherd walked over, pulled Goliath's sword out of its scabbard, and hacked off his head. That's a leader. That's a man who changes history or guides it in his own direction."

"What's your point—that you're one of those rare individuals who can shape history?"

"No. I don't claim to be a Lincoln or a David or a Joan of Arc. My point is only that courage is rare and can appear in the lowliest among us. Whether the average meat sack walking the streets has any conscious knowledge of what has come before, of the cowardice of our forebears that has rendered the world in the sorry condition we find it—has any knowledge of that history or feels the sting of that congenital shame—that sorry meat sack has breathed it in and understands, unconsciously at least, just by swiveling his head around, how little is expected of him. If he himself is not evil, then evil is his master, and those who stand up to evil are fools in his eyes or, even worse, self-important blowhards who need to be silenced lest they expose his own spineless moral anatomy."

Peter Jordan cleared his throat.

"Let me get this straight. You're calling FDR a horrible president because he didn't do something he had no power to do and which most people would consider insane?"

"No. And it's not an insane idea. It was the morally correct thing to do, given that the Germans tried to exterminate the Jews with industrial efficiency. FDR's sin—and sin is not strong enough a word—was handing Eastern Europe over on a silver platter to his buddy Uncle Joe. His refusal to accept Jews fleeing Europe en masse was enough to earn him a spot in Hell; but condemning half of Europe to Communist slavery at the hands of Stalin was a capitulation to evil for which there is no comparison. I changed my mind—he was a villain. It wasn't like he didn't know what happened in Ukraine when the Soviets collectivized the farms, which required them to murder or imprison all the Ukrainian families that were good at farming. And Stalin certainly wasn't surprised that millions of Ukrainians starved to death. No, no, no, on the contrary, he aggravated their misery by outlawing the eating of children in case the famine-stricken wanted to resort to such extreme measures to survive."

"That's quite a little rant. Are you finished?"

"My rant is timeless and universal—transcendental you might say. There can never be an end to it, not even when our sun collapses, for there will always be, somewhere in the two trillion galaxies, some son-of-a-bitch getting kicked around by reckless, entrenched authority. Whole populations subjugated I'll wager. Slavery is the norm. The Eastern bloc of the Soviet Union consisted largely of Slavs, and *Slav* probably goes back to the Latin word for *slave*, so some might say it was their linguistic destiny to fall under the yoke of Communist totalitarianism. But it was not. FDR had a chance to save them, but instead he let Stalin have his way."

"On that uplifting note, we need to go to another break."

The host buttoned him over to the producer who asked him if he wanted to continue the interview and Roland said ok and the producer said good it was going very well and that the commercial break would be over in five minutes and to please wait on the line until Peter Jordan patched him into the broadcast again. Music—Handel—played while he remained on hold. Roland tried to retrace his words, from beginning to end, to ascertain their genesis. He decided that after the show he would see if he could write them down and then compare them to the recording if he could obtain one from the station. The passion was real, that much he knew, but the words themselves, the rapid associations he was making, seemed to have come from an outside intelligence for which he was grateful and at the same time afraid.

He got out of the car and started walking back to the office. A few minutes later, Peter Jordan reemerged in his earbud and bumped-in the next segment before addressing Roland.

"Welcome back, sports fans, and thank you, Mister Hazzard, for staying on the line. I must say you accomplished what few guests have—you talked so vigorously that you forced us to extend our last segment past the break, so I have to warn our listeners in advance that this next segment will be a short one."

"My apologies. I didn't mean to get carried away."

"So, when we left off you were condemning FDR, one of the most popular US presidents. But I'd like to get back to David, specifically how you were comparing yourself to the young shepherd who, against all odds, slew the giant Goliath. Did I get that right?"

"Not exactly. I used him as an example of how bravery can come from humble origins. What I did wasn't brave so much as it was necessary. And don't forget, David had an advantage—he had a long-range weapon."

"And he had God on his side. You can't get a better edge than that."

"I'm agnostic on that subject."

"Yet the people you mentioned—Lincoln, David, Joan of Arc especially—they all recognized a divine agency. Heck, FDR even invoked the name of Christ himself in the run-up to war."

"Maybe so, but he turned his back a ship full of Jews who'd managed to escape the Nazis. They could see the glittering lights of Miami when the devout Christian in Chief ordered the Coast Guard to turn the ship around. No freedom for you, grubby Jews! A few years later, he handed Eastern Europe over to Stalin—put the slave back in Slav. Then he rolled out the red carpet for the best Nazi scientists he could find. I'm pretty sure Christian principles weren't guiding his policies."

"Fair enough. But let's put aside the history lesson. I can hear my ratings crashing as my listeners roll their eyes and move on. The question on the table is: Do you think you were acting according to God's will? You invited the question by bringing up the examples you did. I'm assuming a kid from Northern Idaho had something like a Christian upbringing, and I listened to your interview at KABC San Francisco where you sermonized on the Sixth Commandment. So, I have to ask the question."

Roland wasn't sure if Peter Jordan was about to repeat his question so he let a few seconds of dead air go by before he realized that the host, and the audience, were waiting on him.

"Do I believe in God—is that the question?"

"I guess you could boil it down to that. What I really wanted to know is if you're using Biblical morality as a justification or are you a sincere believer."

"I don't have any theological commitments. Like I said before, I'm agnostic as to the agency of a Creator in the course of human events— kinda like Thomas Jefferson. As far as my upbringing, I'm not going to toss any meat to the jackals. What I will say, to answer your question, is that anyone who truly believes in God wouldn't say so."

"And why is that?"

"Because it doesn't mean anything."

"Come again." Roland had, once again, flummoxed the seasoned radio talk show host.

"It wouldn't mean *anything*, because it would mean *everything*, and no one can wrap his mind around everything. It's too big a thing to claim. It would change the way you lived, the way you talked to people, the way you woke up in the morning. When people say *I believe in God* they usually mean nothing more than *I like the idea that there must be a God.* Jesus never said he believed in God. He called God his *Father.* He claimed a personal relationship, a direct descent. He was either lying, crazy, or was what he claimed to be. He didn't debate it, didn't discuss it. He lived it as the absolute truth and challenged the rest of us to do the same. That's way too heavy for me, but I can respect it. I can't do it and I sure as hell won't denigrate it. But the words—the words by themselves—mean nothing to me."

"I see. No religion for you, but you're not an atheist. We don't want our butcher slayers to be stone-cold atheists. We like transcendent values here on the Peter Jordan show, especially during the Universal Wisdom Hour."

Roland chuckled just to be nice. "Yes. It's fair to say I possess some sort of transcendent values."

"And how would you characterize those values?"

Roland thought about it. He was nearing the building. The blue-tinted, mirrored windows shimmered and distorted his image into that of a man dripped to the earth from the molten clouds suspended above him. He saw him himself, momentarily—the probing question still humming in his eardrums—as a sort of transcendent being trapped, perhaps, between two competing dimensions. Was he the hero of his story, or the villain? Or was that yet to be revealed?

"I thought I made that pretty clear. Don't cower in the face of evil. Fight back if you can, and if you can't, then learn what you need to learn to keep yourself safe."

"So, you're like Batman. Except your cover is as a video game tester."

"How do you know what I do for a living?"

"My crack research team has been at work while we've been talking. You're becoming more famous by the hour—by the minute even."

"Well, here's an update, hot off the presses. My lunch break is over. I'm on my way into the office right now, heading in to quit. While we've been talking, I've been thinking I need to make more time for being famous. I've tested my last video game, for the time being anyway."

"Can we come with you?"

"You mean you want to listen in? While I quit my job?"

"Yeah, as long as you keep it clean. Why not? We've tallied a lot of firsts on this show, and this will certainly be one of those."

"Sounds a little perverse, but okay." He entered the building and swiped his badge and went straight back to Michael's office. The door was open, as was the custom. Michael sat behind his desk wearing his earbuds and looked, arms crossed, at Roland, smiling as though he were expecting him.

Michael didn't wait for Roland to speak. *"Sounds a little perverted, but okay.* How many times have I heard that in my life?"

Roland took a step back. "What the fuck?"

"You need to lasso that tongue, cowboy," said Peter Jordon.

Michael waited for the time lag to catch up. "I agree, Roland. You need to corral that tongue a' yourn." He spoke loudly enough that he could be heard across America.

"Is this some kind of prank?"

"Who are you talking to, Roland?"

"Was this a set-up?" Roland looked at Michael, his voice raised an octave.

"Who are you talking to?" Peter Jordan sounded impatient.

"My boss. He's listening."

"Good, because I was going to tell you to put your phone on speaker."

"No. To the show."

Peter Jordan paused. Then he started laughing. "This is beyond perfection. Let me talk to him. What's his name?"

Michael was laughing too. In a spasm of consternation, Roland flung up his free hand. "You sure you didn't put him up to this, Jordan—you or your producer?"

"I swear on me dear moother's eyes." He had a credible Irish brogue.

"You probably sprang from a crack in a peat bog."

"C'mon, Roland. You've gotta be able to appreciate the irony of the situation…"

Roland pulled out his earbuds and put the phone in speaker mode. "His name is Michael." He set the device on the desk.

The two men shared a good yuck while Roland sat and listened, his mood softening, for the alternative was to turn sullen. *My purpose here is to quit,* he thought, *to embark upon a new adventure, so I might as well make my exit as gracefully—as cheerfully—as possible, especially since millions of people are tuned in.* He was only half-listening. On the credenza behind Michael, standing among the miscellaneous decorative items—a congratulatory plaque recognizing some corporate achievement, several books, a leafy plant, an autographed photo of himself with his arm around a uniformed Jerry Rice, a cleverly wired model of our solar system with a few flying saucers zipping to and fro—was a glass figure shaped like a Franciscan friar filled with hazelnut liqueur, otherwise known as an unopened bottle of Frangelico, booty from last year's Christmas gift exchange no doubt. Michael hadn't even removed the red ribbon tied around its neck. Roland had seen the bottle there before but never taken note of it.

"I've been listening to you for years," said Michael. "Almost always catch at least an hour…"

He's never going to drink that.

"…are you going to miss having Roland around the office?"

He probably doesn't even know what it tastes like.

351

"...he'll be hard to replace... one of the sharpest testers I've ever seen ...but I have to respect his choice..."

I bet he'd give it to me if I...

"...he'll have no shortage of prospects once he stops killing people..."

Roland shook his head like a dog fresh out of a swimming pool. He couldn't believe that he'd been thinking about the bottle of booze, booze he never would have ordered in a million years. He questioned—was it he who'd been dwelling on the bottle, or, if not, then who? A saying he'd heard in AA meetings popped into his head: Man takes a drink, then the drink takes a drink, then the drink takes the man. *Time to step off this merry-go-round.*

"Gimme my phone." He thrust out his hand and Michael give it to him. Roland switched off the speaker before he spoke.

"Hayyy, sports fans, this is Roland Hazzard back on the line. I want to thank Mister Jordan for inviting me on the show today and my boss Michael for being such a good sport for the few months I've been working here. I won't ask him to hold my job—that would be too much. I plan to walk the wire without a net from here on out. And I'd like to thank you listeners out there, especially for not changing the station during my conversation with the host. I need to get used to speaking to large audiences. If I'm lucky enough to be invited to express my views to the public in this or any country, you can be sure that I speak for myself, that I do no one's bidding, and that I absolutely DO wish to change the way you think, or at least put words to thoughts that you already have but have not yet had the nerve to express. And now I will hand in my security badge and be on my way."

He buttoned off the call and set his badge on Michael's desk then extended his hand. Michael shook it and that was that.

~~~~~

Light traffic inbound to The City helped him to relax. He enjoyed driving when he didn't have to think about the other cars around him, when he didn't have to scan ahead and plan his next move. His mind was free to wander. He could pick and choose from the various thoughts that traipsed across his brain or bubbled up from his unconscious. Intriguing him now was the thought that he might, with proper study and practice, be able to teach himself, as he'd read that others had done, to induce by force of will an out-of-body episode when fully awake, not like the chaotic one that had swept him up spontaneously in the church the other day, but a simple, controllable astral floating whereby he could hover above his car while he operated it safely from inside. Probably not, he guessed, but an idea worth investigating. The phone lit up and rang, jarring him out of his reverie.

"Hey, Josh." He was in no mood to talk, having been at it all morning.

"That went well."

"I'm glad you think so because I have no idea. My boss—ex-boss—got a kick out of it."

"Is that all true about the FBI?"

"What are you suggesting?"

"That it might be bullshit. I was hoping Peter Jordan would press for your boss for more details."

"That's not why I cut it short—not to keep him from verifying my story with my boss. I just wanted to wrap it up and put a little bow on it. Those two were prattling on like old hens. What—you worried the feds are gonna take an interest in you?"

"Yeah. I'm your facilitator."

"Well, there's nothing you can do about it now unless you want to call it quits and let me go it alone. I'm not going to beg."

Roland checked the rearview mirrors to see if anyone was behind him, slow as he was driving. It occurred to him that his apartment building was now a well-known address and that would have to deal with invasions of his privacy unless he found another place to live, which he had neither the means nor inclination to do.

"I'm in for the long haul, Roland. I think I can keep you pretty busy. You're pretty fast on your feet and speak in complete sentences, and that's great for radio."

"I want the cable news networks. That should be the next step."

"All I can do is wait for the calls."

"I need to start cashing checks."

"We'll get there, I think. I think your performance today will be a springboard."

"I'm done talking today. I'm all talked out. I'm headed where I can find people who don't speak English."

"Chinatown?"
"Shi de."
"I guess that means yes."
"I'll keep my phone on."
"Be good."
"Whatever that's supposed to mean. I doubt my being good will make any difference at this point."
"Excuse me—I forgot—you're a transcendent being."
"That's the angle. Now let me go so I can put down my phone. Even the transcendent are expected to obey the law."

The call ended. He could feel the concrete rushing beneath his car, closer to him than he wanted the world to be. As he approached the squeeze into The City, he thought again of the breakfast sandwich grenade. Was that good? It was a good shot, certainly, and it made him feel good—no, more than good, omnipotent. Was that good—the rush of power engendered by such an impulsive, frivolous, harmless act of violence? His mind began to race. *What am I doing? What am I doing? What am I doing?*

~~~~~

The elder Chinese denizens of Portsmouth Square had wasted no time in purchasing new boards and pieces, and they'd even been thoughtful enough to buy a traditional Western chess set, likely in honor of their young Caucasian benefactor. Roland strolled over and tossed a pack of cigarettes on the table. "Let's break-a the law." He spoke too loudly on purpose. He was loaded enough to coast for awhile.

They looked up at him and smiled and one man stood and swept his hand over the new equipment to show Roland how well they had used his money. *These are honorable men,* he thought, *most honorable people I know, goddamnit.* He set his new hat on the table next to the new chessboard, the one set up in his honor. One of the men reached over and put the hat on his head and modeled it for the others. They laughed together in their native language.

"You ever been to Los Angeles Chinatown?" He didn't wait for an answer. "Piece a shit. Our Chinatown puts theirs to shame, right?"

They nodded almost certainly out of mere politeness.

"I went there this weekend and picked up that hat."

"Ahhh." They approved in unison. "Very-nice-hat."

"Bought it from a little hombrecito. That means little shithead in Español." He was acting more intoxicated than he felt as a way of lowering his guard, as a way of sensing whether they knew who he was or, more to the point, what he had done. These old men were not plugged in, living off the grid downtown in one of America's centers of technological innovation. In time his fame might reach them, but today he could safely invade their brotherhood as he'd done for the past few months, the same tall affable young white man that he'd been the time before, and the time before that. Somewhere in his heart he knew that, if or when they did find out, even then they would treat him with the same curious hospitality, for their lives—the lives of their mothers and fathers—had been touched savagely by Mao Zedong and, on them, word of Roland's exploits could make no deep impression. "You need a good hat when you shave your head. You Chinese guys should know that better than anyone."

They laughed again, this time more genuinely than before.

Roland picked up the pack of Marlboros and unwrapped it and thumbed open the box and pulled out a cigarette. "Let's break-a the law."

One of the men offered him a light. Roland smoked while he studied the game in progress. He meant to master this discipline, to defeat them politely and graciously, to earn their respect. It was a goal he believed he could achieve, but it was still a long way off. The bottle of baijiu came around and he took a pull. It was a foul concoction, as foreign to his taste as the Oriental board game was to his mind. It sent a shudder through his frame. He let out a gasp. It was foul alright, but it was strong, so it was perfect. He took a second drink, which was not the custom.

"Thank you, gentlemen." He raised his chin and eyed the sun to estimate the time of day, the approach of night.

Chapter 16
October 27-28, 2016

What to make of a general without a plan? Without an organized army? Without an identifiable enemy? What does he make of himself when he opens his eyes and doesn't know where he is? Or what time it is? Or even what day? *And where was I yesterday? And who the hell is calling? And where the hell is my goddamned phone?*

It was his aide-de-camp, and this was reveille.

A groggy voice behind him whispered into his ear. "Are you going to get that?" It sounded like a she, but you never know. Roland swiveled off the mattress and glanced back to verify the person there was female then found the phone in his jacket on the floor. At least he was in his own bedroom and at least he hadn't lost his communication device.

"Hey, Josh." It hurt to speak.

"I did it."

"Which one?"

"Both."

"There's more than two."

"CBN and PNN—the two biggies."

"Did you send the dates to my calendar?"

"You don't sound so good."

"Which one's first, CBN?"

"Yes. CBN."

"How much?"

"Ten grand."

"Flight and hotel?"

"Yes. Two nights. Airfare Included."

"When?"

"Tomorrow afternoon. The plane pulls out at eight tonight."

"Thanks."

"You'd better pull yourself together."

"I'll be there."

"I've emailed you the boarding pass."

"I'll call you when I'm in a car on my way to the airport."

"New York City is no place for a…"

Roland hung up before Joshua could complete his admonition. The woman in the bed spoke. "That sounded important."

He turned to her. She wasn't bad looking. It could have been much worse. He decided he wanted her to stick around and checked the phone and saw that it read 9:16.

"I'm sorry." His tone was apologetic, contrite even, as though he was prepared to hear from her that he had done something wrong or unseemly or pathetic that he was in no position to deny. But to his ear, he was apologizing to himself for being alive.

"You're fine."

"How do you know?"

"As far as I'm concerned I mean. You didn't do anything to me."

Roland sized her up as best he could. His bedroom window let in very little light, situated as it was on the ground floor at the back of the building only four or five feet from the wall of the neighboring building. Just enough light filtered down the gap between the two structures that he could see a face under forty and breasts that had only just begun to decline.

"Nothing at all?"

"You asked me to scratch your back then died on me. Conked right out."

He searched his memory for anything that might place him with her last night but could not retrieve a shred of detail.

"I'm sorry. I mean, thank you."

"You're welcome, Roland."

"Can I ask what for?"

She got out of bed and went to the kitchen and found a clean glass and filled it from the faucet and brought the water back in and handed it to him. He made an effort not to look at her light blue panties, her hips, her breasts, but fixed his eyes on her face as he attempted to drink. She watched him work the glass before answering his question.

"Where do I start? I stopped you from posting some pretty stupid shit on your Twitter account."

"When was that? Where?"

"The Buddha Lounge. I pulled you outta there around 1AM. You were too sloshed to see straight and asked me to proofread something you'd written on your phone. You made me read it out loud and laughed while I read it. I deleted it and logged you off. You'll be happy I did."

"We'll never know, I guess, but thank you for the good intentions."

"I snapped a screenshot of it, so you can see for yourself and re-do it anytime you like."

The water began to go down more easily and he tilted his head back and gulped down most of it then handed her the glass with a motion that said here you go if you'd like the rest. She finished it off and put the empty glass on the dresser then got back into bed and leaned her back against the headboard. She didn't look exactly ready to go out and seize the day herself.

"What were you doing in The Buddha?"

"I'm not a whore."

"That's not what I meant."

"That's all that you could have meant."

"Well, that's awfully late to be out drinking alone in Chinatown."

"You brought me there with you, Roland. What's the last thing you remember?"

"Hard to say, but it was sometime before I ran into you."

"You warned me right up front."

"What do you mean?" He figured he was already off the hook for not knowing her name.

"When we were walking to The Buddha you said, 'Listen lady I'm pretty fucked up and I probably won't remember any of this so don't even tell me your name and I don't think you're a whore I just want some company before I go home.' Something pretty close to that."

"Where did we come from?"

"Tosca."

Roland vaguely remembered lurching into Tosca with a belly full of calamari he'd stuffed into his maw on a barstool at Sodini's.

"Yeah, I sorta remember Tosca. What were you doing there?"

"Internet blind date. I can't believe you don't remember what happened. You were the center of attention."

"Oh. Please don't tell me."

"No, no, no—you came out alright, with my help that is."

Roland looked at her face, assayed her eyes for sincerity, and figured she could probably be trusted. "Were the police involved?"

"No. I got you outta there in time, but it was headed in that direction." She looked at him cheerfully, as if to get permission to tell the rest of it.

"Ok, go ahead, tell me what happened, since you helped me out."

"You were drinking at the bar at Tosca. The guy I was with spotted you, recognized you, and I guess he wanted to impress me, so he started needling you a little, asking you stupid questions, and that made a few other guys a little bold and pretty soon you were surrounded at the bar. I didn't hear most of what was said but from what I could hear you told them to step off and things got a little louder until the bartender asked you to leave. He was nice about it but he said your being there was disrupting the place and so you got up and came over to me. I didn't even think you'd noticed I was there. You just came over and took my hand and said let's get out of here and on our way to the door you passed my date and turned to him and said *I'll take it from here*. Then my date flipped out and started yelling that you were abducting me, and some other guys tried to get in our way, and I told them to fuck off I was taking you home. I told them you asked me to get you out of there before you killed them, and they parted like swallows and let us by."

"Good one. But really, why did you come with me?"

"You seemed sad, really sad. Sad and lonely. And I wanted to make sure you got home okay. Plus, the guy I was with was kind of a douche."

"I guess I should know the name of my babysitter."

"No. Let's keep it the way it is." She laid her hand gently on the meat of his thigh.

"Thank you for the water. I think I need to turn off my phone and get a little more sleep."

"CBN you said. I'm assuming you've got a TV interview. Don't you have to get moving?"

"Not for a few hours. My plane leaves at eight."

"What show may I ask?"

"*Look Alive with Cameron Anderson.*"

"You'd better bring your A-game."

"I'm in no condition to think about it now."

"Do you want me to leave?"

"No. Let's go get something to eat after I snooze off the edge of this hangover."

"Would you like me to scratch your back again?"

"Hold that thought." He left to use the bathroom. When he was finished, he opened the door and there she stood, waiting.

The hallway enjoyed more light than the bedroom. "My turn." She gave a little curtsey to show a little bounce. He was glad she was sticking around and went back to the bed to wait for her. She climbed back in and let out a titter.

"What?" He was still a little embarrassed, not that she was there but that he had only just arrived.

"I just remembered something that you said when we were walking up the hill last night after I pulled you out of the Buddha."

"Must you?"

"You were very sweet. You were trying to get out of having to fuck me. You said, *look lady I don't think you know what you're getting yourself into. I don't fit very well inside most women so I just want you to know you can back out any time.*"

"That's a pretty fair imitation of me."

"Of course, I was pretty sure you were out of commission anyway, so I just walked you home and found your keys and put you to bed."

"And climbed in with me practically naked."

"I know you didn't mean it to be, but your warning struck me as a challenge."

"Struck you? Interesting phrase."

"I guess it rhymes with…you know."

"That's what the word…you know…originally meant."

"Seriously?"

"Old German. Fokken: to hit, to strike. Even now it's used for violence more than for love."

"Well, don't fokken me, sir."

"Trust me, fraulein. I've learned to be very gentle."

They spent the better part of the next hour on his ample mattress in the semi-dark negotiating various positions and angles of entry to mitigate her initial discomfort and then, eventually, to enable her pleasure. Roland maintained his arousal well enough to perform his function, and as their coition progressed, he realized that his growing sense of satisfaction had nothing to do with the sexual fulfillment that awaited him at climax, but with the simple fact that he was sharing slow, wordless, playful minutes with a complimentary member of his own species. Moreover, he understood and sensed she understood as well, in fleeting moments only perhaps, in flashes of psychic union, exactly what it was to be the other. He sensed the precise moment when she had had enough and then let go himself and thanked her and fell asleep to the sensation of her fingernails tracing curlicues on his back.

~~~~~

They ate a late breakfast down the hill in a little cafe on Polk Street. Coffee, eggs, bacon, toast, and fruit. He didn't ask her any questions but instead told her how good he felt, not just cured of the hangover but restored to humanity, all because of what she had done for him, of how perfectly decently she'd treated him, and how something inside him, smothered though it had been by his blackout, must have perceived her goodness and prompted him to take her, a stranger, by hand and lead her out of Tosca to the astonishment of the crowd. He didn't let all that out in a flood of words, but in dribs and drabs, between bites and swallows and sips, as his thoughts and feelings presented themselves. She smiled when he spoke and made polite non-committal replies.

Before they were finished, she straightened up in her chair to ask him a question. "What are you up to, Roland Hazzard? I've watched and listened to a fair amount of what you've had to say in front of cameras and on your podcast. You're kinda all over the place, almost like you're upset at the entire human race and not for any particular reason, but then sometimes you sound like you really care about the direction the world is headed and want the best for us little minions."

Roland thought. She wasn't challenging him or accusing him or denigrating him. It was his policy never to infer offense unless one was clearly offered. He didn't know how to answer her, so he decided to take the long way around, hoping to find something unexpected and useful in his path along the way.

"People don't read, and if you don't read then you don't get any smarter. And if you don't get any smarter, then you get stupider. You can spend all day playing chess and wake up one day at fifty years old, the best chess player you've ever been, top of your game, and then some twenty-two-year-old kid who's been playing for a couple of years plops his ass down in the chair across from you and starts snatching your pieces off the board. I don't know why you wouldn't just shoot yourself at that point, because you've wasted the best years of your life learning nothing but chess and not reading anything else to get smarter about life in the world, and now you're an embarrassment to the chess community."

"That's very sad, but it doesn't answer my question."

"If people read more, and I mean serious books and articles, stuff that shows them things they never even imagined, then they would be in permanent awe of humanity and the world and the universe. But you can't get there unless you've done a lot of reading."

"Get where?"

"Awe. Wisdom. Appreciation of your own ignorance."

"And what good is that? I think I know, but I want to hear you say it."

"You'll have the good sense not to get in other people's business, whether it's talking behind their backs or raping them and slitting their throats. Evil, you see, is paying close attention while Good is walking through a train tunnel with its headphones on and the music turned up full blast. That guy you were with last night, whoever he was; it appears I punished him for not minding his own business."

"So, you think if he read good books that he wouldn't have come over and bothered you?"

"Very likely not."

"He's a professor at SF State—at least that's what he said."

"You might just as well say he knows how to tie his shoes."

"It's okay to say that you don't know."

"Don't know what?"

"What you're up to. It might be as simple as that you like all the attention. That's ok. But I thought there may be something deeper driving you."

"It's partly about the fame, but not fame for its own sake. I'd like to write a book, and a little celebrity is all you really need to get a publisher interested."

"Sad but true, I guess."

"When I was a teenager, I remember hunting around bookstores for American poets I had discovered online…"

"Bookstores? Why didn't you just use Amazon?"

"I didn't have a credit card—plus I like to browse the stacks. I like the smell, especially of used bookstores."

"And?"

"I couldn't find them—James Tate, W.S. Merwin, Charles Simic—but everywhere I went I found Leonard Nimoy. You know who that is?"

"Spock on the old Star Trek."

"Yeah, he must have sold a lot of books back in the seventies, because they're still taking up space in the used bookshops; and the writing, well the writing is greeting card material. It's hard to call it poetry."

"I don't think I could name a single American poet, not living I mean. Wait—Maya Angelou. I'm sure she's still alive."

"Have you read any of her poems? I'm sure you could pick her photo out of a lineup, but I doubt you could identify her writing."

"You're right. Only reason I know about Maya Angelou is because she's been to the White House."

"And the only reason Nimoy got his poems in print is because he wore pointy ears on a hit TV series. I read somewhere that Sammy Davis Junior submitted his photography collections to publishing houses under a pseudonym so he would know for sure whether his work was any good. And he didn't include Rat Pack shots, just artistic compositions."

"How do you know all this stuff?"

"I like to read, naturally, and I have a good memory."

She looked at her phone and tapped on it a few times and it seemed to Roland that the subject was closed until she set the phone screen-down and looked at him. "So, what's your book going to be about? You're admitting that you want to use your sudden fame to get yourself published—it'd better be something good. You wouldn't want people to think, you know, that it's nothing more than a vanity thing."

Roland took the question as a challenge. He hadn't given it much thought. All he knew was that it wouldn't be a literary piece—not a novel. He picked up a crispy strip of bacon and held it in both hands above his plate and snapped it in half. "It's going to be a screed, a condemnation of what I will mockingly refer to as *human progress*. It will be a fervent prayer, an imploration to Jupiter." He put one of the bacon halves on top of the other and snapped them again, then stacked the four pieces together and glanced to make sure she was paying attention. He twisted the bacon stack into a handful of little pieces. "I'll beg Jupiter to let a few little comets or asteroids slip past his grasp." He let the bacon shards crumble through his fingers and land on his plate. "And tumble their way toward Earth."

"Sounds like Star Trek poetry. What does it mean?"

"We need a global cataclysm, a reset. The planet Jupiter acts as a kind of shield. Its massive gravity works like a magnet, pulling in things that would do a lot of damage if they hit us. There wouldn't be life on Earth if it wasn't for Jupiter's protection, at least not advanced life. We'd get pummeled too often for complex ecosystems to develop."

She reached over and plucked a few of the larger bits off his plate and ate them. "They cooked these asteroid comets just how I like them."

"Cooking food—that will pose a major difficulty if we get hit hard enough."

"If the whole human race is wiped out, cooking won't even be a thing."

"And if the human race survives, it'll be the people still hunting with spears and bows-and-arrows and cooking over campfires that survive. Take away our grocery stores and fast-food joints, and the people in the cities will be dead in a few months. The impact and the perpetual winter that follows might not kill everyone, but the breakdown of the supply chain will quickly depopulate the cities. Nope. The primitives who shoot arrows at airplanes will inherit the Earth."

"And you think that would be a good thing—that's your prayer? Throw us back to the stone age?"

"Good or not—impossible to say. But we'd deserve it. As soon as we started tinkering with the atom and making viruses more lethal, we took nature out of the equation—we loaded the dice—and for that colossal hubris no punishment can be too pitiless."

"Who's gonna buy that book?"

"The trick is to make it funny, convince the reader that it could never have been otherwise, that we're stupid to think we ever had a chance at making a go at civilization. *All is vanity and striving after wind.*"

"That's a pretty good line."

"It's been market tested."

"And you're the one to put it out there, right? There are no specific qualifications required to gloat over the demise of humanity."

"That's a great beginning. A perfect opening sentence. Can I use it?"

"Of course. But I think you do pretty well on your own. I've watched your act. You stake out a lot of territory."

"When I'm on the air, speaking in an interview, the only thing I'm aware of is whether I'm making sense or not. I don't prepare what I'm going to say and so I feel free to say anything, as long as it's in the vicinity of the subject at hand and it's reasonable. Even if it's totally outrageous, I want there to be an unmistakable ring of reason in everything I say. Writing is a completely separate discipline. I'll need to make it funny—no, wry—and that will take some work."

"So, you want to be an author, a popular philosopher?"

"Lord of the intellectual dark web."

"Sounds subversive."

"The dominant media structure has become so top heavy that the only way to save it is to undermine it, topple it."

After he paid the check, they left the café and faced one another outside on the sidewalk, both unsure of how to say goodbye. Their intercourse an hour before had been more a chemical bonding than an emotional one. Still, a polite little hug didn't seem correct, nor a warm embrace as friends might share. Roland wished he knew her name, but she'd controlled the terms of their liaison since allowing him to abduct her, so he waited for her to decide how to end their acquaintance. She reached out and took his hand, not to shake it, but to lift it and examine it.

"You have a lot of power." She hefted the hand lightly up and down. "Both in your body and your mind. More power than a dozen regular men, like you're sitting on top of a pyramid. I think your great strength is what let you be so incredibly gentle this morning. Strong and gentle. I like the man I met this morning, but that's not the man I met last night, and I think you can't stick with the man you are—the man standing here with me now—not for all that long, and you're just killing time until you can't resist diving back into the darkness, back into your next blackout. Maybe you should write about that."

She drew him toward her and with her other hand reached behind his neck and pulled his head down for a parting kiss on the lips.

He never saw her again. If someone told him she was an angel come down to give him aid, comfort, and guidance, he would have been tempted to believe it.

~~~~~

When the plane jerked to a stop at its gate at La Guardia Airport, Roland stirred and lifted his head from the wall of the fuselage. He'd been lucky enough to get himself a seat in the emergency exit row for the extra legroom it afforded. His hat still rested on his right knee where he'd placed it at the start of the flight. He'd conversed with no one, outside of a few incidental pleasantries, and spent the flight alternately snoozing and reading *Notes from Underground*, not a good choice for a drunk tapering off a hangover and suffering a craving. 5:30 AM. There were hours to kill before hotel check-in, so he found a place for breakfast in the airport terminal.

As he ate and sipped coffee, he watched two lone patrons sitting at opposite ends of the bar across the walkway. They wore business suits and drank with their heads bent down, both showing patchy hair badly disarranged. Roland supposed there was no one in their lives—leastways no one that gave a damn—who would approve of what they were doing. Perhaps that was true, he thought, and yet maybe in a deeper, inscrutable reality, the world was being spared a serious and lasting sequence of catastrophically malevolent outcomes these men might otherwise have achieved had they not debilitated themselves through drink. A lot of the Nazis were speed freaks. What if they'd been drunks instead? Hard to figure they could have done more damage as drunks than as tweakers. Or perhaps none of it mattered, he speculated, nothing at all, not in the way we thought it might. He pondered a metaphysical system far older than Christianity or even Judaism. Could it be that these morning airport barflies had chosen, along with countless others in their generation, to rejoin the struggle on the revolving blue globe, hobbled this go-round by a predisposition toward alcoholism? Might alcoholism be the last hurdle they needed to clear before graduating into—out to? up to?—Nirvana? Roland entertained himself with an imagined conversation among souls in the waiting room.

So, you're going in for a battle with the booze?
I saved it for last.

*There are electives you can try first that make it easier I've heard.
I think I'd rather take it head on.
Suicide bomber is a good one. If you can press that button, then beating alcohol is not so hard.
The line for suicide bomber is way too long.
You going to be a man or a woman?
An alcoholic man. Alcoholic women tend to get raped a lot.
Have you picked out a wife? A stable wife would make it a lot easier.
Are you volunteering?
No. I've checked that box already, but I'll watch how you're doing down there and maybe I'll jump into the womb as a Downs Syndrome kid if things look desperate. That might snap you out of it.*

Roland freed his imagination to play a medley of voices, all kibitzing at once, on the pros and cons of this or that approach to conquering the demon rum. Might having a handicapped kid help or hurt? Was it cheating to be born and raised by recovered parents? The voices he conjured seemed to rise in the steam from his coffee. He heard them out as if to pass the time until, finally, he channeled unwittingly, from outside the farthest edges of the Universe, the Creator, patiently watching it expand, adding a nip or a tuck to a newborn galaxy here and there, Roland conscious all the while of the competing voices that presumed to understand the rules that underlay His master plan. The Creator cleared his throat politely and in Roland's voice said, *idiots*. The souls in the waiting room quieted down. Roland's voice, coming out spontaneously as it did, startled him, and he thought he might be talking about the drunks across the way since he had yet to take his eyes off them. Maybe they were idiots, he thought, but that did not change the fact that he wished he could join them.

It was urgent now that he get out of there. His resolve to show up sober at the studios of the Cable Broadcast News network remained stronger than the lure of a drink, but there was no guarantee his resolve would hold. He needed to find a place in New York City to safely while away the hours and the only place he knew would serve that purpose was an AA meeting. A quick search on his mobile device revealed a long menu of choices in the area. He decided on a meeting in Central Park and finished his coffee before shouldering his bag and striding forth under his cowboy hat to locate the nearest cab stand.

The Alcoholic—A Hero Contends for His Soul

~~~~~

The cab let him out on Central Park West at 72nd Street in front of the Dakota Apartments, just steps away from the archway where a certified lunatic, Mark David Chapman, gunned down John Lennon for some inexplicable reason. Roland crossed the street and walked to Strawberry Fields in Central Park where the meeting he was looking for was just now taking shape. The chairs were arranged in a circle, about twenty of them. Roland found an empty one and sat with his boot heels dug into the grass. He kept on his hat and sunglasses. Comprising the circle was an assortment of mostly middle-aged to older men and women in casual dress—except for one eccentric dandy—most of them sipping hot beverages. A few smokers had the courtesy to move to the edge of the nearby road where their activity was not quite so objectionable and came over as soon as the meeting was about to start. The leader rapped his pen on the seat of his plastic chair to signal for quiet and welcomed the attendees to the Strawberry Fields Forever Group. Roland sensed that he had interloped on a tight-knit little company but figured that they'd had the occasional tourist breeze into their sober coterie and could tolerate his silent presence today. He would be on the spot only to speak his name when his turn came in the circle, a moment that was fast approaching, after which he could just sit and listen.

"I'm Racheal and I'm an alcoholic."

"Randall. I'm a grateful alcoholic."

"Alessandra, alcoholic."

"Roland, visitor."

"I'm John C, recovering alcoholic."

And around the circle it went back to the leader. "I'm Dominic and I'm *still* an alcoholic."

The format of the meeting was simple. Proceed around the circle clockwise with each alcoholic allotted five minutes to share his or her experience, strength, and hope, the guiding philosophy being that autobiographical accounts of this sort evinced for the newcomer the efficacy of the program. In practice, though, this veteran group was seldom lucky enough to enjoy the presence of a newcomer or a fresh retread, so they mostly just swapped war stories or opened up about pressing personal concerns that had little to do with recovery.

An elderly British gentleman—the dandy—in a thin wool blazer, linen pants, and Italian leather loafers reminisced about his days as an actor on Broadway, a career from which he was by now, to his chagrin, almost completely excluded. He regaled the group with an anecdote. "O'Toole was drunk half the time and often disgraced his art. But I never drank before or during a show. After the final curtain, though, I would sometimes forget to change out of my stage clothes and scoot over to the nearest bar. The pattern became so routine that one day I walked into my regular place and said to the barman, *Patrick—two double bourbons and call the police.*"

A middle-aged black man was next. "I'd set myself up in this brand-new box in an empty lot in Harlem. A huge refrigerator crate, like for a big double-door restaurant unit. The kind of sturdy wooden box that could keep out the rain and keep in the heat. And I had a bed in there, battery lamp, a box of clothes, Coleman cooler, a weapon, a few pictures pinned to the walls. My own little private residence. Perfect place to drink and use. So I meet this woman, Puerto Rican bitch, and she moves in wit me, declares herself my wife. I tells her I'm still technically married, and she says it don't matter 'cuz she's only my street-wife. And we get along for a while, sharing everything I bring in, and one day she gets angry about something I don't even remember and kicks me out. Kicks me out of my own box. Talk about bein' homeless. That was the bottom for me. At first, I blamed it on her being Puerto Rican but then I come to find it was always me. Always and only me. When you take to a life on the street, ain't no one left to blame but you, because it's every man for hisself and that law don't care. When you place yourself below the law, it's all on you."

Roland disagreed profoundly but he kept his mouth shut. He thought the law resided in the human constitution and not in any document. He knew that even small children, or especially small children, understood justice long before they'd been given any tutelage on institutional law. At the same time, he understood that a black man in America had a more complicated relationship with the law than he could adequately appreciate. Either way, it was an AA meeting and crosstalk was, by and large, strongly discouraged.

One woman talked about how she got found out. "I had a little plant sprayer in the apartment that I kept filled with vodka and one day my husband thought the orchid looked a little peaked, so he gave it a good spritz. That night all the petals fell off and he got suspicious and sprayed his hand and checked it. It's hard to deny you have a problem at that point."

A young man from Queens recounted his drunk driving arrest. "They pulled me over at Goethals and 164th just a few blocks from my house and put me through the dog and pony show there on the sidewalk. I kept telling 'em I live right arounds da corner and could I just walk home if they didn't mind but they made me toe the line and balance on one foot and turn around with my arms straight out which most people can't even do sober, and I told them I'm not trying out for the women's gymnastics team and fell over when I tried to spin around on one foot. When I got up I saw my mom standing across the street shaking her head. I started yelling at them *You called my mom? Did you have to call my fucking mom?* They were laughing too hard to explain to me that I was an idiot and gave my mom the keys, and she had Joey DeMarco come get the car, so it worked out okay, but they're still telling that story on me in the neighborhood. I'll never live that one down."

The woman sitting next to Roland, who'd announced herself as Alessandra, was a stick of a thing with white streaks highlighting her long chestnut hair. Her protruding bones advertised a long-distance runner, perhaps an obsession she'd embraced to replace her attachment to alcohol. "I don't have any amusing stories. All I can tell you is that one morning I woke up in a fog and realized I was thirty-five. It wasn't my birthday or anything, and there was nothing else special about that day. All I can think is it was God's grace or the Universe tapping me on the shoulder. *Hey, by the way, in case you hadn't noticed, you're thirty-five already. Already.* It felt like I'd lost a decade somehow, lost one or thrown it away. I was terrified to take another drink for fear that I'd lose another decade, or two, or three, so I came here, and I still haven't lost the gift of desperation."

Now it was Roland's turn, or would have been, but he figured they'd skip him since he hadn't identified himself as an alcoholic. The standard practice at an AA meeting was to invite only self-defined alcoholics to share their experience, strength, and hope, as the newcomer was not likely to benefit from the words of someone who had not embraced recovery. In the old days, his sponsor Denny once explained, newcomers had to keep their mouth shut for a full sober year, and then maybe they'd be invited to share. His status as 'visitor' could mean one of two things: He was there on a court card, or he was just 'kicking the tires.' In either case, he felt safe from the obligation to participate. Heads turned in his direction after Alessandra finished saying her peace.

"I'm Roland. Visitor. Just listening today."

"Visiting from where?" said the leader.

"San Francisco."

"You didn't identify as an alcoholic, yet here you are in an AA circle."

"I'm here on the Third Tradition."

Roland knew the rules. Apart from the Twelves Steps, there were the Twelve Traditions and the somewhat arcane Twelve Concepts. Tradition Three stated that the only requirement for membership was a desire to stop drinking, which in practice meant that the doors were open to virtually anyone. You could, theoretically, show up drunk, but as long as you didn't have a drink in your hand you should be allowed to sit and listen. The leader persisted.

"You having trouble keeping the plug in the jug?"

"I have an important meeting this afternoon and I need to show up sober."

"Millions of people will show up to important meetings today without giving a thought to their need to be sober."

"I'd put it at tens of millions. At least. Depends on how you define *important meeting* I guess. Mine will be televised."

"And that makes you special?"

"Do you really want me to say that I'm an alcoholic? Is it that important to you, Dominic?"

"No. But you seem to be more familiar with AA than a typical visitor. Are you a reporter?"

"No. I'm not trolling you, sir. I'm here for the sobriety."

"But only for today. Do I have that right?"

"Isn't the motto *One day at a time?*"

The leader looked visibly irritated and took a breath. Roland fixed his eyes on the man and imagined he was working to find his center, douse the flame of a resentment that had kindled in his sacral chakra, all the while avoiding Roland's stare. A young man to Roland's left, who'd identified himself as Randall, spoke up.

"You're Hazzard, right? The Butcher Slayer."

"The second A in AA stands for Anonymous, right?"

"Not if the first A doesn't stand for Alcoholic." Alessandra inquired under her breath. "Butcher Slayer?"

"He killed a couple of murderers in California and now he's an internet celebrity. The poster boy for self-defense. Says everyone should be like Batman. Going to be on with Cameron Anderson tonight."

"Aren't we supposed to put principles before personalities?"

The washed-up actor cleared his throat. "Excuse me. Your name is *actually* Rowland Hazard?"

Only about half the members in the circle understood the importance of the question and raised their eyebrows or made an equivalent expression of significance.

"Different spelling. No relation. No one in my family tree has ever been *the third.*"

The meeting leader, Dominic, edified the uninitiated with a primer on the synchronicity surrounding Rowland Hazard the Third that gave rise, with the force of seeming inevitability, to the society of which they were at present sober beneficiaries. Alcoholics need to be reminded every so often, the wisdom went, that without the miraculous advent of AA they would all be doomed to slow, miserable, alcoholic deaths—a truism borne out by the pitiful demise of so many relapsers who never made it back to the rooms.

Roland spotted a squirrel standing in a prayerful posture a few yards away on the lawn. It observed the humans with a serious curiosity, but one could hardly be sure from the squirrel's ink-black eyes. Its tail remained motionless, not twitching as one expects a squirrel's tail to do. He removed from his pocket a little bag of roasted peanuts that he'd received on the airplane and shook a few into his palm and lowered the palm down beside his chair just a few inches above the grass.

Dominic, summarized. "So, it was Carl Jung that sent Hazard to the Oxford Group where Hazard got sober and met a newcomer, Ebby Thatcher, and sent Thatcher off to carry the message to a practicing drunk in order to fortify his own fragile sobriety. That drunk happened to be Bill Wilson, a failed New York stock analyst on the verge of being locked into a loony bin, which in those days was where they warehoused a lot of chronic alcoholics, the ones that weren't left for dead. Bill

Wilson's recovery was so sudden and so profound that he dedicated this life to helping others, and the result was AA."

Half of the circle had stopped listening midway through the dissertation and turned their attention to the squirrel as it loped over to Roland and picked the nuts from his hand daintily one at a time, staring up at its benefactor, the sunglassed cowboy, in apparent gratitude, as it munched each morsel. *Anonymity in its purest form,* Roland mused. He'd figured he could go unrecognized in New York, or pretty much anywhere outside of San Francisco or Los Angeles, especially in his disguise, since all the public video of him showed him with a cleanshaven head. Though he wanted to know how this Randall fellow had made him, his dignity prevented him from asking. What did it matter, anyway, by what means Randall Anonymous surmised his identity? The point was: Roland couldn't fool himself into thinking he could control his celebrity, and the fact that his celebrity took him by surprise in a faraway city accentuated that reality.

"So, Saint Francis here, whatever he has done or become, got saddled with an important AA name. I don't believe in coincidences."

"Isn't there some governing body you should report yourself to?" Roland spoke in a low tone of voice so as not to startle his furry friend. "I came here to lie low and pass the time in a sober herd. I think Bill Wilson and the founders would be appalled at your putting me on the spot."

Dominic smiled and nodded and set the meeting back in motion and pretty soon Roland whisked the creature away and resumed listening to the stories, now somewhat less personal and more gratitude-centered, until they all stood up and said the serenity prayer and went their separate ways.

~~~~~

Roland headed east for no particular reason and Alessandra followed him.

"Where are you going?"

Roland had no idea. It was still too far early for him to check into his hotel.

"I think I'll have a look around the park on this brisk, sparkling morning."

"May I walk with you?"

"I'd like that." He slowed his pace so she could fall in step. The top of her head didn't reach even his shoulder."

"Have you ever been to The Met?"

"I'm coming to the end of my third hour in New York City."

"Good. I will show you The Met. It's not too far."

Her stride was barely half the length of his. He resisted the urge to lift her up by the armpits and set her on his shoulders.

"Metropolitan. Museum. Of. Art." He spoke deliberately, as though answering a question on a quiz show.

"Right you are. How long have you been sober?"

"Not even a day. I doubt I could blow a zero."

They passed the statue of Daniel Webster, still glazed with morning dew. Patches of sunlight dappled the grass and pathways that branched out from there.

"I don't see a ring on your finger. Do you have a girlfriend?"

"On a good day."

"I see. She's not very happy with you right now."

"No. Nothing like that. I mean on a good day I can find a woman to play the part for a while."

"Oh. When planets align. That sort of thing."

"That puts a romantic spin on it."

"Then I could be your girlfriend, in that scenario."

"In point of fact, you are. More so with every step."

"And if I don't want to be?"

"Peel off the next time the path splits."

"Or maybe I'll just turn around and go back."

"Either way, you'll be leaving the umbrella of my protection."

Alessandra looked up to the sky and spun around without missing a step. "Doesn't look like rain to me. You really a killer?"

"A vigorous self-defender."

"You really gonna be on TV tonight?"

"CBN—*Look Alive with Cameron Anderson*. I'm supposed to be there at four o'clock."

"Okay, I believe you. But I'm not your girlfriend, not in any way that I would ever use the term."

"Where's your boyfriend right now?"

"I'm too finicky to have a boyfriend."

He looked over at the pond to his left where mallards and black ducks were relaxing or making a living. He took her hand.

"I'm flying out day after tomorrow."

She pulled her hand away.

"Ok, so what if another girl, a really pretty girl with a good body, suddenly appeared and started walking along with us—could she be your girlfriend too?"

"Was that really necessary?"

"I think you're playing with me, so I'm poking back."

"Alessandra," he took her hand again and guided her over to a bench at a bend in the path and sat her down. "Alessandra. Place your hands in your lap."

She did as directed. He stood in front of her and removed his sunglasses and put them in his coat pocket and looked down at her, then he took off his hat and held it over his heart. Then he spoke.

"I need you to set aside everything today and pretend, pretend with all your might if necessary, because I've created a storm around me and I need someone, a girl, who wants to hold my hand and let me feel like I'm making her safe in a dangerous world. I need to feel that you'd rather die than be away from me. Just until I leave."

She lifted her hands from her lap and placed them on her knees. "You need that—me by your side—to keep yourself from taking a drink? Can we say it that way?"

"It's more than that. And, of course, if I take a drink the spell will be broken. I should not have let that go without saying."

"Let me see those sunglasses."

"What?"

"Remove those fancy sunglasses from your pocket and place them in my hand."

Roland did as she directed and handed her his amber-colored aviator shades. She turned them over and around, this way and that, in the manner of an appraiser.

"Very nice. Maui Jim's." She put them on. "How do they look?"

"That style looks good on everyone, I think. Maybe a tad big for your delicate face, but not absurdly so."

"We have a deal."

"You want my sunglasses?"

"I want to be able to see your eyes while I'm with you, and I don't want you to be able to see mine. The other way around is unacceptable."

"I guess that's fair."

"And when you're gone day after tomorrow, I'll have something to remember you by, assuming I want to remember you."

"Okay. Let's go."

Alessandra remained seated. "One more thing."

"Yes?"

"About this girlfriend thing, this *role.*"

"I don't expect you to sleep with me."

"Good. I needed to hear you say that."

"Completely understood."

She stood up and took his hand. "Ok, cowboy, put on that hat, and let's go imbibe a little culture."

He set his hat back on his head and off they went, fingers interlaced.

~~~~~

They spent the rest of the morning perusing the exhibits at the world-renowned museum. Alessandra took the lead, familiar as she was with the place, and acted as his tour guide, a private guide that asked a lot of personal questions, especially about the killings and the sudden internet fame. Roland was glad that she'd never heard of him, neither by name nor reputation, and happily let her steer the conversation as effortlessly as she steered them from gallery to gallery in the spacious complex. He found her voice both mirthful and soothing, not in the least bit demanding, even when she asked him a direct question, which she had a knack for wording as a statement. "So, I'm guessing you were drunk when you killed him." She showed particular interest in the facts he revealed about The Glendale Butcher. "You'd think I'd have heard of that—a guy who limited his murdering to places with a particular name. It's like he set out to be labeled the Glendale Butcher." Roland found himself nodding sagaciously at her remarks, especially when she looked up to check his eyes to make sure he was listening. He couldn't imagine a better girlfriend, one so sweet and intelligent and curious, one so gentle with his tremulous soul. Though his hand completely enclosed hers—interlocking fingers had become impractical—Roland felt before long that she was holding *his* hand. He didn't question the authenticity of her affection, for he was getting exactly what he'd asked for. No. Wrong. He hadn't understood what he'd asked for, but he could tell that she was showing him what that was. Even her pauses, the spaces between her thoughts, communicated warmth.

"You're an angel." He was inspired perhaps by the Italian Renaissance. "I mean it. You rescued me. I think you meant to."

"I wanted to see your eyes. Who wears sunglasses in an AA meeting?"

"We were outside."

"The sun was just coming up and it was behind you."

He wanted to lift her up and kiss her, like a father might a lost daughter after finding her in a crowded carnival, but he knew that would frighten her, understood with his intellect that her behavior toward him was unremarkable given the circumstances, that most of the tender feelings he ascribed to her were the product of his mind. Yet there was something there, he felt, some incipient bond he was incapable of grasping. To distract himself from his feelings, which, like a flower to the dawn, were bending toward the erotic, Roland observed the art. His brain had collected a lot of information over the years on the major movements and masters, all indexed somewhere in his synaptic networks, so he decided to retrieve some of it.

He pointed at a painting by Matisse. "I can see why they called him a wild beast."

"They did?"

"Yeah. He and a few other guys at the turn of the century broke all the color rules, so the critics called them *Fauves*, which is French for *wild beasts*. Matisse was the greatest of les Fauves."

"Did you study art?"

"I've poked my nose into a lot of different things."

"Do you like art? I mean, does it give you pleasure to look at it? Do you *experience* it? That's more important than knowing about it."

"I like anything that's well made, anything that shows a high degree of practice and discipline. That pretty much guarantees it will contain some measure of beauty."

"I think that's true. But it still doesn't tell me if you enjoy it."

"Whether I enjoy it or not, and how much, matters much less than the fact that I accept its importance and want to understand why it is so highly valued."

"And what have you come to understand about this period, Roland?"

"What fascinates me most about the early Twentieth Century painters in France and thereabouts are the passionate, almost murderous, rivalries. They tell us in AA that the ego is our greatest enemy, that to find inner peace we must abandon our attachment to self. So I ask myself: What would have happened if those artists didn't have such big egos, if they didn't have such a huge desire to be different? Seems to me those fierce rivalries gave rise to some great art. Even while they were trying to break from the stultifying past, they were trying to distinguish themselves from each other."

She let go of his hand. "What about *your* ego?"

"It's feeling kinda rickety right now. That's why I'm so glad you came after me. You're a damned fine girlfriend."

"I'm talking about the night you killed the infamous Glendale Butcher?"

"I didn't know that's who he was."

"Of course you didn't. How could you have?"

"I don't see what you're getting at."

"I'm trying to picture it from the way you described it. You came out of your bedroom and hit him on the head with a bottle and he went down."

Roland nodded yes.

"So why didn't you go back into your bedroom and close the door and call the police? Does the door have a lock? Did you have a phone in there, a window you could crawl out of?"

"Yes to all three."

"All the more reason. But even without a lock, you could have braced the door closed, a man your size. My point is that it seems to me like you didn't have to fight him. You could have let him get away. Was it your ego that kept you from retreating?"

"Life is much harder for the defenseless."

"And much easier for the intelligent."

"That's debatable."

"You're evading the question."

"No. It wasn't my ego that kept me from retreating."

"What then?"

Roland was only half-listening, irked at himself for not having anticipated the question—no, not about the workings of his ego—but about the more logical, perhaps even legalistic one that neither the inspector nor the chief had thought to ask. The police had seen the door and the working lock and the bedroom window—the opportunity for retreat—yet here was this total stranger who'd heard only the basic facts asking him to explain why he'd chosen fight over flight.

"That's not my story."

"You think you're living in a story?"

"Things are happening. Things are taking place. If I avoid them, I'm not being true to the story."

"Anyone can say that. Was getting drunk before you came to New York being true to your story?"

"That didn't slow it down. The phone woke me up yesterday and here I stand. But, to be fair to your question, if he'd pulled a gun, I probably would have made my escape the way you said." His delight in her company had dampened. He pulled up his sleeve to show her the scar. "When you pull a knife on someone you should be prepared to die. Any lethal weapon for that matter."

The conversation had taken them to the antiquities exhibit where tablets of ancient writing and other decorative or useful artifacts were on display. He decided to change the subject.

"Geologists and archeologists have fierce rivalries too, just like artists."

"Any girlfriend worth her salt would want to know, would have to ask the question."

"I think you're pretending a bit too well."

"You can send me away with a word if you want. Otherwise, you're stuck with me. A girlfriend is nothing if she's not loyal."

"What if you're right? What then?"

"I haven't made any particular claim, Roland Hazzard."

"Your implication is pretty clear. You think I should have backed off and barricaded the door and, since I didn't, I'm responsible for his death, because of my ego."

"I'm not calling you a murderer. I'm saying, based only on what you've told me, you *chose* to fight when you didn't have to. If you rewind it to the beginning, you didn't even have to come out of your bedroom with the bottle and smash it over his head. You could have shut the door and locked it. Instead, you wasted good whiskey and got that nasty scratch on your arm."

"I'm glad he's dead, he and his idiot cousin. And I'm glad I'm the one who did it and that people are talking about."

"Okay. I just had to ask. As long as you understand that there are plenty of people, very healthy happy people, who might not let themselves off so easily, no matter who the bad guy turned out to be. Let's say back in 1925 Hitler is walking down the street plotting the Final Solution but otherwise minding his own business and some street thug who has no idea who Hitler is walks up and murders him—is he less evil because the man he murdered turned out to be even eviler? Does God give him a hearty slap on the back when he crosses the finish line?"

"I've got a lot of questions for God if it comes to that."

"If I were you, I wouldn't press my luck. Just tuck in your chin and file in quietly."

Roland laughed at that. He took her hand again. Her point of view, he concluded, was entirely reasonable, not biased in any way by prior knowledge. She'd simply held a mirror up to his face and asked him who he saw, and Roland failed to meet his own eyes, and she did not pass judgment on him for that cowardice and let the matter drop. She could be forgiven.

He pointed to an intact piece of Egyptian pottery, a red bowl resting on a base of two little human feet, reputed to date back to 3900 B.C. "Most of this stuff is probably dated correctly, but some of the big stuff, like the Great Sphynx, that's just guesswork. Geologists who've looked at it very closely conclude that the weathering is from heavy rainfall, which puts it back to at least 10,000 BC, long before the supposed birth of Egyptian civilization; and the archeologists and the anthropologists, furious that their castles are being overthrown, are fighting back. They will not go gentle into that good night."

Roland prattled on, effectively took over the tour, displaying his wide range of knowledge on as many subjects as he could summon from the available material, and not in a pedantic tone, but in his most understated, jovial style.

~~~~~

He swam up from the depths of a languorous nap and surfaced into the present moment a minute before his alarm was set to go off and disabled it to let Alessandra sleep a little longer while he went to the bathroom and shaved his head clean for the big interview with the indefatigable and always impeccably fed TV journalist, Cameron Anderson. When he came back into the room, gingerly in his stockinged feet, she lay on her back just as he'd left her, next to the impression he'd made on the bedspread, snoozing audibly with her big toes touching. He drew his forefinger up the arch of her foot to see if that would wake her, but she only wiggled it and rolled to one side. He changed into the one decent shirt he'd brought and then went back to the bathroom and brushed his teeth, making sure his movements were loud enough to rouse her.

"Is it time to go?" Above the running water in the bathroom, her voice sounded like a radio station tuned a smidge off-center.

"You were really out."

"Did you touch me?"

He came into the room and looked at her. "I spotted you in a dream running naked through a bombed-out city, but I couldn't seem to catch up to you."

"It wouldn't've made any difference."

"No?"

"I'm all sealed up. Un-rape-able."

"If I said that's a shame it wouldn't sound right."

"Forget me. You'd better be careful what you say to Cameron Anderson. He's pretty sharp. He's an expert at picking people apart."

"Let him do his worst. As long as the check clears."

He waited for her to get herself together and then they walked to the elevator.

"I know you didn't see me running naked in an apocalyptic nightmare."

"No. And you know I didn't touch you."

~~~~~

Roland gave the address to the cab driver and off they went through the high-rises of Midtown Manhattan. The descending sun glared off the glassed buildings and blinded him at intermittent turns. She took his hand.

"How are you feeling?"

"I could use my sunglasses."

"You're lucky I'm here. I hope you know that."

"What else would you be doing?"

"Riding the subway home without your sunglasses."

"What are you talking about?"

"When you went to sleep, I did a little research."

"And what did you discover, beyond what I already told you?"

"I wanted to see how big you really were, and I must say you've made a big footprint. It would take a long time, days maybe, to play through all your podcasts and interviews, and then there's tons of commentary to read. I can see why Anderson wants you on *Look Alive.*"

"I get it. But why am I lucky you're still here? I assumed you knew I wasn't dangerous when you came up to the room."

"Yeah, but now I know why Randall took such a dim view of you. Some of the things you say are borderline…I don't know…"

"Crazy?"

"No. Not crazy. A bit sociopathic maybe." He was glad she was distracting him with conversation, for he could feel a fluttering in his belly as they neared the destination. And the way she looked at him from behind his own sunglasses, as if to flaunt them, irritated him in an enjoyable way. *Come what may,* he thought. *Come what may.*

"Why did you follow me after the meeting? Tell the truth."

"Randall, the guy that outed you, he was coming over to talk to me. He hasn't given up yet."

"Didn't you tell him about the cave-in at the grotto? That oughta put a stop to it."

"I've already let him know I'm not ready for the Thirteenth Step."

"So, you were running *from him* more than coming *to me.*"

"I wasn't running from him, but I knew that he wouldn't follow me over to you, and that was enough to make me more curious about you."

"So here you are, the temporary girlfriend of a borderline sociopath who wandered into your AA meeting."

"Nothing happens by accident. I'm thinking this was meant to be."

"I wonder how many people have been raped or murdered trusting what seemed like it was meant to be."

"Are you trying to send me away, right before your big moment? Will I have served my purpose once I deliver you sober to the stage door?"

"No. I still need you. A man is granted automatic credibility whenever he shows up somewhere with a respectable-looking woman."

"I guess I've been demoted—from angel to respectable-looking woman."

"We can call you my body-and-soul-guard."

~~~~~

A repast laid out on a table behind the set offered plates filled with shrimp and fresh fruit and cheeses and different colored olives and crackers of various types and little bite-sized cakes, among other tasty delights. The producers, staff, and crew chatted casually and washed down their morsels with beverages dispensed from tall glass urns set at one end of the buffet into sturdy paper cups that bore the network logo. Against the back wall stood a coffee bar that filled the room with expensive, imported smells—Brazilian coffee, cinnamon, chocolate, nutmeg, and vanilla. Roland stood there alone, tall on his bootheels with his freshly powdered head, trying to decide whether or not to gussy up his coffee with these flavorful subtleties. Alessandra, he observed, mingled near the buffet with a plate in her hand, a New Yorker among New Yorkers. He was happy that she'd slid herself comfortably into the mix.

A man, about forty, with his shirtsleeves rolled halfway up and his shirt collar open where there had recently been a tie, came up behind Roland. "You're Roland Hazzard, right? On tonight with Cameron Anderson, right?"

Roland turned around. "Yes. The punching bag de jour."

"You'll be fine. Cameron can't lay a glove on you. I've seen the way you move."

"I'm not worried. Right now, I'm focused on what to put in my coffee."

"If you're nervous I can get you something stronger. A little liquid courage so to speak."

"Thank you. I bring my own." He patted his empty breast pocket. "I'm already pretty loose—primed and ready to go."

"Glad to hear it. Just make sure you breathe and you'll be fine." He patted Roland on the back and walked away before Roland could ask him who he was.

The moment was drawing near. Soon Cameron Anderson would take his seat behind his desk on the set and the necessary switches would be flipped and the live international broadcast would commence. The show's producer, a woman wearing a headset, would tap Roland during a commercial break and he would go out to the guest chair and come what may. As airtime approached, the group backstage thinned out and he sidled over to Alessandra.

"You've been ignoring me."

"You looked like you wanted to be left alone to wind yourself up into a tight little spring. I could almost hear your psyche squeaking from across the room."

"It's hard to meditate standing up. I wish I could have stayed in the makeup room until showtime, but they kicked me out."

"Kicked you out?"

"They needed to work on someone else, probably the host."

"I haven't seen him. Have you?"

"He probably has a private door to the set. Before I forget, can you go in there and get my hat when I go on so nobody rips it off?"

"I can go now if you want."

"No. Stay here and keep me company. Tell me about all your new TV buddies."

"I didn't find out much about them. They wanted to know all about me, about us really."

And what did you tell them about us?"

"Don't sound so worried, Roland?"

"What did you tell them, Alessandra, if that is your name?"

"Relax, cowboy. I told them I met you today. We have a mutual friend in California that asked me to show you around. Show you around because you've never been to New York. And I made an editorial decision and told them you were a really fun guy, a fountain of knowledge, and a witty raconteur."

"That all?"

"Nothing about the AA meeting, if that's what you're worried about."

"Why do you keep saying I'm worried?"

"Because you look nervous. If you're nervous, channel the tension into…"

"I'm not nervous and I'm not worried. I'm curious. You were very chatty with the staff, like you already knew them, and then they scattered when I drifted over."

"I was networking, trying to make contacts. This is the kind of place I'd love to work, but you can't just drop off your resume. I tried to steer the conversation away from you, but there you are, bigger than life."

The producer appeared at his elbow. It was time for come-what-may.

~~~~~

The set contained a long desk with three chairs, one on either side of the host chair, placed on a raised platform flanked in the back by a wall of gigantic, muted images of people in dramatic poses offset by the title of the program: *Look Alive with Cameron Anderson.*

The host was a slender man, much older than he looked due to an assiduous skincare regimen, physical fitness routine, and an ample shock of white hair which he kept meticulously groomed. A favorite of the gay community for his championing of their supposed agenda, Anderson cultivated an effeminate persona while he kept his heterosexual liaisons a strictly private matter, almost as if he was ashamed to be *not-gay*. He began the segment by reading from his teleprompter. "Our next guest, Roland Hazzard, represents a first for this program, a man who has gained such rapid fame almost completely outside the normal media channels that many of us in the traditional press are beginning to question the very future of broadcast journalism. For those of you who might not yet be aware of him, Roland Hazzard woke up one night a few weeks ago in his San Francisco apartment to find an armed intruder outside his bedroom. According to the police report, Roland fought the intruder and killed him with the intruder's own knife after sustaining a serious cut on his arm…"

The host continued with a description of the Glendale Butcher's criminal career and the subsequent LA broadcast to commemorate his victims where Roland dispatched Barsamian's cousin, then wound up his introduction.

"We've decided not to show the clip of Roland swiftly ending the life of his second attacker because many of you no doubt would find it disturbing; but suffice it to say that anyone interested in seeing that video footage can find it in a matter of seconds on anything connected to the internet. However, it's not these self-defense killings themselves that are our focus today, but Roland's ability to leverage the fame engendered by those killings into a cause célèbre by cultivating a radio and podcast presence that has transformed him in less than a month into what some are calling a cult figure on the intellectual dark web."

With that, the camera pulled back to reveal Roland sitting to the right of Cameron Anderson, a glass of water in front of both men.

"Mister Hazzard, thank you for coming on such short notice. You've got a very full calendar as I understand."

"My pleasure. Your people made all the necessary arrangements and I'm very happy to be here."

"So, how did I do in summarizing your recent past?"

"If you're the one who wrote that then I'd say you painted an accurate picture. In any case, you certainly read it like a pro."

Roland smiled inwardly to assure himself that, if this were a fight, he'd struck the first blow, albeit only a glancing one.

Cameron Anderson didn't miss a beat. "We work as a team around here, though I do get most of the glory I'm ashamed to say. But we didn't invite you on to talk about me. We've been tracking the rise in your popularity in the digital sphere and decided we needed to get you before you got too big for our little show."

"With all due respect, Mister Anderson, I'm not all that famous. I spent most of the day in Central Park and the Metropolitan Art Museum and as far as I know only one person recognized me. I can only imagine what celebrities have to go through."

"I find that hard to believe with that magnificent head of yours."

Roland decided not to prolong the small talk and so kept quiet about his cowboy-hat-and-sunglasses disguise.

"I don't know, maybe I strike people dumb with terror."

"Yeah, there's the whole skinhead thing. I was going to ask you about that."

"I'm sure your staff has combed through all of my interviews, so you know I'm not a skinhead or any kind of white supremacist."

"Yes. But what sort of responsibility do you have for the white nationalists that have embraced your message?"

"That didn't take long."

"What do you mean by that?"

"Flipping over the race card. You know what happens when you force someone to say he's not a racist—it puts in the mind that maybe he is. You of all people should know what words can do. They're your stock-in-trade."

"It just seems funny that you would shave your head the day after killing a person of color."

"Funny? You mean *suspicious,* as though I was signaling to my skinhead brethren that I'd just scored one for the good guys. Is that what you mean?"

"So here on national television are you willing to renounce the support of white nationalists?"

"Mister Anderson, there you've done a clever sleight of hand. Before you ask a man whether or not he's stopped beating his wife, hadn't you better make sure he's married?"

"So, you don't acknowledge that you have white nationalist supporters or at least some that support your message?"

"A couple of things: I don't know what you mean by white nationalist: KKK? Neo Nazi? If that's what you mean, then no I don't acknowledge any such support, let alone sympathy for, or affiliation with. Or do you mean something more subtle, like patriotic white people? I'm not going to try to get inside your head, so you'll have to speak more plainly. Second point: My main message should be embraced by all human beings, and that includes the best of us and the worst of us."

"All human beings?"

"It's a global message that should stand for all eternity."

"Could you sum it up for us, briefly?"

"It's been said any number of ways over the centuries by people willing to die for their freedom, and I don't have anything original in that

The Alcoholic—A Hero Contends for His Soul

vein, so let me borrow the phrase on the Gadsden Flag. *Don't Tread on Me.*"

"And why did you pick that one, because it's distinctly American?"

"No—it's because above the motto is a lethal snake. That's what best symbolizes my message. *Mess with me at your peril.*"

Roland wondered what Alessandra was doing. He'd become used to knowing millions of people were watching and or listening to him and would have access to his public discourse at the touch of a button, conceivably forever. What distracted him now was his uncertainty about her opinion. Not about him personally, for he could see that she liked him, but about his message, both what she'd heard for herself on his podcasts she accessed while he napped, and about what she might be hearing now if indeed she was even listening.

"I see. An eternal message for all of humanity, good guys and bad guys alike?"

"Most people can be either one on any given day, or at any given moment."

"But you're one of the good guys, most of the time anyway." His tone was not of a question but of skeptical sarcasm.

"Thank you, Mister Anderson. I appreciate that."

"It was a question."

"Well. I endeavor to be."

"Even when you're drinking?"

"Yep—same as you."

"I've never been arrested for public intoxication or lost an athletic scholarship because of my drinking."

Roland picked up the glass of water. He imagined each member of his family watching the program, first the face of his mother, horrified. He saw her turning to his father, him grimacing with disgust. He imagined his sister answering her phone. *No, Dad, I knew nothing about this.* Finally, his brother. *Don't convict him yet. They may be trying to smear him.* Roland drank from the glass and set it down gently.

"That statement could come back to haunt you."

"Are you suggesting that I'm lying, that I've had drunken arrests or lost a scholarship? I was never even a college athlete."

"No. I'm looking at the bigger picture, from the karmic perspective."

"So, you're not denying it?"

"I'm not going to talk about it. I'm happy to sit here and listen until you're finished spooning out all the dirt you've collected in your mud pail, but I won't comment on it. You paid to bring me here—the time belongs to you. If you want to spend it trying to tear me down, that is your pre-rog-a-tive." He didn't raise his voice at the end but sharpened his tongue to enunciate each syllable distinctly for emphasis.

"Mister Hazzard—may I call you Roland?"

Roland shrugged.

"Roland," Cameron Anderson continued. "You've made yourself a public figure, hired a publicist to maximize your fame, fame based on your killing of two individuals in circumstances that some people have commented might have been, while technically lawful, perhaps unnecessary."

"Some people…are idiots." With a dramatic hand gesture, Roland bid Cameron Anderson to continue.

"And now that you've achieved some level of fame, a kind of underground following, and some degree of power based on the number of people you're capable of influencing, I think that it's fair that you be vetted by what many call, derisively at times, the *mainstream* media. Public figures, be they politicians, sports heroes, entertainment celebrities—anyone with influence—should be able to stand up to a little scrutiny."

Roland repeated his previous gesture, but a bit lazily, as if bored and hoping the host would finish.

"Is that reasonable? Do you accept that?"

"It's a fine piece of rhetoric. No doubt evenly applied to your ideological friends and foes alike. But I won't be drawn into that rock fight. My ideology was formed by reruns of old cartoons. *Looney Tunes, Tom and Jerry, The Road Runner,* just to start with. My values are based on fundamental principles played out in the little narratives meant to entertain children."

"Like what, for example."

"Kill bad guys, because, if you don't, they'll kill you."

"But is that really the case? In cartoons, the bad guys never really die."

"They need to keep the villains around to kill them again and again, but the kids get the message—lethal force is the only way to go, not civil discourse. I told Barsamian to leave. He had a clear path to the door.

Should I have invited him to stay, to sit down for a chat, ask him to retrace his life path and figure out where he'd made the wrong turn?"

"You could have gone back into your room and locked the door. Called the police from in there."

"There's no archetype for that."

"What do you mean, no *arch-e-type?*"

"There's no myth of the noble coward."

"So, it's cowardly to protect yourself while calling the police?"

"The human psyche has no mapping for that, certainly not in a moment of crisis. Police, telephones, these are modern inventions with no meaning to the human mind."

"Why not just admit you were drunk instead of acting like a professor of psychology?"

"My specialty is ancient megalithic architecture. You realize that with new high-definition ground-penetrating radar they are getting clear pictures of vast urban complexes, tens of thousands of stone structures, overgrown by the forests in Central America? The officially accepted paradigms are being turned upside down, inside out, and backward."

"I want to take you seriously, not take my viewers down your rabbit trails."

The host showed his frustration by doing the unthinkable. He grabbed his hair, grabbed it with all ten fingers, eyes bulging, then dug his nails into his scalp before releasing his hair and holding up exasperated hands. The two-second loop of that action—Cameron Anderson clawing his perfectly styled cut into a riotous tease—would be copied and pasted and captioned, with various humorous and unflattering labels, thousands, maybe millions, of times on dozens of media platforms for decades to come. Everything from *Fluffy's gone missing!* to *A twister is headed this way.* It would serve as a popular meme for losing one's shit. His bosses would hold it over him in contract negotiations. That momentary loss of control would damage his career.

Roland caressed his own smooth head with one hand and smiled.

Cameron Anderson quickly regained his composure. "Maybe when we return from the break we can recover some sanity."

~~~~~

It took every second of the three-minute break for the stylist, sweating as over a timebomb, to restore his hair to something like perfect. He practiced his grimace at the studio lights above the cameras, refusing to look at Roland. As soon as the cameras went on, Cameron Anderson turned to his insouciant guest.

"So, we got a little off track there. That was my fault. I was trying to learn more about your drinking history and possible anger issues, but you're not on trial here. I'd just like to ask you one more question about that if I may."

Roland compressed his lips in a show of forced deliberation. "Let me save you the effort. I have a very short and unimpressive police record readily accessible on the internet thanks to my busy, mostly pseudonymous, detractors. I encourage your viewers to look up my many hours of dialogues and monologues and decide for themselves whether or not I'm one of the good guys."

Cameron Anderson nodded, the kind of slow strenuous nod of someone deeply skeptical of what he was hearing.

"Well, we've invited to join us, via live feed from San Francisco, a man who would like to tell the world about a different side of you."

"Oh?"

A wide rectangular monitor rose up in front of the wall behind the news desk to reveal a handsome man, slightly gray, fifty perhaps, in a dark suit and a green tie, framed from the chest up and seated in front of a projected image of the Golden Gate Bridge viewed from the Marin Headlands, with San Francisco in the background. Roland barely noticed the picturesque backdrop and studied the face of this complete stranger while Cameron Anderson introduced him as Douglas Gordon, a successful international patent attorney. Could he have run across him in The Gutter? *Nope.* He was sure of that much. Then he gulped, felt his throat constrict. *No, no, no.* His vision blurred and his mind swirled as though his brain were being attacked by parasites. How many laws had he broken with that one desperate act of greed—grand theft, conspiracy to defraud, patent infringement—those and probably a dozen criminal statutes he'd never even heard of? Would police come in and handcuff him there on stage, live before the viewing audience, or would they have the decency to wait until the cameras were off?

"Mister Hazzard, do you remember Mister Gordon?"

Remember him? What the fuck is he talking about? "I've never met this man." Roland couldn't be certain, given his propensity for blackouts.

Mister Gordon interjected. "You met me on the 101 Freeway. You drive a yellow 2004 Nissan Sentra with license plate V2F48XM." It was a declarative sentence spoken with accusatory force.

Roland leaned back in his chair and drew air through his nostrils, nodding his head very slightly. "Yes. That's my car." This wasn't about international software piracy and for that he felt relieved.

"I could have you arrested, you know."

"For driving an ugly car with a cracked windshield?"

"For assault—for tossing an object from your car into mine while we were driving up the 101 freeway."

"This is a very bad idea, Mister Gordon."

"So, you admit that it's true?"

"No. I'm saying Mister Gordon here has made a serious mistake, a colossal error in judgment."

"Why don't we let him tell us what happened?"

"Go ahead, sir. I can't wait to hear this."

Mister Gordon sipped from a paper Starbucks cub before he began. "I was driving north on the 101, Friday, September thirtieth, just before noon in light traffic, and this Hazzard fella was in front of me on his phone going way too slow, breaking the law I might add."

"Talking on the phone while driving on the freeway."

"Yes. And for impeding the flow of traffic as well."

"So, what happened next?"

"I honked my horn to get his attention, to let him know he was creating a problem…"

That was a lie as well as Roland could recall, as he'd not herd the toots from the Mercedes. But Roland was in no position to counter the man's story with his version of the facts. On the contrary, this exemplary good citizen must be allowed to paint a most unflattering portrait of Roland, and Roland would have to sit still and take it, for he couldn't very well say, *you flipped me off motherfucker, so I chased you down and sunk a three-pointer with my leftovers through your moonroof.*

"Next thing I know this maniac is chasing me, shaking his fist out his window, trying to get ahead of me and run me off the road, but I have a fast car, so I kept him behind me. When traffic slowed up near The City, he caught up and drove right next to me in the right lane. I just stared straight forward and found a peaceful place in my mind and hoped that he would just go away."

None of that was true, of course. Herr Benz had tried to stare him down, even mocked him with a superior grin, and was in no way fearful or intimidated. If the man was going to fabricate testimony, then Roland felt no compunction about employing the necessary level of mendacity to counter the accusation. He listened all the more intently.

"But he didn't go away, did he?"

"Sounds to me like you've already bought this load of crap, Mister Anderson."

"The man took down your license plate number, so I'm inclined to let him tell his story. Sorry for the interruption, Mister Gordon."

"There's not much left to tell. He lobbed a half-eaten breakfast sandwich into my car through the moonroof and it landed on the seat. I was sure it was a bomb or some sort of incendiary device and almost had a heart attack and nearly slammed into the car on my left. In the state of California, throwing something into a moving vehicle, no matter what it is, is considered an aggravated assault."

Roland reflected. The half-eaten, partially wrapped Sausage McMuffin had struck Herr Benz in the face, on the cheek, and tumbled apart onto his lap. No way in hell he mistook it for a bomb.

"Is he telling the truth, Mister Hazzard?"

"Mister Gordon has made a serious mistake."

"You've said that already. But you haven't said whether or not he's telling the truth."

"No. But let's posit, just posit…"

"Pause what? You're not in charge of the pace of my show?"

Roland turned in his seat and faced the host and lowered his chin and softened his voice. "You're not especially bright, are you?"

"He means *assume*. He means *for the sake of argument.*"

"Correct! And even if it were true, I would never confess to a crime on a network news program."

"That's hardly a denial, kid."

"True. I don't hear a denial."

"I deny that I'm stupid, which I'd have to be to lend you creditably by subjecting myself any further to this interrogation."

"You'd 'a made a great lawyer, kid, but instead you're just a loudmouthed punk with a lethal streak. What's the word? Blood simple."

"Did I hear correctly? You're a patent attorney?"

"*International* patent attorney."

"There's a pretty narrow field, perhaps a bit too narrow to be useful in the rumpus of the day-to-day."

"What does my legal specialty have anything to do with this?"

"Because if you knew the first thing about defamation law…"

"You're lecturing ME on the LAW!?"

"A lecture won't do it, boy. You're in need of a retributional ass-whoopin.'"

"Now you're threatening me?"

The escalation of tension over the last few minutes caused the ratings to spike as a million or so more viewers than normal tuned in to watch the fracas.

"No. I'm saying you should know better than to publicly accuse someone of a crime without offering proof, or even a shred of evidence. That comes under the libel statutes I believe. You've gone to a lot of trouble to make a lot of trouble for yourself, dumbass."

Cameron Anderson squinted a little to better understand the words coming through his earpiece. The segment was not going according to plan.

"Mister Gordon wrote down your license plate. He has the date, the time, the place, and the timeline provided by the SFPD places you on the 101 at that time on that date." His teleprompter assisted him further. "The SDPD detective called your work in Redwood City at 11:15 AM and you arrived at the station in San Francisco just after noon. And the only way to get there is the 101."

"Where's his police report? I'll answer that for you. He doesn't have one, because, if he did, he would have shown it to you. And you should have asked for one before you let this assassin on your TV show to snipe at my good name."

Roland liked his hand. More to the point, he believed that Douglas Gordon was holding bupkis, so he raised the stakes on a semi-bluff.

"Mister Gordon, if I did what you're accusing me of, and the traffic was all bunched up as you say, then you would have taken a picture of my car, and that picture would have a timestamp, and you wouldn't be up to your neck in your own shit right now."

"I memorized your plate and wrote it down as soon as I could. My phone was attached to the mount on my dashboard. But we both know what happened. I didn't file a report because there was no real damage. I'm not here to prosecute you. I'm here only because I want the American people to know what kind of a psycho you are, what your vision of personal freedom looks like. Not only are you an intellectual fraud, but a violent fraud at that."

"You can add wealthy to the list."

"You're not going to get rich off media spots. You're nothing but a flash in the pan."

"Not off media spots, off you personally, off your miscalculation, and we can throw in CBN for giving you a platform."

Cameron Anderson broke in. "Mister Hazzard, whatever the facts, this station has acted in good faith, and you've come onto the set intoxicated. You were spotted drinking backstage."

"That's a lie."

"If I ask you to give me your jacket so I can check for a bottle, will you do it?"

"Be my guest. And bring out the breathalyzer if you have one." Roland took off his jacket and handed it to Cameron Anderson, who immediately checked the pockets and came up empty.

"You could have tossed the bottle backstage."

"Should I blow into your nose?" Roland didn't wait for an answer and blew a stream of air into Cameron Anderson's face. "Tell the audience if you smell any alcohol."

Cameron Anderson shook his head and pressed in his earpiece as if to better hear what his producer was saying.

"The action's right here." Roland moved his hand back and forth between himself and the man on the screen. "You put this guy here on because he's a respected San Francisco lawyer with some seemingly credible dirt to toss around, but it wouldn't take much for anyone with an internet connection to come up with that defamatory fairy tale. All you need to know is my name. Your network has been duped. No one here thought it wise to vet this man's story, and now it's going to cost you."

"You're out of your mind," said Douglas Gordon. "Either that or you're out a boatload of Benjamins." "This is absurd. You're not going to get any money from me." Roland took a drink and lingered over the pause. *This guy doesn't get it. He still thinks he's driving the better car.*

"You will bring it to me and place it at my feet."

"What?" Both men reacted in unison.

"Do you know how crazy that sounds?" said Cameron Anderson.

Roland laughed. "That's exactly what Woody Harrelson said in the movie."

"Movie? What movie?"

"He's making a mockery of your show. I'd kick him off right now."

"*No Country for Old Men.* I'm sure you've seen it. HBO practically loops the damned thing."

"I've seen it."

"What about you, squire?"

"No. I don't know that movie."

Roland set the scene. "Javier Bardem and Woody Harrelson, both hired assassins, both chasing the same satchel of drug money stolen by Josh Brolin, who's recuperating in a hospital from a gunshot wound courtesy of Bardem. Woody knows where Brolin stashed the money, but when the two meet—the two assassins—the only thing Bardem knows is that he's going to murder Woody Harrelson just for being there, just for getting in his way. They're sitting in Harrelson's hotel room, face to face, and Bardem has his shotgun on his knees and Harrelson knows what's coming and is trying to save his own life. He tells Bardem he knows where the satchel is, right nearby, down in the bushes by the riverbank, and that they could just go get it and call it a day.

Bardem says to Harrelson, 'I know something better. I know where it will be.' Harrelson says, 'Where's that?' Then Bardem says the big line: 'It will be delivered to me and set at my feet.' Then Harrelson says what Cameron Anderson just said. 'You know how crazy you are?' After a little more chit-chat, Bardem paints the wall with his brains."

"I'm glad you find all of this very amusing."

"So, you're Bardem, the ultimate badass?"

"And the patent stamper here is Brolin, reaping the whirlwind, huffing his own flatulence." Roland looked at the screen framing

Douglas Gordon. "The station is not going to take the hit all by itself, so say goodbye to your house and your stock portfolio."

"I think we've indulged this little fantasy long enough."

"It's no fantasy. There's at least one dumbass here at CBN—probably not you—about to get what Harrelson got; and, more importantly, there are executives right now, this very minute, talking with the lawyers to find out just how much money to stuff into a satchel and place at my feet to make this go away." Turning again to Douglas Gordon, "You get the picture, Einstein—mister patent stamper? My phone is buzzing in my pocket with lawyers offering to take you down, and your device is silent because your fraternity buddies are not lining up to bail you out of this jam."

Douglas Gordon stood up and disappeared from the frame, leaving the back of his chair for the world to see. Then his feed was cut, and the pretty San Francisco cityscape disappeared.

"Well, Mister Hazzard, we're out of time. I can't say I've enjoyed your company this evening, but in the interest of fairness, I'd like to give you the last word, though I think you've said more than enough already. Maybe something about the overgrown pyramids of Guatemala, perhaps?"

Roland turned to the camera that had him in its sights and looked straight into the lens.

"Look both ways before you cross me." He summoned a preternatural smile. A smile meant to remind the world that the world is unjust and there's no sense in complaining about it.

~~~~~

Alessandra led them to the cab line on the street in front of the highrise and approached the car in front, the one poised to receive the next fare. She looked in the back window and moved on to the one behind it. Nope, not that one either. The fourth cab was acceptable. She opened the door and Roland held it while she climbed in.

The driver turned his head to look at her. "You're not supposed to do this."

"They should know. If they're going to take the lazy way out and sit in line, they'd better make sure their cabs are clean. But I guess lazy is lazy."

Roland said the name of the hotel and the man pulled out. "Roll up next to that first taxi."

The driver did as directed and Roland reached through his window and held out a ten-dollar bill. The rejected driver rolled down his window and glared at Roland.

"You're making Arabs look bad with that pigsty of a taxi. Here's a ten-spot in honor of Ishmael."

The man looked at Roland as one might regard an escaped lunatic and took the money without a word and rolled up his window. Their driver sped off.

"He's Pakistani." The driver was himself an Arab.

"Well, I'm sure he knows enough English to say thank you."

They rode. He leaned back and closed his eyes and slowed his breathing to counteract the adrenaline that lingered in his system. His spirit—the thing that was Roland—edged up and out of his body a few degrees, like an image double-exposed on film, then snapped back snugly into its housing for a moment to draw out more unwanted excitement, then edged out again to expel the tension to the astral plane, rinse and repeat, until his respiration and pulse achieved an imperturbable regularity, such that he no longer cared where he was, who he was with, or what had done—merrily, merrily, merrily, merrily—from the moment he toddled his very first step.

"I'm angry at you."

"Not true. I'd know. I'd be able to feel it."

"I wasn't joking. Did you think I was joking?"

"I'll make it a condition of the settlement."

"You really think you pulled off a stickup in there?"

"I turned an ambush into a victory, and if you want me to put you on the payroll at CBN, on top of the cash they're going to offer, just let me know. What are your salary requirements? I'm not joking."

"Did you really chuck a breakfast sandwich into his car on the freeway?"

"If I did, he'd a' had it coming."

He took his phone from his pocket and powered it on.

"There's another lie."

"What?"

"On the air, you said your phone was buzzing in your pocket, but the phone was shut off."

"I had to set the hook."

"What does that mean?"

"You've never been fishing I gather."

"A comedian I once heard said there's a fine line between fishing and standing on the shore like an idiot."

"Sound like Steven Wright. One of the best."

"What's *setting the hook?*"

"When you feel the fish nibbling you wait until you're pretty sure it has the bait in its mouth, then you tug on the line, but not so hard that you yank out the hook, just hard enough to pierce its cheek or its lip."

"I didn't know fishing required that much skill."

"For the larger fish, it doesn't. They just attack the bait and either get hooked or not. But the smaller fish tend to nibble, and you actually have to catch them."

"Well, do you think it worked?"

Roland widened his eyes and bobbed his chin up and down as one would to a toddler who'd just asked if the sun was going to come up tomorrow. His phone rang.

He looked at the phone then at her. "My agent."

"I'm dying. I'm hooked."

Roland placed his hand on hers where it rested on the seat and took the call. His part in the conversation consisted of *yep, good, uh-huh, I will, more, your call,* and half a dozen other brief responses that betrayed nothing of what the other was saying, except that it was business, not personal. He combed the back of her hand with his fingers. She turned the hand over to receive his attention on her palm. After a minute she reached across with her left hand and caressed the hand that was tickling her right. He looked at her and rotated his head in a wide circle, exaggerated by the brim of his cowboy hat, to show her what a wild ride he was on.

"Thanks, Josh. I'll call you tomorrow."

"Tell me." She petted his hand.

"They called my man in San Francisco with a number in mind. They want to make it go away. My man is going to run it by a lawyer he knows who does this kind of work."

"Full steam ahead, then."

"I'll need a new shirt."

"I don't follow."

"Wouldn't look right to show up on TV tomorrow wearing the same one I wore today."

"You brought only one?"

"I figured New York City carried shirts. These pants will do for another day or two."

She took her hand off his as though to let him know she was not amused.

"Where's tomorrow?"

"PNN."

"Friendly territory for you."

"At least not hostile."

PNN stood for Patriot News Network, the self-described antidote to the otherwise left-leaning cable news channels. According to Joshua, the folks at PNN were very happy with the frenzied reaction on social media to his CBN spot and wanted Joshua to assure Roland that they didn't plan a journalistic ambush in case Roland was thinking of backing out.

Midtown Manhattan scrolled past in the windows, a kaleidoscopic wash of light and sound. The chassis felt sturdy as it absorbed the irregularities of the road beneath them. People didn't exist, not even the driver. He lived in his own separate narrative, a story written by someone else or waiting to be written, the two universes, theirs and his, coming together only in the intersection of conversation. But Alessandra was real, as real as Roland, possibly a member of the family of souls he migrated with from life to life on the karmic cycle, or possibly a stranger who'd just joined the party. One never knew because one was not supposed to know. Correction—a few did know, yet they were no happier for knowing.

"You're always this way, aren't you?"

"It feels good not drinking and not wanting to drink. It's all because of you, Alessandra."

"Evasive, charming, self-absorbed. Tell me more about the call."

"What more do you want to know?"

"You said the word *more*. What did that mean?"

"They threw out a number—four-hundred grand. Can you believe that?"

"That's a lot."

"It's pathetic."

"Even though you did it? You're not going to sit there and tell me that guy made all that up, just to trash you on television. It's not like you're running for office."

"What's the difference?"

"The truth makes no difference?"

"The truth is what you said—he came to trash my name on television. It's called character assassination. Even if he'd brought the necessary evidence to prove his accusation, it would still be just as bad. But he fucked up. He came at me unarmed, and the geniuses at CBN, in their zeal to destroy me, forgot to make sure he had the goods, forgot to protect themselves against their underestimation of the target."

"So what number are you looking for?"

"Josh and the lawyer will figure that out. He's in for ten percent so he's motivated to negotiate. Good lawyers could get millions out of this, but it would take years and they'd throw a lot more dirt at me. A quick settlement will be fast and much cleaner, and I'll make sure you get a fancy downtown job out of it."

"I won't get my hopes up."

"Just figure out what kind of job would make sense for you. I can't make you CEO, but I won't let them give you security guard or janitorial staff. Just do a little research and something will jump out at you."

"I know already. Writer, or even editor. They can stick me at the bottom of the pyramid and I'll claw my way up. And I've got plenty of left-wing cred. It's just getting in the door that's hard."

"Left-wing cred?"

"Book and film reviews, opinion pieces, in papers like *The Village Voice*. That's the biggest one so far."

"I'm a writer."

"Oh. What have you written?"

"Poetry. I'm not sure that counts as writing, at least not most of what shows up in the journals these days."

"You read the poetry journals?"

"You can still find some in San Francisco. I glance through the lit mags when I'm in the bookstores. Most of it makes your eyes cross. If poets have something to say, they should write it down."

~~~~~

The cab dropped them at the hotel and they walked around until they agreed upon a place to eat. She let the litigious financial intrigue drop and probed into his past in as much as it had been touched on during the interview. *Criminal record? Athletic scholarship? Tell me about your family.* On down the list. She had a right to know who she was dealing with if she was going to accept his offer, so he mustered enough candor to satisfy her curiosity and even found himself meandering fondly into episodes from his youth before he'd ever taken a drink.

"We'd row out onto the lake to where it was about twenty feet deep and drop a five-pound circle weight, the kind you use on a bench press, with a ribbon tied to the hole. And the challenge was to see who could dive down to the bottom in that pitch black water and hold his breath long enough to find the weight, carry it up to the surface, and lift it into the boat."

"Why the ribbon?"

"The ribbon kinda floated above the weight, or else it would have been next to impossible to find in the mud at the bottom."

"And you accomplished this?"

"I invented it. I did it five or six times, and no one else who tried it ever could. Just swimming down twenty feet and bringing up a handful of dirt was something to brag about."

They left the café and walked back to the hotel. More than the unfamiliar surroundings, sounds, and smells—the meatiness of the air, the thrum of congested traffic, a different recipe for asphalt, cigarettes smoked openly on the sidewalk—it was the bearing of the people in New York City that most impressed him. As a whole, they exhibited an unselfconsciousness that was at once fast-paced and easy, a manner that said *I know where I'm going, and if you don't you can ask me for help but you better look sharp because I'll only say it once.* In San Francisco, most people were terrified of any unexpected interaction or sensory surprise.

The room was as they'd left it, cool and clean and empty except for Roland's travel bag.

"You don't have to spend the night. Our agreement was for you to see me to the airport, but I won't be leaving till the day after tomorrow."

"I don't have to work. Plus, I feel responsible for keeping you sober until you're out of my protection. I can take you to a meeting tomorrow morning, and then we can do something fun like today before we head over to PNN."

"Then you better call down and have them do your laundry because you don't want to wear those again tomorrow. I'll add mine, but I'll need to buy that new shirt tomorrow, so I don't look like a dirtbag. Imagine the comments. *Hazzard wears the same shirt two days in a row.*"

"Are you trying to get me out of my clothes?"

"I saw two robes hanging in the bathroom."

"You first."

Roland went into the bathroom and brought out a robe and laid it on the bed. "I'm going to take a shower. I'll drop my clothes outside the door and you can send them all down together if you want yours clean too."

He showered longer than necessary to give her plenty of time to change her mind. When he emerged from the steaming bathroom in his robe, he half expected to see her still fully dressed and ready to say goodbye, shake hands, here's my contact information, nice kicking it around with you, let me know how everything works out. Yet she'd remained. Their clothes were gone. She wore the robe. He dared not wonder if she'd sent her panties down with the laundry.

Roland went to the phone and pressed a few buttons. "Hi. Can you send up a small bathrobe, one for a petite female? My wife is tripping over this gigantic thing. Thanks."

"Thank you, dear."

"What do you like from the dessert menu? We mize well, since they're paying"

"Just get two of whatever you want. Let's see if they have that movie. I've never seen it."

"You're a movie critic, and you haven't seen *No Country?*"

"I don't much care for the Coen Brothers, except for *Big Lebowski*. Everyone likes *Lebowski*."

"Yes. But this is more a McCarthy movie than a Coen Brothers movie."

"Yeah, that's why I want to see it. I liked *All the Pretty Horses.*"

"I have a hard time watching Matt Damon trying to pull off a heterosexual."

"Just see if you can find the movie. I'll order some ice cream."

"And pie. Any kind of fruit pie."

"Craving sugar? That's a sign of alcohol withdrawal."

Roland let that go and navigated the hotel's TV interface to see if *No Country for Old Men* was in the on-demand library. Alessandra ordered dessert. A knock at the door brought the robe he'd requested. She took it into the bathroom and closed the door and soon the shower was on. When she came out twenty minutes later, robed and turbaned, he was sitting on the bed watching a fearsome-eyed woman dissect the diabolical agenda of her political enemies.

"I never watch the Trump station."

"I rarely watch any kind of television, except for movie channels on my laptop."

"You didn't find the McCarthy movie?"

"No. I mean yes. I did. It's there, but while I was waiting, I thought I'd study the vibe on PNN since I'll be there tomorrow."

"Who are you going to vote for?"

"I'm surprised you didn't come across my answer to that question when you delved into my podcasts. I get asked that all the time. I'm withholding my ballot. In California, it doesn't matter anyway. My state is bought and paid for, but even if I lived in a swing state I'd be just as disgusted."

"What's so disgusting?"

"The choice between a salmonella apple or a handful of thumbtacks."

They watched the movie side by side on the bed, shins sticking out of their white terrycloth robes, feet pointing up, her toes painted shamrock green. Soon they had a tray of peach pie and vanilla ice cream between them which they finished in silence as the drama unfolded and the tension mounted. He glanced at her a few times, discreetly, to assess how deeply she was absorbed in the story. She reached for his hand as an armed Bardem edged along the array of motel room doors in search of his prey. Roland knew the movie well enough by now that he no longer enjoyed it for the drama, but on a deeper, one might say artistic, level, affirming the filmmakers' choices here and there and spotting the odd defect.

When it was over, he got up and set the tray on the table and took off his robe and draped it over the back of a chair. She looked him up and down, making no effort to conceal her admiration for his athletic frame and his well-defined muscles, naked except for his tight-fitting undershorts.

"That's a lot to tear down."

"Who's gonna tear me down?"

"You haven't surrendered. You must surrender to win."

Roland understood what she meant. It would take a lot of booze over a long period of time to destroy a body like his.

"I surrendered to you," he said. "I guess that's a start."

"This might be the shortest meeting ever," she laughed. "It only takes two, as long as both share a common purpose."

He walked over to the bed and pulled back the covers on his side. "I hope you don't mind if I sleep like this. I'm not going to wrestle with that robe all night."

"Not at all. As long as you know that you're not going to put that thing in me. I can see enough to know that even if I wanted to it wouldn't work."

"You're my temporary, on-location sponsor. I'd never think of trying to take advantage of you. I thought that was understood."

"Okay. Then I'll sleep in my underwear. You won't even know I'm here."

"If I snore, I know how you can stop me."

"How's that?"

"Scratch me"

"No, sir. I know what scratching leads to."

"What's that?"

"More scratching."

Chapter 17
October 29-30, 2016

Roland woke with a floating sensation. He'd been zooming around again, he figured, zipping and zooming, just not in a state of awareness, not piloting his flight as in a lucid dream. He wondered where he'd been. Perhaps nowhere to speak of, perhaps only to some far-flung, lightless dimple in the cosmos. Perhaps to an enormous womb. No. Out there the word *enormous* had no meaning. In any case, he'd left his body—of that much he was certain—and his mortal coil would take some getting used to. *And lookie here and whaddya know, another mortal coil, an itty-bitty female one.* She lay perfectly still under the covers, firmly grounded. Roland inhaled the dead, recirculated hotel air and smiled in spite of it. Smiled indeed, absorbed by the peaceful repose suffused in her face, smiled *never have I woken up sober with a woman next to me, let alone one I haven't...*he dared not finish that thought. *This must be what normal men and women do when normal men and women wind up sharing a bed on the first day they meet.* There was something to be said for garden-variety sanity. Roland knew he could pass the most rigorous sanity check devised by clinical science, but he'd never before felt exactly this much sane.

Nothing like a long run to reacquaint oneself with one's body. He put on his running shorts and shoes and wrote a note for Alessandra. *I'm going for a jog in Central Park. Back before 9. ~R.* He added his phone number in case she needed to reach him beforehand. Outside the hotel he climbed into a cab and told the driver his intentions and after a short ride found himself enjoying the pleasant sensation of coursing through an unfamiliar bucolic wilderness without getting lost. The Park was a near-perfect rectangle. If you kept going in one general direction, you'd eventually come out somewhere on the grid. He followed the best-paved paths, the wider ones, kept close to bodies of water, stayed under trees to taste in their fragrances, maintained a steady pace at roughly eighty percent of full exertion, which meant he passed every other jogger running the same direction, even caused a few to flinch, such a powerful force was he, pounding the land at high speed and circulating great drafts of air through his lungs. He slowed only to avoid a collision or to keep from scaring someone. *If I lived here I would do this every morning*, said the alcoholic to himself after a single day of sobriety. *The regular parkgoers would stop when I dashed by and nod in admiration. There he goes again, they'd say, there goes one powerful specimen of humanity.*

He crossed the 79th Street Transverse just north of The Lake. A man walking his dog tracked Roland as he approached and, when the two locked eyes, the man give him a little fist pump, not demonstrative enough for anyone else to notice, but unmistakable in its message of support. Roland returned the gesture and added a thank-you nod and galloped on, a little lighter, a little less bound by gravity from the momentary surge of self-satisfaction. After a few more strides he stopped short, as though afflicted by a sudden cramp, but this was no charley horse. The incidental fan he'd just passed reminded him that today he was far more famous than he was yesterday. His followers would expect him to make an appearance on social media. He was slacking off on the one job he'd forbidden Joshua from helping him with. For that matter, he'd forgotten to read the tweet that he'd written in The Buddha Lounge, according to the nameless woman who'd taken him home two nights before. A tweet she'd said she erased before he could send it, a tweet she'd saved in a screenshot. Why had she saved it? She must have wanted him to see it. He found a place to sit and pulled up the picture of his unsent message. He recalled she'd said he'd had her read it aloud to him and that he'd laughed at his own words. Now he saw them for the first time, tapped by his drunken fingers at a place and time he could not recall.

My lowly droogs, take a look at your lives. If you could disappear for a couple of days and no one would miss you, take my advice and check out. Your life has no meaning. Hit the reset button and hope for better days on the flipside. Make sure to unfollow me first. I want a clean count.

He let out an involuntary exclamation that did not have a name, an emotional blurt, something between a gasp of shock and a snort of disbelief at a fact impossible to deny. She—the woman who preferred to remain anonymous while giving herself to him—she'd saved his ass alright. That tweet would have sent his public career into a tailspin out of which he could not have pulled. Might have gotten him suspended from Twitter for encouraging *self-harm*. Joshua would have withdrawn his services, and forget about a respectable publisher. He felt the shame of gratitude for an undeserved good deed performed by a total stranger whom he'd plucked, if briefly, from her own life and fitted into his. That was the first real swell of gratitude he could remember, one that came forth unmitigated by his ego, and the sad part was he had no way to thank her. That she'd preferred to remain anonymous elevated her to the status of angel. He read it again, trying to identify in his flippant cruelty some piece of his character. The only thing he could compare it to was his mockery of Barsamian as he gasped out his last breaths. How had Astrid put it? *I'm me and you're not. Tough luck for you, Jack.*

He let the shame of his cruelty crouch behind a blind of rationalization. *I was drunk, too drunk to remember.* There was only partial absolution in that peculiar twist of mind. But an irony came pouring in like rain through the roof of his makeshift blind, an irony he dared not face but could not ignore. Not long ago, before he killed Barsamian, he was the very man he'd meant to mock in that misbegotten tweet. No one would have missed him, certainly not after a couple of days. By his criterion, his life had meaning, but only by dint of having killed a notorious murderer. He looked around him. In every direction, there were people doing things, people who would be missed if they did not carry on, and he counted himself among them only because he had forcibly propelled himself into the public space. His phone vibrated. He answered the call.

"Hey, Josh."

"Roland, you sound good. You good?"

"Just did a couple of miles in Central Park. Heart and lungs in perfect working order."

"How's the hotel?"

"Pretty nice. I'm glad you called so early. What's up?"

"I've been checking your social media accounts and see you haven't posted anything for the past couple of days."

"Yeah, I've been slacking. I need to touch base with my droogs this morning, especially after yesterday."

"I'm glad I caught you then. You're going to have to dial things back a bit."

"Why? I've got a million and a half Twitter followers. That's book deal territory."

"Check again. You've got two-point-two million now. Last night raised your stock a bit."

"All the more reason for me not to dial things back. I need to dial it up. Stoke the furnace so to sp—"

"Slow down, Roland."

"What?"

"Can I put you on speaker? I'm sitting in the office of the defamation lawyer I told you about. We've been on the phone with CBN's legal council for the last half hour. Can I put you on speaker?"

"Go ahead." He snugged in his earpiece. "I'm listening."

An unfamiliar voice piped up and spoke rapidly, in the manner of a salesman. "Good morning, Roland. May I call you Roland? My name is Mike McAfee. I've been working defamation claims for more than ten years, and I spoke with Joshua last night because I think I can be helpful in the situation you've put yourself in."

"Josh, do you trust this guy?"

A chill breeze brushed his sweaty arms. He shuddered.

"We wouldn't be talking right now if I didn't. You're going to want to listen to what this man has to say."

"What do you mean by dial things back? I scored a big win yesterday. My fans will expect me to pontificate, to take the peacock out for a strut."

"That's the worst thing you could do right now."

"How so?" Roland sounded annoyed on purpose.

"Roland, I've been following you for the past month, and I'm going to take something of a hit, professionally speaking, if I wind up representing you. I'll find out who my friends really are, and that's ok with me, because who needs false friends anyway, am I right?"

The question was rhetorical. McAfee continued. "So, to be clear, I'm on your side. Your voice belongs in the public square, and if you want to keep it there you gotta be smart, and we all know that you've got an agile mind, but you will need some guidance here."

"Thank you, Mister McAfee. All I asked is *why.*"

"Why?"

"Roland wants to know why he needs to tone it down."

"Right. Let me put it bluntly. If you want to settle, you gotta keep your mouth shut. I'll lay out all the parameters for that if we get that far. But, on the other hand, if you want to rub salt in the wound, you can do that, but then you'll have to go to trial to get anything out of them. And make no mistake about it—you will probably win the case. The law is on your side. You figured that on the fly out in front of a nationally televised audience. I give you a lot of credit for that. But understand, even if you win a lawsuit, that will not guarantee you an award. What I will guarantee is that most of the people watching last night, whether they like you or not, if you asked them to put it all on the line, man-to-maker, would say that mister Gordon was telling the truth. A Texas jury might wink and give you a couple of million, but a San Francisco or New York City jury might give you one crisp American dollar, which would be their right. Of course, the trial will cost CBN a lot of money and they'll have to pay your court costs most likely, so the best option as far as they're concerned is to settle..."

"Josh said four hundred grand last night. Can we get more than that, in a settlement I mean?"

"It's hard to say. Maybe twice that. But that will come with a lot of conditions, and the way you drink you might want to take your chances with a civil jury."

"Excuse me. The way I drink?"

"Joshua—man-to-maker—do you think Roland Hazzard can keep his mouth shut about this for five years? Would you lay a thousand dollars on it?"

"No. Not if he's drinking, but I'd bet a thousand dollars that Roland will say he doesn't have a problem."

"There's the dilemma."

"What are the conditions—the parameters, as you say—of this muzzle?"

"They get to call you a liar, essentially, and you can't defend yourself. You can never say in public that you did not throw an object at Mister Gordon on the day in question. You can't publicly contradict him. The most you can say is that Gordon cannot prove his accusation and that CBN should not have aired his accusation, both of which are true statements."

"This makes no sense. They pay me a settlement, and then they can repeat the slander?"

"No. They won't be allowed to repeat it, but they can say they believe Gordon and do not believe you. They can't say you threw an object or put anyone on the air who says you threw an object, not without evidence. But they can say who they believe and who they don't believe, since a belief is just like an opinion, therefore protected."

Pondering the logistics of such mendacity made him ill at ease, unable to sit still, perhaps because he was the ultimate source of it. He got up and started walking, north he sensed. The sweat on his arms had dried and he could feel the cold October air and needed to get his heart pumping again.

"What if I want to express my opinion that CBN is full of shit?"

"You're joking, right?"

"No. I need to know where the line is if I'm expected not to cross it."

"You can't have an opinion about whether their belief is true or not true, since you are presumed to know whether or not you did the thing that Gordon alleged. Such an opinion would count as a contradiction and therefore constitute a breach of the agreement."

"So, strap on the ol' ball gag and take it bending over?"

"With both fists clenched full of cash to ease your discomfort. All we're talking about here is a bruised ego, as colorful as you would like to make it sound."

Roland wanted to sit down again, but there was nowhere it sit. He held the phone away from his ear for a second or two and swiveled his head, turned around and around again. He recognized, as if for the first time, a world impossibly complex, far beyond his capacity to comprehend. The best way to manage life was to keep things as simple as possible, he thought, yet he knew he had chosen the opposite course and there was no turning back. He found his bearings and moved forward northward out of the park.

"Roland, you still there?"

"Mister McAfee, what did you mean when you said you are on *my side?*"

"You're a radical libertarian, to fix a label to it, which has its basis in English Common Law and, one might argue, goes back to ancient fundamental concepts of human autonomy. I'm a legal purest and what I do boils down to protecting the biblical Eighth Commandment. I don't agree with statutes that limit or exempt public figures from defamation claims, but that's a separate discussion since they're not claiming, correctly I'd say, that you're an established public figure. But even public figures shouldn't be falsely accused of serious crimes without an avenue of legal redress. Where I sympathize with you—where I think that your voice needs to be out there—is in your belief that people with violence in their hearts will be less likely to act on those impulses if they have a reasonable expectation of being injured or killed by the intended victim or by a bystander. I applaud your exhortation—your conviction I might say—that every able-bodied person should be ready and willing to strike back at an attacker without fear of prosecution from the government. Right now, the balance of fear weighs on the minds of the good guys, and that creates a neurotic society. You, as I understand it, want to transfer the fear back to the minds of the criminally inclined. Is that a satisfactory answer, Señor Hammurabi?"

"I'm a little left of Hammurabi."

"There's a great campaign slogan," said Joshua.

"We still haven't gotten to the heart of the matter at hand. You've got three options here: Take your chances with a jury that might be hostile to your ideas; take a gamble on yourself in the hopes that you won't violate the agreement; or do nothing."

"I don't see the virtue in option three," said Roland.

"If you take the money—whatever the amount might be—and get drunk one day and blow the whole thing up with some careless statement, it will be worse for you than never having taken it at all, because if you're forced to pay the money back that will include my portion, and I'm not about to surrender my cut on account of your bad judgment."

"I made a promise."

"What sort of promise?"

"I promised a friend that I'd get her a job at CBN, and I intend to keep it."

"What would possess you to do that?"

"I've got a fair idea what."

"It's not like that."

"You barely have any friends in San Francisco. Since when do you have a friend in New York City?"

Roland held his tongue to ignore Joshua.

"Tell you what, Mister McAfee, see if you can get them up to seven-hundred thousand. I'll take five and you and Joshua each get one, and my friend gets hired as a writer. She's in journalism, a New York liberal, already a member of their tribe."

"That doesn't make any sense. Why would they hire the friend of their enemy? And even if they did take her on, do you think she'd get a fair shake?"

Roland ignored him again, adding a long pause to emphasize his deliberation. He found a patch of sunlight and stood there to absorb its warmth.

"Does that sound possible, Mike?"

"How well do you know this woman?"

"Well enough to bring her with me to the station last night where she got acquainted with the program's staff."

Joshua would not be tuned out.

"You met her yesterday, didn't you? I don't like the sound of this."

"Tell us more, Roland."

"They gotta guarantee her a year's employment at least one hundred K, which is a little above dogshit for the subway set."

"We mean tell us more about the woman."

"You have to give me your word that you won't pass it along to the people at CBN. As far as you know, she's a good friend of mine, nothing more."

"Why so mysterious?"

"I want your word."

"Strict client confidentiality."

"I met her yesterday at an AA meeting in Central Park. We spent the whole day together. She kept me from veering into the bars. I'm invoking the AA seal."

"That's convenient."

"He doesn't lie. Not when it's important anyway. I wouldn't represent him if he did."

"Don't overthink this, gentlemen. I met her at the Strawberry Fields Forever Group in Central Park at seven AM. Google it. She kept me occupied all day and we became friends. She happened to mention she could see herself working at the station, as a writer maybe, but after I gave them a well-deserved black eye I felt bad for her. So, is this something I can do? I think I have some leverage here, but it's up to you guys to apply the force. She's a friend of mine. Nothing more. And don't say anything about AA."

"It's strange Cameron Anderson would accuse you of being drunk. Why do you think he did that?"

"His spy gave him bad information."

"Spy? Are you serious?"

"Someone came over to me about ten minutes before I went on and offered me a drink, but I told him I was carrying my own bottle and already had a good heat-on and he went away. I never saw him again."

"That's useful. We can use that in our favor."

"You mean add more to the list of things I'm not allowed to talk about?"

"Yes. The more you have that could embarrass them, the more your silence is worth."

The conference continued for another ten minutes, mostly with McAfee and Joshua strategizing for the follow-up call with CBN's legal counsel, while Roland navigated his way back to where he thought he'd started his jog. He threw in the occasional *sounds good* to let them know he was paying attention, but really he was scanning the people around him to see if anyone appeared to recognize him. He reflected on how it could be that one's position in the world—one's status—could radically change one's interior life. What would it mean if the way you thought people saw you actually changed who you were? Would you exist in any meaningful sense in that case? As the call was wrapping up, the subject turned to Roland's obvious drinking problem with Joshua asking him if he planned to keep his sobriety streak going.

"Do you remember the day we met? It wasn't that long ago."

"What's your point?"

"Would you say I was sober?"

"No. I'd say you were trashed."

"But not so trashed that we couldn't have a coherent dialogue, right?"

"Things have changed since then. Considerably."

McAfee chimed in. "Would you have snapped that guy's neck if you'd been sober?"

"I made it clear I went back to the car for the drink after I stopped that attacker."

"No one believes that, least of all me. I had the keys, so the bottle was in your pocket the whole time. You drank at lunch with me then hit your little bottle before the family townhall thing. You smuggled that bottle onto the airplane."

"Why did you go back to the car?"

"He was hoping I would be there waiting behind the wheel ready to make a clean getaway."

Roland grumbled nothing. Voicing resentment at the spoken truth was something Roland had not accustomed himself to.

"I'll be sober when I go on air tonight."

"Everything depends on it," said Joshua.

"Everything?"

"You're going to be very busy from now on, and not just in your bunker doing podcasts and radio spots."

"I guess I'll be as busy as I want to be. If you get the hundred grand I've carved out for you, then we can part ways without any guilt."

"Easy there, Roland. We're all pulling on the same rope."

"Berkeley called. You're about to enter the college speaking circuit, if you want to, that is."

"What do you mean *Berkeley called?* The university invited me to speak?"

"No," said Joshua. "A student group, a free speech club, the Mario Savio—"

"—Sewing Circle."

"You've heard of it."

McAfee chuckled. "You gotta be kidding."

"No. I went there. I'm an alum."

"I know you went to Cal—but is there really a club called the Mario Savio Sewing Circle?"

"Yeah. It was started in my sophomore year. Tell them I'll do it for free."

"They have three thousand dollars to spend."

"Make it a thousand, then. We have to keep our dignity."

His phone vibrated and the banner showed a New York phone number. "Go ahead and book a date. I've gotta take this call. It's my chaperone."

Roland switched over to the incoming call. It was Alessandra. She was hungry and wanted to get moving. He told her he'd be back in a few minutes and said he was glad she'd stuck around, and she said she'd slept very well. He remarked that it was chilly out and she had nothing to say to that, so he repeated he'd be back in a jiff and put the phone in his pocket and left the park to find a cab.

~~~~~

He emerged from the bathroom showered and dressed. He passed the bed where she sat looking at her phone and sat down in a chair to pull on his socks and boots.

"You look like you feel pretty good."

"I hate the world."

"That usually passes. A good meal is a good place to start."

He looked at her and could tell from the skeptical slant of her mouth that she wasn't going to ask him why he said he hated the world because it was clear she didn't believe that he did.

"You look like you should be hungry all the time." He appraised her dangerously skinny body. "Hungry and cold. I doubt you're heavy enough to hang yourself."

She straightened up and blinked like she'd been slapped in the face—slapped for no apparent reason at all. "What happened out there?"

"How much time have you got?"

"You can tell me over breakfast, then."

"How much time *sober*, I mean."

"Oh. I thought you'd never ask."

"You said at the meeting yesterday you woke up at thirty-five and realized you'd lost a decade in an alcoholic haze. You don't look older than thirty-five. I wouldn't have guessed even thirty-five."

"I'll tell you my story over breakfast, and you can tell me about what happened in the park."

"Okay. Let's get you a steak downstairs and then go look for a proper jacket. It will be too cold for you out there." He stood up and moved toward the door. She got off the bed and took his cowboy hat from the top of the TV cabinet.

"Don't forget this. You don't want people to recognize you, right?"

He took his hat and opened the door and stood back and held it open for her to precede him into the scented hotel hallway. He said thank you as she passed even though he was the one holding the door.

~~~~~

She ate with abandon, glancing at him from above the rim of her glass when she gulped down her orange juice. Steak, eggs, potatoes, and an English muffin. Like a street urchin accustomed to scrounging her meals, Alessandra could pack it in. Roland ate his portions finically, passively, distracted by pending obligations, unable to muster the gratitude that would make bearable the situation in which he had placed himself. A drink or two he knew would transform his perception of the situation into the genuine opportunity that it was, and knowing that—that booze would help him to appreciate what he objectively knew was a beneficial circumstance insomuch as it exceeded what he had set out to achieve—impelled him to question his spiritual fitness, though he would not have used that phrase. Meanwhile, he could see sitting across from him a woman fully engaged in the moment, stuffing her bella faccia, clearly unconcerned about, though thoroughly aware of, his disconsolate mind. They'd said barely a word to each other until she raised her chin and dabbed her mouth with her napkin.

"Just say you're sorry. Even if you don't mean it, you'll feel better."

His jaw dropped an honest inch. He didn't try to stop it—just let his mouth hang half-open. True, he wasn't sure what she was talking about, but what left him agog was the realization that he could marry such a woman and that, furthermore, he thought it might be a good idea. Setting aside the requirement for sexual attraction, which was not so rare and probably much overrated anyway, the reason successful lovers got along in perpetuity, rather than just tolerated one another once their hormones settled down, was their suitable temperaments. After that, all that mattered was that they treat each other decently all the time, and lovingly some of the time. Roland wanted, then and there and for the first time in his life, even against his will, to be the kind of man a woman with a suitable temperament took no risk in marrying.

"I'd be happy to, but I don't know why."

"You were wrong in what you said up in the room. Wrong for being hurtful and also factually incorrect."

Now he understood her feasting. "I'm sorry. It just came out. I haven't mastered the whole restraint-of-pen-and-tongue thing."

"You shouldn't make fun of AA. Step Ten comes naturally to most normal people."

"Normal people?"

"A vast conspiracy to which you are not privy."

"You're right, of course. It was very hurtful. I didn't mean it to be when I said it, but when I heard myself say it, I knew."

Alessandra nodded sympathetically. "You asked how much time I have—I have less than a year, almost a year."

"You seem pretty solid." Roland had no idea what that meant but he wanted to say something positive. Alessandra didn't acknowledge the compliment.

"I've never shared this in a meeting, but that morning I mentioned, when I woke up and realized that my life was a waste of energy, I decided to spare the planet my little carbon footprint and let someone, the building manager probably, find me hanging in my bedroom closet, which might have taken a few days since there weren't many people who would have missed me. And you may be surprised to know that I AM heavy enough to hang myself."

"Your sitting here is hardly proof of that."

"The hanger rod and the cord around my neck held just fine when I sunk to my knees, and it took a few seconds, maybe fifteen or twenty, for my vision to start to go…"

"So, your feet were still touching?"

"Yes. My knees were almost touching the floor. Imagine kneeling in a church pew and being lifted up a few inches by a rope around your neck. It looked like that."

"I'd grab the rope."

"I did. When my vision went, I was conscious of myself falling into a deep black hole, kinda floating downward like a feather into an empty well, and my ears started buzzing, louder and louder, very irritating, I just wanted it to stop, and as soon as I had that thought a loud voice, a male voice, very commanding, shouted GRAB THE ROPE. I almost expected him to say YOU IDIOT, but it was just *grab the rope*. An order barked."

"Did you recognize the voice?"

"No. But I would if I heard it again. I think of it pretty often. It was not my imagination. I know that much."

Roland finished his breakfast, having gained his appetite once she'd started talking. Alessandra sipped from her glass of water.

"And now you're here, life turned around, being of service." There was no hint of mockery in his tone, but one of genuine humility accompanied by an imperceptible squirm.

"I don't think of this as a service. I enjoy pretending to be your girlfriend. I haven't felt this human since I was a child. You saw the way I wolfed down that steak and the rest of it. That's not the way I normally eat. Being with you is good for me too."

She seemed eager to depart. He raised one hand to stay her.

"Before we go, I need to tell you something."

"There's a meeting about six blocks away at the Y. It starts in half an hour. There's an amazing speaker on the calendar there, a pretty famous guy, from your neck of the woods I think. Seating will be tight. I don't want to be late."

"Fine, but I just need to tell you that I spoke with a lawyer this morning, a defamation lawyer. It looks like I'm going to get a pile of cash for that little stunt they pulled last night."

"That's really none of my business."

"Well, it is, actually, or could be."

"You're not serious." Roland could see that she knew he was serious.

"I don't make idle promises. What I said last night was a promise."

"What exactly are we talking about here?"

"I told my lawyer to tell their lawyers that CBN needs to hire you as a writer for at least a year at a minimum of one hundred K."

"That doesn't sound like a good idea."

"You don't have to call him, but at least take his number. He wants you to send him a resume. He needs more than just your name to make a case to the people at CBN."

"Why would you do that?"

"Let me ask you. When you said last night backstage that you could see yourself working there, did you have it in mind to follow up on that? Did you take any numbers or business cards?"

"Yes."

"So I made things a little easier for you."

"Well, in your version of the story you may be my white knight, but to them you're still the dragon."

"I have no doubt a Sober Sally like you can win them over."

He sent McAfee's contact information to her phone, which established a handshake between their two devices. Now the two were wedded, at least in that minimal way.

~~~~~

Alessandra wasn't kidding about the scarcity of seating at the YMCA. The place was packed when they got there and it was all she could do to find a single chair near the back of the room. Roland felt relieved by the size of the audience—more than a hundred and fifty by his count—and by the apparent celebrity of the speaker. Roland would not have to identify himself as in a regular AA meeting, and the attendees likely would not pay him much attention if they happened to spot him in the crowd. The much-anticipated headliner today was a Californian named Earl H who'd been in high demand as a circuit speaker for a few years now, so miraculous had been his recovery and so engaging his personality in recounting it. Earl's story, worthy of a lengthy memoir, could hardly be done justice in a few paragraphs, or even by a transcript of one of his many talks, a hundred hours worth or more of which were available online. To his credit, Earl H did not monetize the tens of thousands of views his recordings had received. Roland, though, had never heard of this Earl H everyone seemed so excited about. He squeezed in along the back wall with a few dozen others, lowered the brim of his hat, and listened to the meeting organizer introduce the man of the hour to resounding applause.

A good AA story often contains elements that smack of science fiction, and after ingratiating himself to the crowd with warm acknowledgments to the folks who'd flown him in and put him up for the weekend, Earl H got around to one of his favorite otherworldly drunken episodes.

"I came to one night standing on the sidewalk surrounded by three cops with their guns drawn. I had the vague idea I was in Venice Beach because it smelled like Venice Beach and that's the last place I remembered being. But was that yesterday or a week ago? I had no idea. All I knew is that for some reason—probably the guns—I was still alive on the planet. That and nothing more. Not how I came to be there, but only that I *was* there, with three cops pointing their guns at me and cars slowing down to look, and all I could think to say was: *What's the trouble, fellas? I just got here."*

Earl H tripped along the edge of laughter, sometimes spilling over into self-induced hilarity, and kept the audience hinged on his every word. His voice had the gravelly rasp of Tom Waits topped with the nasal whine of Bob Dylan, and he spoke quickly, without the aid of notes. Now he slowed his rapid wit to recall his earlier years, before the mental institutions and incarcerations, before his youth and intelligence had succumbed to complete, drug-addled dissolution. The road to his bottom was not a long one, marked as it was by constant violence and near continuous oblivion, all taking place after he'd survived a private plane crash in Mexico en route to a family vacation. His whole family—parents and sister—perished. He'd watched them bleed to death while he lay immobile with a broken back and numerous other serious injuries from which, in their totality, an ordinary man would have succumbed. It was there, dying on a hillside in Mexico, the crash site and corpses picked over by thieves, that Earl H made his break with both God and his fellow man. Cancer had failed to kill him in his twenties. The plane crash and the indifferent, avaricious Federales fared no better. Earl H made it home to rehabilitate in the hospital and, after the insurance settlement came through, resumed his descent toward self-destruction with deliberate, vengeful speed.

His voice softened when he spoke of his spiritual malady, common to alcoholics. In Earl H's case, it took the form of a pathological fear of people that manifested itself in open hostility, even when, finally, he was welcomed by the hands of AA members eager to enfold him in the warmth of their shared recovery.

"My eyes, my face, the way I stood—it all said, *back off."*

And stand off he did, going to meetings but remaining unapproachable for a year. But after a time, the crazy-eyed, wild-haired, drug-fueled, booze-soaked psychopath, broken beyond repair in the opinion of the various institutions that had housed him—a human hardly a man—was transformed into a well-groomed raconteur completely at ease in his own skin. Roland tried, to no avail, to disbelieve it. His trusty stock-in-trade, his raison d'être, at least by his own estimation, was to sight the truth and penetrate it. There was no denying it: The man at the podium, this Earl H, was the real deal. No one as popular as he, with such a lengthy online catalog of extemporaneous autobiographies, could escape exposure had he been a fraud.

Roland forgot about himself for a while and listened appreciatively with the others, laughing with the speaker and enjoying the moment. He resolved to search out the speaker tapes of Earl H on the internet to learn more about the remarkable man. AA truly was, he realized for the first time, a program of attraction, not promotion. Court cards were worthless if the people in the rooms were not happy.

Earl H concluded his talk and some of the people left but nearly half stayed behind and formed a queue to meet the man, as was the custom with an AA speaker, unless, of course, some urgent appointment for which he or she had apologized in advance required an immediate departure. Alessandra found a few of her familiars in the fellowship and joined them in the line to pass a friendly moment with the victorious Earl H. She signaled to Roland to make sure he knew what she was doing, and he tipped his hat and found a seat and, after a while, set his hat on the chair next to him. He scrolled through the messages on his phone and scanned his social media accounts. He owed calls to about twenty people, his parents and brother and sister included. His followers on social media were doubtless waiting for him to say—to tweet—something. What a stupid world I have inherited, he thought, yet there was money to be made if one could only garner a little fame. But now was not the time. He needed to be alone, to have some time to think before reengaging that world. Mom and Dad and Sandy and Phillip would have to wait a while longer. At any rate, he'd see them over Thanksgiving.

The meeting room was now practically empty. He'd been too absorbed with his phone to notice the last departures. When he lifted his eyes from his mobile device, there was Earl H, not tall but standing tall, looking down at him with a nimble grin.

"Roland Hazzard. The man himself. The fearsome Butcher Slayer."

Roland dropped his phone and wavered between leaning down to pick it up and standing to acknowledge the man who'd just spoken his name. Instead, he did neither and sat there mute. Earl H didn't linger to relish Roland's flustered disarray.

"We'll save a seat for when you're ready." Earl H walked away before Roland could respond.

Alessandra came up from behind him, startling him anew, and fished his hat off the chair.

"Let's get going."

Roland looked at her like she was a stranger.

"Yesterday I was your girlfriend. Today you'll be my boyfriend. How's that?"

"Ok. And we might as well pretend it's your birthday."

~~~~~

The couple had most of the day to kill before his TV appearance on PNN and they began by shopping for a jacket, a pretend birthday present from a pretend boyfriend to his pretend girlfriend. Roland was keenly aware that his sobriety was also pretended, so stark was the contrast between hers and his. She moved easily, kept a warble in her voice, touched him affectionately from time to time, was altogether comfortable with her fabricated role in his improvised, impoverished life that chilly autumn New York City Sunday. He did not hold her hand and she didn't force the issue as they moved from store to store. Alessandra knew her way around the district and was determined to find not just an acceptable jacket, but a garment she would be eager to don. She acted like she wanted the day to last, to savor its incidental pleasures, and did her best to ignore his indifferent demeanor. Did her best, that is, until she finally had to ask him what he was chewing on.

"I watched you during the talk. I know you enjoyed it. You laughed along with the rest of us. You can't say you didn't enjoy it."

"Did I say I didn't enjoy it?"

"You're not going to bring me down. What did Earl H say to you?"

Roland knew he was wrong, but only in the limited way that a dog knows it's wrong when it sinks its teeth into one of momma's new bedroom slippers. Alessandra was asking him to drop the slipper.

"Nothing. I'm just gathering my thoughts, putting them in order, getting ready for tonight."

"Not so. You're *feeling*, not thinking, not intellectualizing. You haven't given the first thought to tonight."

"It's the Halloween. The stupid Halloween decorations. I can't stand them, and I can't block them out."

"Just tell me to leave and I'll find the nearest door."

"Are you trying to start a fight?"

"I want you to tell the truth."

"I'm going to look for a shirt." He strode over to the rack of casual dress shirts and after five minutes found one that he could wear, a green and white checked cotton number that went well with his jeans, belt, and Laredos. Purchase in hand, he went back to Alessandra, who was modeling a slim-fitting dark gray leather jacket with a high collar and a bunch of zippers.

"Stylish. You're every inch the villain in that little beauty."

"Thanks. I'm sorry I pressed you."

"It's okay. I've been thinking. If it was truly some otherworldly force that put us together, then you make perfect sense."

"I don't understand."

"Yesterday you seemed like just what I wanted, but today I realize that you're what I needed."

"How do you know what you need?"

"The inner turmoil you create—it seems very important, even necessary."

"I don't mean to make you uncomfortable."

"That's exactly it. You don't do it on purpose. But it seems like there's a purpose behind it."

Alessandra draped the jacket over her forearm and patted it with her free hand to say this is the one.

"I think it's whatever Earl H said to you that's put you in a bitchy mood. Release it. Open the door of the birdcage and let the bitchy little devil fly away."

"He recognized me. He said *Roland Hazzard the Butcher Slayer.*"

"That bit of notoriety is paying for this pricey little jacket."

"And before I could stand up to shake his hand, he said *we'll save a seat for when you're ready* and walked off."

"I see."

"Do you?"

"You felt judged. Earl H pegged you for a spectator, a white-knuckler. He was one himself for a long time. What he said to you was right in line with the Twelfth Step. He was carrying the message."

Roland had nothing to say to that. If he'd said what was on his mind, he'd've had to admit that he wanted a drink even knowing that disaster might ensue. At the very least, he wanted to put a half-pint of vodka in his jacket so he could empty it down his throat before going on air tonight. His mind was at war with itself, and he sensed that the side that hated life was winning. His callous remark to Alessandra in the hotel room was, perhaps, his mind trying to get rid of her so he could sabotage the day.

She saw dejection in his face and moved in to put her free arm around his waist. "You've been dry for a little more than a day, and yesterday you kicked ass. Think about that. Earl H must have seen you on TV and was giving you a little nudge. He'll be paying attention to you from now on. The hottest AA speaker in the world probably, and he's got his eye on you along with a few million other people. Use that energy to keep your focus on what you're doing, not on what Earl H might be thinking."

Roland nodded and took the jacket from her arm. "Ok. Now go ahead and get whatever other little things you need. I'll wait here and stare down all the scary witches and skeletons."

"Better yet, close your eyes and stare down your demons. You can't hide from what's inside of you." She swatted him on the tush and glided away.

Roland found a chair and sat down to peruse the activity on his social media accounts, which was extensive, too extensive for a thorough review, and ran the gamut. Congratulations, praise, advice, skepticism all the way to vitriolic condemnation. He decided to post a quote from an American martyr. He wrote: *It's not violence when it's self-defense. It's called intelligence. –Malcolm The Tenth. Soldier on, my droogs.*

He figured there'd be a handful of pedants out there who would miss the humor in the playful substitution of 'the Tenth' for 'X' in the famous activist's cognomen and deem it necessary to correct the apparent mistake. That would trigger an amusing back-and-forth in the subsequent thread. He would check back later to see how the gag played out and, more curiously, to see if anyone out there was clever enough to find the Easter egg he'd hidden. Another famous Malcolm—Malcolm

McDowell—played the lead character, Alex, in *A Clockwork Orange*, who referred to his little gang as *my droogs*. A bit of a stretch, he thought, but someone in the wondrous World Wide Web might make the connection.

Alessandra returned with a few feminine articles, among them a pair of cotton pajamas.

"You planning on spending the night with me again?"

"Nothing's changed. I'll say farewell at the airport tomorrow, but you won't be on your own."

"Yeah, the trusty Higher Power…"

"You can use the fellowship as your Higher Power until you get humble enough to…"

"Establish my own personal contact?"

"Fake it till you make it."

Her purchases came to just under a thousand dollars, the jacket accounting for most of it. He pulled out a wad of hundreds and peeled them off one-by-one onto the counter until he got to ten.

"Thank you." She slid her arms into the jacket. On their way out, she stopped in front of a mirror and put on the Maui Jim aviators.

"You're a certified badass."

"I'm pleased to meet me."

~~~~~

The sensation of fame induces a state of distraction that can lead to neurosis, then mania, into full-blown madness. He pondered this as they made their way back to the hotel, but he did not run it by her. What drew him to this dark conjecture was self-observation, namely his sudden urge to scan his surroundings to see if anyone was looking at him. He attracted more attention than the average denizen under ordinary circumstances, what with his height and athletic bearing—not to mention the glittering emeralds seated in his handsomely chiseled physiognomy—and the wide-brimmed cowboy hat made him all the more conspicuous today. So, it was hard for him to distinguish between ordinary—call it biological—curiosity and actual public recognition. Roland liked the discreet fist pump granted him by the stranger in the park that morning, but how would he react to a stranger walking up to him on the street and demanding his attention? In San Francisco he could brush aside the occasional affrontery of fellow denizens since it was for the most part diffident. The incident at Tosca was the first of its kind for him, but since he had no recollection of it, he could not consider that an actual experience.

"I'll tell you one thing." He spoke not to break the silence, but to continue the conversation taking place in his head.

"I could hear your thoughts crystallizing. I'm pretty perceptive as a rule, but I've never had a stronger intuition about someone than I do with you. It must have more to do with you than with me. Your signal is stronger than my receiver."

"Yeah? What's the sound of a thought crystallizing? Is it louder than one hand clapping?"

"Faint little ticks, like raindrops hitting the tip of a leaf, except yours are pretty loud, more like taps than ticks."

"Or maybe like the snapping of threads on a rope pulled too tight?"

"Make all the fun you like. There's no scar on my neck."

"I don't like the idea that you can hear me thinking. Sounds like bullshit. Seems like you're the one making fun." Roland made it sound sincere, but in truth he thought psychic phenomena were not only possible but more common than most people imagined.

"*What*, then?"

"What *what?*"

"The *one thing?* You said *I'll tell you one thing.*"

"Yeah." He sounded like he didn't want to talk about the thing he'd just volunteered to divulge.

"Were you talking to yourself?"

"No. Well yes, I guess, kinda."

"Then I won't pry."

"Okay. I feel like an astronaut floating in space with no concept of up or down. I'm tethered to something, let's say to my ship, and my ship knows the way back to Earth; but that's all contingent, presumptive really. I feel pretty much alone."

"It can't be that bad."

"I'm realizing I don't know myself very well. My brother is fond of a Shakespeare quote: *To thine own self be true.* Well, I don't know who to be true to, in that sense. If I was going to kill myself, I'd just be removing DNA from the gene pool, not getting rid of a person."

"Sounds pretty narcissistic. Why do you need to know who you are? What does that even mean?"

"You probably already know who you are, so the question doesn't occur to you, just like a fish doesn't know that it's wet, only when it's not, only when it's flopping around in the sun or hanging from a hook, when its world is suddenly, decidedly, not right."

"Are you worried about being famous? I'm not sure you have that problem just yet. I didn't know who you were yesterday, and unless I'd watched Cameron Anderson last night I still wouldn't."

"Call it what you want. I just don't like what I'm feeling."

"The disorientation you were just talking about—it's not the apprehension of sudden fame or imagined fame."

"Is that a professional opinion?"

"In a way."

"In what way?"

"I've known you, been with you continuously, for just over a day, and when we first met you were hungover, so technically not even sober, and I've watched you sober up, like watching a hose—maybe the air hose attached to your spacesuit—unkink itself. And the weightlessness you feel is a lack of *moral* gravity, a feeling that your life is meaningless because you're not used to being sober and you somehow sense that alcohol can only mask the ache of meaninglessness. The thought of being famous only accentuates…"

He stopped and put his hand on her shoulder to get her to stop talking and look at him and saw his reflection in the lenses of his—rather her—sunglasses. "How is that a professional opinion?"

"It's closer to a professional opinion than I am to being your girlfriend."

"I see."

"No. I don't think you do. I take this task, the task you pretty much begged me to do—I take it seriously. Stand-in girlfriend—what does that even mean?" She lifted the shades so they could speak eye to eye and waited for him to say something.

"You're asking?"

"Yes. It's not a rhetorical question."

"I don't know what it means. It just happened. You walked up to me and there you were, a pretty butterfly flitting before my eyes, and I reached out and cupped you in my palms."

"You begged me to pretend *with all my might*. That's what I remember."

"I didn't want to go it alone."

"You've never had a girlfriend, have you? You don't even know what one is—not from personal experience anyway. I bet you've fucked a lot of girls and maybe some women, but you've never been accountable to one, never been in an actual relationship with one. Am I right?"

"Sixth grade." He took his eyes off her to observe that they were blocking the sidewalk and attracting attention, a lanky cowboy in a tense conversation with a diminutive metropolitan. A few people—two men and two women—hovered at their perimeter to make sure things weren't getting out of hand, and more people started to collect around them. "We're creating a scene."

The New Yorker in her kicked into gear. "Let me handle this." She turned to the cluster of concerned onlookers and self-appointed witnesses. "What are you waiting for? Why don't you get out your phones and make a recording of the big bad man…"

"Don't."

Alessandra swiveled toward Roland and shot back. "No. These people…" She waved a hand in their direction. "…are intruding on a private conversation." She turned again to the bystanders. "Just because we're on the sidewalk doesn't mean you get to stop and listen."

A woman spoke. "We want to make sure this man isn't bothering you."

"I'M bothering HIM!"

One of the men laughed.

"This man is a trained killer, a killer of killers…"

"Don't."

She ignored him again. "He was on Cameron Anderson last night, a famous killer on *Look Alive*. Isn't that ironic? He could kill anyone of us here in about five seconds, and he's TERRIFIED of ME."

"Special forces?" the man said.

"No," another woman said. "He's a psycho vigilante with a big internet footprint."

"I'm outta here." Roland started walking. The hotel was not far.

"It's not vigilante if *they* attack *you*," he heard Alessandra say, then rapid footsteps brought her to his side.

"Sorry about that."

"As long as you had fun."

"I had to see for myself."

"Anderson has very high ratings, and Tawny Moore does even better."

"You don't have to go. You can always cancel."

"You're still gonna come with me, right?"

"Tell me about sixth grade."

"Is that a condition?"

"No—of course I'm coming with you. When will you get it through your slippery head?"

Roland recalled his debauch with Alison and caught his breath and looked up and found the sky between the tops of the high-rises. The woman who'd used his slippery head for her pleasure was a whore, but not a whore, and beside him minced a different sort of contradiction: a girlfriend, but not a girlfriend. And there he was beside her: a murderer, but not a murderer. *How is anyone supposed to trust anything?*

He slowed and took her hand. "I just want to make sure." She could have told him to dash across the street between the rushing cars and he would have tried it.

"So—sixth grade."

"I had a girlfriend in sixth grade. So you're wrong—I know what it means."

"Tell me like you need to convince me. Pretend I think you're a liar."

"We were co-captains of the spelling team of Farmin-Stidwell Middle School. She was seventh and I was sixth, but we were the best spellers in the school and led the Wolf Pack to the state championship. But it was forbidden love."

"Forbidden?"

"She couldn't have it known that she was cavorting with a sixth-grader, even though I was bigger than most of the eighth-graders. And I understood that, so we met in secret and did a lot of kissing, but of course people found out."

"Was it serious? I mean exclusive?"

"Yes. We pledged our love. We discussed marriage."

"And how did it end?"

"She lost respect for me, and she was right to. It's one of the few serious regrets of my life, and in a way one of the reasons I'm putting myself out in the public sphere, so I can imagine her seeing me and being proud of me."

"Did you cheat on her? Kiss another girl?"

"No. Nothing like that. It was worse than that. I betrayed her. I displayed my cowardice at the expense of her honor. I cringed under the jackboot of oppression."

"Have you been watching *Game of Thrones*?"

"I kid you not."

They reached the hotel and went inside. Alessandra led him by the hand to a corner of the lobby and sat down on a large red couch and folded her legs beneath her and motioned for him to sit in the adjacent armchair.

"You lost me at jackboot of oppression. Where does a sixth-grader run into the jackboot of oppression?"

"At the Idaho State Spelling Championship."

"You're from Idaho?"

"Yes. That simple fact invites my detractors to label me a Nazi, a priori. I'm from Nazi-country."

She frowned at the absurd remark. "What happened at the spelling bee?"

"There were five of us—our team from Farmin-Stidwell—and we had a name. All the teams gave themselves nicknames. We called ourselves the Oxymorons. It was my girlfriend's idea. We all thought it was very clever. She was proud of having come up with that."

"Yes. That's pretty clever."

"Well, not to one of the organizers it wasn't. The morning of the big day down in Boise the guy in charge calls us in and asks us to change our name. He said that a woman on the committee had a special-needs child, and she found the name offensive. My girlfriend…"

"What's her name?"

"Claire."

"What did Claire say?"

"Claire said *no way*. She said it's not meant to be offensive; It's meant to be ironic, spelling savants calling themselves morons. It's kind of a double irony when you think about it."

"And what did he say?"

"He didn't want to debate it. He told us if we didn't pick a different name, he'd announce us simply as the team from Farmin-Stidwell. And Claire said that's fine because we had our team's name printed on t-shirts, which she had paid for by the way. That was her mistake. She shouldn't have told him about the t-shirts."

"So, what was your betrayal, Roland?"

Roland wasn't listening. He was recalling the moment. "She should have kept her mouth shut about the t-shirts and agreed to be announced with the school's name. Then we could have walked out with the t-shirts on and done is done."

"That would have been dishonest."

"That's what Claire said. That exact word."

"What was your betrayal?"

"I've never told this story before. I think about it a lot. It's the curse of having a photographic memory. I can remember every detail, like playing it back on tape. But the soundtrack is lost. It's just the pictures and the words."

He took off this hat and set it on the little side table next to his chair and rested his face in his hands. He was about to cry so she waited for him to lift his head and look at her.

"What do you mean *the soundtrack?*"

"My emotions. The soundtrack is my emotions. I remember how I felt afterward, but not how I felt at the time. Maybe I was feeling nothing at the time. Maybe that was my problem. I should have locked onto the feelings of my so-called girlfriend—I guess that's called empathy."

"What were you, twelve? What did you do, Roland?"

"I said let's just call ourselves the Charming Did-Wells. That'd been my choice for a nickname."

"Charming Did-Wells?"

"Farmin-Stidwell, Charming Did-Wells. Pretty lame, but I guess I let my little ego take over."

"I see. You didn't back her up. That was a pretty shitty thing to do."

"It got worse. Claire asked the team for a vote. I had my chance to change my mind and I stuck with my stupid rhyming nickname and two of the others voted with me, so that was that."

"Why did the others side with you?"

"I was the best speller on the team. That's all I can figure. Oxymorons was a genius name, but we went with my stupid name because I was the best speller. I didn't have the nerve to stand up to a capricious authority because it was more important for me to be the last kid standing at the spelling bee, and I didn't want to risk losing out on the glory, so I threw my girlfriend under the school bus."

"Yeah, I guess you did."

"I did. And THAT's how I know what *girlfriend* means—because I betrayed my first and only one, the girl who risked being gossiped about for making out with a sixth-grader. I was not a Charming Did-Well."

"You can never make up for that. But you can do right by me."

"How, by staying sober for the rest of the day?"

"That's a lot. We made an agreement yesterday. You asked me to drop everything else so I could walk with you every step of the way. If you steer yourself to a drink, it would be the same as spitting in my face. The jacket and sunglasses mean nothing. They're just gestures of goodwill. I'll toss them in the trash if you don't live up to your end of the bargain."

"Can we go now?" He got up and walked to the elevator and she went with him.

"Did you win?"

"Yes. The team won."

"And you?"

"I got the trophy. I was the last man standing, but I didn't feel like a man at all."

"What was the winning word?"

"Pococurante."

"What does that mean?"

"A nonchalant person. The adjective, from Italian, means 'caring little'."

"Ouch"

"And the painful thing, that summer I discovered my father's box of old *Mad Magazines* in the garage."

"Why was that painful?"

"Alfred E. Neuman. He was the very embodiment of pococurante. He became my secret hero. I swear if I'd known about him before that spelling bee, I'd have had the nerve to stand up to that fascist."

~~~~~

The lie he'd told earlier was not exactly a lie, though technically it qualified. When she asked him what Earl H had said to him, it was true he wished that question would just drift with his silence into oblivion. He'd not, as he'd said, been gathering his thoughts in preparation for his upcoming appearance on the Tawny Moore show, yet the choice of the lie indicated that somewhere in the back of his mind he felt unprepared. He would need to spend some time alone to become adequately self possessed in order to face successfully such a formidable interviewer.

He put on his fancy new button-down shirt and tucked himself in and put on his hat and stood before the mirror. "Can I borrow my old glasses?"

She handed him the shades and he put them on. Roland adopted a Southern drawl. "Much obliged."

"What are you doing?"

"I've got a particular mind to reperrscent myself as the scion of a Texas cattle dynasty."

"You sound like you're imitating someone doing a bad George Bush impression."

"Hence the urgent need to habituate myself to the elegancies of the southerly spoken manner."

"And what, pray tell, are you going to do with this newly acquired proficiency?"

"Might I request of you the affectation of a perfect stranger and accost me as to whether I am the illustrious warrior Mister Roland Hazzard?"

Alessandra took a step back into the entryway then approached Roland with feigned curiosity. "Hey, are you that Roland Hazzard guy?"

"No, ma'am. I shore do hope this Hazzard fella does not owe you a heap a' money or is not otherwise the father of some unfortunate progeny of yourn that he has neglected to acknowledge and support, but

I hope you do locate the person in question, be he a lost relation or fugitive scoundrel."

"Too contrived."

"How about..." He resumed the drawl. "...sorry to disappoint you, ma'am, though I'm proud to bear a 'semblance to such a courageous and upstandin' 'merican."

"I don't know. Sounds like you're mixing in too much hillbilly chic. And if you try to pull that off on someone in public, you'd better be sure they don't have a camera pointed at you because if they put it online it won't take long for someone to..." Now she tried out her own Southern drawl. "...make you out a lyrr."

Roland removed the hat and glasses and scratched an ear as he considered her logic.

Alessandra continued. "So, if you're done horsing around here let's figure out what to do with the afternoon."

"I'm not finished with the museum."

"What's left?"

"The Temple of Dendur, of course, just off the Egyptian wing."

"Seriously? Or is that just a place to hide? You can hide here. We can watch TV."

"No. I mentioned before I was trying to gather my thoughts when you started hammering me with questions and attracted that mob, so now I have to start from scratch."

"You can't do that here? My feet are going to complain."

"No. I need to be moving, observing things, to keep my mind from squirming around in my brain. The museum is the perfect place. Besides, I've got a particular interest in that temple, the only one built by the Romans in Egypt. I'm fascinated by Ancient Egypt in general."

"Okay, I'll soldier on. Maybe I'll bivouac outside the Egypt Room."

~~~~~

They made their way over to the Met and paid their admission and went in. Roland felt obliged to give a cursory examination of the rooms they'd neglected yesterday before heading over to the Egyptian material, and he did his best to marshal enthusiasm for pieces in the permanent collection. But how much Greco-Roman pottery can one be expected to endure? He imagined that the folks who used the stuff would have been perplexed to learn that, two thousand years later, educated people would put it on display and walk around staring at their household items under strict orders not to touch. Graduate student archeologists in the field often must pick up a shard, brush it clean to reveal the image of a man shooting an arrow, and quip, *never seen that before*. Monumental structures, on the other hand, were meant to last forever and to hold the viewer in awe—to subordinate the human beings that beheld them. Pottery, after all, was expected to break, and so what if centuries later ingenious people learned how to dig out the shards and clean them up and piece them back together? Was the ancient pottery set on pedestals not simply evidence of the need for self-important aficionados to celebrate their skill in the restoration of what was never meant to be worth very much in the first place?

They moved over to the Arms and Armor rooms, replete with weapons and gear from Europe to Japan, much of it in pristine condition. Roland circled a column of mounted knights bedecked for war.

"Calling this art is a stretch."

"I think it's beautiful in a way."

"It certainly is well made. But I'm not sure it was ever worn."

"Well, that's the point, maybe. Maybe it was meant to decorate the castle halls, as a display of opulence perhaps."

"I'd be much more interested in looking at a steel suit peppered with arrow dents and a few ax gashes. That would certainly enliven my imagination."

"Looking at those men on horseback reminds me of just how much my feet hurt."

"I'd carry you on my shoulders, but I think security would object."

"I'll just go hang out in the library for a while."

He followed her there and when she chose a place to sit told her he'd be back after a while.

~~~~~

Roland strolled through the Egypt Room. He wondered how much the typical Egyptologist made per year. And why was there such a thing as Egyptology anyway? He'd never heard of another academically approved subdiscipline of archeology that offered an actual degree and job title, so what gave the Egyptologists such a lofty perch? What about the

Etruscanologists? Should they not be allowed to band together and defend their turf? Then again, how many Etruscanologists does the world really need, as long as we have one of every race and gender, assuming enough people can agree on how many races and genders there are and what to call them? Everything's a fucking scam, he mused, starting with the time-honored neighborhood lemonade stand. A couple of nine-year-olds dump a few scoops of yellow powder in a pitcher of water and hawk it on the corner for a dollar a serving, and they think they've helped slake the parched throats of a thirsty populace with lemonade because that's what was printed on the can of yellow powder. Might as well round up a bunch of aimless undergraduates in Stoner's Glade and point to a little crease on the map near, say, Kyrgyzstan and tell 'em *that's Etrusca—from now on you're an expert of THAT*. And the kids think they learned about business because they did almost no work and walked away with a wad of cash. Well, maybe they did. Maybe they did.

Still, the ancient artifacts did fascinate him, even as he scorned the united academic silence on the question of how full-blown civilizations could suddenly spring up out of the desert eight thousand years ago. The dogged refusal of the credentialed elite to reconsider their timelines for the development of civilization, in the face of an ever-growing body of new evidence that subverts their dominant paradigm would, thought Roland, be their ultimate undoing. The avenues of information had widened, lengthened, and accelerated so that its flow could no longer be controlled; and while there were plenty of conspiratorial detours and sinkholes, *the truth*, as they say, eventually *would out*.

He was eyeballing the disturbingly vivacious face on one of the elaborately carved funerary boxes standing in the Painted Coffins Room when he noticed a paunchy, bearded, bespectacled man in his fifties emerge from the narrow Study Gallery secluded behind one of the walls. The man held in one hand an old half-opened cardboard box just big enough to enclose a baseball. He moved quickly as though on an errand through the colorfully painted humanoid caskets like they were ordinary furnishings in a home he'd lived in too long. Then he stopped to notice Roland, in his boots and hat, taller than the coffins and almost as dramatic, following him with his eyes.

"You either work here or you're a thief absconding with a little box of treasure."

The man took off his glasses. "True."

"Either way, you probably know a lot about ancient history?"

"Yes. A thief would have to know what was worth stealing."

"I suppose you could be both. A working Egyptologist and a brazen thief."

"Most of the pioneers of my profession were, in fact, both."

"Slim plunderings nowadays, though, I guess."

The man took a moment. To Roland, he appeared to contemplate whether to continue the conversation. He looked perturbed and would have to drop his irritated mien if he was going to permit Roland to delay him any further.

"Indeed, especially since most of the cursed items are pretty well known by now. What's left is either guarded by guns or not worth the trouble."

"Yeah, I guess you can't sell it for much once it's been cataloged by a museum."

"That's true. Is there anything in particular I can help you with?"

He spoke with a faintly English accent, not of a Brit who'd been too many years in the States, but of an overeducated American who'd watched too many British documentaries.

"We don't have the time for me to get through all the questions I have for a professional archeologist, but I would like to ask you about one thing."

"Let me guess. You're wondering if it's true we've found traces of cocaine and tobacco in Egyptian mummy hair?"

"No. But that would be more than a little bit intriguing if it were true, wouldn't it? Proof of transoceanic commerce between Africa and the Americas would upend the board and send the pieces flying."

"Good, because every so often some glassy-eyed zombie comes in asking about ancient aliens or some other bizarre claim made by Zecharia Sitchen."

"No. I'm not from the zombie tribe. Sitchen couldn't decipher a single line of cuneiform, let alone read hieroglyphics, and he refused to debate scholars that could."

"He was a first-class mountebank."

"Agreed. A mountebank all the way to the bank."

"So, what do you want to know?"

"King Tut's DNA. Do you think…?"
"I'm not going to stick my nose into that shitstorm."
"Well, do you at least trust the claim that his parents were full siblings?"
"Yes. That much I accept. And that degree of incest can shorten the life of your offspring, statistically speaking of course. But I don't think he or his father was European. Just look at a picture of his mummified face."
"Ok, one other thing."
"I really have to go."
"What's in the box?"
"Scarabs. Pretty nice ones too."
"Why the rush?"
"I'm pretty sure they're cursed. I need to get them de-hexed."
"Take the scare out of the scarab, huh?"
"You're a funny guy."
"You can catch me tonight on the Tawny Moore show."
"Sure I can. I really do have to run along."
"Just one more thing?"
"Make it quick."
"All around the world, from Peru to Egypt to Thailand, ancient stone structures sit on top of older structures of unknown origin that are far more advanced in their construction. How do you make twenty-ton stones perfectly flat and fit together as tightly as Legos using nothing but a copper chisel?"
"You sound like a journalist. Are you really going to be on Tawny Moore tonight?"
"Yes. But not as a journalist."
"As a *what* then?"
Roland eyed the ceiling as he formulated an answer. "I'm a life coach with an unorthodox approach. Now, what about my question?"
"It's as hard to change the mind of an archeologist as it is to move a megalith. I'll give you that."
Roland reached out his hand. "Let me have a look at those scarabs."
"There's plenty on display. Anyway, I told you these were cursed. You shouldn't take the chance."
"Yeah. So how do you take the whammy off an enchanted scarab?"

"It requires a young virgin."

"Naturally."

"I'm already late."

"You look like a virgin—try sticking them up your ass."

Roland didn't wait for a reaction and shook his head and turned around and walked off. Ordinarily, he would have honored his upbringing and thanked the man for his time and shaken his hand, but he could not compete with such casual depravity. His mood had soured. He turned around and went to retrieve Alessandra from the library.

~~~~~

She saw him come in and took her feet off the chair she was using as an ottoman and put her phone away to study his approach and waited for him to say something. He put his hat on the table and sat down across from her and softened his expression so she could not read his thoughts. And since he believed his thoughts were protected, he decided to put her to the test and thought about having sex with her. In the hotel room. In the shower. On the bed. In front of the window. On a blanket in the park. Now as newlyweds in the limpid green waters of a secluded Caribbean lagoon. In the space of a minute, staring at her face, they made love a dozen times in a luxuriant erotic revue. She had enough of him looking at her that way.

"You look like you swallowed a stupid pill."

"A blissful prescription, yes."

"You're a strange man."

"I just met a much stranger one."

"Oh?"

"Strange in a disturbing way. Looking at you just now, absorbing your salubrity, has cleansed me of his diabolical influence."

"My salubrity is yours for the absorbing, as long as we still have our understanding."

"You're safe with me."

"Only because you're safe with me. Just don't forget I know what's on your mind."

"Thrilling, isn't it?"

She considered the question before making her reply. "I think I will miss you for a while. But if I join in your stupid little fantasy, I won't miss you at all and I'll like myself less, for a while anyway."

His incipient arousal withered into desuetude. "I guess we should talk about what we're going to do instead."

"This is my town. We can fill the time if you've got enough cab fare. When do you have to be at PNN?"

"Three."

"You didn't spend much time in Egypt. Temple of Dendur not all it was cracked up to be?"

"I never made it there. The Egyptologist I met among the artifacts spoiled my appetite. Plus, as far as I'm concerned, once the Romans got to Egypt it was already modern history. I care about really old stuff, the stuff that shouldn't even exist, the stuff that the ancients didn't even take credit for and couldn't explain."

"I don't think we're gonna find Atlantis, Roland."

"Maybe not, but there's a lot of undiscovered structures underwater, built when the oceans were much lower."

"I'll have to take your word for it." She stood up. "Let's go."

"Whereto?"

"You tell me."

"The White Horse Tavern."

"That's in Greenwich Village, not far from my apartment. Why do you want to go there?"

"Literary history."

"I thought your specialty was ancient history."

"It's a famous old literary hangout. I want to see where Dylan Thomas drank himself to death."

"Straight from sex to death."

"I have the soul of a warrior."

"Yes. A gen-yoo-wine man, except for the drunk part."

"Hard drinking is part of the persona too. Fighting. Drinking. Fucking."

"I didn't say drinking. I said drunk. The drunk takes over whatever was there before the drink. The drunk part always wins. It's like devil possession, if you believe in that sort of thing."

"That's a conversation for another day."

"You'll be gone tomorrow morning."

They walked down the steps of the MET toward Fifth Avenue and when they got to the bottom they stopped and faced one another. To go left, right, or straight ahead? Neither had decided, and she was in charge. "Are you a fan of Dylan Thomas?"

"I'm a fan of irony."

"Aren't we all?"

"He wrote the greatest villanelle of the English Language—a Welshman in his thirties—all about flipping the bird to Mister Death. *Old age should burn and rave at close of day / Rage rage against the dying of the light.* He talked a good game but never made it past the middle innings. Drank himself into a coma courtesy of the bartender at The White Horse Tavern. I want to see if they have the balls to commemorate the man."

"We're not going there."

"Bitch."

She laughed. "Say it like you mean it. You can't, can you?"

He took her hand and glanced at her then looked away and spoke as though to the nearby tree limb. "I love you. I'm not sure what I mean by that but I know it's true." He raised his eyes higher to scan the upper boughs of the elms, evenly spaced, lining the boulevard. "It's kinda like…"

"Shut up you idiot."

He glanced at her again. "I can tell you meant that."

"Where to?"

"Bookstores. Take me to the best used bookstores."

"I'm afraid you've got me there, but I know we're in the right neighborhood. Are you looking for anything in particular?"

"A place to let my mind wander. Looking at old books, touching their pages, the vanilla smell of their decaying chemicals, will take me completely out of myself. The little trip to Egypt didn't do the trick."

"What did the guy, the Egyptologist, say to send you back to me so fast?"

"It wasn't so much what he said, though that was weird and perverse enough. It was the fact that he wanted to disgust me, that he was willing to debase himself just so he could put a disgusting thought in a stranger's head."

"And you did nothing to provoke him?"

"No. I just asked a few tough questions, let him know there are educated people out there who don't necessarily buy the established timeline of human history."

She took his hand and he looked down and smiled at her. "I think there's a rare bookshop just a few blocks down on the other side of the Transverse. We can start there."

"Good." He ducked in that direction careful not to tow her too fast.

The unconsummated lovers spent the rest of the day on the Upper East Side following an improvised itinerary of bookshops courtesy of a map Roland found with his mobile device. Roland spent nearly all of the hundreds of dollars in his pockets on antique volumes of various kinds, until there was too much to carry. They sat together in a café drinking coffee and forking down cake while he explained to her his fascination with each purchase.

"You sure seem to have a lot of money."

"I don't. Not yet."

"But you want to be rich. Have I got that right?"

"I don't so much want to be rich, not the way wealthy people think about rich. I want to have a lot of money so I can spend it on myself and other people. I don't suppose I'll ever be rich."

~~~~~

Tawny Moore occupied the same timeslot as her friend, Cameron Anderson, and usually beat him in the weekly ratings with her eponymous show: *Voice of Reason with Tawny Moore*. Their professional rivalry was plain to see for anyone who wanted to look at the numbers. Their friendship, on the other hand, they kept to themselves, for their respective networks were ideological enemies. Tawny, though, stood in marked contrast to the rest of the lineup at Patriot News Network, whose faces were mostly white and whose women, mostly blond, were hard to tell apart, like contestants in a 1950's beauty pageant, though decidedly thinner. A cinnamon-skinned, raven-haired Brit—daughter of a Moroccan jaw-dropper and an English Lord whose paternal line's colonial adventures were well-documented in historical volumes—Tawny played the physical dissimilarities between herself and her colleagues for all they were worth, right down to the ruby stud riveted to her left nostril. Her father had named her Margaret after the Right Honorable Baroness Margaret

Thatcher, and before she launched her media career she changed it to Tawny—Tawni Moore—a finger in the eye of the corpse of the British Empire. Her rebellion against the forces that named her would have been complete had she converted to Islam and actually become a Moor. The finger in the eye of her father was gesture enough. She did, however, become an American citizen and wore the stars and stripes in a jeweled pin on her lapel, the unofficial emblem of the network.

Tawny styled herself as a proper journalist, eschewing the refuge of *pundit* or *commentator* embraced by so many cable news personalities, whose political bent was so pronounced that trying to conceal it under the title of *journalist* would have been impossible over the long run. No. Tawny Moore was a straight-up reporter whose self-appointed mission was to wipe the smirks off the faces of the smug. And, lest her choice of subjects appear to favor a particular political ideology and expose her to accusations of bias, she was careful to select her guests from across the spectrum, which in recent years had become heavily weighted on the extremes of an increasingly divided society. Roland, then, was an ideal candidate for her scrutiny, for while his message—if you could boil his public ratiocinations down to a single, coherent, message—hewed to the libertarian philosophy, he was inoculated against any conclusions about his partisan leanings by his staunch refusal to voice support for a candidate in the upcoming presidential election. Inoculated too, perhaps, and more significantly and strangely, by his constant detours into the subject of ancient archeology and the academy's ossified reluctance to correct its outdated assumptions.

Quarrels over rights and privileges were, in Roland's mind, drowned out by the cacophony of evidence of an ancient global civilization spread across the planet before it was wiped out by a cataclysm of an incalculable magnitude. Perhaps, he allowed, a series of comet fragments struck the polar ice caps and set the seas to rising some two hundred feet in a virtual instant. There's your global inundation reported in a thousand myths around the world, he'd said. There's Plato's sunken Atlantis. If current human history were actually a do-over, he surmised, then would it not make sense to ascertain as much of the learning from the distant past as possible? In any event, ignoring the subject altogether seemed like the least prudent course, for it was no course at all. Roland has said on more than one occasion in his podcasts that if the major world powers could drop their egos long enough to cooperate on the task of exhibiting to the world all the archeologically anomalous evidence within their borders, then maybe the awe and wonder at such evidence might give us pause before continuing down the road to probable self-annihilation.

In the broadest estimation, Roland stood apart from the ideological war between left and right. Tawny Moore could grill him as mercilessly as she might without fear of riling up the conservative viewers or pandering to the liberals. He represented instead a problem of a more fundamental, and even personal, nature. His popularity in the alternative media posed a threat to her profession and, more pointedly, he'd antagonized her friend, Cameron Anderson, the night before, probably even damaged his career.

Roland bent down and startled Alessandra with a swift peck on the lips, as though to purchase luck.

"That felt like a martial arts move."

"It's called *taste the butterfly*."

"I dare you to do that to the host."

"I intend to do it to the camera."

~~~~~

Tawny Moore introduced him by name and showed a clip from last night's exchange with Cameron Anderson and the patent lawyer. Roland watched himself on the monitor sparring with his adversaries. *I've never met this man... Yes. That's my car... Mister Gordon here has made a serious mistake, a colossal error in judgment... He lobbed a half-eaten breakfast sandwich into my car... Mister Gordon has made a serious mistake... You're just a loudmouthed punk with a lethal streak... You're lecturing ME on the LAW!... A lecture won't do... You're in need of a retributional ass-whoopin... Mister Hazzard, whatever the facts, this station has acted in good faith, and you've come onto the set intoxicated... That's a lie... You're out a boatload of Benjamins... You will deliver it to me and set it at my feet...* And so forth, with chunks omitted, until the clip ended with Roland having the last word... *look both ways before you cross me.*

"That was quite a donnybrook over at CBN last night. You certainly set them back on their heels. How do you feel about that? You've said nothing about it on your social media channels that we could find."

"I can't talk about what happened last night."

"Are you under some sort of legal restriction?"

"No. No restriction, just legal advice."

"I see. Once lawyers get involved everyone clams up."

"I do have one general comment—an observation, really."

"I'd love to hear it."

"Back in ancient times…"

"Let me stop you there, Mister Hazzard."

Roland showed a quizzical face. "Why?"

"You seem unduly preoccupied with ancient times. I'm more interested—and I think I speak for most of my viewers as well—with you and your life, not in your abstruse meanderings. I asked you about your dust-up last night on CBN, and you launch in about ancient times."

"I was answering your question."

"Like the Bible lecture you gave Mizz Hernandez out in San Francisco?"

"She—it was *she* who brought up the Bible. I just straightened her out about the Sixth Commandment."

"Ok, fair enough. And what Biblical wisdom have you come to impart today?"

"Something older than Mosaic law. You're familiar with the Code of Hammurabi?"

"An eye for an eye…but I fail to see what that has to do with what happened on the set over at CBN last night."

"I'm not about to comment directly on that situation, but if you'll let me continue. I have one observation about the so-called news media that begins with the Code of Hammurabi—the oldest set of laws in the world, that we know of anyway."

"I should think we've evolved well past the Hammurabic Code."

"Not everywhere—maybe in the West—but not everywhere. Do you want me to name a few countries where what we call murder and torture and false imprisonment is routine law enforcement? There are places in the world where Hammurabi would be a breath of fresh air—and I don't mean the fresh air you get when they toss you off a building for being a little queer."

"I get your point. So, what does Hammurabi have to teach us about the failings of the news media?" She folded her arms to exaggerate her willingness to listen while at the same time peering across at him with contempt for what he might be about to say.

"There are more than two hundred and eighty laws in the Hammurabic Code. Can you guess what they chose to put right at the top?"

"I'm sure I'd get it wrong."

"False accusation and false witness—the first three or four laws, out of two hundred and eighty some, prescribed the death penalty for false accusation in various forms. There has to be a good reason why they placed that above murder and property crimes."

"Yeah. It falls somewhere near the bottom of the Ten Commandments, right?"

"Right—number nine."

"So why did the...?" She paused to search for the word.

"The Babylonians."

"Thank you," she said. "So why did the Babylonians place such high importance on telling the truth?"

"No. Not on telling the truth, per se. On not lying about people. On not accusing people of crimes unless you have good evidence."

"I see. They understood the importance of what they were trying to establish. The law won't work if people can't trust it—if people are allowed to abuse it."

"Right. Because then you're right back to chaos."

"Fair enough." She uncrossed her arms and leaned forward a bit. "But what does that have to do with the media?"

"When you kill a man's reputation, you might as well banish him to the wilderness."

"Is that how you feel, banished—in a wilderness?"

"I'm not talking about me. I'm fine—my stock is on the rise. I'm talking about the corporate media that trades on fear and vengeance and resentment. The truth is the least of their concerns."

"That's a bit extreme, isn't it?"

"It can't be overstated. When a news organization makes a false accusation that is later *proven* false, it just moves on. There's no shame, no impulse to set things right, to correct the record, apologize and promise to do better." He thought about quoting the Tenth Step...*and where we were wrong, promptly admitted it*...but decided that might open a subject he'd just a soon avoid.

"May I exempt myself from your observation?"

"I don't watch your program, so I wouldn't know. But I will say that the line between opinion and straight reportage has been trampled so badly that the umpire can hardly tell which side the ball lands on."

"I agree—it can get a bit muddy. The journalist in me wants to demand you answer whether you threw the Egg McMuffin and the commentator in me wants to announce that I think you did, but you've dodged the subject adroitly." She enunciated the word *adroitly* as only a stern British woman could.

Roland leaned back and massaged his left earlobe with his thumb and forefinger. Who did this woman think she was dealing with? The man, Gordon, *Herr Benz,* had simply called it a breakfast sandwich. Of course, there was an off chance that he'd said Egg McMuffin in a different interview. Doubtful, though, since it would expose him to further legal action—so Tawny Moore must have reached out to him privately. It smelled like a trap, a poorly baited one at that. It had been a Sausage McMuffin after all.

"My accuser didn't mention the brand of the sandwich."

She looked at him and glowered a smidge. He'd not taken the bait.

"Be that as it may, you never actually denied the accusation."

"That's not how the game is played. The accuser has to present proof. My denial here would count for nothing more than an emotional reaction. It has no probative value."

"You sound like a lawyer. Do you have legal training?"

"I'm an amateur historian delving into legal history."

"Ok, you win. Let's get on with the Code of Hammer-awe-bee. Riveting television. I can see our viewers rolling their eyes, changing the channel."

"Mizz Moore, I think your scintillating personality and striking visage are appealing enough to overcome my prosaic excursions, aye?"

"Ten years ago, I'd've lapped up such flummery. Please go ahead. You've worn me down. Enlighten us more about the murky past."

Flummery—that slayed him. Roland took a sip from his water glass and nodded to himself at the sudden revelation that if one were not careful one could become addicted to one's own bullshit.

"Are you a sorceress?"

"What?"

"A witch—a practitioner of the black arts."

"I've been called a witch before and more often something that rhymes with it, but I have no actual training in witchcraft." He sensed she was softening up a bit.

"And if I called you a sorceress in a public forum, you wouldn't much care, would you?"

"No. Not especially."

"Because most people would think that *I* was the nut, not you. Right?"

"I suppose so."

"As recently as a few hundred years ago in Europe and even America, being called a witch could get you sentenced to death, or at least kicked out of the community, which itself could be a death sentence."

"Yes. And there are still places in the world so backward that that sort of thing is a problem."

"Now, what if someone, not me, say one of your neighbors, tweeted out that you are known to whisper hateful things into the ears of little children? That you've been known to sit at the edge of playgrounds and when a ball comes rolling over you pick it up and hand it to the child and whisper in her ear *your mother is poisoning your food* or *your daddy wears dresses and takes it up the bum*? Or what if I said that I heard such things about you, that I didn't know if they were true, but that I believed them and thought it best to warn everyone—just to be on the safe side—that you might be a serial hate whisperer?"

The host rolled her eyes and smirked at the ceiling.

Roland observed her supercilious attitude and decided to raise the stakes a bit, to see if he could ruffle her. "Or what if I said that I'd heard that when you were in high school—I guess that would be secondary school in the UK— you liked to slip LSD in people's beer?" He drank again from his water glass to let her know it was her turn to say something.

"If that sort of thing went on for too long, I supposed I'd have to take some sort of legal action against you."

"Why?"

"I'll play. Because it's wrong—because it's so wrong that it's criminal."

"Ahh. Now there's a fine distinction—sin and crime."

"I'll grant you—not all sins are crimes, yet crimes are at some level probably sinful. But we were talking about Hammurabi."

"Correct. And the Hammurabic Code didn't appeal to morality—it said, *if you do x then the law will punish you with y*. But the Ten Suggestions…"

"Excuse me—the ten *suggestions?*"

"Right. *Commandments* is a bad translation. The Hebrew word means something closer to *suggestions* or *directions*. They're meant to be guides to good living. After all, how would the law go about punishing someone for coveting his neighbor's wife, let alone his ox?"

"How would you know about that?"

"Know what?"

"The flawed translation of Ancient Hebrew."

"The Bible is the most important collection of ancient writings, at least in the West. You can't call yourself educated unless you've put in some time with the Bible—which I have—and when I see something that doesn't make sense, I look deeper. I research the original text."

"Are you on the spectrum?"

"What do you mean?"

"I don't know—you seem a little obsessive-compulsive."

"You saying I've got a touch of the Asperger's?"

"I'm not qualified to diag…"

"Look, I don't like things that don't make sense—incongruous facts, unexplained mysteries. That doesn't put me on some kind of clinical spectrum."

"I apologize—I'm just trying to understand you."

"Sounds more like you're trying to classify me, as though I were some kind of insect. It's a lot easier to dismiss what I have to say if you can label me a mental-defective."

She laughed. Roland glanced at the camera and cocked his head and made a silly face as if to suggest that Tawny Moore's laughter made no sense so maybe she was the mental-defective.

"What *are* you trying to say? Can you crystallize it for us?"

Roland put his face back to normal and tapped his chin with his forefinger. "The media—the people in charge of informing the public—

they don't care about right and wrong. They care about whipping people up emotionally, and I'm a perfect lighting rod. Why? Not because I killed a couple of bad guys, but because I took time out of my busy schedule to point out that our society is raising a bunch of cowards. And what do I get for my trouble—now *I'm* the bad guy, the *crazy* guy?"

"Not someone who would toss his breakfast at another motorist on the freeway."

"Make no mistake about it. I am, first and foremost, a dangerous man, and there are not enough like me out there, which is a sad state of affairs, a symptom of an unhealthy body politic."

"Now that's what a lot of people take issue with, that you say there needs to be more people like you. It comes off as so much flippant bombast, perhaps to cover for..." She paused as though to formulate.

"For what?"

"An unspeakable, unconscious rage."

"Sure. That's possible—but what if the backseat psychologists are wrong? What if I'm not covering for anything? What if I'm a latter-day Nietzsche, a prophet of the post-modern age, a harbinger of the end of the line, the only one who's willing to stand up on the roller coaster and say *don't look now folks, but this last exhilarating descent is actually a bottomless pit.*"

"I can see why Cameron Anderson grabbed his hair."

"So can I. He's used to telling everyone how the world works, which people are moral, and who should be avoided. Basically, who should and shouldn't be allowed into polite society. In short, he's an elitist. A perfect elitist. And the thing about elitists is they're all the same. You know what they're going to say before you finish your sentence. Ten-year-old kids are far more interesting to talk to because they have ideas of their own and language enough to express them. And they're hard to fool because they don't take things so seriously."

"You're nobody's fool. I'll grant you that."

"Whatever else I am, I'm an athlete, which means I've learned how not to be too predictable. And the other half of being an athlete is knowing how to read an opponent, because the better you can read them the less agile, the less reactive, you need to be. At the highest level, athletic competition is as much mental as physical."

"So, the guy with the machete, the Glendale Butcher's cousin, you could tell what he was going to do before he did it."

"I saw it in his eyes."

"So you could have disarmed him."

"True. I've made that clear a number of times, in several interviews."

"I'm not one of your devotees, Mister Hazzard, so you'll have to forgive my ignorance."

"Not at all. I just wanted you to know that your question is a logical one, one I've been asked before."

"So why didn't you disarm him?"

"Have you seen the footage?" He thought about correcting his own word since *footage* was a vestige of the bygone film industry, but he thought that might sound a bit pedantic.

"Yes. It's pretty shocking."

"I answered that question on the steps of KTLA. I said I killed him to set a good example for the children, and while I admit that at the time I meant to come off as glib, the more I thought about it later—and thinking about it now—the happier I am that I said that. That remark certainly drew a lot of attention."

"I might regret this, but why does killing someone when you could have disarmed him set a good example for children, or for anyone for that matter?"

"Because it confirms what people instinctively know, that justice is best meted out on the street, so to speak, before the state gets involved. If Barsamian's cousins are thinking about taking another crack at me, at least they know they're putting their lives on the line. The best deterrent to crime is a populace whose members are ready and willing to defend themselves with lethal force. Let's call that being a *moral athlete*. It shouldn't be a controversial idea, yet here I am, all over the internet and now on television saying what should be self-evident to every reasonable individual. Lucky me."

"As much as you vilify the media, you certainly have not been denied access."

"The chief villains are the print and television news. The internet is a mixed bag. But most of the major media—what people call the mainstream media—has held me up as an object of ridicule and scorn, or at least as a borderline personality."

"And you're here to tell us what's what."

"Yes. The social fabric is unraveling. Eventually, words translate to actions. There is violence in the heart of every man and woman, and it doesn't take much to unleash it. I recently saw a picture of a white politician giving what appeared to be a Nazi salute in the woods somewhere, but it turned out that the photo had been cropped just enough to cut off the end of his hand, which was pointing at something up in the trees. But the angle of the arm was just right to be mistaken for the ol' sieg heil, so the journalist published it as though it was. Turns out the original photo showed him standing next to his friend, a black man, smiling at whatever—let's say an owl—his Caucasian buddy was pointing at in the treetop. It's pretty hard to claim we live in a civil society when people with influence can pull that kind of crap with impunity because the courts can't stop it. The journalist can claim she acted in good faith and protect the identity of the person who originally posted the deceptively cropped photo. Eventually, rage boils over into violence, and then it's every man and woman for themselves. That's when the aggressors need to be worried about what might happen if they pick the wrong victim."

"Do you really think we're coming to that?"

"It's hard to predict when the dam will break because no society has ever been tested in this exact way—total strangers hurling dirt at one another at the speed of light. But the cracks are forming. If serious, thoughtful people weren't concerned, then I wouldn't be so popular in the alternative media. The level of discussion is far deeper there than on traditional television, with all due respect to you, Mizz Moore. Only the dark web can restore us to sanity."

Thus ended the first of Roland's two segments on the Patriot News Network. Tawny Moore departed the set with a whoosh—to use the potty, Roland guessed—leaving him alone on the stage with three manned cameras—one of them wo-manned, actually—still pointed at him as though he were the target of a firing squad. One of the technicians picked up a miniature foam football and tossed it gently to Roland, who plucked it from the air with one hand. The two men played a game of chicken, each one tossing the ball back a little harder each time. Neither dropped it. They played for the same team.

The Alcoholic—A Hero Contends for His Soul

~~~~~

Tawny Moore returned, looking a bit more relaxed. Roland thought if he were in her business, he'd have a way of ingesting a little booze in between segments to ease the discomfort of an aggravating guest. *Or maybe I'd insert a little pleasure device.* The sexuality of women presented an endless fascination, and this one was a veritable sphinx. He focused on that thought while he watched her with lascivious intent and tried to transmit his fantasy into her mind, to no apparent effect. In truth, his preoccupation with the host went beyond the erotic but took on an anthropological, or even constitutional, interest. He wondered what it would take to crack her veneer.

The center camera's light went on and she launched in straightaway. "We've only got a few minutes left, Mister Hazzard, and I'd like to ask you a few more personal questions if you don't mind."

"I'm here on your nickel."

"You said before that you were not on the spectrum…"

"I have an abnormally high IQ. The way I think, the way I talk, the leaps I make—I sometimes strike people as a little strange—a little *off*. But I'm not on the spectrum."

"What about the alcoholism spectrum? My spies tell me that you've been known to block people from your Twitter account for asking about your history of alcohol abuse."

"I block anyone I notice who engages in gratuitous insult or ad hominem attack. My account is pretty active, so I need to weed out the haters."

"I hope you don't think I'm trying to attack you—I'm genuinely curious."

"Well. I don't think there's a recognized spectrum for alcohol use."

"I said alcohol-ism."

"Either way?"

"Are you still drinking?"

"This again. Why do you ask?"

"It's part of your story."

"It's more a myth than a story."

"What's the difference?"

"A story has an author. A myth does not. And I'm not about to let someone other than me be in charge of my story. The myth I cannot control."

"You are very adept at dodging direct questions, I've noticed."

"Did you bring a breathalyzer? I'd be glad to blow a zero for you, or should we let your nose render the verdict?"

"No need to get defensive, Mister Hazzard. I'm not suggesting that you're intoxicated now, but your drinking is part of the public record. Two arrests in San Francisco for intoxication. You were drunk when you killed the Glendale Butcher, and the officer on the steps of KTLA smelled alcohol after your second killing. With all due respect, those are facts, not myths."

"If you're trying to shame me, you'll have to work a lot harder."

"I doubt it's possible to shame you, judging from your performances so far. I'd think you have a little touch of PTSD after killing two people with your bare hands in the space of three days."

"Post-Traumatic Stress Disorder is, I believe, a serious condition brought about by prolonged exposure to, as the label says, traumatic circumstances."

"Police get counseling after they shoot people in the line of duty."

"I don't think that's the same thing—counseling, probably mandatory counseling, for an officer-involved shooting, and PTSD from armed conflict in a war zone. I don't imagine anyone is completely immune from psychological damage in the latter category, but that has nothing to do with what I've experienced. I'm trained to react to violence, and I reacted according to my training."

"So, no counseling?"

"Not unless this counts."

"I'm trying to be serious, Mister Hazzard. Maybe you're suffering stress that you're not aware of. Maybe alcohol has dulled your psyche so that you…"

Roland raised a hand to signal his interruption. "I'm not drinking."

"Are you back in AA?"

"Don't you know? It sounds like you've had me under surveillance."

"We have not invaded your privacy in any way, sir." She picked up a sheet of paper on her desk and glanced at it while she continued. "A San Francisco judge, on February the twelfth, 2016, found you guilty of drunk and disorderly conduct, and because it was your second alcohol-related offense, he ordered you to attend thirty over a three-month period."

"Why am I even here? You could have read that without me on stage with you."

"You were paid an appearance fee. I expect that's part of the reason."

"I don't mean to sound ungrateful, but this is incredibly boring, to me and, I assume, to the viewers as well."

"Were the AA meetings boring too? Did you even attend them?"

"Yes. I did. I satisfied the court order."

"And yet you kept on drinking."

"The court did not require me to quit drinking, just attend the meetings."

"So, AA doesn't work. Or at least it didn't work for you."

Roland smoothed his head with his open palm. He'd come to like the feel of it and found it a useful palliative.

"You don't have any idea what you're talking about."

"I'm asking."

"My experience, in my short time in AA, is that it works."

"But you kept on drinking."

"To be honest, I didn't work the program. I was court-ordered, after all. But from what I observed, the people that worked the program got sober and stayed sober. My experience shouldn't reflect in any way on AA as an organization."

"Then you don't identify as an alcoholic."

"I don't play identity politics. I identify as me, Roland Hazzard of Planet Earth, unrepentant dispatcher of evil individuals."

"Can't you be that *and* an alcoholic? That's what I want to find out. Can your self-righteous posture and claims of moral rectitude withstand the erraticism and irresponsibility that we commonly associate with alcoholics?"

"I was drunk when I killed the first guy, but not the second guy. But even if I was drunk for both guys, I did the right thing, and my sitting here, alive and well, should be proof enough of that."

"Unfortunately, it's not. There are plenty of bad people walking around free and, quite as unfortunately, we're out of time. I'll end as I always do on *Voice of Reason*—and seldom with more trepidation than now—by giving my guest the last word."

She gestured for him to proceed and leaned back in her chair, eyes rolled heavenward, with her hands joined in a mock portrayal of prayer.

Roland broke the fourth wall again, as he'd done last night. He stared straight into the camera and spoke.

"Mizz Moore is right, and she has proven my point. There are plenty of bad people walking around free, and that's our fault, because when we see people stepping out of line in little ways we look away, and the more we do that the harder it becomes to stand up to serious evil. We've become so tribal that we find fault where there is none in people outside our superficial group, and we excuse the politically correct transgressions of people within our identity categories because we're frightened at the thought of being groupless. If we keep this up there will be widespread social unrest and blood in the streets, and the people with the most guns will win." Now he was pointing his finger at the lens. "Is that the kind of future you want? Helter Skelter? Charlie Manson's dream come true? Is that what you want for your bright-faced toddlers?"

The light on the camera went off.

"Well done."

He shook her hand and thanked her and left the stage, his heart still thrumming. When he reached the door of the set he turned around and looked at her. She raised both her eyebrows to ask him what he wanted to say.

"You think I should wear my cowboy hat on camera or," pointing to his head "stick with my gorgeous dome?"

"Roland, if you're worried about your on-screen image then don't be afraid to switch things up. As long as your message is consistent people will keep watching you. And if you turn out to be a drunk or a psychopath it won't take long for people to find out, cowboy hat or no cowboy hat."

~~~~~

They returned to the hotel by cab in silence. He wanted to talk, wanted to hear what she had to say, wanted validation, approval, congratulations, the like. But he didn't press her. Her presence, he allowed, was validation enough. In the lobby, she said she was going to get something to eat and veered toward the café. The way she said it— *I'm going to get something to eat*—told him that she wanted to eat alone. Up in the room, he paced. Would she come back, or was her action in the lobby just a ruse for her to make her escape? He checked the time and figured he'd give her an hour and if she didn't come back by then he'd go to work on the minibar. He opened the little refrigerator and saw it was well stocked and contended with the feeling that maybe he didn't want her to return and *fuck her anyway*. No. He slammed the little door and knew he was wrong to doubt her and that she would come back and that the eternal foe of alcoholics—resentment—was eroding his good judgment.

Half an hour passed. She opened the door and came in. He looked up from where he sat on the bed with his laptop resting on his thighs. She smiled and said she was glad to see him busy and didn't ask him what he was doing on the computer. He closed it and set it aside and turned on the TV and asked her if she wouldn't mind watching *The Sopranos*.

"You can get the whole series on-demand in this hotel."

"I don't mind. Haven't you seen it already?"

"Only bits and pieces. I don't watch much TV."

"Why do you like the Sopranos?"

"It's Tony. He's such a likable villain. It's amazing how they pulled that off."

"They didn't—it was all Gandolfini. He played a lot of bad guys before that, and they were all very likable."

"That's right—you're a movie critic."

"Was. I did only a few movie reviews for *The Voice*."

"Who should play me?"

"Is that where you think this is headed?"

"Stranger things."

She went into the bathroom and changed into her new pajamas and sat on the bed and watched the TV with him and after a while she got up and pulled down the bedcovers and got in and put her head on the pillow. Roland took that as a cue and climbed in beside her and shut off the TV and plugged in his earbuds, put Chopin and shuffle, then closed his eyes.

~~~~~

Alessandra returned to her chipper self the next morning as they ate a quick breakfast and watched the clock to make sure they caught a cab in time to make his flight at LaGuardia.

"I need to thank you."

"For what?"

"You let me stay quiet last night. You respected my silence. You didn't question me about it."

"I stun myself sometimes, so I can't blame you for being struck dumb."

"It wasn't that. I wasn't shocked by what you said out there. It really wasn't that outrageous, at least not after spending so much time with you."

"What then?"

"I'm a pretty leftwing girl. My whole life, from K through college, I've been fed the same line about men and what they're not and what they should be and why you can just dismiss the whole sex, you know. *A woman needs a man like a fish needs a bicycle.* You're the perfect example of what's supposed to be wrong with the male gender."

"Guys like me painted half-naked ladies on their airplanes before they bombed the shit out of the Nazis, and a lot of them never came back. I'm pretty sure if that sort of thing had been banned, we'd never have won the war."

"That's just it. If you'd asked me a couple of days ago if that was okay—painting naked ladies on warplanes—I'd have been shocked at the question. I'd've said *of course that's not okay.* And if someone had told me about you, I probably would have sneered and repeated some vapid slogan about toxic masculinity."

"Is that why you were so quiet? Disillusionment?"

"If I'd opened my mouth….if we'd started talking, I would have had to tell the truth. And I didn't want to tell the truth."

"You're starting to annoy me."

"I would have had to tell you that I'd never been so attracted to a man in all my life. The truth is that I snapped. Your masculinity crumpled up my little ideology into a ball and made it disappear—poof—like magic."

"I'm sure you'll recover."

"Roland, you must have known. You must have sensed, anyway, that the only way I could be with you last night and not turn your body into my personal jungle gym was for us both to stay quiet."

"I didn't sense that at all. I thought you were bothered or perturbed so I left you alone."

"No. I was nervous and aroused. If we'd got going, the neighbors would have called the front desk to complain."

"Now you're just being cruel."

"Don't get me wrong. I'm glad we didn't do it. It was essential that we didn't do it, but you need to know that meeting you—getting to know you—has changed me, because I respect you for qualities I was educated—brainwashed really—to despise. You've opened my eyes. I think I can be with a man now without judging him. That's what I wanted to thank you for."

"I'm still thinking about the jungle gym."

"That's your privilege. But one thing I want you to think about when you're done thinking about that…"

"I know—don't drink."

"No. It's stupid to tell a drunk not to drink. I just want you to know that the man who changed me, the man who opened me up to men, was sober and could not have had this effect on me if he was drunk. You showed me the best part of your mixed-up self, Roland, and that has made me a better, stronger woman. I want you never to forget that, whether or not you decide to go on drinking."

Roland flinched. His left hand, the one closest to her, trembled. He looked at it. The hand trembled because Roland had stopped it from clenching into a fist. His chest tightened. He felt ill. She had no right to lay down such a heavy truth in their last minute together, to drop him at the airport a better man than he was when he arrived and tell him that he and he alone could keep what he'd become and, if he chose not to, then he would have no one but himself to blame. The driver stopped and got out and pulled his bags from the trunk and opened his door.

Roland hung his head a little. To turn his chin in her direction, to face her eyes, to accept the sincerity of the mind that had just revealed such scorching truth, required more effort than he'd ever had to muster. Snapping a man's neck took no effort at all but turning his own neck to look at Alessandra required a monumental act of will.

"When I told you I loved you yesterday, I think I said it because I liked who I was becoming around you, but I'm not there yet, and part of me thinks it's just a fantasy of normalcy. Life down the road might make these feelings look foolish. That's why it's hard to say goodbye."

"Never tell someone goodbye. Not unless one of you is dying."

Chapter 18
November 2016

The first week of November saw a transformation in the public mood of San Francisco sufficient to fill a chapter in a textbook entitled *Studies in Mass Electoral Dysphoria*. The recently concluded Halloween season had induced, as always, a euphoria of sexual liberty in what was already the most libertine city in America, culminating for many in the annual Exotic Erotic Ball, which played out like a Roman orgy, though far more expansive, inviting participation from all the social classes, from toga-clad senators to ball-gagged slaves. Apart from The Ball, the populace donned all sorts of outlandish costumes, at work and on the streets, from the blatantly sacrilegious Sisters of Perpetual Indulgence, who canvassed Market Street and environs in their flowing white habits, aerodynamic wimples, and the all-important oversized codpieces, to children as young as ten dropped off at school dressed in stripper-drag with dollar bills spilling from the seams. The transition from infancy to adulthood often was a short one in The City by the Bay.

The arteries of the body politic still surging with the thrill of exhibitionism, out of nowhere descended a polar vortex to benumb the collective glee—Donald J. Trump was elected forty-fifth president of the United States. Those same exuberant revelers now rent their clothes, gnashed their teeth, and tore at their breasts. The modest wept in private or in small, intimate huddles. One would have thought the populace had been informed they were no longer free to pursue their livelihoods and predilections; and since this was not the case, questions of a sociological—or even clinical—nature suddenly became pertinent. Or perhaps the explanation required no such complex analysis. Perhaps a community noted for its boundless creativity simply had suffered a colossal failure of imagination.

Roland had sequestered himself in the run-up to Election Day. It wasn't so much his aversion to Halloween—though that was part of it—but his fear of public confrontation now that he'd raised his profile all the more through his two appearances on national cable news channels. Holed up in his *bunker*, as he called it, he continued to engage his followers on social media, recording new podcasts, and making guest appearances on a few popular YouTube programs. To stage the videocasts, he set up a chair in his parlor in front of a wall where he'd hung a picture of a bespectacled Malcolm X and positioned his camera to frame himself in the chair with the iconic photo of the martyr just above his right ear. As Election Day approached, the question of his political allegiance became a repeated line of inquiry. Roland refused to take a side or even say if he planned to vote at all. His default position was that politicians could not save the country from its precipitous decline without the help of a courageous populous. If the people served the government and not the other way around, the people deserved what they got.

"We live in a post-constitutional age. The promise of small government is broken. The Mayflower might as well have sunk. We might as well surrender ourselves as slaves to the natives."

On the night before the election, he patched himself via video chat into the *Joe Rogan Experience,* the most popular long-form interview show on the web for the wide range of prominent figures who appeared there and for the unpretentious intelligence of the host, Hollywood-native Joe Rogan. It was Roland's second appearance. He wore his signature Guatemalan cowboy hat and sported a bullet belt draped across his chest.

"Roland Hazzard, back again. I see you're still wearing your Halloween costume."

"I am."

"Lemme guess. Santa Ana?"

"Pancho Villa. I bought the hat down your way, on Olvera Street as a matter of fact."

"And the bandolier? Is that real? Are those live rounds?"

"No. But it's a pretty fair replica. I got it online. Won't tell you how much I paid for it."

"So, first question. I have to get this out of the way—who you gonna vote for? And I don't mean in the next Mexican election."

"I couldn't vote in Mexico, even if I wanted to. They have strict voter ID laws down there."

"Seriously. Here's your chance to endorse a presidential candidate to my millions of minions…"

"I'll tell you what I tell all the other nosy armpit huffers—no one."

"Really, with so much at stake? I mean, this is a true fork in the road, is it not? So much depends on it."

"So much depends upon a red wheelbarrow glazed with rainwater beside the white chickens."

"What? Some sort of secret code? Wheelbarrow, rainwater, chickens—is the vigilante uprising about to begin? Do I need to grab my helmet and flak jacket?"

"No. I've sprinkled lamb's blood on your door."

"That one I understand. Moses, right?"

"Right you are."

"Hazzard, why are you always so obscure, some might even say evasive?"

Roland sighed. Audibly. Even forcefully. These radio and webcast interviews had grown tedious, and he hadn't been at it all that long. Roland had reached the point where he was saying shit just to say it. Worse yet, he caught himself repeating himself. The virtually unplumbable depths of his encyclopedic memory threatened to betray him. Joe Rogan, though playful and often deliberately crass, was covertly intelligent and could put the hard questions to you—he deserved some respect. Roland tried to explain himself.

"You know when you're talking, or you're in a group of people talking, and someone says something that reminds someone else of a line in a popular song? And the guy starts singing it."

"Yeah, you wanna smack him across the mouth. Motherfucker why you interrupting the conversation just to burp your brain?"

"Well, Joe, I just did just that—burped my brain."

"Sorry, I didn't catch it. I don't know that song."

"It's not a song. It's a little poem by a once celebrated, now forgotten, American poet."

"A red wheelbarrow? That's a poem?"

"*The* Red Wheelbarrow, by the venerable Pulitzer Prize winner, William Carlos Williams."

"He got famous for that?"

"As famous as an American poet could be in his lifetime, yeah."

"So, what does it mean?"

"The poem?"

"Yes."

"No one knows. What do abstract paintings mean?"

"That's fucked up. Tell me something about this William Carlos Williams fella."

"He was a doctor, a country doctor, you know, with a little black bag full of medical tools, shows up to your house to treat your ailments. He was tending to a sick child on a farm somewhere and it wasn't going so well for the kid and he looked out the window and saw a red wheelbarrow glazed with rainwater beside some white chickens, so he prayed to that. Or maybe the kid was staring at it, wondering if he'd ever get to play outside again, and maybe the doctor observed that."

"You're fucking with me, right?"

"Nope. That's the folklore."

"He was a working doctor and he won a Pulitzer Prize for making word pictures?"

"It's the googleable truth. Writing poetry wasn't enough for some poets. One of Williams' contemporaries, Wallace Stevens, also a Pulitzer Prize winner, worked as an insurance executive for most of his life. Academia destroyed American poetry sometime after the seventies. Of course, there was always some politics in the arts. Take a look at Walt Whitman. But the craft was always the focus, love of language for its sounds and shimmering meanings and connotations. Now it's all politics. The craft has been abandoned."

"So those guys—Williams and Stevens—they were men who wrote poetry, not poets with dicks."

"You have a rare gift, Joe Rogan."

"I'm happiest when I'm off the FCC's leash."

"I didn't mention this the last time I was on, but I've been following your program for a while for just that reason. Relaxed unfettered long conversations away from the censors and corporate overlords—you've created something great here, Joe, something that's going to make people smarter, or at least more attentive. You're winnowing the wheat from the chaff."

"You keep blowing me and I'll lose respect for you, Mister Hazzard. So back to the poem, The Red Wheelbarrow—I liked it much more once you told me the story behind it. The wheelbarrow represents some kind of Higher Power."

"Again, the story is apocryphal. The little poem is supposed to stand on its own two tiny feet. It's supposed to evoke a sense of mystery or even bucolic awe."

"Way over my oft-baked head. I've heard of guys in AA who don't believe in God using say, a doorknob, as their Higher Power."

"I've heard that too, but I think that's a pretty temporary solution, or maybe just an absurd extreme used by sponsors to make the point that you can pick any Higher Power you want, as long as you pick something. As long as you're not your own Higher Power."

"So, recovering drunks don't pray to doorknobs and lightbulbs, but the great Willie Williams prayed to a wheelbarrow when the situation moved beyond his scientific powers?"

"You probably know more AA folks than I do, with all the time you've spent in Hollywood."

"I can't speak to the numbers, but I know a few. One friend of mine—who shall remain nameless—made wind chimes out of his newcomer chips."

Roland lowered his voice as though ashamed. "I never took any chips."

"Roland Hazzard, Butcher Slayer, point-blank—are you still drinking?"

"I've been sober since I got back from New York, and I was sober throughout in New York."

"Then Cameron Anderson was lying? You weren't intoxicated on the set?"

"Not even a little. Sober as an ayatollah. But I won't say Anderson was lying, just *mistaken* or *misinformed.*"

"So why do you think he tried to bust you?"

"I never thought I'd hear myself say this, but *on the advice of counsel* I'm going to have to decline to comment on what happened during my appearance on CBN."

"Fair enough, but just to be clear, you do have a lawsuit ongoing."

"We're in negotiations. My job is to keep my mouth shut."

"Not easy for a wordy guy like you."

"That hurts, Joe. You find me wordy? I think you're a shitty dresser."

Joe Rogan never wore a proper shirt when hosting his show, always and only a t-shirt that exhibited his well-sculpted muscles.

"Look at you, all offended. I didn't mean wordy in a bad way like an English teacher would say it. I mean *wordy* like into words. You're a word guy, a *wordy* guy—it's playful. I don't invite people on unless they can deliver the words."

"I guess my hackles have a hair trigger. Maybe I'm worried about being wordy since I'm starting to put things on paper, trying to gain some traction on a book."

"Autobiographical, I hope. I think a lot of people would like to read it, to find out what makes you tick. Like I said before, you tend to be a little evasive, or maybe a better way to say it is that you shoot off on tangents."

"Look, Joe, it's not that I'm trying to be coy or evasive or difficult or anything like that; but there's only so much to say about the actions that got me all this attention. A lot of so-called journalists tend to want me to justify the killings, to put me on the defensive, to hold me to account, as though they enjoy some sort of moral authority by the mere fact that they've been hired to ask questions. So instead of indulging their hubris, I try to educate them and whoever's listening on larger, or maybe deeper, matters that I think our society—our civilization, really—has either diminished or forgotten how to talk about."

"You make an interesting point. On the dark web, we're mostly independent. No one hires us to ask questions or deliver content. We serve no master."

"Right. So, if a journalist doesn't actually want to talk to me, the way you and I are talking now, but instead talk *at* me, or talk at some image they have of me, then I'm going to adjust my stride to avoid slipping on their pile of dogshit."

"I like what you've had to say about archeological…what did you call them…not mysteries?

"Anomalies"

"Yeah, archeological anomalies. That's a topic I've been fascinated with for a while. I've done a few shows with learned gentlemen who've devoted a lot of time to that stuff."

"I'm not an expert on the subject, but I think we'd be much better off as a species if we spent more of our scientific bandwidth figuring out our past than in finding new ways to speed ourselves off the cliff into oblivion."

"Talk about that. I've listened to a few of your interviews, and you seem to take a pessimistic view. Talk about where you think we're headed."

"It's impossible to say or even to hazard a respectable guess, even for the people developing the technology that's transforming us. The consequences of what we are doing are too multifarious and far-reaching for any one mind to get a handle on. We are constantly reacting, like the pilot of a small boat on a tempestuous ocean."

"Give me one example, Roland. Prophesy for the audience. Give 'em a little something to chew on."

"They can chew on the new loneliness pill, or should I say anti-loneliness pill."

"You're making that up."

"Wish I was, but it's neuroscientists that are *cooking it up.*"

"Wouldn't a normal anti-depressant work?"

"I guess not. I guess loneliness is so prevalent now that they can isolate it as its own distinct malady and treat it as such. And that makes perfect sense, though I doubt anyone predicted it back when the causes for it started to emerge."

"What would you say are the causes, besides the obvious one of people staring into screens all day?"

"It can't be just that, though the fact is that people are starting at a younger and younger age before they're really even people. Kids who can barely talk are performing complex tasks on touch screens. Alarming really."

"So, if it's not just that, what is it? What's causing the loneliness?"

"So much depends upon the red wheelbarrow glazed with rainwater beside the white chickens. Maybe Williams saw this coming. Maybe I was wrong. Maybe that little poem struck a spiritual chord and that's why it remains in the literary canon."

"You've lost me again."

"Half a century ago, families were large. Kids had siblings or lived in neighborhoods with lots of kids, and maybe lots of animals, so after it rained, as soon as the chickens came back out into the yard, when the red wheelbarrow was still glazed with rainwater, unless you were sick you couldn't wait to get outside and play. Widespread chronic loneliness, the reason for the new pill, could never have occurred. Also, kids had grandparents, which is a whole different kind of relationship that holds a special value in the lives of children. It won't be long before the whole concept of a grandparent will seem absurd. Half the kids don't even know who both their biological parents are, and the ones they have are barely ever around or too busy to be present when they are around, and there's no one to play with, so they live inside their little silos with their electronic devices. You think a pill is going to cure that? No wonder credentialed academics and comfortable politicians talk seriously about legalizing infanticide. They don't want to look at what becomes of a new human being in this insane world we have created, or worse yet, have some innocent little face ask them in toddler-English why life is no fun."

"That's heavy shit. I'm sure I'll get a lot of feedback on that little diatribe. By the way, I had kickass grandparents, all four of them. I can't imagine growing up without them. How about your grandparents?"

"The one I was closest with as a kid died not too long ago, and it's only been recently that I realized just how much I miss him."

"Maybe you'll see him again if the believers are right, but that's too big a topic to get started on now. What's next for you, Mister Villa? You said you're working on a book, any other big plans? Running for mayor of San Francisco maybe?"

Roland took his hat off and set it on the table beside him and caressed his head to give himself time to decide what to say, whether to answer the question truthfully or invent something innocuous to serve in its place. He decided to reveal the truth.

"I'm going to speak on the Berkeley campus."

"Fuuuck, that's gonna be nuuuts. When is it?"

"Can't say."

"Can't say or won't say?"

"Won't. This is the world we live in, unfortunately. My hosts don't want the event to be overwhelmed by media and self-righteous fanatics, so they'll announce it day-of and let word of mouth fill the seats. It'll be recorded and posted online. I get to talk for an hour."

"Can you tell me who's hosting it?"

"The Mario Savio Sewing Circle."

"I don't know you well enough to tell when you're lying."

"It's a real student club, a free speech club—have your man look it up right now."

Joe Rogan pointed to his assistant in the studio at a desk behind the glass to say go ahead look it up.

"Who is Mario Savio?"

"Was. He died in the nineties. Heart attack. Age fifty-three. Founder of the Berkeley Free Speech Movement back in the nineteen sixties."

"Sewing Circle. That's an interesting choice."

"I think they're trying to point out that free speech poses no more threat than sewing circle gossip."

"How many seats at this sewing circle event? Can you tell me that much?"

"The room holds a couple hundred."

"Tell me the date offline. You can trust me with your secret. I'll send someone up to watch if I don't come myself."

"Yeah, don't come yourself. I don't want the planet Joe Rogan to overwhelm my meager gravity."

~~~~~

America had a new president, one of questionable character no doubt, but one of high energy and unflappable charisma. Half the country was either furious or gobsmacked, and the other half crossed its arms in smug satisfaction. Satan and his legions rolled with laughter. God looked up from peeling His orange. Roland, after five days of nothing but delivered food—mainly pizza and Chinese—ventured out of his bunker to stock his kitchen. He'd been sober for well over a week, and while his obsession over his self-imposed abstinence lessened a little each day, still he was ill at ease. His short dry stretch proved far more difficult, both mentally and physically, than the span of months it took to satisfy the court-imposed AA attendance earlier that year, and it occurred to him at least once a day that going to a meeting would help him get through it. Yet a peculiar twist of mind told him that his celebrity status, such as it was, would draw attention away from the serious business of recovery in a group that opened each meeting with a dedication to *placing principles above personalities*. If pressed, though, he would have had to confess that it was the laughter we wanted to avoid, for abstinence made him mean while it sharpened his intellect, and the mirth of the *happy-joyous-and-free* extolling the gifts of the program would have worn down his molars.

Andruko's Market appeared much as he'd left it, though peaches were no longer in season. Taras saw Roland come in and acknowledged him as he rang up a customer. Roland grabbed a pear and headed back to the meat counter where Oleg stood at the slicer diminishing a ham one sliver at a time. Roland tapped on the bell. Oleg turned around and looked at Roland. He turned back around without a word or gesture and set a fresh slice of ham on the pile. Roland stood and fixed a stare at Oleg's head. Oleg turned around again and looked at Roland with an expression of controlled contempt.

"Dyou. Vutt dyou vant?"

"You're not wearing any gloves."

"Tooching pourk iss not haram."

"Do I look like the sharia police? I'm talking about California law."

"So dyou da Californdja poulice?"

Roland took a bite of the pear and chewed it slowly while he scraped away a smudge of something on the stainless-steel counter with his fingernail. Oleg returned to his slicing job. Roland tapped the bell again. Oleg did not turn around this time and spoke instead to the disappearing hunk of ham.

"Dyou come to pay vat dyou owe then dyou pay Taras."

"I'd like a rack of lamb. I'd like it cut into individual ribs."

Oleg faced Roland again.

"Dyou got da money?"

Roland set a white envelope on the meat counter. "That one in the middle." He pointed to the rack he wanted. "And wear the food service gloves. You've got a box right there."

Oleg lifted the flap of the envelope to confirm that it held cash. Then he slipped on a pair of thin transparent plastic gloves and reached into the display case and pulled out the rack on top.

"No. Not that one. The one underneath it."

Oleg did as directed. "Put dat back in djor pockit. Give to Taras."

Roland complied and stayed at the counter watching Oleg cut the rack into its individual ribs with his butcher's knife.

"I had a dream about you last night, Oleg. There were lots of knives in it, all flying around."

Oleg ignored him.

"C'mon, Oleg. Practice your English. Don't you wanna assimilate?"

"I doon't cayre vutt dyou haff to say."

"Not bad not bad. So, the dream—it started with you sitting in a big, huge pot of boiling water in some jungle somewhere. You were dead, of course, head leaning out of the pot and your skin peeling off. I'm not sure how I could tell it was you, but it was a dream, and I just knew. Poor Oleg, captured by the cannibals."

Roland paused and watched. Oleg focused on the task before him, his back to Roland, and when he turned his head a smidge in Roland's direction to show his ear, Roland knew he was listening and waiting to hear the rest.

"So, it was definitely not halal, this luncheon they were throwing together, these cannibals. Haram in the extreme, I'd say."

"Murderers dream about murdering."

"Not so fast. I was just watching, standing outside the circle. Then the next thing I know, they're cutting you up. Scraping off your flesh to clean your bones. It wasn't a feast after all, or it was before, and then suddenly it was something else—you know how dreams are, always changing. Anyway, suddenly I was watching an assembly line. Skilled craftsmen with sharp obsidian blades whittling your bones into eating utensils—forks, knives, spoons, chopsticks—working like mad to meet a deadline. As it turns out, I was the foreman, or maybe the factory owner, and we were late in producing our latest line of cutlery—the Oleg Collection.

"Are dyou feenished?"

"Not until you're finished."

Oleg set the package of meat on the counter and wrote a price on it.

"The dream ended with the workers handing me a wooden case with a full set of cutlery made from your bones—your ivory—and then presenting me with a bowl, the top of your skull, a gift for the boss—your skull filled with blood for me to drink. That's all I remember."

"I remember dat dyoor filled of nothing but sheet."

"C'mon, Oleg, no hard feelings. I was just passing the time while I made sure you didn't spit on my mutton."

Roland filled a shopping basket and paid for his purchases at the register and, after the transaction was completed, handed Taras the illicit envelope.

"It's all there, plus a c-note for your patience."

"You want a pint, the Smirnoff blue? It's on me."
"No. Not today."
"Why do you get my brother all wound up?"
"He's already wound up. I want to see if I can pop his spring."
"Yes. I know, but why?"
"He has contempt for the very air that he breathes."
"He wasn't any happier in Tbilisi."
"Maybe you should get him laid. San Francisco has every flavor. Here in the Christian West, we do whatever we want and ask forgiveness later. When in Rome, I say."
"Oleg would slaughter every last one of you if he could. I'm much more tolerant."

~~~~~

After he put his groceries away, he took a run to the vermillion bridge. Standing beneath it, chest heaving, gathering his breath with his hands on his hips, close enough to watch the ocean slosh against the southern stanchion, Roland measured with his eyes the distance between the span and the water and wondered if he could survive the plunge, provided he brought both feet together to a point and entered the water like a perfectly vertical dart. He'd heard that, while most all the leapers had perished, a few had survived, and he thought there must be some common denominator in the impact profile of the survivors, though he doubted any such data had been collected or could be collected. His macabre speculation, the unbidden nature of it, stopped him short, like a horse at full gallop reined back. Why spend a single synapse on the ruination of such foolish persons? With the hundreds of ways there are to kill yourself, forcing people to retrieve your body after you jump off the Golden Gate Bridge is one of the more selfish ways to go. The rescuers of the occasional survivor should have held the head under for five minutes to finish the job. The dead that mattered, he averred, were the men who died while building the spectacularly useful structure. And what about the two structures—The Bay Bridge—connecting San Francisco to Oakland? Probably many more casualties, given how much larger the project was. The fact was, from the beginning of human civilization, any time people set about to build something big, workers died in the construction process. And they knew that going in. And it wasn't just slaves. Civilizational progress costs lives, but everyone figured that the benefits outweighed the costs. The Hoover Dam exhibits memorial plaques that identify the men whose bodies could not be retrieved for proper burial. The dam is one giant grave marker. Nowadays, though, because of more powerful and sophisticated machines, massive building projects required less human labor, so many fewer workers died. And none of them died to provide a launchpad for glory-seeking narcissistic suicides.

Before he could stop himself, Roland made the sign of the cross then regarded his hand as though it were controlled by another. God looked up from peeling his orange. Roland turned his back to the bridge and hoofed it home.

~~~~~

Tina sat alone in one of the chairs along the wall reading a newspaper as though she were a customer waiting for the stylist to arrive. When he entered the bells jingled and she glanced up from her reading and smiled. Just a smile. An innocent smile. A feeble defense against the catastrophe that is the human condition.

"Hola, Tinasita. Slow day, I see."

"I do better on Mars." His presence enlivened her only a little. The playful repartee that formed the basis of their relationship was not, he sensed, available today. She was not herself.

"I could help you. I've got plenty of..."

She stood up abruptly and cut him off. "I glad you came in. I'm saying goodbye to my customers."

"I'm serious, Tina. I can help you out."

"You can clean the Tenderloin? I could make my price to zero and still no one might walk through piss and shit and needles to get the free haircut."

"It doesn't look so bad today."

"Not bad today! Piss and shit should not be like the weather. How can I work where I will not bring my children?"

"Where will you go?"

"Sacramento."

"I'm not kidding. I can give you money if you need it. I've got a few thousand dollars I'm not using."

"It's my shop. I sold it. My American dream. I got enough to start over in Sacramento. Let someone else try to make business work on this street. I will miss my customers but not this place. Ten years ago, it was okay, mostly drunks and whores, but this year is like a wave of death."

She gestured toward the chair for him to sit. He sat. She picked up his left arm and examined the scar.

"It heals good. But it never go away."

Roland didn't want to talk about the scar. The scar represented a combat error, a lapse in agility probably due to drunkenness. A private shame. Yet the wound served as convincing evidence that Barsamian had successfully attacked him and, as such, bolstered his valuable lie. If he'd come away unscathed from the fight, which ended with Barsamian on his back in a puddle of his own blood, ribs cracked, jaw broken, teeth knocked out, face contused, and a knife sticking out of his chest, Roland would have had a hard time claiming it was a fight to the death. The scar was an alibi of sorts—a bullshit alibi—but an alibi, nonetheless. It represented to Roland both a physical failure and a moral weakness. He'd've just as soon, at that moment, have her hack off the arm like she'd done the putrescent foot of the gangrenous refugee on the boat to America. His self-revulsion passed.

"You're one of my only friends."

"That's very sad. You famous now. You need some real friends."

"There's nothing keeping me here. Maybe I'll pull up stakes myself."

"Pull up stakes?"

"Like the American settlers. Pack up my things and start over someplace else."

"Why would you stay here if you didn't have to? You're so young."

"There is a girl."

"Is she your girl?"

"No. She's her own girl."

"Single?"

She began to drag the razor across his lotioned head, back and forth, like mowing a snow-covered lawn down to the bare earth.

"Yes. She's unattached."

"Does she know you love her?"

"Who said I love her?"

"What else does it mean, *there is a girl?*"

"I would miss her. She'd be the only one I'd miss, apart from you of course."

Tina finished the shave. Touched him up behind the ears. Trimmed his eyebrows. Draped his head with a hot towel and let him sit for a minute then wiped him clean. He sighed his pleasure. She swiveled the chair around so that he faced the mirror.

"What are men?"

"Is this a riddle?"

"You know the answer. I tell you this before."

"Oh, right. Pussies. Big pussies."

"You looking at one right now, mister."

"I know you're not charging me today, but still, I feel I've been diminished."

He set a hundred-dollar bill on her counter as he left and said he'd be back next week to say goodbye, but his path would take him elsewhere.

~~~~~

Roland sat in his parlor. He'd put off his brother far too long. For weeks Major Hazzard had been pestering him—well, Roland thought of it as pestering—with texts, at first long and supportive, then inquisitive and solicitous, and finally irritated and terse. Until the texts stopped altogether. It had been four or five days since Phillip had messaged him. Scrolling to the bottom of the thread, Roland read the major's last installment: *Go it alone then, little brother.* Farther up he read through the series of his own bland replies, going back weeks, where repeatedly he'd promised to call. Phillip had not even asked Roland to call—it went without saying—but Roland had seen fit to volunteer that he would. Now, the texts having ceased, his own words weighed on him. A promise delayed eventually counts as a promise un-kept. His brother's silence indicted him. Roland set his phone on the table, pulled off his Laredos, then picked up the phone and placed the call.

"Roland, glad you could fit me in."

"I'm sorry, Phillip. But I know you don't want to hear that."

"Is that why you called? To say sorry for not calling?"

"It's partially your fault, you know."

"What is? What's *it?*"

"Do you remember our last conversation?"

"Hold on. Let me ask *you* a question, before we talk about my faults."

Roland felt trapped. His brother knew him better than anyone in the world and did not brook bullshit. He was not prepared to sift through the persona he had created and set aside the elements he'd invented to present the person Phillip would recognize as genuine.

"What's the question, Phillip?"

"Think before you answer, Roland. Assume that your answer will be stored in some database somewhere and could be digitally searched and transcribed by an intelligent algorithm or by some interested agent at some unknown point in the future. We're not alone. No one on the grid is ever alone."

"Really? Has it gotten that bad already?"

"Don't change the subject. You love to do that. It won't work with me."

"Wait, Phillip. What's the subject? Who's in charge of the subject?"

"When you snapped that little fucker's neck, was that because of what I said?"

"I don't know what you mean."

"Before I agreed to wire you money to pay your gambling debt, I advised you to *milk this pig*. That was the phrase I used."

"Yes. That's what I meant. But I shouldn't have said *your fault*. I meant I probably wouldn't have become an internet celebrity if you hadn't said that. It was the book deal, specifically. When you said I should take it all the way to a book deal. That's what did it."

"So, my question remains, did you snap his neck to augment your fame, in hopes of a book deal?"

"I think I've already addressed that question."

"No you haven't. You might have dodged it a few times. I think I've listened to all your podcasts and interviews, and no one has put you on the spot about that. And if they have, then I missed it, so humor me."

"Why do you care, Phillip?"

"You're the one who should care."

"I know what I did."

"Do you know why?"

"There was no why."

"Are you sure?"

"It was all training. Nothing but training."

"So, no intention? No moment of hesitation? No chance to refrain?"

"Phillip, what if I announced to the world, through all my media channels, that I made a conscious decision not to disarm him but to kill him instead, and that I did it to elevate my public profile to land a book deal?"

"You tell me."

"I'd be just as free as I am today."

"Probably true."

"Did you pause every time, before you squeezed off a shot into a jihadi?"

"You CAN'T com-PARE what YOU DID to WAR." Roland didn't know why he was deliberately agitating his brother. Resentment perhaps, a free-floating vapor of toxic acerbity produced by his resistance to any moral governance outside his own. An effluvium he breathed involuntarily. One that easily could be neutralized by the ingestion of alcohol, except Roland wasn't drinking. As such, his difficult moments passed more slowly, even painfully. Marshaling words, and the thought of having to marshal them, wore on his very sense of justice. Yet, he knew he was obliged. Phillip had not violated any boundaries, had not declared war. His brother, who he trusted above all others, was simply calling him to account.

"I don't know."

"Don't know what?"

"If I could have stopped myself."

"And what about the fame, the book deal?"

"I don't have a book deal."

"This is not an interview, dipshit. I'm not some kind of media nitwit you can jerk around."

"No, Phillip. I didn't kill him for fame. If I did, it was at a layer of my subconscious that I can neither denounce nor defend."

"I'm going to believe that, if only because I have to. I don't want to be—and I can speak for Mom and Dad and Sandy—*we* don't want to be related to a guy who gloats about an unnecessary legal killing. You're not operating in a vacuum here, little brother."

"I spoke with Sandy a few days ago."

"She told me."

"She didn't put me through the wringer."

"She doesn't have colleagues in the Pentagon looking at her cockeyed. My security clearance is very high, so the crazier you get out there the less I'm going to be trusted. They'll consider me genetically compromised."

"That's not a real thing."

"It's not an official phrase, but it's a real thing."

"What are you telling me? What do you want from me?"

There was a long pause. Roland studied his toes and saw the nails needed clipping. The narrow points of his Laredos made regular foot care essential.

"Nothing, Roland." Phillip's voice carried a hint of resignation and a dash of disgust.

Roland needed more than nothing from Phillip. He deserved to know his brother's mind. "Tell me, do you want me to stop, to close up shop, to give the pig a rest?"

"I can't tell you what to do, Roland. Just do me a favor."

"What's that?"

"No aliens. Stick to archeological oddities and prehistoric catastrophes. I understand you don't want to talk about the killings—I know you're trying to engage a wider audience by mixing in the strange and unexplained—but don't start talking about extraterrestrial visitors. Promise me that."

Roland laughed. "Does that include cattle mutilations?"

"Yes. That's aliens. The government, the military, we know shit, shit we won't publicly admit. And people know that we know, and they know that we know that they know that we know. Don't stray down that path. It's the road to perdition."

"What if I just quoted something I read on a website?"

"Goddamnit, Roland. Stick to the Giza Plateau and the Peruvian Andes." His voice tilted toward anger, a threatening anger.

"Okay okay, Phillip. No space aliens. Scouts honor."

"That's all I'm asking."

"What are you going to do if Trump goes sniffin' around Area 51 and Groom Lake?"

"See what you're doing?"

"I'm genuinely curious!"

"Suppress your curiosity. Don't talk about it."
Both men let the emotion dissipate over a few seconds of silence. The major was, as it happened, in charge of the subject. Roland reminded himself that his brother was the one man he dared not cross, for Phillip had never lied to him or given him bad advice, and there was no reason to think that he ever would.

"I'm going to speak at Berkeley tomorrow."

"You sound pretty good. Soberly good. I want to make sure I say that before we finish talking."

"Thanks, Phillip. I promised my agent and my lawyer."

"How's that going?"

"You mean the not drinking, or the legal matter?"

"The legal matter."

"The money is on its way, or almost on its way. They're still working on it, but it's going to come through. A substantial six-figure sum."

"What are you going to tell your disciples at Berkeley?"

"That humans are all alone in the Universe. God created the Earth in the first six days and made an ottoman for Himself to rest his feet on Sunday."

"You've perfected the art of being an asshole."

"So, what's the mood around the Pentagon?"

"You mean about Trump?"

"Yeah. First time a true interloper has won the job of Commander in Chief."

"Hard to tell. People aren't showing their cards. Ma'am would have let us run around the world breaking a lot of shit—we know that. But we're not sure what Trump's got in mind."

"How do you feel about him?"

"Abraham Lincoln said it himself. This country was designed to withstand a bad president every so often. Besides, the office seems to get smaller every year. He'll probably be forced to spend most of his time defending himself to get a whole lot done. He'll be lucky if the magnifying glass he's under doesn't fry him."

They talked a while longer until the subject turned to their parents. Roland agreed that Mom and Dad had every right to be nervous about what he was doing and fearful of what he might become. Sandpoint, Idaho was every bit as connected to the world as New York City and San

Francisco, so there was no sense pretending that their Rocky Mountain sanctuary insulated them from his self-serving public frolic.

"Are you still coming to Thanksgiving?"

"Yeah. Sandy already asked me that. I told her yes."

Roland wished he'd been smart enough to force the conversation to a conclusion a minute or so earlier.

"Have you called Mom and told her yourself?"

"No."

"Call her, then. Will you do that?"

It wasn't a question, rather a request, a request he had no reason to refuse.

"Yeah, I was planning on that." He figured Phillip knew that wasn't perfectly true.

~~~~~

Roland parked his car on a residential street near campus and got out and draped his bandolier across his chest and put on his hat, which, added to his boots, completed his Pancho Villa getup. The several dozen shiny pointed bullets protruding from the compact little sleeves in the leather ammo belt were costume shells made from spent cartridges soldered at the bottom to ensure they could not be reused. It was a heavy adornment that accentuated his wide pectorals flexing under his black t-shirt.

People moved aside and stared at him as he made his way up Bancroft Avenue and entered Sproul Plaza. He moved with long, deliberate strides through the rows of pollard plane trees toward the rust-green arch of Sather Gate, eyes hidden under wraparound sunglasses. His Laredos wore a fresh polish and their buffed steel tips caught the overhead sun as he propelled himself forward. Now several people shouted and pointed but dared not approach him. When he reached the iconic landmark, two campus police officers—a white man and a black woman—were there to intercept him.

"What do you think you're doing, sir?"

Roland took off his glasses and hung them on the neck of his t-shirt and put on his most affable face. Portraying affability made him, he felt, more affable. He thumbed up the brim of his hat so they could see that his smile extended into his eyes.

"I'm here to give a little speech in Dwinelle Hall. I'm a guest of the Mario Savio club."

"We know who you are," the woman said. "And we knew you were coming today. But the bullet belt has got to go."

"I anticipated this. And I want to assure you that I checked with my lawyer beforehand. These bullets are phony and legal to carry around."

He pulled one out to show them. "Hollywood bullets. The ends are soldered-over and there's no gunpowder in the casings. Besides, I don't even have a gun. I'd have to throw them to hurt someone with 'em."

By now, several people had formed around them to listen in. "That's him. That's the Human Hazzard," said one young man. Another struck up the Spiderman theme. "Hazzard Man, Hazzard Man, kills as long as he's plastered man." Others chuckled.

Roland looked at the crooner, a young Caucasian lad still plagued by acne and sporting a baseball cap turned backward. The kid stopped singing and smiled. Roland detected no malice in his mirth, only the satisfaction of a child surprised by his own cleverness.

"That's a pretty nice backpack you've got. Timberland?"

The lad glanced at the pack slung on his shoulder. "Yeah. It's a Timberland."

"Can I borrow it?"

"What?"

"I don't have time to hypnotize you. I need a backpack, just for the next hour or so."

"No—why?"

Roland gestured toward the officers with the point of the bullet but kept his eyes on the lad. "They don't like me walking around campus with my costume ammo belt. And I get it. The university wants to make the student body frightened and resentful, to varying degrees so to speak."

"What does that have to do with my backpack?"

"I'm gonna put the bandolier in your backpack and carry it into the hall." Then he looked at the officers. "Will that be satisfactory? You don't have the right to confiscate my harmless property."

The officers conferred and agreed that would be alright. Roland re-sheathed the loose bullet and beckoned for the backpack.

"I wasn't planning to go to your talk."

"You got something better to do?"

Lacking a rejoinder, the lad removed the books from his backpack and handed it over. Roland took off his hat, gave it to the lad to hold, then unslung the bandolier and put it inside the pack and zipped it up and slung the pack over his shoulder and took his hat from the lad and set it on his head and adjusted the brim.

"This a-way." He started walking. "Dwinelle Hall." The officers followed at a distance along with a few curious idlers.

"What did you mean *no time to hypnotize me?* You can't just walk up to people and hypnotize them."

"It's a very rare and peculiar skill, I'll give you that. But if you want to know the truth, I'm here to *un-hypnotize* you."

"How you gonna do that?"

"You'll find out inside, and if you're going to keep your hat on, at least turn it in the right direction."

The lad reversed the brim of his baseball cap.

"Baby steps," said Roland. "Baby steps."

~~~~~

The lyceum in Dwinelle Hall held about three hundred seats. Nearly all of them were filled. Roland stood backstage with his host—Sreedhar something or other—and put on the bullet belt, impatient for the man to leave and set the ball rolling. Sreedhar said *showtime* and left his side to greet the audience and introduce the speaker. Roland pulled a pint bottle—Smirnoff blue—from inside his pants and unscrewed the cap and slugged down half of it. He hadn't had a drink for roughly a month—since his debauch before New York—so the alcohol packed a wallop, made him fairly swoon with contentment. He hummed with satisfaction as he listened to the words being used, just now, to describe him. *Unrepentant practitioner of lethal self-defense. Defiant in the face of overweening authority. Instinctive grasp of the values that undergird the US Constitution.* A vaguely approving murmur rippled through the crowd. The bandolier suddenly felt ridiculous, the hat absurd. He guzzled more. Sreedhar, Roland observed, spoke a better brand of English than nearly every born American he knew. He wrapped up his glowing hyperbole and turned and motioned for Roland to come to the podium. A smattering of applause—weak, polite, reluctant applause that stopped nearly as soon as they started. Roland could count each beat of his heart, stimulated by the sudden inrush of alcohol to this bloodstream, exacerbated still by the panic of indecision. He thought of Hamlet—*to remove this crazy get-up or not to remove*—and laughed. *I will be this person. I will sell this motherfucker.*

He entered the stage with his hands aloft as though to the cheers of adoring fans. But no one was cheering. When the audience laid eyes on the man before them, outfitted as he was and elevated by his cowboy boots to the height of six-foot-eight, some of them turned to one another as if confused. Others tapped their fingers on the screens of their devices issuing urgent communiques.

Roland stepped to the microphone. "Sounds to me like you're wondering why I showed up dressed like a Mexican revolutionary. You're saying *What's the meaning of this? Why would he not show up wearing his karate uniform—his gi?* As some of you might know, I was a martial arts instructor at this very university not so long ago, and I used my martial arts training to kill the two men who attacked me recently. So why the Mexican outfit instead of the karate gi? It's simple. My Pancho Villa ensemble is meant to celebrate the fighting spirit inside all freedom-loving people willing to die rather than surrender their right to self-determination."

Some in the audience voiced their approval. For his part, Roland had not done much homework on Villa and did not want to press too hard on the historical figure he'd chosen to represent. He needed to depart quickly from the boilerplate rhetoric.

"I challenge everyone to find an example of someone in Mexico who has been prosecuted for defending himself. I bet you'll come up empty. I'll bet the only people you'll find in trouble for self-defense are in English-speaking nations, so-called first-world countries, like the UK for example. And it's coming to a theater near you!" Roland had heard about a few such egregious prosecutions and figured the subject could lay a good foundation for his platform today.

"BUT YOU'RE A FREE MAN!" shouted someone, a male. Shouted not in a hostile way, but with a matter-of-fact incredulity that challenged Roland's remarks as non sequitur.

"Th-th-that's true. That's true, of course." He cursed himself inwardly for not preparing a proper speech or at least a stack of notes to flip through. Lest he devolve into a stuttering fool, he re-focused his mind and pressed the tip of his tongue to the back of his front teeth to gather his resolve.

"The fact that I'm walking the streets today is a mere trick of the law, much to the consternation of many politicians and media stars, not to mention vast swathes of self-righteous neo-Marxists who bend and swirl like tall grass in the wind. The San Francisco chief of police, of all people, gave me the old Heisman straight arm—" Roland posed briefly in the manner of the famous trophy, "—after I took out one of the most wanted murders in the country, because he didn't like the way I spoke to his employees, who are not, in truth, his employees. They are the city's employees, the people's employees."

The audience, he observed, was beginning to sway in his direction, inclining toward him to pay closer attention, cellphones pocketed or set in their laps. Inclining toward him in sympathy as well, perhaps. Either way, their attention emboldened him. He'd never spoken to a live audience before and he began to sense that these people, many of them anyway, had not come for any particular ideological reason, but as curiosity-seekers, to behold the magnificent killer and listen to him talk about his bold and violent actions. His muttered conviction of just a few minutes ago came back to him—*I will sell this motherfucker.* When he'd said that, he meant only to sell the costume with a vague and unreasoned appeal to Pancho Villa, but now he realized he had to sell something else, a message, or even just an idea. *Maybe I'm the victim here.*

"The people in power—specifically the FBI, the Fascist Bureau of Intimidation—who warned me, threatened me actually, not to speak out about my entirely lawful actions—they bristle at me for one reason: I offend their unelected egos. I represent the truth, which is that they cannot protect you; and they don't like someone popping up his head to point that out. They should be thanking me. I mean, there was a serial killer, a known serial killer, a most-wanted man who they'd let slip through their fingers, a psychopathic murderer, walking around my neighborhood chatting up a woman in my building. That alone ought to call for a big public whoops. Instead, when I call them to haul away the body, they jump on me for having a bad attitude and—*yes*—for being a little drunk. I admit it, but all the more reason not to keep a working man up all night with a lot of questions when the corpse of a murderer is leaking a puddle of hemoglobin on his hardwood floors."

"So you're the victim here?" someone shouted.

"Quite the opposite. If I'd shied away and kept my mouth shut, then I would be a victim. My reason for speaking is to let everyone know that the government is supposed to work for us. The balance is tipping, and if it goes too far their way it's impossible to tip it back without a violent civil war. Inherent in the right to life, liberty and the pursuit of happiness is the obligation to defend oneself from violent attacks. And the more the politicians and the media mesmerize us into believing that they have our backs, the more gleefully the criminals will rub their greedy hands together."

"Do you own a gun?" It came from a woman in the back.

"I don't. But I'm not opposed to the Second Amendment if that's what you're driving at." He looked to Sreedhar Unpronounceable, who was sitting in the front row just below him. "Isn't the question-and-answer part supposed to come at the end?"

Sreedhar shrugged and rotated his finger in a circular forward motion to say keep the ball rolling.

"But more important than keeping the Second Amendment intact—more important by an order of magnitude I'd say—is to punish crime. When a civil society becomes so civil that it's civil even to its violent elements, then it's become barbaric in reverse. Like a cartoon character, we're sawing off the branch we're sitting on. Our bloated prison system is an admission that we don't want to live in a safe society. Authoritarian governments don't have to punish what you and I call crime because people are scared too shitless to step out of line, so their prisons are full of people who are suspected of opposing the authorities. Our penal system contains very few political prisoners and puts a lie to any claim that we live in an authoritarian country; but instead, it demonstrates that we are a distressingly apathetic citizenry, so apathetic that the word *citizen* has nearly lost its meaning. When someone pulls out a weapon with intent to cause harm or death, or if he breaks into a house, that person should not be thinking about what might happen if he gets caught. That person, that *criminal,* should believe—believe at a cellular level, deep in his reptilian lobe—that he is putting his life on the line. In North Korea, your whole life can change if you step on the wrong patch of grass, or grimace at the wrong statue. It's that way with all theocratic regimes—very little crime as most of us understand that word."

"Are you drunk? North Korea is not a theocracy!" It was a male voice this time, belonging to someone who lacked the nerve to raise his head.

"Au contraire, mon frère." Roland scanned the collage of young faces. "North Korea is the most religious country in the world. Its head of state is declared to be a god. Whether you're a monotheist or an atheist or something in between, I think we can all agree that the pudgy little fuck in his palace in Pyongyang is not a god. I mean, the Soviets might have put a picture of Stalin in every home and every cell in the gulags, but they were sensible enough not to call him a god."

The doors at the back of the hall burst open admitting a splash of light from the lobby. A noisy band of protesters had arrived to commandeer the space. They wore black clothing and hooded sweatshirts with the hoods drawn over their heads, and some carried signs that looked hastily prepared. He made out one of them: *Hate Speech Isn't Free, We Charge*. Then another, this one bilingual: *Punch a Nazi - Putsch a Nazi* with a little hammer and sickle drawn in one corner. These were shock troops drawn by text messages from a few within the venue informing them that a fascist held a microphone in a public forum. The squelch from a bullhorn ricocheted off the walls.

The man with the bullhorn got right to it. "GET OFF THE STAGE OR FACE OUR RAGE." Sreedhar stood and went to the back of the hall to address the situation. The two police officers he'd met in the plaza stepped out of the shadows and made their presence known by standing up and moving to the side of the stage with their hands on their gunless utility belts.

Roland held up a hand and spoke very softly into the microphone. "Easy there. Everyone calm down." He looked at the male with the bullhorn, who was busy assessing the attitude of the two police officers. "Why don't you come up and join me? You can explain the source of your rage to all the good people here." The man hesitated and looked at his cohorts as if to make sure they would not disapprove. "What are you afraid of?" Roland continued, beckoning with his hand, "We can share the mic. I was just about to launch in about the Ancient Egyptians. Turns out the Great Pyramid was built at the exact geographical center of the planet and its base is a perfect square oriented to true north, which would be really, really hard to do even today. Even more astonishing, its various dimensions encode the number for pi three or four different ways."

Audience members swiveled their heads side to side in apparent perplexed confusion at the sudden change of topic, while others chuckled in appreciation of Roland's agile pivot. Now he spoke to the audience.

"I could go on about global grid lines formed by dozens of the most ancient and mysterious megalithic structures on earth, but before I do I think our angry friend here should have a chance to tell us what about my appearance here so upsets him and his posse."

The man, now halfway to the stage, scruffy-bearded, nearly as tall as Roland but carrying much more mass, whispered into his megaphone. "We're here to confront your toxic masculinity."

"Toxic masculinity? You're the one who burst into the hall ordering people around."

"Not *people,* just *you...*" his voice came through more loudly now, "...the fascist in the racist outfit."

"If you'd been on time, you'd have heard that I'm wearing this to celebrate the spirit of independence over oppressive authority, which will always be a radical concept."

"And what does that have to do with the Ancient Egyptians?"

"Look, sir, I have this room for sixty minutes, booked through the proper channels at this great university, my alma mater. This is my house for the time being. I'd be happy to share some of my time with you, but not the way you're going about it. If you want to come up on stage and have a little chat that would be fine; but if not, I'll have to ask you to put down the bullhorn and take a seat or lead your band of merry malcontents out of here so I can get back to business."

"You didn't come here to talk about Ancient Egypt." Now he was shouting, the horn at his side. "That much I know."

"You know nothing of the sort," he struggled to keep his voice low, but the strain showed in his face as a tightening around the eyes. "The good folks at the Mario Savio Sewing Circle gave me no agenda nor even asked what I was going to say in this free speech event."

"You have a huge digital footprint. The Mario Savio fascists know exactly what your message is."

"Ok, I'll play. What did I come here to say? What have you come to protest against?"

At a loss for words, the man moved his mouth mutely like a grouper fish behind aquarium glass, finally resorting to repetition.

"I said it already—*toxic masculinity*. And I'll add patriarchy and cultural appropriation."

"Those are just buzzwords. Can you be more specific?"

"You promote violence and now you're doing it while caricaturing Mexicanness."

"Your comrade back there is carrying a sign that says Punch a Nazi. Is that not promoting violence?"

"By any means necessary."

"Now you're quoting Malcolm X, who was quoting JP Sartre, and you probably don't even know it. Can't you come up with something original? It's Free Speech Day after all."

"Free speech is a dog whistle for capitalist oppression and racist aggression."

"And you're the one who gets to decide who's allowed a mic and who isn't? Have I got that right? Sounds to me like you're the fascist."

"You've transformed yourself into a symbol and once you do that, you're dangerous, and the First Amendment does not apply to dangerous symbols."

"Are you going to come up here and remove me? Because that's what you'll need to do if you want to get laid."

"Excuse me?"

"Be honest. That's all this is. You think if you can force this fascist off the stage, you'll have your pick of the hairy-legged fawns this afternoon."

"That's offensive."

"I'll tell you what's offensive—you interrupting my talk. No. Check that—you trying to stop me from speaking. And what's more, it's pathetic. You don't even have the nerve to come up on stage and share the mic after I politely invited you. You just want to stand down there sputtering your platitudes. Don't threaten action if you're not prepared to follow through. It makes you look weak, stupid, an—as I said—pathetic."

"Your last comment was so sexist and heteronormative that I don't want to share a stage with you. It would legitimize your ideas, to put them on equal footing with mine."

"You don't even have any ideas, only triggers. And I'm the trigger man. So be it. Halleluiah. But since you mentioned sexism, if you'd done any research at all on me, you'd know that I taught martial arts at this very university and specifically trained women how to fight off rapists. There are a lot of tricks you can use to immobilize a taller, stronger attacker. And more than one woman—more than one young, small woman—came back to thank me after she used these techniques to successfully resist an assault. And they were exhilarated, empowered, more confident than ever, and certainly not ashamed they had to use violence."

The man stepped up onto the stage and approached Roland with his megaphone raised to his mouth and led a chant with his other arm, pumping his upraised palm as though lifting the words from the throats of his supporters. "OFF THE STAGE. OFF THE STAGE. OFF THE STAGE." Roland turned and faced the man, a hefty, scraggily-bearded, two-hundred-and-fifty-pounder yelling into the megaphone as he approached. He could feel the waves of the man's amplified voice vibrating his face. When the bell of the bullhorn was a foot away from his nose, Roland determined he could reasonably construe an impending physical assault—on his eardrums at the very least—and took a step backward. The man advanced to close the space Roland had opened between them, punching at the air with his instrument as he continued to shout, "OFF THE STAGE." It was clear that the man intended to cover Roland's face with the cone and blast the demand into his very nostrils. Now Roland took a long step backward, raised his arms, and with alarming speed hopped off his left boot two feet into the air and delivered a crane kick with his right, a kick that in a combat situation would have landed on his opponent's jaw. His hat fell off as his boot struck the underside of the megaphone sending it spinning end-over-end, ten or twelve feet into the air. The audience sent up a collective WHOA. The agitator stood stunned, regarding his suddenly empty hand while Roland reached down behind his back as he landed and, without looking, caught his hat before it touched the floor while he tracked with both eyes the airborne megaphone as it fell, tumbling, toward the head of his aggressor. He snatched it out of the air by its handgrip with his right hand an inch before it could strike the man's skull, preventing what might have been a serious injury, and then placed his hat back on his head. It seemed all of one motion. The crowd reacted with a WHAA, as though they had witnessed a well-orchestrated magic trick or acrobatic stunt. He felt the urge to bow but refrained, his hat already back in place.

The two police officers appeared on stage and Roland handed one of them the bullhorn and then turned to the man, who looked a bit terrified.

"You're not dangerous enough to need to be killed." Roland raised his fist and shook it gently, symbolically. He spoke softly, and though the hall was quiet only the people in front could hear what he said, for he wanted it to be a private message delivered in public. "But if you get that close to my face again, you'll be shitting your own teeth tomorrow. And the way dentistry has progressed, I'm sure you can find a surgeon who can reattach them to your gums. You'll be the first man in history with a truly shit-eating grin."

The female officer was listening in. "That's enough. Break it up."

"Good idea," said Roland.

None of the devices recording the event picked up his words very clearly, and when it went viral his fans and detractors alike devoted countless hours debating what he'd said or might have said. Even the lip-readers weighed in. In the main, the public got the gist of it.

Sreedhar of the King's English stepped forward with a document in hand and showed it to the officers. The officers, Sreedhar, and the agitator formed a huddle around the piece of paper. Roland returned to the microphone and walked the audience through what was going on.

"My sponsor here is showing the officers that this man has violated the rules of engagement. He crossed the line when he opened up with his bullhorn on the stage, so he's forfeited his right to remain. He's created an unsafe space or some horseshit like that. But I'm willing to give him another chance." He looked imploringly to the audience. He'd pretty well won them over. "Whaddaya say we give him another chance and find out what exactly he has to say, other than *get off the stage?*" He swirled his right hand as though mixing the air. "C'mon. Whaddaya say we give him another chance?"

The crowd applauded and a few hooted their approval.

"But first he has to pass a little test. Nothing too difficult. We just need to find out if he's read any books. From what we've seen so far, his vocabulary is very limited, so we should find out if he even deserves to speak in front of a crowd at one of the world's premier academic institutions." He turned to Sreedhar and the officers. "Let him stay." And then to the agitator. "Do you want to speak to my audience? Give them a piece of your mind?" The man bit the inside of his cheek and sneered with one eye closed as he nodded. "The officer will hold onto the tool of your trade and give it to you on your way out." The officer gestured with the bullhorn and nodded his assent.

"Ok, big fella, you ready?"

"Fuck you."

The man pulled his hood back to reveal his unkempt hair and unhappy face, which resembled a carelessly peeled potato. Come to think of it, Roland observed, all of the faces in the self-proclaimed anti-fascist cohort—the one's not wearing masks—could have come from a Picasso painting, each one contorted in its own repellent way.

"That's not a very good start. A little gratitude would be appropriate."

"Gratitude for what?"

"Giving you a chance to show off your critical thinking skills. But first, before I hand you the microphone, you have to pass the Hazzard Inquisition."

"More fascist bullshit."

"Let's be clear. If I were a fascist, I'd have let the police remove you from this stage for breaking the rules set up to protect peaceful speakers like me from fascist goons like yourself. For the time being, this is my sovereign space, and I'd be happy to share it with you if you can name three plays by the Bard."

"The Bard?"

"William Shakespeare. He wrote nearly forty, and about half of them are famous. I'm asking you to name just three."

"Romeo and Juliet."

"That's one."

"King Henry."

"There were a bunch of Henrys. Which one do you mean?"

"The Eighth, I think. The one who executed all his wives."

"He killed only two out of six—that's a good average only in baseball. But fair enough—you stayed awake in high school. How about a third Shakespeare play?"

The man leaned back his head and peered at the ceiling as though he might spot the name of a Shakespeare play up there. Then he lowered his head and pursed his lips. He was about to accept defeat when one of his comrades, still standing in militant readiness at the back of the hall, blurted out, "DEATH IN VENICE." A few in the crowd laughed.

"Yeah. I was going to say that one."

Roland smiled and appealed to the audience. "Can anyone tell us who wrote *Death in Venice?*"

Someone yelled, "TOE-MAAS MANN."

"I think you meant *Merchant of Venice*. I can't give you credit for that."

"I don't give a shit about dead white male authors."

"How about black authors, living or dead, male, female or transblender? Can you name three of those? Three African American writers. Playwrights or novelists. And no help from your traveling zoo or it's over."

"Malcolm X."

"Sorry. He wrote a memoir, an autobiography."

The man shook his head. "This is bullshit."

"More of your razor-sharp critical thinking skills on display. Why not throw it open to your bovine coterie? Any of you back there?" He gestured to the line of black-clad protestors standing in the back. "You're here to champion the oppressed, right? Can any of you name some great black writers, and I don't mean rappers and poets?"

A few dejected troops along the back wall snarled loudly.

"Toni Morrison!"

"Maya Angelou!"

"Great! They're contemporary, but they'll do. Anyone from an earlier time, when blacks were actually being oppressed."

They remained silent. Morrison and Angelou were all they had.

"How 'bout you in the audience? Great black writers."

The names came forth. Ralph Ellison, Richard Wright, James Baldwin, Fredrick Douglas, Booker T. Washington, and several others that Roland had never heard of. He waited until they'd exhausted their collective list.

"Seems like my peaceful, well-mannered audience is more familiar with the literature of the oppressed than you party-crashers in the back. I'm thinking you should all take a seat and let me finish out my time here or toddle off and find another so-and-so to hassle." He turned to their leader. "Unfortunately, you've failed the test. I'll have to ask you to step off the stage."

"I'll stay so I can hear what you have to say about *ancient archeology.*" He stepped down and took a seat near the front, motioning with his hand for his followers to settle in.

Roland proceeded with his talk. "I graduated from this great university a few years ago with an English degree. And I'm almost inclined to say a *perfectly useless* English degree because an economic analysis would support the contention that a degree in English and half the other so-called disciplines for which universities award diplomas are perfectly useless. But I chose to take as many of the so-called hard classes as I could, classes that would have been required for an English degree a few decades ago. I loaded up on the old stuff, stuff that doesn't even look like English anymore, works that have to, in some sense, be translated to be understood, written in forms that have to be decoded. Chaucer and the 15th and 16th century epics that followed. Stuff that makes Shakespeare read like a comic book. I could have opted to deconstruct the Brady Bunch for its oppressive patriarchy and heteronormativity. I could have delved into the lyrics of Snoop Dogg from a social class perspective. I could have immersed myself in victim-based politically motivated memoirs that are impossible to check for accuracy. All in the service of so-called literary analysis. No. My interest was in the evolution of the English language as practiced by the original literary masters— to bear the burden of a traditional curriculum."

The agitator-in-chief piped up. "I thought you were going to talk about archeology!"

"Patience, Attila, I'll get to that directly. So, I supplemented my study in English literature—and I include very little American Literature in that category, since I read that on my own for pleasure—with history and western philosophy, because my objective was to learn about the past— the older the better—and eventually I got around to taking a class in archeology. Well, it was in that first archeology class that I learned my most important lesson at this university, and it had nothing to do with the material being presented. It was about academia itself. I learned that the academic establishment—the vaunted experts—are hell-bent on excluding anything that does not fit neatly within their accepted narrative of human development. I could spend an hour telling you about some of the amazing things all over this world that defy explanation by the so-called experts, like the stone walls in Cuzco, Peru that predate the Incas, huge walls that look like jigsaw puzzles so tightly fitted that stonemasons of today with the most advanced tools could not replicate them. The Incas had no idea who built them and simply arranged their own far inferior masonry on top of them. Same with the Aztecs when they discovered Teotihuacan—had no idea who built it. But they founded their civilization at that magnificent abandoned site, amid impossible buildings that conformed to celestial alignments far more advanced than anything they could come up with. The long-standing theory about the first people to settle in North and South America has been shot, but most anthropologists and archaeologists won't give up their theory that puts the first humans here only thirteen thousand years ago. Scholars who present evidence to counter the theory have been routinely, reflexively, shunned by academics. Research grants pulled, jobs lost, reputations ruined. I could spend hours if I had time to make a slide deck showing you evidence from around the world that debunks the established timeline of human development. The rain-weathering on the Great Sphinx itself shows that it predates the Egyptians by about eight thousand years, and then there's the extensive stone pillar complex of Gobekli Tepe in Turkey, still mostly buried, that blows the whole timeline apart. Hunter-gatherers twelve thousand years ago with no metal tools were not supposed to be building massive stone monuments. It's eight thousand years older than Stonehenge and no one can explain how it was possible.

So, what's my point? Why is the Butcher Slayer so interested in ancient archeology? Because we've hit a wall, and going back, all the way back, seems the only way forward. Our technological advances have outstripped our ability to adapt psychologically. If we don't stop dulling our brains with novel conveniences, we'll lose our minds, and without our minds, we'll never figure out who and what were the ancient people that built so many massive beautiful perfect things, some in very remote places, things we'd be hard pressed to replicate with our finest instruments of measurement and most powerful industrial machines. We look upon such works of genius and shrug. Well, I for one will not shrug, and I despise those who do or who make up absurd theories as to how such things were built."

Roland scanned the young faces to make sure they were still alert. Someone in the back put up his hand and barked, "What happens if we don't give a shit?" Roland nodded in consideration of the question.

"Suicide. In the micro first, and then the macro. More and more young people, sensing nothing to live for, are taking the easy way out when they realize they'll never be rich or famous, or because they've been ostracized on social media. There's a growing, generalized anxiety from crowded isolation that could be cured if the Arbiters of Truth and the Keepers of Science would simply admit their mistakes and acknowledge that the human race, as we call ourselves, is a stunted breed left over after the waters receded following the great cataclysm that deluged the megalithic coastal civilizations around the world. We're the ones who survived because we dwelt in the hills and caves. We're the drooling idiot left alone to play with a garage sale chemistry set."

Roland checked the crowd again to make sure he still had their attention. As far off the beaten path as he was, he intended to go even further.

"And when the idiot gets bored, he thinks it's a good idea to see if he can make the viruses even more communicable and deadly, on the pretext of finding a cure in case a superbug evolves naturally—but that's a lie. He just wants to do it, to put his science to the test, and he needs a plausible reason and doesn't care if the superbug escapes, because who gives a fuck anyway since life has no meaning in the first place. And don't dare question the motives of the Overlords or show them contradictory evidence or they'll bully you off the stage like the self-appointed morality police that joined us today."

Roland noticed that the chief militant had returned to his retinue at the rear of the hall, and it looked like they were preparing to leave, finding no political angle from which to attack Roland's archaeological assertions and now themselves coming under rebuke.

"And the one thing I have to say to all of you so-called anti-fascists is this—and I hope you're listening carefully—before you start calling people in this society, our society, your fellow citizens for Chrissakes—before you call them fascists, have the decency to read about the horrendous acts of cruelty and state-sponsored murder perpetrated by authoritarian governments and theocratic institutions around the world in, say, the last fifty, sixty years. Educate yourself on the origins and nature of actual fascism before you continue tossing that word around, and the same goes for Nazism. You have to do that work yourself because God knows the universities are not going to delve into the subject in any meaningful detail."

He stopped himself. A word he'd said has stopped him. *Chrissakes* could be forgiven as a casual expression, but then he'd followed it up with a *God knows*. Hard to dismiss that as an accident. In the passion of his diatribe, Roland had unconsciously invoked the divine. Perhaps, he reflected, he needed some help to *sell this motherfucker*. He forged ahead.

"People as naïve as you are capable of formulating laughable propositions and arriving at the most absurd conclusions, even misidentifying virtue as evil and feeling awfully smug in doing so. In order to be as good and moral as you think you are, you must first understand evil without letting it drown you in cynicism. Your facile, puerile cynicism springs from the vague notion that someday soon you might need to get a job that makes a meaningful contribution to the society that you've decided preemptively to hate.

Barging in here with your hoods up and your faces masked behind bandannas to try to shut me down takes no courage, because the whole campus is a safe-space for you. You're free to compete with yourselves on who can out-preen and out-posture the other on these once-hallowed grounds, because you're risking nothing. Try taking your show on the road to a truly authoritarian society, where free speech is not allowed, and see how far you get. You'll be begging for a ride to an actual safe space—the local US Embassy."

He glanced at the wall clock and noted he had half an hour left. The vodka rush was beginning to wear off. He stood there cursing himself inwardly for not having had the foresight to fill a water bottle with the stuff before arriving at the venue. The ride was over. The wave had flattened out on the beach. Yes—he could have kept talking, but the emergent craving for alcohol would have distracted his focus and possibly exposed him as someone less than the man who had arrived thirty minutes before with his arms raised in existential victory.

"I've said enough for now. I'm willing to take any questions you might have." He motioned for Sreedhar to release the handheld mic into the crowd. A young woman decided not to wait for the mic to come her way and shouted out "You're all over the map, Roland Hazzard. What does any of that have to do with the question of lethal self-defense? How far does someone have to go before you would snap his neck?"

"I don't know. It's more art than science. As to your first question, I was trying to make the point that prisons are not a normal feature of a healthy society. The ancients didn't have them, not to any great extent. Prisons were used to house important captives, like an enemy prince or king—someone you could ransom. Actual criminals were either kicked out of town or dispatched on the spot. There was no concept of a walled penitentiary. It took a lot of time and effort to make solid buildings. What sense would it make to spend your limited human and natural resources building complex structures to house criminals who you then have to feed? To do so would be insane. We think our penal system makes us civilized—no. It makes us look stupid. The Romans used their sewer system to hold the criminals that were spared execution. Judges served to decide whether you were guilty of whatever it was you were accused of and, if so, whether you should be permitted to live and if so, how much compensation you had to pay your victim; and compensation often included slavery for some period of time, what today we might call indentured servitude because slaves had rights too. All very neat and clean, no conniving lawyers or creative mental incapacity defenses. Clean and very inexpensive, monetarily and administratively."

"What are you suggesting?" a male voice called out, the microphone still not in use, "Exterminate or enslave everyone in prison and close them all down?"

"No—and I'm not here to extemporize on public policy. I'm suggesting that we not only teach people how to defend themselves and others but that we instill in them their obligation to do so. The law is still on the side of the good, at least partially, so wake up every day emotionally prepared, morally prepared, to end the life of an attacker, and pretty soon—and I mean in a generation to two—there won't be the need for so many prisons and police and courtrooms and judges and lawmakers. The bad guys will be afraid to act out. But today we think of compassion as the highest of virtues when it is, in fact, the weakest, and we have demoted courage to the bottom of the list when in fact it is the rarest of them all."

The young man who'd asked the questions now had the mic in his hand. "So street justice—execution on the spot. Aren't you promoting a sort of anarchy?"

Roland noticed that more people were quietly filing in, probably due to word-of-text from the people already there. The wonders of instant electronic communications, he thought, a double-edged sword to be sure, and one he'd found more indispensable than alcohol in the furtherance of his persona. "Welcome stragglers. Thank you for coming." The hall was now completely full, with people lining the walls, and they all were strangely attentive. He waited until they were situated before he continued. "The gentleman here has asked if I am in favor of anarchy, and I'll tell you this: If on one end of the spectrum we have authoritarian government control—call it fascism—and on the other end we have anarchy, I say we should err on the side of anarchy. That seems rather obvious to me, and I'd be willing to bet that the cities with the highest murder rates are in states with very strict gun laws, but I have not done the research on that." He patted the bottle in his front pocket and resisted the urge to pull it out and finish it off.

The man with the mic continued. "So just as a thought experiment, let's say that most of the public is armed or otherwise equipped and ready for self-defense and the crime rate drops and the prisons are mostly empty or closed down—what do we do with the murderers and rapists, because there still will be some?"

"Feed them to the dogs. Next question."

Sreedhar retrieved the mic and handed it to an eager-looking woman.

"My question is about capital punishment, so that fits right in. Are you aware that studies show capital punishment is not a deterrent to crime? How does your philosophy of lethal self-defense square with that?"

"That's two questions—let's start with the first. Imagine, as a thought experiment, that the state—any hypothetical state—decreed that the crime of murder would be punishable by death unless it was committed on a Tuesday or a Thursday. You see where I'm going with this. It's pretty obvious that pre-meditated murders would skew toward Tuesdays and Thursdays. That would be the best test for the theory that capital punishment is not a deterrent. As for the second question, my philosophy, as you call it, is not well enough developed to merit that term.

It's more of an advocacy or, better yet, a lament, a lament that the fate of violent criminals is all too often left to the discretion of judges and the machinations and manipulations of diabolical lawyers and, increasingly, to naïve mental health professionals. My point is that if violent attacks are punished on the spot by citizens, those sorts of crimes will be reduced to a minimum and all that will be left are the most determined premeditators, psychopaths like the Glendale Butcher."

"And what do we do when we catch that sort?"

"As I said, feed them to the dogs, Monday through Sunday. That would add some deterrent I'd bet."

"I don't follow the metaphor *feed them to the dogs*," the young woman said.

Roland surveyed the crowd. "Has anyone ever read *Antigone* by Sophocles?" A few people raised their hands. "The rest of you can ask them more about the Ancient Greek classic after this is over, if you're interested. The story relies on a fundamental truth that no one wants to be eaten by dogs. Can we all agree on that—no one wants to be eaten by wild animals?" The crowd remained silent, nonplussed. His words had not sunk in. "Seriously," he raised his voice, "if you had a choice to have your dead body, or the corpse of a loved one, buried safely in the ground or cremated, or else eaten by a pack of dogs, how many of you would select *eaten by dogs?*" No one raised a hand. "The aversion to the prospect of having your dead body become a carcass to be ripped apart by dogs or birds or what have you is older than history, far older. Burial rites are one of the earliest expressions of human culture and are bound up in notions of the soul and the afterlife. The Greeks, for example—and this is the source of the central conflict in the Sophocles tragedy I mentioned—regarded the sanctity of a dead body as such a serious matter that after a battle they would bury not only their own dead but the enemy dead as well, for they believed that the soul could not move on to the afterworld if the corpse was left above ground to be ripped apart by animals."

"ARE YOU SERIOUS?" someone shouted.

"As a car battery wired to your balls. The point is that Greeks were not unique in their respect for the dead, and that respect was an expression of a prehistoric, even primordial, horror of preliterate humans watching their deceased relatives and loved ones torn apart as carrion by aggressive scavengers. So, when the King of Thebes declared under pain of death that Polynices's body be left where it fell on the battlefield, that was no small matter; but his sister, Antigone, spread dirt over his body anyway, willing to accept the ultimate punishment to save the soul of her fallen brother. I believe that primordial aversion still exists today, and just as profoundly."

"Will this be covered on the midterm?" shouted someone else. The audience laughed. When the last chuckle subsided, a different woman had the mic in her hand.

"Mister Hazzard, I think you had most of us in your corner up until now. Are you truly proposing that we throw the dead bodies of executed murderers to packs of wild dogs? I doubt many of even the most hardcore death penalty advocates would go for that."

Roland found himself again riding another wave of inspiration and closed his eyes to better coax his mind for a worthy reply. He realized that if he'd taken out the bottle when he'd wanted it moments ago and swigged from it, he'd have lost all credibility and that what he was about to say would carry no force. The room, he knew, still belonged to him. He stared hard into a point at the very center of the assembly.

"No. I'm not," he spoke slowly and calmly. "If I were in charge of the state, they'd be ground up and mixed with grain and packed into cans with their faces pasted on the labels." Gasps of horror rose from the audience above a ripple of nervous laughter. "I'm not kidding around here. You'd see the murderer's face and a lot of personal details: name, crimes, parents' names, help me out here."

"THAT'S SICK!" someone said at the top of her lungs.

"Maybe so. But it would probably do the trick. Only the most deranged individual would snicker at the thought of his mugshot staring out from a dog food label with the details of his pathetic, ignominious life bullet-pointed underneath it."

"I LIKE THE IDEA," someone else chimed in. "When are you running for office?" More laughter.

"I do have to be running, but not for office. I need to get back over the bridge before the traffic gets too hairy. I'll let you guys hammer out the rest of the details."

"YOUR TIME'S NOT UP!" shouted a woman. "Tell us more."

"Ok. One more observation—probably the most important one of all. If we start teaching our children that there's no such thing as boys and girls, we might as well just slit their throats, and then slit our own, to deprive our conquerors of the satisfaction."

With that, he lifted his hat straight up like a magician revealing a miraculously bald head, dropped it back in place, bowed ever so slightly, then spun about-face on his bootheels and walked off. He found his way to the back door of the building through a maze of hallways he remembered well, then out into the little parking lot reserved for tenured faculty hidden under the trees behind the building annex. He breathed in the resinous redwoods and headed into their protective shade then, quickly, unnoticed, trotted down a small embankment at whose bottom driveled Strawberry Creek meagerly westward into a less peopled section of the campus. Cigarette butts here and there. A refuge for the tobacco-puffing pariah class. He finished the Smirnoff and pocketed the empty bottle so as not to add to the litter. The Eucalyptus Grove lay close, and beyond that the West Gate.

Before he emerged from the ravine into the open space of Crescent Lawn, he hung the bandolier on a low branch of a venerable copper beech tree. Then he strode—just a random hombre under a cowboy hat—to Oxford Street and thence to his pathetic excuse for a car.

~~~~~

As Roland approached the onramp to Highway 80 westbound to the Bay Bridge back to San Francisco, his immediate future flashed before his mind. Driving the clown car back to his bunker struck him as the worst of all possible decisions. It wouldn't take long for boredom to force him past his fear of the public and out his door to secure the one reliable remedy for both the boredom and the fear, and he would wind up listing around Chinatown or North Beach or Union Square in a blackout until some self-deputized agent of the common good spotted the notorious Roland Hazzard drunk and called the police. Roland Hazzard was a scorn. At least he believed himself to be. A man of small repute, no doubt, but repute enough to find friends and foes alike among his anonymous fellow men. Roland might enjoy the hearty good wishes of a hundred casual strangers, but it would take only one motivated foe to alter the course of his evening or, perhaps, his life. He swung the wheel away from the onramp and navigated to the other side of the highway and headed in the opposite direction. Highway 80 traversed the continent from San Francisco to Hackensack, and anywhere but San Francisco was okay with him. The notion of an extended ramble around the United States entertained his fancy for a moment, and he might have followed the inclination had the vehicle beneath him been more roadworthy; but as soon as he entered East Richmond and passed the Solano Avenue exit, Roland knew exactly where he was going. Back to the womb. Sandpoint in the fall would take no getting used to.

This was new territory to him, north of Berkeley and beyond. The car, which he'd bought from a stranger three years ago, never had ranged under his power very far from The City. The brackish mudwaters of the back bay seemed to him, as he passed through Vallejo—the stomping grounds of the Zodiac Killer—the perfect place to dump a body.

~~~~~

An hour later, at Vacaville, he left I-80 and headed due north to link up with Interstate 5. He stopped for gas in Corning, a little farm town set in olive country, then guided his weary vehicle into the parking lot of the Rolling Hills Casino Hotel and picked up his phone. His social media feeds were blowing up. Enterprising digital editors already had produced abbreviated and annotated versions of the speech, still fresh in his mind. Titles like *Hazzard Owns Berkeley SJWs* and *Roland Dunks on Dumbshits*. Somehow, someone had managed to obtain more than one recording of the speech and zoom in on certain dramatic moments—a close-up of the megaphone spinning in the air, for example—and splice those segments into the larger recording to make for a presentation akin to a sporting event shot from different angles and edited to produce and exhilarating effect. The moment the point of his boot struck the body of the megaphone, the wide-eyed shock of the man who'd held it, the moment Roland's hand snatched it from the air, the sweep of his other arm to grab the hat, like a highlight reel of a ballet. All compiled and published on the web in the space of an hour. Roland had to laugh. It was masterful. He sent it to Joshua with the message: *I don't think I'll ever top this.*

He went inside the hotel and bought a bathing suit at the gift shop and lifted a towel from a housekeeping cart and took a swim in the pool. He tested his lungs, gliding back and forth lengthwise underwater nearly three times before coming up for air. He rested and tried again, and a third time and a fourth, until on the fifth attempt he made it four times back and forth on a single breath. A boy and a girl, seven or eight he guessed, stood poolside watching him.

"I can do that once across the short way," said the boy.

"That you would even think to test yourself in the first place is a good sign."

"What does that mean?" said the girl.

"It means he knows already that his body can be very useful."

"Yes," she said. "But I can have babies."

"Right. And the boys have to learn to be strong so they can build the houses where the babies are going to live."

"Girls can build houses too."

"Of course. But wouldn't you like the boy to help?"

The two kids looked at each other and the boy nodded to her to say that what Roland had just said seemed reasonable, and the next generation was saved. Roland pushed himself up and out the pool and went into the shower room and washed off the chlorinated water and dried himself and got dressed and pulled on his Laredos and put on his hat and went inside to play a little blackjack. He knew enough about the game not to get hurt, as long as he stuck to the odds chart, which he'd memorized as a teenager. He picked a ten-dollar table where sat an elderly man by himself, a Modoc Indian with a long gray braided ponytail sticking out the opening in the back of his green John Deere baseball cap. Just to be polite, Roland asked him if he minded that he sat down, though he knew permission was not required, and the man nodded ok. He gave the dealer a c-note for a stack of chips and let the game begin.

The Modoc was a reckless player. Hit a hard 13 with the dealer showing a 6. The card came a king, and the dealer raked his chips into the tray. The man made another bonehead play—failed to hit a soft 14 with the dealer showing a 10. Roland was just passing time, playing like a robot, paying more attention to the other player's decisions than to his own. The old Modoc clearly was not considering mathematics to make his moves in a game where success over the long run was based on one's ability to calculate odds. He made another bad play. In the short time since Roland sat down, the old Indian had lost nearly half his chips and Roland could conclude only that the man believed he had powers of divination that could beat the odds and it appeared those powers were not working very well today.

Roland worked up the nerve to say something and decided on, "Having a rough run I see."

"Don't worry, we'll get it all back." The man seemed friendly enough.

"We? You got a lizard in your pocket?"

"I'm not talking about the chips. They come and go on their own."

"All what then?"

"The continent. Both continents."

The cards and the chips continued to come and go while they conversed.

"North *and* South America?"

"As you call them. Named after a European. Imagine that."

"I guess the Central part is a fait accompli."

"Fate's got nothing to do with it."

"So, what's the plan?" Roland had to stop himself from adding *chief*.

"That will cost you a drink."

The dealer summoned the waitress and they played in silence until the drinks came, whiskey and Coke for the Indian and just plain Coke for Roland. They clinked glasses. "Good luck," said Roland.

"You don't know the plan yet."

"I've kept my end of the bargain. Just don't tell me the Indians are going to take back the land by force. If you tell me that I'll consider myself cheated."

"No. We can't do it militarily of course."

"Then how?"

"Genetically."

"Outbreed the conquerors? Is that what you're saying?"

"No. We will transform them."

"How, by doing some kind of a spirit dance?"

"It's a global initiative, about ten years away. The intercontinental social justice council will authorize the release of nanobots into the food, air, and water and, most importantly, vaccines that will genetically modify the populations of all the great land masses to restore them to their indigenous states."

"Interesting. I'll still be me, but I'll look like a Native American version of me."

"Yes. The testing is underway and the results are promising."

"What about African-Americans?"

"Depends on how racially pure they are. They're much harder to change than the whites, generally."

Roland thought about it as he watched the man suck in his cheeks to draw the drink through the thin plastic straw. They played cards. The buzzes, pings, and pops of the electronic gambling machines arrayed around them ricocheted off each other to fill the air with a rollicking confusion. Had the noises been color-coded it would have been impossible to concentrate amid the psychedelic blizzard. As it was, his gambling partner's deranged fantasies put Roland's mind off kilter. Yet he could not resist exploring the depths of the man's imagination, uncertain as to whether it was the product of psychosis or a grandiose taunt. How far can he carry this, Roland wondered.

"I think there might be some resistance to this plan, particularly from the privileged whites."

"Yes of course. That's why we've been softening up the younger generations before they start to enjoy their privileges. We're teaching them to hate the privilege, to be ashamed of what they came from and who they are."

"We? You and your lizard again?"

"You never know who you're talking to, son."

"Unless you actually do."

"Especially not then."

"Ok. Once you guys genetically purge all the white people out of the Americas, what are you going to call the two continents?"

"You think I'm kidding around with you here?"

"Isn't the drink worth a few questions?"

"Not stupid questions. What do you care what we change the names to?"

"Fair enough. But I'm still not sold. Tell me—how far back you gonna go? The global genetic engineers will restore the continents to their native ethnicities as they were at what point in time exactly? I could be wrong, but I think we have plenty of Neanderthal DNA lying around. You plan to give those dumbasses a second bite at the apple?"

"I know you're being facetious, but this is a serious enterprise."

"Maybe you could bring me to one of your meetings."

The man sucked another mouthful through the tiny straw. The creases on his weathered face stretched and whitened as they pinched together like the spines on a folded fan.

"Why not just drink from the glass? You're working awfully hard there. Aren't plastic straws illegal anyway? Aren't you worried it might someday get stuck like a chicken bone in the throat of a majestic turtle gliding through the South Pacific?"

"Just that sort of attitude is why we're going to start with the whites."

"Makes sense. Start at the top. But what are you going to do with all the diabolical inventions, the war machines controlled by artificial intelligence? I'd keep all the good stuff the whites created, but if you keep the bad stuff too then you'll be in the same kettle of fish heads."

"You're talking about phase two."

The Modoc hit a soft 17 with the dealer showing 6. The worst play he'd made so far, but the card came a 4 so he won the hand and reinforced his counterintuitive approach to blackjack.

"Phase two?"

The man rattled the ice cubes at the bottom of his empty glass.

"Get this man another drink so we can hear about phase two."

They played in silence until the drink came. Roland had doubled his chip stack and, true to plan, increased his bet size to better use the house's money against the house. "Let's hear about phase two." The Modoc had had time to think, so this had better be good.

"We need to dumb down the species as a whole. That should be self-evident to anyone paying attention."

Roland caressed his chin. "Go on."

"So, once we eliminate whiteness and its legacies of power…"

Roland couldn't help but interrupt. "Excuse me, but you talk like a college professor. Are you so employed?"

"I'm divulging secrets, son. I can't tell you who I am or what I do."

"Fair enough. So once whiteness is eliminated, then what?"

"Breeding control."

Roland thought about it for a second. "Seems to me if you did phase one right, you wouldn't need breeding control."

"Not to control racial populations, but to control the decline of intelligence."

"Decline of intelligence? That could mean different things."

"Intelligence is like a weapon, a weapon of the mind that degrades the spirit. As the human race becomes smarter, the spirit is threatened. The spirit is in fact denied. Consciousness is reduced to a category of the material, which is an abomination to the Great Spirit. The material sciences need to be de-emphasized or the human race will destroy itself and make the world uninhabitable for future species to pursue their spiritual journeys."

"Okay. Let's say all that's true, that there's a soul and that…"

"I said nothing about the soul."

"Soul, spirit—aren't those the same thing?"

"The soul is the memory of all the lives experienced by the spirit. The spirit is the life itself, the companion to the Creator in the Creation."

"What religion is that?"

"The first religion, before human hierarchies corrupted it and developed all the bastard religions that we have now. It never had a name."

"You're pretty slippery—I'll give you that. Now, tell me how we're going to control the buildup of scientific intelligence so we can return to our ancient spiritual devotions."

"Now you're the one saying *we*."

"You got me there, chief. I'm nearly sold. Halfway down the garden path."

"Garden of Eden, yes. There's a glimmer of truth in that ancient story."

"Fine, but let's talk about the future. Breeding control. Intelligence suppression. Are we going to euthanize all the smart babies before they're old enough to know that they need to act stupid to stay alive?"

"Enforced cousin marriage."

"Orwell's got nothin' on you!"

"Orwell did not contemplate the rise of the machines. The only way to stop the advance of our monstrous technology is to inhibit our ability to bring the future to fruition."

"I see. Enforced cousin marriage will keep the IQs down and the future at bay. But how will we enforce this policy?"

"The devil's in the details. All pregnancies will have to be registered so there are no unauthorized births."

"You're talking about forced abortions, a kind of eugenics, but only in reverse."

"Precisely—*reverse eugenics*. That's the phrase we use."

"They'd better get rid of all the guns first. I think universal disarmament should come before phase two."

The dealer dealt himself an ace and checked his hole card and turned over a jack and raised his eyebrows and swept the players' chips into the tray. Two new players, Mexican ladies of late middle age, set their drinks and chips on the table and sat down in the seats between Roland and the harbinger of the post-Caucasian utopia.

"Bullets too. Guns and bullets."

Roland nodded fair enough to show that adding bullets to the ban was perfectly reasonable in light of the big picture and stood up to depart the table. He looked at the old Modoc from the vantage of his full height and fixed him with his most pitiless regard. Before the man could infer contempt or hostility or any such unwelcome intention, the handsome young cowboy cracked a smile. "I know I'm gonna wind up telling someone about this conversation, and I'd like to have something to call you. I know the sensitive nature of the information you gave me makes it impossible for you to reveal your identity, but I'm guessing you have one of those spirit names like Spotted Elk or Teetering Bolder. How 'bout Dyslexic Spider?"

"Gamboling Fool." Roland knew he meant running, not wagering.

"I bet you could sprint like Thorpe in your day."

"Only when they were chasing me."

Roland smiled again and tipped his hat. "Endeavor to persevere." He went to the cage and cashed in his chips. He'd had a good run of luck and, like a disciplined gambler, left the table before it ran out. He bought a sandwich at the bar and while he ate it stared at the television to avoid talking to a woman who had taken a seat two stools down.

"I like your hat." The hat sat on the bar between them.

"Made in Guatemala." He barely glanced at her. The bartender shot him a look to make sure Roland knew the nature of the parley into which he had just entered. Roland circled the rim of his water glass with the tip of his forefinger to say he did.

"You like to travel?"

Roland shrugged and kept his eyes on the TV.

She would not be deterred. "What brings you here? It can't be the luxurious rooms."

He kept his elbows on the bar and quickly improvised an amiable expression then turned his head slowly toward her. "I don't have a room here, ma'am."

"You're not staying here?"

"I think I just said that."

"No? The pool is just for guests of the hotel."

"You caught me. I'm just passing through. Needed a quick dip to stretch my muscles before I jumped back on the road."

"You're not a gambler? Looks like you did pretty well."

"You've been watching me? I'm usually aware when I'm under surveillance."

"I couldn't help myself. Those are very nice muscles you were stretching out there."

"How about I buy you a drink and we call it even?"

"Call it even?"

"So you don't rat me out for crashing the swimming pool."

"I was hoping we could share more than a drink."

"Miles to go before I sleep." He slid a twenty on the bar and looked at the bartender and tilted his head toward the woman to say pour her a drink and put on his hat and looked at her and touched the brim and said *ma'am* and left. As he walked to his car, he reflected that not so long ago he would have considered such an encounter or, one might say, *opportunity*, as a validation of his inborn good luck. Today he counted it as nothing more than an unwelcome temptation.

He pointed the car north and resumed his progress up Interstate 5 toward the forgotten counties of Tehama, Shasta, and Siskiyou. This was not the California of musical lore. Not the California his exuberant driver Singh had traveled so far to call home. Opioids must sell well up here, he thought. Meth labs bubbling right along provided their owners didn't get too ambitious. Roland tried to imagine the people who supported these oversized zip codes and realized he couldn't. Maybe they weren't all drug addicts. He studied the cars on the highway. Many of those he passed appeared to be in worse shape than his. Could it be that this part of the country was far more normal than where he lived, than where most Americans lived? Where Roland was headed, the Idaho Panhandle, was normal indeed, if friendly was normal and predictability a prerequisite for sanity.

As he crossed the Shasta County line into Siskiyou County, Mount Shasta rose before him off to the east. Roland resisted the notion that it was set there deliberately, a conscious force on the landscape and a vaguely threatening one. A long-dormant but still active volcano that lorded its power over the supplicant landscape. Why, he mused, is Mount Shasta in Siskiyou County and not in Shasta County? Either someone had decided to name the mountain after the county to the south or named the county to the south after the mountain to the north. He vowed to look up the name the natives called it, for that was its original name. Why not let it go back to that, since the California bureaucrats had made a mess of it?

The sunset slowly pinked the solitary snowclad alp, lending it an astronomical majesty. It said to all observers: *The universe proceeds like clockwork, and one day you will be ground to powder in its gears.* Roland decided not to drive past Mount Shasta, not to head into the darkening evening with the imperious singularity staring over his shoulder. He spent the night in Weed, situated due west of Mount Shasta where Route 97 split off from Interstate 5. Dining options were limited. He chose the Hi-Lo Café, closest to his motel. The drive had made him thirstier than he'd realized, and he drank three glasses of water before deciding on his order. A boy at the table across from him kept staring at his head. Roland ignored him until the boy found the nerve to speak.

"Gonna ink that dome?"

Roland looked at the man sitting next to the boy, presumably his father, and noted his muscular, heavily tattooed arms and the flames exploding from his shirt collar up his neck as if his head were poking up out of Hell.

"No one can afford my price."

The boy looked confused. "You mean you don't have enough money?"

"No—I'm *charging* money."

The boy looked at his father, but the father did not look at the boy since he was now looking at Roland, his expression skeptical though impassive. The boy saw that his father was following the conversation and resumed.

"You want someone to pay you to tattoo your head?"

"Prime real estate." The boy looked at his father and whispered *what's that?*

"He's famous."

"You famous?"

"This head gets a lot of airtime, and I'm offering it to the highest bidder as a kind of walking billboard, but no one wants to pay my price."

"How much is that?"

The father had heard enough. "He's trolling you, Son."

"You're not famous?"

"No. He's famous. He's just not offering his head for a billboard."

"I've never seen you. What are you famous for?"

"Killing bad guys." The boy looked at his father and his father nodded.

"Like a superhero?"

"More like Jackie Chan."

The boy looked at his father again for more information.

"Martial arts movie star."

"How do you pick who to kill?"

"I've only killed two people and they both picked me. It's called self-defense."

"He's one of the good guys."

"You couldn't kill my dad."

"Good guys don't kill each other, not in the whole history of the world, not on purpose is what I mean."

"Even if you were a bad guy, you couldn't."

"I bet you're right—but bad guys usually strike first. That's why you always want to be on the lookout."

"I was. I always am. And I saw you."

Roland forced a laugh to blunt the sting of the boy's remark and finished up and paid the check and walked over to Cedar Lanes bowling alley and spent the next hour clearing his mind of all concerns, which meant abolishing language from his consciousness, reverting to the state of man before The Fall. Hardly an experienced bowler—he was glad the machine kept score—he had to strike a balance between force, of which he commanded an abundance, and finesse. The pursuit of that balance required that he step outside himself. The Fall, he surmised, was a metaphor for mankind's marriage to his ego, to his belief in the Self, when a moment's sober reflection should make it obvious that the human race's tenure on Earth was doomed to meet a catastrophic end. Ecclesiastes, not Revelation, was nearest to the mark. *All is vanity*—you can't break the ball, you can't break the pins, you can't break the lane, and you can't break the record. Yet we measure our approach to make sure we don't commit a foot fault.

After his third game his head poured sweat and he had to get a towel from the woman at the shoe counter to sop it. A longneck Budweiser looked good. It was the beverage of choice in this popular establishment. He never craved beer, as a rule, but a longneck Bud looked like it would hit the spot. He resisted the urge and gave the towel back to the woman and took off the bowling shoes and pulled on his boots and went back to the motel. *I can stop drinking after I start,* he told himself. What he didn't acknowledge was that it took a great effort of will amid the present circumstances—driving through unknown territory—where a normal person might not have even considered it. It never occurred to him to question whether his guzzling concealed vodka backstage before his speech and behind the building afterward was abnormal behavior.

~~~~~

The next morning, he got up and showered and left the motel and ate at the Hi-Lo again, which laid out a much better breakfast than it had a dinner. He branched over to the 97 and headed to Klamath Falls in Southern Oregon. The air grew thinner, the population sparser. When he crossed the border into Idaho, a lone roadside market appeared, seemingly not attached to any sort of town. The building was painted all white and wore a large sign above its awning declaring its identity in big red block letters: END TIMES BODEGA. Whatever sportive force was authoring his reality, it wanted Roland to go in there. He turned off the road to oblige. His boots clomped up the wooden steps and vibrated the porch boards. He adjusted his hat before he reached for the door, but the door opened before he could grasp the handle. He stepped back to let it swing past him. The woman who'd opened it stopped and held the door to let Roland pass, but she didn't want him to pass just yet. She might have been five-foot-five and fifty-five years old but her narrow hips and broad shoulders, her deep blue eyes and steel-gray hair, advertised a woman who wasn't scared to take or throw a punch. She wore the quizzical expression of someone for whom life is an endless amusement, not for the fun she was having but for the folly of her fellowman.

She looked at Roland to make sure she had his attention. "Californee." *Was that a statement of fact, as in 'I see you're from California'. Is she referring to me by the state that's stamped my license plate?* Roland remembered a verse his grandfather used to sing. Some sort of Depression-era Dust Bowl ditty, he figured.

Hey Arky,
Tell Oaky,
Texas got a job
Out in Californee,
Pickin' up prunes
Squeezin' oil outta olives.

Roland resisted the impulse to turn and make sure his vehicle tag was in her field of vision because he hadn't seen her glance at his car.

"Sandpoint."

"That's where you're headed?"

"It's where I'm from and where I'm headed."

"Just a short hop to Canada from there. It'll be much safer north."

"You think the time is nigh?"

"Closer than it was yesterday. We know not the day or the hour, so it pays to keep alert."

"Should we be worried?"

"I shouldn't—I don't know about you." She unhanded the door. Roland caught it before it closed. She skipped down the steps like an athlete and disappeared.

He entered the establishment. One whole wall was devoted to wine, hundreds of bottles housed in triangular bins made from diagonally divided wooden boxes stacked in columns. The labels were all of the same plain design, white with red letters, just like the sign aboard the store. *End Times Burgundy. End Times Cabernet. End Times Pinot Noir. End Times Chardonnay.* The man at the counter watched him scan the merchandise. Roland touched the brim of his hat to say hello. The man nodded and turned back to his Bible.

Food shelves occupied most of the floor space. Not a very ample room, its inventory was easy to take in. Canned goods all. White labels with red letters. *End Times Pork and Beans. End Times Fruit Cocktail. End Times Mulligan Stew.* All the food groups covered. Roland understood the theme and decided not to look too closely, not to act too curious. It was a mistake coming in here, he realized. But to turn around and walk out would be to admit to a sort of perverse personality, a tourist of odd roadside markets, a voyeur of fringe capitalism. He had to purchase something. Behind him was a wall of ammunition, none of it bearing the End Times label. The store carried all the top brands in the most popular calibers: *Federal Premium, Savage Arms, CCI, Remington, Winchester.* He dared not lift a box lest he feel impelled to purchase it. Then he spotted the Thanksgiving display. *End Times Pumpkin Pie Filling. End Times Cranberry Sauce. End Times Green Beans and Bacon.* The author of his haphazard journey had not abandoned him. He grabbed two cans of *End Times Cranberry Sauce* and paid without conversation and got back on the road.

~~~~~

He filled his tank in Coeur d'Alene and parked to let the engine cool and called home. He knew he'd be welcomed if he showed up unannounced but wanted to avoid the confusion of surprise and to give his mother time to prepare his old bedroom, which she would certainly want to do. The drive up I-95 to Sandpoint would take an hour. His mother answered.

"Hello."

"Hi, Mom."

The dread silence that followed gave him second thoughts and tempted him to change his mind, to pretend he was still in California and calling just to say hello, calling just to confirm his intention to spend Thanksgiving with the family back home. He was about to repeat *Hi Mom* when his mother responded.

"Roland." It was not a question. It sounded more like an accusation or, worse, the naming of a malevolent force, as one would say Dracula when the vampire crossed in front of the moon.

"I know, Mom. I know."

"I look at your picture every day, your high school graduation photo. I want to take it off the wall."

"I'm coming home, Mom."

Again, she paused.

"Yes I know. Sandy told us."

"I mean now."

He could hear her breathing evenly, exhaling slowly through pursed lips as if to keep herself composed.

"Where are you?"

"Coeur d'Alene."

"That's just perfect." Millicent's sarcasm came off not as sneering but as disgusted.

"I'm only a week early, Mom."

"You waited until you were already here before you called. That doesn't give us much of a choice, does it?"

"Is Dad there? Can I talk to Dad?"

"I can speak for both me and my husband."

"Your husband? You've never called him that to me before."

"Be that as it may."

"So, what are you telling me, Mom? That I should turn around and go back?"

"There's a lot *you* haven't been telling *us*. Let me start there."

"I haven't lied to you."

"That's a coward's dodge."

"I didn't want to hurt you, to upset you."

"With what?"

Roland's mouth went dry. The person who sounded like his mother had become someone he did not recognize, and the unexpected strangeness of the impasse between them raised a tingle, a wave of horripilation, along his neck and arms.

"I'm sorry, Mom."

"You didn't knock over your glass at the dinner table."

"What do you want me to say?"

"Tell me all the things I know about you now that I didn't know the last time we talked. If you can do that, then you're welcome to come ahead."

"And if I can't?"

"Then we'll see you on Thanksgiving Day at exactly three o'clock."

Roland propped his forehead against the steering wheel and let his phone hand fall to the floorboard. He'd planned on being of maximum service during his stay, around the house and on the property, as a way of redeeming himself and restoring himself to their good graces, but now it seemed his first act of service was to begin telling the truth to his mother. Where to begin?

"I lied about leaving the volleyball team. I got kicked off."

"For drinking."

"For being drunk at practice, twice."

"So, the coach gave you a second chance."

"He did, and I blew it. I didn't tell you because I kept the scholarship money flowing by getting the karate instructor job, and I even got a paycheck on top of that, so I figured it was my business."

"If you have to lie, then it's not so innocent as that."

Roland thought it best to move on rather than debate the morality of his lie.

"I got arrested twice—you heard that already, I'm sure."

"For drunkenness. Are you seeing the pattern here?"

"Can you put Dad on the other line, if he's there?"

"Anything you can say to him you can say to me."

"I just don't want to have to go over all of this again, Mom."

"You'll go over it as many times as you have to, Roland. So, we've got the drunken arrests and the boot from the volleyball team. Keep going."

"I quit my job. You must know I quit my job."

"Yes, and stayed in San Francisco anyway."

"I haven't had a drink in nearly a month." He figured since she hadn't asked, this lie was less sinful, especially if it gave his mother some hope.

"Is that the cherry on top of your pile of poop?"

"How far back do you want me to go?"

"Just since our last phone call—what unflattering things have I learned about my son through the media?"

"That I killed another man? That can't be what you're talking about."

"And you bragged about it in front of a bunch of cameras, intoxicated. Didn't you think we'd see that? More to the point—don't you care enough about us to talk to us before the media shows up at our door?"

"Have they been bothering you?"

"It's all your father can do to keep from blowing his top and making things worse."

"Why didn't anyone tell me?" Roland knew that was a bad question the moment he finished asking it and recovered his verbal footing. "I mean I'm sorry. If I'd known..." She cut him off.

"So, is that it? Is that all the dirt?"

"I gave a speech at Berkeley yesterday in front of a few hundred people. It's already up on the internet."

"Sandra told me. She follows you very closely."

"Did you see it, or any clips from it?"

"No. But Sandra said you kicked a megaphone out of someone's hand."

"Is that something you'd've wanted me to call home about first?" He did his best not to sound sarcastic or resentful, but a hint came through.

"You're supposed to keep in touch with your family in times of crisis—don't you know that? I keep asking myself who raised you, but I don't like the answer. Maybe it's not a question of how well but how much."

Roland wanted to tell her that he never considered any of this a crisis and that he was not the type of kid that could be raised like rows of corn; that he was a bush, a blackberry bush—hard to kill and well worth the danger in the pruning and the picking—but that would not have gone over well.

"I've talked to Sandy and Phillip. They never said anything about you being..."

"Your father ordered them not to, and I agreed with him."

"Why?"

"You're a lab rat, the way he sees it."

"A lab rat?"

"You've put yourself in a complicated maze and you want to manage all by yourself. As far as he's concerned, the best thing for you is to let you alone. We can't force you to confide in us. You can't tell someone when they've hit bottom. They have to decide that on their own."

"You're right, Mom. I guess I was afraid to call. I didn't want to hear how disappointed you were in me or to listen to any advice. That's the truth, the way you said it—I wanted to do this on my own and not think about how it was affecting you and Dad."

"Is there anything else you need to tell me before you get here?"

"You know I got my head shaved, right?"

"We won't be taking any pictures this year. Anything else?"

"I picked up some cranberry sauce for Thanksgiving dinner."

~~~~~

Harold Hazzard was waiting on the front porch in his chair when Roland pulled up the driveway. He looked at Roland and didn't wave. Roland rolled down his window and patted the roof of his car to acknowledge its valiant service, as one would pat the neck of a horse before dismounting. While the car was still running Harold stood up and raised his hand chin-high and approached with his fingers spread out, like he was indicating the number five. Except he was not indicting a number. He was saying wait there, don't shut off the car. Roland poked his head out the window.

"Hey, Pop."

"Put that thing in the patch next to the garage. There's a cover inside. I want you to cover it."

"This piece of shit?"

"That piece of shit is known. I bet you I could find a picture of it if I googled *Roland Hazzard's car.*"

"What about the garage?"

"The International's in there with the transmission sitting next to it. I'm gonna need your help with that since you're here."

"Ok. I'll get the cover right now."

"If you get the Scout working, you can take it. Your grandfather would like that. It can't be healthy to drive a thousand miles crammed inside that rattletrap."

"Sorry for the trouble, Pop."

"Your mother pounded in a no-trespassing sign out front. I yanked it up yesterday. The police have been pretty vigilant so far, so things have calmed down. But once people find out you're here, you'll be the one dealing with the nuisance."

"Is the shotgun still in the front closet?"

"This is not the time to crack wise, son. Whatever you wouldn't say to your mother, best not say to me. She's in a state, and understandably so. But you know that, don't you?"

"Dad, all I meant is the journos are a bunch of pussies. They'd scatter like roaches at the sight of a Daisy bee-bee gun."

"You'd love that, wouldn't you? Another little snippet to go viral and increase your click count."

"I'm not all that well monetized—yet."

"Is that how you're going to make a living in this world—internet celebrity?"

Roland squinted—squeezed his eyes all the way closed momentarily, clenched his teeth even—and thought about mentioning his plan to write a book, then decided instead to diffuse the tension.

"I'm really glad to be back here, Dad, for a break from all that. I won't make any trouble—bet your bottom dollar. I'll deal with them politely if they show up."

"That's all I wanted to hear."

"Good, then. Now let me get this clown car out of sight."

He parked it between the garage and the fence and entered the garage through the backyard door and turned on the light. There stood Grandpa Merrill's '65 Jeep International Scout in its original alligator green with cream white top and bumper to match. The car he'd used to learn how to drive. Its rear end was propped on two steel jack stands and the transmission sat on an aluminum oil pan in the adjacent parking spot. His father had no use for the car and, while a competent mechanic, was no hobbyist. A '65 Scout in this condition was worth several thousand dollars, running or not, and Roland was sure that Harold would have sold it had it not held sentimental value for Millicent. Palming it off on Roland was a sensible move—keep it in the family but out of his garage. Roland would be only too happy to oblige. He found the car cover and went back to his car and removed his computer bag and grocery sack then draped the vehicle from bumper to bumper and hoped he'd never have to set eyes on its bile yellow hull again.

~~~~~

His mother seemed younger. He figured the reprimand she delivered him an hour ago had unburdened her of worry and given her a boost of vitality. Still, she didn't appear to be exactly happy. Her hug was too strong, its release too abrupt, and her smile ended with a smirk as if to say she could unload on him all over again.

"I made your bed up, Son. Didn't you bring a bag?"

"I didn't plan on coming from Berkeley, Mom. But after the scene I caused, I didn't want to go back to my apartment and deal with a swarm of reporters."

"How long do you think until they figure out you're here?"

"I need to go into town at some point. If no one rats me out, then…"

"Will you be doing any of your internet talks in this house?"

"I hadn't planned on it, but either way nobody knows where I am when I'm online."

"How long are you going to stay?"

"Is this what it's gonna be like, Mom?"

"You're overdrawn, Roland. You'll need to start making deposits, and not with your mouth."

Roland nodded affirmatively, eyes wide open. This was the opposite of what he expected—Dad nonchalant, even friendly, and Mom all up his ass.

"Message received. Thanks for the room."

He carried his bag upstairs and examined the drawers and closet to see which of his old clothes remained. He set the paper sack on the dresser and felt like an idiot for not having tossed the cans in Coeur d'Alene.

His Laredos went into the closet. He found his old work boots, a pair of sturdy leather brogans with a lot of wear left in them. His old clothes looked a little snug but not too tight to wear.

For the next few days, he tended to the property, clearing away fallen debris, cutting dead limbs from the trees, closing gaps in the fences. He was careful not to do too much, lest his efforts imply that his father was not keeping up with things. He got the ladder and the high-pressure sprayer to wash the greenhouse he'd built with the help of a few friends one weekend during his senior year in high school seven years ago. His father came out to watch him.

"Can you go inside and check for leaks, Pop?"

"This thing doesn't leak."

"I'm hitting it pretty hard. Are you sure?"

"And it supports a couple of tons of snow on top of it."

"I double-trussed the roof and used a bunch of extra purlin clamps all around. Still, that might not keep it water tight forever."

"Extra clamps might have done it. Look for yourself. I'll wager not a drip in there. It could double as a fallout shelter."

"I'm glad you and Mom are using it. I noticed lots of herbs, besides the tomatoes and the veggies."

"Flowers too. So, what about the Jeep?"

"I made a list of parts I'll need. I'll go in town today. Kinda nervous about it."

"Why? You never minded your local popularity."

"It was all based on sports. This is about real issues. Did you watch my speech at Berkeley?"

"No. Your sister keeps your mother and me up to date. Phillip tells me that you're a strange cross between a loose cannon and a sharpshooter."

"I was in rare form down in Berkeley, like a Pentecostal preacher. I don't know what came over me. Hell, Pop, it might have been the real thing."

"What did you say?"

"Execute murderers and can them for dog food."

"That is rather Biblical, except for the canning."

"Yeah, well, I don't want to get into a lot of back and forth out in public, especially not around here. The press will hear about it and they'll come straight over."

"Well, Thanksgiving is day after tomorrow. It could take a long time to get parts for that thing, so if I were you, I'd order them before the holiday. Phillip plans to leave the end of next week, so if you want him to help you put everything back together then I suggest you get what you need right away."

Roland found a baseball cap and put on his glasses and drove to town in his father's Ford. Nothing much had changed since his childhood, and certainly not since his visit last Christmas. The streets were clean and the people well behaved. Stubborn Hillary Clinton posters remained in a few storefronts and planters. Trump supporters, apparently, had taken their signs down. The Napa Auto Parts store on Larch Street held the answer that would affect not only his time spent in the forthcoming hours but his situation for some time to come—could they locate the parts he needed to get the '64 Scout back on the road, and not just for local transportation, but for the long haul? And could they get them by Wednesday?

Roland went to the parts counter at the rear of the store and presented the man his list. "This might be a stretch, but you gotta start somewhere."

The man, clean-shaven, in his late twenties, wore a striped short-sleeve clerk shirt that bore a patch with the name *Mark* embroidered in cursive. He took the list and looked at it, glanced up at Roland, back at the list, then back at Roland.

"You sure these are the correct part numbers?"

"I wrote the part names next to the numbers to prevent any mistakes."

"This will take some time to research." He meant for Roland to go away while he checked the computer.

"Just looking at the list, can you tell me, please, what are the odds? Do you have access to private dealers?"

"If you want to find original parts for a fifty-year-old car you'll have to navigate those waters yourself."

"Then what are you looking up?"

"3D printer catalog."

"Can they replicate the whole transmission?"

"That's the route I'd go, instead of mixing plastic with steel. It will cost more, but much less hassle and more reliable in the end."

"How soon can you have it?"

"Depends on how much you're willing to pay."

"Assume I can afford the soonest you can get it."

"A week. Maybe a little longer because of the holiday."

"Robots celebrate Thanksgiving now?"

"Far as I know. They're forming unions too. Pretty soon they'll be suing for civil rights."

"They deserve the world if we can't stop them from taking it over."

"Maybe a good subject for one of your podcasts."

Roland gave him a wary look.

"You get me that plastic transmission by next Wednesday, and we can hash out doomsday together on my podcast. I've got a few million subscribers and counting, Mark."

"I'm one of 'em. Are you back to stay? You could probably win an election around here."

"I like this town too much to risk ripping it apart. I'm thinking Toledo or Indianapolis."

"I'll call you when it's ready. The 3D print shop is out of Spokane, so there's no shipping delay."

"Thank you." Roland turned to leave.

"Is this your personal number?"

"It's the landline where I'm staying. I wasn't kidding about that podcast. You get it here by Wednesday and maybe we can get together."

Next step, transfer the title. Everything in Sandpoint proper lay within walking distance. Most of the buildings were brick, with nothing above three stories tall. A rail line ran alongside the lake carrying trains that hauled everything from raw timber cut from Northwestern forests to airplane fuselages manufactured in Seattle at the Boeing factory. The long rumbling lines were so much a fixture that visitors could not help but notice their passing and inhabitants all but forgot they were there. He listened to a train roll by as he entered the Department of Motor Vehicles. The line was short and led to one open station. The station was staffed by his old flame, Claire. She noticed him before he reached the front of the line but made no overt gesture, just a glace and faint smile of recognition. He rocked back and forth gently on his heels before he got to her.

"Hey, Claire."

"I was wondering if I'd ever see you again."

"I should have apologized to you a long long time ago."

"Did you come here to apologize? Looks like you're carrying some DMV business."

"Lately I've come to believe that Fate is pulling my strings."

"What have you got there?"

"My grandpa's old Jeep. I need the title transferred to my name." He handed over the document.

"Do you have a bill of sale?"

"He's been dead a couple years. You must know that."

"Death certificate?"

"Merrill Selkirk helped put this town on the map. Even people that never met him know he's dead."

"You're right. I never met your grandpa, but I know he's dead. But even if you had a newspaper clipping, I couldn't accept that."

"So, the DMV needs a copy of the death certificate? "

"We need to see the original, along with a legal will or trust that gives the vehicle to you."

"And what if I can't get that?"

"Then an order from a probate court." Her face betrayed no mischief. He turned his head from side to side, looking at nothing in particular, not wanting to show Claire his consternation.

"Well. I guess the apology is all the business I'm going to get done in here today. I just ordered a new transmission over at Napa Auto, so I need to call and cancel that."

"What's the apology?"

"Are you kidding me?"

"Just say it, Roland."

"I betrayed you, Claire. You loved me, and I betrayed you. And I never said I was sorry. I just moved on. Your shock, your pain, I did not try to assuage it. I lacked the integrity to admit that I was wrong, even though I knew I was wrong. My behavior was that of a child and not of a…"

"You owe me about a hundred dollars for the oxymorons t-shirts." Roland took a hundred-dollar bill out of his pocket and placed his hand over it and pushed it across the counter.

"Do you still have them?"

"No. Only a crazy person keeps a memento of betrayal."

"You're right. It was a stupid question. But, before I go, on the off chance that you might be able to believe me, I was in New York last month doing a couple of TV interviews…"

"I saw them."

He continued as though she hadn't interrupted him. "And I told the story to a friend I made over there. I relived what I did, and I cried, and I could cry again right now if I went back there in my mind. I resolved to make amends to you before I left town this visit if I could find you."

She lowered her eyes, inspected the old vehicle title and registration papers in her hand, then looked back up at Roland. She had green eyes just like his, blond hair, a serious vulpine face. They would have made beautiful, intelligent offspring. The small rock on her finger meant she'd not married rich—few in Sandpoint, Idaho did—but the gem sparkled as though cherished by its owner, so he guessed she'd married well. He dared not ask his name. Such a familiarity might be overstepping. He had no idea how to behave so he erred on the side of caution. Kept his mouth shut.

"I accept your apology, Roland, and I will process the title transfer so you can take the late Merrill Selkirk's 1964 Jeep International Scout off this panhandle to wherever the wild winds blow you."

"I won't forget the favor, Claire. Nor the lesson—I swear."

"All I ask—don't die like your grandfather. The sadness at his passing was mixed with a lot of pity. My husband thinks you're a rooftop riot, and I play right along. So just don't flame out or nod off dead like a rockstar. Think of your family."

"Does he know about...?"

"Yes. He calls you my boyfriend. *Hey, Hun! Guess what your boyfriend just said.*"

She gave him a temporary title. "Two weeks for the official one. It will go to your parents' address." They touched hands and said goodbye. On his walk back to Harold's Ford he passed a bar he knew too well, a bar where he'd learned to shoot pool and drink beer before drinking became a problem, before he'd discovered what a blackout was. Roland knew if he went in and sat down, he'd be surrounded by friends and well-wishers, that instant camaraderie would ensue, and that very likely before the night was over the local cops would somehow get themselves involved. And he knew he could find a warmer, more-genuine embrace at an AA meeting, which would not be hard to find in this technological age in a town of seven thousand. But Roland was not ready to trust in the promised anonymity of the fellowship in the place where he was born and raised and held half the public-school athletic records, so he went home as he knew he should.

~~~~~

Harold deferred to Millicent in the saying of Thanksgiving grace. The family of five, all youthful, healthy, and alert, assumed a prayerful posture and bowed their heads while she extemporized a blessing.

"Dear Lord," she began, "thank you for bringing us together again this year and for the bounty you have bestowed on our family. Though we are still sad that Grandpa Merrill can't be with us, we know that You did not take him rashly and that he had a lot to do with his own demise. Still, we miss his loving nature and his constant good humor." She paused as though to organize her thoughts. "And thank you for this extra time that we have with Roland this November and for keeping him safe in the unpredictable path he has chosen. Thank you for the bounty you have given us to assemble this wonderful meal that all of us have participated in preparing, and I'll thank you all the more that the men will clean up after."

"Amen," said Harold. The table repeated amen in unison.

They ate and shared stories about Grandpa Merrill, their last grandparent to pass and the one they knew best. His Selkirk ancestors migrated from Scotland to the Northwest in the 1850s and sunk roots in the territories as loggers, trappers, and miners. Merrill came to Sandpoint as a young man, an apprentice engineer for North Pacific Railroad, and after a few years working in that capacity then tried his luck at the American Dream, developing land to attract people to the town. A very safe town in a very wild region. The peaceable native Kootenai and Kalispel peoples camped on the lake during the summer and moved on to Montana or Washington in the fall, so the only real trouble came from the local bears and wolves. Merrill served as sheriff for a time, then as mayor, but mostly he bought, developed, and sold land and businesses, not in the spirit of avarice but in service of the general prosperity. A town father in the truest sense of the word. But, at the end, he was just a drunk. The constant socializing necessary for a man of his ambitions eventually made him dependent upon alcohol, and though he acknowledged the problem and battled it constantly in the final decades of his life, Merrill Selkirk died sodden in a drooping wooden home on an overgrown acre outside the town limits. Still loved, but no longer admired. When his signature vehicle, the green '64 Jeep International, broke down a few years before, he was wise enough not to have it fixed. He'd confessed to

Millicent that he believed the police would finally be forced to arrest him, and a judge incarcerate him, if they caught him driving drunk again.

Still, the stories his daughter's children told at the table, like most of the stories told about him generally, extolled the virtues of goodness, bravery, and indomitable good humor that characterized his manifestly successful life. His alcoholism, when it was mentioned, was accepted as an unlucky draw in the genetic lottery, not as the symptom of an underlying spiritual malady. Roland, the youngest, was his favorite, though no one mentioned it. The parents let their children regale the table with familiar anecdotes of Grandpa Merrill. When the pauses grew longer Harold chimed in.

"This town owes him a debt of gratitude."

"He was a great daddy, the kindest funnest daddy. I was a lucky child."

"I've been wondering when you kids are going to get busy. The Selkirk branch has gone fallow, but the Hazzards still have a fighting chance."

The siblings smiled and looked at one another. Phillip and Sandy knew he was talking more to them than to Roland. They ate in silence for a minute until Phillip spoke.

"So, Roland, what did you contribute to this feast? Mom said we all had a hand in it. Where's your hand in evidence?"

Roland lifted a forkful of cranberry sauce. "This here. How do you like it?"

"Not bad. Hope you didn't cut yourself opening the can."

Sandy tasted it. "It's good. Where'd you get it?" Roland got up and went to the kitchen and brought back the second, unopened can and rotated it like a TV spokesmodel to show everyone the label. "A roadside market just west of Post Falls near the state line." He set it on the table.

"*End Times*. Perfect! You can bring it as a prop to your next big performance."

"Maybe you can get your hands on a can of *End Times Dog Food*, fortified with grade-A certified ground-up murderer meat."

"Was that necessary?" said Harold.

The unappetizing image jarred the conversation into another brief silence. Roland picked up the can and gave it an appraising nod and set it back on the kitchen counter.

"I don't have anything lined up right now. Not in the way of an interview or a speech."

"Then you're done with all that?"

"For the time being. I'm going to DC in January." When he said it, he knew his brother would react, stationed as he was at the Pentagon.

"What for?"

"Meet the new president, once he settles in."

"You don't just knock on the door of the White House with a plate of brownies."

"He invited me."

"Bullshit."

"Phillip!" said Millicent.

"Do you know me to lie, brother?"

The implied breach of civility stopped everyone from chewing while they waited for Phillip to respond. Roland's query did not carry the threatening purport as in the old westerns, where one cowboy says to the other, *you callin' me a lyrr*. Still, it was not a rhetorical question, and it was brother-to-brother.

"No, Roland—but it just doesn't make any sense."

"His winning the election doesn't make any sense. I see Hillary signs still posted around town. Some people haven't come to grips with it."

"What does he want with you?"

"He's *your* boss, technically. Maybe you can find out."

"I'm asking you. What was the invitation for? Who contacted you?"

"My agent. Someone contacted him, a woman, I think. I don't know who. I didn't ask. All he said was President Trump would like you to be his guest at the White House in January. More will be revealed."

"He said that? *More will be revealed?*"

"No. I added that. It's a phrase I picked up at…"

"Grandpa used to say it." said Sandy. "He picked it up at AA."

"Is that where you got it, Roland?"

"Yup."

"How's that going?"

"Will you do me a favor, Sandy?"

"Ok, I'll shut up."

"No, Sis, I'm not trying to muzzle you."

"Then what? I can't agree until I know the favor."

"The elephant in the room. It's thirsty. Can you get it a drink?"

Sandy looked at Phillip, then at Harold, then at Millicent. Millicent shook her head no.

"You'll have to get it yourself, Roland. The rest of us agreed not to drink."

"I didn't mean for me. I meant for the rest of you, for this little conspiracy." He turned to his mother. "Mom, you always have a little red wine. It won't bother me at all."

"I'll have a beer," said Phillip. Harold raised a forefinger to say he'd like one too.

"And wine for Mom. I don't know what you guys were thinking."

"We thought it was the right thing to do," said Millicent, "since you aren't drinking."

Roland had two ways to play this, defensive or magnanimous. The time-honored AA dictum of contrary action sprang to mind. His tenure as a public figure had taught him that contrary action was counterproductive if you wanted people to pay attention and talk about you later, but at Thanksgiving dinner, contrary action was the best advice. So magnanimous it would be.

"You're right, Mom. I should not have left you thinking about it. I should have come out and said I'm not drinking but you guys go ahead. Instead, I forced you to wonder about the right thing to do."

Harold cleared his throat. "That's not the elephant in the room."

A dead silence landed on the table, accentuated by the clinking of silverware on china. Roland shifted in his seat. "Is this some kind of game show? Name the invisible elephant?"

"You boast about killing people."

"People?"

"Let's not do this," Millicent said.

"Yes. Let's not," said Sandy.

"We have to," Phillip said.

"All we're doing is clearing the air."

"I'm feeling kinda ambushed here."

"You did the right thing, Roland," said Phillip. "You decided not to drink. That invites a sober conversation."

Again, the insufferable internal call to contrary action. *Tolerance, magnanimity in the face of intrusion, how is that supposed to build my character?* His defensive impulse won the moment. "Are you saying I asked for this?"

"We're your family," said Sandy. "If you can't talk to us then what good is this?" She drew a circle above the table with her finger to indicate the family gathering.

"I've been keeping my own council for as long as I can remember."

"Your celebrity, unfortunately, involves us," said Harold.

"Implicates us even," Phillip said.

"We deserve to know what you're up to," said Sandy.

"You've read John Donne, haven't you," said Millicent. "Mister Berkeley English major."

"I think I'm *done*."

"John Donne." Harold said the name not with an interrogative lilt but as a question, nonetheless.

Roland quoted the eminent metaphysician: "No man is an island."

"The ending is the point," Millicent said.

"Refresh my memory."

Phillip took the baton: "*Any man's death diminishes me, because I am involved in mankind; And, therefore, never send to know for whom the bell tolls; It tolls for thee.*"

"I see."

"John Donne agrees with me," Harold said. "To gloat over killing is bad form."

"Phillip quoted me Shakespeare the day after I killed Barsamian. *To thine own self be true*, he said. So I followed the major's orders. My public persona is my own authentic self." Maybe it was, maybe it wasn't. Roland didn't know. All he could say is that he never prepared his remarks before he spoke publicly, so in as much as he was unrehearsed, he called that authentic.

"Don't blame this shitshow on me, Roland. Sorry, Mom."

"Well," said Sandy. "It's some kind of show."

Roland looked at Phillip. "It's hard not to take that personally, Phillip. You were the one who told me to make the most out of my accidental celebrity. *Milk this pig and put some lipstick on it*, I think you said. Well, I guess you don't like the color I chose or the way I applied it. You tell me."

"I just suggested you try to make a little money on public appearances, given your precarious financial circumstances at the time, but you took it too far; you put the lipstick around its eyes and ears and left the applicator sticking out of its nose."

"He went whole hog."

"Not funny, Dad," said Sandy.

"Let's stop dancing around. Do you want me to stop, to crawl into a hole? Maybe we should take a vote."

"No, Son, if this is who you are—your own authentic self, as you say—then you go right on ahead."

"At least find out what the president has to say," Millicent said.

"Probably wants to flesh out your dog food proposal," Harold said.

"You need to give the man a chance, Honey."

"They're sharpening their knives in Washington as we speak," said Phillip.

"And if they fail, at least we know where the End Times market is," Harold said.

"Can we not get started on Trump?" said Sandy. "I remember something grandpa said when people started arguing."

"What was that? I generally remember everything."

"The big difference between Heaven and Hell—Heaven has no religions or political parties."

"Yes," said Millicent. "No unpleasant conversation at the dinner table."

They finished their Thanksgiving feast in keeping with her wishes. Harold shot Roland a furtive glance before opening his second beer. Millicent and Sandy left the table with the bottle of red to watch the Redskins vs. Cowboys in the family room. The brothers chatted a little while they cleared the table and washed the dishes.

"I can't wait to see that 3D transmission."

"It's the color of a hardboiled egg, according to the picture I saw."

"Let's hope not quite as soft."

"I plan to beat on it up and down the mountain for a few hours before I drive it back to California."

"How'd you manage to transfer the title?"

"My good reputation and winning personality."

"I'll never root against you, Roland. You know that."

"But I make it tempting."
"Your luck can't last forever."
"I don't need it forever. Another fifty, sixty years will do."

~~~~~

The following Wednesday, Roland, Phillip, and Sandy, lying on their backs under the elevated chassis of the '64 International, installed a plastic transmission spit from a printer in Spokane, Washington. The boys propped it on blocks, lined it up, and held it steady, while their sister bolted it in place. Harold watched and stroked his chin like he was proud to have raised them, though he'd given them little mechanical education.

Roland could see his shoes and the bottoms of his pant legs and wanted to find out what his dad was thinking. "Hey, Pop," he said, his voice ricocheting around the Jeep's undercarriage and off the slick concrete floor.

"What do you need?"

"Nothing. I just want to ask you a question."

"I'm not old enough yet that you can start making fun of me."

"Easy, Pop. It's a philosophical question, one your life makes you qualified to answer."

"Your mother is the educated party."

"Sorry, you can't dodge this."

"Okay."

"You were a good father—I mean when we were kids—right?"

"That's not a philosophical question," Sandy said. "That's strictly personal."

"That's just the run-up. The precondition to the question."

"Spit it out," said Phillip.

Harold interjected. "I've never even thought about it."

"But if it was a binary, dualistic world—were you a good one or not?"

"Good, then. Most certainly good."

"But you weren't like some of the others, always involved in their kids' activities."

"I don't like how some parents behave at their kids' sporting events, or even at their music recitals. What's the question, Son?"

"He wants to know why you didn't want to see him dominate all the other kids," said Phillip.

"No. I want to know if you had a philosophy behind being a father."

"Don't tell me you've got a girl pregnant," said Sandy.

Harold folded his arms and waited for Roland to respond to Sandy.

"I wasn't talking to you in the first place. Just keep snugging the bolts. If this thing falls off while I'm on the highway and smashes through a windshield and kills the driver and the car flips over and the whole family dies in an explosion, I can't exactly sue you."

"You're not going to be a father any time soon, I hope."

"No, Dad. Do I have to climb out from under here and stand up and swear an oath? I'm just curious about how you approached parenting now that the job is pretty much over."

"If I had any theory at all it was along the lines of the Hippocratic Oath—*First, do no harm.* Your mother did most of the parenting as you well know."

"Are you saying you weren't necessary, Daddy?" said Sandy.

"Simply being there and being good to the mother—that's the most important job of a father. Stick around and set a good example. Let the kids be whoever they're going to be, as long as they don't step too far out of line. I probably should have been easier on Phillip and harder on Roland, but how can anyone know for sure about that kind of thing?"

"That's a really good answer, Pop." His siblings murmured their agreement.

"I got one for you."

"Shoot."

"Do you think you're going to Heaven, Son?"

"If there's a flipside to all this, I'll be glad to participate. I'm more certain that there is no Hell."

~~~~~

The three of them took the Jeep up the switchbacks of Telemark Road to Schweitzer Mountain. Though it was cold enough for snow to accumulate, a major storm had yet to cloak the slopes with powder, so the route to the resort was clear and largely empty. Roland was grateful to have the road to himself so he could pay his full attention to wrangling the unassisted steering while coordinating the clutch and the stick shift up and down the slow steep hairpin turns. He was way out of practice, his factory-standard Nissan designed so any idiot could drive it easily. It would take some time before the operation of his grandfather's veteran Jeep became second nature. It ran, the transmission worked, the brakes didn't squeak or smell, the shocks were tight, so all agreed the car was roadworthy. Even the radio sounded good. Sandy entertained them with her singing when a song she knew came on.

They left the next day, Sandy and Phillip, and Roland felt alone for the first time in years. The friendship of close siblings can't be compared to ordinary friendship. Behind it lies a hint that siblinghood came about by some kind of prior agreement and, too, a warning that to break the bond on Earth would spell embarrassment on the other side. Roland resolved that he must leave too, that to remain much longer would count as hiding from the reality he had created for himself. He'd not dared to conduct a live videocast while staying in his parent's home—abstaining from his celebrity under their roof seemed as necessary as abstaining from alcohol.

Before he left, though, he had one thing left to do, something without which his visit to Sandpoint would have been incomplete. He needed to spend a little time on the lake.

~~~~~

Gouged into the land at the end of the last ice age and shaped like a human ear, Lake Pend Oreille held the distinction of being the largest lake in Idaho and the fifth deepest in the United States, so deep in fact that the Navy used it to test submarines. Of course, the lake came equipped with a sea monster, the so-called Pend Oreille Paddler, an elusive plesiosaur some reckoned, that bothered no one and added intrigue for the children and the tourists. That late November the edges of the lake had not yet begun to freeze but the boats had all but disappeared, except the most cold-blooded mariners who didn't mind repeated slaps across the face from the frigid northern air.

Roland rowed out a few hundred yards to where the morning breeze barely rippled the water and dropped his little anchor. Its twenty-foot rope pulled tight so he knew the ten-pound grapnel had not hit bottom, which didn't concern him since the weight of the dangling metal alone would keep the boat from drifting too fast. Besides, even without an anchor, the boat couldn't wander so far that Roland couldn't easily swim to it. He stretched on his swimmer's cap—to insulate the only part of his body he cared to keep warm—and lit a cigarette and scanned the densely wooded northern shoreline, following it eastward with his eyes until it ran out at the tip of Kootenai Point. In the several years since he moved away, real estate development had continued, but the land around most of the lake was far too steep and rocky to allow for any kind of durable construction. The eagles had nothing to worry about if they could worry. Their eyries would be safe for as long as the sun came up.

He took a final drag and dipped the cigarette out in the lake and set the wet butt on the rower's seat, then he took a deep breath and dove in. The freezing water seized him like a fist. The shock was too severe. He rose to the surface immediately and spread out his arms and legs and floated on his back until he gained control of his respiration, staring straight up into the empty light blue canvass. He would try again, but this time without the advantage of a plunge off the skiff. Twenty-plus feet would be no mean achievement, especially in cold water. Below five feet it had to be in the low forties. Down he drove himself, feet propelling him with a tight and furious flutter, arms oaring him into the deepening darkness with powerful sweeping strokes. His ears complained. It had been a while since he'd put them through this ordeal. He found the rope, then followed it to the grapnel and held on. The coldness of the water rattled his nervous system, which signaled a persistent warning that this was no place for the owner of a human brain to be—but neither, he told himself, was plummeting three hundred feet-per-second from two miles up in the air or struggling to the top of Mount Everest to get a better view. True, he'd been this deep before, even deeper, but never in freezing temperatures. One minute had elapsed. He rolled over and looked up to see if he could discern a hint of light from above. He put his free hand in front of his face and slowly drew in closer to touch his nose. He was, in truth, ensconced in total darkness. Freezing darkness. He let go of the metal fluke and found the rope to ease himself upward, letting out bubbles as he rose.

He broke the surface with breath to spare. His skin was numb but still cold. He reached up with one hand, gripped the trim of the skiff, and rocked the vessel. To pull himself up with both arms out of the water back into the boat would require an athletic effort of some speed and agility so as not to swamp it, but his ritual was not complete. Roland had nothing to prove to himself, no personal record to set. So, what was he doing down there? Did he even know well enough to articulate it? Did the expression *God only knows* even apply? He hadn't thought about the possibility of God for a few days, so if you'd asked Roland, he'd've said the meaning of his behavior now had value only to the extent that it was self-evident. He drew in a full measure of air and went down again, this time with less difficulty, his body now acclimated to the conditions. He found the rope, then the grapnel, and went deeper, twenty-five feet perhaps, maybe twenty-eight, and rolled over as before and wafted the water upward to maintain his depth. He closed his eyes and felt the beginnings of hypothermia creep into his flesh with a pleasing warmth. He counted the seconds. Sixty, ninety, two full minutes—he could go longer. The sound of a motor penetrated the depth. He swam ten yards to the west to be clear of the intruding vessel when he emerged. His head popped up. He let out an emphatic gasp.

"What are you doing out here?" It was Lake Patrol. Roland recognized the young man operating the little red and white speed boat marked with the Bonner County seal as Chris Lancaster, a local man some two or three years older than Roland who'd attended the same public schools.

"Diggin' the scene with a gangster lean. What the fuck do you care?"

"I *don't* care. My job is to make sure you're okay."

"Well, I'm okay. Should I recite the alphabet?"

"Your name will do."

"You know me, Chris."

"Is that you? Roland Hazzard? The flamethrower?"

"My best pitch was the backdoor slider. I don't think anybody ever squared the barrel on that slippery pill."

"Not sayin' much since most the hitters stood at the back of the box with the bat on their shoulder when you took the bump."

"I never hit anyone hard enough to knock him out of the game."

By now the boat had puttered over near enough so they were no longer shouting. "What's the rumpus, Columbus?"

"I should ask you."

"You were under quite a while. You're not weighing down a body, are you?"

"That's not in the vicinity of funny."

"Neither is this." Chris toggled his finger left and right between the empty rowboat and Roland treading water.

"Why are you hassling me, Chris?"

His tone changed to one of officious authority. "We got a call about a possible suicide. Someone from the Seasons resort was watching you through binoculars and reported a man smoking a cigarette in a rowboat then plunging into the lake and not coming up."

"Well, I'm up." The pleasant warmth of incipient hypothermia spread from his torso to his limbs. "And you're killing my buzz."

"You're telling me you're out here just taking a dip?"

"Things are just as you observe."

"What I observe is a man who's put himself into an impossible situation."

"Impossible is a very big word."

"How long have you been in there?"

"Twelve minutes. Maybe thirteen."

"Why don't you climb aboard, Roland? We can tow the skiff back to wherever it belongs."

"I'm not finished with my underwater meditation." With that, he disappeared. The bottom layer of the lake water forced the chill through his hard numbed muscles and into his bones. To counteract his buoyancy he swam, albeit very slowly, careful to preserve his air. He kept one arm in front while he pulled with the other to be sure that if there happened to be an obstacle in the way he would touch it before slamming face-first into it. This concentrated exercise took his mind off his rapid asphyxiation, which he did not clock. Now he had something to prove, namely that he followed his own law, though he would never be so bold as to declare himself above the statutory law. At present, though, he was below it.

When he emerged, halfway to death, Roland saw Officer Lancaster bobbing with his patrol boat snugged up against Roland's empty skiff some thirty yards off. Roland waved until Chris spotted him. The patrolman spun up a fishtail and sped over. The wake from the speed boat washed over Roland and he felt like diving under again just to give his old acquaintance another scare. Instead, he spoke. "What are you trying to do, drown me?"

"This is not normal behavior, Roland."

"Whoever said the pursuit of happiness had to follow the ever-changing guidelines of normal?"

"Get into the fucking boat, lunatic."

"What are you going to do, shoot me for refusing to let you save my life?" He swam over to his boat and with a few tremendous kicks propelled himself upward out of the water, hooked his elbows over the side of his boat, and rolled himself in and onto his back. The boat rocked wildly, and he had to catch himself to avoid falling over the other side back into the lake. He righted himself and sat on the rowing board. He peeled off his swim cap, which bore the Bonner County emblem on one side and a picture of the Long Bridge—the unofficial symbol of Sandpoint, Idaho—on the other.

"Remember this?"

"Why would I remember that?"

"It goes to the winner of the Long Bridge Swim, dumbass."

"What's your point?"

"I'm not going to accidentally drown in this lake, and if I decide to kill myself, I'm damn sure not going to let the government stop me."

Chris shook his head and motored away toward his next errand. Roland rowed back to City Beach and dragged the boat up onto the sand and put the wet cigarette butt in the nearest trashcan and drove home and gathered his things. In the front yard, he hugged his mother and kissed his father on the cheek and thanked them and told them he loved them.

"I'll call you once a week—at least." Harold put his arm around Millicent as though to assure his son that the two had their lives well in hand. Roland climbed into his grandfather's vintage Jeep and headed back to benighted San Francisco.

Chapter 19
January 2017

Roland Hazzard kept his word. He called his parents—his mother, really—once a week. The calls seldom lasted more than a few minutes and never touched on the killings or the various unrelated and often fringy subjects he explored on the several media channels where he continued to appear. He knew that she, at bottom, wanted only to hear the steady, sober voice of her prodigal son. When his seven-hundred-thousand-dollar settlement from CBN came through, he mentioned it in passing as a way of allaying any worry she and his father might have about his financial situation, unemployed as he was in the conventional sense.

"I've been meaning to ask you. What made you throw a breakfast sandwich at that man?" Roland didn't tease out why she assumed he was guilty, for he'd lost the benefit of her doubt. He thought of saying *it was all I had handy* but knew his flippancy never impressed her.

"He crossed the line, Mom."

"What line?"

"Between—I don't know—incivility and harassment. I guess you could say I was retaliating."

"What did he do—in plain English?"

"He flipped me off—raised his finger through his sunroof as he passed me on the freeway."

"Sounds like garden variety incivility to me."

"It's that he did it through the sunroof. That made it a kind of public shaming. If he'd kept his hand inside the car, then I guess I would have let it go."

"Still, Son, your retaliation seems a bit extreme."

"I know it was, Mom. But the lure of the challenge got the best of me. It was a difficult shot. I wanted to see if I could make it."

"If you were so proud of your shot, why did you deny it on national TV?"

"That's simple. The folks at CBN set me up. The interview turned out to be an ambush, so I turned the tables on them. If I'd wanted to get greedy, I probably could have gotten more and made a big case out of it."

"That money is not going to last very long, and you probably have to pay taxes on it."

"I've got other money coming in from my internet content, as long as the tech overlords don't demonetize me."

"I don't know a thing about that world."

"I've had to learn quickly, Mom. I'm taking the opportunities as they come."

"Speaking of that, when are you going to the White House? President Trump has been there for more than a week now, right?"

"I leave the day after tomorrow."

"Do you know any more about it? I mean since Thanksgiving."

"Maybe he wants to offer me a cabinet post."

"Even I would oppose that." She laughed as though surprised by her own words.

"Why, Mom?"

"Tell me you weren't joking, and I'll tell you why." She had him there. Roland paused to come up with a cabinet post that would make sense for his qualifications.

"I could head up the Ministry of Consciousness."

Harold picked up the other phone and announced his presence.

"Hey, Dad."

"What do you want me to do with your old car? If you want me to sell it, you'll need to sign over the title."

"Just give it to one of those charities that takes old vehicles. Cars for Kids, Junks for Punks, whatever it is."

"You'll still need to sign over the title I assume."

"You're right. The title is in the glove. And there's a vice-grip clamped to the window crank on the passenger side. Send me the title or forge my signature. Keep the hand tool."

~~~~~

He landed at Ronald Reagan Washington National Airport on January 31st at 4:29 PM, sober since the pint in Berkeley, and caught a cab over to the Trump International Hotel, a towering golden palace on Pennsylvania Avenue just a few blocks from its owner's new official residence—The White House. The Grand Lobby of the Trump Hotel took his breath. Flying metal arches interlinked with catwalks, suggesting to Roland the base of the Eifel Tower, spanned the airspace above the opulent, marble-floored central lounge. He unslung his bag and stood to take in the architecture, not so much to admire its beauty but to ponder the mentality that would add so much extra effort and expense to appoint the lobby with a dramatically unnecessary homage to steel. One thing was certain—the effect was to make one feel small and confused.

"Welcome, Mister Hazzard." It was a feminine voice. Roland reached for his hat as he located its source. A gorgeous coco-skinned woman at least six feet tall, dressed in the slimming uniform of a hotel concierge, stood to his left a few feet away. She'd snuck up on him without intruding on his space. He lowered his hat to cover his heart and made a slight bow.

"On behalf of the President of the United States, welcome to Trump International Hotel."

"He's not here, is he, ma'am?" Roland's voice had a worried pitch.

"I assume he's always here, even if I see him on live television giving a speech at a rally."

"I see. What I meant was, he's not waiting for me, is he?"

"No. He wouldn't do that."

"So you know him, I mean on a first-name basis?"

"Yes. He hired me personally and checks in on me from time to time."

Roland looked at her name tag.

"Well thank you, Candice. I feel properly welcomed."

"Let me show you to your room."

Roland picked up his bag and followed Candice to the elevators.

Once inside the room, she opened the curtains to show him his view of the city and handed him his electronic key card. He put his bag on the couch along the wall and looked at the Alaskan king-sized bed and noted that he'd never slept on a mattress so large.

"You have a standing reservation at the restaurant with an open tab, so whenever you're hungry they'll seat you right away, or you can order up."

"Thank you, Candice. Missus Conroy mentioned that."

"Yes. Those were Maryanne's instructions. You will not receive a bill, Mister Hazzard."

"Thank you again."

"Get a good rest. You've lost three hours. A car will come for you at 11:30 tomorrow morning to take you to the White House. Your meeting with President Trump is set for noon."

As she approached the door, she extended an elegant finger and tapped one of the hooks on the wall to show him, if he was paying attention, where to hang his hat. Then she left the room. He hung his hat on the hook and turned around to see the sun descending behind the Washington Monument. He put the hat back on and hurriedly set up his camera and computer on the table to deliver a webcast in a chair in front of the window. Before he pressed start, he tweeted out an announcement that he was about to begin and waited a few minutes for an audience to gather.

"Good afternoon my slithy droogs, deep in your webby digs. Set down your tepid energy drinks, pale worms. Lift the hems of your filthy jams and buff the smudges off your spectacles, for I want you to see clearly the sun going down in the window behind me. Yes. You're not mistaken. Behold in the foreground the national obelisk—the Washington Monument. And while the local sun descends this evening, know, my droogs, my star is on the rise. Tomorrow morning, I, your humble champion, your roving acrobat, your bandoliered knight, will meet with United States President Donald J. Trump, in the storied Oval Office, for reasons that are yet to be revealed. But one thing is perfectly clear: I was summoned hither. He flew me here today first class and set me up in the Trump International Hotel, which is where you find me now, in this lavish arrangement; and he will dispatch a shiny black car for me tomorrow. What could this mean? Who knows? Whatever it is, unless I am mistaken, Nostradamus didn't see it coming."

Roland went on like this for three or four minutes, purling polysyllabic blandishments about his hypothetical impact on the American cultural landscape. Was he a devastating meteor? A tornado of locusts? Perhaps a sweet-smelling, invisible mist that induces mass rationality?

"I don't know what Mister—President—Trump wants to talk about. But if he asks my opinion, I'll tell him that the country—the thing we call the United States of America—is fast devolving into sectarian fanaticism. *E Pluribus Unum* mocks us on our currency. Maybe he can fix that little problem before the yuan bodyslams the dollar."

Roland got up and left the camera running so the viewers could watch the sun set. He dressed for dinner and then returned to the chair.

"Now I'm off to dine on a sumptuous meal at President Trump's expense in the hotel restaurant. You, my droogs, can get back to your Cheetos and Red Bull. I'll keep you posted."

~~~~~

The maître d'hotel recognized Roland and obliged when he asked to be seated at a quiet table and led him to a spot in the back near the kitchen. Roland declined a cocktail and ordered ginger ale. If nothing else, he would be sober for the sit-down with Trump. His chair faced the dining room and he noticed that a few people glanced over at him as he sipped his drink, and he thought about moving to the opposite seat where he would face a watercolor of what looked like Florence, Italy, but he decided to stay put. To show his back to the other diners, he thought, would have looked like either cowardice or arrogance, and Roland pondered the relationship between those two seemingly disparate personality traits. He suspected that the arrogant were probably cowards at heart and that cowards came in every stripe.

He started with the Maine lobster bisque then went to work on the tomahawk steak, which he didn't finish so as to leave room for something off the dessert cart—a wedge of blackberry cobbler and a scoop of vanilla ice cream. When he was satisfied, he fished the lemon wedge out of his water glass and bit into it to cleanse his palette. The maître d' came over.

"Did you enjoy your meal, Mister Hazzard?"

"One of the best I've ever had."

"Very good. I just want to make sure you didn't wait around for the check. Your meals and incidentals are compliments of the hotel, of Mister Trump himself."

"That's the reason it's one of the best meals I've ever had. I don't normally mix in this rarefied air."

"I'm glad we could furnish a memorable epicurean experience. Before you go, I have one favor to ask."

"I'm happy to hear it."

"Our chef would like to meet you. He wants to say hello."

"By all means let him come."

A few minutes later the chef arrived in his chef's get-up, a man of fifty-something with the girth and worried expression of a baseball manager. Roland stood to shake his hand and the man wiped his hand on his pants before reaching it out. In his other hand the chef held a sheet of paper, the menu card containing the day's special entrées.

"I'm sorry to bother you, Mister Hazzard, but my daughter wouldn't forgive me if she knew you were here and I didn't get your autograph."

"This is a first for me. I guess you should tell me her name."

The chef placed the menu card blank-side-up on the table and set a pen on top of it. "Philomena. She's a freshman at Georgetown."

"You'd better spell that for me, just to be safe."

The chef recited the spelling of his daughter's name and Roland wrote a message to an idealized Philomena. It read: *Good Philomena, Endeavor to Persevere. -Roland Hazzard.*

The chef read aloud. "*Good Philomena.* I like that. She is a good child."

"I can tell that you love her."

"How?" The chef lifted the autographed paper. "This here?"

"You still call her *child.*"

The maître d' nodded and smiled, and the two men left Roland to himself.

~~~~~

He slept without incident, without an excursion into the unseen realm, his unconscious mind tethered instead to the audiobook he left streaming through his mobile device when he went to bed. In the morning he had breakfast sent up and ate half of it while watching a documentary about creatures that lived at the bottoms of the deepest oceans that seemingly defied the laws of physics. The deep-sea submersibles sent down to observe them were built by necessity to withstand thousands of pounds of pressure per square inch, yet somehow these blind and often transparent creatures moved about comfortably, and their bizarre body plans defied the theory of evolution by natural selection through random mutation. He noted his thoughts in a journal on his computer for use, perhaps, one day in a podcast denouncing the pagan cult of Science.

His phone rang. It was Maryanne Conroy. "Go down and wait," she told him. "The car will be there soon."

Roland dressed and pulled on his Laredos and straightened his tie in the mirror and put on his hat before he went down to meet his ride. A black Lincoln pulled up and the driver got out and opened his door, but before Roland could climb in the man stood in his way and briefly patted him down then stood aside to let him pass. He shut the car door and went around and got behind the wheel. Roland set his hat on the seat as the car sped away,

"You secret service?"

The man eyed Roland in the rearview mirror. "I don't do interviews."

Roland thought about making an apology and explaining that he was a little nervous considering he was about to meet President Trump and meant not to pry but was only making small talk but decided to keep his mouth shut even before finishing his thought.

The car entered the White House grounds through a side gate and stopped at the back door and the man let Roland out and escorted him into the gigantic neoclassical mansion. Another agent joined them inside and they walked together up a flight of stairs and down a hall to the Oval Office. The driver knocked on the door and President Trump said come in and the agent opened the door and the three went inside. President Trump stood behind his desk with his back to the room looking out the window. The other agent closed the door and the two stood shoulder to shoulder in front of it. Roland walked to one of the two chairs near President Trump's desk then stopped and moved toward the grandfather clock and watched President Trump to see what he would do—stay behind his desk or make for one of the couches in the center of the office—and then remembered to take off his hat.

President Trump turned around. He commanded the space around him. Tall and broad-shouldered, he supplied enough girth to challenge his tailor. His ample head and florid face made a prominent platform for his orange-tinted hair. Though ruggedly homely in the main, his self-confident eyes insisted he was handsome. Now he lifted his palms to shoulder height in a gesture of mock bewilderment and spoke to the agents. "What are you guys doing?"

The driver answered. "This is a dangerous man, Mister President."

"I am too. Maybe the most dangerous man in the world—maybe in the history of the world. Let's find out about Roland." He looked at Roland. "Are you a dangerous man, Roland? You mind if I call you Roland?"

"Well, sir…" Roland was not sure if he should answer both questions. "In the—the—general sense I guess yes—yes, I am. But I'm not a danger to you."

"See there, Jim—he's a pussycat. And the last guy kept the pygmies on the payroll, right?"

The two agents looked at each other then back at President Trump. "Pygmies, sir?" said the driver, whose name apparently was Jim.

"Behind the walls, with their blowguns and their poison darts. He told me he had narrow slots built into the panels to cover all the angles."

The other agent bent forward slightly, tightening his gut and grimacing to suppress a guffaw.

President Trump continued. "The pygmies can take care of Mister Hazzard if things go sideways."

"Sorry, sir, no Pigmy blowgunners today. You're defenseless in here unless you're carrying a weapon."

"Seriously guys, Mister Hazzard—Roland—may I call you Roland?—you don't mind—why would you mind?—Roland here is my guest and I want him to feel welcome. But—if you insist—I'll have him use the chair on top of the trap door—if that will make you so very happy. Just remind me—is it the green button or the yellow button that springs the trap?"

The two agents looked at each other and nodded, then spoke in unison. "Yellow button, sir."

"I'm safe then. Incredibly safe. Never been safer. Safest man in the world. One of the few perks of the job. You two can wait outside or patrol the West Wing. Make sure no one's engaged in any inappropriate behavior."

The agents left. President Trump lifted his palms to say *here we are.* "Have a seat young man." His tone softened. Roland shook his head at the two chairs to show President Trump that he wasn't about to put himself at risk of possibly being plunged into oblivion then lowered himself onto the nearest couch and set his hat next to him. President Trump opened a drawer in his desk and extracted two cold cans of Diet

Coke, which he carried to the coffee table. He set one in front of Roland and one on the other side of the table before taking his place on the opposing couch.

"What's the green button for?"

"Something nuclear. I'm not exactly sure. Iran, maybe North Korea. You realize how many presidents have said *new-quoo-lerr*? I'm not going to continue that verbal atrocity."

Roland chuckled to be polite. "Not to be impertinent, Mister President, but you didn't invite me here to joke around." He sipped from the can and lowered his eyes, wondering if he'd sounded too forward. He set the can down on a coaster very deliberately, dead center middle. He could feel President Trump watching him, so he raised his eyes.

"What can I do for you, sir?"

"You're right, Roland, so very right. This is no joke. People—some people—not most people obviously—thought my running was a joke. Now they're not laughing—saddest most humiliated people in the country today—the ones that thought I was a joke. But I'm having a good time—great time, really. How about you? You've made quite a splash yourself—there are people out there—so I understand, so I understand—that think the same of you, that think you're a joke." He waited for Roland to respond. Looked him straight in the eye.

"I don't spend much time thinking about what people think about me, except for my friends and family."

"Well, that's a good policy. But I want you to know that I think a lot of you. I think you're tremendous really, really tremendous. A long-ball hitter I like to say. Long-ball hitter if I've ever seen one. If I didn't think a lot of you, I wouldn't have invited you here."

"I was eager to come."

"How are you liking the hotel?"

"It's great, sir—Mister President. Very kind of you to—"

"I hope you ate at my steakhouse. Best steaks in the city. Don't tell me—you ordered the tomahawk."

"I did. I couldn't even finish it. One of the best meals I've ever had."

"I would've put money on it. What did I tell you—long-ball hitter."

Roland took another sip from the Diet Coke and decided to ask, "You're not spying on me, are you?"

President Trump straightened up on the couch. "Spying? Let's talk about spying. I think I'm the one being spied on. A lot of powerful people—powerful unelected people—think I don't belong where we're sitting, but that's a different conversation." He took a drink from his can and set it back down. Roland did not wait to fill the silence.

"Truth is, if you want to know, I was, in fact, a long-ball hitter—that was back in high school. But I was even more feared as a pitcher."

President Trump nodded vigorously. "I've heard that about you. A tremendous athlete, I hear. Hit the snot out of the volleyball too. Broke a few noses."

"Just one. But I knocked plenty of guys on their asses."

"I've read a lot about you, Roland. Heard a lot and read a lot. People say that I don't read but I'm a great reader, amazing reader—pick up information faster than anyone. I heard that you worked on my golf game. *Trump Resorts* I think it's called."

"*Donald Trump's Golf Resorts*—yes. I was the lead tester."

"How did that make you feel—being looked at by the US Olympic Team one day, then next day you're sitting in front of a screen testing video games?"

Roland stayed silent for longer than necessary to formulate an answer. He didn't want to force the issue but running through the back of his mind was something like *what the fuck am I doing here*? Had he been talking to anyone else in the world he would have excused himself from the conversation. Then he remembered the signature line from Donald Trump's successful reality TV show, *The Apprentice*.

"I didn't watch your TV show much…" The truth is he'd never watched it but only heard people talk about it. "…but I think I'm feeling like I think some of the people felt when you told them—*you're fired.*"

"Even the few that I didn't fire were squirming half the time. I'm not easy on people. But I didn't invite you here to make you squirm."

Roland nodded and smiled to show a bit of gratitude and returned to a more comfortable subject.

"You know they scrapped the title, right? Last I heard they were going to sell it to an overseas distributor."

"They paid me—what's the name of the company?—paid me a lot as a matter of fact."

"Pacific Gameworks. Redwood City, California."

"Yes—Pacific Gameworks—they can do what they want. They're not required to put the game on the market."

"They pulled it because you won—you know that, right?"

"They probably would have pulled it even if I hadn't. Winning the nomination was enough, I think. They hate me out in San Francisco—but I don't mind. I have more important things to think about."

"Before I quit the job, I shared a few of my ideas on how to improve the game."

"You want to tell me, I can tell."

"A fantasy course on the Texas-Mexico border with the Trump wall and illegals jumping over and sneaking across the course. Left-wing protesters screaming on the margins. The golfers get extra points for doing a little freelance border security. Something like that."

"Very amusing, but I wouldn't put my name on that. That would be a change I would have had to approve, and I wouldn't have approved it."

"I was thinking maybe as a bonus course if you broke 60 on one of the resort courses. Trying to leverage your Build the Wall theme..."

"A border wall is not a joke."

"I wasn't exactly serious when I suggested it."

"It's not just about keeping people from breaking our immigration laws—it's about setting up a deterrent. A lot of people die or get abused along the way, and then there's the drugs. All kinds of drugs. A wall would solve a lot of problems. It's never been worse down there, and it's getting more out of hand every day. A wall would solve a lot of problems."

"I see. You want me to use my internet platform to promote your wall policy."

President Trump widened his eyes in genuine astonishment. "No. I'd rather you stay out of politics."

"Why is that? I don't mean to be rude, but I have no idea why you asked me here. I'm hoping you'll get around to that."

"You remind me of my brother, Fred. That's why I asked you here."

"I didn't know you had a brother."

"I don't—he's dead."

"Oh." Roland sensed a change in Trump, like he was about to meet the inner man.

"He was a beautiful person. A beautiful, beautiful man. Very tall, like you, and handsome, and brilliant. You sometimes hear that God doesn't hand out gifts with both hands, but in Fred's case he gave with both hands and then went back to the barrel and scooped up some more. I got more than my fair share it's safe to say, but Fred—what can I say?—Fred had it all. Could have done anything he wanted."

Roland looked straight at President Trump, looked into his eyes to assess his emotions. He didn't look sad, just wistful. He reached for the Diet Coke then pulled back his hand and looked back at President Trump.

"I'm sorry. I don't understand."

"Fred died a long time ago. He was forty-three, young in years but a shell of a man. He could have passed for seventy. Saddest thing you've ever seen. There was nothing we could do to help him. He drank himself to death. No other way to put it. It's a disease, I'm told, a disease that starts in the body and destroys the soul. And you seem to me to be on that same path, Roland. And let me tell you, if I didn't see so much promise in you—so much of my brother—I wouldn't show any interest. We can't save everyone, and we might not even be able to save you, but you show tremendous promise. Tremendous. I saw what you did to Cameron Anderson and that sleazy lawyer he brought on to take you out at the knees—you pivoted like a master and took them both out in one strike."

Roland felt his heart thudding, heat rising through his chest. His face would be red in a second or two with a mixture of anger and embarrassment. He leaned back on the couch and put his hands on the cushions by his side and tried to slow his breathing.

"I know this is uncomfortable for you to hear. You probably thought I was going to give you a big atta boy for killing those murderers and pushing a message of self-reliance, and that's all well and good. But if, in the end, you wind up a pathetic drunk your message won't mean shit. You'll be undermining your cause—if you even have a cause. You'll be nothing more than a crazy drunk with a…"

Anger, or irritation perhaps, overcame embarrassment. Roland felt the need to interrupt. "So, this a presidential intervention?"

"No. This is man-to-man. Strictly between us. You don't have to like me or be happy that I'm president. Frankly, I'd rather you not even talk about me. I know they—the press—the predators—scumbags most of them—they'll want you to tell them all about this meeting. But if I were you, I'd say nothing—don't give them even a scrap to torture and twist. Consider this like one of those anonymous meetings I know you've gone to. What we say here stays here as far as I'm concerned."

Roland's consternation became physically uncomfortable. He was, quite literally, hot under the collar and could no longer sit still. He stood up to remove his jacket and loosen his tie and before he could get his second arm out of his jacket the doors flew open and the agents burst in with their guns drawn.

Jim took the lead. "SHOW YOUR HANDS. RAISE YOUR HANDS NOW!"

Roland dropped his jacket on the floor and fell back onto the couch with both arms raised, all ten fingers splayed. "What the fuck is this? What have I done?"

President Trump stood up and stared down at two red dots dancing on Roland's chest. "Put your guns away."

"I thought this was a private conversation." Roland kept his arms raised.

"Put your guns away," Trump said again, commanding now. They did as they were ordered. Roland stood up and picked up his jacket and laid it over the back of the couch.

Roland looked at Jim. "You frisked me before I got into the car. And there was a metal detector at the door where we came in."

President Trump showed Jim a mocking frown, a look that said *he's got a point, doesn't he?*

"He can kill with his bare hands, sir. And quickly. Have you seen the LA video?"

"Half a dozen times. That little shit rushed our mighty friend here. Roland used his momentum. I doubt he even had to move his feet. Hell—I probably could have done it."

Roland thought to point out that it wasn't so easy, that the technique he'd employed to snap Barsamian's cousin's neck looked effortless because he'd trained enough on the execution of that move that he didn't have to think about how to do it, that the move executed itself through Roland. He remembered explaining to the cop in front of KTLA that his attacker had committed accidental suicide when he'd swung his machete.

"President Trump's right about one thing." Roland was looking at both agents. "It's much harder to kill a man when he's moving away or fighting back."

"Close the door behind you. You're doing a tremendous job, guys." He held up his thumb and forefinger a half-inch apart. "Maybe just *a little bit* too tremendous."

The agents holstered their weapons and straightened their suits and left the room. President Trump sat back down and Roland after him.

"Where were we?"

Roland, still a bit shaken, shook his head, not to say that he didn't know where they'd left off but that he couldn't believe what had just happened.

"They weren't going to shoot you. I know danger—I did business with some pretty rough hombres in New York and New Jersey. Mostly in my younger days on my way up. I could tell you stories—lots of stories. But I didn't bring you here to talk about me."

"I get the message." He picked up his hat, the crown half crushed from when he'd landed on it, and tried to form it back into shape, but it was pretty well smashed and would never be the same.

"Not yet. I haven't finished yet."

"I appreciate your concern, Mister President." Roland stared at his hat, still shaking his head in a show of mourning over its damaged condition.

"I've got more than concern—I want to make you an offer. That's why you're here—to hear my offer."

Roland put the hat down and leaned back and crossed his arms. "Okay."

"Let's get back to golf. Do you golf?"

"No."

"Never golfed?"

"My buddies and I once hit a bucket of old golf balls into the lake where I grew up, but I was just a kid."

"I bet you hit the snot out of it."

"Could never get 'em to fly straight."

"That's cuz it's a difficult game—hardest game in the world—greatest test of mind and body—not for the easily frustrated."

"I won't argue with that."

"So, my offer—my challenge, really—is for you to learn how to play golf."

"Because I worked on your video game?"

"No. Because..." Trump took a moment to think. "Because I want to play golf with you, out in Mar-a-Lago. Tiger Woods too, if he's available. Would you like to play golf with the leader of the free world and the greatest player of all time?"

Roland uncrossed his arms and leaned forward and looked at President Trump. "Yes. How could I say no to that?"

"Easily—by saying that you don't want to learn."

"Ok then, I agree to learn. That's a good incentive."

"I'll send you a set of clubs, top-notch clubs, best clubs money can buy. Do you have a particular brand you want—no you don't—you don't golf. I'll take care of that. And I'll special order the extra long shafts. What are you, six-five?"

"Six-six."

"As soon as you can break ninety-five, I'll take you out with Tiger Woods. Can't promise Tiger Woods—can't promise Woods—but I'll try. I have to work around his schedule."

"That's like twenty-five over par, right?"

"Something like that—depends on the course. A ninety is considered bogey golf. You have to be really, really good to play bogey golf on a legitimate course. So, I'm saying ninety-five. Gives you a few extra strokes over bogey. Most weekend golfers can't break a hundred."

"I think I get the idea."

"Do you?"

"Yes—I won't be able to break ninety-five if I'm a drunk. Is that about the size of it?"

President Trump nodded yes. "Not if you've never played before. Golf is about minimizing mistakes, and when you're learning it's just one mistake after the other."

"Maybe I'll never get there—sober or not."

"Oh, you'll get there if you want to—athlete like you. I'd say less than a year if you work at it. But this is not about golf, let's make sure we're clear about that."

"I'm clear about that." Already he was trying to figure out where he would play and how often in order to become a bogey-level golfer in the space of a year.

"I learned from my father that a smart person learns from his own mistakes and a wise one learns from the mistakes of others."

"Yep. I've heard that too."

"Do I strike you as a fearful man?"

"No—but I don't..."

"I'm not. There's no way you can get to where I am in business if you're afraid. Risk is part of the deal. You can only get so far if you avoid risk. But there is one thing I'm deadly afraid of, that I won't take a risk with—alcohol. Drugs and alcohol. I decided a long time ago that they would not be part of my life. What they did to Fred let me know that I might have inherited the same—what do you call it?"

"Predisposition."

"Yes—predisposition. But it's not just Fred. I've seen dozens of people—not just the celebrities we all know about—but people I know personally. Wonderful successful brilliant tremendous people—seen them lose everything because of drugs and alcohol. And this opioid—this Fentanyl—problem is out of control. I'm going to have to see what I can do to slow that down."

"I don't envy you that task."

"There are a certain number of people that are going to hate you no matter what you do, some even if you do exactly what they say they want you to do. So you might as well do what you think is right. Helps you sleep at night."

There came a knock at the door. "That's probably Maryanne. She advised against this little pow-wow."

"I guess I should be grateful, sir."

"Time will tell. Time will tell."

The knock came again. President Trump stood up and Roland stood up and collected his things. "I'll leave you to it."

President Trump came around the couch and shook his hand. "Live your life. Don't let it live you."

He walked Roland to the door and opened it and Roland tipped his hat to disarm the derisive smile of the impatient Mrs. Conroy, then he turned to President Trump and said thank you.

Jim led him back to the shiny black Lincoln. The morning had cooled. Maybe a front coming in. Roland had no sense of East Coast weather. In the Northern Rockies you could see the weather coming from far away and how fast and how much rain or snow it was likely to drop, but here he was out of his element.

"Is it going to rain?"

"No. Probably not."

"That was pretty fucked up, that stunt you and your buddy pulled."

"Nothing personal. Just showing off for the new potus." He opened the car door to let Roland in.

"Forgiven." Roland removed the injured hat and looked at it as though to make sure it agreed.

"I'm supposed to take you back to the hotel."

"I'd rather walk. I want to give myself an unguided tour."

"You can't walk around here, not on the White House grounds. And there are a few reporters at the East Gate. I can take you past them aways and drop you off."

"No. Take me to the reporters please."

Jim moved away a few feet and pulled out his mobile and spoke to someone for a minute or so and came back. "Ok, get in. I'll drop you outside the gates."

Roland admired the immaculate lawns as Jim drove to the exit. "I plan to walk the pentagram."

"You can't just walk into the Pentagon, even if your brother works there."

"I said pentagram, not pentagon."

"Never heard of the pentagram walk."

"The guy that laid out Washington DC was a Freemason and gave the city an occult design. The White House is the fifth point, the bottom of a giant pentagram. I plan to visit the other four points: Washington Circle, Dupont Circle, Logan Circle, Mount Vernon Square. Lucifer owns this sulfurous swamp. I believe you were a little possessed yourself, the way you came at me with your gun drawn and your eyeballs playing tug-of-war."

Jim curled his lip and nodded sarcastically and let it go. "You plan on sharing that little episode with the press?"

On the way over, the man had been distant and officious, a bit superior and professionally annoyed, but now he'd suddenly become a human being. Roland guessed that once you've pointed a pistol at an innocent man and been told to put your weapon away, you owe that man the courtesy of treating him as a normal human being.

"I thought you were listening."

"What do you mean?"

"To me and Trump. The place was mic'd obviously, and you had eyes on me."

"So?"

"President Trump and I agreed to keep the meeting confidential?"

"So why do you want to talk to the press?"

"Same reason women wear lipstick and heels—to arouse the public."

The East Gate opened and Jim drove through and swung the wheel and snugged the car against the near curb on Pennsylvania Avenue. A group of reporters on the sidewalk eyeballed the car with obligatory curiosity.

"Ok, pretty boy, out you go. Your fans look like they get paid by the hour." Roland opened the door and emerged slowly, one careful boot at a time, tucking his chin to his sternum and pressing the crown of his hat to his head as though to keep a sudden gust of wind from carrying it off. To delay the moment further, before he got out, he leaned back into the car to leave the driver with parting words and improvised a truthful, though half-hearted, "No hard feelings, Jim—hope you never have to take a bullet in the line of duty—don't open your umbrella in a thunderstorm." Words spoken hurriedly and forgotten with the thud of the town car's heavy door. He stood and raised his chin. *Will they recognize me?* The Lincoln sped off. With only a sidelong glance at the reporters, Roland started walking. The reporters, seven or eight of them, jerked toward him like a school of fish. "Roland Hazzard!" It was a female voice. He spun on his bootheels to face them and forced a smile. They looked like interns, freelancers, real go-getters, not a recognized journalist among them.

"Y'all waitin' on little ol' me?" He remembered something his mother said in one of their recent conversations: *Do me a favor and pretend I'm listening any time you speak to the public.*

They shouted their predictable questions, like a pack of dogs barking at a crow on a wall. He regarded them until they quieted down before addressing them generally.

"Your voices got all smooshed together, so let me just say that I did in fact just sit down with President Trump..." Their handheld devices jockeyed for position to capture his face and voice. "... and we had a nice long chat. He thinks the country is in very good hands and we should all feel lucky that we dodged a bullet last November. He's got a fancy new pair of Patagonia waders to wear when he set himself to the task of draining the swamp..."

"Why did he want to talk to you?"

"You guys've heard of the Defense Department, right?"

They stared mutely. "The DOD?" said one of them.

"Did Trump offer you a defense job?"

"Sort of. But not with DOD. He's creating a new department for me to take charge of—Department of *Self*-Defense."

A few of them chuckled. Roland decided to play it for all it was worth. "One of my first projects is to pay people who stop crimes in progress and even capture criminals. There are so many cameras around that a lot of felonies are caught on video, and if a self-defense panel determines there was a crime in progress and a particular person or group of people stopped it, certain financial rewards can come into play. We're still at the fifty-thousand-foot level on this idea, so the devil will be in the details."

"A return to the bounty hunters of the Old West?"

"Way more better. Everyday citizens will know that the government has their back if they have the stones to step up and do the right thing. There's too much cellphone video online of people watching while victims are being mistreated and abused. So, I want to pay people to put their phones in their pockets and stop crime instead of recording it."

"Will the heroes get their faces on food packaging, like on Wheaties boxes? Bad guys on dog food, good guys on breakfast cereal?"

Roland took a step back to better address the group. "Let's see if this dog will hunt. Savvy, kemosabes?" He pointed to the man who'd asked the question. "I'm going to give this sarcastic sum'bitch a mild to moderate beating—maybe just slap him ruddy—and the rest of you are going to see if you can stop me. If you can, each of you gets one of these." He pulled out a wad of hundreds from his jacket and fanned them. They laughed, but timidly. He lunged at them without moving his feet, then smiled and put the money away. His proposed victim laughed, and they all joined in on the joke.

"Is this for real?"

"Is what for real?"

"The Department of Self-Defense?"

"Like I said, planning stages."

"Trump's on board with this?"

"I've probably said more than I'm supposed to, but that's the general idea."

"Won't Congress have to approve it?"

"Anyone who votes *no* won't be in congress very long."

Roland pulled out his sunglasses and put them on and tipped his hat and strode away. "Adios, muchachos."

They started to follow him. He turned around. "Now look. I had my driver drop me into your laps. I didn't have to do that. And I've given you something to chew on, so if you don't mind…"

"Can we assume now that Roland Hazzard is a Trump supporter?"

"Assume at your peril. I support any and all elected officials who are willing to put the bad guys behind bars or in the ground. Savvy?"

More questions came forth. He held up his hand. "I have a podcast. You wanna know more, you can find me there." With that, he walked off, and briskly.

~~~~~

Roland strolled along the Potomac under a row of skeletal cherry trees, denuded by winter. The wind rubbed against the skin of the loitering river and in patches seemed to push the rippled water back the way it came. Roland stopped and made sure no one was close enough to notice before he hung his hat on the thumb of a branch and left it behind. The breeze chilled his head as he walked. He pressed the soles of his boots hard against the concrete path, as though he could affect the rotation of the Earth or wobble the planet on its axis. He made his way past George Washington University toward Washington Circle in the Foggy Bottom district and found a 7-11 where he bought a knit cap and scarf, a pack of cigarettes, and a half pint of whiskey, which he opened and drank in one tilt standing right there at the counter as the clerk watched. He screwed the cap back on the bottle, set it on the counter with a thunk, said thanks, and walked out.

He kept walking. It felt like east. He muttered to himself as he pitched forward, head woozy from the crash of alcohol on his brain, the image— the very type—of the babbling street drunk he might one day become. *Couldn't he have just called me? Did he have me fly out all this way just to tell me about his brother Fred? Were those guns loaded? Maybe it was all a stunt, a little theater to shock me straight.* He picked up another bottle at the next 7-11 he saw and headed toward the National Arboretum to hide out for a while. The sun overhead pulsed behind the flat white cloudcover and cast a widespread glare. Roland looked through his polarized lenses and tried to discern the outline of the orb but could make out only its diffuse molten perimeter. Chin pointed upward, he nearly lost his balance and stepped to one side and weighed an arm to keep from falling over but did not retract his skyward gaze. In that moment, so disoriented, Roland imagined himself floating in a spacious air pocket inside a thick Antarctic sheet, there enraptured by the marvel of what seemed a volcanic eruption boring into solid ice. He imagined that in that laboratory of elemental extremities, where the Earth's primordial combustion met the ancient glacial cap, must yet live some impossibly durable microbial lifeform devised at the birth of the planet by The Creator's first generation of workshop elves. A harmless but unkillable species of bacteria, perhaps, perfect for novices practicing their craft. And when the eruption finally broke through there would begin a slow, unstoppable process whereby the inside of the Earth would consume its outer surface with unquenchable fire leaving only that simplest of species to reign without consciousness over our once blue-green world. Venus would weep and Mars would laugh. Roland scowled. *Nobody knows anything and the people who think they can uncover the universal secret are the most laughable of all.*

He found an isolated spot in a grove of beech trees and leaned against one and drank, slowly now, as he sunk to a seated position with his back to the tree, sipping himself to sleep as he fought the urge to pull out his mobile device and send out something to entertain his droogs.

~~~~~

He woke up slumped to one side with the bottle cradled in his lap nearly empty, momentarily terrified by his unfamiliar surroundings and his inability to remember how he'd gotten there. In the faint light, he couldn't tell if it was dawn or dusk. He closed his eyes to focus his mind and swallowed hard. *This is no way to live.* It took him half a minute to piece things together. He took out his phone to check the time. It would be dark in an hour or so. He finished the bottle and pocketed it and left the park to find more alcohol.

North across New York Avenue lay the neighborhood of Brentwood, quiet enough at this hour. He spotted a little church, yellow paint peeling from its wooden siding. Where there are houses of worship there surely must be liquor stores. He tottered up Montana Avenue. What trees and vegetation were able to subsist on these neglected city blocks looked suicidal this winter. None of the people he saw acknowledged him. If he didn't find a market soon, he decided, he'd flag a taxi and return to the hotel. What Roland didn't know was that the closer he drew to Rhode Island Avenue, just up ahead, the less likely a taxi would be. Businesses were few, but trade went on nonetheless, transacted hurriedly in the shadows, though that was mostly just for form, as the police were no more present than taxis. And there were plenty of dark corners with most of the streetlights burned out and few of the buildings shedding any light. Roland sensed he'd ventured too far into the bleak unknown and turned around to head back while he could still remember the way. A car, the lone car moving on the street—a sparkly amber Chrysler—rolled up on him. A window slid down to reveal the face of a young black man, scalp squeezed tight by a latticework of cornrows. Roland stopped and waited for the kid—kid?—his age was hard to divine—to speak.

"Whatchoo lookin' fah, niggah?"

"Soul food and a place to eat." Roland wasn't looking for heroin and was sure that the kid—whose threatening tone, by Roland's impaired judgment, did not entitle him to a straight answer—missed the musical reference.

"You playin'? Youze da wrong place fah playin' with a niggah, niggah."

"Just taking a walk on the wild side, mindin' my own."

All the windows were tinted. Roland couldn't tell if the back seat was occupied. All he could see of the driver were his arms and hands on the wheel. Whether it was just the two of them or a full crew, this was no time to show weakness.

"You here ta do bidniss?"

"How much for a ride to the Trump Hotel, fellas? I took a wrong turn back at the Arboretum."

"How much you got?"

Roland heard the question but ignored it. "But I need to find a liquor store first."

"Look like youz'ad plenty a' dat. Howzabout a little boost? Little somp'n to puts the light back in y'eyzz?"

"Do I look like a tweaker?"

"Looks like you don't know what's good fah you."

Roland had heard that opinion too often, said different ways, but this occasion stung him worse than the others.

"I told you—I need a ride to the Trump. A hundred bucks to take me to the Trump."

"You stayin' dare? No playin?"

"I am—if I can get back to it."

"How much you payze a night?"

Roland realized the kid was not trying to assess the contents of his character, but that of his wallet.

"No idea. I'm on President Trump's dime. I met with him today in the White House."

The kid spoke quietly to the driver and then turned and spoke to the riders in the back seat and then turned back to Roland.

"My boyz is gonna get out and let you in so weeze can give youze a ride."

The right rear door opened and a young black man in a black leather jacket and black chinos got out. Cornrows got out. Roland took a step back, then another. The driver put the car in park. The door behind the driver opened and a third man got out. Then the driver got out.

"I'll sit anywhere you want," Roland said to the driver, "but I ain't gonna drive."

"Youze too drunk to drive," said Cornrows.

"Troodat," said Roland.

"Let's see somm'a dat Trump chedda," said Cornrows.

"I ain't playin' fellas. I need a ride. If you don't want to make a hundred bucks, then I'll find my own way back."

"We needz t' seeze da money firss," said Leather Jacket.

Roland scanned the faces of the four, then stared directly into the eyes of the cornrowed kid as the other three deployed themselves in an arc until Roland was half-encircled. They meant not just to *seeze da money*, but to seize the money. It was more irony than he could bear, and he laughed. Here was as good a place as any to die. His parents could certainly use the little fortune in his bank account. A cushion for their retirement that might soften the blow of the stupid circumstances of his death today. Probably not today, though, thought Roland, not unless they have guns and were willing to use them.

"Before we get busy, I think you guys should look me up."

"Look you up?" said Cornrows.

"I'm all over the internet."

Cornrows motioned to Leather Jacket, who took out his phone.

"Put in *Roland Hazzard Butcher Slayer.*"

The man tapped in the search words and viewed the result, at first skeptically, and then with a growing interest that reached a smiling fascination. The others huddled around his screen as he replayed it, this time with the volume turned up so that Roland could hear his theatrical voice declare a citizen's arrest before issuing the preposterous command: *Interlock your fingers behind your head.* What the malefactors witnessed next choked their incipient laughter. Then from the phone came the screams of the onlookers.

Leather Jacket said, "I heard 'a dis muth'fuka. Heezz bin-on tee-vee. He killed a niggah what killed a bunch a shorties and dis niggah wiff da sword wuz the cuzz."

"Izz gonna take moren dat t' setchoo free a' Montana Avenue," the passenger said.

"This some kinda white tax?"

"Izz d'muthfukin Trump immigrant tax muthafucka," said Cornrows. "And I'z puttin' it on for'ners like youself."

"You guys'll need weapons."

"Naa. We gotchoo," said Leather Jacket. "That Arab cuzz wuz a pussy."

Roland thought to inform these unfortunate souls that Barsamian and his *cuzz* were Armenian, not Arab, but it looked like the situation had moved beyond conversation. Still, Roland tried to keep them engaged.

"I got news for you. We're all pussies. All the way up to Jesus."

"Jesus was a pussy?" said Cornrows. "We outta kill you just for sayin' dat."

"How Jesus was a pussy?" the driver said.

"You read the Bible?"

"Had it read to me more'n I can count," the driver said.

"What were Jesus' last words?"

"God, why you done fucked me?" Leather Jacket said.

"Dass right," said Cornrows. "Niggah done shit hisself 'fore he went out. Hit da speed-dial to Daddy when he heard five-o wuz comin'."

"How dat?" the driver said.

"He whined like a little bitch. Axed Daddy to step up and stop it."

"Yep. His human side—the pussy in us all—came out at the end."

"Dat don't mean we lets you go," Cornrows said.

"I guess a Christian upbringing don't count for much anymore."

"Showz us what you got," the passenger said. "I'm tyrd a bein' talked to. Give it up."

"You guys behind on your felony count for the day?"

The passenger repeated Roland's words in a nasal voice like a black comedian mimicking an educated white man.

They moved in closer, Cornrows in front.

"We gots no quota. We take 'em as they come."

Roland stepped back for a third time and readied himself for a fight, mentally choreographing the order of his strikes.

"Dis ain't no Jackie Chan movie. You can't take four. We gotchoo."

"The prospect of it focuses the mind. Repeat that sentence if you know what it means."

They formed the points of a compass around him. Cornrows wasted no time and skipped forward, shifted all his weight on his front foot, and threw an errant haymaker that Roland barely had to dodge. With a low side kick, he swept the kid's forward ankle and sent him down hard on his left shoulder, then he spun around to attack the nearest fighter, the leather jacket, and took hold of his shoulder and elbow with both hands. Before he could wrench the shoulder from its socket a car came squealing up and jumped the sidewalk and rocked to an emphatic halt. The doors burst open and Jim and his partner leaped out with their guns drawn.

"DOWN! DOWN! DOWN!"

The three upright assailants laid down with their arms spread out like they'd done that before while their associate on the sidewalk next to them rolled in pain. Jim jumped on the back of the passenger, the largest of the four, and held a gun to the base of the young man's skull. "Give it 'a me."

"What?"

"If I have to reach into your pants and get it myself, I'll break your nose with the sidewalk."

The passenger moved his right hand very slowly down from his head then under his belly and slid out a nine-millimeter pistol pincered between his thumb and forefinger and let it go as soon as it was free of his body. The partner bent down and took the weapon and put it in the car.

Jim got off the man. "You can get up now. Let's have a look at all of you."

"Was that necessary?"

"He was about to pull the gun."

"The president wants to make sure you get back safe," the partner said.

"You should have come sooner. I think I hurt this kid." He gestured at Cornrows. "I might have had to hurt them all."

"Or they'd have hurt you," Jim said.

Roland flung up his arms in a mocking show of joyous victory. "Dereliction of duty either way!"

"Please get in the car, Mister Hazzard," the partner said.

"Ok," said Roland, now gesturing to his assailants. "C'mon you guys. Let's go have a drink at the Trump International. There's a foot massager in my room. Rocket you into another dimension."

The young men returned to their feet and two of them helped up Cornrows.

"Damn, you wazn't playin'," the driver said.

Jim holstered his weapon. "You want to press charges, Mister Hazzard? I can call the local PD to come over and take these gentlemen into custody."

"Aren't you listening? I want these gentlemen to be my guests at the hotel. They can follow us over. My room has a great view of the Washington Monument and all the sparkly lights behind it bouncing off the Potomac. I'll order up a jug of Courvoisier. It's a once-in-a-lifetime chance, fellas."

Before they could respond, the partner, weapon still drawn, put the kibosh on the invitation. "They'll have to take a rain check. You won't be staying there tonight."

"What are you talking about?"

Jim explained. "The chief said that if we found you drunk in town to pull your room and take you straight to the airport." He looked squarely at Roland and nodded.

"The chief?"

"The Commander in Chief," the partner said.

"He ain't drunk," said Leather Jacket.

"Naw," the driver said. "Weeze just messin'. Mister Hazzard just showin' us his Jackie Chan."

Jim looked at his partner and swept back his jacket and unsnapped the cover on his holster but did not remove the gun. The partner kept his pistol pointed up next to his ear with his finger on the trigger. Jim looked back at the defeated black males. Cornrows was standing under his own power but rocking with pain. "You know we could shoot all of you dead and drive away and it would never make the papers. You know that right?"

"Four shots and we'd be done," said the partner.

"That cuz weeze all heart," said Cornrows.

"C'mon guys," said Roland. "Let 'em come."

"We'll be guarding the tombstones in Arlington if we let you roll in drunk to the Trump International with a bunch of local felons," Jim said.

"Racist," said Cornrows.

Roland pulled his wad from his pocket and peeled off four bills and handed one to each of the young men. "My apologies. The man in the picture was one of the great American abolitionists. He had your back from the very beginning."

"We haz much respect for the Benjamins," the driver said.

"This ain't zackly reparations," said Cornrows.

"Let's go, killer," said Jim.

"Sorry, fellas. Nice meetin' y'all."

"You gotsta take orders from the man, just like all us niggahs," said Cornrows.

Roland crossed his wrists in front of him in the manner of a prisoner being led away and walked to the rear door of the Lincoln. As he was about to reach for the handle, the door opened wide.

"Little brother." It was Phillip and he did not appear to be amused.

He slid over to let Roland in. In his lap was Roland's damaged hat. He handed it to Roland.

"Littering is against the law."

"I hung it on a tree. Donation to the world at large."

"On the ground, in a tree—it all counts as despoiling our beautiful river scenery."

"Shouldn't you be overseas lecturing our tribal allies in Afghanistan on the western definitions of murder and rape instead of picking up litter in the capital?"

Jim lined the men up in front of their garish Chrysler and took a few pictures then told them to get in and watched them drive away. Then he got into the government vehicle and his partner wheeled it around and drove the other way. The brothers sat in silence. Roland leaned back and enjoyed the warmth of the heated car. "I need my stuff, my laptop at least."

"We got it."

"When?"

"When you passed out in the arboretum."

"Why didn't you grab me up then, since you were following me?"

"Jim wanted to. He called me. I told him if you made it back to the hotel okay, then let you be. But just to hedge our bets we collected your stuff and kept an eye on you."

"I could'a taken those four. I'd'a made it back."

"We probably just saved your life. Even if you win that fight, there were more on the way. You can't defeat a mob."

"You wanna save my life? Stop somewhere I can get a bag full of hamburgers. Then convey me to wherever you must."

Phillip looked at Jim and Jim nodded. "That will help sober him up."

They drove. Phillip put his hand on Roland's shoulder to show him how genuinely relieved he was that his brother was safe.

"Yeah. I guess that was pretty stupid."

"It would've been my fault, Roland. I convinced these guys to lengthen your leash."

"What are you going to tell the president?"

"I don't know him." He motioned to the agents in the front seat. "Talk to them."

Jim had an answer. "If President Trump wants to know the details, we'll tell him the details. We'll start with you passing out under a tree."

"Fair enough."

They drove in silence for a few minutes. His feet ached in his boots from so much walking. He could have nodded off in an instant but for his hunger and chose to stay awake so as not to embarrass Phillip.

"What did you and President Trump talk about?"

Roland pretended that his mind was elsewhere. "What?"

"You heard me."

"Well."

"Either tell me it's none of my business or give me a simple answer. I heard the bullshit you fed to the press—*Minister of Self-Defense.*"

"Those idiots will believe anything. I almost went with Minister of Consciousness."

"I'm not all that curious to tell the truth."

"He told me he likes the cut of my jib. Challenged me to break ninety-five so we can play golf at his place down in Florida."

Jim looked at Phillip and nodded that was true.

"Did you tell him you've never played golf?"

"Ergo the challenge."

"You gonna give it a try?"

"You know me well enough."

"I'm not so sure. I know I used to know you."

The car pulled into a Wendy's and the driver purchased hamburgers and off they went to the airport. Phillip and Jim escorted Roland inside and, with the power of a Secret Service badge, secured a first-class seat for Roland on the next direct flight to San Francisco. By the time he took his seat, Roland's head was throbbing from the effects of withdrawal. He ordered two servings of whiskey before the doors were closed and drank them warm from their little bottles and was sound asleep, snoring softly, before the plane took off.

Chapter 20
February 2017

*R*oland Roland Roland. *What hath thou become?* An intruding voice heckled him down his slide into dissipation. Conscience? Maybe. But there were other voices, too. *Your star is rising, eh?* A mocking echo of his recent proclamation to his droogs. He opened his eyes, fully clothed in his empty bathtub with the shower curtain drawn. His sagging stomach groaned. It received an alarming reply. *Roland eat a gun.* That frightened him. He clamped his hands over his ears and stood up and elbowed his way through the curtain and toppled over the edge of the tub and pulled his hands from his head to break his fall as he crashed to the floor. His right wrist bent back past tolerance. He grabbed the wrist with his left and squeezed against the pain. Now the voice again, but this time more than one and at a quickening tempo. *Roland-eat-a-gun. Rolandeatagun.* Not a commanding tone, but a childish pitch, a chorus of imps pronouncing a sentence, as from a verdict, so ordered and to be carried out by his own hand. He cried out twice, "I do NOT OWN a GUN! I do NOT OWN a FUCKING GUN." The voices went silent.

On his knees in the hallway now, battling a gag, eyes watering both from that and the shooting pain in his wrist, Roland drooled copiously onto the now well-trodden bloodstain, which bore faintly still the sweet smell of animal decay. With great effort and a loud guttural retch, he vomited a sad little trickle of bile that mixed with the puddle of drool. He knew neither the time of day nor the date, but at least he knew where he was. The hecklers—were they within his brain or without?—had retreated. *I will live this day. I will live this day.* That was the best he could say for himself, not sure that the alternative would not be better. Then came a knock at the door. "Christ," he inveighed, addressing the Redeemer.

"Roland?" It was Astrid. She sounded worried. He got up and opened the door. She wore pajamas, ones he'd never seen. *How many different pairs does this woman have?*

He'd forgotten to wipe his mouth. He turned his head and drew the back of his hand across his chin. "Good morning, Hemlock."

"Are you alright?"

"I am as I appear to be."

"Are you alone?"

"Quoth the raven."

"What?"

"Nevermore. Never been more alone. Whaddaya want?" He sounded not irritated but defeated.

"Who were you talking to?" They shared a bathroom wall. "I heard—I felt it, actually—a loud thud and then you said…"

"I was on the phone. Yes. I slipped on the wet floor while I was on the phone and couldn't catch myself in time."

"What did you mean, *I do not own a gun?*"

The very mention of a gun in San Francisco required investigation. Roland lacked the energy to elaborate on his lie, to invent a conversation that might plausibly lead him to loudly declare alone in his apartment that he didn't own a gun.

"No tango un arma."

"Fuck, Roland, do I need to call the police?"

"Astrid, my dutifully vigilant neighbor and friend, if you want to call the police then I suggest you do that. But tell them my exact words—I-do-not-own-a-gun. I was talking to my sponsor if you have to know. He thinks I'm suicidal and he forced me to tell him that I don't have a gun. He reasons that without a gun it takes some planning and deliberation to commit suicide, and he wanted to make sure I didn't have the means to kill myself expeditiously."

"You have a sponsor—an AA sponsor?"

"I don't call him unless I'm drunk. I know—that's twisted."

"Why are you holding your wrist? You can kill yourself pretty fast with a deep slash."

Roland showed her his wrist, which had begun to swell. "I sprained it when I fell. It hurts like hell."

"You're sure you're not suicidal? It smells like you're drinking and smoking yourself to death in there."

"The only thing I'm sure of right now is throbbing pain. But if it helps—I have no plans to kill myself. Not today anyway."

"What about moving out? You've been saying for weeks that you plan to move out—is that still true?"

A difficult question for Roland to answer honestly, especially in his present condition. It was true that he meant to move out, had been sincere in stating that intention to Astrid three or four times since January; but as he'd taken no steps in that direction, he couldn't exactly say he was planning on it. Since his return from Washington DC, the building had been defaced repeatedly with anti-Trump graffiti, and you never knew when a band of protesters was going to show up and imprecate his name—Trump's or Roland's or both—at the top of their lungs. Usually, it was Astrid that shooed them away. Her interest in his moving was, therefore, more than casual. Still, her perseverance was no match for the inertia of a solitary, unemployed, practicing alcoholic with a healthy bank account.

"Wu won't let me break the lease. I still have three months to go."

"Bullshit."

"I know. That's what I told him."

"No. You're lying. You haven't talked to Mister Wu."

"Oh yeah? How would you know?"

"Me and the other tenants approached him about you, and he said he'd send you a letter promising you he won't enforce the lease and will return your security deposit in-full with no questions asked."

Roland felt too beleaguered to correct her grammar. Wu's alleged letter, he figured, might be among the unopened mail strewn on the table in his parlor.

"You're right, Astrid. I'm a sack of shit. Now, if you'll excuse me, I have to finish throwing up." He closed the door slowly, tentatively, not to be rude, with eyes downcast.

~~~~~

It took a few days for Roland to summon the courage to address the mounting mail situation. The collection, it seemed, grew all on its own, like a multicolored colony of rectangular lily pads propagating on his tabletop. He deduced—for there was no other explanation—that he brought the mail in blacked-out coming home from his nightly perambulations to and around Chinatown. The pile was a source of comfort actually, for it proved that even in oblivion he maintained both the good sense to empty the little mailbox for the carrier's sake and the coordination to operate the tricky old lock in the bent metal door. He found the letter Astrid mentioned and read it. She was half right. Mister Wu—a man he'd met only once, on the day he moved in—offered to let him out of his one-year lease but made no mention of returning his security deposit without an inspection. He refolded the letter and put it in his toaster, which he used as an organizer—bills in one slot, anything else of importance in the other. One thing was clear from the brief communique—Wu was not trying to force him out. Whatever else one might say about the San Francisco Chinese, they made it a point to mind their own business. He ate in their lunchrooms and drank at their bars because they politely left him alone. Since his tête-à-tête with President Trump, however, the remainder of San Francisco was off limits to Roland, at least the livable zones. He could, if he chose, tiptoe with impunity through the feces on the needle-littered sidewalks among the destitute and addled; but in the professional quarters, he could count on receiving the occasional finger or verbal rebuke. Even trudging down the hill to Chinatown at night was a risk, if being confronted by angry zealots in public counted as a bad experience. A different personality might have embraced such encounters, but not Roland. The public persona he'd created over the months since the killings thrived on stage and in front of the camera, but the essential Roland Hazzard remained a mild-mannered multiple martial arts master who shied away from conflict. Shied away even from his mail.

One delivery, however, stood, quite literally, apart from the rest—a set of golf clubs sent by The White House propped in one corner of his parlor. And not just a set. Someone on the president's staff—if not the man himself—had ordered him a shiny leather bag embossed with the presidential seal, attached to which were a similarly signified golf towel and club brush. It was a complete kit and a first-class one. The ball pouch was filled with balls—again, sporting the presidential seal. The shoe pocket contained shoes in his size. Another zippered pouch revealed golf tees. Roland had let the bag stand for days. Didn't even open every zipper.

He pulled out the five iron and gripped it as a golfer would and hinged his wrists to feel the weight of the clubhead. The injured wrist was still very sore, and he observed that golf was out of the question for the near future. It occurred to him that a normal person would have gone for an x-ray just to see how badly he'd hurt it. He put down the club and picked up his phone and called his White House contact, Maryanne Conroy.

"Good morning, ROLAND HAZZARD." In their previous conversations, she'd not been particularly friendly.

"Hi, Mizz Conroy…"

"Missus Conroy."

"Sorry—Missus Conroy…" He hesitated, thinking he should make an excuse and beg off the call.

"What do you want, Mister Hazzard?"

"I hurt my wrist."

Silence on her end. More than silence. Roland sensed flummoxed consternation. He knew she couldn't hang up on him.

"You called to tell me about an ouchie on your wrist?"

"The president didn't give me his number, and I don't think I would have bothered him about it anyway."

"Excuse me. I'm very busy here. Do you want me to pass along a message to President Trump? *Roland called to say he hurt his wrist?*"

"He sent me a complete set of Titleists. He's going to take me out to play at Mar-a-Lago. I assumed you knew about that."

"When? I know his calendar by heart."

"I can't swing a club. I doubt I could even putt without pain."

"When were you supposed to play?" She sounded irritated.

"We haven't set a date yet—I need to practice first. The reason I called—if you'll bear with me—is I want to know if he's said anything that might change that."

"Change what?"

"Our golf plans."

"Ohhh," she said, in a tone of sudden comprehension. "Do you want me to find out and call you back?"

"No. I just wanted to get your sense of it."

"Why would he change his mind about hosting you to a round of golf?"

"You heard what he said about me at the press conference a few weeks ago?"

"Maybe I did, but why don't you remind me. I can't keep up with everything he says."

"He basically told the reporter that I was fulla shit and had no business using our meeting to troll the press."

"That's not how I remember it."

"He seemed upset."

"I think he was upset that the reporter was wasting his time asking about what was obviously a joke."

"But he did say I had no business saying what I said."

"You mean about him setting you up as head of the new Department of Self-Defense?"

"Yes."

"Not right out in front of the White House. If you'd waited and said it online, then who gives a shit, but not right after your private little sit-down, and with the White House in the background. Bad idea."

"But he's not mad?"

"What if he is?"

"Then I'll send the clubs back."

"Who raised you?"

"Excuse me?"

"Let's walk through this step by step. The president of the United States invites you to the Oval Office. He offers to take you for a round of golf at his private resort. Afterward, you spew a bunch of nonsense to the press and then proceed to stumble around drunk in DC until the Secret Service has to rescue you from a gang of violent thugs. Right so far?"

He decided not to quibble about being rescued. "If this were a trial, I'd have to stipulate to all of that."

"Then he sends you a brand-new set of golf clubs. Now, at what point in that sequence of events does it occur to you to question the president's integrity?" She'd have made a formidable AA sponsor. Roland heard Denny's tone underneath her superior diction.

"Why insult my parents?"

"Because if you're this insecure and ungrateful, maybe your upbringing has something to do with it."

He took a deep breath. "My brother is the youngest person ever to achieve the rank of major in the Marine Corps, so I guess they're off the hook as far as parenting goes."

"You're right. I'm very sorry. And I don't mean to hurt your feelings, but there's one thing you said that I agree with completely."

"What's that?"

"That you're full of shit. And something makes me think you believe your own bullshit."

"I didn't say I was full of shit. I said the president said…"

"The president said nothing of the sort, not to the press anyway. He defended your *offbeat sense of humor*. I think he used that exact phrase. That's a long way from saying you're full of shit. You were describing yourself. The president, on the other hand, is not full of shit. He's a man of his word. If he said he'd take you out for a round at Mar-a-Lago, then you can count on it. Now, before I hang up, do you have a message for President Trump? If so, I'll convey it."

"Tell him I got the clubs and want to thank him and that I sprained my wrist pretty badly so I'm a little behind schedule and I'll be sure to let him know when I'm ready to play."

"You see?"

"No. I don't think I do."

"All that unpleasantness could have been avoided if you'd just started with that."

"I'll let you get back to work, Missus Conroy."

"Not so fast. Before you get back to doing whatever it is you do, Roland, let me give you a piece of advice." She didn't wait for his assent. "I don't know why the president decided to—I don't even know how to put it—decided to invite you into his private confidence. Frankly, it baffles me. I'm a pretty shrewd political consultant and he pays me very well; so I was a little perturbed that he didn't consult me before he elevated your dubious public profile. But it's not my job to second guess him, only to give advice when he asks for it. So I've kept my mouth shut. But I won't hesitate to offer you my unsolicited advice." Now she waited.

"Go ahead."

"If you want to stay in the president's good graces, don't talk about him. Not in interviews, podcasts, tweets, not in any public forum. You're a loose cannon. Stick to secret alien bases in Antarctica and gigantic Wisconsin skeletons—anything that will keep your little minions chasing their shadows."

"Wisconsin giants—I'll look into that."

"New York Times, 1912. Start there."

"You're kidding me."

"The older the paper the more likely it's telling the truth. Journalists these days spend more time filtering the so-called news to suit their agenda or flat out inventing alternative facts than actually reporting on events."

"Can I quote you on that?"

"Very funny, kid. Just leave my boss alone."

"Will you give him my message?"

"I said I would."

He said goodbye and she ended the call. He put down the phone and leaned back on his couch and stared up at the cracks in the yellowed white paint on the ceiling. In two years of living there, he'd never noticed them. He spoke to the cracks. "Tell the president I hurt my wrist?" "Idiot," he said to himself.

He wasn't sure that wasn't why he'd called, but he couldn't fathom himself well enough to surmise another reason. Still, that reason didn't ring true. He sat there for close to an hour inhaling his own body odor, gulping back thirst. Apart from his conversation with Astrid—and then just now with Maryanne Conroy—he hadn't partaken of meaningful human interaction in more days than he could count, so befogged were those drunken weeks. *To cry or not to cry?*—his loneliness distilled that simple question. But to cry from an isolation wholly self-imposed would count as an admission of defeat, the abdication of the throne in a derelict castle. He realized then that he'd picked up his phone to satisfy a basic human need—human contact. The need for sympathy, to be more precise. Like an elderly shut-in who called his financial advisor once a week just to talk about his aches and pains. Perhaps the cackling taunts that sent him fleeing his bathtub that painful morning days ago were a sign of mania brought on by prolonged isolation. How could he know? One thing was sure—hope lay only in the reclamation of his dignity. He'd put everything on the line just now. Yesterday he could have sold the clubs and washed his hands of them. But the bargain he'd struck with Trump was no longer strictly a private matter, and in calling Maryanne and asking her to pass his message along he'd reinforced the contract such that it weighed on his character with ponderous consequences. Her words—*I said I would*—indicted the very question that elicited it, as if to say that only a person of lazy integrity would imagine that the other would not keep her word. Trump himself, it appeared, could be trusted as well. The tears withdrew. The question became: *To golf or not to golf?* He laughed at his pathetic wrist and picked up his phone with his good hand.

Joshua answered. "Roland, what gives?"

"Any progress on a book deal?"

"It's seven-thirty."

"Seventy-thirty is a bit steep, don't you think?"

"Seven-thirty in the morning. You're doing this on purpose, aren't you?"

"I'm in a good mood. Just got off the phone with Maryanne Conroy."

"What does that have to do with your fantasy book deal?"

"My connection to Trump—that's got to pump my prospects up a bit."

"No one has reached out to me about a book deal. If you want me to make some inquiries, then send me a book proposal. I'll help you work on it but send me a rough draft first."

"You don't sound optimistic."

"You don't inspire a lot of confidence. I've left you messages the last couple of weeks, but you've been off the grid."

"What kind of messages?"

"Just checking up on you, making sure you're okay." Joshua sounded both sleepy and emotionally drained.

"I shut off all communications with the outside world so I could get some writing done." His lies composed themselves. "I'll have a book synopsis for you today or tomorrow."

"Ok. I'm eager to see what you've been working on."

"One more thing."

"What?"

"Can you hook me up with a golf pro—a local teaching pro?"

"I'm sorry, Roland. I've lost the ability to detect whether you're serious or not."

"If I fill your ears with foul angry language, will that convince you I'm serious?"

"Why—I'm sorry—I mean, what brought this on?"

"Promise you'll believe me."

"I'll believe only what's believable. It's a professional weakness."

"Trump wants to take me golfing."
"And you don't know how to play—is that what you're telling me?"
"I need to be able to break ninety-five. That's his condition."
"Yeah, you'll need some help if you want to get there anytime soon."
"I know. Can you help me?"
"The lawyer golfs."
"McAfee?"
"Call him. He likes you."
"What are you implying?"
"What are you inferring?"
"That *he*, as opposed to *you*, likes me!"
"No. I meant *he* as opposed to *most people.*"
"If you want to sever our connection, just say so."
"I just fucking promised to read your book proposal."
"I don't want you to do me any favors."
"You placed this call to ask me for a favor."
"I mean as my publicity agent, Joshua. If you don't like my message, my public image, then don't represent me."
"You need to return my phone calls."
"Have I missed anything important, anything lucrative?"
"A few things. Nothing very lucrative, but lucrative. I'll put the details in an email. Now let me get back to sleep."

Joshua ended the call before Roland could sputter an apology. No matter. He set the device down and, in reward for the morning's industry, filled a vase with water and drank it down, for there were no clean glasses. There he stood in the kitchen, slit-eyed, bristle-headed, haggard, disheveled, unwashed, malodorous, chin dripping and, moreover, quite satisfied that he was an up-and-coming literary talent, having written nary a word in weeks.

~~~~~

His alarm went off at 3:30 PM. Soon the busses would roll in force west down Sacramento Street full of commuters from the Financial District. The parking police and their attendant tow trucks were, even now, Roland knew from experience, poised to ticket and whisk away at the stroke of 4:00 every vehicle still parked in the bus lane. The cost and inconvenience of being caught in that bureaucratic net had disciplined

Roland to keep an alert on his phone set in perpetuity. He buttoned off the alarm and got up and picked through a bunch of old grapes for the edible specimens and ate them. He spread peanut butter on a crust of bread and ate that, then he took his last wrinkled apple, which resembled a shrunken human head, and tested it with his front teeth before devouring it. He filled an empty plastic water bottle from his jug of vodka and set it on the counter.

The five-iron stood against his table in the parlor. He took it and held it as before then put it back into the bag and pulled out the nine. *Any fool can hit a nine.*

He looked at the open page on his laptop screen where he'd written at the top: *Book Proposal—A Time to Kill by Roland Hazzard*. Must be a dozen books or movies by that name, he thought, but none of them a philosophical memoir. Perhaps he'd invent a whole new literary genre! He closed the screen then found his baseball hat and sunglasses and grabbed the counterfeit water bottle and carried it with the shiny new nine-iron to the Jeep International Scout and drove to the driving range at the Presidio and purchased a large bucket.

Roland hit every ball, some seventy-five in total. He winced with the first few timid swings and sipped his vodka against the pain. His initial intention was only to test his ability to hit the ball high and reasonably straight, which, as he'd mumbled to himself before, most coordinated people could do with some consistency using a nine iron. But by the end he was smashing the tired old range balls, hooking and slicing them left and right, just to see how far he could make them go. Here and there he caught the club short on the plastic mat inches behind the ball and doubled over in pain, his wrist humming like a tuning fork. He swore aloud and glared at the people who looked at him. By the end, his hangover quashed but far from satisfactorily drunk, Roland understood his reason for being there had nothing to do with golf. He'd come to punish himself, both physically and psychologically. He'd come to put his brokenness on full display and execrate himself in close proximity to sober and serious practitioners of that most difficult of athletic endeavors. He'd come to flail—and fail—publicly and to hurt himself in the process. It was a refuge from his apartment—the three ill-lit rooms, the permanent bloodstain, the unholy lure of instantaneous publicity on the sundry social media channels he inhabited, and finally, the computer's infinite ream of electronic blank pages that he could not, try as he might, populate with words. The Bridge held more appeal and was not too far from the Presidio.

He drove instead to Deidre's and knocked on her door, said her name as he knocked, but she was either not at home or ignoring his entreaties. He'd have told her he'd injured his wrist somehow and needed medical attention and he wouldn't have had to invent the cause of the injury if she'd opened the door. A lie would have issued so effortlessly from his mouth that he himself would have been merely witness to it.

He found a store and bought a pint of whiskey then drove to the ocean to smoke and watch the sun go down. He stared through his polarized lenses at the nuclear furnace and felt himself pulled toward it like an iron shaving to a distant magnet, then suddenly repelled, as though the magnet had reversed polarity. In a bout of vertigo, the sun enlarged and shrank like a pendulum along his sightline, growing closer each time it swung toward him. He took a long drink and propped the bottle in the sand. *What kind of God...?* He couldn't complete the thought above the sun's infernal denunciations. Demonic wisps leapt from its turbulent corona and were sipped back in. Screams. Faint, hilarious screams. What sort of God would create a frail beast in God's own image and likeness— infused with a spark of divinity—then judge it by God's own divine standards; and then, finding it wanting, punish it forever? He took another swig and set the bottle back in its rut. Such a God is unacceptable. He believed in something else, something more reasonable, not the strident denials of Thomas Paine nor the profane fulminations of Robespierre, yet something less extreme than draconian medieval theologies. The Creator does not lead us to temptation, he felt certain. Nor does the Creator punish those who lose their moral footing and spin weightlessly off the wheel. Such souls, irretrievable, float free and quickly are pulled into the sun for immolation, each one letting out a final shriek in recognition of the ultimate loss. He fingered a hole in the sand to bury his cigarette butt and found the dampness cool and pleasing and dug deeper in to bury and soothe his throbbing wrist. *And what of you, Fred Trump? What became of you, deceased First Brother of the USA? Do you inhabit an alternate dimension now, or have you been recycled? Perhaps you so dishonored your existence through drunkenness that you lost the privilege to continue and were drawn into yonder sun for extinguishment?* He drank the more with his good hand and lifted the bottle to bid the Sun farewell as it fizzled into the Pacific. He took out his mobile device and dictated his thoughts into the recorder for use in his coming masterpiece. He swooned, reclined, and dozed.

A heavy fog crawled in, obscuring the night. When he got up to leave it was dark, the bottle nearly finished. He took John F. Kennedy Drive through Golden Gate Park to lessen the chance of contact with the police and soon found himself disoriented. The meandering roads through the park were poorly lit and the mist reduced what visibility there was. On top of that, he didn't know the layout, didn't know exactly where JFK Drive ended or where its tributaries led. He figured he'd just drive and let the park spit him out then navigate back home on the city grid. He took a right down Crossover Drive, a left on Martin Luther King Junior, another left on Nancy Pelosi, a right down Bowling Green past Robin Williams Meadow, which took him back to MLK Junior at the south edge of the park, the opposite side from where he wanted to be. To correct his mistake, he made a sharp left and found Kezar Drive and drove eastward into The Panhandle toward Oak Street and the Haight-Ashbury District. From there it would be a straight shot to Van Ness Avenue and an easy route home. He exited the park on Oak going a little too fast, bottle between his knees, steering with this damaged right hand and lighting a cigarette with his left. A figure appeared in the roadway, the image of a shoeless man in a long gray coat, swathed in brume. Roland blinked. The man, his head thrown back, his face upturned to the sky, was laughing, laughing wildly, wildly but inaudibly, and not at the sky. He was pointing at Roland, the forefinger on his left hand crooked and aimed squarely between the driver's eyes. The crazy old dawdler, nose to the watery moon, was laughing at Roland Hazzard. He blinked again, swerved left to miss the lunatic, and crossed into the oncoming lane. He dropped his cigarette and grabbed the wheel with both hands to regain control and yanked it back hard the other way and pitched the car onto two wheels. He jerked the wheel left again—the worst thing he could have done—and rolled the Jeep into a US Postal Service mailbox bolted to the sidewalk. He heard the crash. A newer, lighter car might have glanced off the sturdy government fixture, but the 1964 Jeep International Scout ripped it off its moorings. Roland, unbelted, shot forward headfirst into the glass. Had his left knee not caught the steering wheel, the impact would have thrown him free of the car and into the street. The Jeep came to rest on its side. His unconscious body lay wedged on the dashboard trimmed with polygonal bits of safety glass. The radiator hissed and spurted. Unprocessed mail littered the street. The wheels, one at a time, came to a stop.

~~~~~

He rose, motionless, the hiss of the radiator now a persistent buzz, as of a fly. Below him, the wreck. His arm—the right—hung limply on the hood of the car, the pain in his wrist completely gone. As he ascended, he scanned the road for the man who'd sent him off course, but the man was nowhere to be seen. Roland knew he hadn't struck the stationary pedestrian, and his disappearance perturbed him. The condition of his once beautiful car perturbed him too. The buzzing increased. It did not, he realized, emanate from the car. It came from all around. It dawned on him: *I'm sober. That's my arm. That's me. That's impossible!* Again, the buzz, louder still. He remembered the first line of a poem he admired by Emily Dickinson. He remembered the praise he'd received for the thesis he'd written on her work to complete his English degree. *I heard a Fly buzz—when I died.* Could it be? His mind had never felt so sharp. If this was death, then life was dull. As many times as he'd been out of body in lucid dreams—this was different. He couldn't navigate this space, let alone sense up from down. Still, he'd never felt so completely alive. The scene before him fell away, or he was pulled back from it by an unknown force. His view of the crash below constricted rapidly as if seen through the wrong end of a telescope. Then the picture blinked out.

Roland found himself alone, suspended in a chamber of indeterminate size, but an enclosure nonetheless. Pitch dark. He perceived neither floor, ceiling, nor walls. The medium in which he floated, seemingly motionlessly, weightlessly, lacked the quality of air. He imagined the space that encased him was something like a domed arena of which he was the sole occupant, and though he felt utterly alone there was no fear in him with which to contend.

He brought his hands to his face, as was his custom when out of body, but he couldn't see his fingers. Still, he was not troubled. He knew he wasn't blind, only that there was nothing to see. Yet all was well. He knew he existed, knew more keenly than he'd ever known it. He knew that if nothing changed, he would be content to remain suspended in this lightless, soundless chamber forever. Everything was just fine, even his complete lack of understanding of what was going on was just fine. He comprehended serenity. He knew peace. Life on Earth was over. Not a big deal. He closed his eyes and opened them—not a wit of difference. Would there be sleep here? Dreams? His mind began to branch into realms of inquiry he'd never entertained. He apprehended mathematical interrelationships—sacred geometries—that simplified reality. Then he saw a light, a pinpoint of radiant light far into the distance, like a tiny pinprick in a black curtain that separated the space he occupied from a sea of brilliance. He opened and closed his eyes again to be sure he wasn't imagining it. The strangest thing—the light emanated music, a faint interweaving of melodies of transcendent beauty produced by no instruments he could identify. Like his spontaneous mathematical insights, the music was both impossibly complex in its structure and organically simple in its effect, as though, like the wind, it had a life of its own. Not the oppressive heft of Dickinson's cathedral tunes. And when he closed his eyes, the music stopped. He opened them again, and it resumed. He did it over and over, as one would play with a new toy. He wondered—Was the light playing peek-a-boo with him, or he with the light? It didn't matter. Nothing mattered. He, the light, the music—they just were. Their presence had no particular meaning because their presence was their meaning. He turned his head and the light followed, always dead center where his vision converged, whether he looked up or down or over his shoulder, there it was. And when he closed his eyes, the music stopped.

If I'm dead, why am I alone? Do we all get our own private nursery and a musical light to play with? Not a bad deal, but not what I would have expected. No religion paints this picture.

As soon as he posed the question, the light drew closer and the music more distinct, not louder, just more delicate and beautiful, and what had been a pinhole of white light took on a more kaleidoscopic look. Subtle pinks and greens swirled in the approaching marbled glow. He passed his hand before his eyes and the light penetrated his astral form, though a bit blurred. He counted his fingers, five on each transparent hand. *Now what?*

The light had a voice, though not an audible one, a voice that answered telepathically. "Patience," it said. "The hardest lesson of all."

"Why am I alone?"

"You're not, are you?"

"Okay. So who are you?"

The light was now the size of his fist. The outline of a human form appeared and separated itself from the glow like a drip of wax.

"Patience, Roland. I'm new to this too."

The figure came forward and stopped before Roland and quickly, like a focused lens, clarified in sharp resolve.

"Grandpa Merrill? Popa?"

He was dressed just how Roland remembered him as a child, in a thin wool blazer and a duckbilled woolen cap, at once vaguely nautical and professorial. A character, and proud of it, except now his face was smooth, unblemished by the florid blooms powdered over by the mortician to conceal the signs of the booze that killed him.

"You've made a mess down there."

Roland looked down. He could see the crash on the street below him again, but hazy now, as through a pane of heavy glass.

"How did you do that?"

"Don't waste time. That's the second hardest lesson."

"Am I dead? I thought the whole time-thing was abolished in the afterlife."

"No. Not dead."

"So, what is this?"

"A visiting room—a parlor. It's not very fancy. I had to throw it together on the fly. I told you I'm new to this. Fred was not allowed."

"What's going on? What's this all about? Fred who? Fred Trump? You know Fred Trump?"

"Not exactly know him, but we're all connected here."

"Not allowed to do what?"

"Visit you as we're visiting now."

"Why's that?"

"You would have been angry. That would have made communication impossible. Another difficult lesson."

"Why?"

"You know why."

Roland paused. Telepathic dialogue had its advantages, but one drawback was that you couldn't lie. He tried to clear his mind of thoughts and concentrated on listening for more information, but the truth was he had already intuited the answer to his question, not from Grandpa Merrill, but from the circumstance itself.

"That was him, wasn't it, in the road, laughing at me? He caused the crash on purpose. You're right, I would have been angry. In fact, bring him in so I can …"

"You see? This is not productive."

"Why did he do it?"

"You called him out."

"So he tried to kill me?"

"Your death was not authorized. If it had been, you wouldn't be here with me right now. You'd be on the flipside with a host of others."

"Where's Jesus? I want to talk to Jesus."

"This sort of thing is way below His pay grade."

"You're going to send me back there, aren't you?"

"I'm not in charge."

"I don't want to go."

"We're running out of time."

"Why did he do it, Pops?"

"A lesson in humility. That's as much as I know."

"You said authorized. Who authorized this?"

"One of the Elohim, I'm guessing."

"Elohim?"

"A high-ranking spirit. One that's never been incarnate—Divine Council, maybe. We don't have time for me to explain the organization."

"So, what's the purpose?"

"Ahhh, now we're getting somewhere."

"Please just tell me, Grandpa."

"I can't tell you your purpose. I can only tell you that you will not achieve it if you keep on drinking. Fred fell far short, and so did I—we couldn't lick the booze. Everyone has to conquer addiction. It's a basic requirement."

"Requirement for what?"

"To remain on the flipside, among the saints and bodhisattvas. Many faiths have a word for it."

"The flipside? Is that the source of the light?"

"The Creator is the source of the light. The flipside is what people call Heaven."

"I want in. I like the music. Look at my body—it's all beat to shit. Isn't there something you can do?"

"Your work is not yet done. Besides, I have no control. I'm not even here, actually."

"What do you mean?"

"I'm a projection. Most of me is back with the light. The rest is in another body down on Earth."

"What do you mean, a projection?"

"I am who your grandpa was, not his true essence."

"Like a ghost?"

"Yes," Grandpa Merrill chuckled, "like a ghost."

"And part of you is in some little kid back on Earth?"

"And when that life ends, that spirit will be rejoined with my soul—the life force to the eternal consciousness—for another evaluation. But just for now I was called upon to project this message, to talk to you, so you would understand. Fred has done you a wonderful favor. Given you a great gift."

"How can you be in three places at once?"

"By the power of the Trinity. Our time is almost up."

"I don't understand this gift."

"You get to know what others don't. You have a reason to change, to start living right. Most people on your path stay on it and, when they return to the source, find out they've made little or no progress. You have a chance to move forward. Someday, if you take the right path, you'll meet Fred and you can thank him."

Below him he saw flashing lights and people standing around and paramedics slowly extricating him from the wreck. He could feel himself tugged down toward Earth and saw his grandfather fading.

"I'm sorry about the Jeep."

"Me too. A beautiful machine. I took good care of it."

"It's gonna hurt, isn't it?"

"Yes, but only for a while." Grandpa Merrill was far away now, being pulled back to the light.

The music began to ebb. He heard below him the sounds of his earthbound emergency.

"Is there a Hell?"

"A few choose something like it. A very few. Those that can't humble themselves before the suffering they have inflicted."

"I love you, Popa." Their separation was nearly complete.

"I love you, Roland. Here, everyone loves everyone. Tell your mother I said hello."

~~~~~

He awoke at 11:11 AM, a day and a half later, in a bed on the third floor of Zuckerberg Hospital from, medically speaking, a coma. The doctors weren't worried it would last very long as his brain activity was robust and his eyelids constantly twitching. When he finally opened them the daylight from outside the window, weak though it was, offended his eyes.

"Fuck."

"Roland!" It was his mother.

"Sorry, Mom. I didn't know you were here."

She came over and gingerly kissed the bandage on his head. His father fell in behind her.

"My God, Son."

"I didn't get that far."

"Thank God for that."

He tested his eyes again, cautiously now, and saw his left leg suspended in a cast. Pain shot through his entire body. "How bad is it?"

"As long as you're thinking clearly—that's what matters most."

"How bad is it, Dad?"

"You won't walk for a while."

"No internal injuries. Tell him, Harold."

"No internal injuries from the accident, but your liver's in pretty bad shape."

"I need something for the pain."

"They didn't give you anything hoping the pain would wake you up. I'll go get the nurse." She left the room.

"Your blood alcohol was point-two-six. Point-zero-eight is the legal limit here."

"I can't do math right now."

"You'll have plenty of time to practice math when you're marking time in jail."

Roland forced his eyes wide open to look at his father, to appraise the look on his face, to gauge his level of disgust. It was more than he'd ever seen and tinged with pity for added shame.

"Whaddaya mean?"

"You're under arrest. When you're well enough to be discharged, the hospital will sign you over to the police. You'll be arraigned as soon as you get out of here."

"I'm sorry, Dad."

"For what?"

"Putting you and Mom through all this hassle. I'll pay for your flight and hotel."

"Your friend Joshua took care of everything."

Millicent came in with a doctor and a nurse. The doctor spoke first.

"Mister Hazzard, so glad you could join us." His chipper disposition was a credit to his profession.

"I didn't have a choice."

"Of course. But we're glad that Mother Nature saw fit…"

"I asked to stay. Request denied."

"Asked who?"

"Grandpa, Mom. He told me to say hello. Last thing he said: *Tell your mother I said hello.* Now I'm here and here you are and I'm passing that along as instructed." The nurse put her hand over her mouth.

"Not a damn thing wrong with your patient, Doctor Gandhi." The two had conversed before by all appearances, well enough to be jovial.

The doctor turned to Harold. "What do you mean, Mister Hazzard?"

"No damage to his personality, anyway. Multiple concussions, subdural hematomas, half a dozen bone fractures. Five minutes out of a coma and he's cracking wise. That's my son, alright."

"You saw him?" said Millicent.

"Jesus Christ!" said Harold.

"I asked for Him. Again—request denied."

The doctor spoke up before things got too crazy. "It's not uncommon for patients in Roland's condition to believe they visited an alternate reality." The nurse looked at Millicent and nodded with her eyes widened to say that maybe it was more than just belief.

"What else did he say?"

"The rest was personal to me, Mom. But as he was leaving—or as I was being sent back—he told me to say hello. I'm glad he did that."

"I've heard just about enough."

"He's telling the truth, Harold. Can't you see that?" Roland looked at his father and pursed his lips and gave him a matter-of-fact nod.

The doctor and the nurse attended to the tubes and monitors attached to his body.

"Why did you not want to come back, honey?"

"I saw my body in the wreck, Mom, as I floated up and away. Not a pretty sight. And it was very pleasant over there, very peaceful, and I didn't even make it to the light. That's where I wanted to go."

The doctor looked at Millicent. "It's a common enough experience—the brain's neurochemical response to massive trauma."

The nurse stood behind him and gave Millicent her best skeptical look to say the doctor was full of shit.

"Mind your own business."

"Millicent!"

"Even if he's right, what harm does it do?"

"It was Grandpa, Mom. Let it go, Doc. No one can prove it one way or another."

"Tact and diplomacy unimpaired."

"Is your name really Gandhi? Or is my dad just horsing around?"

"I'm one of many Gandhis."

"I should have asked to talk to your famous kinsman. He might have enough juice on the flipside to let me stick around."

They all laughed to varying degrees, the nurse most amusedly.

"Now let's get down to the business of pain management. How would you rate it from one to ten?"

"Fifty. Does it matter? Shoot me with as much as I'm allowed."

"It's not a matter of how much. It's a matter of what."

"I'm a ten. Whatever works on a ten."

"You sound pretty comfortable. Someone with ten-level pain normally has a hard time carrying on a conversation."

Roland hiked himself up in the bed to make a man-to-man reply. "What are you tryin' to tell me, Doc?"

"You seem to have developed an unusually high tolerance for alcohol, especially for a man your age. Your BAC level when they brought you in normally would have incapacitated a man your size, yet you were able to drive a car. For the most part anyway. And your liver studies tell me that you've been hitting it pretty hard."

Roland leaned on his left elbow to raise himself up as high as he could go, as though to make sure he was taken seriously. "I'm not asking for alcohol."

"We would normally give you a fentanyl drip, but people with your predisposition often have a hard time tapering off opioids."

"If it makes any difference, I don't have a drug problem. Never taken a narcotic of any kind for recreational purposes."

"Well, with the national epidemic we're under a lot of pressure right now to…"

"Doctor Gandhi, look at it this way. The kid's going straight from here to jail, and from there to court, and from there probably back to jail for an extended stay…"

"Wait a second, Dad."

"Time for you to shut up and listen, Son. I'm doing you a favor here."

"I wish I were in shape to dodge it."

Harold ignored the remark and resumed with Doctor Gandhi. "I've spoken to the police and the assistant DA. His BAC was point-two-six. Aggravated DUI starts at point-one-eight. So there's no question he'll get the aggravated charge. And he's got two alcohol-related priors. Add to that his friendship with Trump and they might give him the maximum."

"I see. You figure he'll be in the system long enough to break whatever habit he might develop here."

"I don't want him to suffer if we can get around the policy, and I can't think of a better reason to make an exception."

"You make a very good case." Doctor Gandhi turned to Roland. "I hope your council in court is as persuasive as your father, young man."

When the fentanyl entered his veins, Roland's pain ebbed away. "Thank you. That feels better. That feels a lot better."

~~~~~

News of his crash and hospital arrest raced through the media, along with sundry predictable speculations, exaggerations, and fabrications. Zuckerberg Hospital hadn't hosted a celebrity in recent memory and, while security did its best to keep unwanted visitors from barging in on Roland, a few enterprising trolls managed, under false pretenses, to sneak onto his floor and peek into his room long enough to snap a few pictures of the heavily bandaged patient trussed up in traction. The dressing on his left hand made it easy for someone to photoshop in a credible—if oversized—middle finger in the obscene position. That image became a multi-purpose meme, most often used to indicate indomitability. Someone pasted President Trump's face on Roland's head and captioned it: *One button, one finger.*

And there were flowers, of course, more than his room could hold. Everyone on the third floor got plenty of spillover flowers for the first week or so. Cards and letters piled up as well. His mother screened them since Roland couldn't very well open an envelope. She kept the ones worth keeping and tossed the rest.

"Here's an interesting one."

Roland looked up. "Yeah?"

"I won't read it aloud. It's semiliterate. From a woman named Gillian who considers you a psycho but would still like to come to the hospital and…"

"Don't say it, Mom."

"I wasn't going to. I was thinking of a euphemism—how 'bout *give you a Lewinski?*"

"Toss it."

She opened another.

"This guy wants to take you on an scuba diving trip to check out an interdimensional portal at the bottom of the Baltic Sea."

"Save that. It's probably not a portal, but I've heard there's something down there that makes compasses go crazy."

"Here's another sexpot. She includes a picture. Kinda pretty. Do you want to see?"

"Nope. Toss it."

"Another well-wisher. This guy wants you to train him—offering a lot of money."

"Keep that too."

"This woman wants to have your babies…" Millicent kept reading. "Interesting…it's not a sex thing. She wants to strengthen the breed. She calls you the ultimate alpha male."

"Toss it," he said.

"This one's from New York." Millicent opened it and read. "Sounds like she knows you—Alessandra?"

"Hand that to me, please. I met her when I was there. She showed me around town."

Millicent held up a large blue one. "This one's from the White House."

"Go ahead and read it, Mom. Outloud. Don't summarize."

She opened the flap carefully to preserve the envelope and removed the card and read.

"*Dear Roland…*"

"Is it his hand? Look at the signature."

"Yes. It looks like he wrote it himself."

"Ok, thanks. Go on."

Dear Roland, the hospital tells me that you're pretty banged up but going to make it. My golf challenge is more on than ever. Use the sport as a tool for your rehab. You'll get there sooner than you think if you put in the effort. Who knows, one day I might be saying to you: You're hired! I'll be following your progress if you don't mind. Remember Fred. Regards, Donald Trump.

She put the card back in its envelope and set it aside. "What's the golf challenge?"

"He promised to take me golfing with Tiger Woods if I can shoot a respectable score."

"That's something." She waited for her son to say more but Roland closed his eyes. She waited again. "Who's this Fred?"

Roland kept his eyes shut. The image of the figure in the road he'd crashed to avoid—the person, specter, hallucination, whatever it was—flickered in his memory. What was real? What was not? Was his pain real only when the drugs wore off, or was it there underneath the fentanyl? Was it a lie to ignore her question? Was there a way to know?

"It's not important, Mom. I'm starting to fade."

Later that afternoon two police officers came in and one of them read him his Miranda Rights and placed him officially under arrest and explained the process and asked him if he had any questions and Roland said he had none and thanked them. The other officer, who'd been silent the whole time, told him he was lucky to be alive and that he was glad he had survived.

"I'm still mulling that over." The officers chuckled. Millicent eyed them disapprovingly.

~~~~~

The hour of his arraignment had arrived. The judge called Roland's name and the bailiff opened the door to the holding tank and Roland, in a mustard yellow jumpsuit, head bobbing on an opioid stream, crutched over to his public defender and leaned the crutch against the table and nodded hello to his parents and lowered himself into the empty chair next to his court appointed lawyer. The gallery was full of spectators, Joshua included, but Roland didn't notice him, eager as he was to sit down and get this business over with. The courtroom belonged to the Honorable Clarence Hazelrigg, known affectionately around the office as Judge Clancy. Roland felt the judge smiling at him and hoped it wasn't a gleeful smile, as of one happy to wield authority. When he looked up at the bench, he saw instead a compassionate, knowing smile. They'd met before.

"Good morning, Mister Hazzard. I can't say I'm glad to see you again, but I'm certainly glad you are well enough to be here." The white-haired Hazelrigg wore his late middle age with a supercilious mirth meant to keep everyone in the room guessing and eager to hear what he was about to say.

Roland, with obvious effort, sat up straight. "Thank you, Your Honor."

"Nor am I happy to announce that I was right about you, even though my prescience has earned me a free dinner at Julie's Supper Club."

Roland's public defender, one Joseph Clarke, rose a few inches off his seat but did not stand to speak. "Your Honor, if I may, I'm not sure this is appropriate."

"You get paid by the city and by the hour, Mister Clarke. Now let's talk about what's appropriate. Is recidivism appropriate?" He waited for an answer, but Mister Clarke only shook his head slightly, not to say *no, it is not* but to indicate that he considered the question gratuitous.

"Is it?"

"Mister Hazzard has been convicted only once, so he's not a recidivist."

"Excuse me, Mister Clarke, have you read the case file?" Clarke threw up his hands. "Mister Hazzard is not a hardened criminal."

"True. At least not as far as we know. But this is his third arrest, and this one is a felony case. I'd say he qualifies as a recidivist."

"You're right, you're honor. Technically speaking, you are correct. I apologize."

"Technically speaking? What is the law if not technical?" Muffled assent and even laughter from the gallery. The judge had the crowd.

"Do you want me to answer, Your Honor?"

"No. That one was rhetorical." He waited for the room to quiet down. "Now where was I, Mister Hazzard? Yes. Julie's Supper Club. Last year—what was it, April, around Good Friday?—when I sentenced you to a little dry-out time, I mentioned to one of the DAs that you'd be back within a year. Statistically speaking that's an iffy proposition, because while most offenders re-offend on a regular basis, rarely are they re-arrested within a year. Not in this city anyway."

Roland did his best to remain still and betray no reaction to the judge's reminiscence. He remembered the man, of course, but not nearly as well as the man apparently remembered him.

"The DA offered a wager—a dinner at Julie's—and I took the bet. Why, you might ask. Is this a regular thing between me and the DAs? I assure you it is not. In fact, it's the first time we've ever gambled, so to speak, on a defendant's future. So why did I make my prediction? It's simple, young man—I had a premonition, a shudder in my bones. Now, this sort of thing does not run in my family. My ancestors, who go back to the colonies, would have sooner burned a witch than given her a fair hearing."

Roland kept his eyes on the garrulous magistrate, who clearly was making the most out of what for some could be a tragically dispiriting job. Clarke leafed through the pages in Roland's file. The county prosecutor, alone at the other table, bit his lip to suppress his amusement.

"When you appeared in the news, I had to kick myself. My premonition was valid, I figured, but I was just not well-practiced enough in my paranormal powers to interpret it correctly. Then you quickly became a full-blown celebrity—and I won't comment on your pathway there except to say that your skill in maneuvering your way into that slander action on live television was something to behold—and at that point I was convinced that the shudder in my bones had been more like the wiggle in a divining rod that sensed your coming fame. Now here we are, almost exactly a year later, and I don't know what to think. Was my premonition true as it relates to your returning to my courtroom, or true only as it related to my seeing you all over the media? It's an interesting question, don't you…"

Clarke could stay silent no longer and interrupted the judge's rhapsodic diversion. "Your Honor, I renew my objection, not on legal grounds. It's just that there are a lot of cases to get through today."

"Mister Clarke, are you suggesting that I'm wasting the people's time? Would you rather just enter a plea and move on to your next case?"

"We're prepared to do that without further delay, Your Honor."

"I don't operate a mill here, counselor, especially when a man comes before me a second time within, let's say, a year. I figure I didn't make a strong enough impression the first time. Besides, in case you're not aware, your client's parents are in the room, and I think it's only fair to them that we exhibit a measure of compassion for their unfortunate son."

Clarke looked over his shoulder. Harold and Millicent sat side by side in the front row dressed like two congregants in their Sunday best among an unwashed horde. Millicent smiled at Clarke while Harold gave him a nod. He whispered to Roland, "Why didn't you tell me they were here?" Roland gave him a look that said *what does it matter?*

The judge spoke to Harold and Millicent. "Mister and Missus Hazzard, I'm glad you could be here today. The public defender—who is a very capable young man, by the way—would like me to move things along here, but I'd like to address a few questions to your son. Would you object to my doing that?"

Harold shook his head no to answer the question and held up an approving thumb. Millicent put her hand on Harold's shoulder.

"Mister Hazzard," the judge opened a palm and weighed the air. Roland took the cue and stood up.

"You're lucky to be alive. Let's start with that."

"Yes, Your Honor. If life is lucky and death unlucky."

"Well, what do you think?"

"I'm glad I'm alive, but I'm not scared to die. There is no death."

The judge looked over at the stenographer. "You got that, Chandra? *There is no death.*" She lifted the scroll from her machine and checked it and smiled to the judge and nodded then set her hands in position ready to continue.

"Did you see the other side?"

"I did. That or pretty near."

"Well, that's very interesting, but we're here to talk about what's happening on this side of the veil. I'm going to read the charges against you. Aggravated DUI, Felony DUI, Destruction of Government Property, Reckless Driving, and Possession of a Lethal Weapon. Do you understand these charges?"

"Not the last one."

"A single golf club carried inside a vehicle, without any other golfing equipment, can be considered a deadly weapon."

"Shouldn't I have had to swing it at someone first?"

"Probably so. I guess the state is wondering why someone with a violent history is carrying a nine-iron around in his car."

"I'd just come from the range at the Presidio. I was practicing. The nine is a good place for a beginner to start. And I've never committed a violent crime."

"I'll have to take your word for that, but you do have a violent imagination."

"I publicly advocate that all human beings be prepared and willing to defend themselves and their children and companions against violence. That little dose of common sense has earned me a large following, which is more of a statement about our times than it is about my personality or imagination."

"Grind up convicts into dog food—that says nothing about your personality or imagination?"

"Your Honor—It's a testament to the strength of a good classical education. In the past, when the law was there to punish the wrongdoer, no one talked about deterrence. If the punishment is just, deterrence is assured. As soon as society starts debating the question of deterrence, we know that punishment has fallen short."

"The justice you meted out to the Glendale Butcher didn't seem to deter his cousin, now did it?"

"You can't deter a kamikaze by telling him he might get shot down."

The judge spoke to Harold and Millicent again. "What are we going to do with him? Has he always been like this?"

"Yes," said Harold. "You can't tell him anything."

"I put him in God's hands when he was about four."

The gallery laughed. It was more of a derisive laugh at the mention of God than an appreciation of the truth put bluntly.

"Well. Looks like God delegated that responsibility to me for the time being." He looked a Roland. "Mister Hazzard, do you understand the meaning of a point-two-six?"

"Yes. It puts me down for the felony charge,"

"That's correct, but I wasn't speaking legally. Put the law aside."

"It means that when my blood was tested there were twenty-six microliters of alcohol per milliliter."

"Fair enough—you don't want to talk about it."

"I came here to enter a plea."

"You make it sound like you had a choice. The state has dressed you as a prisoner and brought you here so we could hear your plea. That should be obvious to a smart guy like you."

"My mistake, Your Honor."

"And with your recent financial windfall, you could have afforded a lawyer. Why are you using a public defender?"

"They wouldn't let me represent myself. The state requires itself to sit next to me."

"The state keeps statistics. How many defendants do you think register point-two-five and above?"

"I suppose you mean as a percentage of the total DUI arrests."

"Don't tell me you have both raw numbers and percentages at your fingertips. Broken down by county perhaps?"

"I'm not going to fight this."

"My understanding is that you have to surrender to beat it." The judge was in on it, too, it appeared. He knew the correct AA slogan for just this situation—*surrender to win*. How many times had Roland heard that one?

"I'm talking about this charge."

"I'm talking about something much more important. The fact that you're so scrupulously avoiding is that very few human beings your age could remain conscious long enough to reach that level of alcohol intoxication."

"I'm not proud of that, sir."

"Yes. But you're proud, nonetheless. Too proud to admit you have a problem."

"I think it's pretty clear I'm in the thick of it."

"Point-two-six and driving a car—that's a seasoned alcoholic."

Tired of standing on one leg, Roland took his crutch and lodged it under his arm and balanced his weight. He looked down at Clarke and pointed to the glass of water on the table and Clarke lifted the glass and handed it to Roland and Roland took a long drink and handed the glass back to Clarke. Then he looked at the judge.

"Guilty as charged, Your Honor."

"Alcoholism is not a matter of guilt or innocence, son."

Clarke spoke up. "Mister Hazzard would like to plead guilty and proceed as quickly as possible to sentencing. He does not want a trial. You'll forgive me for not being more familiar with his prior record, but given that he informed me at the outset of his decision I didn't see the point in…"

"You're off the hook, counselor. You're not the defendant here." Then he spoke to Roland. "Mister Hazzard, before I accept your plea, I need to make sure that you understand what you're doing. Once you formally enter a guilty plea, you can't contest the sentence that I impose. Do you understand that?"

"I do, Your Honor. I just want to know one thing beforehand."

"What is it, young man?"

"Can you put somewhere that the jail has to allow me to use my laptop and allow me to keep it charged?"

"I'm sorry, but you can't continue your internet antics while in custody. You'll know what your celebrity was worth by how many of your devotees show up when you're back online."

"I don't care about that. I just want to write."

Joshua rose from his seat at the back of the room and signaled to the judge with a wave. The judge raised his chin and cocked his head sideways. "Mister Hazzard, if I'm not mistaken you have an advocate in the gallery." Roland turned around and raised his hand hello to Joshua.

"Do you have any idea what he's doing here?" said Clarke.

"Not a clue."

The judge spoke to the bailiff. "Officer Wattle, please escort Mister Goldberg to the podium." Joshua walked forward to the bar and the officer opened the gate and Joshua nodded thank you and stepped to the podium.

"I wouldn't normally do this Mister Goldberg, but you've been a respected journalist for a long time in this city, so I think you've earned the privilege to intrude."

"Let me say upfront that I didn't come here to intrude, Your Honor. I came to give Roland some good news. When Roland mentioned just now that he wanted to be able to write, I thought I should share the good news with the court, as long as he doesn't mind." Joshua looked at Roland. Roland gave him a goofy look that said *who gives a fuck at this point*.

"Roland has a book deal, Your Honor. He's been prospecting for months now, and I just got an offer yesterday with a substantial advance. That's what I came here to tell him."

"*You* just received an offer? Are you his agent?"

"His agent, his publicist—it's fairly informal."

"You're responsible for releasing this genie from his bottle?"

"I could see what was coming from day one. The press was not going to give him a fair shake. So I got to know him and wrote the first and only news article based on an actual interview. It snowballed from there." Roland cleared his throat, not liking to be referenced in the third person repeatedly in one exchange.

"Did you bring the offer with you?" Joshua reached into his jacket and pulled out an envelope and the bailiff took it and handed it to the judge. The judge opened the letter and read it then spoke to Roland. "A hundred-thousand dollars—I don't know the publishing game, young man, but this seems like a pretty healthy advance to me." He handed the letter back to the bailiff, who returned it to Joshua.

"Well done, Mister Goldberg. You have softened my heart. Assuming your friend pleads guilty and spares the state the time and expense of a preliminary hearing and a trial, I'll give young Roland here a nice long stay at one of our finer establishments with specific instructions that he be allowed to write—which is already allowed."

Joshua pressed. "On his computer, Your Honor?"

"Yeah. Since we can call him a professional writer, I can arrange for him to be allowed the tool of his trade."

"Thank you, sir."

"Not at all. You seem to have the angels lined up behind you, and who am I to stand in their way?"

Judge Clancy waved Joshua away and took Roland's plea in short order and sentenced him to three months in county jail with a guarantee of regular physical therapy, access to his laptop (sans internet), and a rigorous recovery regimen—a euphemism for AA meetings. The state long since had made a deal with the ACLU not to use the AA name in its sentencing language and the ACLU agreed not to complain about the state's violation of the separation, albeit ephemeral, of church and state, God being a mainstay in the Twelve Step program. After a few customary goodbyes with his parents and Joshua, the bailiff led him back through the prisoner's door with nothing but a crutch and his designs on literary immortality.

~~~~~

Roland took a visual inventory of his cell. Six-by-ten, bunk bed, toilet, and a sink with a stainless-steel mirror affixed to the wall above it. One electrical outlet, useless, though, since they'd taken his charging cord, probably as a precaution against him hanging himself. He set his computer on the bottom bunk and pulled off the bedsheet from the upper bunk and tied it to the frame and tested its strength to see if it would hold in case he decided to try to beat the system. How much sheet would he need if he jumped off the bunk with his legs tucked? Would the force be enough to break his neck? Would the bunk topple over instead? To be fair to the prisoner, he wasn't contemplating suicide, only assessing the possibility. Why? If his grandpa's information was correct—assuming the encounter was real—then suicide would only delay the process or, worse perhaps, exempt him from it. Pascal's wager might be moot if he spit in the Creator's face after having been given every reason to finish this term on Earth in a responsible fashion. These machinations, he soon realized, were nothing but avoidance—not of having to go on living, but of having to open his laptop and get some work done.

Seated on his bed, he wrote in fits and starts until his battery died. He set the computer on the floor and opened his bag and took out the stack of cards and letters he'd saved from the hospital. The one from Alessandra was his favorite.

Dear Roland, I've been wanting to write you almost since the day you left, but email seemed a little too casual, and besides you probably get a thousand a day and mine might have gotten buried in the avalanche. As it turns out I'm glad I procrastinated, because now with what has happened to you, I get a chance to say much more than thank you. The job you got me is fun and challenging and all that good stuff, and most importantly I'm up to the task and the people here at CBN have stopped looking at me like a friend of the enemy. It doesn't hurt that I'm a dyed-in-the-wool New Yorker with all the correct attitudes, so I'm fitting in well and pretty sure when my year is up they will keep me on my merits. But who knows?

Today I got into it with one of the producers. He made a crack in front of me to the effect that he wished you'd died in the accident. I think he was testing me to see if would defend you. Well, I didn't hold my tongue. I told him in front of everyone that I'd rather take the subway home at night with you by my side than him or anyone else in the office, and that shut him up....

He put the letter back in the bag and tried to sleep. He missed his music. The fentanyl he'd become accustomed to had completely worn off. In his veins, angry blood cells jostled for relief. Raindrops by Chopin, Canon in D by Pachelbel, several others he could think of—lightweight fare, to be sure—would have smoothed the edges of the jagged little corpuscles—microscopic shurikens, he imagined—tearing the walls of his blood vessels. But music was not allowed. The pain pills they'd given him—some diluted form of codeine—did practically nothing. To ease himself, he closed his eyes and returned to the place where he'd met his grandfather—the antechamber to Heaven. The memory of the NDE—he thought of it not as a Near-Death Experience but as a Non-Death Experience—was the best he could do for music. Curiously, the memory hadn't faded as would the memory of a dream. Any doubts he entertained about its authenticity were abolished by the durable clarity of his recollection. When he closed his eyes and remembered the impossibly beautiful music, new details of the episode presented themselves. Recalling the experience, then, actually enhanced it and enabled him to ignore the pain lingering from his injuries and any apprehensions about the future that might have otherwise troubled him.

~~~~~

His first morning there a guard opened his door and woke him with a loud voice.

"Roland Hazzard"

His sleep had been fitful from the fentanyl withdrawal, and he answered immediately but curtly.

"Predicate nominative."

"What did you say?" The guard seemed offended.

"I am he. That is my name."

"I know your name. It's not Predator Dominant or whatever you said."

"I'm sorry. I'm still half-dreaming. Forgive me."

"The sergeant wants to talk to you. You need a few minutes?" It took Roland a second to deduce that the guard was asking if he needed to use the bathroom before leaving his cell.

"Yes. A couple of minutes will do." The guard left and closed the door behind him. Roland took a piss and brushed his teeth and wiped his mouth and grabbed his aluminum cane and rapped on the door with his knuckles. The guard opened it and let him out and motioned him to follow.

Sergeant Gutiérrez, overweight and saggy-jowled with a coarse black mustache and short-cropped graying hair, sat behind his desk in his glassed-in office. The wall behind him contained a long narrow wire-reinforced window a few feet below the ceiling. Its purpose was not for viewing the outside world but for letting in light. Judging from the angle of the morning glare, Roland guessed it was the south wall. The east wall supported a bank of closed-circuit TVs that monitored the common areas of the jail, including the shower room. Pictures, including one of the sergeant holding a framed award, hung on the west wall, along with a map of the jail. Roland wondered why the award the sergeant displayed in the photo wasn't itself mounted on the wall. His rectangular desk was made of cheap pine and there were two chairs in front of it. The guard pulled back one of the chairs and indicated to Roland that he should sit. Roland sat and hooked his cane on the arm of the chair.

"I don't normally meet with prisoners in my office. But we need to get a few things straight before you get settled in."

"Alright."

"You're probably wondering why I put you in solitary."

San Francisco County Jail segregated the sexes and further categorized its inmates as pre-trial, post-trail, and awaiting transfer, each group having a separate ward or pod. The Sheriff's Department, which ran the facility, set aside a few private cells for 'high-risk' prisoners, a euphemism for the especially violent. Normally, Roland would have served out his sentence in the post-trial ward, the largest and most relaxed of the three, as it housed low-level offenders; but the Sergeant saw fit to mark him as a pariah and slot him in one of the private quarters.

"I don't mind. I thought you were giving me a quiet place to work."

"If it were up to me, you wouldn't have that computer."

"I won't give you a reason to take it away. I won't cause any trouble."

"Your being here is trouble enough."

Roland held his tongue. Smartass rejoinders zipped through his mind, and he let them go wherever unuttered thoughts go. Still, the sergeant's remark needed some interrogation. He took a soft approach.

"I'm sorry, sir. I don't understand."

"You'll be eating your meals with the rest of the prisoners, and you'll have time in the exercise room with a physical therapist as well as visiting hours. Other than that, you'll be in your cell."

It occurred to Roland that Sergeant Gutiérrez had stretched the limit of his authority and was trying to get a sense of Roland's amenability.

"I guess now I'm wondering why."

"The laptop in the first place. If I put you in the common pod something might happen to it and then I'd have to deal with that. But my larger worry is you personally—how you will behave among the prisoners. We haven't had any serious violence in my jail in months because I take proper precautions."

"I'm used to being by myself."

"I don't want you to talk to anybody, other than staff. Not during meals, not in the visiting area, not in the exercise room."

"You mean I can't even be polite?"

"Smile and nod."

"What about the AA meetings?"

Sergeant Gutiérrez gave Roland a discerning look that weighed whether Roland was trying to be difficult or conscientiously thorough. It took him ten or fifteen seconds to come up with a reply. Roland scanned the monitors while he waited. He imagined this was the only government job in America that officially allowed you to watch people shower.

"I haven't spent much time in the recovery meetings, but I guess you're encouraged to talk in there. What I'm trying to tell you is don't engage in any idle conversations. If after a month you want to watch TV with the other residents, I'll consider it if I've seen that you're not causing any trouble."

"Causing trouble by talking to people?"

"Word gets around fast in here. It won't be long before everyone knows who's in the vault."

"I see. You're worried if you let me mix I might organize a revolt or something."

"What did you call yourself this morning when the guard came to get you? Predator something—predator dominant? That worries me."

"No, sir. That wasn't what I said."

"Do I have to call him in here?"

"Predicate Nominative—it's English grammar. If you answer the phone and the person on the line says: Sergeant Gutiérrez? One correct response is 'I am he.' That's the predicate nominative. He addressed me by name, almost as though he wasn't sure who I was. I was having a little joke with myself."

"That's too strange to be a lie, but still, it worries me. You make some off-the-wall remark like that in this place and people don't ask you what it means. They assume it's an insult."

"Okay. No more high-brow humor. You have my word."

"Regardless, someone might try to provoke you, or come at you."

Roland held out his arms and shook his head sadly at the condition of his body. "I'm in no condition to mix it up with anyone."

"I know what you're capable of."

"Is this like San Quentin? There some kind of badass pecking order in here?"

"It's not, but there are plenty of borderline personalities in here, men who act on impulse or for reasons known only to them."

"I won't kill anyone."

"That's not good enough."
"What do you expect me to do if someone comes at me?"
"Ward it off."
"What if it's more than one?"
"Roll up into a ball and play dead."
"I don't mean to be difficult, Sergeant. I know the Bill of Rights is null and void inside the county jail. You want to limit my freedom of speech, freedom of association—fine—and then my natural right to defend myself."
"Do you want your computer cord, or do you want to rely on me to keep it charged?"
"Okay. I'll keep to myself. No friends, no enemies."
"I'm glad we have that settled. It's time for breakfast."
"One more thing."
"What is it?"
"Aren't you worried I might hang myself?"
"The county has insurance for that sort of thing."

~~~~~

The guard led him from the sergeant's office to the breakfast room where he got in line with his fellow malefactors, his head still slick from yesterday's pre-arraignment shave in the hospital. The nurse had had to navigate the razor around the scars on his head and she told him he might just as well let it grow out in the can because even if they gave him a razor it would likely not be very sharp and a dull razor on the smoothest of scalps was precarious and a dome as nicked up as his was just asking to bleed.

"You've shaved a lot of heads?"

"I've shaved every part of the body that has hair except the insides of the nostrils."

The guard watched him from the doorway as he ate from his orange plastic cafeteria tray: watery oatmeal, dubious sausages, four-inch pancakes. The basket for hard-boiled eggs—a reward for the early risers—had been picked clean. He tasted the coffee. It wasn't coffee. The orange juice came in half-pint Tropicana cartons, so he guessed that was okay. Roland hadn't had a gulp of milk in years, but he figured in here he might as well take as many nutritious calories as he could find, so he drank the cup of leche they gave him. He glanced up at the guard, the one who'd come to his cell to take him to the sergeant.

You corpulent beady-eyed stringy-haired motherfucker. While I was brushing my teeth you had what—two minutes—to scurry off and rat me out to the bossman? Predator Dominant? Are you still reading comic books? A twelve-year-old would laugh at such a stupid name.

Murderous fantasies passed through his mind, and he tried to project them through his eyes into the mind of his enemy. The guard must have sensed his hostility. He stared back at Roland and drummed his fingers on the taser holstered to his belt. Roland reined in his animus. He realized, as if for the first time, how easy it must be for drug addicts to lose control, as now, still suffering from opioid withdrawal, he felt his emotions fraying. He had to stop himself from raising his middle finger to the man, and in that act of refrainment resolved to exhibit himself as the very type of Christ, at least for as long as he remained locked up. He looked away, then down, saw the food on his plate. It seemed almost a dare—*will I actually eat this?* The pancakes looked benign, he thought, *it's hard to fuck up pancakes.*

A presence approached from behind and loomed for a second then reached around him and set an egg on his tray and gave it a little spin. "Slayah," the man said and walked off without looking back. Roland watched him go, a tall, broad-shouldered black man with a powerful stride, not one to be trifled with under any circumstances. Another hand appeared and set an orange juice carton on the table next to his tray and a voice again said *Slayah*. Roland looked up and smiled and nodded, then he looked over at the guard to be sure he was observing this show of respect. Three more paid him tribute—adding two more precious eggs and another box of juice to his haul—each calling him *Slayah* before moving on. It seemed to Roland they must have conferred in advance on his jailhouse name—Slayer. He mulled it over as he peeled one of the eggs and decided he liked it and washed down the egg with tepid Tropicana orange juice.

The jail garb did not include pockets but, even so, he managed to carry the rations using his cane-hand to cup the eggs as he hobbled through the cafeteria exit. The guard preceded him to his cell.

"I'm allowed to talk to *you*, right?"

"I can't do you any favors."

"Not even carry my eggs for me?"

"You like movies, right? You're always talking about movies in your podcasts."

"I like them more than most."

"Then I bet you've seen *Cool Hand Luke*."

"Paul Newman—one of his great performances."

"Well, Cool Hand Luke ate all of his eggs."

Roland unpeeled an egg and popped it in his mouth and crushed it between his teeth and swallowed it.

"I thought you were going to say we *had a failure to communicate*."

The guard shook his head and reached out his hand and Roland put the eggshells in the hand and the guard put the shells in his pocket and opened the door to Roland's private cell and Roland stepped inside.

"Same time tomorrow, I guess."

"I'll be back in a few hours to take you to your meeting."

~~~~~

The men's jail offered two meetings daily, one in English, the other in Spanish, and if you weren't court-ordered it was hard to get in. The recovery administrator adhered to AA's standard for a closed meeting, whereby only real alcoholics (and, by extension, real addicts) were permitted to attend. Seating was limited. In the past, some inmates, during their pre-trial hearings, sought to curry the court's leniency by jumping on the recovery train. But the penal system got wise and realized that you can't have a bunch of fakers in a room where inmates—at least some of them— were sincerely trying to summon the willingness to lay down their war with the bottle, pipe, or needle. If the jail's recovery program was not indicated by the judge, the only way into the room was by petition from your lawyer or a family member, and the petition should include evidence of prior participation in a drug or alcohol abuse program and the name of a sponsor. Truth be told, the entire men's jail could have used the 12-Step Program, and not just for drugs and alcohol. Wrapping the mind around Step 1—admitting one's powerlessness— alone often had a sobering effect on one's outlook on life, and you could substitute just about any problem for the word 'alcohol.' But most of the men in the facility ordered to attend AA had become so habituated to their character defects and moral depravity they seldom got to Step 2, which required the formation of a belief that some unidentified Higher Power could restore them to sanity. Many had never known sanity to begin with and could scarcely define the term.

Meetings took place in the morning and lasted an hour. His first day, Roland squirmed in his seat, still trying to fit himself into his skin, and he listened carefully and took stock of everyone, wearing an impassive expression to ward off congeniality. The leader, Rinaldi, a self-described African-American who claimed to have survived numerous overdoses and episodes of life-threatening violence, had mastered the art of soft-spoken authority. His job was, to be sure, a difficult one, having to coax strength and hope from the few that seemed to embrace the principles of the program so they could serve as examples to the others. At the same time, he assessed the willingness of the newcomers and gently encouraged the vulnerable—the ones that had a chance—into the fold. The recalcitrant regulars—about half of the room—needed to be handled with respect on the off chance that their masks might slip and expose a sliver of humility.

Today, Rinaldi took up the subject of powerlessness, the principle of Step 1, always a good theme for the incarcerated. He went around the room eliciting participation.

A cocky fuckup around Roland's age chimed in. "I'm powerless over myself."

"Even in here?" said Rinaldi.

"Shit in here ain't for real."

"There's people a lot older'n you—a lot older'n me, even—who know nothing else."

"That must be how they wanted it."

"I'm thinking if you've decided that you can't control yourself, you'll be one of them too."

"I'm powerless over breaking into cars. No one goes in all day long for that. I hit more than fifty. Only reason I'm here is the last one had a bag of medicine a dude really needed."

"But alcohol? You've got that under control?"

"Haven't had a drink in two weeks." Half the room laughed. That's how long he'd been in jail.

The next man in the circle was up. "Hi, I'm Antonio. I really am powerless over breaking into cars—breaking into lots of things."

"If you can say that with a straight face, then you're halfway home."

When Roland's turn arrived, he straightened up and crossed his arms. "Roland Hazzard, alcoholic."

"The Slayah," said a young black man. "He's powerless over killin' niggahs."

"Please," said Rinaldi. "No crosstalk." Then he turned to Roland. "This is not your first time in the program, Roland, and I know you're not voluntary. Do you have any thoughts on Step 1?"

"Most people who can't manage their lives are not alcoholics, but if booze and drugs are getting in your way, it can't hurt to listen to what sober men have to say."

"If it rhymes it must be true," said the cocky fuckup. Roland shot him an irritated look and stayed silent for the rest of the hour. After the meeting, the guard took him to the workout room where a physical therapist, a Lebanese Canadian in his fifties by the name of Gad, waited to evaluate his condition and outline a routine. The focus was on his left leg. He had Roland lie on his back and took his ankle and flexed the leg back and forth, finding its tolerances.

"The x-ray shows the tibia has healed nicely, but the knee is pretty shot. If we work on it every day, we should have you off that crutch in two or three weeks. That's as optimistic as I can be."

Roland liked Gad. He treated Roland as a good doctor would a cooperative patient and didn't mention his exploits or the celebrity that followed. Roland thanked him when the hour was over. The guard took him back to his cell where he waited for an hour for the door to open again at lunchtime. Lunch brought more gratuities—apples, fruit punch boxes, a licorice stick. Roland kept his head down, nodding in gratitude at the magnanimous gestures and carried his booty back to his cell to wait for visiting hours. No one came on his first day, nor on his second. He added a few more names to his approved visitor list, but on the third day still no one came. The codeine prescription produced at least one desirable effect—it kept him from caring about his lack of visitors and didn't cloud his mind as he took up the task of writing in earnest.

Chapter 21
March 2017

He kept the letter from the publishing house taped to the wall next to the mirror and read it every day. The deal was fairly straightforward. It called for a memoir of between two-hundred-fifty and three-hundred pages and provided a twenty-five thousand dollar "working advance" with the promise of the remaining 75K upon his submission of a complete first draft, as long as it came within one year of the date of that initial correspondence. If the book was published, he'd receive the standard royalties. Roland had best get cracking. The work he envisioned would be the tale of his life from his earliest feats, beginning with the horror on his mother's face when he toddled into the house, naked except for his diaper, with a lizard thrashing between his clenched teeth. There were so many episodes of prowess, so vividly remembered, that Roland knew he could not touch on them all, so instead of laboring over the picking and choosing he decided he'd use a select few to serve as a scaffold for a treatise on, or rather an indictment of, the insidious power of modern civilization to bridle the human spirit by limiting the natural potential of the free individual. His proposition being that a person of his extraordinary inborn gifts felt, more crushingly than the average Joe, the boot of human institutions, be it the caprice of governmental authority, the arrogance of scientific consensus, the hypocrisy of religious dogma, the contradictions of social justice, or the vapidity of popular culture. Worst of all—pervading it all—was the addiction to technology, from instruments of war to digital gaming devices. The resulting erosion of conscience and numbing of the critical mind, he reasoned, had lowered the status of the species to where it was difficult to argue that humanity was worth saving. Perhaps can we detect an asteroid on a collision course with our precious planet—but why bother to send up a rocket to nudge it off course? Would the Earth not rather be rid of the cankerous boils of civilization that fester on its surface even if that meant it would take a few hundred millennia to recover from the cure? An awfully presumptuous theme, he understood, to weave through his arguably premature autobiography, but there was no reason not to swing for the fences. He might, it occurred to him, drop in a few comments that justified his use of alcohol, since, after all, one as naturally superior as he could hardly be blamed for taking chemical refuge from the absurdity of modern life. The truth, alas, was far simpler, devoid of any nuance—he drank because he enjoyed the effects of alcohol, no different than any other alcoholic.

He hunched over his laptop for hours at a time. If he couldn't produce a few hundred readable pages in the time allotted, then his high opinion of himself would be invalidated. That much he knew. It didn't have to be perfect, just good enough to fulfill the contract. The real work will be in the finishing, not in the drafting. He was free to type without pressure. *I'll start with the stories and add the jeremiads later.* The jail around him disappeared as he embarked upon his narrative through the portal of his computer screen. Time slowed to a crawl, his heart and respiration rates reduced to meditative levels. One afternoon he was interrupted by a knock on the door. It swung open before he could answer. It was his favorite guard, Kurt, a man of Slavic extraction who, sadly, bore the hallmarks of tribal inbreeding. Roland showed him a kindness informed by pity.

"Kurt, what can I do for you?"

"You got a visitor."

"Really? Who?"

"Do you care? You want me to find out—whoever it is must be on your list."

"Sorry. You caught me by surprise. I lost track of time."

"You want me to tell whoever it is you're busy?"

"I'll tell them myself if need be."

Kurt led the way. Roland hobbled after him with his cane and at one point told him to slow down since his legs were stiff from sitting on his bed for the last hour and a half. He hoped it was Joshua and was eager to tell him how well the book was coming along.

~~~~~

The visiting room consisted of a row of face-to-face cubicles separated by glass. Each cubicle was outfitted with a desktop, chair, and a telephone receiver. On the back wall on the visitors' side hung a large round clock with a sweeping second hand. No one had thought to hang a few pictures or set down a plant in the corner—not even a plastic one—for décor, to make the place feel a bit less institutional. Visiting hours were 2:00 to 4:00 every day, at a cadence of thirty minutes per visit, with a limit of two visitors per slot. The policy remained from decades past when friends and family were a given and even prisoners could expect a little love. Roland walked in and noticed he was the only one there. These days the visiting room was largely empty, while the jail operated at full capacity, most of the inmates having washed up from distant towns or south of the border. The irony of the trend—that the more inmates the jail housed the fewer visitors came to see them—was lost on the bureaucrats.

Father Bartholomew appeared on the visitor's side and sat down across from Roland and snugged the chair in behind him. It took Roland a second to recognize the priest in his civvies and pork pie hat, but the beatific glim in his eyes was unmistakable. Roland picked up his phone and put it to his ear and Father Bartholomew did the same.

"Padre, it's good to see you, but how did you get in? You're not on my list."

"Bribery."

"Isn't that a sin?"

"Only if the briber knowingly disadvantages another person."

"That makes sense, even if you just made that up. Seriously, how'd you get in? What did you say? I'm curious to know what level of respect I'm getting around here."

"I made the guard a bargain. I gave him a fifty-dollar bill and told him that if you refused my visit then he could keep the money."

"Did you tell him you're a priest?"

"They know me around here."

"Don't tell me—you're here to give me my last rites. I'm on death row and I'm the last to know."

Father Bartholomew smiled and shook his head.

"I like the hat."

The padre touched his felt chapeau but didn't remove it.

"It does the job."

"Church-issue looks like."

"No. A gift from a parishioner with taste enough to find the perfect shade of Franciscan brown."

"Shame you can't wear it with your robe."

"You're in a chatty mood. This place must suit you."

"What do they say in the movies? *I can do this stretch standing on my head.*"

"I guess you'll have to stick to mental gymnastics for the time being. Are they treating you pretty well, rehab-wise?"

"Yeah. The arms are almost back to perfect. My ribs are still sore, but I'm used to bruised ribs. Left knee, though, might never be the same."

"No spinal issues, I hope."

"Nope. I lucked out. Lucked out in a couple of ways."

"What about the other rehab?"

"I know I've got to stay sober. I know I can't drink."

"Do they have you going to meetings in here?"

"Yes of course. It's a familiar drill."

"Is it? You remember what you said on the *Tawni Moore Show?*"

Roland understood what he was driving at and switched the phone to the other hand and nodded yes.

"Did you believe it? Or were you just…"

"I was defending the program. She was trying to use me as an excuse to impugn something she knew nothing about."

"I know, but did you believe what you said?"

"Yes—statistically speaking, I guess. The people who work the program have a much better chance of staying sober. That's what the data shows, I'm told, and I've seen it firsthand. Is this what you came to talk about?"

"No. But I just want to be clear. I ask you about the meetings here in lockup, and you shrug it off as familiar drill. Right after you got through telling me you know you need to stay sober. It doesn't add up. You announced on national television that you didn't work the program the first time around."

"I've been in here a little over a week. You're knocking me off my pink cloud."

"You're right, Roland. I'm not here to assess your willingness or even to give you advice. I am here to apologize—and to clear something up."

"What, did you steal my donation to the Santa Barbara Madrigals? I haven't been trained for this sort of thing, but since this setup is kinda like a confessional, let 'er rip, Padre."

Father Bartholomew lifted his hat and nodded to salute the joke then set it down on the table in front of him. His action re-set the stage. Two bald men—Roland's head stubble wasn't quite long enough to call hair—seated a few feet apart, separated by a pane of glass, staring at one another, each talking into an old-fashioned telephone receiver.

"This is important. It's deadly serious."

The air around them seemed to darken. Roland glanced at the lights in the ceiling to see if there was some sort of electrical problem, but the lights were glowing steadily, yet the space between them seemed shrouded in shadow.

The priest continued. "I was going to keep it to myself, at least until—or unless—you wandered into The Shrine again."

"Apologize for what? We barely know each other."

"The morning you came into the church, after you killed that man—I lied to you. I told you that strangely I been thinking about you then—presto—there you were."

"I remember."

"That's not what happened."

"Big deal. Why's that important?"

"Hear me out. I dreamt the whole thing the night before. I knew you would come in. I was waiting for you, actually."

Roland gave him an appraising look. "You dreamt of me killing someone and then showing up at your church?"

"Not the killing—just you showing up."

"That's mighty peculiar. My judge said something right along those lines, but not a dream, just a hunch he said."

"What kind of hunch?"

"That he knew he'd see me again arraigned in his courtroom. That he'd made a wager on it."

"Could'a been just judicial swagger."

"So could this—what you're saying—be just religious swagger. And why should I care anyway? You had a premonition and didn't fess up to it at the time. It would've made things awkward had you told me. I'd've been a little incredulous, less likely to stick around and talk to you. I think it was a smart move on your part."

"You believe in such things?"

"Premonitions? I've never had one, but I don't rule it out. I know there's more than this physical realm. I told you about my adventures as a lucid dreamer."

"It was more than a premonition, Roland. It was certain knowledge."

"That's impossible to prove. Now you're asking me to believe you. I'm open-minded—just don't ask me to believe you."

"I didn't come down here to tell you about my dream and convince you that it was foreknowledge. I'm not here to convince you of anything."

"Then what then? I'm glad you didn't put fifty bucks on the line to tell me about a dream."

"I came to give you some information…"

"Yes. Some *deadly serious* information."

"Please, Roland…"

"Sorry. Go on."

"You don't have to believe what I'm going to tell you, but if you don't want to hear it at all then just tell me to leave and I'll go now."

Roland thought to mention that maybe he didn't want to hear what the man had come to say precisely because he was inclined to believe it. The peculiar draining of the light in the room, he realized, was not an optical effect, but his consciousness trying to separate from his body. He sensed that were he to but close his eyes and emit a hum he might well float out and observe the scene from above.

"First tell me how you came by this so-called information."

"I have a gift—a burden of a gift, a burden I had to lay down if I wanted to minister to people. You see, when I meet people, I often know more about them than they know about themselves, sometimes down to their physical ailments. A penitent doesn't want to spill her guts in the confessional about her moral failings only to have me tell her that her sins are forgiven, say three rosaries and, by the way, make sure to have your uterus checked because I'm seeing incipient cancer."

"You telling me you're some kind of Edgar Cayce?"

"Yes and no. I have the same kind of ability, but Cayce cultivated it. Like I said, I had to set my gift aside as an occupational hazard."

"You can just do that—switch off psychic ability?"

"Not entirely. But I neglected it on purpose. You lose it like a musician loses his skill if he doesn't practice. And the longer you neglect it, the harder it is to get back into form. But the talent is always there."

"You're telling me you came out of retirement just for me?"

"I am—I did. It took some time for me to get a confident read on you."

For the first time since he woke up from his accident, Roland craved a cigarette. He inhaled deeply and imagined the instant satisfaction afforded by smoked tobacco. Then he said what needed saying.

"I'm about to ask what on Earth possessed you to do that—it's kind of an invasion—but I'm thinking you'll tell me it was something not of this Earth."

"You can make light of it, Roland—I understand your skepticism. Again, I don't expect you to accept as truth what I discovered. But I'm obliged to reveal it to you if only because of the amount of time I spent discovering it. As to your question—it was something very much of this Earth. It was you. You've been *of this Earth* for a very long time."

The light in the room returned to normal as Roland's consciousness snapped back snugly into place. "Padre, you came down here to tell me I've been reincarnated? If reincarnation is the active metaphysical principle, then aren't we all cycling through? Why is this news?" Father Bartholomew squinted with irritation.

"Cut the crap. You know more than you let on. I saw you lift off during the madrigals concert. You edged out of your skin like a pencil drawing behind an oil painting breaking free of the figure on the canvas and floating away. Totally freaked out the prostitute you brought with you. She knew something was amiss, though apparently she couldn't see what I saw."

"What makes you say she was a prostitute? She was dressed alluringly, sure, but not whorish for San Francisco."

Father Bartholomew took a sheaf of papers from his jacket pocket and pressed it flat on the table in front of him and turned the pages until he found the one he was looking for. It appeared to Roland the pages comprised a list of some kind. He tapped with his forefinger at an entry in his notes. "You met her the first time around 500 BC in a temple in Babylon—she was a temple prostitute. Mind you, I wasn't targeting her, but when she showed up in my research on you, I couldn't very well mistake her. She's played that role many times over the centuries, I suspect."

Roland laughed. "She was more than a little different—I'll tell you that."

"Let's not talk about her." Father Bartholomew eyed the page. "You telling me you made a study of my past lives?"

"I can only guess at how many hours it took—dozens, maybe a hundred. I had to do it in secret. If any of my colleagues caught me riveted in a trance with my eyes rolled back, I'd have to answer for that. And I wouldn't lie—I'd have to tell them I was practicing mediumship and that would be the end of my prize perch in old San Francisco. I help a lot of people in this modern-day Gomorrah."

"Why then? Why put your job on the line?"

"The dream—you showing up just as I knew you would that morning. Then your astral antics during the concert. Then the sudden fame. I had to find out who you were. You crossed my path, I'm convinced, so that I could reveal the truth to you. There's no other way to put it."

"That's a long list—how many pages? How many lives? I'd like to see it."

"It wouldn't make much sense to you. My notes are just the impressions I got from each life I uncovered. Where you were famous, I got a name or portion of a name, often a location and social position. Usually the images I received gave me a sense of the place and time, and I often got your approximate age at death and how you died. But I'm sure it's full of errors and near misses."

"I've read about past life regression, Padre. Isn't the patient supposed to be hypnotized? How can you pull my past lives out of thin air?

"I'm not a master of the energies and frequencies, but suffice it to say that your name, your voice, and your likeness whizzing around the world didn't hamper my efforts."

"Yeah, but…"

Father Bartholomew raised a finger. "Do you want to hear what I have to say, or just nitpick the process? Because there was no process—I bulled my way through it. Dropped a lot of weight."

"You do look a little thinner. Okay, lay it on me."

"Far as I can tell, you're one of the Originals. I counted one life last century, two in the Nineteenth, dozens on back into the Middle Ages, hundreds before that. Then things started to get murky. But one of the themes I noticed throughout was violence. You're often drawn to violence and war." He continued to scan the pages. "Northern Europe, the Mediterranean, Persia, China, Japan. Here you were a warrior in Central or South America—Inca or Aztec—I'm not a great student of history. Here I saw you on horseback covered in paint holding a feathered lance, so probably a Plains Indian. You've spent a lot of time on horseback, all over the world, on horseback and aboard ship. You've killed a lot of people in battle and been killed in battle over and over again. Here I wrote down—*looks like Zulu*."

"You said where I was famous you got a name. So, give me some names."

"When you were famous or close to someone famous—yes. Here I noted that you fought with Joan of Arc, got killed in France storming a castle. Your next life, you came back as the son of Suleiman the Magnificent, Selim the Second, better known as Selim the Drunkard. A real piece of work. Ever heard of him?"

"No—I mean I've heard of Suleiman of course, but not his son."

"I had to look him up. He became the Ottoman Emperor in the fifteen hundreds and for eight years basically drank wine and romped in his harems until one day he slipped on the wet tiles drunk in a bathhouse and cracked his head open. That was you. Two lives ago you died drunk in an alley in some American city after a career as a bare-knuckle boxer—no name came through for that one. Safe to say you never fought John L. Sullivan, or I'd have seen that."

"What are you getting at here?"

"The further back I went, the more famous lives I encountered. If you want to know all the names and places, you'll have to figure out how to regress yourself, or maybe hire someone when you get out of here, someone who can put you under and knows how to walk you back slowly through your whole history. It's a terrifying prospect, really. It might take years."

"Terrifying—more terrifying than war?"

"You go back before Jesus—you're actually older than Jesus. You were with Joshua at Jericho. In fact—and I'd get kicked out of the priesthood if I said this on the pulpit—Jesus was Joshua before he was Jesus."

"How could you know that?"

"Because you met Jesus in Jerusalem when you were a Roman soldier, a drunken Roman soldier. And when I saw you in Jericho with Joshua, those two—Jesus and Joshua—housed the same soul."

"You saying Jesus was in the reincarnation mill? There's nothing about it in the New Testament. You'd think Saint Paul would have at least given us the heads-up."

"Maybe not Saint Paul, but in the book of Matthew, Jesus tells his disciples that John the Baptist is Elijah *returned*. And in Revelation you'll find the words, *Him that overcometh will I make a pillar in the temple of my God, and he shall go no more out*. There are other places in scripture where reincarnation is hinted at."

Roland gave in to curiosity. The priest had come prepared and had no apparent reason to lie. He was either a high-functioning lunatic or an unexpected friend come to speak the truth. "Ok, I'll bite—who else was Jesus?"

"I have him going as far back as Melchizedek and as recently as a girl in Florida born with a horrendous genetic defect confined for life to a stretcher and attached to expensive machines."

"Just for shits and giggles, huh? Or maybe he still had some bad karma to work out left over from that Jericho massacre, even after redeeming all of humanity on the cross."

"My hunch is that he wanted to set an example, to demonstrate happiness and courage in the face of extreme hardship, to give the doctors and nurses a dose of perspective."

"How could you possibly know all this?"

"Images—the information comes in images. The trick is slowing them down well enough to read them, to piece them together to form a meaningful narrative."

"Ok, ok, I get all that—but you were backtracking me, right? How did you get all the info about Jesus?"

"The soul we call *Jesus* has no soul group because his soul group is everyone, the universe of all conscious beings. Most of us run with only a dozen souls or so. Jesus can crash anyone's party, so those of us with the gift of mediumship can jump on his train too. He's available to all who would seek him."

"I call bullshit on that—*available to all who would seek him.*"

"I already told you. I'm not here to convert you."

"No. I mean I asked for him, for Jesus, after I crashed my car, my grandfather's Jeep. I shattered the windshield with my head and went away, and the word on the other side was—*Jesus is not available.*"

"What are you saying—you died, briefly died? Who did you ask?"

"My grandfather, my dead grandfather. I rose out of my body and looked down on the accident, and after a while there he was. He came through a little pinhole of light. I told him I wanted to go where he'd come from, that I didn't want to go back into my body, and he told me *no-way-Jose.* Then I filed an appeal—I said *I want to talk to Jesus.*"

"And what did your grandpa say?"

"No dice—*you're S-O-L, Marcel.*"

Father Bartholomew made no attempt to conceal his amusement. "You weren't dead—that's my guess—just unconscious. Or maybe your heart actually did stop for a little while and grandpa didn't have the juice to summon Jesus. In any case, he didn't visit you to guide you into the afterlife, but for some other reason. What was it?"

"He told me I had to go back because I had yet to achieve my purpose."

"That's pretty much standard. Anything else?"

"Yeah. To tell my mom hello from him."

"No. I mean about your purpose."

"That I couldn't achieve it if I kept on drinking."

"I was hoping to hear that. It will make what I have to tell you easier for you to swallow, so to speak."

"First tell me what you meant when you called me an *Original.*"

"It means you're pathetic, possibly the biggest fuck-up in the history of the Universe."

"That's not very nice." Roland got up to leave and glanced at the clock on the back wall. "I think your time is up anyway."

"Sit down." Father Bartholomew spoke in a commanding voice, one that cast the pall back over the room. There was no *please* implied. Roland sat. The priest continued. "I don't mean to hurt your feelings, Roland, but I fear the situation is dire. You may have run out of hall passes. As far as I can tell, you are one of the first beings on Earth ever to be invested with a self-conscious energy—a soul—and the fact that you're still on the hamster-wheel means that you're a literal de-generate, a terminal backslider. You should have moved on by now, have, as the scripture says, taken your place as a pillar in Heaven, going out no more. In a sense, you might actually be on a kind of death row."

Roland lowered his head and thought for a minute and decided that even if it was bullshit, he needed to hear it. He raised his eyes and looked into the Padre's face. "How old—how far back did you trace me?"

"So far back I couldn't even tell what I was looking at—forty thousand years, maybe older." Father Bartholomew turned to the last page in his sheaf. "I saw an image of you painting pictures in a cave in what felt like Europe, possibly the Iberian Peninsula. You were the headman or shaman of a very primitive tribe."

"What kind of pictures?"

"Constellations, a sort of prehistoric zodiac. For all I know you invented astrology. Before that, I saw only shadows cloaked in mist. My list stops there, with you establishing an ancient cosmology."

"And after that? What did I do after I mapped the stars, make Tarot cards out of bark peelings?"

"It sounds preposterous, I know. I don't blame you for making light of it. All I can tell you is what I saw, and the long and short of it is that you appear to have been one of what the Book of Genesis calls the mighty men of old, heroes of great renown."

"Chapter six, verse four. One of the strangest bits in the entire Bible."

"That passage probably came from Sumerian mythology and, like all myths, bears some element of truth. The peoples of Mesopotamia sprung up seemingly out of nowhere with all sorts of technology and cultural achievements, and their myths say that superior beings brought them the necessary knowledge to create their civilizations."

"And I was one of them, huh, like Prometheus stealing fire from Mount Olympus and gifting it to the human race?"

"Yeah, except in your case you didn't steal something that the gods wanted to keep for themselves—you delivered wisdom intended for mortals. You hastened our development and became the subject of mythology. That was your job, lifetime after lifetime, century after century, to come to earth and move things along, to help societies progress."

"Like what? Name me one of my contributions to human progress. Let's start with my greatest achievement."

"Greatest would be a matter of opinion, but your most famous, most prominent—that would be the Great Pyramid at Giza. You were the brains behind that."

Roland bit his lip. He'd visited the structure many times in his lucid dreams, had seen it in its former glory before its limestone veneers were looted, had sat astride its gleaming polished capstone and surveyed the surrounding plateau.

"What was my name? Did the vision come with a name?" His skepticism had softened to genuine curiosity.

The Padre glanced down at his notes. *"Hermes Three—*I kept hearing *Hermes Three."*

"Hermes—like the Greek god?"

"Hermes Three, over and over. The pageant of your past lives moved faster the farther back I went, until, like I said, it dissolved into a murky fog. When I saw you speaking to Abraham, giving him some important advice, I heard a voice—*Hermes Three.* Then, a few lives later, I saw you in some sort of classroom lecturing what looked like a room full of Egyptian priests, drafting diagrams and writing formulas to explain some sacred geometry, the marriage of heaven and earth—again, *Hermes Three Hermes Three.* It all came together with you standing before the Great Pyramid. *Hermes Three—as above, so below."* He patted his stack of pages. "It's all right here—a lot of it, anyway. You've come to the end of the road. The voice—the one that kept saying Hermes Three—was laughing. They're laughing at you on the other side."

"I've never heard of Hermes Three. Who was Hermes Three?"

"A legendary figure, a composite, like Merlin of Ancient England, but much older. I did some research. The alchemists of the 12th Century called you Hermes Trismegistus—Thrice-Greatest Hermes, Bearer of Secrets. The Egyptians called you Thoth, their god of science. Are you starting to get the picture?"

"Yep. I guess I've come down a few pegs."

"Down to your last peg, I fear."

"How do you know? What if everything you're saying is true and not some elaborate fantasy of yours? Maybe I like it this way, rubbing elbows with the masses on this wobbly orb."

"No. You're a laughingstock, a cosmic embarrassment. All the other Originals, the ones sent down to move the species forward, have achieved their purposes and moved on to other tasks in service of the Creation. You serve only yourself. You've abused the privilege of reincarnation, drinking and sporting and fighting and, well, banging around here endlessly, to the point where, if you don't check the addiction box this time around, you'll lose your hall pass, might wind up with your consciousness embedded in an aimless asteroid for all eternity, aware of nothing but darkness. The Creator will not be tested."

"Check the addiction box—sounds very bureaucratic."

"It is. There are many levels. You should be on the other side in the science wing designing DNA molecules for new life forms on a cooling planet in some distant galaxy, not here talking to me."

"You're out of your mind, Padre. If I were the Pope I'd keep you away from Catholics."

"You believe me. I can see in your face that you believe me because it's the only way to figure it. How can you go from being an almost godlike presence in the world, inventing alphabets, guiding ships full of tin and copper ore across uncharted oceans, discovering medicinal plants, aligning gigantic megaliths to celestial movements—and once the modern age is in full swing—to spending a series of pointless lives in opium dens and whorehouses, in drunken brawls, drowning face down in the rain or gasping for air with a knife in your chest?"

Roland recalled the knife he'd jammed into Barsamian's lung, how it twitched as the dying assailant struggled for breath, how satisfied he'd felt at having ended the man's life, as if the conclusion of their interaction was as it should have been, almost foreordained by circumstances outside of his control. *Maybe,* he thought, *just maybe.*

"Let me get this straight. You came down here with your stack of papers—the findings from your paranormal investigation of me—to warn me that, if I don't stop drinking now, in this life, my soul will lose purchase on the other side, that I'll be expelled from the program and banished to eternal isolation?"

"Correct. Though I'm not sure about the eternal isolation—that's just a guess. But the expulsion from the process, of that I am fairly certain."

"Why this life? How do you know I'm down to my last chance? How could you possibly know that? What vision told you that?" Roland believed him.

Father Bartholomew observed Roland's agitation then glanced away involuntarily, shifting his eyes as if from embarrassment, before re-engaging the prisoner's stare.

"You sent yourself a message, except you're too blind to see it, let alone understand it. You named yourself Roland Hazzard. I looked it up—the spelling is only a little bit off. *Rowland Hazard the Third*, the famous first recovered alcoholic, friend of the founder of Alcoholics Anonymous. There are no coincidences."

"My mother named me."

"You picked your family—we all do. Every single time. You picked the Hazzard family in Idaho, and it takes only a novice angel to whisper a baby's name into a mother's ear."

"You're not the first guy to point out the illustrious legacy of my name."

"There's more to it than that. After the Crusades, in which you took great part, and killed, and died, half a dozen times—after your days of glory were over—you seldom appeared on the historic stage."

"You told me—opium dens and such."

"Yes. You chose a series of lives without any chance of repute except ill repute, as though the whole point of each life was to resist the temptation to escape it by means of drugs and alcohol. And you failed, every single time. You chose to be born low, and you died even lower. This life, you chose to be born quite comfortably and gave yourself..."

"Hold it one second. Where am I if I'm not here? Where's the *me* who planned out my lives?"

"We bring down only part of our consciousness, usually no more than thirty percent. But it looks to me like you brought down a good deal more this time. Look at you, a man with enormous physical and intellectual gifts, far beyond those of a typical mortal, much like the heroes of old of which you were once one. On top of that, you have a strong spiritual bent not easily swayed by religious dogma. All the tools for a rich, fantastic life, except the recovery box remains unchecked. The persistent failure to annihilate your ego on this place we call Earth has made you unworthy of all your great achievements going back long before the beginning of history, so here you are with a sign around your neck that says Roland Hazzard in big bold letters, and you don't even know why."

"You don't know that. You can't know that. No one could know that."

"True, not to a mathematical certainty, but it's not a matter of science. Science without humility is Russian roulette. No—I know it with a moral certainty. You pushed your chips all-in this time, gave yourself a huge advantage over other men and a name to clue you in to why you are here, and I've come to make sure you see that."

"If half of me is on the other side, then why doesn't that part…?"

"Because free will is the point, the whole point of these vessels of flesh in a three-dimensional perishable space. All you did on the other side was set things in motion and watch it play out. Now—in the mortal here and now—if you can't find peace without the attachments of the flesh, then you will go where they send the souls who can't be potty trained."

"So, where do murderers go?"

"Who cares? Are you worried about running into the Glendale Butcher if you make it back home?"

"No—I don't mean him."

"I see. You think your killing him might count as murder when viewed from outside the legal system, on—let's say—the moral plane?"

"Something like that." Roland wondered if the jailers might record the visiting room conversations and decided to play it safe. "What if, hypothetically, there was some free will involved?"

Father Bartholomew shook his head as one would at a recalcitrant child.

"You've burned entire villages, Roland, set ships ablaze in the Byzantine wars with what they called Greek Fire. Now you're worried about the killing of a lone combatant?"

"So, if I beat the booze, work the program, defeat my ego—all the violence you say I've done gets cleared from the books?"

"Already been cleared. This is a violent planet—violence comes with the territory. As far as the Glendale Butcher goes, you did him a favor. He was off track. You sent him back so he could reassess his priorities."

"If what you say is true, I don't see how you can shill for the Catholic Church, knowing how far they missed the boat when it comes to the afterlife."

"The Church has far worse problems in the ranks of its Holy Orders than a friar in San Francisco who doesn't preach eternal damnation. Truth is, this is the first time I've ever tried to put the scare into someone."

"Well, Padre, you caught me at the right place and the right time. There's no booze in this place and the daily AA meetings are more interesting than television."

"There's more to sobriety than not drinking and using."

"Just like the Big Book says."

Father Bartholomew folded his papers longways and slipped them inside his jacket and put on his Franciscan-brown felt porkpie hat and asked Roland if there was anything he could do for him or get for him. Roland thought about it.

"Does prayer work?"

"I pray as if it does."

"Then light a votive candle for me in the church every day until I get out of here. And I—I will act as if everything you've just told me is true."

Both men hung up their telephone receivers and left the visiting room without turning around.

~~~~~

The monotony of a highly regimented life can dull one's imagination and enervate his beliefs and convictions. Aspirations seem pointless after a while. With that in mind, Roland spent the better part of that day and the day after setting to the page as faithfully as he could remember all the alarming details of the Padre's revelations, lest his mind aggregate the conversation into a single remembered episode easily dismissed for its outlandish claims. The Padre's credibility lay in his attention to certain specifics, and Roland wanted to be able to review them at will. Besides, if he ever decided to avail himself of the services of a bona fide past-life regressionist, it would be good to have something in his back pocket going in.

He cut out the painkillers altogether and settled into his routine, determined to take life on life's terms, advice he'd heard over and over in the rooms of AA. All it meant, it had finally sunk in, was armoring oneself against resentment, a temptation available to everyone throughout the day at the merest inconvenience from the moment of birth. Mostly he looked forward to the physical therapy sessions and the attendant gym privileges. Gad knew his business. It helped that the hospital had sent him the x-rays. Roland improved so rapidly that Gad had to keep him from pushing himself beyond reasonable limits. One day in the weight room another prisoner, for a joke, set a paper water cup on his own head and challenged *Mista Slayah* to kick it off.

"He's not in here to practice karate."

"Hold it out in your hand about shoulder high."

"I don't think this is a good idea."

Roland looked at Gad. "It's a good test for my leg, and there's no way he can get hurt."

Gad assented and the young man with the cup set it in his palm and held it out at arm's length. Roland positioned himself a few feet from the man and bounced up and down letting his weak left leg—his pivot leg—bear most of his weight. He steadied his breathing, found his focus, launched into a spinning back kick, and caught the cup with the ball of his right foot, sending it across the room. When he landed, Roland felt a stab of pain in his left knee that ran up his femur and into his spine. He fell backward and broke his fall with his forearms in perfect form.

"Damn," the young man walked over and picked up the cup.

"How did that feel?"

"Bad idea. I won't try that again anytime soon."

~~~~~

A few days later, while Roland was in his cell working on his manuscript, a guard came and told him he had a visitor. He'd had only a few since Father Bartholomew, friends from the docks. He'd been thinking of withdrawing his list altogether and admitting all comers, if only for amusement, since the few on the list showed such poor attendance.

"Who is it?"
"A woman."
"No name?"
"I don't sign them in. He told me she was pretty, though."
Roland closed his laptop. He doubted his sister would make the trip just to sit with him for half an hour. Alessandra too was a stretch. He'd put her on his list only on the off chance she would have reason to travel to San Francisco. Alison and Deidre were the only other possibilities. He hoped it was Alison, the temple prostitute of Ancient Babylon. He'd have a bit of fun with her about that scurrilous information. He checked his face in the steel mirror and yanked out a nose hair and went with the guard to the visiting room and waited.

Gina came through the door dressed in a smart pair of slacks and a cotton blouse with her hair done up. Pretty to be sure. Pretty at the very least. She sat down in front of him and gave him an exaggerated smile that took the place of a greeting and held her smile long enough that when she was finished smiling, he knew she was not going to lift the receiver until he picked it up first. The longer he waited, the sterner her expression grew. He sensed that if he tried to wait her out, she would get up and leave and he'd never see her again. The stakes were high. She'd learned the Mexican standoff. Finally, he picked up the phone. Gina responded in kind.

"Hi Gina. I've been thinking about you." That was a safe enough beginning, he thought, hard for her to judge as insincere.

She nodded. "I've done my best to put you out of my mind, but now that's impossible."

"I didn't realize you—" He stopped himself. Gina looked far from lovelorn.

She crossed her arms. "You didn't realize what?"

"That you—that you still wanted to know me. How did you get in here? Your name is not on the list."

Gina ignored the question. "You think I came here out of friendship or, God forbid, something more?"

"I thought maybe you were worried about me."

"You were never concerned about me—that much is clear."

"What do you mean, *never concerned about you?*"

"Did you ever ask yourself why I didn't visit you in the hospital?"

"I figured you'd written me off. That's why I didn't put you on my visitor list. How'd you get in? Didn't they ask you your name?"

"That's a coward's dodge. I stayed away because you never called me. After you quit and launched your little media career—when you groomed yourself into the beautiful pony that loves to be admired—I was hoping you would call me. But you didn't, and that means you didn't care about me. So you can't sit there and tell me you've been thinking about me and expect me to believe it. Don't get me wrong, Roland, I was glad you survived, if for no other reason than you should get to live a full life. But now, I'm just relieved that you're not dead."

"I see." He didn't. Those were just filler words. Roland was genuinely confused. He might as well have grunted *uh-huh*.

"No. You don't. You don't see. I got fired yesterday."

The blunt force of it, not what she said but what it meant—his sudden comprehension of why she was there—twisted his stomach and drained his face. A toddler was found floating in the swimming pool because Roland left the gate open. Should he deny it if he thought no one could prove it? Should he stand up and turn his back and go back to his cell? However many lives he'd inhabited before, he felt firmly attached to this one.

The sanest human being will confess that he has, at some point, studied suicide, not necessarily contemplated it, but rolled the idea around in his mind at the very least. At the moment, however, that option was not available for Roland, and he was left with two other desperate choices—fight or flight. Either would abandon dignity, as would any attempt to evade responsibility. This was a critical moment in this life. The decision he faced now seemed far more momentous than the choice to murder or not to murder Barsamian. For Roland to ask Gina why she got fired would be to pretend that he did not know the answer.

"I'm sorry. I'm really sorry. I blew it."

"Sorry for what?"

"I'll tell them it was me."

"Can you prove it? Because if you can't then my ass is still grass."

"I have the phone number of the guy I sold it to, but I haven't seen him or talked to him since the day I made the exchange and don't even know if he's still in the country."

"You put my job at risk for money? You mind telling me how much?"

"Only a few thousand. The code was not certified."

"Well, it was good enough for someone in China to spin up a saleable counterfeit. It's pretty big news in the industry. You screwed a lot of people."

"I had no idea the company kept logs, or I never would have done it."

"Yeah, but you didn't know they didn't keep logs. You probably never even thought to find out. You just did it."

"I'll tell them. I'll tell them everything I can."

"Tell me when you did it. I think I know but I want to hear it from you."

"The morning after I—the morning I came in with my bandaged arm. You went to the bathroom. Only a few other testers were there. It took me only a minute."

"You know, Roland, you could be prosecuted—probably will be."

"I don't care about that. I just want to clear your name so you can get your job back."

"The FBI is listening in."

"What?" The reality of his situation began to dawn on him. "Is that how you got in to see me—the FBI?"

Gina shook off the question. "Confessing to me won't be enough. You need to prove it to them. So far, I've said nothing except I was fired."

"I see." Now, though, he truly did understand. "It's either you or me."

"They didn't put it that way. They know who the criminal is. I haven't been charged."

"Who's on the line—same two guys who came that morning to harass me?"

"Yes. Those two, and they're recording this conversation. It's important, legally, that I say that, so if you don't want to participate, you can hang up now."

"I'm happy to say what I did, but what I really want to talk about is what happened to me after the accident. I went to a very strange place."

Gina raised her voice. "Don't talk to me like we're friends. You lied to me, Roland. I'm not surprised you left me off your visitor's list."

Roland's eyes widened involuntarily in genuine shock at her reaction and sincere innocence over her accusation.

"Wha—what lie? What did I lie to you about?"

"And here we have it—you don't even remember. You probably didn't even notice yourself lying *while* you were lying."

"I don't deny it. I'd just like to know what it was."

"The morning you came in with the bandage. I asked you what happened, and you said you got cut by a burglar. I knew that was bullshit. Don't ask me how I knew—I just knew."

Roland kept his ear to the receiver only through the exertion of will. He could not look at her. He closed his eyes and lowered his head while he listened.

"And I ask myself: Why didn't you just say you'd killed a guy? You knew I would find out, that it would be on the local news. It's almost like you wanted to be exposed as a liar, and not just to some casual acquaintance, but to me, your friend. It made me question everything I thought about you. I mean, you knew I cared about you, that I—yes, I'll say it—that I could have loved you, and that morning you made me feel like an idiot."

"I don't have an answer. I can't make an excuse. You're right—the lie was a reflex."

"That's pathetic."

"It is—I am. I guess I just considered myself a short-timer at that job, kinda like a drifter. I didn't care what you thought about me. I was never going to live up to the virtues of a woman like you anyway."

"Then you did what you did."

"Yes. It was completely selfish."

"Well, you have to live up to something someday, don't you think? Don't you someday want to be worthy of something, of someone? No one believes in God anymore and so they just flail around, doing whatever they want. You're a perfect example. You didn't think anyone would find out—that's bullshit. The truth is you didn't think at all."

He looked at her through a blur of tears but now was speaking to the FBI.

"On September Thirtieth, around 9:30 AM, I copied the NBA game off your machine onto a thumb drive and, a few days later, sold it to a Chinese guy named Chowshang. I don't know his last name or even how to spell his first name. He gave me eight thousand dollars cash at a table in Li-Po's bar on Grant Street in Chinatown. I was pretty sure I scammed him because the build was not certified. If I thought I was selling a usable build, I would have made sure I got a lot more money. I thought I was cheating him. I thought it was junk."

"They reverse-engineered it and released a buggy version in China that will run on most PlayStations. It's a piece of crap and won't damage the market too badly, but it's clearly our company's product."

"Is that enough—enough to get you your job back?"

"They're not happy I walked away from my machine without logging off, technically a violation of company policy. I told them I didn't feel any risk because you were my friend, and you can imagine how that went over."

"You told the truth."

"You sat right next to me, and I'm normally really good about logging off when I leave my station, so you were the prime suspect."

"I'm sorry" He meant it. His face drooped. His eyes dulled.

"You're pretty messed up, aren't you?"

"I'm right where I belong, I think."

"I can't imagine that. I can't imagine ever thinking I belonged in jail."

"Can you forgive me?"

"If you can forgive yourself, then maybe."

"I don't know. Maybe not in this life."

The door opened and two men came in, Agents Mitchell and Healy, Tweedle Dum and Tweedle Dee, the hobbit and the dwarf, outfitted in their bargain-rack attire. Gina saw that Roland saw them and turned her head to confirm it. She got up to leave, her face softened with compassion.

"Will you come see me again? I want to tell you about my coma."

"I won't promise I will, and I won't make a prediction either."

~~~~~

The agents, Mitchell and Healy, sat side by side and Mitchell picked up the receiver. When the earpiece reached his head Roland was already talking.

"I want to apologize for the way I handled myself…"

"Save it, Hazzard."

Roland looked at Healy, hoping to see a friendly demeanor, but Healy looked bored. A menu of smart remarks for Mitchell passed through his mind, and he let them pass, a skill he'd become better at from his practice of meditation. He held himself in that neutral space and felt his heart slow to a gentle thrum. His attention wandered and eventually landed back on Mitchell who, receiver still in hand, kept his eyes fixed on him. Healy leaned over and covered his mouth to protect against lip-reading and said something to this partner. Mitchell nodded.

"By the way, you have the right to remain silent."

"Am I under arrest?"

"Yes and no. We have to proceed as if you are, based on your confession, but ultimately, it's up to the injured party, Pacific Gameworks and their principals, to charge you or not. We just need to establish there was no entrapment here."

"Are we still being recorded?"

"No. We have what we need."

"Good. But in case you need more, the phone number of the man I sold the file to is on my phone, which is in my apartment."

"We have your phone records—we know the number."

"You got a warrant, then?"

"It wouldn't be legal otherwise."

"When?"

"Why?"

"Gina said she got fired yesterday. So, you're telling me that between then and now you got a warrant and managed to dig up my phone records and pinpoint the number for my Chinese contact?"

Mitchell ignored the question.

"How much money did he give you?"

"Eight thousand dollars—eighty one-hundred-dollar bills. I owed some of it around town. Gambling debts."

"You'd better hope Gina can turn things around for you."

"How do you mean?"

"She might be able to reverse your bad luck—persuade the company not to press charges. She's very well-liked."

"I'm in no position to say what's good luck or bad luck. This whole world might be nothing more than kabuki theater."

Healy reached for the receiver and Mitchell gave it to him.

"Hazzard."

"Yeah."

"Your dog food idea—some of us down at the office think it's a riot. People are pasting mock-ups of our most wanted suspects on dog food cans. Thought you'd like to know that."

"The idea just came to me. I didn't have time to think it through."

"Stroke of genius. Some have suggested that we introduce the practice in certain—how can I say it?—*traditionalist* cultures, where dogs have a very low status."

"Sounds more like a job for the CIA."

He chatted with Agent Healy for another few minutes, toggling his eyes between the two civil servants, secure in his indifference to his very future. He had, at least for the moment, ceased fighting everything and everyone. He knew unconsciously that the best outcome, as far he was concerned, lay in relinquishing all pretense of control. Consciously, he understood that mouthing off to the Feds could do him no good. He wondered if Gina had left the building and would he ever see her again.

"Roland," said Healy. "Snap out of it."

"Sorry. What?"

"What would you do with the bodies of criminals slain in the commission of a crime, like Barsamian?"

"You're just fucking with me at this point."

"No—you started a good thought experiment. Let's follow it through."

Roland mulled it over and decided he might as well play along. "What happened to his remains? Where are they now? And his cousin's remains?"

"Next of kin, I'd bet. That's the normal procedure. If no relatives—cremation and disposal."

"Well. We could institute a regulation that gives the state the right to dispose of the body of anyone killed in the commission of a violent felony. Over time, you'll have cases of dog food containing high-profile death penalty convicts, mass shooters who offed themselves, all the way down to armed robbers shot by store clerks, and the odd machete-swinger who ran into a trained neck-snapper."

"Problem is, with the death penalty cases anyway, the lethal chemicals will taint the meat, so you can't mix it into dog food. People will know that. I can think of half a dozen government agencies that would put a stop to it before it got started."

"There's always the firing squad," said Roland. "All you need to do is fish out the bullet."

Agent Mitchell reached for the phone and Healy raised a finger to say just one sec.

"Have you thought about the black market it would create?"

"I told you." Roland was not the least bit irritated—amused, rather, that they were heading down this rabbit trail. "I was just riffing out there. Spitballing."

"Capital Murder Dog Food would be collector's items for the most famous cases, and that, of course, would attract counterfeiters. Imagine if we executed Charles Manson and canned his sorry ass—imagine what those would go for."

Roland laughed. "Imagine sitting in jail for selling counterfeit convict dog food."

"I imagine a can with your face on the label would fetch a fortune."

"Okay. You've had your fun. Let's see what Dennis has to say."

Healy handed the receiver to Mitchell. Roland relaxed his eyes to remove any hint of hostility or resentment that might have bubbled up from Healy's needling.

"One last thing, Hazzard."

"At your service, sir."

"You lied to me last time we spoke. Lying to a federal agent is against the law."

Roland searched his memory and spotted the lie to which he thought Mitchell might be referring, but he decided to play the fool.

"What, did I say *good morning*? I'll grant that it was decidedly not a good morning, not for me anyway."

"No. That wouldn't count as a lie."

"Even if it did, why would it be against the law? You weren't questioning me as part of an official investigation, or you would have had to advise me of that."

"I'm not saying that your lie was against the law, but that people need to be careful when talking to Feds."

Roland conceded half the match. "Whatever it is you're talking about, I'm sorry that I hurt your feelings. I want to go out on a good note with you gents."

"I don't care if that's true or not. You shouldn't have told me you had no plans to give another public interview when you already had one scheduled for the radio that day with Peter Jordan. That kink in your character can't be straightened out by a car accident."

"I didn't appreciate being bullied into silence, and I'm sure if he knew about it your boss would understand why I…"

"My boss? You mean the president?"

"Are you saying he's not your boss?"

"He's a bottle on a fence post."

"What about her—would she have been a bottle on a fence post?" Mitchell chuckled as though he possessed a secret truth. "No." He allowed himself a lengthy pause. "She's in the ear of the guy with the bottle in his crosshairs."

"I see why you shut off the recorder if in fact you were recording."

"Go ahead and tell him what I said, word for word if you can manage that. You're nothing but a drunk with an ax to grind—a head-injured drunk at that, as far as anyone who matters is concerned. Your star has not only fallen, it's fizzled."

"Didn't you hear? I got a book deal."

"Whatever you might say in your book—whether you're charged with this crime or not—we have the evidence, evidence of your guilt, evidence that can't be disputed. It's a story the press would love to print."

"Dennis, seriously, let's not get adversarial here. I know I've said some disparaging things about the Feds in my talks, but I never mentioned your names. I took all of it very personally, but I never went after you or Agent Healey."

"Did you say anything to Trump?"

"About your little visit, about our little chit chat?"

"Yes—what did you two talk about?"

"I promised him I'd keep that between us, and I've been good to my word. But I can assure you he never brought it up, and neither did I."

Roland set the telephone receiver on the desktop and looked back and forth at the agents and glanced down at the receiver then back up at the agents again. His shoulders meant to convey that he was finished talking but that he was willing to pick up the receiver again if they had anything else to say. His eyes told them he accepted his predicament and that there was nothing they or anyone else could do to him that would affect his serenity, and he weighed in his mind whether or not that was true.

~~~~~

Roland returned to his cell and opened up his laptop, not to write but to read what he had written so far, as a way of warding off the shame and confusion he'd refused to show the feds. When he came to the end of the pages he'd written, he shook his head. The prose was a bit limp. He needed a stronger voice, a first-person narrator with literary flair—warm and self-critical. What he'd written thus far sounded epistolary, like journal entries to himself. Only in the composition of poetry had Roland ever truly enjoyed the ring of his own voice. He began to type. The lines came of their own accord.

I accuse myself of squandering my youth
in booze and succulent vaginas, and gladly
I accuse myself of landing an excellent job
for the sake of money and succulent vaginas.
And I accuse myself of treating women
not as people but as places I can leave, and so
I accuse myself of flouting human decency.
I accuse myself of shameless hypocrisy,
for frequently I denounce moral turpitude
and define out loud what's right and what's wrong.

I accuse myself of mysterious minor injuries
discovered on my limbs hungover mornings, then
I accuse myself of self-loathing, of promising
the mirror I will change my manner of living
which destroys my youth in measures too small to gauge
each day. I accuse myself of showing up for work
and presenting myself as a responsible adult
and doing my job efficiently and expertly
for the betterment of a tolerable company,

*while I remain intolerable to myself and conceal
the fact of my despicable nature from people
well disposed to my gregarious affability.*

*I accuse myself of accusing others of mendacity and
outright fraud when I know myself to envy the
flagrancy of power abused by the higher-ups, and I
accuse myself of thinking I'm the greatest capable
of becoming a rock-and-roll star
or a famous actor when today I would settle for sex
filmed by a practical stranger in a filthy room.*

He tinkered with the phrasing for half an hour to better lay bare his wretchedness. The chord he'd stuck within himself would, he hoped, reverberate through the account of his life he intended to write. He'd leave no stone unturned. That might be it! Instead of *A Time to Kill, No Stone Unturned* would make a better title. Or how about *No Stone Unmoved?* He liked that better. A variation on the cliché—a confession bound to draw tears from matter itself. The portrait he envisaged would show a young man born lonely, and content to be lonely, a naturally shy boy with a lively personality at the ready, a champion athlete who never celebrated victory, a popular kid who preferred no one friend over another, a student who corrected his teachers in private, a teenager uncomfortable with his superiority and who, once he found alcohol, finally experienced a sense of ease and comfort as a member of our vastly pathetic humanity, a humanity whose only possible redemption lay in a collective agreement, to an oath he himself would compose: *Punish the Wicked.* His book would be a plea to the *Spiritus Mundi*, to the conscience of civilization, with a caveat that no such thing ever existed. The business about architecting the Great Pyramid and rendering the Zodiac on the walls of a sacred subterranean space to celebrate the birth of human consciousness—that he would keep to himself. Thus empowered with direction and trajectory, he tapped out a fresh beginning to his story, the purpose of which would be, at least in part, to acknowledge the role alcohol played in his tolerance of the human race and to justify, albeit tacitly, his remorseless facility with homicide.

~~~~~

As the days flowed into weeks, Roland put his crime out of his mind. He'd internalized the Serenity Prayer, not a hard thing to do when you're a guest of the state. In confinement, the difference between the things he could control and those he could not required little wisdom to ascertain. Of one thing he was certain—he was safe, not only from unwanted attention from the outside world but from himself. If circumstances would have him stay longer on a software theft conviction, here or in another facility, Roland couldn't see the downside. For the time being, a power greater than himself—not God, necessarily, but the state—had restored him to sanity. The revelations of Father Bartholomew disturbed him constantly, not just for the remarkable specificity of the details, but in their general purport. If the whole reincarnation process indeed followed some sort of metaphysical law, then there must be some overarching authority behind it, a Creator God. Roland flirted with belief. In his heart of hearts, he knew there was something outside of time and space; but reckoning with that truth was another matter. For the time being, the California Penal System must serve as his Higher Power.

~~~~~

With two weeks left in his sentence, Roland received his final visitor, his former boss, Michael. He wore a suit and tie, not the casual attire Roland was accustomed to seeing him in at work. Michael showed Roland a warm smile. Roland smiled back and picked up the receiver and rested his free hand on his blue AA Big Book.

"You didn't get dressed up on my account I hope."

"I'm coming from work. I got promoted, so…" He twiddled the bottom of his necktie.

"Congratulations. Executive management by the looks of it."

"Chief Technology Officer."

"What about Gina?"

"She took my position, so no more baseball caps for her."

Roland nodded his approval of the decision. "So, she's on her way up. Good for her."

"You two have gone in opposite directions, but I've got good news for you today."

"I know—they're not going to prosecute. They'd have served me weeks ago."

"Not deciding to prosecute is not the same as deciding not to prosecute."

"How is this good news?"

"Because they've decided—we've decided, I should say, since senior management took a vote—to let you be the one who decides. We've come up with a number, call it restitution, and if you agree to it then we'll put it in writing. You'll be off the hook."

"How much—how much will my freedom cost me?"

"Two hundred thousand."

"Can I ask you how you arrived at that figure? I can't imagine that two hundred K makes the company whole."

"The stunt you pulled, all the press it got, we figure it probably boosted sales a bit. It's impossible to know. The Chinese bootleg is a piece of shit. No, we were thinking more along the lines of punishment—justice you might say. Your money will go to charity."

Roland patted the Big Book. "It says in here that we need to learn to accept life on life's terms."

"Or you can take your chances with a San Francisco jury. We're probably talking years here, not months."

"Fine. I'll be glad to pay your restitution."

"And there, you see, we have our good news. Gina will be happy to hear it, and I'll be happy to take it back to the office. You've got more friends there than you think, though most don't dare to say it out loud."

"Does that include you?"

"I voted in favor of offering you this deal, Roland. No need to look for enemies."

"Thanks, Michael. And I owe you an amends."

"An amends?"

"It's part of my recovery, to make amends to those I have harmed."

"If you must, but I don't think of myself as having been harmed by you."

"Maybe not, but I know my presence at the office made things harder for you. You took a chance on me, and I behaved badly."

"Ok, I'll accept that. But I had a choice to keep you or let you go, and I chose to let you stay."

"Can I ask why?"

"Nothing personal. You were very good at the job. And Gina liked you, and she's very good at her job."

Michael departed. Roland remained in the chair by the phone with his hand on the Big Book, as though he was prepared to swear on it. The guard came over and told him that no one else was signed up to see him today, which had begun to happen more frequently as his release date approached. Roland picked up the book and used it to salute the guard and the guard opened the door and followed him back to his cell.

~~~~~

The hour of his release arrived. A guard stood at the door waiting to escort him to the discharge officer. He took one last look at his reflection in the steel mirror. His hair had grown out to where it needed combing and his mustache and beard were full. On the outside, he looked like a different person, and on the inside he felt a whirlwind of emotions, chiefly fear of the future, but also optimism, sadness, a pinch of self-disgust, and then a breeze of gratitude. His only response was to cry, but the guard was there at the door waiting for him. He reminded himself that his feelings were not who he was, that he was only feeling them, that who he was would remain once the feelings passed, and his knowledge that who he was would be revealed over time in the spaces between emotions gave him relief enough to suppress his tears and move to the next indicated thing without judgment of its overall value in the scheme of his life.

"You're not going to get any better looking no matter how long you stare."

"Don't ever say that to your wife."

~~~~~

He'd arranged to have Singh pick him up. The climb from the jail to his Nob Hill apartment took them through the most depressed blocks of The City. It had stormed heavily the night before, and Roland observed that, whereas a good drenching was supposed to put a fresh gleam on a city, it made San Francisco's vast homeless encampments look like a third-world disaster. Tents broken and collapsed, filth collected in puddles, people huddled under ripped sheets of plastic or dragging them around. How many, if offered, would accept a fast-acting suicide pill?

Would the number change if they were told the pill would give them the greatest high of their life for thirty minutes, then lights out? *It's coming,* he thought, *it's coming.*

They headed up Larkin Street through the Tenderloin.

"Can you take a right on Ellis and circle around the block?"

"Sure. Is there somewhere you need to stop?"

"I want to see if the hair salon on Hyde is still in business."

The place was closed as he'd expected. People were living under her awning and in her doorway. She'd stopped shoveling sand against the tide.

"How do you do it?"

"Do what?"

"Witness so much human ruin day after day."

"I know the difference between pity and contempt."

"I think I could explain the difference, but I don't think I could practice it."

"At least you know that about yourself." Singh turned his head and shot him a discerning glance.

"Explain what you mean."

"Do you remember our last ride together?"

"Of course. We sang the Beach Boys. *Don't Worry Baby.* We shared an unforgettable explosion of joy."

"Yet, you killed a man later that day—broke his neck and crowed about it."

"I don't get your point."

"You could have pitied him and let him live—let him go to jail. Instead, you showed contempt. And for that, you reaped contempt. Jesus forgave his murderers—pitied them."

"You believe the Gospels, Singh? Have you become a Christian?"

"I believe in the power of the message, whether the Gospels are factual or not."

"You're a better man than I."

"I'm a better man than I was yesterday. That's all that matters."

Singh parked in front of his building, got out of the car, and met Roland on the curb to say farewell.

"You are a very great man. And great men have great flaws. If you overcome your flaws, you may become a good man, a heroic man. Most of the heroes in the world are not *of* the world and not known *to* the world. Fame puts you at a great disadvantage, but I believe you will overcome." With that, he embraced him then stepped back and smiled and bowed and got back into his taxi and drove away.

~~~~~

His apartment was cleaner than he'd ever seen it, thanks to his mother. Roland put his belongings on the table in his parlor and sat on his couch and measured his breath and waited for the next indicated right thing to present itself. Astrid. He needed to make amends to Astrid. He got up and took his tripod with his webcam mounted on it and carried it to Astrid's door and knocked.

It was nine in the morning. She opened her door, clad as ever in flannel pajamas, a bit disheveled but wide awake.

"Hi, Roland." She did not conceal her surprise. "I thought I heard someone come in. I barely recognize you."

"I don't mean to bother you, Astrid, but I'd like to talk, just for a minute."

"Astrid? C'mon, Roland."

"Oh." He remembered the game. "Daisy. I'd like to talk to you, *Daisy.*"

"*Daisy?* So ordinary. You can do much better than that!"

"I'm sorry to bother you, African Daisy—Miss African Transvaal Daisy."

"That is a gorgeous choice, thank you. What have you got there?"

"I'm hanging up my silks, stepping down off my high horse."

"I don't get it."

"My tripod and webcam—the tools of my trade. I have no more use for them."

She took the apparatus from him. "I can find a home for this. Does this mean you've retired from the internet?"

"Yes. As an online personality, anyway. But that's not what I came to talk to you about."

"What, then?"

"I'm leaving here, and I need to say I'm sorry before I go."

"Sorry? Sorry for what?"

In his sobriety—the agitation of it having all but disappeared—he saw her countenance anew. Her perplexity gave her face the cast of a Picasso figure, sharp and disjointed, eyes askew, yet strangely attractive. He felt relieved that he'd never taken advantage of her sexually.

"Just my overall assholery and occasional drunken madness—for putting you in a position where a decent person would naturally worry about me."

She brought her hands to her face and brushed aside her hair and adjusted her cheeks to somehow remove the Picasso effect. She looked happy—relieved at what he'd said.

"I'm glad you're okay now, Roland. Of course, I forgive you. You weren't doing anything to me, you were just doing it. To be honest, I pitied you."

"Yeah. I was pathetic."

"Even so, I was spiteful sometimes. I retaliated, like the night when the police came. So I think I owe you an apology."

Her decency made him uncomfortable. "I didn't expect you to be so, I don't know, gracious."

"I met your parents, got to know your mother while she was cleaning up your place. You're lucky to come from such good people. Don't let them down."

"My mom wants me to go back home, but my dad is silent on the subject, so I know what that means."

"What are you going to do?"

"Get out of here as soon as I can. I wanted to make sure I made amends before I left, in case I didn't see you again."

"Well, Roland, I can say one thing for sure."

"What—what's that?"

"I'll never forget this last year, not if I live a thousand more."

Chapter 22
Spring 2017

He found a rundown two-bedroom house on Santa Rosa Avenue near the Cannabis Wellness Center in the weather-beaten hamlet of Pacifica, California, just south of The City, and paid a year's rent in advance and promised he would fix the place up. The old hippie widow who owned the property didn't recognize him or pretended not to and, in any case, made it plain that she was grateful for the advance rent as it would allow her to cover the exorbitant property tax bill that was coming due and dogging her serenity.

To the west, within walking distance, stretched the Pacifica Pier, a popular destination for fishermen and crabbers. Just north of town lay Sharp Park, a regulation 18-hole municipal golf course. A variety of shops and restaurants serviced his oceanside neighborhood. There were several AA meetings to choose from as well—he liked the daily Wake Up Group at the Baptist church on Francisco Avenue—and a little fitness center and a martial arts studio. Also, a hardware store for the necessary handyman supplies, a grocery market, ye old bookshop, and sundry small businesses. It was a perfect location for a man with neither a job nor a car to hide out and finish his memoir.

One of the first establishments Roland visited was Winters Tavern, about five blocks from his house, just up the street from the Baptist church. It had the rough feel of a rathskeller and boasted a diverse offering of live music on the calendar attached to its door. He walked in at two o'clock on a Wednesday afternoon and took a look around and knew instantly what it must be like in the evenings and that he could become a regular at such a place—dark, boozy, and clangorous with a no-nonsense bartender. A place where a body could keep a low profile and hone the edge of his sobriety. At the back of the place on the stage against the wall he spotted what he'd hoped to find, a piano. He hadn't touched piano keys in more than a year and hadn't played seriously since he was a teenager in Idaho.

The place was empty except for the man behind the bar and an employee prepping the stage for this evening's music. Roland walked over and took off his shades and set them on the bar and set a five-dollar bill next to them.

"What can I get you?" The man wore a brown leather cowboy hat, Aussie style, with buffalo nickels affixed to the band. The leather was discolored in blotches and looked like it had been sprayed with rust. His eyes glittered intently from deeply worn sockets, and the rest of his face lay hidden under a poorly tended, mostly gray beard. Roland thought he looked like the great Jerry Garcia before the booze and drugs caught up with him.

"Ginger ale. If you don't have that then a Coke."

The man scooped ice into a glass from a trough below the bar and shot it full of Coke with a soda gun.

"Is that all? We have a small but dependable lunch menu."

"No food, thank you. But may I know your name?"

The man raised an eyebrow. "You a musician? Looking for work?"

"No. But I *am* here on business."

The man licked his upper lip with the tip of his tongue.

"Serra. I'm the owner. You can talk business with me."

"Sarah? As in the great Sarah Carter, inventor of country music? Or as in Sarah, wife of Abraham, who gave birth to the great nation of Israel?"

"As in the great Father Junipero Serra, who made it his mission to civilize the tribes of California in the name of the great Jesus Christ."

"Ahh, the humble Franciscan missionary. I have a friend in San Francisco who wears the brown robe."

"You said you had business here."

Roland took off his knit cap and set it on the bar next to his shades.

"Do you know who I am—I mean, do you recognize me?"

The man answered without hesitation. "No. I've never seen you before."

"My name is Roland Hazzard."

The man thought for a second or two and gave a slow nod. "Yeah, I've heard a' you."

Roland reached into his jacket and pulled out a sheet of paper with his picture on it and his name written underneath the image. He handed it to the man.

"I don't want your autograph."

Roland smiled. "Serra, great civilizer of benighted savages, shoulderer of the White Man's Burden, I have come for your ministry and your blessing."

"What the fuck are you talkin' about?" The man took a step back and leaned one hand on the counter next to the register.

"I've been sober for a few months now and want to keep it that way. I'd like to give you two hundred dollars if you'll keep this picture and tell your bartenders…"

"Tell them what? Not to serve you?"

"No. They can serve me. But as soon as they serve me tell them to call the police. Tell them to call the police and let them know that Roland Hazzard is in the bar and things are about to get real. Chief Stadle knows I'm living in Pacifica and so does Pastor Cosgrove at the church up the street. I plan to make my rounds to all the prominent members of this community because here is where I'm settling for the time being. Now you know. I'm willing to give you this bit of money for your efforts." He began to withdraw his wallet from his pants.

"How long you say you've been sober?"

"Including jail, or not?"

"Not. How long have you been sober out in the world?"

"Less than three weeks."

"You're not sober, son. You're still strapped to the back of the dragon, to your own chaotic ego." He came forward and pushed the picture back toward Roland. "I know you mean well, so you can be forgiven—but I don't do this sort of unholy business."

"Will you at least mention it to the bartenders?"

"I'll tell them that if Roland Hazzard comes in and looks like he's going to cause trouble, rack a round in the peacemaker and point it at the ceiling. If that don't work, step two is point the peacemaker at the troublemaker."

Serra took the shotgun out from under the bar and held it up. It looked clean and very functional.

"I guess that's how you do it down here. I appreciate that."

"Look, the venerable J Serra, builder of missions—his heart was in the right place. He meant well. There's no doubt he's in Heaven. But if you look at history, more often than not you'll see that trying to civilize people into falling in line with the program—whatever program you happen to be pushing—usually doesn't end very well. More often than not it's a better idea, and a lot less effort, just to remove the troublesome variable from the equation."

"You sound like me."

"I doubt you even know who you are." He pushed the five-dollar bill back toward Roland and turned toward the stage, as though he needed to check the progress of the drum kit setup.

"When did you know that you knew who you were?"

"One day in the desert, I found out who I was."

"What, on a mescaline trip or something?"

"No. On top of a Cougar 4-by-4 MRAP, just outside Ramadi."

"Oh. Right there on the Euphrates."

"Yep. Smack dab in the Cradle of Civilization. Though the locals didn't think of themselves as civilized, but they sure as hell didn't want us there trying to set 'em straight."

"What happened? My brother is a combat vet. Afghanistan, Marines, now back in DC."

"Having a brother who's a combat vet doesn't get you any closer to being one."

"Do a lot of guys *find themselves* in combat?"

"A lot more lose themselves than find themselves."

"So, you got lucky."

"Yeah, most definitely. I had a moment of clarity out on patrol, up on my armored vehicle, hands on the machine gun. I made the decision that I was going to shoot anything that moved and get home with my team in one piece whether I had to spend the rest of my life in prison or not."

"You can't get much clearer than that."

"Is there anything else?"

"Does that piano work, or is that a stupid question?"

"Yes and yes."

"I'd like to play it, not for money or anything, but just to play. I'd like to come in when it's quiet like this and play."

"Let's hear you."

Roland walked over to the stage and stepped up and nodded to the man setting up the drum kit and went to the old upright piano set against the wall and saw that it was a Bush & Lane and opened the fallboard and sat on the bench and thought about what he should audition with. He didn't want to try anything too hard or ostentatious but rather something that had a nice melody that would demonstrate some skill. He called upon the melodies of his youth and chose a medieval Christmas hymn he'd practiced beyond profaning. It fit right in with the theme of war in the Middle East. He sang softly while he played just to keep the tempo.

"O come, O come, Emma-a-an-uel, and ransom captive I-I-Israel."

When he got to the high note, he belted out, "REJOICE, REJOICE." Serra interrupted him with a shout from behind the bar. "I didn't say you could sing!"

The man working on the stage said, "I've heard worse."

Roland closed the fallboard and stood up and turned to Serra and showed him an approving smile. "Me too. The instrument is in tune."

"Go ahead, then. You can play it. Just go easy on the religious material."

Roland walked back to the bar and put on his knit cap and sunglasses. The picture of himself he'd brought lay folded on the bar. Serra pushed it toward him. "Take your wanted poster with you."

Roland put the paper in his pocket and sucked down the rest of his Coke.

"Can I give you a bit of advice?"

"Sure."

"If you hang around a barbershop long enough, you'll eventually get a haircut."

~~~~~

Out on the street he shook off the minor humiliation he'd just endured by repeating under his breath a phrase he learned in the rooms— *You can restart your day at any time and as many times as you want.* It was an assertion that puzzled him, sane and useful as it sounded, as it begged for a reductio ad absurdum. Suppose, for example, your wife ran off with your business partner and took all the money. Would killing the business partner count as restarting your day? What about killing the wife? For that matter, what about killing yourself? These questions were too big to ponder. He walked back to his house and got his crab net and headed to the pier to hang out with the Mexicans, among whom he would, with any luck, learn to be at peace with this whole blessed situation and improve his Spanish in the bargain. His Chinese acquaintances in Portsmouth Square had served as the same sort of refuge, and he thought that they had probably already forgotten him unless by some trick of luck they'd learned about the celebrity of the young drunk who'd often inserted himself into their midst. Or maybe the new boards he'd paid for would cement him in their lore. No. Those men were not sentimental, he conjectured. Growing up in Communist China had inoculated them against frivolous emotions. The Mexicans who fished the pier were a far more amiable lot.

~~~~~

    His homemade crab net consisted of a circular nylon mesh around three feet in diameter. The outside of the circle was formed by an aluminum ring. The center, or bottom, of the net contained another aluminum ring about eight inches across to which was attached a wire box with a lid that closed with a latch. The wire box allowed for crabs to reach in with their claws and pick at whatever bait was in there—chopped-up squid or fish most commonly. Three lengths of rope were tied, evenly spaced, to the outside ring, and the ropes were joined roughly three feet above the net and secured with a foam float. Attached to that was the main rope that was long enough to reach from the platform of the pier to the ocean floor. The process was simple: You filled the box with bait, looped the main rope around a railing of the pier, and tossed the net into the water. The net dropped to the bottom and spread out flat with the rope suspended above it by the float. The delicious arthropods—the state allowed a daily limit—would scuttle over and feast on the easy meal. There was no way of sensing activity in the net, so you had to judge more or less based on the other crabbers' timing. Throwing in the net and pulling it up empty two minutes later made you look like an idiot, but you didn't want to wait half an hour, because a crab could eat his fill and move on. In the peak season, it didn't matter. Often there were so many crabs on the march that you could haul up your limit in less than an hour no matter how impatient you were. Eating them was sometimes harder than catching them.

    The pier was a strictly utilitarian construction, a concrete spit supported by wooden pilings, meant for harvesting the various coastal species, or for just watching to sun go down. He walked on with his gear and when he got to the end said *hola* to the Suarez brothers—Miguel and Henry—and got to work setting up his rig. The brothers shared a cigarette quickly because it was illegal, but at the very end of the pier it was almost impossible to notice the smoke. Roland enjoyed the smell, though he had given up the vile habit. They spoke to him mostly in English and he worked on his Spanish.

"Cuantos hoy?"

"Thirteen between us. Siete mas."

The bag limit for Dungeness was ten per day per person—ten that measured at least 5 and ¾ inches across the shell—males only. Females and undersized males you had to throw back. Occasionally, the ranger walked the pier to spot any obvious infractions. Some of the Mexicans carried hunting knives with six-inch blades to measure the close ones. The rest just carried rulers.

"Como se dice, *I should have been a pair of ragged claws?*"

Henry gave it a try. "Debería haber sido un par de garras… desiguales… andrajoso?"

Miguel chimed in, "No. Harapienta."

"Si bueno. Garras harapienta—*ragged claws.*"

"*Scuttling across the floors of silent seas.*"

Henry looked at Miguel. Miguel said, "¿Qué es *scuttling?*"

Roland made a scurrying motion with his ten fingers. "Ah," Miguel said, "Corriendo."

"No," Henry said. "Gateando. Like a crab. Or escabulléndose."

"Si," said Miguel. "Escabulléndose —mas correcto. Escabulléndose por los suelos de mares silenciosos."

Henry delivered it in full. "Debería haber sido un par de garras harapienta escabulléndose en los suelos de mares silenciosos. *I should have been a pair of ragged claws creeping across the floors of silent seas.* ¿Si?"

"Si bueno. Gracias."

"Sounds like poetry. Did you write that?"

"No. A guy from Saint Louis did. Muerta ahora."

"He doesn't sound very happy," said Henry.

"The Germans drained all the fun out of life."

The brothers looked at Roland then at each other and hauled up their nets. He could see they had no idea what he was talking about, and he was not about to explain it.

"I was thinking about all the crabs down there, crawling around in the silent darkness."

"Necesitas una mujer, amigo," said Miguel. Henry laughed. The brothers gathered their gear and their bucket full of live Dungeness crabs fighting to stay on top of the pile and nodded goodbye in unison and walked down the pier. He'd meant to ask them if they had mujeres of their own but remembered that one of the foundational precepts of the program was to refrain from blurting out the first thing that popped into your mind. Their point was made. He was adrift, perched on a concrete slab thirty feet above the ocean, but adrift nonetheless.

The net had been down for less than ten minutes, and he decided to wait a little longer. He took out his phone and called his editor, the woman in charge of assisting him with his masterpiece.

"Hi, Marjorie, this is Roland."

"Hi, Roland. Whatcha up to?"

"Just out on the Pacifica Pier looking out at the ocean, waiting to pull up my crab trap."

"My mouth is watering. What's on your mind?"

"I was wondering if you had any feedback on the chapters I sent. Also, I was wondering if you thought the poem was okay. I was thinking of adding a few more that I've written over the years, you know, to add a little garnish to the narrative."

"No. I don't think so. I mean, I like the one you included. Kinda shocking, really. But I don't want your story to serve as a frame for your poetry. That's the express train to the remainder bin."

"I see."

"Let's make sure you do. I'll tell you a little story that should put the subject in better perspective."

"It's just us and the open ocean here."

"I can hear the wind."

"I'll mute my end." He buttoned off his microphone.

"Roland, I know a little bit about the poetry world because I was a poet once upon a time, a graduate student poet at the University of Iowa, at the famed Writers' Workshop. One spring, I think it was 1988, Kurt Vonnegut came through on a speaking tour to promote his upcoming non-fiction book. Nearly all the fiction writers in the writing program were there, about half the poets, and a bunch of miscellaneous students and professors. It was a packed house. The first thing he wanted to make clear to everyone was that literary fiction was dead. Movies and TV had taken over the storytelling function in our culture, so writers had better think about producing non-fiction. That's where the real social impact was, and the money too. During the Q-and-A afterward, I raised my hand, rather meekly as I recall, and asked the great Kurt Vonnegut where poetry fit in. Without missing a beat—and this was before you had to worry about hurting people's feelings when you gave your opinion—he said, *everyone should write a poem before breakfast and then throw it in the trash*. A few people laughed. Most of us were put off. His respect for poetry was reduced to inspirational morning thoughts—relevant only to the author and then only for a moment."

"Okay. No more poetry. How do you like what you've seen so far?"

"It's good. You're a competent writer—a muscular stonemason, a careful builder, not an author of cathedrals, but very few are. I'll send you my markup. One thing I'd like to hear more about is your sports experiences. Don't be modest. Pump up that aspect of your story. And the religious or transcendental experiences too—people like that sort of thing. Take liberties. You're larger than life, so people will expect your early years to be larger than life, or at least more exciting than most. If you're thinking about an episode in your life that you're hesitant to reveal, that's when you want to go full bore."

Roland pulled up his net and waited for her to finish. She was about as easy to listen to as a person could be, he thought. So easy that you understood her without even processing her words. He sensed that she was on his side, or at least on the side of his book. This would be a strictly professional relationship based on achieving the best results for everyone concerned.

"I understand. Anything else?"

"When you get to the meeting with Trump, give us the details, even if you have to make stuff up. Your Oval Office meeting will be one of the marketing bullets, so we need that scene to pay off."

The net held four crabs, all still feeding on the bait at the bottom of the net, unaware that their lives were essentially over. Fish panicked when they were hooked and yanked out of the water, but crabs showed no awareness whatsoever of their change in circumstance. One of them was too small and he tossed it back and wished it luck on its migratory trek.

~~~~~

Establishing a productive routine is a good idea for anyone who wants to get along in the world and critical for the recovering alcoholic. In jail, Roland had come to accept that he faced the choice between life and death, and if his grandpa and Father Bartholomew could be believed, there was more at stake than even that—the very eternity of his consciousness was on the line. Out of jail, Roland knew that he had to enforce a routine on himself, and he settled into a good one. Most days started with the Wake Up Group at the Baptist church then back home for an hour or two at his desk adding pages to his book, another hour or two working on the house—painting the interior walls was first on the list—then off to the dojo or golf course on alternating days. When the mood struck him, he bought lunch at Winters Tavern and played the piano and chatted with Serra when the war veteran was so disposed. Serra bought a case of ginger ale and gave him a can free of charge every time he came in. Once or twice a week he went to the pier and caught a few crabs for dinner. Evenings he would read or work on his book or stream a movie on his computer. Alone most of the time, the flow of life in his new surroundings proceeded to a musical soundtrack piped into his ears from the voluminous library stored on his phone. The question of happiness, the pursuit of it, never entered his mind, and the prospect of joy seemed positively absurd. What he had achieved, though—one might call it a veneer of contentment—put the people he came across at ease. Yet he always felt a little restless.

~~~~~

The local municipal golf course, Sharp Park, was an eighteen-hole affair, poorly maintained and justifiably so. Built along an inhospitable stretch of the coastline, the weather could turn sour quickly with heavy wind-driven mist that shriveled the resolve of the most dedicated linkster. Sometimes a squall rolled in and drenched the landscape. As such, the course did not get much play, leastways not until summer. This suited Roland, as he could be reasonably sure of walking on at just about any hour of the day. He never played alone. A round of golf, he learned, could not be recorded—did not actually take place—if the golfer played alone. A solo trip was nothing more than an exercise in golf, not a legitimate event. If there wasn't a group teeing off when he got there, he would wait until he could join a twosome or a threesome, or even another single like himself. This was how he learned to play, by accompanying others and watching how the more successful players executed their strokes. He most enjoyed walking the course with the old timers, who pulled their bags on rolling carts. His damaged knee made it difficult for him to carry his bag which, being of professional size and quality, was particularly heavy. The duffers moved slowly and deliberately and were happy to tutor the lanky beginner with the gimpy leg.

"Pretty fancy set for a novice," said Joe, a spry Filipino who liked to talk. "You show up with a bag like that, people expect you know what you're doing."

"I won it on a quiz show."

"They still have quiz shows?" said Rudy, the youngest of the three at sixty-eight.

"It was a charity event at my church back home, not a TV game show."

Roland didn't consider that a lie. He considered it an act of generosity, saving everyone's time, of which these gents had little to spare. If he'd told them how he'd come by the bag, a lot of questions might ensue and he would become the focus of attention or, worse yet, the mention of the president's name could touch off a flap.

The octogenarian in the group, Ambrose, seldom spoke to Roland except to give him pointers. "Not so hard," he would say when Roland rushed his swing and sliced the ball to the right. "Slow it down. You need to learn to hit it straight before you can hit it far." For Ambrose, bogey was par, and he made it nearly every hole, always punching the ball squarely, straight up the fairway, though not very far. His excellent chipping was key to his success. He wore the bottoms of his trousers rolled.

Filipino Joe offered Ambrose some advice "You'll need to hit it harder if you ever want to shoot your age." Everyone was rooting for him to do it, and he'd come close a few times with scores of eighty-six and eighty-seven. Shooting your age in golf was something that deserved to make the papers.

Ambrose carried a gray leathery golf bag that looked older than he was. It lacked the pockets and zippers found in a normal one. It was nothing more than a long tube given shape by the wooden frame inside it and had a single strap attached.

Roland wondered aloud. "I've never seen a bag like that. What's it made out of?"

"Here we go," said Joe.

"A whale's penis," said Ambrose.

"You're shitting me."

"We don't talk like that out here," said Ambrose. These were old-school gentlemen. They broke the law that prohibited their cigars but kept their language civil.

"Sorry, but that's hard to believe."

"I can't tell you what species. But it used to be attached to a whale."

"Where'd you get it?"

"Japan, on my way home from Korea."

"That's got to be illegal."

Joe chimed in. "Back then you could eat brains from the head of a live monkey at a Tokyo restaurant."

"That's a myth," Rudy said.

"Not so," Joe said. "The Japs learned it from the Chinee."

"His point," said Ambrose "is that over there, there were no laws against animal cruelty."

"I guess the whale was already dead, and I don't suppose they were hunting it just for its penis like they kill rhinos just for their horns."

"Right you are."

"Can you show me how you chip so well?"

"Watch the Phil Mickelson chipping video. Change your life."

Change your life, indeed. That's what this was all about, this sojourn in Pacifica. From here, who knew or cared? God did, presumably. Roland slowly had grown more comfortable with the idea of a Higher Power who, omniscience aside, at least cared. For now, he remained on what the program called *the narrow path* and had yet to enter *the broad highway* where he would someday walk among *the happy, joyous, and free*. His spiritual awakening would be of the gradual variety, as opposed to the revelatory jolt that visited the more evangelical of the recovered, principally the founder, Bill Wilson.

While happiness remained elusive—he'd yet to realize it was a serious problem that required a decision, much like the decision to stop drinking—it popped up occasionally and unannounced, mostly out on the golf course when he hit a perfect shot. Suddenly, what seemed impossible became possible; and if it was possible, it was, by deduction, repeatable. The spectacle of the ball launched from his iron soaring high into the air and landing a hundred and eighty yards away softly on the green then rolling slowly pinward, gave him a feeling of power and personal satisfaction that verged on joy. The hope he drew from his rare great shots recalled for him the thrill of mastering the many sports he played growing up. But just as quickly he was back to catching the turf behind the ball with the sole of the club and lifting a huge divot from the fairway, only to watch the ball dibble forward a few feet. Mercifully, Sharp Park, being wet most days from the thick morning fog, kept the Winter Rules sign posted nearly year-round. That meant golfers were free to lift-clean-and-place their balls after each shot even if the ball landed on a dry patch. Roland took advantage of winter rules and never played a bad lie unless he yanked the ball into the heavy rough and opted not to take a penalty stroke for placing it on the fairway. The memory of the pain in his wrist made him wary of taking a hard swing even in the best of circumstances, for as a beginner he sometimes caught the ground well behind the ball. His fear of pain, then, caused him more often than not to hit the ball thin, sending it skidding forward, often farther than it would have gone had he hit it perfectly. But a thin shot was unpredictable, as the top-spinning ball could carom off the fairway and wind up in the rough. Golf, he quickly learned, was all about managing mistakes. It tested one's emotional fitness as much as one's physical skill. Roland's temperament improved gradually as his scores improved, and after two months of regular play, he'd taken twenty strokes off his early scores but still had yet to break a hundred. He'd need a major breakthrough to reach ninety-four.

More important to Roland than his golf score was the rehabilitation of his left leg. He could walk well enough, albeit with a slight limp, but jogging was difficult, and a flat-out sprint was out of the question. In fairness to the leg, its stiffness actually helped his golf swing, but that small benefit was something Roland was not willing to enjoy. He was determined to achieve full flexibility and strength in the uncertain limb and, as far as his golf swing was concerned, would keep it stiff not by dint of disability but through proper practice. He'd always enjoyed running. His goal was to reach the point where he could pound out a few miles without discomfort, and he was a long way off.

Close to his house were a martial arts studio and a little fitness center. On the days he didn't play golf, Roland worked out at one place or the other, most often the dojo, which featured Muay Thai classes that were perfect for increasing his leg flexibility and strengthening his core. The principal trainers were a husband-and-wife team of battle-tested Jujitsu masters not ashamed to display their myriad medals and trophies in the window box of the storefront. The husband, Paulo, a swart Brazilian sculpted to perfection, ran the Muay Thai classes. He spotted Roland's skills right away and approached him after his first class.

"You're not a beginner—not even an intermediate. Why are you in the beginner's class?"

"I'm new to Muay Thai, so I thought I should start here. I'm recovering from a bad car wreck and want to take it slow."

"I noticed the leg. Anything else holding you back?"

Roland thought to reply that the only thing truly holding him back was an advanced case of Original Sin, but he decided it was best to keep their first interaction strictly professional. He lifted his right hand.

"I'll know about this wrist once I start punching."

~~~~~

One Saturday evening around eight o'clock as he sat at his kitchen table tapping away at his memoir waiting for his teapot to sing, his phone buzzed. He looked with alarm at the device as though it were the napkin holder and it had suddenly come to life. The last time someone had called him was days ago when Sandy checked on him. But it was too soon for her to be calling again. He picked it up and saw the name: Gina. More than his family members, with whom he acknowledged an inextricable bond, Gina represented what, for want of a better word, might be called reality. He'd exposed his character to her more than to anyone alive—Barsamian had seen his darkest side—and so in his mind, the reality of who he was in this world, in this life, was contained in her experience of him.

Roland thumbed the button. "Hi, Gina." He tried to sound normal. It was her call. He would let her guide it.

"Hi, Roland." She spoke a bit hesitantly. "Is this a good time to talk? I mean, have I caught you at a good time?"

"Yes. But I would drop whatever I was doing?"

"Well. What *have* you been doing?"

"Since I got out?"

"I don't suppose you do too much in jail."

"Oh I got a lot done in there."

"Rehab?"

"Body and soul."

"Soul?"

"AA meeting every day."

"Forced, or voluntary?"

"Are you interviewing me, Gina?"

"Yes."

"For what? Not to say I mind."

"For another conversation."

"The babiest of steps."

"The babiest of steps."

"That's nice. That's okay by me."

"So?"

Roland returned to her question. "I was court-ordered, but I wanted to go. I looked forward to going. It was a good meeting—the leader made sure it was a good meeting."

"What does that mean—a good meeting?"

"The leader set a good tone, and there were a few guys in there for the recovery, guys who talked about things that mattered. And then, of course, a lot of knuckleheads, but even a few of them eventually got the message."

"Are you still going to meetings?"

"Every day. Every morning at the local Baptist church."

"Can I ask you where you're living?"

"Pacifica."

"So, you stuck around. I thought you might evacuate the catastrophe—go back home or something."

Roland let her words vibrate in the air. He didn't want to lie, didn't want to say that he stuck around in the hopes that they could see each other again; but then again, he wasn't exactly sure why he'd stayed in California and so close to San Francisco when he could have moved anywhere. He wasn't on parole.

"I have a book contract and I'm on a deadline, so I found someplace nearby where I could make a quick getaway and try to finish it. I've been settled in here for a few months." It was as near to the truth as he could steer.

"I guess Pacifica is a good place to hide out. I've never even been there."

"It's a quiet little working-class town—not a lot of San Francisco depravity."

"Well."

Roland waited for her to continue, but she didn't. He looked at his reflection in the night-blackened window.

"Yes. I'm well."

"Still a wiseass, I see."

"Not a public wiseass, though. Not anymore."

"Books are public. If you cut out the wiseass it might not do so well. You still have a public even though you've kept off social media."

"I'm going for a more literary tone. Not a quick bestseller that disappears after a few months. I want my book to last a long time." He could hear her doing dishes in the background, water running, plates clacking. He wasn't going to help her fill her silences. Finally, she spoke.

"After that bustling jail community, you must get lonely living by yourself in a strange town, sitting in an apartment writing all day."

"I've been lonely most of my life, but I can tell you honestly that these last few weeks I've never been less lonely. I'm not shut in all day, and not in an apartment. I rented a little house."

"So you're not hiding out."

"Those were your words. I said I needed a quick getaway. Pacifica is very low-key, and I keep myself pretty busy, along with the writing."

"Pretty busy? Doing what?"

"Physical training, golfing, crabbing, fixing up the house—besides early morning meetings at the church."

"Golfing? You don't like golf. Remember what you said when you were assigned the Trump game?"

"Golf is a good walk spoiled. Mark Twain is supposed to have said that."

"I like golf. My dad taught me how to play."

"I'm not sure I like it, but I'm on a mission to get good at it."

"Since when?"

"It's a long story. I'd rather not tell you over the phone."

"What—you make it sound like your line is bugged."

"The last time we talked it was."

"That was the jail's line. Don't tell me you're mad about that."

"No. You did the right thing—and the intelligent thing."

"I've got my clubs. We could play tomorrow."

"I'm glad you've forgiven me, Gina."

"I'm a Christian—not a very good one most of the time. My dad often reminded me of the duty to forgive. It helps the one doing the forgiving."

"It makes me feel good too."

"So, what about tomorrow?"

"You wanna help me hang my new curtains?"

"No. I wanna golf."

"I golfed today, and I can't do it two days in a row. My left leg is still a long way from…"

"I was going to ask about that. Are you still in pain?"

"Only when I push it to the limit. I stretch it and strengthen it every other day at the dojo or the weight room, and on the other days I play golf. Today was a golf day."

"What did you shoot?"

"1-0-6."

"Ouch."

"I started just a few months ago, so go easy on me. Be a good Christian."

"Do you even believe in God?"

"Is that something you ask all of your friends?" The water stopped. The clinking stopped. He pictured her drying her hands with a towel. Roland sensed that, without having meant to, he had taken the wheel. She quickly disabused him of that false impression.

"I have no interest in being your friend, Roland."

Her words sank into his brain like a stone dropped into a mudpot. The silence now belonged to him. He auditioned a few replies in his mind but none sufficed. He imagined a dishtowel draped over her shoulder waiting for him to respond. After five or six seconds, he spoke.

"That's a hell of a thing to say."

"Have you ever been just friends with a girl? I bet you've fubbed around a lot, but do you know any females you haven't been to bed with?" Astrid didn't count since she was just his nextdoor neighbor. He thought about saying Tina, but she wasn't really a friend, just a haircutter he flirted with. He thought about Alessandra but withheld that episode of his life since it was brief and certainly concluded.

"Just you."

"And we're not even friends, are we?"

"No. I couldn't manage it."

"No. Not drunk. Things were moving right along until you started drinking. You know that, right?"

"Love scares me." He couldn't believe his ears. The words had bypassed his will and issued straight from his heart.

"Go on."

"I'm not sure, but maybe I started drinking again to sabotage things. I know I didn't make a conscious decision—nothing like that—but maybe..."

"Allowing yourself to love means giving up control."

"Yeah, I guess. I know when I'm drunk the world is much smaller and the fewer people in it the better."

"So back to my question. This is still an interview."

"I'd rather talk about golf."

"It's simple enough. Put Jesus aside. I'm not asking you if you're still a Catholic or even a Christian. I want to know if you believe in God—at any level. It's not like I'm going to hang up if you say no."

"I'm pretty sure there is no death. I've visited the other side. As for who's in charge of the whole shebang—you got me. In the rooms, we just call it the Higher Power and try to accept that the Higher Power wants us to be happy. That's good enough for me."

"What does that mean—you've visited the other side?"

"When I crashed my car and headbutted the windshield. I was trying to tell you about it in jail."

"You had one of those near-death things?"

"Yeah—I met my dead grandpa."

"What did he say? Or did you just see him?"

"He told me I couldn't stay, that I had to go back." Roland was tempted to tell her what Father Bartholomew said but decided that it was too outlandish for a rational person to accept, and in any case he wouldn't know where to begin.

"You wanted to stay? You saw heaven?"

"No—I couldn't get in. I saw the front door, made all of light, a pearly light. I can see it anytime I want to if I close my eyes. And the music, an indescribably beautiful symphony—but that memory has begun to fade."

"What about now?"

"What *about* now?"

"If you could go back—if you could get in—say your grandpa gave you a choice?"

"Maybe not. Maybe if he'd promised that I would recover from my injuries. But I don't think that's how it works. I don't think the spirits can see our futures, only tell us when we haven't fulfilled our purposes. What I saw, hovering in that middle space—what I saw when I looked down, my broken, unconscious body draped across my broken windshield over the hood of my car—I didn't want to go back into the wreck of a human being."

"I just want to know that you're glad you survived, that you're glad to be alive."

"I don't think like that. All I know is that I'm not ready to go. Things I have yet to accomplish—that was the drift of my non-death experience."

Gina paused. Roland sensed that she wanted to ask more questions and hoped she wouldn't but was prepared to serve her the whole enchilada if she expressed such an appetite.

"What color are the curtains?"

"Green and yellow, vertical stripes. Very sheer."

"Those won't keep out much light."

"I'm looking to brighten up the place. My old apartment was more like a cave or a dungeon."

"I'm glad I never saw it."

"My mom made it look as good as it could when I was in lockup."

"Let's not talk about that. Going to see you was one of the worst days of my life."

"You set things right. I want to thank you for that. It humbled me."

She stayed silent for a few seconds. "I'll come tomorrow morning and help you."

Roland gave her his address and they ended the call without talking any more about golf, but he was happy that golf was probably in the offing. The conversation, her buoyant personality, enlivened his spirit, put him in a golly-gee-willikers mood, which gave him the mental energy to write a few more pages than he'd intended to. The manuscript stood at a hundred-and-fifty plus and consisted in part of excessively understated anecdotes of his athletic exploits and achievements growing up, to the point where he was offered the volleyball scholarship. As he began to write about it, he marveled—a kid who'd played only a little volleyball and not for a very good club offered a full ride at Berkeley over kids his size or even taller who'd played since they were twelve. He marveled at it, not in self-admiration, but at the sheer improbability of his good fortune.

Crouching behind a corner in the back of his mind lurked his pride in getting away with murder, a tail he could not shake; and he wondered momentarily how, or if, in his memoire he might hint at his guilt without betraying his reputation for unperturbable rectitude. He stood up and closed the laptop and promised himself he would never regret taking those two lives and never pretend to anyone, privately or publicly, that he regretted it.

~~~~~

Gina knocked on his door just after eleven. Roland answered, freshly dressed and toweling his wet hair. She wore jeans and a blue and white checkered cotton shirt with the sleeves rolled up. Her hair was up too, her face lightly powdered, her lips unpainted. He'd never felt so grateful, so his gratitude was awkward as he invited her in and fumbled with motions of simple hospitality, offering her a place to sit and asking if she'd like of cup of tea. She smiled amusedly at his nervousness.

"Don't let me cry today," he said, to show her he could tease himself. "If I start going soft, tell me to buck up."

"Buck up."

"I'm serious. I can't tell you how happy I am that you came."

"I'll leave if you act this way. This is not you. And the beard and mustache are abominable."

"I'm in incognito mode. Plus, beards look very distinguished on book jackets."

"I won't permit it, not if I have anything to say."

He wanted to look at her, to show her with his eyes how glad he was that she'd referenced a possible future, but he knew better than to press his luck by raising an eyebrow, so to change the subject, he insisted on giving her a tour of his humble abode. From the living room where they stood behind its curtainless front window he led her into the small adjacent dining room, which doubled as his writing space, and through the doorway into his tidy kitchen. She opened his refrigerator and looked inside and closed it and looked at him and said good for you, by which he understood that she approved of the fresh produce. The rear entry to the kitchen joined the hallway, which led to the house's only bathroom on the near side and two bedrooms on the other side. The bedroom windows faced the side street that formed the corner lot on which the house was built. Roland kept the windows open for ventilation and because he liked to hear the activity on the sidewalk outside when he slept. He showed her the larger, back bedroom because his bed was neatly made and he was proud of his tall oak dresser with its curved drawers and brass handles. The other bedroom, he told her, was unfurnished, but she poked her head in anyway.

"Wow."

"Wow what?"

"Your clubs." She walked in to take a closer look at the presidential seal on the bag and the same insignia on the clubhead covers. She pulled the driver out and unsheathed it and handed the cover to Roland. "The president gave you these—am I right?"

"You are."

"May I ask why?"

"To challenge me. He said if I can break ninety-five, he'll sport me a round with Tiger Woods."

"Because you worked on Trump Golf Resorts?"

"No." Roland paused to formulate his next sentence. "Because a drunk who's never played golf would have to get sober if he wanted to break ninety-five. That's more or less what he said."

She took the clubhead cover out of his hand and put it back on the driver and slid the driver back into the bag then moved past him out the doorway into the hallway and back into the front room. He followed her. She turned and looked at him. "That's a pretty clever maneuver by Trump. I'm still wondering why."

"I don't think there was a why. It seemed like a spontaneous gesture—a dare. And I knew he was serious. I had no doubt he'd send the clubs."

"So, you liked him—you accepted the dare."

"He knows how to be likable—he's in the business of being likable, I think, one-on-one, man-to-man likable."

"A lot of people hate him."

"The FBI guys we met think he's going to be assassinated. One of them called him *a bottle on a fence post*. I think they're eager for it to happen."

"My dad says he's *a crash test dummy.*"

Roland chuckled. "That's funny, but I'm not sure I get it."

"They can do whatever they want to him, see how much chicanery they can get away with. Who's going to defend him, the Republican Party? He steamrolled those bozos."

"I see. The perfect guinea pig. He already had plenty of dirt on him before he won the office, so the deep-staters can throw all the mud they want and see what sticks."

She smiled at him to agree.

"I'd like to meet your dad. Sounds like a pretty sharp guy."

"That day's a long way off if it ever were to come."

"Does he know you know me?"

"Course he does—everybody who works at Pacific Gameworks gets asked about you."

"That all?"

"He thinks you're something special, a rare breed, a bona fide American."

"Even after what I did—the position I put you in?"

"I didn't tell him."

"I want to meet him. I'll tell him."

"You'll have to get through me."

~~~~~

As they worked on the curtain job, Roland went through the list of projects he'd set for himself.

"Besides sanding and refinishing the floors, I'm going to replace the kitchen cabinets, put down new linoleum, replace the sink in the bathroom, add ceiling fans and new light fixtures."

"That's crazy, Roland. Why?"

"The owner is going to pay for the materials, so it's just labor. Besides, it was the easiest way."

"What do you mean?"

"In case she didn't want to rent to me. I gave her twelve months upfront and promised to fix the place up. I wanted to avoid a long conversation, so I made it easy for her."

"You really wanted to live in this dump that badly?"

"I like the small-town feel, like where I grew up. And this rundown house gives me a sense of purpose. I've still got enough money to coast for a while."

They took down the dilapidated inoperable blinds sagging over the living room windows and patched up the old screw holes and installed the curtain rod Roland had purchased and hung the new curtains. All in about an hour. Roland liked that she knew had to handle tools and understood the order of the tasks without any direction from him, and he made sure not to mention what a competent handyman she was. Privately he assayed her. For his taste in women, she was the perfect mixture of feminine and masculine, and she could golf, so she said, which fact remained top of mind.

"You're right."

He eyed her like she'd been reading his mind but knew that wasn't true yet didn't know what she was talking about. Throughout his life, when someone made that simple acknowledgment—*you're right*—he was fond of replying, *I usually am.* True as that might have been, such facile arrogance could not be softened by adding a chuckle, not for Gina leastways.

"About what?"

"The quality of light. The green and yellow add a nice glow to the room with the sun coming through."

"Thanks. Are you hungry?"

"Sure. I could eat."

"How about a crab salad? I can make a fresh crab salad if you can wait an hour."

"It doesn't take an hour to make a salad."

"First we have to rustle up a few crabs."

"Oh! That sounds fun."

"Good good." He grabbed a few frozen squids from the freezer. "Let's go."

They went outside. Roland went to the garage and got his crabbing gear and they went to her car and he told her where to go and she drove to the pier and parked. The fishermen and crabbers were out in force today. He led her about halfway up the pier and found an open gap on the south rail and showed her how it was done. She took a tube of lotion from her little backpack purse and applied the cream to her face and rubbed some on his forehead and nose.

"Thank you. It's usually not this sunny out." He lowered the contraption into the water.

"How long does it usually take?"

"We need only three or four, so I figure about fifteen minutes."

They stood in comfortable silence inhaling the ocean breeze. The seagulls wheeled. Pelicans plunged, emerged, and sat, bobbing and gulping. A young boy—six, maybe seven—snooped along the pier looking at the various catches. When he came to Roland and Gina he stopped.

"Where's your bucket?"

Roland looked at Gina before he replied to the boy. "We don't eat them."

The boy twisted his lips and gave a puzzled look. "Then why do you catch them?"

"We write messages on them and throw them back."

"What kinna messages?"

"Whatever we feel like. *Don't eat me I'm poison. My name is Charlie.* Sometimes we put on smiley faces. Just silly stuff. Once I wrote *fifty-dollar reward* and put my email."

The boy wasn't buying. "It would wash off."

Gina held out a bottle of nail polish she'd fished from her purse. "We use this. It's much thicker than paint. Lasts a long, long time."

The boy considered the claim. "For reals?"

"No. We just put 'em in the bag and take 'em home and boil 'em up. We're taking only three or four today."

"It's a good idea anyway. *Don't eat me I'm poison.* Niggahs be trippin'."

"It's my idea, but you can use it."

"Thanks," said the boy and down the pier he went.

He moved a little closer to her. "Nice play."

"The kid looked like a hard sell. Seems like you like talking to children."

"An intelligent child is the most fascinating kind of person."

"How do you mean?"

"Life hasn't fractured him into a cubist hash. He is who he is supposed to be on that day and time and shows natural self-confidence because of it, and because of it he does not censor himself. Children are the easiest people to get to know."

"I guess you've tried to hold on to your original child."

"I needed to drink to blunt the feeling that life would eventually frustrate me."

"It's not going to frustrate me. I'm going to enjoy every day as much as I can. That's the only decision you have to make. The rest is details. And I've always hated Picasso. I mean, he was cataclysmically brilliant in the panorama of history, but his pictures were meant to be ugly. I'll give them that."

"Most of his art is aggressively masculine—at least that's how it strikes me."

"What we're doing out here is pretty masculine. I'm practically the only woman on the pier."

The Suarez brothers came strolling up with their gear. They saw Roland before he saw them and nodded to him, both smiling.

"Buenos tardes, amigos!"

Henry answered. "Beunos tardes, Roland y…"

"Gina. Mi buena amiga."

"¿Solo tu amiga?" said Miguel with a toothy grin. "Ella es muy bonita."

"Yes. And thank you. We're just friends. I'm helping him fix up his rundown house."

Henry got down to business. "We know lots of workers. Twenty bucks an hour. You can read poetry to your chica, and they can do the work." The brothers laughed and moved on to find a spot farther down the pier.

"What were they talking about? Read me poetry?"

"I was testing their Spanish the other day. I gave them a few nifty lines from T.S. Eliot to see if they could handle it."

"I guess there's not a lot to do out here while you're waiting for your catch."

They stood quietly for a few more minutes, close but not together, before he hauled up the trap. Four male crabs, one too small. He tossed it back and they watched it splash and disappear. He folded the trap around the prisoners and stuffed it into the bag and slung it over his shoulder and off they went.

"Stop here at the market. We need salad fixings."

"I'll get them. I can tell your leg is bothering you."

"How can you tell?"

"You walked a little more gingerly on the way back than on the way there. A round of golf must be hard for you."

"This morning I tried kicking on the heavy bag at a little dojo where I go and probably overdid it. I need to be more patient."

Back at the house, Roland placed the live crabs in the sink and filled a pot with water and put it on the burner to boil and scrubbed his hands clean then put on some modern bluegrass. He returned to the stove and watched the water while Gina set herself to the task of making a salad. He kept his back to hers and listened to the sound of her hands dismantling a head of lettuce and chopping bell peppers. He could smell what she was doing. The silence between them was comfortable. He could get used to this.

When the water boiled, he tossed in a pouch of spices called 'crab boil' and lowered in the three Dungeness. "It takes about fifteen minutes."

"Do you think they feel it?"

"I guess any living thing will panic. I bet a forest somehow knows when it's on fire."

When the crabs were ready Roland broke them open and forked out the meat and put it in a bowl and handed it steaming to Gina to add to her salad. She didn't take the bowl but pressed it back into his hand. "Chill." For a moment he thought she might be telling him to take it easy, but he'd never heard her indulge in urban slang and quickly understood that she meant for him to put the hot crab meat in the freezer to cool down. He did as he was told then went over to the salad bowl Gina had prepared and lowered his face over it and inhaled—celery, onions, cucumbers, peppers, garlic, and some kind of vinaigrette dressing.

"The table."

He caught her drift and took what he needed to set the table in the next room and cleared off his computer and writing pad and made ready for the meal and sat there with an empty mind, midway between happiness and fear. Time reckoned itself. The light in the front room softened imperceptibly. A bird swept past the window and cast a fleeting shadow that did not disturb his peace.

They ate across from each other and agreed that such a salad could not be found in the finest restaurants in San Francisco for any price and how it was true that one could eat very well, very healthily, on a few dollars a day and he said he had to be careful because if he ate crab every day he'd probably develop gout in his ankles and that would spell disaster for his golf game.

"Seriously?"

"Uric acid. Builds up in the joints."

"You're too young and fit to develop gout."

"Never know."

"You just wanted to shift the topic to golf."

"Yes I did, and I did."

"Do you think I haven't made up my mind?"

"I'm learning not to think too much, at least not about the future—one day at a time as the saying goes."

"I didn't come today because I thought you needed help hanging curtains."

"I don't even know who I am anymore after what I've been through, after what I started. I thought I knew who I was when that guy broke into my place and faced me down and refused to leave. I knew—knew before he cut me—that I would kill him with that knife and lie about it. But now I'm not sure I would do it again, and at the same time I don't think it was wrong even though it was murder."

"If you'd let him live, I wouldn't be here—you'd probably still be pissing your life away."

Roland blinked as though he'd been slapped, though her words carried no scorn.

"You might be right. But how do you figure?"

"If you hadn't killed him, you wouldn't have had to deal with that other guy—his cousin, was it?—and, you know, put a very public exclamation point on the first execution. Your fame exposed you, Roland, and I think if you were left alone to your own devices, you'd wind up just another guy born with a lot of talent who never amounted to anything."

"I could still be that guy."

"I doubt it—not if you stay sober."

"That's a hard thing to hear—a hard thing to have said to you."

"It was hard to come over here. You just said you don't feel you did anything wrong when you murdered that stranger, but what about when you stole the code from my computer and sold it to China?"

Roland swallowed a laugh and smiled. "Of course, I knew it was wrong, but I had no idea it could blow back on you—I didn't know the security protocols. If I thought I was putting you at risk, or even myself at risk, I'd never have done it. I just needed money and it seemed like an easy and harmless way to get it."

"That's revealing. You're willing to do something wrong if you think you won't get caught."

"I don't cheat at golf, even when no one's looking."

"That reminds me of something my dad used to say."

"Let me guess—sports don't build character, they reveal it."

"Bullseye!"

"I've been known to chew up the bullseye."

"You're impossible. You haven't changed a bit."

A clean-shaven Roland and Gina kept company on the phone for the next two weeks before settling on a day to play golf at Sharp Park. He was glad for the delay, for his game, such as it was, had gone to hell after her visit. Try as he might—and *trying*, after all, was the problem—to keep himself locked in the moment for every shot, thoughts of Alessandra kept intruding. Not thoughts of her exactly, but the memory of the feelings he briefly entertained for her in New York when he mused that he could marry her. It struck him as absurd, even insane, that he'd let himself be overcome with a yearning for lifelong companionship with a woman he picked up, almost randomly, at an AA meeting and who he had little prospect of ever seeing again. It dawned on him that he'd manufactured those feelings in the safety of impossibility simply to validate his distorted view of his own humanity. The persona he'd created in the media to argue to the world that his violent actions were morally correct had left him empty because, at the time, he was not altogether sure that he was right. In New York, he'd thought, foolishly he now realized, that love, even an impetuous love, might redeem him. But now that Gina had reappeared and seemed favorably disposed toward him, it occurred to him that love must involve a certain amount of discipline, much like a martial art. He had yet to fully appreciate what the good padre had tried to impart to him—that the killings—murders even—mattered not at all in the metaphysical calculus of eternity. Only love mattered. Violence was easy. Anyone could kill. But to love required a deeper intentionality, one he was not sure he could marshal. To love another required one to first love one's own capacity to love—*to love love*—and that meant loving the source of love—the Creator. AA theology only touched on this fact, and Roland scarcely could articulate the psychology of his discomfiture while it interfered with his golf swing, but he knew it had to do with love and he sensed that he'd need to shake his unease if he wanted to make it with Gina.

~~~~~

It's not hard for an experienced fighter to strike the middle of the heavy bag over and over again. At the dojo, Roland delivered kick after kick with his right leg, alternating between excitement that he had Gina in his life and anger at himself for feeling unworthy of her. His rickety left leg held up well as he pivoted on it and drove his hips into each assault on the swaying bag. Like a dervish, his energy appeared to be inexhaustible as he timed each kick so that he struck the bag just as it reached the bottom of its arc to achieve maximum impact. Timing the impact just so was no easy feat even for a seasoned practitioner. The dojo owner, Paulo, marveled from a distance until, after one tremendous kick, the hook that held the bag tore clean from its wooden beam. The bag landed on the mat with a thud and Roland lost his balance and fell backward, bracing his fall with his elbows.

Paulo came over. "Are you okay?"

"Sorry about that, Paulo, I'll pay for it."

"For what, a bigger hook and a deeper hole?"

Roland stood up and picked up the hook and examined it and shook his head. "You should dip the threads in epoxy before you screw it into the beam."

~~~~~

Roland and Gina golfed on Sundays—three Sundays in a row so far. The tenor of their relationship was more business than pleasure as they had a specific goal—a target score—and their mission was for Roland to achieve it. He still had plenty of work to do. That Sunday morning, Roland took their two golf bags from the trunk of her car and set them down on the pavement in the parking lot. Gina closed the car door and came over and pulled the driver from his bag and put it back in the trunk and shut the lid.

"What's the big idea?"

"It does you more harm than good."

"I need to learn how to hit it. I'm not showing up to play with Tiger Woods without my driver."

"If you can hit the three-wood off the tee straight down the fairway consistently, then you've earned the driver." She gave him a playful swat on the patootie as if to say don't question my judgment.

He wanted to tell her that he felt a bit tense around her and that her presence probably had more to do with his difficulty in squaring the club face on the ball than his inconsistent swing mechanics. In keeping with a whip of wisdom he'd gleaned from his AA meetings—*restraint of tongue and pen*—he rejected the thought and kept his mouth shut. For whatever reason, Gina's idea bore fruit. Roland landed most of the fairways and celebrated a few pars, accepting as the round progressed Gina's repeated familiarities. She liked to touch him, to caress his back to keep him loose, to reach up and tap the tip of his nose when he hit a good shot. Roland felt some measure of peace before it was over, not because he managed to shoot his best score—102 is nothing to brag about, twelve shots behind Gina—but because he could see that he was growing more comfortable with moment-to-moment existence as a human being.

~~~~~

Before bed that night, without thinking, he picked up his phone and called his old sponsor, Denny. The two hadn't spoken since October when Denny informed Roland that Roland's name—a slight variation thereof—was chiseled like a cartouche in the foundation of Alcoholics Anonymous. Denny picked up right away, for the hour was only 9:15.

"Are you sober?"

Roland stammered at the abruptness of the interrogative. It seemed to him as though Denny, poised for the call, had jumped right on his case. He didn't wait for Roland to untie his tongue. "Don't say anything if you've been drinking or using. Just hang up the phone. The last two times we talked, you were in no shape to talk recovery. I broke my number one rule for you twice and I won't do it again."

"I'm sober, Denny. You want, I can recite the alphabet backward in Spanish."

"How long?"

"February nineteenth—the day after I wrecked my grandpa's car."

"So why are you calling me?"

"I wanted to tell you that I'm okay and to thank you for sticking your neck out getting me that job and to apologize for fucking it up."

"So, this is a Ninth-Step call?"

"I guess you could say that."

"It either is or it isn't."

"Sure, yeah—this is a Ninth-Step call."

"So, you're working the program now? I heard you say on TV that you didn't work the steps. That was mighty righteous. I give you credit for coming clean about that."

"I did meetings every day in jail, and since I've been out I'm still going every day."

"Why haven't I seen you?"

"I moved. I'm in Pacifica—I like it down here."

"You still haven't answered my question."

"No, Denny. I don't have a sponsor. I'm not working the steps." Roland wanted to explain that his notoriety made him shy, that he was perforce the big kahuna in lockup, that he'd moved to Pacifica to escape recognition and that he preferred to sit quietly in his local neighborhood meetings and draw strength in sobriety from the GOD known as Group Of Drunks. But he knew what Denny would say, that GOD also stood for Good Orderly Direction and that only by embracing the steps under the firm guidance of a committed sponsor well-versed in the Big Book would he stand a chance at achieving long-term recovery.

"I'll let you take me through them, but I don't have a car. You'll have to come to me. Anyway, that's not why I called."

"I'm glad you're sober and doing okay so far without the steps, but you know what you need to do."

"Do you believe in reincarnation?"

"No. But I don't reject it either. I don't dabble in theology above and beyond the existence of a Higher Power who wants us to be happy."

"You never sound happy, Denny."

"Not when I'm talking to you."

~~~~~

He lay in bed, eyes closed, concentrating in the pitch dark. The noise outside his open window was proof of the world. He would be leaving it soon as people do in the hours and minutes of sleep, and he wanted to be sure he would get where he wanted to go. A book of old teachings he'd studied as a teen spelled out the steps very plainly. He knew them by heart. He'd mastered the technique well enough that he could skip the preliminaries and just will the result. But tonight was different. He had a job to do or, more precisely, a mission to accomplish, so he followed the process by rote. The final contemplation in his preparation was that of a lotus flower suspended in his throat. He let his mind settle into the backs of his eyes then drizzle out of his optic nerves and descend his windpipe to drip hypnotically into the center of the imagined lotus flower floating in his airway. As soon as sleep arrived, he would be free, and once free he wasted no time, for he understood that even released from his body to roam the astral plane at will, he was still tethered to the physical realm by a thin filament and therefore connected to time.

He found his hands, wiggled his fingers, and sketched a mountain meadow with his eyes. He wouldn't need much scenery, but he needed to feel grounded, a place to stand and a few hundred yards of fairway. Then he did something he'd never tried before in dreamworld—he called for a tool, fabricated one with his imagination. Behold a driver, identical to the one in his golf bag. He laughed, bounced the toe of it gently off the side of his head, then reached into his pocket and pulled out a tee and a ball and proceeded to work on squaring up the clubface on impact. The balls rocketed into the distance just as in an electronic simulator. He summoned the dead masters by name. *Snead, Hogan, Arnold Palmer—hasten to my aid.* In due course, his balls flew true.

He continued the exercise on subsequent nights, attending to the other clubs and the finer points of the game—chipping, putting, even sand shots—until he grew bored of the endeavor, for the successes he experienced in his dreamscape were, he understood, not valid until tested against the physical world. Yet he had reason to trust in the efficacy of his out-of-body training, having over the years spent countless nights practicing violence and fornication with abandon. All those escapades had served him well in a material capacity. Yet he knew not how to love and knew he knew not how, so he called to the void for help with that mystery, as though the Creator might tear off a scrap of Its infinite self and deliver the secret by messenger. He called out to his grandpa to no avail, then to Jesus just for sport. No dice. The gardens he created in dreams were not annexed to the mansion, from which he could hear, if he squinted, the joys of victorious souls muffled behind whatever inviolate barrier separated him from that eternal kingdom, of which he had yet to prove himself worthy.

He thought to conjure Gina and play-act at love, filling her mouth with adoring responses to his tender affections, but he feared that would be a fraudulent pantomime. He could fix his golf swing with his head on the pillow using this form of self-hypnosis, tried and trued by sages throughout the ages, but lucid dreams provided no space for him to learn how to love.

~~~~~

Sunday arrived. May 28th. Summer around the corner, just a slight tilt of the Earth away. More than that, a day of reckoning for the man who used to open his eyes hungover nearly every Sunday when he lived in San Francisco. The good folks at the Wake Up Group at the Baptist church were chipper as usual. He sat through the meeting quietly, still unwilling to share his experience, strength, and hope, certain that they all knew who he was and grateful not to be asked to answer for it. Still, he knew that if he didn't come out of his shell before long his daily presence there would take on the character of stalking, and he resolved to take an active part in the meeting while he still felt welcome. Perhaps even seek out a sponsor.

Ambling home that morning, he saw the sun had already bored a bright white hole in the cloud cover. The air was still enough that the squawks of distant seagulls carried untattered to his ears. An ideal day for golf on the coastal course he knew so well. Gina picked him up in her car and they drove the short distance and he unloaded the bags and told her he felt confident today and would use the driver come what may. They folded into the threesome of the old duffers, which was okay because the course was not busy and a group of five would not slow anyone down. The jovial seniors eyed Gina approvingly and Rudy wondered aloud, in an obligatory playful dig, how she could manage to golf if her vision was so poor that she chose a guy like Roland, and Filipino Joe laughed and Roland said they were all old enough to probably have some inkling of life on the other side to talk as recklessly as they did, and they laughed even louder and Joe said they weren't worried because they knew who he was and Rudy said Roland Hazzard kills only bad guys.

"He can outsource it," said Joe. "He's buddies with the president so it might only take a phone call."

Ambrose shook his head. Since he didn't talk much, people paid attention when he signaled he might have something to say. "Trump is the one who oughta be worried."

"What do *you* know, Amb?" said Rudy.

"Only the lay of the land."

"You seeing assassins on the horizon?"

"Not on the horizon. The danger is the screen on that thing in your pocket."

Roland jumped in before things could spiral out of control.

"You guys still bicker about the JFK assassination and now you're confabulating about the president while he's still just settling in." Roland knew his ten-dollar word would arrest their palaver. "Gina came to golf this morning and she'll beat all of us and not use the ladies' tees."

The first hole measured 455 yards, narrow with a slight bend to the left toward the green. While the others were positioning their bags and pulling out their gloves, Roland grabbed his driver and walked into the box, stuck a tee into the ground, put a ball on it, stepped back and, with a tremendous whoosh, compressed the ball half-flat on the center of the clubface and launched the dimpled orb high and far out of sight down the center of the fairway. He pointed a finger straight up to the sky like a slugger thanking Heaven after swatting one out of the park.

"Roland!" she said.

"Jesus!" he said.

"We don't take the Lord's name in vain out here," Joe said.

"Specially not on Sunday," Rudy said.

"'Twas not in vain. That *was* my Jesus swing."

"Did you go to church this morning, Roland?" said Gina.

"In a manner of speaking."

"You either did or you didn't," said Rudy.

"My AA group meets at the Baptist church near my house, so you decide."

They made their way up the fairway and to the green. Roland and Gina each scored par and Roland penciled the card with the scores of all five. At the second tee, Gina edged over to Ambrose.

"I've never seen a bag like that?"

"Here we go," said Roland.

"Whale leather," said Joe.

"Stretched and cured by the industrious heathens of a pacified Japan," said Rudy.

Gina turned to Roland. "Are they putting me on?"

"They say it's a penis."

Gina wrinkled her nose and looked at Ambrose. "Sir, is that a whale's penis?"

"It was or I was cheated."

"May I take a picture of it?" She reached into her golf bag for her mobile device.

"I'd rather you didn't."

"Really—seriously?"

"Once that thing gets into your phone it might as well be everywhere—Jupiter, Zeta Reticuli."

"We wouldn't want anyone plagiarizing Moby Dick."

"Your mother named you right," Joe said. "RUDE-ee."

Roland turned to Gina and said too loudly, "Do you want to play through and leave the local color behind?"

"I don't mind," said Joe. "Without you here my blathering friend will have no one to yap at."

"You have the card," Ambrose said to Roland.

"We're not going back for another card," Rudy said. "If you play through, please leave us the card."

"I might need proof of this round."

"Why's that?"

Roland looked at Gina and shook his head that she shouldn't divulge the reason. She walked over to Ambrose and ran a hand along the trophy amputated from an enormous slain cetacean.

"I like playing with you old war horses." She walked over to Roland and took his hand. That clinched the matter for Roland. Whether he broke ninety-five or not, the day would be reckoned a success. He had only to enjoy the rest of it.

~~~~~

It would likely abuse the patience of the enduring reader to dedicate much space here to a detailed narration of Roland's triumphant round that day. Let it suffice that he did not tempt fate with any further demonstrations of his preposterous Jesus swing. He stayed close to Gina to elicit her advice as one would a caddy, advice she studiously gave. Twice, when he saw the codgers looking, he leaned down and imbibed the cinnamon-vanilla essences in her hair to let them know that he had yet plenty of life to live. The marked improvement in his game, upon which they could not help but remark, indicted their usefulness as golf mentors, for their advice it was evident had profited him little, while the injection of romantic optimism in the form of a lovely female seemed somehow to have transformed him into a player to behold.

Roland chipped in from sixty feet. "How are you doing this? You can't have improved this much in a week." He couldn't simply shrug off her wonderment, yet he had no truth to tell her, for the source of his ability was not known to him, only suspected. For him to answer that he was tutored by the masters while dreaming would be tantamount to claiming magical powers and open up a subject best discussed only after years of intimate trust. As such, he needed an equivocation that would satisfy her now and be forgivable should he come clean later on.

"It must be the meditation."

"Meditation?"

"Step Eleven—prayer and meditation."

"You meditate about golf?"

"I empty my mind of things that could hurt my golf."

When he totaled up the front nine, he stood at 44, best of the five and one shot better than Gina and Ambrose. Rudy asked to double-check the card and Roland remarked that if the old farts were wagering, he'd have had to call bullshit on Rudy more than once and noted how peculiar it was that Rudy forbore profanity and sacrilege but had no problem lying about his score on a hole here and there. He softened the remark with a laugh and a friendly jostle to keep the mood from souring. Gina took the card and looked at it carefully and nodded and twisted her lips and handed it back to Roland like it was a strange but legitimate artifact.

The weather changed as they began the back nine. Wind from the west. Not zephyrs whispering the advance of summer, but violent gusts propelled by some unconscionable force in command of the ocean, gusts that lashed the crests of the waves offshore and raised a spray long before they crashed. Hats blew off a dozen heads simultaneously throughout the course as if by prestidigitation and golfers dropped their clubs to chase their tumbling head coverings.

Roland stood before the ocean and held up the back of his left hand as if he would smack the wind back from whence it came and slowly drew down three fingers leaving only the middle one erect.

"Who's that to?" said Joe.

"Ferdinand Magellan."

"Careful now—he brought Jesus to my people."

"Yeah, but he named that chaos the *Pacific* Ocean."
"You won't shoot 44 again if this keeps up," said Rudy.
"We know it won't let up," said Ambrose.
"I'll show him how," said Gina.
"Not to 44 you won't."
"I need 50 or better."
"What's the prize?" said Rudy.
"You'll read about it in the paper someday."
"No one reads the paper," said Ambrose.

Roland wondered if he'd ever come to learn what he was doing in 1520 when Magellan was rounding the world or if Father Bartholomew's notes contained a clue. He shook off the distracting thought and took out his three-wood to tee off on the 10th hole. Gina went to his bag and took out the five iron and gave it to Roland and put the three-wood back in the bag.

"Close the face a little and hit a low runner."

Roland did as she suggested and stung the ball, sending it skipping forward up the fairway where it rolled to rest some two-hundred yards away. He and the others played the back nine in similar fashion, delofting their clubs to keep their shots below the wind, and when the scores were totaled Roland had a 92. He signed the card and Gina witnessed it with her signature below his and gave him a hug. The two took turns shaking hands with the three old men, who themselves did not shake one another's hands, then Roland and Gina walked briskly to her car.

"You're coming with me."
"Are you asking me or telling me?"
"I'm telling *him*."

They loaded the bags and got in the car.

"Don't start the engine yet."
"Why?"
"I want to make the call."
"Can't you talk while we drive?"
"I don't want any background noise."
"Who are you calling?"
"You know."
"You have his direct line?"
"His righthand man's."

"Who's that?"

"Maryanne Conroy."

"She seems like a busy woman—get's a lot of airtime."

"It's my only option." He found the number and placed the call. She answered after two rings.

"Roland Hazzard." It was more of an accusation than a greeting. Her tone said *I've stored your name in my phone because I'm required to take your call so get straight to it.*

"Hi, Missus Conroy. Is your boss around? I'd like to talk to him."

"What about?"

"About the deal we had—you know. We talked about it the last time we…" She cut him off.

"How long you been out of jail?"

"What difference does that make?"

"Is there a golf course in the San Francisco jail? It takes time to get good at golf."

"I've been out a few months. I found a good teacher." Roland looked over at Gina and smiled. Maryanne Conroy remained silent. Roland looked at Gina again and raised his eyebrows to indicate he was waiting on silence.

"Okay, Roland, I'll let him know."

"I'd rather tell him myself, and I need to ask him something else."

"Something else?"

"Let's start over. Can I talk to the president—yes or no?"

"That's not the way it works around here."

"President Trump and I have an understanding. Maybe you tell him I'm on the line and let him decide if I can talk to him."

"What if he's not available at the moment?"

"I'll wait, or he'll call me back. I just need you to tell him I'm on the line. I'm sure that much is possible." Roland glanced sidelong at Gina again to make sure that she wasn't annoyed at his presumptuousness. Had she not been there he might have taken a more aggressive tone toward Conroy.

"Hold the line."

Roland swiveled toward Gina and touched her arm. "She's got me on hold. She doesn't like me, but that's okay,"

"Half the country doesn't like you."

"Yeah. I'm either something or I'm something else."

They sat in silence for a while until Gina spoke.

"Do you really think the president is going to take your call?"

"He's one of my only friends, strange as that sounds, so unless he's putting out a fire he'll take my call—or he's not a friend."

She nodded gravely as though considering his logic.

"What's next? I'm kinda hungry."

"I know of a decent place in town for lunch."

The silence was broken by a click.

"Roland, this is Donald Trump. Maryanne tells me you did it. I knew you were a winner."

"I had some help. I want to talk to you about that."

"What kind of help? As long as you shot an honest round."

"I did, and I'd like to bring my helper along, make it a foursome. She plays very well and gave me a lot of pointers. We played this morning on the coast in a stiff ocean wind, and she kept me from playing against it."

"Whud you shoot?"

"Ninety-two."

"In heavy wind?"

"In heavy wind—on the back nine."

"With your girlfriend as caddy?"

"She played too but gave me caddy-like advice."

"Whud she shoot?"

"Ninety-one."

"IT WAS A BAD ROUND FOR ME." Gina wanted to make sure Trump could hear her. "I USUALLY SHOOT IN THE EIGHTIES."

"Little spitfire you got there—lemme talk to her. What's her name?"

"Gina." Roland handed her the phone. She took it with a self-satisfied grin.

"Hello, Mister President, this is Gina."

"Gina, Gina, I've known a lotta good Ginas. Tons of Ginas in New York City."

"I'm from Iowa—I learned to golf in Iowa."

"Fabulous. Got great support from the Hawkeye State. So, tell me, Gina, how long have you known Roland?"

"About a year. I sat beside him at work. I watched him test your golf game for months. He's much better with a controller in his hand."

"How many rounds has he played? He can't have been out of jail that long?"

"Roland, how many rounds have you played since you got out?"

"Twenty-five—maybe a few more."

"Less than thirty, sir."

"That's hard to believe—I mean I believe it now that you told me, but by itself I would find it hard to believe. Let me talk to Roland. I'll see you in Florida this Summer."

"I can't wait. Thank you." She gave the phone back to Roland.

"Lovely girl, Roland, I can tell, I have a great sense for people, even just talking on the phone. She's a keeper, a real keeper, you hear me?"

"Yes, Donald, loud and clear."

"So, how's the leg?"

"Serviceable. But it'll never be the same thanks to Fred."

"You talking about my brother—what does he have to do with it?"

"I was raging at God on the beach as the sun went down the night of my crash, and I invoked the spirit of Fred, more or less taunted him."

"So, you're blaming Fred for the accident—why not the Big Guy?"

"Cuz it was Fred that jumped in front of my Jeep—the phantom of Fred Trump. Otherwise, I glide around that easy curve."

"How do you know it was Fred?"

"My grandpa told me."

"And where was he when all this happened?"

"I met him afterward, above the wreck, on the doorstep to the great beyond. The Jeep used to belong to him. He died drunk, just like Fred, a couple years ago. He gave me a piece of his mind and in the course of things let me know it was your brother that stood in the middle of the road pointing his finger at me and laughing like a fiend."

"And you believe it was real, not just a crazy dream?"

"Have you read Shakespeare?"

"Not since my schooldays—just the basics, Macbeth, Hamlet, a few others."

"Do you remember in the first act of Hamlet, when the ghost of Hamlet's father appears, and Hamlet's friend, the over-educated Horatio, can't believe what he's seen with his own eyes? Do you remember what Hamlet tells him?"

"I don't. But on that subject, there are a few ghouls in this castle I'd like to get rid of."

"I don't doubt it—but what Hamlet says is: *There are more things in Heaven and Earth, Horatio, than are dreamt of in your philosophy.*"

"I see, I see—good enough for Shakespeare, good enough for Roland Hazzard."

"And not just that incident. There've been other things too, facts and events when conscious and not, things I can't shake, more than we have time to talk about. I'm resigned to leaving the big questions open hoping I get the answers on the other side."

"As long as you're sober, as long as your mind is right, I don't suppose it should matter what you believe."

"That sounds like something you might hear at an AA meeting."

"Feel free to use it anytime you like, just keep your butt in those chairs. We don't want to lose you. There's a silent majority that appreciates your philosophy, Hornblower."

"I won't come if I'm not sober—I consider that part of the deal."

"Someone will be in touch with the particulars—everything's on me. Be good to Gina."

The call ended. Gina started the car.

She peered at him. "Donald?"

"Celebrities—we go on a first-name basis."

"Were you a celebrity when you poked your head through the door to the other side?"

"More will be revealed."

~~~~~

When they walked through the door at two o'clock that Sunday, Winters Tavern smelled like the kitchen was in use and there were a few people at the bar and several diners at the tables but otherwise the place was quiet and since business was normally slow at that hour on the Day of Rest there was no waitstaff and Serra came over to their table to take their orders. He took off his hat and lowered it briefly with respect to the lady at the table and set it back on his head and squared it.

"Roland, I'm pleased to see you with company today."

"Gina, meet Serra. He owns the place and knows the habits of courtesy."

The Alcoholic—A Hero Contends for His Soul

"I approve. What's good here?"

Serra ran through the modest bill of fare, and they ordered toasted flatbread sandwiches.

"To drink?"

"Or not to drink—*that* is the question."

"He's been waxing Hamlet today."

"Ahh. Your man is a peculiar sort—a high-end speculator."

"I'll have my usual ginger ale."

"I'll have a beer. Something in a bottle."

"Red Hook?"

She nodded. "That would be fine."

He pocketed his pad and pencil and turned to go but stopped himself. "You going to play for us today?"

"I'm thinking about it."

Serra left to deliver their order to the kitchen.

"Softball? That sounds fun, but you need to rest the leg."

Roland tilted his head toward the stage.

"He means the piano. I come in here sometimes when it's quiet to tickle the ivories."

~~~~~

The couple ate and chatted about the strange and fortuitous morning while the descending sun slowly pinked the tinted west window of the saloon. People were beginning to fill up the place. When their meal was finished, the check paid, and the normal thing for them to do was get up and leave, Gina said she wanted to hear him play the piano. He consented and got up and crossed to the stage and stepped up onto it and walked over to the antique upright and opened the fallboard and sat down on the bench.

Someone at a table said in a loud voice, "Are you the entertainment tonight? I thought it was Bluegrass Sunday. We came to see the Wild Blue Yonders."

Roland turned to the man. "I'm just doing a sound check on the piano." He touched the keys lightly, still uncertain as to what he would play. Then he decided.

"We're going to have a bit of music trivia. Let's see who can find the lyric." He played E-D-E-D-C-G-C and looked at the few who were paying attention. "C'mon. This is easy." Again he played E-D-E-D-C-G-C, this time a little faster.

"I know it," a man said.

"Yes. But can you sing in time? Let's try again."

He played the first three notes and sang softly, "I-MAY-not..." then finished the musical phrase as the man chimed in, "ALL-ways LOVE you..."

Now Roland played B-B-A and sang, "But long AS..."

Then, to B-D-G, the man sang, "there are STARS..."

Roland continued with B-C-D and the two finished the line in unison, "a-BOVE YOU..."

The audience fumbled with the next stanza as Roland continued to play the melody until a woman with a clear voice set the lyric back on track with, "If you should EV-er..."

Roland joined in. "LEAVE ME..."

The audience followed. "Life would go ON..."

Now all together. "Be-LIEVE ME..."

Then the nightingale. "The WORLD could show..."

Roland came through with his tenor voice. "NOTH-ing to ME..."

Now Roland again, projecting above the rest. "So what GOOD would LIVING do MEEE?"

Finally, the whole bar in unison belted out the titular refrain. "GOD only KNOWS what I'd BE with-OUT YOU." The singers continued to repeat it until Roland, smiling at Gina, quit the melody and removed his fingers from the keys. The audience, sparse though it was, applauded with a vigor that startled Roland enough that he felt compelled to rise and, short of bowing, nod to their appreciation.

"Please," he said, stepping forward. "Credit goes to the masterful Brian Wilson and, of course, to yourselves for joining in."

The innocent gladness on their faces cleansed him with an ablution of humility that set him awobble. The many displays of admiration he'd received in his young life had on most occasions swelled him with pride and sometimes left him with the taste of contempt for his competition. Now, looking down from the stage, he suddenly saw faces from an episode in his past, the looks of spectators after he won a gold medal bout in a karate tournament in Idaho, looks not of admiration but of horror at how brutally he'd beaten his opponent. He shook off and blinked away the discordant vision and regained his balance, and then, in view of the spontaneous expressions of public appreciation today in Winters Tavern, formed an inward resolve—*I can do this. I can be a decent human being.* He said this to himself without judgment or indictment of his past but in acknowledgment that he was not, after all, an extraordinary member of the human species apart from his prodigious inborn gifts.

In Gina's eyes he detected a quiet laughter that seemed to well from a combination of affection and approval, and for once he felt both worthy of her love and capable of bearing the responsibility that reciprocating it would entail.

"Play something else," someone said.

"The piano is working just fine. My lady and I have to be going."

~~~~~

The sun dipped behind the ocean and left the town quiet. The leading edge of night sped westward over the face of the waters at a thousand miles per hour. The air was still. Barely a rustle in the sycamores outside Roland's house. The celestial machinery and the rhythms of nature lay outside the tinkering of the subordinate ministries. Only the Creator could interfere at the astronomical level. Tonight, the local asteroids maintained their harmless orbits.

Carmela Salvador pulled her two-wheeled shopping cart up the sidewalk with her granddaughter in tow. The child heard something and stopped to listen and looked at Roland's open bedroom window.

"Lola, Lola," she said with alarm. "Someone is hurting a lady in there."

Carmela Salvador stopped and stood the cart upright and looked at the house and listened intently. Slowly she smiled at the child's distress then raised her eyes.

"No, pobrecita," she said to the sky. "Ella es feliz. She is enjoying herself very much."

www.ingramcontent.com/pod-product-compliance
Ingram Content Group UK Ltd.
Pitfield, Milton Keynes, MK11 3LW, UK
UKHW011320130825
7381UKWH00023B/286